John Grisham

THE BRETHREN

A PAINTED HOUSE

ARROW

This edition published in 2003 by Arrow Books,
an imprint of Random House UK Ltd,
20 Vauxhall Bridge Road, London SW1V 2SA

Printed and bound in Great Britain by
Cox & Wyman Ltd, Reading, Berkshire

THE BRETHREN

ONE

For the weekly docket the court jester wore his standard garb of well-used and deeply faded maroon pajamas and lavender terry-cloth shower shoes with no socks. He wasn't the only inmate who went about his daily business in his pajamas, but no one else dared wear lavender shoes. His name was T. Karl, and he'd once owned banks in Boston.

The pajamas and shoes weren't nearly as troubling as the wig. It parted at the middle and rolled in layers downward, over his ears, with tight curls coiling off into three directions, and fell heavily onto his shoulders. It was a bright gray, almost white, and fashioned after the Old English magistrate's wigs from centuries earlier. A friend on the outside had found it at a secondhand costume store in Manhattan, in the Village.

T. Karl wore it to court with great pride, and, odd as it was, it had, with time, become part of the show. The other inmates kept their distance from T. Karl anyway, wig or not.

He stood behind his flimsy folding table in the prison cafeteria, tapped a plastic mallet that served

1

as a gavel, cleared his squeaky throat, and announced with great dignity: 'Hear ye, hear ye, hear ye. The Inferior Federal Court of North Florida is now in session. Please rise.'

No one moved, or at least no one made an effort to stand. Thirty inmates lounged in various stages of repose in plastic cafeteria chairs, some looking at the court jester, some chatting away as if he didn't exist.

T. Karl continued: 'Let all ye who search for justice draw nigh and get screwed.'

No laughs. It had been funny months earlier when T. Karl first tried it. Now it was just another part of the show. He sat down carefully, making sure the rows of curls bouncing upon his shoulders were given ample chance to be seen, then he opened a thick red leather book which served as the official record for the court. He took his work very seriously.

Three men entered the room from the kitchen. Two of them wore shoes. One was eating a saltine. The one with no shoes was also bare-legged up to his knees, so that below his robe his spindly legs could be seen. They were smooth and hairless and very brown from the sun. A large tattoo had been applied to his left calf. He was from California.

All three wore old church robes from the same choir, pale green with gold trim. They came from the same store as T. Karl's wig, and had been presented by him as gifts at Christmas. That was how he kept his job as the court's official clerk.

There were a few hisses and jeers from the spectators as the judges ambled across the tile floor, in full regalia, their robes flowing. They took

2

their places behind a long folding table, near T. Karl but not too near, and faced the weekly gathering. The short round one sat in the middle. Joe Roy Spicer was his name, and by default he acted as the Chief Justice of the tribunal. In his previous life, Judge Spicer had been a Justice of the Peace in Mississippi, duly elected by the people of his little county, and sent away when the feds caught him skimming bingo profits from a Shriners club.

'Please be seated,' he said. Not a soul was standing.

The judges adjusted their folding chairs and shook their robes until they fell properly around them. The assistant warden stood to the side, ignored by the inmates. A guard in uniform was with him. The Brethren met once a week with the prison's approval. They heard cases, mediated disputes, settled little fights among the boys, and had generally proved to be a stabilizing factor amid the population.

Spicer looked at the docket, a neat hand-printed sheet of paper prepared by T. Karl, and said, 'Court shall come to order.'

To his right was the Californian, the Honorable Finn Yarber, age sixty, in for two years now with five to go for income tax evasion. A vendetta, he still maintained to anyone who would listen. A crusade by a Republican governor who'd managed to rally the voters in a recall drive to remove Chief Justice Yarber from the California Supreme Court. The rallying point had been Yarber's opposition to the death penalty, and his high-handedness in delaying every execution. Folks wanted blood,

3

Yarber prevented it, the Republicans whipped up a frenzy, and the recall was a smashing success. They pitched him onto the street, where he floundered for a while until the IRS began asking questions. Educated at Stanford, indicted in Sacramento, sentenced in San Francisco, and now serving his time at a federal prison in Florida.

In for two years and Finn was still struggling with the bitterness. He still believed in his own innocence, still dreamed of conquering his enemies. But the dreams were fading. He spent a lot of time on the jogging track, alone, baking in the sun and dreaming of another life.

'First case is Schneiter versus Magruder,' Spicer announced as if a major antitrust trial was about to start.

'Schneiter's not here,' Beech said.

'Where is he?'

'Infirmary. Gallstones again. I just left there.'

Hatlee Beech was the third member of the tribunal. He spent most of his time in the infirmary because of hemorrhoids, or headaches, or swollen glands. Beech was fifty-six, the youngest of the three, and with nine years to go he was convinced he would die in prison. He'd been a federal judge in East Texas, a hardfisted conservative who knew lots of Scripture and liked to quote it during trials. He'd had political ambitions, a nice family, money from his wife's family's oil trust. He also had a drinking problem which no one knew about until he ran over two hikers in Yellowstone. Both died. The car Beech had been driving was owned by a young lady he was not married to. She was found naked in the front seat, too drunk to walk.

4

They sent him away for twelve years.

Joe Roy Spicer, Finn Yarber, Hatlee Beech. The Inferior Court of North Florida, better known as the Brethren around Trumble, a minimum security federal prison with no fences, no guard towers, no razor wire. If you had to do time, do it the federal way, and do it in a place like Trumble.

'Should we default him?' Spicer asked Beech.

'No, just continue it until next week.'

'Okay. I don't suppose he's going anywhere.'

'I object to a continuance,' Magruder said from the crowd.

'Too bad,' said Spicer. 'It's continued until next week.'

Magruder was on his feet. 'That's the third time it's been continued. I'm the plaintiff. I sued him. He runs to the infirmary every time we have a docket.'

'What're ya'll fightin over?' Spicer asked.

'Seventeen dollars and two magazines,' T. Karl said helpfully.

'That much, huh?' Spicer said. Seventeen dollars would get you sued every time at Trumble.

Finn Yarber was already bored. With one hand he stroked his shaggy gray beard, and with the other he raked his long fingernails across the table. Then he popped his toes, loudly, crunching them into the floor in an efficient little workout that grated on the nerves. In his other life, when he had titles – Mr. Chief Justice of the California Supreme Court – he often presided while wearing leather clogs, no socks, so that he could exercise his toes during the dull oral arguments. 'Continue it,' he said.

5

'Justice delayed is justice denied,' Magruder said solemnly.

'Now that's original,' said Beech. 'One more week, then we'll default Schneiter.'

'So ordered,' Spicer said, with great finality. T. Karl made a note in the docket book. Magruder sat down in a huff. He'd filed his complaint in the Inferior Court by handing to T. Karl a one-page summary of his allegations against Schneiter. Only one page. The Brethren didn't tolerate paperwork. One page and you got your day in court. Schneiter had replied with six pages of invective, all of which had been summarily stricken by T. Karl.

The rules were kept simple. Short pleadings. No discovery. Quick justice. Decisions on the spot, and all decisions were binding if both parties submitted to the jurisdiction of the court. No appeals; there was nowhere to take one. Witnesses were not given an oath to tell the truth. Lying was completely expected. It was, after all, a prison.

'What's next?' Spicer asked.

T. Karl hesitated for a second, then said, 'It's the Whiz case.'

Things were suddenly still for a moment, then the plastic cafeteria chairs rattled forward in one noisy offensive. The inmates scooted and shuffled until T. Karl announced, 'That's close enough!' They were less than twenty feet away from the bench.

'We shall maintain decorum!' he proclaimed.

The Whiz matter had been festering for months at Trumble. Whiz was a young Wall Street crook who'd bilked some rich clients. Four million dollars had never been accounted for, and legend held that Whiz had stashed it offshore and managed it from inside Trumble. He had six years left, and would be almost forty when paroled. It was widely assumed that he was quietly serving his time until one glorious day when he would walk free, still a young man, and fly off in a private jet to a beach where the money was waiting.

Inside, the legend only grew, partly because Whiz kept to himself and spent long hours every day studying financials and technical charts and reading impenetrable economic publications. Even the warden had tried to cajole him into sharing market tips.

An ex-lawyer known as Rook had somehow got next to Whiz, and had somehow convinced him to share a small morsel of advice with an investment club that met once a week in the prison chapel. On behalf of the club, Rook was now suing the Whiz for fraud.

Rook took the witness chair, and began his narrative. The usual rules of procedure and evidence were dispensed with so that the truth could be arrived at quickly, whatever form it might take.

'So I go to the Whiz and I ask him what he thinks about ValueNow, a new online company I read about in *Forbes*,' Rook explained. 'It was about to go public, and I liked the idea behind the company. Whiz said he'd check it out for me. I heard nothing. So I went back to him and said, "Hey, Whiz, what about ValueNow?" And he said he thought it was a solid company and the stock would go through the roof.'

'I did not say that,' the Whiz inserted quickly.

He was seated across the room, by himself, his arms folded over the chair in front.

'Yes you did.'

'I did not.'

'Anyway, I go back to the club and tell them that Whiz is high on the deal, so we decide we want to buy some stock in ValueNow. But little guys can't buy because the offering is closed. I go back to Whiz over there and I say, "Look, Whiz, you think you could pull some strings with your buddies on Wall Street and get us a few shares of ValueNow?" And Whiz said he thought he could do that.'

'That's a lie,' said Whiz.

'Quiet,' said Justice Spicer. 'You'll get your chance.'

'He's lying,' Whiz said, as if there was a rule against it.

If Whiz had money, you'd never know it, at least not on the inside. His eight-by-twelve cell was bare except for stacks of financial publications. No stereo, fan, books, cigarettes, none of the usual assets acquired by almost everyone else. This only added to the legend. He was considered a miser, a weird little man who saved every penny and was no doubt stashing everything offshore.

'Anyway,' Rook continued, 'we decided to gamble by taking a big position in ValueNow. Our strategy was to liquidate our holdings and consolidate.'

'Consolidate?' asked Justice Beech. Rook sounded like a portfolio manager who handled billions.

'Right, consolidate. We borrowed all we could

8

from friends and family, and had close to a thousand bucks.'

'A thousand bucks,' repeated Justice Spicer. Not bad for an inside job. 'Then what happened?'

'I told Whiz over there that we were ready to move. Could he get us the stock? This was on a Tuesday. The offering was on a Friday. Whiz said no problem. Said he had a buddy at Goldman Sux or some such place that could take care of us.'

'That's a lie,' Whiz shot from across the room.

'Anyway, on Wednesday I saw Whiz in the east yard, and I asked him about the stock. He said no problem.'

'That's a lie.'

'I got a witness.'

'Who?' asked Justice Spicer.

'Picasso.'

Picasso was sitting behind Rook, as were the other six members of the investment club. Picasso reluctantly waved his hand.

'Is that true?' Spicer asked.

'Yep,' Picasso answered. 'Rook asked about the stock. Whiz said he would get it. No problem.'

Picasso testified in a lot of cases, and had been caught lying more than most inmates.

'Continue,' Spicer said.

'Anyway, Thursday I couldn't find Whiz anywhere. He was hiding from me.'

'I was not.'

'Friday, the stock goes public. It was offered at twenty a share, the price we could've bought it for if Mr. Wall Street over there had done what he promised. It opened at sixty, spent most of the day at eighty, then closed at seventy. Our plans were to

9

sell it as soon as possible. We could've bought fifty shares at twenty, sold them at eighty, and walked away from the deal with three thousand dollars in profits.'

Violence was very rare at Trumble. Three thousand dollars would not get you killed, but some bones might be broken. Whiz had been lucky so far. There'd been no ambush.

'And you think the Whiz owes you these lost profits?' asked ex-Chief Justice Finn Yarber, now plucking his eyebrows.

'Damned right we do. Look, what makes the deal stink even worse is that Whiz bought Value-Now for himself.'

'That's a damned lie,' Whiz said.

'Language, please,' Justice Beech said. If you wanted to lose a case before the Brethren, just offend Beech with your language.

The rumors that Whiz had bought the stock for himself had been started by Rook and his gang. There was no proof of it, but the story had proved irresistible and had been repeated by most inmates so often that it was now established as fact. It fit so nicely.

'Is that all?' Spicer asked Rook.

Rook had other points he wanted to elaborate on, but the Brethren had no patience with windy litigants. Especially ex-lawyers still reliving their glory days. There were at least five of them at Trumble, and they seemed to be on the docket all the time.

'I guess so,' Rook said.

'What do you have to say?' Spicer asked the Whiz.

Whiz stood and took a few steps toward their table. He glared at his accusers, Rook and his gang of losers. Then he addressed the court. 'What's the burden of proof here?'

Justice Spicer immediately lowered his eyes and waited for help. As a Justice of the Peace, he'd had no legal training. He'd never finished high school, then worked for twenty years in his father's country store. That's where the votes came from. Spicer relied on common sense, which was often at odds with the law. Any questions dealing with legal theory would be handled by his two colleagues.

'It's whatever we say it is,' Justice Beech said, relishing a debate with a stockbroker on the court's rules of procedure.

'Clear and convincing proof?' asked the Whiz.

'Could be, but not in this case.'

'Beyond a reasonable doubt?'

'Probably not.'

'Preponderance of the evidence?'

'Now you're getting close.'

'Then, they have no proof,' the Whiz said, waving his hands like a bad actor in a bad TV drama.

'Why don't you just tell us your side of the story?' said Beech.

'I'd love to. ValueNow was a typical online offering, lots of hype, lots of red ink on the books. Sure Rook came to me, but by the time I could make my calls, the offering was closed. I called a friend who told me you couldn't get near the stock. Even the big boys were shut out.'

'Now, how does that happen?' asked Justice Yarber.

The room was quiet. The Whiz was talking money, and everyone was listening.

'Happens all the time in IPOs. That's initial public offerings.'

'We know what an IPO is,' Beech said.

Spicer certainly did not. Didn't have many of those back in rural Mississippi.

The Whiz relaxed, just a little. He could dazzle them for a moment, win this nuisance of a case, then go back to his cave and ignore them.

'The ValueNow IPO was handled by the investment banking firm of Bakin-Kline, a small outfit in San Francisco. Five million shares were offered. Bakin-Kline basically presold the stock to its preferred customers and friends, so that most big investment firms never had a shot at the stock. Happens all the time.'

The judges and the inmates, even the court jester, hung on every word.

He continued. 'It's silly to think that some disbarred yahoo sitting in prison, reading an old copy of *Forbes*, can somehow buy a thousand dollars' worth of ValueNow.'

And at that very moment it did indeed seem very silly. Rook fumed while his club members began quietly blaming him.

'Did you buy any of it?' asked Beech.

'Of course not. I couldn't get near it. And besides, most of the high-tech and online companies are built with funny money. I stay away from them.'

'What do you prefer?' Beech asked quickly, his curiosity getting the better of him.

'Value. The long haul. I'm in no hurry. Look,

this is a bogus case brought by some boys looking for an easy buck.' He waved toward Rook, who was sinking in his chair. The Whiz sounded perfectly believable and legitimate.

Rook's case was built on hearsay, speculation, and the corroboration of Picasso, a notorious liar.

'You got any witnesses?' Spicer asked.

'I don't need any,' the Whiz said and took his seat.

Each of the three justices scribbled something on a slip of paper. Deliberations were quick, verdicts instantaneous. Yarber and Beech slid theirs to Spicer, who announced, 'By a vote of two to one, we find for the defendant. Case dismissed. Who's next?'

The vote was actually unanimous, but every verdict was officially two to one. That allowed each of the three a little wiggle room if later confronted.

But the Brethren were well regarded around Trumble. Their decisions were quick and as fair as they could make them. In fact, they were remarkably accurate in light of the shaky testimony they often heard. Spicer had presided over small cases for years, in the back of his family's country store. He could spot a liar at fifty feet. Beech and Yarber had spent their careers in courtrooms, and had no tolerance for lengthy arguments and delays, the usual tactics.

'That's all today,' T. Karl reported. 'End of docket.'

'Very well. Court is adjourned until next week.'

T. Karl jumped to his feet, his curls again vibrating across his shoulders, and declared, 'Court's adjourned. All rise.'

13

No one stood, no one moved as the Brethren left the room. Rook and his gang were huddled, no doubt planning their next lawsuit. The Whiz left quickly.

The assistant warden and the guard eased away without being seen. The weekly docket was one of the better shows at Trumble.

TWO

Though he'd served in Congress for fourteen years, Aaron Lake still drove his own car around Washington. He didn't need or want a chauffeur, or an aide, or a bodyguard. Sometimes an intern would ride with him and take notes, but for the most part Lake enjoyed the tranquillity of sitting in D.C. traffic while listening to classical guitar on the stereo. Many of his friends, especially those who'd achieved the status of a Mr. Chairman or a Mr. Vice Chairman, had larger cars with drivers. Some even had limos.

Not Lake. It was a waste of time and money and privacy. If he ever sought higher office, he certainly didn't want the baggage of a chauffeur wrapped around his neck. Besides, he enjoyed being alone. His office was a madhouse. He had fifteen people bouncing off the walls, answering phones, opening files, serving the folks back in Arizona who'd sent him to Washington. Two more did nothing but raise money. Three interns managed to further clog his narrow corridors and take up more time than they deserved.

He was single, a widower, with a quaint little

townhouse in Georgetown that he was very fond of. He lived quietly, occasionally stepping into the social scene that had attracted him and his late wife in the early years.

He followed the Beltway, the traffic slow and cautious because of a light snow. He was quickly cleared through CIA security at Langley, and was very pleased to see a preferred parking space waiting for him, along with two plainclothes security personnel.

'Mr. Maynard is waiting,' one of them said gravely, opening his car door while the other took his briefcase. Power did have its perks.

Lake had never met with the CIA director at Langley. They'd conferred twice on the Hill, years earlier, back when the poor guy could get around. Teddy Maynard was in a wheelchair and in constant pain, and even senators got themselves driven out to Langley anytime he needed them. He'd called Lake a half-dozen times in fourteen years, but Maynard was a busy man. His light-lifting was usually handled by associates.

Security barriers collapsed all around the congressman as he and his escorts worked their way into the depths of the CIA headquarters. By the time Lake arrived at Mr. Maynard's suite, he was walking a bit taller, with just a trace of a swagger. He couldn't help it. Power was intoxicating.

Teddy Maynard had sent for him.

Inside the room, a large, square, windowless place known unofficially as the bunker, the Director was sitting alone, looking blankly at a large screen upon which the face of Congressman Aaron Lake was frozen. It was a recent photo, one taken at a black-tie fund-raiser three months earlier where Lake had half a glass of wine, ate baked chicken, no dessert, drove himself home, alone, and went to bed before eleven. The photo was appealing because Lake was so attractive – light red hair with almost no gray, hair that was not colored or tinted, a full hairline, dark blue eyes, square chin, really nice teeth. He was fifty-three years old and aging superbly. He did thirty minutes a day on a rowing machine and his cholesterol was 160. They hadn't found a single bad habit. He enjoyed the company of women, especially when it was important to be seen with one. His steady squeeze was a sixty-year-old widow in Bethesda whose late husband had made a fortune as a lobbyist.

Both his parents were dead. His only child was a schoolteacher in Santa Fe. His wife of twenty-nine years had died in 1996 of ovarian cancer. A year later, his thirteen-year-old spaniel died too, and Congressman Aaron Lake of Arizona truly lived alone. He was Catholic, not that that mattered anymore, and he attended Mass at least once a week. Teddy pushed the button and the face disappeared.

Lake was unknown outside the Beltway, primarily because he'd kept his ego in check. If he had aspirations to higher office, they were closely guarded. His name had been mentioned once as a potential candidate for governor of Arizona, but he enjoyed Washington too much. He loved Georgetown – the crowds, the anonymity, the city life – good restaurants and cramped bookstores and espresso bars. He liked theater and music, and he and his late wife had never missed an event at the Kennedy Center.

On the Hill, Lake was known as a bright and hardworking congressman who was articulate, fiercely honest, and loyal, conscientious to a fault. Because his district was the home of four large defense contractors, he had become an expert on military hard-ware and readiness. He was Chairman of the House Committee on Armed Services, and it was in that capacity that he had come to know Teddy Maynard.

Teddy pushed the button again, and there was Lake's face. For a fifty-year veteran of intelligence wars, Teddy seldom had a knot in his stomach. He'd dodged bullets, hidden under bridges, frozen in mountains, poisoned two Czech spies, shot a traitor in Bonn, learned seven languages, fought the cold war, tried to prevent the next one, had more adventures than any ten agents combined, yet looking at the innocent face of Congressman Aaron Lake he felt a knot.

He – the CIA – was about to do something the agency had never done before.

They'd started with a hundred senators, fifty governors, four hundred and thirty-five congress-men, all the likely suspects, and now there was only one. Representative Aaron Lake of Arizona.

Teddy flicked a button and the wall went blank. His legs were covered with a quilt. He wore the same thing every day – a V-necked navy sweater, white shirt, subdued bow tie. He rolled his wheel-chair to a spot near the door, and prepared to meet his candidate.

★

During the eight minutes Lake was kept waiting, he was served coffee and offered a pastry, which he declined. He was six feet tall, weighed one-seventy, was fastidious about his appearance, and had he taken the pastry Teddy would've been surprised. As far as they could tell, Lake never ate sugar. Never.

His coffee was strong, though, and as he sipped it he reviewed a little research of his own. The purpose of the meeting was to discuss the alarming flow of black market artillery into the Balkans. Lake had two memos, eighty pages of double-spaced data he'd crunched until two in the morning. He wasn't sure why Mr. Maynard wanted him to appear at Langley to discuss such a matter, but he was determined to be prepared.

A soft buzzer sounded, the door opened, and the Director of the CIA rolled out, wrapped in a quilt and looking every day of his seventy-four years. His handshake was firm, though, probably because of the strain of pushing himself around. Lake followed him back into the room, leaving the two college-educated pit bulls to guard the door.

They sat opposite each other, across a very long table that ran to the end of the room where a large white wall served as a screen. After brief preliminaries, Teddy pushed a button and another face appeared. Another button, and the lights grew dim. Lake loved it – push little buttons, high-tech images flash instantly. No doubt the room was wired with enough electronic junk to monitor his pulse from thirty feet.

'Recognize him?' Teddy asked.

'Maybe. I think I've seen the face before.'

19

'He's Natli Chenkov. A former general. Now a member of what's left of the Russian parliament.'

'Also known as Natty,' Lake said proudly.

'That's him. Hard-line Communist, close ties to the military, brilliant mind, huge ego, very ambitious, ruthless, and right now the most dangerous man in the world.'

'Didn't know that.'

A flick, another face, this one of stone under a gaudy military parade hat. 'This is Yuri Goltsin, second in command of what's left of the Russian army. Chenkov and Goltsin have big plans.' Another flick, a map of a section of Russia north of Moscow. 'They're stockpiling arms in this region,' Teddy said. 'They're actually stealing them from themselves, looting the Russian army, but, and more important, they're buying them on the black market.'

'Where's their money coming from?'

'Everywhere. They're swapping oil for Israeli radar. They're trafficking in drugs and buying Chinese tanks through Pakistan. Chenkov has close ties with some mobsters, one of whom recently bought a factory in Malaysia where they make nothing but assault rifles. It's very elaborate. Chenkov has a brain, a very high IQ. He's probably a genius.'

Teddy Maynard was a genius, and if he bestowed that title on another, then Congressman Lake certainly believed it. 'So who gets attacked?'

Teddy dismissed the question because he wasn't ready to answer it. 'See the town of Vologda. It's about five hundred miles east of Moscow. Last week we tracked sixty Vetrov to a warehouse there. As you know, the Vetrov –'

'Is equivalent to our Tomahawk Cruise, but two feet longer.'

'Exactly. That makes three hundred they've moved in during the last ninety days. See the town of Rybinsk, just southwest of Vologda?'

'Known for its plutonium.'

'Yes, tons of it. Enough to make ten thousand nuclear warheads. Chenkov and Goltsin and their people control the entire area.'

'Control?'

'Yes, through a web of regional mobsters and local army units. Chenkov has his people in place.'

'In place for what?'

Teddy squeezed a button and the wall was blank. But the lights stayed dim, so that when he spoke across the table he did so almost from the shadows. 'The coup is right around the corner, Mr. Lake. Our worst fears are coming true. Every aspect of Russian society and culture is cracking and crumbling. Democracy is a joke. Capitalism is a nightmare. We thought we could McDonaldize the damned place, and it's been a disaster. Workers are not getting paid, and they're the lucky ones because they have jobs. Twenty percent do not. Children are dying because there are no medicines. So are many adults. Ten percent of the population are homeless. Twenty percent are hungry. Each day things get worse. The country has been looted by the mobsters. We think at least five hundred billion dollars has been stolen and taken out of the country. There's no relief in sight. The time is perfect for a new strongman, a new

21

dictator who'll promise to lead the people back to stability. The country is crying for leadership, and Mr. Chenkov has decided it's up to him.'

'And he has the army.'

'He has the army, and that's all it takes. The coup will be bloodless because the people are ready for it. They'll embrace Chenkov. He'll lead the parade into Red Square and dare us, the United States, to stand in his way. We'll be the bad guys again.'

'So the cold war is back,' Lake said, his words fading at the end.

'There'll be nothing cold about it. Chenkov wants to expand, to recapture the old Soviet Union. He desperately needs cash, so he'll simply take it in the form of land, factories, oil, crops. He'll start little regional wars, which he'll easily win.' Another map appeared. Phase One of the new world order was presented to Lake. Teddy didn't miss a word. 'I suspect he'll roll through the Baltic States, toppling governments in Estonia, Latvia, Lithuania, etc. Then he'll go to the old Eastern bloc and strike a deal with some of the Communists there.'

The congressman was speechless as he watched Russia expand. Teddy's predictions were so certain, so precise.

'What about the Chinese?' Lake asked.

But Teddy wasn't finished with Eastern Europe. He flicked; the map changed. 'Here's where we get sucked in.'

'Poland?'

'Yep. Happens every time. Poland is now a member of NATO, for some damned reason.

Imagine that. Poland signing on to help protect us and Europe. Chenkov solidifies Russia's old turf, and casts a longing eye westward. Same as Hitler, except he was looking to the east.'

'Why would he want Poland?'

'Why did Hitler want Poland? It was between him and Russia. He hated the Poles, and he was ready to start a war. Chenkov doesn't give a damn about Poland, he just wants to control it. And he wants to destroy NATO.'

'He's willing to risk a third world war?'

Buttons were pushed; the screen became a wall again; lights came on. The audiovisuals were over and it was time for an even more serious conversation. Pain shot through Teddy's legs, and he couldn't keep from frowning.

'I can't answer that,' he said. 'We know a lot, but we don't know what the man's thinking. He's moving very quietly, putting people in place, setting things up. It's not completely unexpected, you know.'

'Of course not. We've had these scenarios for the last eight years, but there's always been hope that it wouldn't happen.'

'It's happening, Congressman. Chenkov and Goltsin are eliminating their opponents as we speak.'

'What's the timetable?'

Teddy shifted again under the quilt, tried another position to stop the pain. 'It's difficult to say. If he's smart, which he certainly is, he'll wait until there's rioting in the streets. I think that a year from now Natty Chenkov will be the most famous man in the world.'

'A year,' Lake said to himself, as if he'd just been given his own death sentence.

There was a long pause as he contemplated the end of the world. Teddy certainly let him. The knot in Teddy's stomach was significantly smaller now. He liked Lake a lot. He was indeed very handsome, and articulate, and smart. They'd made the right choice.

He was electable.

After a round of coffee and a phone call Teddy had to take – it was the Vice President – they reconvened their little conference and moved forward. The congressman was pleased that Teddy had so much time for him. The Russians were coming, yet Teddy seemed so calm.

'I don't have to tell you how unprepared our military is,' he said gravely.

'Unprepared for what? For war?'

'Perhaps. If we are unprepared, then we could well have a war. If we are strong, we avoid war. Right now the Pentagon could not do what it did in the Gulf War in 1991.'

'We're at seventy percent,' Lake said with authority. This was his turf.

'Seventy percent will get us a war, Mr. Lake. A war we cannot win. Chenkov is spending every dime he can steal on new hardware. We're cutting budgets and depleting our military. We want to push buttons and launch smart bombs so that no American blood is shed. Chenkov will have two million hungry soldiers, anxious to fight and die if necessary.'

For a brief moment Lake felt proud. He'd had

24

the guts to vote against the last budget deal because it decreased military spending. The folks back home were upset about it. 'Can't you expose Chenkov now?' he asked.

'No. Absolutely not. We have excellent intelligence. If we react to him, then he'll know that we know. It's the spy game, Mr. Lake. It's too early to make him a monster.'

'So what's your plan?' Lake asked boldly. It was quite presumptuous to ask Teddy about his plans. The meeting had accomplished its purpose. One more congressman had been sufficiently briefed. At any moment Lake could be asked to leave so that another committee chairman of some variety could be shown in.

But Teddy had big plans, and he was anxious to share them. 'The New Hampshire primary is two weeks away. We have four Republicans and three Democrats all saying the same thing. Not a single candidate wants to increase defense spending. We have a budget surplus, miracle of all miracles, and everyone has a hundred ideas about how to spend it. A bunch of imbeciles. Just a few years ago we had huge budget deficits, and Congress spent money faster than it could be printed. Now there's a surplus. They're gorging themselves on the pork.'

Congressman Lake looked away for a second, then decided to let it pass.

'Sorry about that,' Teddy said, catching himself. 'Congress as a whole is irresponsible, but we have many fine congressmen.'

'You don't have to tell me.'

'Anyway, the field is crowded with a bunch of

clones. Two weeks ago we had different front-runners. They're slinging mud and knifing each other, all for the benefit of the country's forty-fourth largest state. It's silly.' Teddy paused and grimaced and tried to reshift his useless legs. 'We need someone new, Mr. Lake, and we think that someone is you.'

Lake's first reaction was to suppress a laugh, which he did by smiling, then coughing. He tried to compose himself, and said, 'You must be kidding.'

'You know I'm not kidding, Mr. Lake,' Teddy said sternly, and there was no doubt that Aaron Lake had walked into a well-laid trap.

Lake cleared his throat and completed the job of composing himself. 'All right, I'm listening.'

'It's very simple. In fact, its simplicity makes it beautiful. You're too late to file for New Hampshire, and it doesn't matter anyway. Let the rest of the pack slug it out there. Wait until it's over, then startle everyone by announcing your candidacy for President. Many will ask, "Who the hell is Aaron Lake?" And that's fine. That's what we want. They'll find out soon enough.

'Initially, your platform will have only one plank. It's all about military spending. You're a doom-sayer, with all sorts of dire predictions about how weak our military is becoming. You'll get every-body's attention when you call for doubling our military spending.'

'Doubling?'

'It works, doesn't it? It got your attention. Double it during your four-year term.'

'But why? We need more military spending, but a twofold increase would be excessive.'

'Not if we're facing another war, Mr. Lake. A war in which we push buttons and launch Tomahawk missiles by the thousands, at a million bucks a pop. Hell, we almost ran out of them last year in that Balkan mess. We can't find enough soldiers and sailors and pilots, Mr. Lake. You know this. The military needs tons of cash to recruit young men. We're low on everything – soldiers, missiles, tanks, planes, carriers. Chenkov is building now. We're not. We're still downsizing, and if we keep it up through another Administration, then we're dead.'

Teddy's voice rose, almost in anger, and when he stopped with 'we're dead,' Aaron Lake could almost feel the earth shake from the bombing.

'Where does the money come from?' he asked.

'Money for what?'

'The military.'

Teddy snorted in disgust, then said, 'Same place it always comes from. Need I remind you, sir, that we have a surplus?'

'We're busy spending the surplus.'

'Of course you are. Listen, Mr. Lake, don't worry about the money. Shortly after you announce, we'll scare the hell out of the American people. They'll think you're half-crazy at first, some kind of wacko from Arizona who wants to build even more bombs. But we'll jolt them. We'll create a crisis on the other side of the world, and suddenly Aaron Lake will be called a visionary. Timing is everything. You make a speech about how weak we are in Asia, few people listen. Then

27

we'll create a situation over there that stops the world, and suddenly everyone wants to talk to you. It will go on like that, throughout the campaign. We'll build the tension on this end. We'll release reports, create situations, manipulate the media, embarrass your opponents. Frankly, Mr. Lake, I don't expect it to be that difficult.'

'You sound like you've been here before.'

'No. We've done some unusual things, all in an effort to protect this country. But we've never tried to swing a presidential election.' Teddy said this with an air of regret.

Lake slowly pushed his chair back, stood, stretched his arms and legs, and walked along the table to the end of the room. His feet were heavier. His pulse was racing. The trap had been sprung; he'd been caught.

He returned to his seat. 'I don't have enough money,' he offered across the table. He knew it was received by someone who'd already thought about it.

Teddy smiled and nodded and pretended to give this some thought. Lake's Georgetown home was worth $400,000. He kept about half that much in mutual funds and another $100,000 in municipal bonds. There were no significant debts. He had $40,000 in his reelection account.

'A rich candidate would not be attractive,' Teddy said, then reached for yet another button. Images returned to the wall, sharp and in color. 'Money will not be a problem, Mr. Lake,' he said, his voice much lighter. 'We'll get the defense contractors to pay for it. Look at that,' he said, waving with his right hand as if Lake wasn't sure what to look at. 'Last year the aerospace and defense industry did almost two hundred billion in business. We'll take just a fraction of that.'

'How much of a fraction?'

'As much as you need. We can realistically collect a hundred million dollars from them.'

'You also can't hide a hundred million dollars.'

'Don't bet on it, Mr. Lake. And don't worry about it. We'll take care of the money. You make the speeches, do the ads, run the campaign. The money will pour in. By the time November gets here, the American voters will be so terrified of Armageddon they won't care how much you've spent. It'll be a landslide.'

So Teddy Maynard was offering a landslide. Lake sat in a stunned but giddy silence and gawked at all that money up there on the wall – $194 billion, defense and aerospace. Last year's military budget was $270 billion. Double that to $540 billion in four years, and the contractors would get fat again. And the workers! Wages soaring through the roof! Jobs for everyone!

Candidate Lake would be embraced by executives with the cash and unions with the votes. The initial shock began to fade, and the simplicity of Teddy's plan became clear. Collect the cash from those who will profit. Scare the voters into racing to the polls. Win in a landslide. And in doing so save the world.

Teddy let him think for a moment, then said, 'We'll do most of it through PACs. The unions, engineers, executives, business coalitions – there's no shortage of political groups already on the books. And we'll form some others.'

29

Lake was already forming them. Hundreds of PACs, all flush with more cash than any election had ever seen. The shock was now completely gone, replaced by the sheer excitement of the idea. A thousand questions raced through his mind: Who'll be my Vice President? Who'll run the campaign? Chief of staff? Where to announce? 'It might work,' he said, under control.

'Oh yes. It'll work, Mr. Lake. Trust me. We've been planning this for some time.'

'How many people know about it?'

'Just a few. You've been carefully chosen, Mr. Lake. We examined many potential candidates, and your name kept rising to the top. We've checked your background.'

'Pretty dull, huh?'

'I suppose. Although your relationship with Ms. Valotti concerns me. She's been divorced twice and likes painkillers.'

'Didn't know I had a relationship with Ms. Valotti.'

'You've been seen with her recently.'

'You guys are watching, aren't you?'

'You expect something less?'

'I guess not.'

'You took her to a black-tie cry-a-thon for oppressed women in Afghanistan. Gimme a break.' Teddy's words were suddenly short and dripping with sarcasm.

'I didn't want to go.'

'Then don't. Stay away from that crap. Leave it for Hollywood. Valotti's nothing but trouble.'

'Anybody else?' Lake asked, more than a little defensive. His private life had been pretty dull since he'd become a widower. He was suddenly proud of it.

'Not really,' Teddy said. 'Ms. Benchly seems to be quite stable and makes a lovely escort.'

'Oh, thank you very much.'

'You'll get hammered on abortion, but you won't be the first.'

'It's a tired issue,' Lake said. And he was tired of grappling with it. He'd been for abortions, against abortions, soft on reproductive rights, tough on reproductive rights, pro-choice, pro-child, anti-women, embraced by the feminists. In his fourteen years on Capitol Hill he'd been chased all over the abortion minefield, getting bloodied with each new strategic move.

Abortion didn't scare him anymore, at least not at the moment. He was much more concerned with the CIA sniffing through his background.

'What about GreenTree?' he asked.

Teddy waved his right hand as if it was nothing. 'Twenty-two years ago. Nobody got convicted. Your partner went bankrupt and got himself indicted, but the jury let him walk. It'll come up; everything will come up. But frankly, Mr. Lake, we'll keep the attention diverted elsewhere. There's an advantage in jumping in at the last minute. The press won't have too much time to dig up dirt.'

'I'm single. We've elected an unmarried president only once.'

'You're a widower, the husband of a very lovely lady who was well respected both here and back home. It won't be an issue. Trust me.'

'So what worries you?'

31

'Nothing, Mr. Lake. Not a thing. You're a solid candidate, very electable. We'll create the issues and the fear, and we'll raise the money.'

Lake stood again, walked around the room rubbing his hair, scratching his chin, trying to clear his head. 'I have a lot of questions,' he said.

'Maybe I can answer some of them. Let's talk again tomorrow, right here, same time. Sleep on it, Mr. Lake. Time is crucial, but I suppose a man should have twenty-four hours before making such a decision.' Teddy actually smiled when he said this.

'That's a wonderful idea. Let me think about it. I'll have an answer tomorrow.'

'No one knows we've had this little chat.'

'Of course not.'

THREE

In terms of space, the law library occupied exactly one fourth of the square footage of the entire Trumble library. It was in a corner, partitioned off by a wall of red brick and glass, tastefully done at taxpayer expense. Inside the law library, shelves of well-used books stood packed together with barely enough room for an inmate to squeeze between them. Around the walls were desks covered with typewriters and computers and sufficient research clutter to resemble any big-firm library.

The Brethren ruled the law library. All inmates were allowed to use it, of course, but there was an unwritten policy that one needed permission to stay there for any length of time. Maybe not permission, but at least notice.

Justice Joe Roy Spicer of Mississippi earned forty cents an hour sweeping the floors and straightening the desks and shelves. He also emptied the trash, and was generally considered to be a pig when it came to his menial tasks. Justice Hatlee Beech of Texas was the official law librarian, and at fifty cents an hour was the highest paid. He was fastidious about 'his volumes,' and often bickered with Spicer about their care. Justice Finn Yarber, once of the California Supreme Court, was paid twenty cents an hour as a computer technician. His pay was at the bottom of the scale because he knew so little about computers.

On a typical day, the three spent between six and eight hours in the law library. If a Trumble inmate had a legal problem, he simply made an appointment with one of the Brethren and visited their little suite. Hatlee Beech was an expert on sentencing and appeals. Finn Yarber did bankruptcies, divorces, and child support cases. Joe Roy Spicer, with no formal legal training, had no real specialty. Nor did he want one. He ran the scams.

Strict rules prohibited the Brethren from charging fees for their legal work, but the strict rules meant little. They were, after all, convicted felons, and if they could quietly pick up some cash on the outside then everyone would be happy. Sentencing was a moneymaker. About a fourth of the inmates who arrived at Trumble had been improperly sentenced. Beech could review the records overnight and find the loopholes. A month earlier, he had knocked four years off the sentence of a young man who'd been given fifteen. The family had agreed to pay, and the Brethren earned $5,000, their biggest fee to date. Spicer arranged the secret deposit through their lawyer in Neptune Beach.

There was a cramped conference room in the back of the law library, behind the shelves and barely visible from the main room. The door to it had a large glass window, but no one bothered to look in. The Brethren retired there for quiet business. They called it their chamber.

Spicer had just met with their lawyer and he had mail, some really good letters. He closed the door and removed an envelope from a file. He waved it for Beech and Yarber to see. 'It's yellow,' he said. 'Ain't that sweet? It's for Ricky.'

'Who's it from?' Yarber asked.

'Curtis from Dallas.'

'The banker?' Beech asked excitedly.

'No, Curtis owns the jewelry stores. Listen.' Spicer unfolded the letter, also on soft yellow stationery. He smiled and cleared his throat and began to read: ' "Dear Ricky: Your letter of January eighth made me cry. I read it three times before I put it down. You poor boy. Why are they keeping you there?" '

'Where is he?' asked Yarber.

'Ricky's locked down in a fancy drug rehab unit his rich uncle is paying for. He's been in for a year, is clean and fully rehabbed, but the terrible people who run the place won't release him until April because they've been collecting twenty thousand dollars a month from his rich uncle, who just wants him locked away and won't send any spending money. Do you remember any of this?'

'Now I do.'

'You helped with the fiction. May I proceed?'

'Please do.'

Spicer continued reading: ' "I'm tempted to fly down there and confront those evil people myself. And your uncle, what a loser! Rich people like him think they can just send money and not get involved. As I told you, my father was quite wealthy, and he was the most miserable person I've ever known. Sure he bought me things – objects

35

that were temporary and meant nothing when they were gone. But he never had time for me. He was a sick man, just like your uncle. I've enclosed a check for a thousand dollars if you need anything from the commissary.

'"Ricky, I can't wait to see you in April. I've already told my wife that there is an international diamond show in Orlando that month, and she has no interest in going with me."'

'April?' asked Beech.

'Yep. Ricky is certain he will be released in April.'

'Ain't that sweet,' Yarber said with a smile. 'And Curtis has a wife and kids?'

'Curtis is fifty-eight, three adult children, two grandchildren.'

'Where's the check?' asked Beech.

Spicer flipped the sheets of stationery and went to page two. '"We have to make certain you can meet me in Orlando,"' he read. '"Are you sure you'll finally be released in April? Please tell me you will. I think about you every hour. I keep your photo hidden in my desk drawer, and when I look into your eyes I know that we should be together."'

'Sick, sick, sick,' Beech said, still smiling. 'And he's from Texas.'

'I'm sure there are a lot of sweet boys in Texas,' Yarber said.

'And none in California?'

'The rest of it is just mush,' Spicer said, scanning quickly. There would be plenty of time to read it later. He held up the $1,000 check for his colleagues to see. In due course, it would be

36

smuggled out to their attorney and he would deposit it in their hidden account.

'When are we gonna bust him?' Yarber asked.

'Let's swap a few more letters. Ricky needs to share some more misery.'

'Maybe one of the guards could beat him up, or something like that,' Beech said.

'They don't have guards,' replied Spicer. 'It's a designer rehab clinic, remember? They have counselors.'

'But it's a lockdown facility, right? That means gates and fences, so surely there's a guard or two around. What if Ricky got attacked in the shower or the locker room by some goon who wanted his body?'

'It can't be a sexual attack,' Yarber said. 'That might scare Curtis. He might think Ricky caught a disease or something.'

And so the fiction went for a few minutes as they created more misery for poor Ricky. His picture had been lifted from the bulletin board of a fellow inmate, copied at a quick print by their lawyer, and had now been sent to more than a dozen pen pals across North America. The photo was of a smiling college grad, in a navy robe with a cap and gown, holding a diploma, a very handsome young man.

It was decided that Beech would work on the new story for a few days, then write a rough draft of the next letter to Curtis. Beech was Ricky, and at that moment their little tormented fictional boy was writing his tales of misery to eight different caring souls. Justice Yarber was Percy, also a young man locked away for drugs but now clean and nearing release and looking for an older sugar daddy with whom to spend meaningful time. Percy had five hooks in the water, and was slowly reeling them in.

Joe Roy Spicer didn't write very well. He coordinated the scam, helped with the fiction, kept the stories straight, and met with the lawyer who brought the mail. And he handled the money.

He pulled out another letter and announced, 'This, Your Honors, is from Quince.'

Everything stopped as Beech and Yarber stared at the letter. Quince was a wealthy banker in a small town in Iowa, according to the six letters he and Ricky had swapped. Like the rest, they'd found him through the personals of a gay magazine now hidden in the law library. He'd been their second catch, the first having become suspicious and disappearing. Quince's photo of himself was a snapshot taken at a lake, with the shirt off, the potbelly, the skinny arms, the receding hairline of a fifty-one-year-old – his family all around him. It was a bad photo, no doubt selected by Quince because it might be difficult to identify him, if anyone ever tried.

'Would you like to read it, Ricky boy?' Spicer asked, handing the letter to Beech, who took it and looked at the envelope. Plain white, no return address, typed lettering.

'Have you read it?' Beech asked.

'No. Go ahead.'

Beech slowly removed the letter, a plain sheet of white paper with tight single-spaced paragraphs produced by an old typewriter. He cleared his voice, and read: ' "Dear Ricky: It's done. I can't believe I did it, but I pulled it off. I used a pay phone and a money order so nothing could be traced – I think my trail is clean. The company you suggested in New York was superb, very discreet and helpful. I have to be honest, Ricky, it scared the hell out of me. Booking a gay cruise is something I never dreamed of doing. And you know what? It was exhilarating. I am so proud of myself. We have a cabin suite, a thousand bucks a night, and I can't wait." '

Beech stopped and glanced above his reading glasses halfway down his nose. Both of his colleagues were smiling, savoring the words.

He continued: ' "We set sail on March tenth, and I have a wonderful idea. I will arrive in Miami on the ninth, so we won't have much time to get together and introduce ourselves. Let's meet on the boat, in our suite. I'll get there first, check in, get the champagne on ice, then wait for you. Won't that be fun, Ricky? We'll have three days to ourselves. I say we don't leave the room." '

Beech couldn't help but smile, and he somehow managed to do so while shaking his head in disgust.

He continued: ' "I am so excited about our little trip. I have finally decided to discover who I really am, and you've given me the courage to take the first step. Though we haven't met, Ricky, I can never thank you enough.

' "Please write me back immediately and confirm. Take care, my Ricky. Love, Quince." '

'I think I'm gonna vomit,' Spicer said, but he wasn't convincing. There was too much to do.

'Let's bust him,' Beech said. The others quickly agreed.

'How much?' asked Yarber.

'At least a hundred thousand,' said Spicer. 'His family has owned banks for two generations. We know his father is still active in the business, so you have to figure the old man might go nuts if his boy gets outed. Quince can't afford to get booted from the family gravy train, so he'll pay whatever we demand. It's a perfect situation.'

Beech was already taking notes. So was Yarber. Spicer began pacing around the small room like a bear stalking prey. The ideas came slowly, the language, the opinions, the strategy, but before long the letter took shape.

In rough draft, Beech read it: '"Dear Quince: So nice to get your letter of January fourteenth. I'm so happy you got the gay cruise booked. It sounds delightful. One problem, though. I won't be able to make it, and there are a couple of reasons for this. One is that I won't be released for a few more years. I'm in a prison, not a drug treatment clinic. And I'm not gay, far from it. I have a wife and two kids, and right now they're having a difficult time financially because I'm sitting here in prison, unable to support them. That's where you come in, Quince. I need some of your money. I want a hundred thousand dollars. We can call it hush money. You send it, and I'll forget the Ricky business and the gay cruise and no one in Bakers, Iowa, will ever know anything about it. Your wife and your children and your father and the rest of your rich family will never know about Ricky. If you don't send the money, then I'll flood your little town with copies of our letters.

' "It's called extortion, Quince, and you're

caught. It's cruel and mean and criminal, and I don't care. I need money, and you have it." '

Beech stopped and looked around the room for approval.

'It's beautiful,' said Spicer, already spending the loot.

'It's nasty,' said Yarber. 'But what if he kills himself?'

'That's a long shot,' said Beech.

They read the letter again, then debated whether the timing was right. They did not mention the illegality of their scam, or the punishment if they got caught. Those discussions had been laid to rest months earlier when Joe Roy Spicer had convinced the other two to join him. The risks were insignificant when weighed against the potential returns. The Quinces who got themselves snared were not likely to run to the police and complain of extortion.

But they hadn't busted anyone yet. They were corresponding with a dozen or so potential victims, all middle-aged men who'd made the mistake of answering this simple ad:

> SWM in 20s looking for kind and
> discreet gentleman in 40s or 50s
> to pen pal with.

One little personal in small print in the back of a gay magazine had yielded sixty responses, and Spicer had the chore of sifting through the rubbish and identifying rich targets. At first he'd found the work disgusting, then he became amused by it. Now it was a business because they were about to extort a hundred thousand bucks from a perfectly innocent man.

Their lawyer would take a third, the usual cut but a frustrating percentage nonetheless. They had no choice. He was a critical player in their crimes.

They worked on the letter to Quince for an hour, then agreed to sleep on it and do a final draft the next day. There was another letter from a man using the pseudonym of Hoover. It was his second, written to Percy, and rambled on for four paragraphs about bird-watching. Yarber would be forced to study birds before writing back as Percy and professing a great interest in the subject. Evidently, Hoover was afraid of his shadow. He revealed nothing personal, and there was no indication of money.

Give him some more rope, the Brethren decided. Talk about birds, then try to nudge him to the subject of physical companionship. If Hoover didn't take the hint, and if he didn't reveal something about his financial situation, then they'd drop him.

Within the Bureau of Prisons, Trumble was officially referred to as a camp. Such a designation meant there were no fences around the grounds, no razor wire, no watchtowers, no guards with rifles waiting to nail escapees. A camp meant minimum security, so that any inmate could simply walk away if he chose. There were a thousand at Trumble, but few walked away.

It was nicer than most public schools. Air-conditioned dorms, clean cafeteria serving three squares a day, a weight room, billiards, cards, racquetball, basketball, volleyball, jogging track, library, chapel, ministers on duty, counselors, caseworkers, unlimited visiting hours.

Trumble was as good as it could get for prisoners, all of whom were classified as low risk. Eighty percent were there for drug crimes. About forty had robbed banks without hurting or really scaring anyone. The rest were white-collar types whose crimes ranged from small-time scams to Dr. Floyd, a surgeon whose office had bilked Medicare out of $6 million over two decades.

Violence was not tolerated at Trumble. Threats were rare. There were plenty of rules and the administration had little trouble enforcing them. If you screwed up, they sent you away, to a medium-security prison, one with razor wire and rough guards.

Trumble's prisoners were content to behave themselves and count their days, the federal way.

Pursuing serious criminal activity on the inside was unheard of, until the arrival of Joe Roy Spicer. Before his fall, Spicer had heard stories about the Angola scam, named for the infamous Louisiana state penitentiary. Some inmates there had perfected the gay-extortion scheme, and before they were caught they had fleeced their victims of $700,000.

Spicer was from a rural county near the Louisiana line, and the Angola scam was a notorious affair in his part of the state. He never dreamed he'd copy it. But he woke up one morning in a federal pen, and decided to shaft every living soul he could get close enough to.

He walked the track every day at 1 P.M., usually

43

alone, always with a pack of Marlboros. He hadn't smoked for ten years before his incarceration; now he was up to two packs a day. So he walked to negate the damage to his lungs. In thirty-four months he'd walked 1,242 miles. And he'd lost twenty pounds, though probably not from exercise, as he liked to claim. The prohibition against beer was more responsible for the weight loss.

Thirty-four months of walking and smoking, twenty-one months to go.

Ninety thousand dollars of the stolen bingo money was literally buried in his backyard, a half a mile behind his house next to a toolshed – entombed in a homemade concrete vault his wife knew nothing about. She'd helped him spend the rest of the loot, $180,000 altogether, though the feds had traced only half of it. They'd bought Cadillacs and flown to Las Vegas, first class out of New Orleans, and they'd been driven around by casino limos and put up in suites.

If he had any dreams left, one was to be a professional gambler, headquartered out of Vegas but known and feared by casinos everywhere. Blackjack was his game, and though he'd lost a ton, he was still convinced he could beat any house. There were casinos in the Caribbean he'd never seen. Asia was heating up. He'd travel the world, first class, with or without his wife, stay in fancy suites, order room service, and terrorize any blackjack dealer dumb enough to deal him cards.

He'd take the $90,000 from his backyard, add it to his share of the Angola scam, and move to Vegas. With or without her. She hadn't been to Trumble in four months, although she used to come every three weeks. He had nightmares of her plowing up the backyard looking for his buried treasure. He was almost convinced she didn't know about the money, but there was room for doubt. He'd been drinking two nights before being shipped off to prison, and had said something about the $90,000. He couldn't remember his exact words. Try as he might, he simply could not recall what he'd told her.

He lit another Marlboro at mile one. Maybe she had a boyfriend now. Rita Spicer was an attractive woman, a little chunky in places but nothing $90,000 couldn't hide. What if she and a new squeeze had found the money and were already spending it? One of Joe Roy's worst recurring nightmares was a scene from a bad movie – Rita and some unknown male with shovels digging like idiots in the rain. Why the rain, he didn't know. But it was always at night, in the middle of a thunderstorm, and the lightning would flash and he would see them slogging their way through the backyard, each time getting nearer and nearer to the toolshed.

In one dream the new mystery boyfriend was on a bulldozer, pushing piles of dirt all over the Spicer farm while Rita stood nearby, pointing here and there with her shovel.

Joe Roy craved the money. He could feel the cash in his hands. He would steal and extort all he could while he counted his days at Trumble, then he would rescue his buried loot and head for Vegas. No one in his hometown would have the pleasure of pointing and whispering and saying,

'There's old Joe Roy. Guess he's out of the pen now.' No sir.

He'd be living the high life. With or without her.

FOUR

Teddy looked at his pill bottles lined along the edge of his table, like little executioners ready to take away his misery. York was seated across from him, reading from his notes.

York said, 'He was on the phone until three this morning, talking to friends in Arizona.'

'Who?'

'Bobby Lander, Jim Gallison, Richard Hassel, the usual gang. His money people.'

'Dale Winer?'

'Yes, him too,' York said, amazed at Teddy's recall. Teddy had his eyes closed now, and was rubbing his temples. Somewhere between them, somewhere deep in his brain, he knew the names of Lake's friends, his contributors, his confidants, his poll workers, and his old high school teachers. All of it neatly tucked away, ready to be used if necessary.

'Anything unusual?'

'No, not really. Just the typical questions you'd expect from a man contemplating such an unexpected move. His friends were surprised, even shocked, and somewhat reluctant, but they'll come around.'

'Did they ask about money?'

'Of course. He was vague, said it would not be a problem, though. They are skeptical.'

'Did he keep our secrets?'

'He certainly did.'

'Was he worried about us listening?'

'I don't think so. He made eleven calls from his office and eight from his home. None from his cell phones.'

'Faxes? E-mail?'

'None. He spent two hours with Schiara, his –'

'Chief of staff.'

'Right. They basically planned the campaign. Schiara wants to run it. They like Nance of Michigan as VP.'

'Not a bad choice.'

'He looks fine. We're already checking him. Had a divorce when he was twenty-three, but that was thirty years ago.'

'Not a problem. Is Lake ready to commit?'

'Oh yes. He's a politician, isn't he? He's been promised the keys to the kingdom. He's already writing speeches.'

Teddy removed a pill from a bottle and swallowed it without the aid of anything liquid. He frowned as if it was bitter. He squeezed the wrinkles in his forehead and said, 'York, tell me we're not missing anything on this guy. No skeletons.'

'No skeletons, Chief. We've examined his dirty underwear for six months. There's nothing that can hurt us.'

'He's not going to marry some fool, is he?'

'No. He dates several women, but nothing serious.'

'No sex with his interns?'

'None. He's clean.'

They were repeating a dialogue they'd had many times. Once more wouldn't hurt.

'No shady financial deals from another lifetime?'

'This is his life, Chief. There's nothing back there.'

'Booze, drugs, prescription pills, gambling on the Internet?'

'No sir. He's very clean, sober, straight, bright, pretty remarkable.'

'Let's talk to him.'

Aaron Lake was once again escorted to the same room deep inside Langley, this time with three handsome young men guarding him as if danger lurked at every corner. He walked even quicker than the day before, his head even taller, his back without the slightest curve. His stature was rising by the hour.

Once again he said hello to Teddy and shook his calloused hand, then followed the quilt-laden wheelchair into the bunker and sat across the table. Pleasantries were exchanged. York watched from a room down the hall where three monitors hooked to hidden cameras relayed every word, every movement. Next to York were two men who spent their time studying tapes of people as they talked and breathed and moved their hands and eyes and heads and feet, in an effort to determine what the speakers really meant.

'Did you sleep much last night?' Teddy asked, managing a smile.

'Yes, actually,' Lake lied.

'Good. I take it you're willing to accept our deal.'

'Deal? I didn't know it was exactly a deal.'

'Oh yes, Mr. Lake, it's exactly a deal. We promise to get you elected, and you promise to double defense spending and get ready for the Russians.'

'Then you have a deal.'

'That's good, Mr. Lake. I'm very pleased. You'll make an excellent candidate and a fine President.'

The words rang through Lake's ears, and he couldn't believe them. President Lake. President Aaron Lake. He'd paced the floor until five that morning trying to convince himself that the White House was being offered to him. It seemed too easy.

And as hard as he tried, he couldn't ignore the trappings. The Oval Office. All those jets and helicopters. The world to be traveled. A hundred aides at his beck and call. State dinners with the most powerful people in the world.

And, above all, a place in history.

Oh yes, Teddy had himself a deal.

'Let's talk about the campaign itself,' Teddy said. 'I think you should announce two days after New Hampshire. Let the dust settle. Let the winners get their fifteen minutes and let the losers sling more mud, then announce.'

'That's pretty fast,' Lake said.

'We don't have a lot of time. We ignore New

Hampshire and get ready for Arizona and Michigan on February twenty-second. It's imperative that you win those two states. When you do, you establish yourself as a serious candidate, and you're set for the month of March.'

'I was thinking of announcing back home, somewhere in Phoenix.'

'Michigan's better. It's a bigger state, fifty-eight delegates, compared to twenty-four for Arizona. You'll be expected to win at home. If you win in Michigan on the same day, then you're a candidate to be reckoned with. Announce in Michigan first, then do it again hours later in your home district.'

'An excellent idea.'

'There's a helicopter plant in Flint, D-L Trilling. They have a large hangar, four thousand workers. The CEO is a man I can talk to.'

'Book it,' Lake said, certain that Teddy had already chatted with the CEO.

'Can you start filming ads day after tomorrow?'

'I can do anything,' Lake said, settling into the passenger's seat. It was becoming obvious who was driving the bus.

'With your approval, we'll hire an outside consulting group to front the ads and publicity. But we have better people here, and they won't cost you anything. Not that money will be a problem, you understand.'

'I think a hundred million should cover things.'

'It should. Anyway, we'll start working on the TV ads today. I think you'll like them. They're total gloom and doom – the miserable shape of our military, all sorts of threats from abroad. Armageddon, that sort of stuff. They'll scare the hell out of people. We'll plug in your name and face and a few brief words, and in no time you'll be the most famous politician in the country.'

'Fame won't win the election.'

'No, it won't. But money will. Money buys television and polls, and that's all it takes.'

'I'd like to think the message is important.'

'Oh, it is, Mr. Lake, and our message is far more important than tax cuts and affirmative action and abortion and trust and family values and all the other silliness we're hearing. Our message is life and death. Our message will change the world and protect our affluence. That's all we really care about.'

Lake was nodding his agreement. Protect the economy, keep the peace, and American voters would elect anyone. 'I have a good man to run the campaign,' Lake said, anxious to offer something.

'Who?'

'Mike Schiara, my chief of staff. He's my closest adviser, a man I trust implicitly.'

'Any experience on the national level?' Teddy asked, knowing full well there was none.

'No, but he's quite capable.'

'That's fine. It's your campaign.'

Lake smiled and nodded at the same time. That was good to hear. He was beginning to wonder.

'What about Vice President?' Teddy asked.

'I have a couple of names. Senator Nance of Michigan is an old friend. There's also Governor Guyce from Texas.'

Teddy received the names with careful deliberation. Not bad selections, really, though Guyce would never work. He was a rich boy who'd skated through college and golfed through his thirties, then spent a fortune of his father's money to purchase the governor's mansion for four years. Besides, they wouldn't have to worry about Texas.

'I like Nance,' Teddy said.

Then Nance it would be, Lake almost said.

They talked about money for an hour, the first wave from the PACs and how to accept instant millions without creating too much suspicion. Then the second wave from the defense contractors. Then the third wave of cash and other untraceables.

There'd be a fourth wave Lake would never know about. Depending on the polls, Teddy Maynard and his organization would be prepared to literally haul boxes filled with cash into union halls and black churches and white VFWs in places like Chicago and Detroit and Memphis and throughout the Deep South. Working with locals they were already identifying, they would be prepared to buy every vote they could find.

The more Teddy pondered his plan, the more convinced he became that the election would be won by Mr. Aaron Lake.

Trevor's little law office was in Neptune Beach, several blocks from Atlantic Beach, though no one could tell where one beach stopped and the other started. Jacksonville was several miles to the west and creeping toward the sea every minute. The office was a converted summer rental, and from his sagging back porch Trevor could see the beach and the ocean and hear the seagulls. Hard to believe he'd been renting the place for twelve years now.

53

Early in the lease he'd enjoyed hiding on the porch, away from the phone and the clients, staring endlessly at the gentle waters of the Atlantic two blocks away.

He was from Scranton, and like all snowbirds, he'd finally grown weary of gazing at the sea, roaming the beaches barefoot, and throwing bread crumbs to the birds. Now he preferred to waste time locked in his office.

Trevor was terrified of courtrooms and judges. While this was unusual and even somewhat honorable, it made for a different style of lawyering. It relegated Trevor to paperwork – real estate closings, wills, leases, zoning – all the mundane, nondazzling, smalltime areas of the profession no one told him about in law school. Occasionally he handled a drug case, never one involving a trial, and it was one of his unfortunate clients at Trumble who'd connected him with the Honorable Joe Roy Spicer. In short order he'd become the official attorney for all three – Spicer, Beech, and Yarber. The Brethren, as even Trevor referred to them.

He was a courier, nothing more or less. He smuggled them letters disguised as official legal documents and thus protected by the lawyer-client privilege. And he sneaked their letters out. He gave them no advice, and they sought none. He ran their bank account offshore and handled phone calls from the families of their clients inside Trumble. He fronted their dirty little deals, and in doing so avoided courtrooms and judges and other lawyers, and this suited Trevor just fine.

He was also a member of their conspiracy, easily

indictable should they ever be exposed, but he wasn't worried. The Angola scam was absolutely brilliant because its victims couldn't complain. For an easy fee with potential rewards, he'd gamble with the Brethren.

He eased from his office without seeing his secretary, then sneaked away in his restored 1970 VW Beetle, no air-conditioning. He drove down First Street toward Atlantic Boulevard, the ocean visible through homes and cottages and rentals. He wore old khakis, a white cotton shirt, a yellow bow tie, a blue seersucker jacket, all of it heavily wrinkled. He passed Pete's Bar and Grill, the oldest watering hole along the beaches and his personal favorite even though the college kids had discovered the place. He had an outstanding and very past-due bar tab there of $361, almost all for Coors longnecks and lemon daiquiris, and he really wanted to clear the debt.

He turned west on Atlantic Boulevard, and began fighting the traffic into Jacksonville. He cursed the sprawl and the congestion and the cars with Canadian plates. Then he was on the bypass, north past the airport and soon deep into the flat Florida countryside.

Fifty minutes later he parked at Trumble. You gotta love the federal system, he told himself again. Lots of parking close to the front entrance, nicely landscaped grounds tended daily by the inmates, and modern, well-kept buildings.

He said, 'Hello, Mackey,' to the white guard at the door, and 'Hello, Vince,' to the black one. Rufus at the front desk X-rayed the briefcase while

Nadine did the paperwork for his visit. 'How're the bass?' he asked Rufus.

'Ain't biting,' Rufus said.

No lawyer in the brief history of Trumble had visited as much as Trevor. They took his picture again, stamped the back of his hand with invisible ink, and led him through two doors and a short hallway. 'Hello, Link,' he said to the next guard.

'Mornin, Trevor,' Link said. Link ran the visitors' area, a large open space with lots of padded chairs and vending machines against one wall, a playground for youngsters, and a small outdoor patio where two people could sit at a picnic table and share a moment. It was cleaned and shined and completely empty. It was a weekday. Traffic picked up on Saturdays and Sundays, but for the rest of the time Link observed an empty area.

They went to the lawyers' room, one of several private cubbyholes with doors that shut and windows through which Link could do his observing, if he were so inclined. Joe Roy Spicer was waiting and reading the daily sports section where he played the odds on college basketball. Trevor and Link stepped into the room together, and very quickly Trevor removed two twenty-dollar bills and handed them to Link. The closed-circuit cameras couldn't see them if they did this just inside the door. As part of the routine, Spicer pretended not to see the transaction.

Then the briefcase was opened and Link made a pretense of looking through it. He did this without touching a thing. Trevor removed a large manila envelope which was sealed and marked in bold

'Legal Papers.' Link took it and squeezed it to make sure it held only papers and not a gun or a bottle of pills, then he gave it back. They'd done this dozens of times.

Trumble regulations required a guard to be present in the room when all papers were removed and all envelopes were opened. But the two twenties got Link outside where he posted himself at the door because there was simply nothing else to guard at the moment. He knew letters were being passed back and forth, and he didn't care. As long as Trevor didn't traffic in weapons or drugs, Link wouldn't get involved. The place had so many silly regulations anyway. He leaned on the door, with his back to it, and before long was drifting into one of his many horse naps, one leg stiff, the other bent at the knee.

In the lawyers' room, little legal work was being done. Spicer was still absorbed in point spreads. Most inmates welcomed their guests. Spicer only tolerated his.

'Got a call last night from the brother of Jeff Daggett,' Trevor said. 'The kid from Coral Gables.'

'I know him,' Spicer said, finally lowering his newspaper because money was on the horizon. 'He got twelve years in a drug conspiracy.'

'Yep. His brother says that there's this ex-federal judge inside Trumble who's looked over his papers and thinks he might be able to knock off a few years. This judge wants a fee, so Daggett calls his brother, who calls me.' Trevor removed his rumpled blue seersucker jacket and flung it on a chair. Spicer hated his bow tie.

'How much can they pay?'

'Have you guys quoted a fee?' Trevor asked.

'Beech may have, I don't know. We try to get five thousand for a two-two-five-five reduction.' Spicer said this as if he had practiced criminal law in the federal courts for years. Truth was, the only time he'd actually seen a federal courtroom was the day he was sentenced.

'I know,' Trevor said. 'I'm not sure they can pay five thousand. The kid had a public defender for a lawyer.'

'Then squeeze whatever you can, but get at least a thousand up front. He's not a bad kid.'

'You're getting soft, Joe Roy.'

'No. I'm getting meaner.'

And in fact he was. Joe Roy was the managing partner of the Brethren. Yarber and Beech had the talent and the training, but they'd been too humiliated by their fall to have any ambition. Spicer, with no training and little talent, possessed enough manipulative skills to keep his colleagues on track. While they brooded, he dreamed of his comeback.

Joe Roy opened a file and withdrew a check. 'Here's a thousand bucks to deposit. Came from a pen pal in Texas named Curtis.'

'What's his potential?'

'Very good, I think. We're ready to bust Quince in Iowa.' Joe Roy withdrew a pretty lavender envelope, tightly sealed and addressed to Quince Garbe in Bakers, Iowa.

'How much?' Trevor asked, taking the envelope.

'A hundred thousand.'

'Wow.'

'He's got it, and he'll pay it. I've given him the wiring instructions. Alert the bank.'

In twenty-three years of practicing law, Trevor had never earned a fee anywhere close to $33,000. Suddenly, he could see it, touch it, and, though he tried not to, he began spending it – $33,000 for doing nothing but shuttling mail.

'You really think this will work?' he asked, mentally paying off the tab at Pete's Bar and telling MasterCard to take this check and shove it. He'd keep the same car, his beloved Beetle, but he might spring for an air conditioner.

'Of course it will,' Spicer said, without a trace of doubt.

He had two more letters, both written by Justice Yarber posing as young Percy in rehab. Trevor took them with anticipation.

'Arkansas is at Kentucky tonight,' Spicer said, returning to his newspaper. 'The line is fourteen. Whatta you think?'

'Much closer than that. Kentucky is very tough at home.'

'Are you in?'

'Are you?'

Trevor had a bookie at Pete's Bar, and though he gambled little he had learned to follow the lead of Justice Spicer.

'I'll put a hundred on Arkansas,' Spicer said.

'I think I will too.'

They played blackjack for half an hour, with Link occasionally glancing in and frowning his disapproval. Cards were prohibited during visitation, but who cared? Joe Roy played the game hard because he was training for his next career. Poker and gin rummy were the favorites in the rec room, and Spicer often had trouble finding a blackjack opponent.

Trevor wasn't particularly good, but he was always willing to play. It was, in Spicer's opinion, his only redeeming quality.

FIVE

The announcement had the festive air of a victory party, with red, white, and blue banners and bunting draped from the ceiling and parade music blasting through the hangar. Every D-L Trilling employee was required to be present, all four thousand of them, and to heighten their spirits they had been promised a full day of extra vacation. Eight hours paid, at an average wage of $22.40, but management didn't care because they had found their man. The hastily built stage was also covered in banners and packed with every suit in the company, all smiling broadly and clapping wildly as the music whipped the crowd into a frenzy. Three days earlier no one had heard of Aaron Lake. Now he was their savior.

He certainly looked like a candidate, with a new slightly trimmer haircut suggested by one consultant and a dark brown suit suggested by another. Only Reagan had been able to wear brown suits, and he'd won two landslides.

When Lake finally appeared, and strode purposefully across the stage, shaking vigorously the hands of corporate honchos he'd never see again, the laborers went wild. The music was carefully ratcheted up a couple of notches by a sound consultant who was a member of a sound team Lake's people had hired for $24,000 for the event. Money was of little concern.

Balloons fell like manna. Some were popped by workers who'd been asked to pop them, so for a few seconds the hangar sounded like the first wave of a ground attack. Get ready for it. Get ready for war. Lake Before It's Too Late.

The Trilling CEO clutched him as if they were fraternity brothers, when in fact they'd met two hours earlier. The CEO then took the podium and waited for the noise to subside. Working with notes he'd been faxed the day before, he began a long-winded and quite generous introduction of Aaron Lake, future President. On cue, the applause interrupted him five times before he finished.

Lake waved like a conquering hero and waited behind the microphone, then with perfect timing stepped forward and said, 'My name is Aaron Lake, and I am now running for President.' More roaring applause. More piped-in parade music. More balloons drifting downward.

When he'd had enough, he launched into his speech. The theme, the platform, the only reason for running was national security, and Lake hammered out the appalling statistics proving just how thoroughly the current Administration had depleted our military. No other issues were really that important, he said bluntly. Lure us into a war we can't win, and we'll forget about the tired old quarrels over abortion, race, guns, affirmative action, taxes. Concerned about family values? Start losing our sons and daughters in combat and you'd see some families with real problems.

Lake was very good. The speech had been written by him, edited by consultants, polished by other professionals, and the night before he'd delivered it to Teddy Maynard, alone, deep inside Langley. Teddy had approved, with minor changes.

Teddy was tucked under his quilts and watching the show with great pride. York was with him, silent as usual. The two often sat alone, staring at screens, watching the world grow more dangerous.

'He's good,' York said quietly at one point.

Teddy nodded, even managing a slight smile.

Halfway through his speech, Lake became wonderfully angry at the Chinese. 'Over a twenty-year period, we allowed them to steal forty percent of our nuclear secrets!' he said, and the laborers hissed.

'Forty percent!' he shouted.

It was closer to fifty, but Teddy chose to downplay it just a little. The CIA had received its share of blame for the Chinese thievery.

For five minutes Aaron Lake blistered the Chinese, and their looting and their unprecedented military buildup. The strategy was Teddy's. Use the Chinese to scare the American voters, not the Russians. Don't tip them. Protect the real threat until later in the campaign.

Lake's timing was near-perfect. His punch line brought down the house. When he promised to double the defense budget in the first four years of his Administration, the four thousand D-L Trilling employees who built military helicopters exploded in a frenzy.

Teddy watched it quietly, very proud of his creation. They had managed to upstage the spectacle in New Hampshire by simply snubbing it. Lake's name had not been on the ballot, and he was the first candidate in decades to be proud of that fact. 'Who needs New Hampshire?' he'd been quoted as saying. 'I'll take the rest of the country.'

Lake signed off amid thunderous applause, and reshook all the hands on the stage. CNN returned to its studio where the talking heads would spend fifteen minutes telling the viewers what they had just witnessed.

On his table, Teddy pushed buttons and the screen changed. 'Here's the finished product,' he said. 'The first installment.'

It was a television ad for candidate Lake, and it began with a brief glimpse of a row of grim Chinese generals standing rigidly at a military parade, watching massive hardware roll by. 'You think the world's a safer place?' a deep, rich ominous voice asked off-camera. Then, glimpses of the world's current madmen, all watching their armies parade by – Hussein, Qaddafi, Milosevic, Kim in North Korea. Even poor Castro, with the last of his ragtag army lumbering through Havana, got a split second of airtime. 'Our military could not now do what it did in 1991 during the Gulf War,' the voice said as gravely as if another war had already been declared. Then a blast, an atomic mushroom, followed by thousands of Indians dancing in the streets. Another blast, and the Pakistanis were dancing next door.

'China wants to invade Taiwan,' the voice continued as a million Chinese soldiers marched in perfect step. 'North Korea wants South Korea,' the voice said, as tanks rolled through the DMZ. 'And the United States is always an easy target.'

The voice changed quickly into one with a high pitch, and the ad shifted to a congressional hearing of some sort, with a heavily bemedaled general lecturing some subcommittee. 'You, the Congress,' he was saying, 'spend less on the military each year. This defense budget is smaller than it was fifteen years ago. You expect us to be ready for war in Korea, the Middle East, and now Eastern Europe, yet our budget keeps shrinking. The situation is critical.' The ad went blank, nothing but a dark screen, then the first voice said, 'Twelve years ago there were two superpowers. Now there are none.' The handsome face of Aaron Lake appeared, and the ad finished with the voice saying, 'Lake, Before It's Too Late.'

'I'm not sure I like it,' York said after a pause.

'Why not?'

'It's so negative.'

'Good. Makes you feel uncomfortable, doesn't it?'

'Very much so.'

'Good. We're going to flood television for a week, and I suspect Lake's soft numbers will get even softer. The ads will make people squirm, and they won't like them.'

York knew what was coming. The people would indeed squirm and dislike the ads, then get the hell

65

scared out of them, and Lake would suddenly become a visionary. Teddy was working on the terror.

There were two TV rooms on each wing at Trumble; two small bare rooms where you could smoke and watch whatever the guards wanted you to watch. No remote – they'd tried that at first but it had caused too much trouble. By far the nastiest disagreements occurred when the boys couldn't agree on what to watch. So the guards made the selections.

Rules prohibited inmates from having their own TVs.

The guard on duty happened to like basketball. There was a college game on ESPN, and the room was packed with inmates. Hatlee Beech hated sports, and he sat alone in the other TV room and watched one banal sitcom after another. When he was on the bench and working twelve hours a day, he had never watched television. Who had the time? He'd had an office in his home where he dictated opinions until late while everyone else was glued to prime time. Now, watching the mindless crap, he realized how lucky he'd been. In so many ways.

He lit a cigarette. He hadn't smoked since college, and for the first two months at Trumble he'd resisted the temptation. Now it helped with the boredom, but only a pack a day. His blood pressure was up and down. Heart disease ran in the family. At fifty-six with nine years to go, he would leave in a box, he was certain.

Three years, one month, one week, and Beech

was still counting the days in as opposed to the days to go. Just four years ago he'd been building his reputation as a tough young federal judge who was going places. Four rotten years. When he traveled from one courthouse to the next in East Texas, he did so with a driver, a secretary, a clerk, and a U.S. Marshal. When he walked into a courtroom people stood out of respect. Lawyers gave him high marks for his fairness and hard work. His wife had been an unpleasant woman, but with her family's oil trust he'd managed to live peacefully with her. The marriage was stable, not exactly warm, but with three fine kids in college they had reason to be proud. They had weathered some rough times and were determined to grow old together. She had the money. He had the status. Together they'd raised a family. Where was there to go?

Certainly not to prison.

Four miserable years.

The drinking came from nowhere. Maybe it was pressure from work, maybe it was to escape his wife's bickering. For years, after law school, he'd been a light social drinker, nothing serious. Certainly not a habit. Once when the kids were small, his wife took them to Italy for two weeks. Beech was left alone, which suited him fine. For some reason he could never determine, or remember, he turned to bourbon. Lots of it, and he never stopped. The bourbon became important. He kept it in his study and sneaked it late at night. They had separate beds so he seldom got caught.

The trip to Yellowstone had been a three-day judicial conference. He'd met the young lady in a bar in Jackson Hole. After hours of drinking they made the sad decision to take a ride. While Hatlee drove she took off her clothes, but for no other reason than to just do it. Sex had not been discussed, and at that point he was completely harmless.

The two hikers were from D.C., just college kids returning from the trails. Both died at the scene, slaughtered on the shoulder of a narrow road by a drunken driver who never saw them. The young lady's car was found in a ditch with Beech hugging the steering wheel, unable to remove himself. She was naked and knocked out.

He remembered nothing. When he awoke hours later he saw for the first time the inside of a cell. 'Better get used to it,' the sheriff had said with a sneer.

Beech called in every favor and pulled every string imaginable, all to no avail. Two young people were dead. He'd been caught with a naked woman. His wife had the oil money so his friends ran like scared dogs. In the end, no one stood up for the Honorable Hatlee Beech.

He was lucky to get twelve years. MADD mothers and SADD students protested outside the courthouse when he made his first official appearance. They wanted a life sentence. Life!

He himself, the Honorable Hatlee Beech, was charged with two counts of manslaughter, and there was no defense. There was enough alcohol in his blood to kill the next guy. A witness said he'd been speeding on the wrong side of the road.

Looking back, he'd been lucky his crime was on federal lands. Otherwise he would have been shipped away to some state pen where things were much tougher. Say what you want, but the feds knew how to run a prison.

He smoked alone in the semidarkness, watching prime-time comedy written by twelve-year-olds, and there was a political ad, one of many those days. It was one Beech had never seen, a menacing little segment with a somber voice predicting doom if we didn't hurry and build more bombs. It was very well done, ran for a minute and a half, cost a bundle, and delivered a message no one wanted to hear. Lake Before It's Too Late.

Who the hell's Aaron Lake?

Beech knew his politics. It had been his passion in another life, and at Trumble he was known as a fellow who watched Washington. He was one of the few who cared what happened there.

Aaron Lake? Beech had missed the guy. What an odd strategy, to enter the race as an unknown after New Hampshire. Never a shortage of clowns who want to be President.

Beech's wife kicked him out before he pled guilty to two counts of manslaughter. Quite naturally, she was angrier over the naked woman than the dead hikers. The kids sided with her because she had the money and because he'd screwed up so badly. It was an easy decision on their part. The divorce was final a week after he arrived at Trumble.

His youngest had been to see him twice in three years, one month, and one week. Both visits were on the sly, lest the mother find out about them. She had prohibited the kids from going to Trumble.

Then he got sued, two wrongful death cases brought by the families. With no friends willing to step forward, he'd tried to defend himself from prison. But there wasn't much to defend. A judgment of $5 million had been entered against him by the trial court. He appealed from Trumble, lost from Trumble, and appealed again.

In the chair beside him, next to his cigarettes, was an envelope brought earlier by Trevor, the lawyer. The court had rejected his final appeal. The judgment was now written in stone.

Didn't really matter, because he'd also filed for bankruptcy. He'd typed the papers himself in the law library and filed them with a pauper's oath, sent them to the same courthouse in Texas where he was once a god.

Convicted, divorced, disbarred, imprisoned, sued, bankrupt.

Most of the losers at Trumble handled their time because their falls had been so short. Most were repeat offenders who'd blown third and fourth chances. Most liked the damned place because it was better than any other prison they'd visited.

But Beech had lost so much, had fallen so far. Just four years ago he'd had a wife with millions and three kids who loved him and a big home in a small town. He was a federal judge, appointed by the President for life, making $140,000 a year, which was a lot less than her oil royalties but still not a bad salary. He got himself called to Washington twice a year for meetings at Justice. Beech had been important.

An old lawyer friend had been to see him twice,

on his way to Miami where he had kids, and he stayed long enough to deliver the gossip. Most of it was worthless, but there was a strong rumor that the ex-Mrs. Beech was now seeing someone else. With a few million bucks and slender hips it was only a matter of time.

Another ad. Lake Before It's Too Late again. This one began with a grainy video of men with guns slithering through the desert, dodging and shooting and undergoing some type of training. Then the sinister face of a terrorist – dark eyes and hair and features, obviously some manner of Islamic radical – and he said in Arabic with English subtitles, 'We will kill Americans wherever we find them. We will die in our holy war against the great Satan.' After that, quick videos of burning buildings. Embassy bombings. A busload of tourists. The remains of a jetliner scattered through a pasture.

A handsome face appeared, Mr. Aaron Lake himself. He looked directly at Hatlee Beech and said, 'I'm Aaron Lake, and you probably don't know me. I'm running for President because I'm scared. Scared of China and Eastern Europe and the Middle East. Scared of a dangerous world. Scared of what's happened to our military. Last year the federal government had a huge surplus, yet spent less on defense than we did fifteen years ago. We're complacent because our economy is strong, but the world today is far more dangerous than we realize. Our enemies are legion, and we cannot protect ourselves. If elected, I will double defense spending during my term of office.'

No smiles, no warmth. Just plain talk from a

71

man who meant what he said. A voice over said, 'Lake, Before It's Too Late.'

Not bad, thought Beech.

He lit another cigarette, his last of the night, and stared at the envelope on the empty chair – $5 million lodged against him by the two families. He'd pay the money if he could. Never saw the kids, not before he killed them. The paper the next day had their happy photos, a boy and a girl. Just college kids, enjoying the summer.

He missed the bourbon.

He could bankrupt half the judgment. The other half was for punitive damages, nonbankruptable. So it would follow wherever he went, which he assumed was nowhere. He'd be sixty-five when his sentence was over, but he'd be dead before then. They'd carry him out of Trumble in a box, send him home to Texas, where they'd bury him behind the little country church where he'd been baptized. Maybe one of the kids would spring for a headstone.

Beech left the room without turning off the TV. It was almost ten, time for lights-out. He bunked with Robbie, a kid from Kentucky who'd broken into 240 houses before they caught him. He sold the guns and microwaves and stereos for cocaine. Robbie was a four-year veteran of Trumble, and because of his seniority he had chosen the bottom bunk. Beech crawled into the top one, said, 'Good night, Robbie,' and turned off the light.

'Night, Hatlee,' came the soft response.

Sometimes they chatted in the dark. The walls were cinderblock, the door was metal, their words were confined to their little room. Robbie was twenty-five and would be forty-five before he left Trumble. Twenty-four years – one for every ten houses.

The time between bed and sleep was the worst of the day. The past came back with a vengeance – the mistakes, the misery, the could-haves and should-haves. Try as he might, Hatlee could not simply close his eyes and go to sleep. He had to punish himself first. There was a grandchild he'd never seen, and he always started with her. Then his three kids. Forget the wife. But he always thought about her money. And the friends. Ah, the friends. Where were they now?

Three years in, and with no future there was only the past. Even poor Robbie below dreamed of a new beginning at the age of forty-five. Not Beech. At times he almost longed for the warm Texas soil, layered upon his body, behind the little church.

Surely someone would buy him a headstone.

SIX

For Quince Garbe, February 3 would be the worst day of his life. It was almost the last, and it would've been had his doctor been in town. He couldn't get a prescription for sleeping pills, and he didn't have the courage to use a gun on himself.

It began pleasantly enough with a late breakfast, a bowl of oatmeal by the fire in the den, alone. His wife of twenty-six years had already left for town, for another day of charity teas and fund-raising and frantic small-town volunteerism that kept her busy and away from him.

It was snowing when he left their large and pretentious banker's home on the edge of Bakers, Iowa, and drove ten minutes to work in his long black Mercedes, eleven years old. He was an important man about town, a Garbe, a member of a family that had owned the bank for generations. He parked in his reserved spot behind the bank, which faced Main Street, and made a quick detour to the post office, something he did twice a week. For years he'd had a private box there, away from his wife and especially away from his secretary.

Because he was rich and few others were in

Bakers, Iowa, he seldom spoke to people on the street. He didn't care what they thought. They worshiped his father and that was enough to keep their business.

But when the old man died, would he have to change his personality? Would he be forced to smile on the sidewalks of Bakers and join the Rotary Club, the one founded by his grandfather?

Quince was tired of being dependent on the whims of the public for his security. He was tired of relying on his father to keep their customers happy. He was tired of banking and tired of Iowa and tired of snow and tired of his wife, and what Quince wanted more than anything that morning in February was a letter from his beloved Ricky. A nice, brief little note confirming their rendezvous.

What Quince really wanted was three warm days on a love boat with Ricky. He might never come back.

Bakers had eighteen thousand people, so the central post office on Main was usually busy. And there was always a different clerk behind the counter. That's how he'd rented the box – he'd waited until a new postal worker was on duty. CMT Investments was the official lessee. He went straight to the box, around a corner to a wall with a hundred others.

There were three letters, and as he snatched them and stuffed them in his coat pocket his heart froze as he saw that one was from Ricky. He hurried onto Main, and minutes later entered his bank, at exactly 10 A.M. His father had been there for four hours, but they had long since stopped bickering over Quince's work schedule. As always, he stopped at his secretary's desk to hurriedly remove his gloves as if important matters were waiting. She handed him his mail, his two phone messages, and reminded him that he had lunch in two hours with a local real estate agent.

He locked his door behind him, flung his gloves one way and his coat the other, and ripped open the letter from Ricky. He sat on his sofa and put on his reading glasses, breathing heavily not from the walk but from anticipation. He was on the verge of arousal when he started reading.

The words hit like bullets. After the second paragraph, he emitted a strange, painful 'Awwww.' Then a couple of 'Oh my gods.' Then a low, hissing 'Sonofabitch.'

Quiet, he told himself, the secretary is always listening. The first reading brought shock, the second disbelief. Reality began settling in with the third reading, and Quince's lip started to quiver. Don't cry, dammit, he told himself.

He threw the letter on the floor and paced around his desk, ignoring as best he could the cheerful faces of his wife and children. Twenty years' worth of class photos and family portraits were lined along his credenza, just under the window. He looked out and watched the snow, now heavier and accumulating on the sidewalks. God how he hated Bakers, Iowa. He'd thought he might leave and escape to the beach, where he could frolic with a handsome young pal and maybe never come home.

Now he would leave under different circumstances.

It was a joke, a hoax, he told himself, but he

instantly knew better. The scam was too tight. The punch line was too perfect. He'd been set up by a professional.

All his life he'd fought his desires. Somehow he'd finally found the nerve to crack the closet door, and now he got shot between the eyes by a con man. Stupid, stupid, stupid. How could this be so difficult?

Random thoughts hit from every direction as he watched the snow. Suicide was the easy answer, but his doctor was gone and he really didn't want to die. At least not at the moment. He wasn't sure where he'd find a hundred thousand bucks he could send off without raising suspicions. The old bastard next door paid him a pittance and kept his thumb on every dime. His wife insisted on balancing their checkbook.There was some money in mutuals, but he couldn't move it without her knowing. The life of a rich banker in Bakers, Iowa, meant a title and a Mercedes and a large mortgaged house and a wife with social activities. Oh how he wanted to escape!

He'd go to Florida anyway, and track the letter somehow, and confront this con man, expose his extortion attempt, find some justice. He, Quince Garbe, had done nothing wrong. Surely a crime was being perpetrated here. Perhaps he could hire an investigator, and maybe a lawyer, and they'd protect him. They'd get to the bottom of this scam.

Even if he found the money, and wired it as instructed, the gate would be opened and Ricky, whoever in hell Ricky was, might want more. What would stop Ricky from extorting again, and again?

If he had guts he'd run off anyway, run to Key

West or some hot spot where it never snowed and live any damn way he wanted to live, and let the pitiful little people of Bakers, Iowa, gossip about him for the next half-century. But he didn't have the guts, and that's what made Quince so sad.

His children were staring at him, freckled smiles with teeth wrapped in silver braces. His heart sank, and he knew he'd find the money and wire it precisely as directed. He had to protect them. They had done nothing wrong.

The bank's stock was worth about $10 million, all of it still tightly controlled by the old man, who at the moment was barking in the hallway. The old man was eighty-one, very much alive but still eighty-one. When he was gone, Quince would have to contend with a sister in Chicago, but the bank would be his. He'd sell the damned thing as fast as he could and leave Bakers with a few million in his pocket. Until then, though, he'd be forced to do what he'd always done, keep the old man content.

Quince's getting yanked out of the closet by some con man would devastate his father, and pretty much take care of the stock. Sister in Chicago would get all of it.

When the barking stopped outside, he eased through the door and passed his secretary for a cup of coffee. He ignored her as he returned to his room, locked his door, read the letter for the fourth time, and collected his thoughts. He'd find the money, and he'd wire it just as instructed, and he'd hope and pray with a fury that Ricky would go away. If not, if he came back for more, Quince would call his doctor and get some pills.

The real estate agent he was meeting for lunch was a high-roller who took chances and cut corners, probably a crook. Quince began to make plans. The two of them would arrange a few shady loans; overappraise some land, lend the money, sell to a strawman, etc. He would know how to do it.

Quince would find the money.

The Lake campaign's doomsday ads landed with a thud, at least in public opinion. Massive polling through the first week showed a dramatic increase in name recognition, from 2 to 20 percent, but the ads were universally disliked. They were frightening and people just didn't want to think about wars and terrorism and old nukes getting hauled across mountains in the dark. People saw the ads (they were impossible to miss), and they heard the message, but most voters simply didn't want to be bothered. They were too busy making money and spending it. When issues were confronted in the midst of a roaring economy, they were limited to the old standbys of family values and tax cuts.

Candidate Lake's early interviewers treated him as just another flake until he announced, live on the air, that his campaign had received in excess of $11 million in less than a week.

'We expect to have twenty million in two weeks,' he said without boasting, and real news started to happen. Teddy Maynard had assured him the money would be there.

Twenty million in two weeks had never been done before, and by the end of that day Washington was consumed with the story. The frenzy reached its peak when Lake was interviewed, live yet again, by two of the three networks on the evening news. He looked great; big smile, smooth words, nice suit and hair. The man was electable.

Final confirmation that Aaron Lake was a serious candidate came late in the day, when one of his opponents took a shot at him. Senator Britt of Maryland had been running for a year and had finished a strong second in New Hampshire. He'd raised $9 million, spent a lot more than that, and was forced to waste half of his time soliciting money rather than campaigning. He was tired of begging, tired of cutting staff, tired of worrying about TV ads, and when a reporter asked him about Lake and his $20 million Britt shot back, 'It's dirty money. No honest candidate can raise that much that fast.' Britt was shaking hands in the rain at the entrance to a chemical plant in Michigan.

The dirty money comment was seized with great gusto by the press and soon splattered all over the place.

Aaron Lake had arrived.

Senator Britt of Maryland had other problems, though he'd tried to forget them.

Nine years earlier he'd toured Southeast Asia to find some facts. As always, he and his colleagues from the Congress flew first class, stayed in nice hotels, and ate lobster, all in an effort to study poverty in the region and to get to the bottom of the raging controversy brought about by Nike and its use of cheap foreign labor. Early in the journey, Britt met a girl in Bangkok, and, feigning illness,

80

decided to stay behind while his buddies continued their fact-finding into Laos and Vietnam.

Her name was Payka, and she was not a prostitute. She was a twenty-year-old secretary in the U.S. embassy in Bangkok, and because she was on his country's payroll Britt felt a slight proprietary interest. He was far away from Maryland, from his wife and five kids and his constituents. Payka was stunning and shapely, and anxious to study in the United States.

What began as a fling quickly turned into a romance, and Senator Britt had to force himself to return to Washington. Two months later he was back in Bangkok on, as he told his wife, pressing but secret business.

In nine months he made four trips to Thailand, all first class, all at taxpayer expense, and even the globe-trotters in the Senate were beginning to whisper. Britt pulled strings with the State Department and Payka appeared to be headed for the United States.

She never made it. During the fourth and final rendezvous, Payka confessed that she was pregnant. She was Catholic and abortion was not an option. Britt stiff-armed her, said he needed time to think, then fled Bangkok in the middle of the night. The fact-finding was over.

Early in his Senate career, Britt, a fiscal hardliner, had grabbed a headline or two by criticizing CIA wastefulness. Teddy Maynard said not a word, but certainly didn't appreciate the grandstanding. The rather thin file on Senator Britt was dusted off and given priority, and when he went to Bangkok for the second time the CIA went with him. Of course he didn't know it, but they sat near him on the flight, first class also, and they had people on the ground in Bangkok. They watched the hotel where the two lovebirds spent three days. They took pictures of them eating in fine restaurants. They saw everything. Britt was oblivious and stupid.

Later, when the child was born, the CIA obtained the hospital records, then the medical records to link the blood and DNA. Payka kept her job at the embassy, so she was easy to find.

When the child was a year old, he was photographed sitting on Payka's knee in a downtown park. More photos followed, and by the time he was four he was beginning to remotely favor Senator Dan Britt of Maryland.

His daddy was long gone. Britt's zeal for finding facts in Southeast Asia had faded dramatically, and he'd turned his attention to other critical areas of the world. In due course he was seized with presidential ambitions, the old senatorial affliction that sooner or later gets them all. He'd never heard from Payka, and that nightmare had been easy to forget.

Britt had five legitimate children, and a wife with a big mouth. They were a team, Senator and Mrs. Britt, both leading the juggernaut of family values and 'We've Got to Save Our Kids!' Together they wrote a book on how to raise children in a sick American culture, though their oldest was only thirteen. When the President was embarrassed by sexual misadventures, Senator Britt became the biggest virgin in Washington.

He and his wife struck a nerve, and the money

rolled in from conservatives. He did well in the Iowa caucuses, ran a close second in New Hampshire, but was running out of money and sinking in the polls.

He would sink even more. After a brutal day of campaigning, his entourage settled into a motel in Dearborn, Michigan, for a short night. It was there that the senator finally came face to face with child number six, though not in person.

The agent's name was McCord, and he'd been following Britt with phony press credentials for a week. He said he worked for a newspaper in Tallahassee, but in fact he'd been a CIA agent for eleven years. There were so many reporters swarming around Britt that no one thought to check.

McCord befriended a senior aide, and over a late drink in the Holiday Inn bar he confessed that he had something in his possession that would destroy candidate Britt. He said it was given to him by a rival camp, Governor Tarry's. It was a notebook, with a bomb on every page: an affidavit from Payka setting forth the broad details of their affair; two photos of the child, the last of which had been taken a month earlier and the child, now seven, looking more and more like his dad; blood and DNA summaries indelibly linking father and son; and travel records which showed in black and white that Senator Britt had burned $38,600 in taxpayers' money to carry on his affair on the other side of the world.

The deal was simple and straightforward: Withdraw from the race immediately, and the story would never be told. McCord, the journalist, was ethical and didn't have the stomach for such trash. Governor Tarry would keep it quiet if Britt disappeared. Quit, and not even Mrs. Britt would know.

Shortly after 1 A.M., in Washington, Teddy Maynard took the call from McCord. The package had been delivered. Britt was planning a press conference for noon the next day.

Teddy had dirt files on hundreds of politicians, past and present. As a group they were an easy bunch to trap. Place a beautiful young woman in their path, and you generally gathered something for the file. If women didn't work, money always did. Watch them travel, watch them crawl in bed with the lobbyists, watch them pander to any foreign government smart enough to send lots of cash to Washington, watch them set up their campaigns and committees to raise funds. Just watch them, and the files always grew thicker. He wished the Russians were so easy.

Though he despised politicians as a group, he did respect a handful of them. Aaron Lake was one. He'd never chased women, never drank much or picked up habits, never seemed preoccupied with cash, never had been inclined to grandstand. The more he watched Lake, the more he liked him.

He took his last pill of the night and rolled himself to bed. So Britt was gone. Good riddance. Too bad he couldn't leak the story anyway. The pious hypocrite deserved a good thrashing. Save it, he told himself. And use it again. President Lake might need Britt one day, and that little boy over in Thailand might come in handy.

SEVEN

Picasso was suing Sherlock and other unnamed defendants for injunctive relief in an effort to stop them from urinating on his roses. A little misdirected urine was not going to upset the balance of life at Trumble, but Picasso also wanted damages in the amount of five hundred dollars. Five hundred dollars was a serious matter.

The dispute had been festering since the past summer, when Picasso caught Sherlock in the act, and the assistant warden had finally intervened. He asked the Brethren to settle the matter. Suit was filed, then Sherlock hired an ex-lawyer named Ratliff, yet another tax evader, to stall, delay, postpone, and file frivolous pleadings, the usual routine for those practicing the art of law on the outside. But Ratliff's tactics didn't sit well with the Brethren, and neither Sherlock nor his lawyer was held in high esteem by the panel.

Picasso's rose garden was a carefully tended patch of dirt next to the gym. It had taken him three years of bureaucratic wars to convince some mid-level paper-pusher in Washington that such a hobby was and always had been therapeutic, since

Picasso suffered from several disorders. Once the garden was approved, the warden quickly signed off, and Picasso dug in with both hands. He got his roses from a supplier in Jacksonville, which in itself took another box of paperwork.

His real job was that of a dishwasher in the cafeteria, for which he earned thirty cents an hour. The warden refused his request to be classified as a gardener, so the roses were deemed a hobby. During the season, Picasso could be seen early and late in his little patch, on all fours, tilling and digging and watering. He even talked to his flowers.

The roses in question were Belinda's Dream, a pale pink rose, not particularly beautiful, but loved by Picasso nonetheless. When they arrived from the supplier everybody at Trumble knew that the Belindas were there. He lovingly planted them in the front and center of his garden.

Sherlock began urinating on them just for the sheer hell of it. He wasn't fond of Picasso anyway because he was a notorious liar, and peeing on the man's roses just seemed appropriate for some reason. Others caught on. Sherlock encouraged them by assuring that they were in fact helping the roses by adding fertilizer.

The Belindas lost their pinkness and began to fade, and Picasso was horrified. An informant left a note under his door, and the secret was out. His beloved garden had become a favorite watering hole. Two days later, he ambushed Sherlock, caught him in the act, and the two chubby middle-aged white men had an ugly wrestling match on the sidewalk.

The plants turned a dull yellow, and Picasso filed suit.

When it finally reached trial, after months of delays by Ratliff, the Brethren were already tired of it. They had quietly preassigned the case to Justice Finn Yarber, whose mother had once raised roses, and after a few hours of research he had informed the other two that urine would, in fact, not change the color of the plants. So two days before the hearing they reached their decision: They would grant the injunction to keep Sherlock and the other pigs from spraying Picasso's roses, but they would not award damages.

For three hours they listened to grown men bicker about who peed where and when, and how often. At times, Picasso, acting as his own attorney, was near tears as he begged his witnesses to squeal on their friends. Ratliff, counsel for the defense, was cruel and abrasive and redundant, and after an hour it was obvious he deserved his disbarment, whatever his crimes may have been.

Justice Spicer passed the time by studying the point spreads on college basketball games. When he couldn't contact Trevor he placed make-believe bets, every game. He was up $3,600 in two months, on paper. He was on a roll, winning at cards, winning at sports, and he had trouble sleeping at night dreaming about his next life, in Vegas or in the Bahamas, doing it as a pro. With or without his wife.

Justice Beech frowned with deep judicial deliberation and appeared to be taking exhaustive notes, when in fact he was drafting another letter to Curtis in Dallas. The Brethren had decided to bait him again. Writing as Ricky, Beech explained that a cruel guard at the rehab unit was threatening all sorts of vile physical attacks unless Ricky could produce some 'protection money.' Ricky needed $5,000 to secure his safety from the beast, and could Curtis lend it to him?

'Could we move this along?' Beech said loudly, interrupting ex-lawyer Ratliff once again. When he was a real judge, Beech had mastered the practice of reading magazines while half-listening to lawyers drone on before juries. A blaring and well-timed admonition from the bench kept everyone sharp.

He wrote: 'It is such a vicious game they play here. We arrive broken into tiny pieces. Slowly, they clean us up, dry us out, put us back together, piece by piece. They clear our heads, teach us discipline and confidence, and prepare us for our return to society. They do a good job of this, yet they allow these ignorant thugs who guard the grounds to threaten us, fragile as we still are, and in doing so break down what we've worked so hard to produce. I am so scared of this man. I hide in my room when I'm supposed to be tanning and lifting weights. I cannot sleep. I long for booze and drugs as a means of escape. Please, Curtis, loan me the $5,000 so I can buy this guy off, so I can complete my rehab and leave here in one piece. When we meet, I want to be healthy and in great shape.'

What would his friends think? The Honorable Hatlee Beech, federal judge, writing prose like a faggot, extorting money out of innocent people.

He had no friends. He had no rules. The law he

once worshiped had placed him where he was, which, at the moment, was in a prison cafeteria wearing a faded green choir robe from a black church, listening to a bunch of angry convicts argue over urine.

'You've already asked that question eight times,' he barked at Ratliff, who'd obviously been watching too many bad lawyer shows on television.

Since the case was Justice Yarber's, he was expected to at least appear as if he were paying attention. He was not, nor was he concerned about appearances. As usual, he was naked under his robe, and he sat with his legs crossed wide, cleaning his long toenails with a plastic fork.

'You think they'd turn brown if I crapped on them?' Sherlock yelled at Picasso, and the cafeteria erupted with laughter.

'Language, please,' Justice Beech admonished.

'Order in the court,' said T. Karl, the court jester, under his bright gray wig. It was not his role in the courtroom to demand order, but it was something he did well and the Brethren let it slide. He rapped his gavel, said, 'Order, gentlemen.'

Beech wrote: 'Please help me, Curtis. I have no one else to turn to. I'm breaking again. I fear another collapse. I fear I will never leave this place. Hurry.'

Spicer put a hundred dollars on Indiana over Purdue, Duke over Clemson, Alabama over Vandy, Wisconsin over Illinois. What did he know about Wisconsin basketball? he asked himself. Didn't matter. He was a professional gambler, and a damned good one. If the $90,000 was still buried behind the toolshed he'd parlay it into a million within a year.

'That's enough,' Beech said, holding up his hands.

'I've heard enough too,' Yarber said, forgetting his toenails and leaning on the table.

The Brethren huddled and deliberated as if the outcome might set a serious precedent, or at least have some profound impact on the future of American jurisprudence. They frowned and scratched their heads and appeared to even argue over the merits of the case. Meanwhile, poor Picasso sat by himself, ready to cry, thoroughly exhausted by Ratliff's tactics.

Justice Yarber cleared his throat and said, 'By a vote of two to one, we have reached a decision. We are issuing an injunction against all inmates urinating on the damned roses. Anyone caught doing so will be fined fifty dollars. No damages will be assessed at this time.'

With perfect timing T. Karl slammed his gavel and yelled, 'Court's adjourned until further notice. All rise.'

Of course, no one moved.

'I want to appeal,' Picasso yelled.

'So do I,' said Sherlock.

'Must be a good decision,' Yarber said, collecting his robe and standing. 'Both sides are unhappy.'

Beech and Spicer stood too, and the Brethren paraded out of the cafeteria. A guard walked into the middle of the litigants and witnesses and said, 'Court's over, boys. Get back to work.'

★

The CEO of Hummand, a company in Seattle which made missiles and radar-jamming machinery, had once been a congressman who'd been quite close to the CIA. Teddy Maynard knew him well. When the CEO announced at a press conference that his company had raised $5 million for the Lake campaign, CNN interrupted a liposuction segment to carry the story Live! Five thousand Hummand workers had written checks for $1,000 each, the maximum allowed under federal law. The CEO had the checks in a box that he showed to the cameras, then he flew with them on a Hummand jet to Washington, where he took them to the Lake headquarters.

Follow the money, and you'll find your winner. Since Lake's announcement, over eleven thousand defense and aerospace workers from thirty states had contributed just over $8 million. The Postal Service was delivering their checks in boxes. Their unions had sent almost that much, with another $2 million promised. Lake's people hired a D.C. accounting firm just to process and count the money.

The Hummand CEO arrived in Washington amid as much fanfare as could be generated. Candidate Lake was on another private jet, a Challenger freshly leased at $400,000 a month. When he landed in Detroit he was met by two black Suburbans, both brand new, both just leased at $1,000 a month each. Lake now had an escort, a group of people moving in sync with him wherever he went, and though he was certain he'd soon get used to it, it was unnerving at first. Strangers around him all the time. Grave young men in dark suits with little microphones in their ears, guns strapped to their bodies. Two Secret Service agents were on the flight with him, and three more waited with the Suburbans.

And he had Floyd from his congressional office. Floyd was a dull-witted young man from a prominent family back in Arizona who was good for nothing but running errands. Now Floyd was a driver. Floyd took the wheel of one Suburban, Lake in the front seat, two agents and a secretary sitting behind. Two aides and three agents piled into the other, and away they went, headed for downtown Detroit where serious local TV journalists were waiting.

Lake had no time for stumping or walking neighborhoods or eating catfish or standing in the rain outside busy factories. He couldn't hike for the cameras or stage town meetings or stand amid rubble in ghettos and decry failed policies. There wasn't enough time to do all the things candidates were expected to do. He was entering late, with no groundwork in place, no grass roots, no local support of any kind. Lake had a handsome face, a pleasant voice, nice suits, an urgent message, and lots of cash.

If buying TV could buy an election, Aaron Lake was about to get himself a new job.

He called Washington, talked to his moneyman, and was given the news about the $5 million announcement. He'd never heard of Hummand. 'Is it a public company?' he asked. No, came the answer. Very private. Just under a billion in annual sales. An innovator in radar jamming. Could make billions if the right man took charge of the military and started spending again.

Nineteen million dollars was now in hand, a record, of course. And they were revising their projections. The Lake campaign would collect thirty million in its first two weeks.

There was no way to spend money that fast.

He folded the cell phone, handed it back to Floyd, who appeared to be lost in traffic. 'From now on we use helicopters,' Lake announced over his shoulder to the secretary, who actually wrote down the directive: Find helicopters.

Lake hid behind his sunglasses and tried to analyze thirty million bucks. The transition from a fiscal conservative to a freewheeling candidate was awkward, but the money had to be spent. It wasn't squeezed from the taxpayers; rather, it was freely given. He could rationalize. Once elected, he'd continue his fight for the workingman.

He thought again about Teddy Maynard, sitting in some dark room deep inside Langley, legs wrapped in a quilt, face squinting from pain, pulling strings only he could pull, making money fall from trees. Lake would never know the things Teddy was doing on his behalf, nor did he want to.

The Director of Middle East Operations was named Lufkin, a twenty-year man Teddy trusted implicitly. Fourteen hours earlier he'd been in Tel Aviv. Now he was in Teddy's war room, somehow looking fresh and alert. His message had to be delivered in person, mouth to mouth, no wires or signals or satellites. And what was said between them would never be repeated. It had been that way for many years.

'An attack on our embassy in Cairo is now imminent,' Lufkin said. No reaction from Teddy; no frown, no surprise, no cutting of the eyes, nothing. He'd gotten such news many times before.

'Yidal?'

'Yes. His top lieutenant was seen in Cairo last week.'

'Seen by whom?'

'The Israelis. They've also followed two truck-loads of explosives from Tripoli. Everything seems to be in place.'

'When?'

'Imminent.'

'How imminent?'

'Within a week, I'd guess.'

Teddy pulled an earlobe and closed his eyes. Lufkin tried not to stare, and he knew better than to ask questions. He would leave soon, and return to the Middle East. And he would wait. The attack on the embassy might proceed with no warning. Dozens would be killed and maimed. A crater in the city would smolder for days, and in Washington fingers would point and accusations would fly. The CIA would be blamed again.

None of it would faze Teddy Maynard. As Lufkin had learned, sometimes Teddy needed the terror to accomplish what he wanted.

Or maybe the embassy would be spared, the attack thwarted by Egyptian commandos working with the United States. The CIA would be praised for its excellent intelligence. That wouldn't faze Teddy either.

'And you're certain?' he asked.

'Yes, as certain as one can be in these situations.'

Lufkin, of course, had no clue that the Director was now plotting to elect a President. Lufkin had barely heard of Aaron Lake. Frankly, he didn't care who won the election. He'd been in the Middle East long enough to know it didn't really matter who set American policy there.

He'd leave in three hours, on the Concorde to Paris, where he'd spend a day before going to Jerusalem.

'Go to Cairo,' Teddy said without opening his eyes.

'Sure. And do what?'

'Wait.'

'Wait for what?'

'Wait for the ground to shake. Stay away from the embassy.'

York's initial reaction was one of horror. 'You can't run this damned ad, Teddy,' he said. 'It's R-rated. I've never seen so much blood.'

'I like that,' Teddy said, pushing a button on the remote. 'An R-rated campaign ad. It's never been done before.'

They watched it again. It began with the sound of a bomb, then footage of the Marine barracks in Beirut; smoke, rubble, chaos, Marines being pulled from debris, mangled bodies, Marines lying dead in a neat row. President Reagan addressing the press and vowing revenge. But the threat

95

sounded hollow. Then the photo of an American soldier standing between two masked gunmen. A heavy, ominous voiceover said, 'Since 1980, hundreds of Americans have been murdered by terrorists around the world.' Another bomb scene, more bloody and dazed survivors, more smoke and chaos. 'We always vow revenge. We always threaten to find and punish those responsible.' Quick clips of President Bush on two separate occasions angrily promising retaliation – another attack, more bodies. Then footage of a terrorist standing in the door of a jetliner, dragging off the body of an American soldier. President Clinton, near tears, his voice ready to crack, saying, 'We will not rest until we find those responsible.' Next the handsome but serious face of Aaron Lake, looking sincerely at the camera, coming into our homes, saying, 'The fact is, we don't retaliate. We react with words, we swagger and threaten, but in reality we bury our dead, then forget about them. The terrorists are winning the war because we have lacked the guts to fight back. When I'm your President, we will use our new military to fight terrorism wherever we find it. No American death will go unanswered. I promise. We will not be humiliated by ragtag little armies hiding in mountains. We will destroy them.'

The ad ran for exactly sixty seconds, cost very little to make because Teddy already had the footage, and would start running during prime time in forty-eight hours.

'I don't know, Teddy,' York said. 'It's gruesome.'

'It's a gruesome world.'

96

Teddy liked the ad and that's all that mattered. Lake had objected to the blood, but came around quickly. His name recognition was up to 30 percent, but his ads were still disliked.

Just wait, Teddy kept telling himself. Wait until there are more bodies.

EIGHT

Trevor was sipping a carry-out double latte from Beach Java and debating whether to add a generous shot or two of Amaretto to help soothe away the morning's cobwebs when the call came. His cramped suite had no intercom system; one was not needed. Jan could simply yell any message down the hall, and he could yell back if he wanted. For eight years he and this particular secretary had been barking at each other.

'It's some bank in the Bahamas!' she announced. He almost spilled the coffee as he lunged for the phone.

It was a Brit whose accent had been softened by the islands. A substantial wire had been received, from a bank in Iowa.

How substantial, he wanted to know, covering his mouth so Jan couldn't hear.

A hundred thousand dollars.

Trevor hung up and added the Amaretto, three shots of it, and sipped the delightful brew while smiling goofily at the wall. In his career he'd never come close to a fee of $33,000. He'd settled a car wreck once for $25,000, taken a fee of $7,500, and within two months had spent all of it.

Jan knew nothing about the offshore account and the scam that diverted money to it, so he was forced to wait an hour, make a bunch of useless phone calls, and try to look busy before announcing he had to take care of some crucial business in downtown Jacksonville, then he was needed at Trumble. She didn't care. He disappeared all the time and she had some reading to keep her occupied.

He raced to the airport, almost missed his shuttle, and drank two beers during the thirty-minute flight to Fort Lauderdale, then two more on the way to Nassau. On the ground, he fell into the back of a cab, a 1974 Cadillac painted gold, without air-conditioning and with a driver who'd also been drinking. The air was hot and wet, the traffic slow, and Trevor's shirt was sticking to his back by the time they stopped downtown near the Geneva Trust Bank Building.

Inside, Mr. Brayshears came forward eventually and led Trevor to his small office. He presented a sheet of paper which gave the bare details: a $100,000 wire originating from the First Iowa Bank in Des Moines, remitter being a faceless entity named CMT Investments. The payee was another generic entity named Boomer Realty, Ltd. Boomer was the name of Joe Roy Spicer's favorite bird dog.

Trevor signed the forms to transfer $25,000 to his own, separate account with Geneva Trust, money he kept hidden from his secretary and from the IRS. The remaining $8,000 was handed to him

99

in a thick envelope, cash. He stuffed it deep into his khaki pants pocket, shook Brayshears' soft little hand, and raced out of the building. He was tempted to stay a couple of days, find a room on the beach, get a chair by the pool, and drink rum until they stopped bringing it to him. The temptation grew to the point that he almost bolted from the gate at the airport and raced to get another cab. But he reached deep, determined not to squander his money this time.

Two hours later he was in the Jacksonville airport, drinking strong coffee, without liquor, and making his plans. He drove to Trumble, arriving at four-thirty, and he waited for Spicer for almost half an hour.

'A pleasant surprise,' Spicer said dryly as he stepped into the attorney-conference room. Trevor had no briefcase to inspect, so the guard patted his pockets and stepped outside. His cash was hidden under the floor mat of his Beetle.

'We received a hundred thousand dollars from Iowa,' Trevor said, glancing at the door.

Spicer was suddenly happy to see his lawyer. He resented the 'we' in Trevor's announcement, and he resented the healthy cut he raked off the top. But the scam wouldn't work without help from the outside, and, as usual, the lawyer was a necessary evil. So far, Trevor could be trusted.

'It's in the Bahamas?'

'Yes. I just left there. The money's tucked away, all sixty-seven thousand of it.'

Spicer breathed deeply and savored the victory. A third of the loot gave him $22,000 and change. It was time to write some more letters!

He reached into the pocket of his olive prison shirt and removed a folded newspaper clipping. He stretched his arms, studied it for a second, then said, 'Duke's at Tech tonight. The line is eleven. Put five thousand bucks on Tech.'

'Five thousand?'

'Yep.'

'I've never put five thousand on a game before.'

'What kinda bookie you got?'

'Small time.'

'Look, if he's a bookie, he can handle the numbers. Call him as soon as you can. He may have to make a few calls, but he can do it.'

'All right, all right.'

'Can you come back tomorrow?'

'Probably.'

'How many other clients have ever paid you thirty-three thousand bucks?'

'None.'

'Right, so be here at four tomorrow. I'll have some mail for you.'

Spicer left him and walked quickly from the administration building with only a nod at a guard in a window. He walked with a purpose across the finely manicured lawn, the Florida sun heating the sidewalk even in February. His colleagues were deep in their unhurried labors in their little library, alone as always, so Spicer did not hesitate to announce: 'We got the hundred thousand from ole Quince in Iowa!'

Beech's hands froze on his keyboard. He peered over his reading glasses, his jaw dropping, and managed to say, 'You're kidding.'

'Nope. Just talked to Trevor. The money was

wired in exactly as instructed, arrived in the Bahamas this morning. Quincy baby came through.'

'Let's hit him again,' Yarber said, before the others could think of it.

'Quince?'

'Sure. The first hundred was easy, let's squeeze him one more time. What could we lose?'

'Not a damned thing,' Spicer said with a smile. He wished he'd said it first.

'How much?' asked Beech.

'Let's try fifty,' Yarber said, pulling numbers from the air as if anything was possible.

The other two nodded and pondered the next fifty thousand, then Spicer took charge and said, 'Look, let's evaluate where we are now. I think Curtis in Dallas is ripe. We'll hit Quince again. This thing is working, and I think we should shift gears, get more aggressive, know what I mean? Let's take each pen pal, analyze them one by one, and step up the pressure.'

Beech turned off his computer and reached for a file. Yarber cleared his small desk. Their little Angola scam had just received a fresh infusion of capital, and the smell of ill-gotten cash was intoxicating.

They began reading all the old letters, and drafting new ones. More victims were needed, they quickly decided. More ads would be placed in the back pages of those magazines.

Trevor made it as far as Pete's Bar and Grill, arriving there just in time for happy hour, which at Pete's began at 5 P.M. and ran until the first fistfight. He found Prep, a thirty-two-year-old sophomore at North Florida, shooting nine-ball for twenty bucks a game. Prep's dwindling trust fund required the family lawyer to pay him $2,000 a month as long as he was enrolled as a full-time student. He'd been a sophomore for eleven years.

Prep was also the busiest bookie at Pete's, and when Trevor whispered that he had serious money to place on the Duke-Tech game, Prep asked, 'How much?'

'Fifteen thousand,' Trevor said, then gulped his longneck beer.

'You serious?' Prep asked, chalking his cue stick and glancing around the smoky table. Trevor had never bet more than a hundred bucks on any game.

'Yep.' Another long pull on the bottle. He was feeling lucky. If Spicer had the guts to lay $5,000 on the game, Trevor would double it. He'd just earned 33,000 tax-free dollars. So what if he lost ten? That much belonged to the IRS anyway.

'I'll have to make a call,' Prep said, pulling out a cell phone.

'Hurry. The game starts in thirty minutes.'

The bartender was a local who'd never left the state of Florida but had somehow developed an intense passion for Australian Rules Football. A game was on from Down Under, and it took a $20 bribe from Trevor to get the channel changed to ACC basketball.

With $15,000 riding on Georgia Tech, there was no way Duke could miss a shot, at least not in the first half. Trevor ate french fries, drank one bottle after another, and tried to ignore Prep, who was standing near a pool table in a dark corner, watching.

In the second half, Trevor almost bribed the bartender to switch back to the Aussie game. He was getting drunker, and with ten minutes to go was openly cursing Joe Roy Spicer to anyone who would listen. What did that redneck know about ACC basketball? Duke led by twenty with nine minutes to go, when Tech's point guard got hot and nailed four straight threes. Trevor had Tech and eleven.

The game was tied with a minute to go. Trevor didn't care who won. He'd beat the spread. He paid his tab, tipped the bartender another $100, then flashed a smart-ass salute to Prep as he walked out the door. Prep flipped him the bird.

In the cool darkness, Trevor skipped along Atlantic Boulevard, away from the lights, past the cheap summer rentals packed tightly together, past the neat little retirement homes with their fresh paint and perfect lawns, down the old wooden steps to the sand, where he took off his shoes and strolled along the edge of the water. The temperature was in the forties, not unusual for Jacksonville in February, and before long his feet were cold and wet.

Not that he felt much – $43,000 in one day, tax-free, all hidden from the government. Last year after expenses he'd cleared $28,000, and that was working practically full time – haggling with clients too poor or too cheap to pay, avoiding courtrooms, dealing with penny-ante real estate agents and bankers, bickering with his secretary, cutting corners on taxes.

Ah, the joy of quick cash. He'd been suspicious of the Brethren's little scam, but now it seemed so brilliant. Extort from those who can't complain. How thoroughly clever.

And since it was working so well, he knew Spicer would turn up the heat. The mail would get heavier, the visits to Trumble more frequent. Hell, he'd be there every day if necessary, hauling letters in and out, bribing guards.

He splashed his feet in the water as the wind picked up and the waves roared in.

Even more clever would be to steal from the extortionists, court-certified crooks who certainly couldn't complain. It was a nasty thought, one he was almost ashamed of, but a valid one nonetheless. All options would be kept open. Since when were thieves known for their loyalty?

He needed a million dollars, nothing more or less. He'd done the math many times, driving to Trumble, drinking at Pete's, sitting at his desk with the door locked. A lousy million bucks, and he could close his sad little office, surrender his law license, buy a sailboat, and spend eternity drifting with the winds around the Caribbean.

He was closer than he would ever be.

Justice Spicer rolled over again on the bottom bunk. Sleep was a rare gift in his tiny room, on his tiny bed with a small, smelly roommate named Alvin snoring above him. Alvin had roamed North America as a hobo for decades, but late in life had grown weary and hungry. His crime had been the robbery of a rural mail carrier in Oklahoma. His apprehension had been aided mightily when Alvin walked into the FBI office in Tulsa and declared, 'I did it.' The FBI scrambled for six hours to find the crime. Even the judge knew Alvin planned it all. He wanted a federal bed, certainly not one provided by the state.

Sleep was even more difficult than usual because Spicer was worried about the lawyer. Now that the scam had hit its stride, there was serious cash lying around. And more on the way. The more Boomer Realty collected in the Bahamas, the more tempting it would become for Trevor. He and he alone could steal their ill-gotten loot and get away with it.

But the scam worked only with an outside conspirator. Someone had to sneak the mail back and forth. Someone had to collect the money.

There had to be a way to bypass the lawyer, and Joe Roy was determined to find it. If he didn't sleep for a month, he didn't care. No slimy lawyer would take a third of his money, then steal the rest.

NINE

Defensepac, or D-PAC as it would quickly and widely become known, made a roaring entry onto the loose and murky field of political finance. No political-action committee in recent history had appeared with as much muscle behind it.

Its seed money came from a Chicago financier named Mitzger, an American with dual Israeli citizenship. He put up the first $1 million, which lasted about a week. Other Jewish high-rollers were quickly brought into the fold, though their identities were shielded by corporations and offshore accounts. Teddy Maynard knew the dangers of having a bunch of rich Jews contribute openly and in an organized fashion to Lake's campaign. He relied on old friends in Tel Aviv to organize the money in New York.

Mitzger was a liberal when it came to politics, but no issue was as dear as the security of Israel. Aaron Lake was much too moderate on social matters, but he was also dead serious about a new military. Middle East stability depended on a strong America, at least in Mitzger's opinion.

He rented a suite at the Willard in D.C. one day,

and by noon the next he had leased an entire floor of an office building near Dulles. His staff from Chicago worked around the clock plowing through the myriad details required to instantly outfit forty thousand square feet with the latest technology. He had a 6 A.M. breakfast with Elaine Tyner, a lawyer/lobbyist from a gigantic Washington firm, one she'd built with her own iron will and lots of oil clients. Tyner was sixty years old and currently regarded as the most powerful lobbyist in town. Over bagels and juice she agreed to represent D-PAC for an initial retainer of $500,000. Her firm would immediately dispatch twenty associates and that many clerks to the new D-PAC offices where one of her partners would take charge. One section would do nothing but raise money. One would analyze congressional support for Lake and begin, gently at first, the delicate process of lining up endorsements from senators and representatives and even governors. It would not be easy; most were already committed to other candidates. Yet another section would do nothing but research – military hardware, its costs, new gadgets, futuristic weapons, Russian and Chinese innovations – anything that candidate Lake might need to know.

Tyner herself would work on raising money from foreign governments, one of her specialties. She was very close to the South Koreans, having been their presence in Washington for the past decade. She knew the diplomats, the businessmen, the big shots. Few countries would sleep easier with a beefed-up United States military than South Korea.

'I feel sure they'll be good for at least five million,' she said confidently. 'Initially, anyway.'

From memory, she made a list of twenty French and British companies that derived at least a fourth of their annual sales from the Pentagon. She'd start working on them immediately.

Tyner was very much the Washington lawyer these days. She hadn't seen a courtroom in fifteen years, and every meaningful world event originated within the Beltway and somehow affected her.

The challenge at hand was unprecedented – electing an unknown, last-minute candidate who, at the moment, enjoyed 30 percent name recognition and 12 percent positives. What their candidate had, though, unlike the other flakes who dropped in and out of the presidential derby, was seemingly unlimited cash. Tyner had been well paid to elect and defeat scores of politicians, and she held the unwavering belief that money would always win. Give her the money, and she could elect or beat anybody.

During the first week of its existence, D-PAC buzzed with unbridled energy. The offices were open twenty-four hours a day as Tyner's people set up shop and charged forward. Those raising money produced an exhaustive computerized list of 310,000 hourly workers in defense and related industries, then hit them hard with a slick mail-out pleading for money. Another list had the names of twenty-eight thousand white-collar defense workers who earned in excess of $50,000 a year. They were mailed a different type of solicitation.

The D-PAC consultants looking for endorsements found the fifty members of Congress with the most defense jobs in their districts. Thirty-seven were up for reelection, which would make the arm-twisting that much easier. D-PAC would go to the grassroots, to the defense workers and their bosses, and orchestrate a massive phone campaign in support of Aaron Lake and more military spending. Six senators from defense-heavy states had tough opponents in November, and Elaine Tyner planned a lunch with each of them.

Unlimited cash cannot go unnoticed for long in Washington. A rookie congressman from Kentucky, one of the lowest of the 435, desperately needed money to fight what appeared to be a losing campaign back home. No one had heard of the poor boy. He hadn't said a word during his first two years, and now his rivals back home had found an attractive opponent. No one would give him money. He heard rumors, tracked down Elaine Tyner, and their conversation went something like this:

'How much money do you need?' she asked.

'A hundred thousand dollars.' He flinched, she did not.

'Can you endorse Aaron Lake for President?'

'I'll endorse anybody if the price is right.'

'Good. We'll give you two hundred thousand and run your campaign.'

'It's all yours.'

Most were not that easy, but D-PAC managed to buy eight endorsements in the first ten days of its existence. All were insignificant congressmen who'd served with Lake and liked him well enough. The strategy was to line them up before the cameras a week or two before big Super Tuesday, March 7. The more the merrier.

Most, however, had already committed to other candidates.

Tyner hurriedly made the rounds, sometimes eating three power meals a day, all happily covered by D-PAC. Her goal was to let the town know that her brand-new client had arrived, had plenty of money, and was backing a dark horse soon to break from the pack. In a city where talk was an industry in itself, she had no trouble spreading her message.

Finn Yarber's wife arrived unannounced at Trumble, her first visit in ten months. She wore fraying leather sandals, a soiled denim skirt, a baggy blouse adorned with beads and feathers, and all sorts of old hippie crap around her neck and wrists and head. She had a gray butch cut and hair under her arms, and looked very much like the tired, worn-out refugee from the sixties that she really was. Finn was less than thrilled when word got to him that his wife was waiting up front.

Her name was Carmen Topolski-Yocoby, a mouthful that she had used as a weapon all of her adult life. She was a radical feminist lawyer in Oakland whose speciality was representing lesbians suing for sexual harassment at work. So every single client was an angry woman battling an angry employer. Work was a bitch.

She had been married to Finn for thirty years – married, but not always living together. He'd lived with other women; she'd lived with other men.

111

Once when they were newlyweds, they lived with an entire houseful of others, different combinations each week. Both came and went. For one six-year stretch they lived together in chaotic monogamy, and produced two children, neither of whom had amounted to much.

They'd met on the battlefields of Berkeley in 1965, both protesting the war and all other evils, both law students, both committed to the high moral ground of social change. They worked diligently to register voters. They fought for the dignity of migrant workers. They got arrested during the Tet Offensive. They chained themselves to redwoods. They fought the Christians in the schools. They sued on behalf of the whales. They marched the streets of San Francisco in every parade, for any and every cause.

And they drank heavily, partied with great enthusiasm, and relished the drug culture; they moved in and out and slept around, and this was okay because they defined their own morality. They were fighting for the Mexicans and the redwoods, dammit! They had to be good people!

Now they were just tired.

She was embarrassed that her husband, a brilliant man who'd somehow stumbled his way onto the California Supreme Court, was now locked away in a federal prison. He was quite relieved that the prison was in Florida and not California; otherwise she might visit more often. His first digs had been near Bakersfield, but he managed to get himself transferred away.

They never wrote each other, never called. She

was passing through because she had a sister in Miami.

'Nice tan,' she said. 'You're looking good.'

And you're shriveling like an old prune, he thought. Damn, she looked ancient and tired.

'How's life?' he asked, not really caring.

'Busy. I'm working too hard.'

'That's good.' Good that she was working and making a living, something she'd done off and on for many years. Finn had five years to go before he could shake Trumble's dust from his gnarled and bare feet. He had no intention of returning to her, or to California. If he survived, something he doubted every day, he'd leave at the age of sixty-five, and his dream was to find a land where the IRS and the FBI and all the rest of those alphabetized government thugs had no jurisdiction. Finn hated his own government so much he planned to renounce his citizenship and find another nationality.

'Are you still drinking?' he asked. He, of course, was not, though he did manage a little pot occasionally from one of the guards.

'I'm still sober, thanks for asking.'

Every question was a barb, every reply a retort. He honestly wondered why she had stopped by. Then he found out.

'I've decided to get a divorce,' she said.

He shrugged as if to say, 'Why bother?' Instead he said, 'Probably not a bad idea.'

'I've found someone else,' she said.

'Male or female?' he asked, more curious than anything else. Nothing would surprise him.

'A younger man.'

113

He shrugged again and almost said, 'Go for it, old girl.'

'He's not the first,' Finn said.

'Let's not go there,' she said.

Fine with Finn. He had always admired her exuberant sexuality, her stamina, but it was difficult to imagine this old woman doing it with any regularity. 'Show me the papers,' he said. 'I'll sign them.'

'They'll be here in a week. It's a clean break, since we own so little these days.'

At the height of his rise to power, Justice Yarber and Ms. Topolski-Yocoby had jointly applied for a mortgage on a home in the marina district of San Francisco. The application, properly sanitized to remove any hint of chauvinism or sexism or racism or ageism, blandly worded by spooked California lawyers terrified of being sued by some offended soul, showed a gap between assets and liabilities of almost a million dollars.

Not that a million dollars had mattered to either one of them. They were too busy fighting timber interests and ruthless farmers, etc. In fact, they'd taken pride in the scantness of their assets.

California was a community property state, which roughly meant an equal split. The divorce papers would be easy to sign, for many reasons.

And there was one reason Finn would never mention. The Angola scam was producing money, hidden and dirty, and off-limits to any and every greedy agency. Ms. Carmen would damned sure never know about it.

Finn wasn't certain how the tentacles of community property might reach a secret bank account in the Bahamas, but he had no plans to find out. Show him the papers, he'd be happy to sign.

They managed to chat a few minutes about old friends, a brief conversation indeed because most friends were gone. When they said good-bye, there was no sadness, no remorse. The marriage had been dead for a long time. They were relieved at its passing.

He wished her well, without so much as a hug, then went to the track, where he stripped to his boxers and walked an hour in the sun.

TEN

Lufkin was finishing his second day in Cairo with dinner at a sidewalk café on Shari' el-Corniche, in the Garden City section of the city. He sipped strong black coffee and watched the merchants close their shops – sellers of rugs and brass pots and leather bags and linens from Pakistan, all for the tourists. Less than twenty feet away, an ancient vendor meticulously folded his tent, then left his spot without a trace.

Lufkin looked very much the part of a modern Arab – white slacks, light khaki jacket, a white vented fedora with the bill down close to his eyes. He watched the world from behind a hat and a pair of sunshades. He kept his face and arms tanned and his dark hair cut very short. He spoke perfect Arabic and moved with ease from Beirut to Damascus to Cairo.

His room was at the Hotel El-Nil on the edge of the Nile River, six crowded blocks away, and as he drifted through the city he was suddenly joined by a tall thin foreigner of some breed with only passable English. They knew each other well enough to trust each other, and continued their walk.

'We think tonight is the night,' the contact said, his eyes also hidden.

'Go on.'

'There's a party at the embassy.'

'I know.'

'Yes, a nice setting. Lots of traffic. The bomb will be in a van.'

'What kind of van?'

'We don't know.'

'Anything else?'

'No,' he said, then vanished in a swarming crowd.

Lufkin drank a Pepsi in a hotel bar, alone, and thought about calling Teddy. But it had been four days since he'd seen him at Langley, and Teddy had made no contact. They'd been through this before. Teddy was not going to intervene. Cairo was a dangerous place for Westerners these days, and no one could effectively blame the CIA for not stopping an attack. There would be the usual grandstanding and finger pointing, but the terror would quickly be shoved into the recesses of the national memory, then forgotten. There was a campaign at hand, and the world moved fast anyway. With so many attacks, and assaults, and mindless violence both at home and abroad, the American people had become hardened. Twenty-four-hour news, nonstop flash points, the world always with a crisis somewhere. Late-breaking stories, a shock here and a shock there, and before long you couldn't keep up with events.

Lufkin left the bar and went to his room. From

his window on the fourth floor the city rambled forever, built helter-skelter over the centuries. The roof of the American embassy was directly in front of him, a mile away.

He opened a paperback Louis L'Amour, and waited for the fireworks.

The truck was a two-ton Volvo panel van, loaded from floor to ceiling with three thousand pounds of plastic explosives made in Romania. Its door happily advertised the services of a well-known caterer in the city, a company which made frequent visits to most of the Western embassies. It was parked near the service entrance, in the basement.

The driver of the truck had been a large, friendly Egyptian called Shake by the Marines who guarded the embassy. Shake passed through often, hauling food and supplies to and from social events. Shake was now dead on the floor of his truck, a bullet in his brain.

At twenty minutes after ten, the bomb was detonated by a remote device, operated by a terrorist hiding across the street. As soon as he pushed the right buttons, he ducked behind a car, afraid to look.

The explosion ripped out supporting columns deep in the basement, so the embassy fell to one side. Debris rained for blocks. Most of the nearby buildings suffered structural damage. Windows within a quarter of a mile were cracked.

Lufkin was napping in his chair when the quake came. He jumped to his feet, walked onto his narrow balcony, and watched the cloud of dust.

The roof of the embassy was no longer visible. Within minutes flames were seen and the interminable sirens began. He propped his chair against the railing of the balcony, and settled in for the duration. There would be no sleep. Six minutes after the explosion, the electricity in Garden City went out, and Cairo was dark except for the orange glow of the American embassy.

He called Teddy.

When the technician, Teddy's sanitizer, assured Lufkin the line was secure, the old man's voice came through as clearly as if they were chatting from New York to Boston. 'Yes, Maynard here.'

'I'm in Cairo, Teddy. Watching our embassy go up in smoke.'

'When did it happen?'

'Less than ten minutes ago.'

'How big –'

'Hard to tell. I'm in a hotel a mile away. Massive, I'd say.'

'Call me in an hour. I'll stay here at the office tonight.'

'Done.'

Teddy rolled himself to a computer, punched a few buttons, and within seconds found Aaron Lake. The candidate was en route from Philadelphia to Atlanta, aboard his shiny new airplane. There was a phone in Lake's pocket, a secure digital unit as slim as a cigarette lighter.

Teddy punched more numbers, the phone was summoned, and Teddy spoke to his monitor. 'Mr. Lake, it's Teddy Maynard.'

Who else could it be? Lake thought. No one else could use the phone.

'Are you alone?' Teddy asked.

'Just a minute.'

Teddy waited, then the voice returned. 'I'm in the kitchen now,' Lake said.

'Your plane has a kitchen?'

'A small one, yes. It's a very nice plane, Mr. Maynard.'

'Good. Listen, sorry to bother you, but I have some news. They bombed the American embassy in Cairo fifteen minutes ago.'

'Who?'

'Don't ask that.'

'Sorry.'

'The press will be all over you. Take a moment, prepare some remarks. It will be a good time to express concern for the victims and their families. Keep the politics to a minimum, but also keep the hard line. Your ads are prophetic now, so your words will be repeated many times.'

'I'll do it right now.'

'Call me when you get to Atlanta.'

'Yes, I will.'

Forty minutes later, Lake and his group landed in Atlanta. The press had been duly notified of his arrival, and with the dust just settling in Cairo, there was a crowd waiting. No live pictures had yet emerged of the embassy, yet several agencies were already reporting that 'hundreds' had been killed.

In the small terminal for private aircraft, Lake stood before an eager group of reporters, some

120

with cameras and mikes, others with slim record-
ers, others still with just plain old notepads. He
spoke solemnly, without notes: 'At this moment,
we should be in prayer for those who've been
injured and killed by this act of war. Our thoughts
and prayers are with them and their families, and
also with the rescue people. I am not going to
politicize this event, but I will say that it is absurd
for this country to once again suffer at the hands of
terrorists. When I am President, no American life
will go unaccounted for. I will use our new military
to track down and annihilate any terrorist group
that preys upon innocent Americans. That's all I
have to say.'

He walked off, ignoring the shouts and questions from the pack of shaggy dogs.

Brilliant, thought Teddy, watching live from his
bunker. Quick, compassionate, yet tough as hell.
Superb! He once again patted himself on the back
for choosing such a wonderful candidate.

When Lufkin called again it was past midnight
in Cairo. The fires had been extinguished and they
were hauling out bodies as fast as they could.
Many were buried in the rubble. He was a block
away, behind an army barricade, watching with
thousands of others. The scene was chaos, smoke
and dust thick in the air. Lufkin had been to
several bomb sites in his career, and this was a bad
one, he reported.

Teddy rolled around his room and poured
another decaf coffee. The Lake terror ads would
begin at prime time. On this very night the
campaign would spend $3 million in a coast-to-
coast deluge of fear and doom. They'd pull the ads

tomorrow, and announce it beforehand. Out of respect for the dead and their families, the Lake campaign would temporarily suspend its little prophecies. And they'd start polling at noon tomorrow, massive polling.

High time candidate Lake's positives shot upward. The Arizona and Michigan primaries were less than a week away.

The first pictures from Cairo were of a harried reporter with his back to an army barricade, soldiers watching him fiercely, as he might get shot if he tried once more to charge forward. Sirens wailed all around; lights flashed. But the reporter knew little. A massive bomb had exploded deep in the embassy at ten-twenty when a party was breaking up; no idea of the casualties, but there'd be plenty, he promised. The area was cordoned off by the army, and for good measure they'd sealed the airspace so, dammit, there'd be no helicopter shots. As of yet, no one had claimed responsibility, but for good measure he gave the names of three radical groups as the usual suspects.

'Could be one of these, could be someone else,' he said helpfully. With no carnage to film, the camera was forced to stay with the reporter, and since he had nothing to say he prattled on about how dangerous the Middle East had become, as if this were breaking news and he was there to report it!

Lufkin called around 8 P.M. D.C. time to tell Teddy that the American ambassador to Egypt could not be located, and they were beginning to fear he might be in the rubble. At least that was the word on the street. While talking to Lufkin on the

122

phone, Teddy watched the muted reporter; a Lake terror ad appeared on another screen. It showed the rubble, the carnage, the bodies, the radicals from some other attack, then the smooth but earnest voice of Aaron Lake promising revenge.

How perfect the timing, Teddy thought.

An aide woke Teddy at midnight with lemon tea and a vegetable sandwich. As he so often did, he'd napped in his wheelchair, the wall of TV screens alive with images but no sound. When the aide left, he pushed a button and listened.

The sun was well up in Cairo. The ambassador had not been found, and it was now being assumed he was somewhere in the rubble.

Teddy had never met the ambassador to Egypt, an absolute unknown anyway, who was now being idolized by the chattering reporters as a great American. His death didn't particularly bother Teddy, though it would increase the criticism of the CIA. It would also add gravity to the attack, which, in the scheme of things, would benefit Aaron Lake.

Sixty-one bodies had been recovered so far. The Egyptian authorities were blaming Yidal, the likeliest of suspects because his little army had bombed three Western embassies in the past sixteen months, and because he was openly calling for war against the United States. The current CIA dossier on Yidal gave him thirty soldiers and an annual budget of around $5 million, almost all originating from Libya and Saudi Arabia. But to the press, the leaks suggested an army of a thousand with unlimited funds with which to terrorize innocent Americans.

The Israelis knew what Yidal had for breakfast and where he ate it. They could've taken him out a dozen times, but so far he'd kept his little war away from them. As long as he killed Americans and Westerners, the Israelis really didn't care. It was to their benefit for the West to loathe the Islamic radicals.

Teddy ate slowly, then napped some more. Lufkin called before noon Cairo time with the news that the bodies of the ambassador and his wife had been found. The count was now at eighty-four; all but eleven were Americans.

The cameras caught up with Aaron Lake outside a plant in Marietta, Georgia, shaking hands in the dark as the shift changed, and when asked about events in Cairo, he said: 'Sixteen months ago these same criminals bombed two of our embassies, killing thirty Americans, and we've done nothing to stop them. They're operating with impunity because we lack the commitment to fight. When I'm President, we'll declare war on these terrorists and stop the killing.'

The tough talk was contagious, and as America woke up to the terrible news in Cairo, the country was also treated to a brash chorus of threats and ultimatums from the other seven candidates. Even the more passive among them now sounded like gunslingers.

ELEVEN

It was snowing again in Iowa, a steady swirl of snow and wind that turned to slush on the streets and sidewalks and made Quince Garbe once again long for a beach. He covered his face on Main Street as if to protect himself, but the truth was he didn't want to speak to anyone. Didn't want anyone to see him darting yet again into the post office.

There was a letter in the box. One of those letters. His jaw fell and his hands froze when he saw it, just lying there with some junk mail, innocent, like a note from an old friend. He glanced over both shoulders – a thief racked with guilt – then yanked it out and thrust it into his coat.

His wife was at the hospital planning a ball for crippled children, so the house was empty except for a maid who spent her day napping down in the laundry room. He hadn't given her a raise in eight years. He took his time driving there, fighting the snow and the drifts, cursing the con man who'd entered his life under the ruse of love, anticipating

125

the letter, which grew heavier near his heart with each passing minute.

No sign of the maid as he entered the front door, making as much noise as possible. He went upstairs to his bedroom, where he locked the door. There was a pistol under the mattress. He flung his overcoat and his gloves onto an armchair, then his jacket, and he sat on the edge of his bed and examined the envelope. Same lavender paper, same handwriting, same everything with a Jacksonville postmark, two days old. He ripped it open and removed a single page.

Dear Quince:

Thanks so much for the money. So that you won't think I'm a total thug, I think you should know the money went to my wife and children. They are suffering so. My incarceration has left them destitute. My wife is clinically depressed and cannot work. My four children are fed by welfare and food stamps.

(A hundred thousand bucks should certainly fatten them up, Quince thought.)

They live in government housing and have no dependable transportation. So, thanks again for your help. Another $50,000 should get them out of debt and start a nice college fund.

Same rules as before; same wiring instructions; same promises to expose your secret life if the money is not received quickly. Do it now, Quince, and I swear this is my last letter.

Thanks again, Quince.

Love, Ricky

He went to the bathroom, to the medicine cabinet, where he found his wife's Valium. He took two, but thought about eating all of them. He needed to lie down but he couldn't use the bed because it would be wrinkled and someone would ask questions. So he stretched himself out on the floor, on the worn but clean carpet, and waited for the pills to work.

He'd begged and scraped and even lied a little to borrow the first installment for Ricky. There was no way he could squeeze another $50,000 from a personal balance sheet already heavily padded and still teetering on the edge of insolvency. His nice large house was choked with a fat mortgage held by his father. His father signed his paychecks. His cars were large and imported, but they had a million miles on them and little value. Who in Bakers, Iowa, would want to buy an eleven-year-old Mercedes?

And what if he managed to somehow steal the money? The criminal otherwise known as Ricky would simply thank him again, then demand more.

It was over.

Time for the pills. Time for the gun.

The phone startled him. Without thinking, he scrambled to his feet and grabbed the receiver. 'Hello,' he grunted.

'Where the hell are you?' It was his father, with a tone he knew so well.

'I'm, uh, not feeling well,' he managed to say,

staring at his watch and now remembering the ten-thirty meeting with a very important inspector from the FDIC.

'I don't give a damn how you feel. Mr. Colthurst from the FDIC has been waiting in my office for fifteen minutes.'

'I'm vomiting, Dad,' he said, and cringed again with the word Dad. Fifty-one years old, still using the word Dad.

'You're lying. Why didn't you call if you're sick? Gladys told me she saw you just before ten walking toward the post office. What the hell's going on here?'

'Excuse me. I gotta go to the toilet. I'll call you later.' He hung up.

The Valium rolled in like a pleasant fog, and he sat on the edge of his bed staring at the lavender squares scattered on the floor. Ideas were slow in coming, hampered by the pills.

He could hide the letters, then kill himself. His suicide note would place the bulk of the blame on his father. Death was not an altogether unpleasant prospect; no more marriage, no more bank, no more Dad, no more Bakers, Iowa, no more hiding in the closet.

But he would miss his children and grandchildren.

And what if this Ricky monster didn't learn of the suicide, and sent another letter, and they found it, and somehow Quince got himself outed anyway, long after his funeral?

The next lousy idea involved a conspiracy with his secretary, a woman he trusted marginally to begin with. He would tell her the truth, then ask

128

her to write a letter to Ricky and break the news of Quince Garbe's suicide. Together, Quince and his secretary could scheme and fake their way through a suicide, and in the process take some measure of revenge against Ricky.

But he'd rather be dead than tell his secretary.

The third idea occurred after the Valium had settled in at full throttle, and it made him smile. Why not try a little honesty? Write a letter to Ricky and plead poverty. Offer another $10,000 and tell him that's all. If Ricky was determined to destroy him, then he, Quince, would have no choice but to come after Ricky. He'd inform the FBI, let them track the letters and the wire transfers, and both men would go down in flames.

He slept on the floor for thirty minutes, then gathered his jacket, gloves, and overcoat. He left the house without seeing the maid. As he drove to town, flush with the desire to confront the truth, he admitted aloud that only the money mattered. His father was eighty-one. The bank's stock was worth about $10 million. Someday it would be his. Stay in the closet until the cash was in hand, then live any way he damned well pleased.

Don't screw up the money.

Coleman Lee owned a taco hut in a strip mall on the outskirts of Gary, Indiana, in a section of town now ruled by the Mexicans. Coleman was forty-eight, with two bad divorces decades earlier, no children, thank God. Because of all the tacos, he was thick and slow, with a drooping stomach and large fleshy cheeks. Coleman was not pretty, but he was certainly lonely.

His employees were mainly young Mexican boys, illegal immigrants, all of whom he, sooner or later, tried to molest, or seduce, or whatever you'd call his clumsy efforts. Rarely was he successful, and his turnover was high. Business was slow too because people talked and Coleman was not well regarded. Who wanted to buy tacos from a pervert?

He rented two small boxes at the post office at the other end of the strip mall – one for his business, the other for his pleasure. He collected porno and gathered it almost daily from the post office. The mail carrier at his apartment was a curious type, and it was best to keep some things as quiet as possible.

He strolled along the dirty sidewalk at the edge of the parking lot, past the discount stores for shoes and cosmetics, past a XXX video dive he'd been banned from, past a welfare office, one brought to the suburbs by a desperate politician looking for votes. The post office was crowded with Mexicans taking their time because it was cold out.

His daily haul was two hard-core magazines sent to him in plain brown wrappers, and a letter which looked vaguely familiar. It was a square yellow envelope, no return address, postmarked in Atlantic Beach, Florida. Ah, yes, he remembered as he held it. Young Percy in rehab.

Back in his cramped little office between the kitchen and the utility room, he quickly flipped through the magazines, saw nothing new, then stacked them in a pile with a hundred others. He opened the letter from Percy. Like the two before,

130

it was handprinted, and addressed to Walt, a name he used to collect all his porn. Walt Lee.

Dear Walt:

I really enjoyed your last letter. I've read it many times. You have a nice way with words. As I told you, I've been here for almost eighteen months, and it gets very lonely. I keep your letters under my mattress, and when I feel really isolated I read them over and over. Where did you learn to write like that? Please send another one as soon as possible.

With a little luck, I'll be released in April. I'm not sure where I'll go or what I'll do. It's frightening, really, to think that I'll just walk out of here after almost two years, and have no one to be with. I hope we're still pen pals by then.

I was wondering, and I really hate to ask this, but since I have no one else I'll do it anyway, and please feel free to say no, it won't hurt our friendship, but could you loan me a thousand bucks? They have this little book and music shop here at the clinic, and they let us buy paperbacks and CDs on credit, and, well, I've been here so long that I've run up quite a tab.

If you can make the loan, I'd really appreciate it. If not, I completely understand.

Thanks for being there, Walt. Please write me soon. I treasure your letters.

Love, Percy

A thousand bucks? What kinda little creep was this? Coleman smelled a con. He ripped the letter into pieces and threw them in the trash.

'A thousand bucks,' he mumbled to himself, reaching for the magazines again.

Curtis was not the real name of the jeweler in Dallas. Curtis worked fine when corresponding with Ricky in rehab, but the real name was Vann Gates.

Mr. Gates was fifty-eight years old, on the surface happily married, the father of three and the grandfather of two, and he and his wife owned six jewelry stores in the Dallas area, all located in malls. On paper they had $2 million, and they'd made it themselves. They had a very nice new home in Highland Park, with separate bedrooms at opposite ends. They met in the kitchen for coffee and in the den for TV and grandkids.

Mr. Gates ventured from the closet now and then, always with excruciating caution. No one had a clue. His correspondence with Ricky was his first attempt at finding love through the want ads, and so far he'd been thrilled with the results. He rented a small box in a post office near one of the malls, and used the name Curtis V. Cates.

The lavender envelope was addressed to Curtis Cates, and as he sat in his car and carefully opened it, he at first had no clue anything was wrong. Just another sweet letter from his beloved Ricky. Lightning hit, though, with the first words:

Dear Vann Gates:
    The party's over, pal. My name ain't Ricky,

and you're not Curtis. I'm not a gay boy looking for love. You, however, have an awful secret, which I'm sure you want to keep. I want to help.

Here's the deal: Wire $100,000 to Geneva Trust Bank, Nassau, Bahamas, account number 144-DXN-9593, for Boomer Realty, Ltd., routing number 392844–22.

Do so immediately! This is not a joke. It's a scam, and you've been hooked. If the money is not received within ten days, I will send to your wife, Ms. Glenda Gates, a little packet filled with copies of all letters, photos, etc.

Wire the money, and I'll simply go away.

Love, Ricky

With time, Vann found the Dallas I-635 loop, and before long he was on the I-820 loop around Fort Worth, then back to Dallas, driving at exactly fifty-five, in the right-hand lane, oblivious to the traffic stacked up behind him. If crying would help, then he would've certainly had a good one. He had no qualms about weeping, especially in the privacy of his Jaguar.

But he was too angry to cry, too bitter to be wounded. And he was too frightened to waste time yearning for someone who did not exist. Action was needed – quick, decisive, secretive.

Heartache, though, overcame him, and he finally pulled onto the shoulder and parked with the engine running. All those wonderful dreams of Ricky, those countless hours staring at his handsome face with his crooked little smile, and reading his letters – sad, funny, desperate, hopeful – how could so many emotions be conveyed with the written word? He'd practically memorized the letters.

And he was just a boy, so young and virile, yet lonely and in need of mature companionship. The Ricky he'd come to love needed the loving embrace of an older man, and Curtis/Vann had been making plans for months. The ploy of a diamond show in Orlando while his wife was in El Paso at her sister's. He'd sweated the details and left no tracks.

He did, finally, cry. Poor Vann shed tears without shame or embarrassment. No one could see him; the other cars were flying past at eighty miles per hour.

He vowed revenge, like any jilted lover. He'd track down this beast, this monster who'd posed as Ricky and broken his heart.

When the sobbing began to subside, he thought of his wife and family and that helped greatly in drying up the tears. She'd get all six stores and the $2 million and the new house with separate bedrooms, and he would get nothing but ridicule and scorn and gossip in a town that loved it so. His children would follow the money, and for the rest of their lives his grandchildren would hear the whispers about their grandfather.

Back in the right lane at fifty-five, back through Mesquite for the second time, reading the letter again as eighteen-wheelers roared past.

There was no one to call, no banker he could trust to check out the account in the Bahamas, no lawyer to run to for advice, no friend to hear his sorry tale.

For a man who'd carefully lived a double life, the money would not be insurmountable. His wife watched every dime, both at home and at the stores, and for that reason Vann had long since mastered the scheme of hiding money. He did it with gems, rubies and pearls and sometimes small diamonds he placed aside and later sold to other dealers for cash. It was common in the business. He had boxes of cash – shoe boxes neatly stacked in a fireproof safe in a mini-storage out in Plano. Post-divorce cash. Cash for the afterlife when he and Ricky would sail the world and spend it all in one endless voyage.

'Sonofabitch!' he said through gritted teeth. And again and again.

Why not write this con man and plead poverty? Or threaten to expose his little extortion scheme? Why not fight back?

Because the sonofabitch knew exactly what he was doing. He'd tracked Vann well enough to learn his real name, and the name of his wife. He knew Vann had the money.

He pulled into his driveway and there was Glenda sweeping the sidewalk. 'Where have you been, honey?' she asked pleasantly.

'Running errands,' he said with a smile.

'Took a long time,' she said, still sweeping.

He was so sick of it. She timed his movements! For thirty years he'd been under her thumb, with a stopwatch clicking in the palm of her hand.

He pecked her on the cheek out of habit, then went to the basement where he locked a door and began to cry again. The house was his prison (with a mortgage of $7,800 a month, it certainly felt like it). She was the guard, the keeper of the keys. His sole means of escape had just collapsed, replaced by a cold-blooded extortionist.

TWELVE

Eighty coffins required a lot of space. They were laid in perfect rows, all neatly wrapped in red, white, and blue, all the same length and width. They'd arrived thirty minutes earlier aboard an Air Force cargo plane, and were removed with great pomp and ceremony. Almost a thousand friends and relatives sat on folding chairs, on the concrete floor of the hangar, and stared in shock at the sea of flags arranged before them. They were outnumbered only by the shaggy dogs, all quarantined behind barricades and military police.

Even for a country well accustomed to foreign policy boondoggles, it was an impressive body count. Eighty Americans, eight Brits, eight Germans – no French because they'd been boycotting Western diplomatic functions in Cairo. Why were eighty Americans still in the embassy after 10 P.M.? That was the question of the hour, and so far no good answer had surfaced. So many of those who made such decisions were now lying in their coffins. The best theory buzzing around D.C. was that the caterer had been late, and the band even later.

But the terrorists had proved all too well that they would strike at any hour, so what difference did it make how late the ambassador and his wife and their staff and colleagues and guests wanted to party?

The second great question of the hour was just exactly why did we have eighty people in our embassy in Cairo to begin with? The State Department had yet to acknowledge the question.

After some mournful music from an Air Force band, the President spoke. His voice broke and he managed to summon a tear or two, but after eight years of such theatrics the act had worn thin. He'd already promised revenge many times, so he dwelt on comfort and sacrifice and the promise of a better life in the hereafter.

The Secretary of State called the names of the dead, a morbid recitation designed to capture the gravity of the moment. The sobbing increased. Then some more music. The longest speech was delivered by the Vice President, fresh from the campaign trail and filled with a newly discovered commitment to eradicate terrorism from the face of the earth. Though he'd never worn a military uniform, he seemed eager to start tossing grenades.

Lake had them all on the run.

Lake watched the grim ceremony while flying from Tucson to Detroit, late for another round of interviews. On board was his pollster, a newly acquired magician who now traveled with him. While Lake and his staff watched the news, the pollster worked feverishly at the small conference

138

table upon which he had two laptops, three phones, and more printouts than any ten people could digest.

The Arizona and Michigan primaries were three days away, and Lake's numbers were climbing, especially in his home state, where he was in a dead heat with the long-established front-runner, Governor Tarry of Indiana. In Michigan, Lake was ten points down, but people were listening. The fiasco in Cairo was working beautifully in his favor.

Governor Tarry was suddenly scrambling for money. Aaron Lake was not. It was coming in faster than he could spend it.

When the Vice President finally finished, Lake left the screen and returned to his leather swivel recliner and picked up a newspaper. A staff member brought him coffee, which he sipped while watching the flatlands of Kansas eight miles below him. Another staff member handed him a message – one that was supposed to require an urgent call from the candidate. Lake glanced around the plane, and counted thirteen people, pilots not included.

For a private man who still missed his wife, Lake was not adjusting well to the complete lack of privacy. He moved with a group, every half hour slotted by someone, every action coordinated by a committee, every interview preceded by written guesses about the questions and suggested responses. He got six hours each night alone, in his hotel room, and damned if the Secret Service wouldn't sleep on the floor if he'd allow it. Because of the fatigue, he slept like an infant. His only true moments of quiet reflection occurred in the bathroom, either in the shower or on the toilet.

But he wasn't kidding himself. He, Aaron Lake, quiet congressman from Arizona, had become an overnight sensation. He was charging while the rest were faltering. Big money was aimed at him. The press followed like bloodhounds. His words got repeated. He had very powerful friends, and as the pieces were falling in place the nomination looked realistic. He hadn't dreamed of such things a month earlier.

Lake was savoring the moment. The campaign was madness, but he could control the tempo of the job itself. Reagan was a nine-to-five President, and he'd been far more effective than Carter, an avid workaholic. Just get to the White House, he told himself over and over, suffer these fools, gut it through the primaries, endure with a smile and a quick wit, and one day very soon he'd sit in the Oval Office, alone, with the world at his feet.

And he would have his privacy.

Teddy sat with York in his bunker, watching the live scene from Andrews Air Force Base. He preferred York's company when things were rough. The accusations had been brutal. Scapegoats were in demand, and many of the idiots chasing the cameras blamed the CIA because that's who they always blamed.

If they only knew.

He'd finally told York of Lufkin's warnings, and York understood completely. Unfortunately, they'd been through this before. When you police the world you lose a lot of cops, and Teddy and

York had shared many sad moments watching the flag-covered coffins roll off the C-130s, evidence of another debacle abroad. The Lake campaign would be Teddy's final effort at saving American lives.

Failure seemed unlikely. D-PAC had collected more than $20 million in two weeks, and was in the process of hauling the money around Washington. Twenty-one congressmen had been recruited for Lake endorsements, at a total cost of $6 million. But the biggest prize so far was Senator Britt, the ex-candidate, the father of a little Thai boy. When he abandoned his quest for the White House he owed close to $4 million, with no viable plan to cover his deficit. Money tends not to follow those who pack up and go home. Elaine Tyner, the lawyer running D-PAC, met with Senator Britt. It took her less than an hour to cut the deal. D-PAC would pay off all his campaign debts, over a three-year period, and he would make a noisy endorsement of Aaron Lake.

'Did we have a projection of casualties?' York asked.

After a while Teddy said, 'No.'

Their conversations were never hurried.

'Why so many?'

'Lots of booze. Happens all the time in the Arab countries. Different culture, life is dull, so when our diplomats throw a party, they throw a good one. Many of the dead were quite drunk.'

Minutes passed. 'Where's Yidal?' asked York.

'Right now he's in Iraq. Yesterday, Tunisia.'

'We really should stop him.'

141

'We will, next year. It'll be a great moment for President Lake.'

Twelve of the sixteen congressmen endorsing Lake wore blue shirts, a fact that was not lost on Elaine Tyner. She counted such things. When a D.C. politician got near a camera, odds were he'd put on his best blue cotton shirt. The other four wore white.

She arranged them before the reporters in a ballroom of the Willard Hotel. The senior member, Representative Thurman of Florida, opened things up by welcoming the press to this very important occasion. Working from prepared notes, he offered his opinions on the current state of world events, commented on things in Cairo and China and Russia, and said that the world was a lot more dangerous than it looked. He rattled off the usual statistics about our reduced military. Then he launched into a long soliloquy about his close friend Aaron Lake, a man he'd served with for ten years and whom he knew better than most. Lake was a man with a message, one we didn't particularly want to hear, but a very important one nonetheless.

Thurman was breaking ranks with Governor Tarry, and though he did so with great reluctance and no small feeling of betrayal, he had become convinced through painful soul-searching that Aaron Lake was needed for the safety of our nation. What Thurman didn't say was that a recent poll showed Lake becoming very popular back in Tampa-St. Pete.

The mike was then passed to a congressman

from California. He covered no new territory, but rambled for ten minutes anyway. In his district north of San Diego were forty-five thousand defense and aerospace workers, and all of them, it seemed, had written or called. He'd been an easy convert; the pressure from home plus $250,000 from Ms. Tyner and D-PAC, and he had his marching orders.

When the questions started, the sixteen bunched together in a tight little pack, all anxious to answer and say something, all afraid their faces might not get wedged into the picture.

Though there were no committee chairmen, the group was not unimpressive. They managed to convey the image that Aaron Lake was a legitimate candidate, a man they knew and trusted. A man the nation needed. A man who could be elected.

The event was well staged and well covered, and instantly made news. Elaine Tyner would trot out five more the following day, then save Senator Britt for the day before big Super Tuesday.

The letter in Ned's glove box was from Percy, young Percy in rehab who got his mail through Laurel Ridge, Post Office Box 4585, Atlantic Beach, FL 32233.

Ned was in Atlantic Beach, had been for two days, with the letter and with the determination to track down young Percy because he smelled a hoax. He had nothing better to do. He was retired with plenty of money, no family to speak of, and besides, it was snowing in Cincinnati. He had a room at the Sea Turtle Inn, on the beach, and at night he hit the bars along Atlantic Boulevard.

He'd found two excellent restaurants, crowded little places with lots of young pretty girls and boys. He'd discovered Pete's Bar and Grill a block away, and for the last two nights he'd staggered from the place, drunk on cold drafts. The Sea Turtle was just around the corner.

During the day Ned watched the post office, a modern brick and glass government job on First Street, parallel to the beach. A small, windowless box midway from the floor, 4585 was on a wall with eighty others, in an area of medium traffic. Ned had inspected the box, tried to open it with keys and wire, and had even asked questions at the front desk. The postal workers had been most unhelpful. Before leaving the first day, he had stuck a two-inch strand of thin black thread to the bottom of the box's door. It was imperceptible to anyone else, but Ned would know if the mail was checked.

He had a letter in there, in a bright red envelope, one he'd mailed three days earlier from Cincinnati, then raced south. In it he'd sent Percy a check for $1,000, money the boy needed for a set of artist's supplies. In an earlier letter, Ned had revealed that he had once owned a modern art gallery in Greenwich Village. It was a lie, he had not, but he doubted everything Percy said too.

Ned had been suspicious from the beginning. Before he answered the solicitation, he had tried to verify Laurel Ridge, the fancy detox unit supposedly holding Percy. There was a telephone, a private number he'd been unable to pry out of directory assistance. There was no street address. Percy had explained in his first letter that the place was top-secret because many of its patients were high-powered corporate executives and top-level government officials, all of whom had, in one way or another, succumbed to chemicals. It sounded good. The boy had a way with words.

And a very pretty face. That's why Ned kept writing. The photo was something he admired every day.

The request for money had caught him by surprise, and since he was bored he decided to make the drive to Jacksonville.

From his spot in the parking lot, low behind the steering wheel of his car, with his back to First Street, he could watch the wall of boxes and the postal customers as they came and went. It was a long shot, but what the hell. He used a small pair of foldable binoculars, and on occasion caught a stare from someone walking by. The task grew monotonous after two days, but as the time passed he became more and more convinced that his letter would be retrieved. Surely someone checked the box at least once every three days. A rehab clinic with patients would get plenty of mail, wouldn't it? Or was it simply a front for a con man who dropped by once a week to check his traps?

The con man showed up late in the afternoon of the third day. He parked a Beetle next to Ned, then ambled into the post office. He wore wrinkled khakis, white shirt, straw hat, bow tie, and had the disheveled air of a would-be beach Bohemian.

Trevor had enjoyed a long midday break at Pete's, then slept off his liquid lunch with an hour nap at his desk, and was just stirring about, making his rounds. He put the key in Box 4585 and

145

removed a handful of correspondence, most of it junk mail, which he threw away as he flipped through the letters on his way out of the building.

Ned watched every move. After three days of tedium, he was thrilled that his surveillance had paid off. He followed the Beetle, and when it parked and the driver walked into a small, run-down law office, Ned drove away, scratching his temple, repeating out loud, 'A lawyer?'

He kept driving, down Highway A1A, along the shore, away from the sprawl of Jacksonville, south through Vilano Beach and Crescent Beach and Beverly Beach and Flagler Beach and finally to a Holiday Inn outside Port Orange. He went to the bar before he went to his room.

It wasn't the first scam he'd flirted with. In fact, it was the second. He'd sniffed the other one out too before any damage was done. Over his third martini he swore it would be his last.

THIRTEEN

The day before the Arizona and Michigan primaries, the Lake campaign unleashed a media blitz, the likes of which had never been seen before in presidential politics. For eighteen hours, the two states were bombarded with one ad after another. Some were fifteen seconds, little softies with not much more than his handsome face and the promises of decisive leadership and a safer world. Others were one-minute documentaries on the dangers of the post-cold war. Still others were macho, in-your-face promises to the terrorists of the world – kill people simply because they are Americans, and you will pay a very dear price. Cairo was still very fresh, and the assurances hit their mark.

The ads were bold, put together by high-powered consultants, and the only downside was oversaturation. But Lake was too new to the scene to bore anyone, not now anyway. His campaign spent $10 million on television in the two states, a staggering amount.

They ran at a slower clip during voting hours on Tuesday, February 22, and when the polls closed the exit analysts predicted Lake would win his home state and run a close second in Michigan. Governor Tarry, after all, was from Indiana, another midwestern state, and he'd spent weeks in Michigan during the previous three months.

Evidently, he hadn't spent enough time there. The voters in Arizona opted for their native son, and those in Michigan liked the new fellow too. Lake got 60 percent at home, and 55 percent in Michigan where Governor Tarry got a paltry 31 percent. The balance was divided among the noncontenders.

It was a devastating loss for Governor Tarry, just two weeks before big Super Tuesday and three weeks before the little one.

Lake watched the vote counting from on board his airplane, en route from Phoenix, where'd he'd voted for himself. An hour from Washington, CNN declared him the surprise winner in Michigan, and his staff opened the champagne. He savored the moment, even allowed himself two glasses.

History was not lost on Lake. No one had ever started so late, and come so far so fast. In the darkened cabin, they watched the analysts on four screens, the experts all marveling at this man Lake and what he'd done. Governor Tarry was gracious, but also worried about the enormous sums of money being spent by his heretofore unknown opponent.

Lake chatted politely with the small group of reporters waiting for him at Reagan National Airport, then rode in yet another black Suburban to his national campaign headquarters where he thanked his highly paid staff and told them to go home and get some sleep.

It was almost midnight when he got to Georgetown, to his quaint little rowhouse on Thirty-fourth, near Wisconsin. Two Secret Service agents got out of the car behind Lake, and two more were waiting on the front steps. He had adamantly refused an official request to put guards inside his home.

'I do not want to see you people lurking around here,' he said harshly at his front door. He resented their presence, didn't know their names, and didn't care if they disliked him. They had no names, as far as he was concerned. They were simply 'You people,' said with as much contempt as possible.

Once he was locked inside, he went upstairs to his bedroom and changed clothes. He turned out the lights as if he were asleep, waited fifteen minutes, then eased downstairs to the den to see if anyone was looking in, then down another flight to the small basement. He climbed through a window, and stepped into the cold night near his tiny patio. He paused, listened, heard nothing, then quietly opened a wooden gate and darted between the two buildings behind his. He surfaced on Thirty-fifth Street, alone, in the dark, dressed like a jogger with a running cap pulled low to his brow. Three minutes later he was on M Street, in the crowds. He found a taxi and disappeared into the night.

Teddy Maynard had gone to sleep reasonably

content with his candidate's first two victories, but he was awakened by the news that something had gone wrong. When he rolled himself into the bunker at ten minutes after 6 A.M., he was more frightened than angry, though his emotions had run the gamut in the past hour. York was waiting, along with a supervisor named Deville, a tiny nervous man who'd obviously been wired for many hours.

'Let's hear it,' Teddy growled, still rolling and looking for coffee.

Deville did the talking. 'At twelve-o-two this morning he said good-bye to the Secret Service and entered his house. At twelve-seventeen he exited through a small window in the basement. We, of course, have wires and timers on every door and window. We've leased a rowhouse across the street, and we were on alert anyway. He hasn't been home in six days.' Deville waved a small pill, the size of an aspirin. 'This is a little device known as a T-Dec. They're in the soles of all of his shoes, including his jogging shoes. So if he's not barefoot we know where he is. Once pressure is applied from the foot, the bug emits a signal that is broadcast for two hundred yards without a transmitter. When pressure is relaxed, it will continue to provide a signal for fifteen minutes. We scrambled and picked him up on M Street. He was dressed in sweats with a cap over his eyes. We had two cars in place when he jumped in a cab. We followed him to Chevy Chase, to a suburban shopping center. While the cab waited, he darted into a place called Mailbox America, one of these new places where you can send and receive mail outside the Postal Service. Some, including this one, are open twenty-four hours for mail pickup. He was inside for less than a minute, just long enough to open his box with a key, remove several pieces of mail, throw it all away, then return to the cab. One of our cars followed him back to M Street, where he got out and sneaked back home. The other car stayed at the mailbox place. We went through the waste can just inside the door, and found six pieces of junk mail, evidently his. The address is A1 Konyers, Box 455, Mailbox America, 39380 Western Avenue, Chevy Chase.'

'So he didn't find what he was looking for?' Teddy asked.

'It looks as though he tossed everything he took from his box. Here's the video.'

A screen dropped from the ceiling as the lights faded. Footage from a video camera zoomed across a parking lot, past the cab, and onto the figure of Aaron Lake in his baggy sweats as he disappeared around a corner inside Mailbox America. Seconds later he reappeared, flipping through letters and papers in his right hand. He stopped briefly at the door and then dumped everything in a tall wastebasket.

'What the hell's he looking for?' Teddy mumbled to himself.

Lake left the building and quickly ducked inside the cab. The video stopped; the lights became brighter.

Deville resumed his narrative. 'We're confident we found the right papers in the trash can. We were there within seconds, and no one else entered the premises while we waited. The time was twelve fifty-eight. An hour later, we entered again and keyed the lock to Box 455, so we'll have access anytime we need it.'

'Check it every day,' Teddy said. 'Inventory every piece of mail. Leave the junk, but when something arrives I want to know it.'

'You got it. Mr. Lake reentered the basement window at one twenty-two and stayed at home for the rest of the night. He's there now.'

'That's all,' Teddy said, and Deville left the room.

A minute passed as Teddy stirred his coffee. 'How many addresses does he have?'

York knew the question was coming. He glanced at some notes. 'He gets most of his personal mail at his home in Georgetown. He has at least two addresses on Capitol Hill, one at his office, the other at the Armed Services Committee. He has three offices back home in Arizona. That's six that we know about.'

'Why would he need a seventh?'

'I don't know the reason, but it can't be good. A man who has nothing to hide does not use an alias or a secret address.'

'When did he rent the box?'

'We're still working on that.'

'Maybe he rented the box after he decided to enter the race. He's got the CIA doing his thinking for him, so maybe he figures we're watching everything too. And he figures he might need a little privacy, thus the box. Maybe it's a girlfriend we missed somehow. Maybe he likes dirty magazines or videos, something that is shipped through the mail.'

After a long pause, York said, 'Could be. What

if the box was rented months ago, long before he entered the race?'

'Then he's not hiding from us. He's hiding from the world, and his secret is truly dreadful.'

They silently contemplated the dreadfulness of Lake's secret, neither wanting to venture a guess. They decided to step up surveillance even more, and to check the mailbox twice a day. Lake would be leaving town in a matter of hours, off to do battle in other primaries, and they would have the box to themselves.

Unless someone else was also checking it for him.

Aaron Lake was the man of the hour in Washington. From his office on Capitol Hill he graciously granted live interviews to the early morning news programs. He received senators and other members of Congress, friends and former enemies alike, all bearing tidings of great joy and congratulations. He had lunch with his campaign staff, and followed it with long meetings on strategy. After a quick dinner with Elaine Tyner, who brought wonderful news of tons of new cash over at D-PAC, he left the city and flew to Syracuse to make plans for the New York primary.

A large crowd welcomed him. He was, after all, now the front-runner.

FOURTEEN

The hangovers were becoming more frequent, and as Trevor opened his eyes for another day he told himself that he simply had to get a grip. You can't lay out at Pete's every night, drinking cheap longnecks with coeds, watching meaningless basketball games just because you've got a thousand bucks on them. Last night it had been Logan State and somebody, some team with green uniforms. Who the hell cared about Logan State?

Joe Roy Spicer, that's who. Spicer put $500 on them, Trevor backed it up with a thousand of his own, and Logan won it for them. In the past week, Spicer had picked ten out of twelve winners. He was up $3,000 in real cash, and Trevor, happily following along, was up $5,500 for himself. His gambling was proving to be much more profitable than his lawyering. And someone else was picking the winners!

He went to the bathroom and splashed water on his face without looking at the mirror. The toilet was still clogged from the day before, and as he stomped around his dirty little house looking for a plunger the phone rang. It was a wife from a previous life, a woman he loathed and one who loathed him, and when he heard her voice he knew she needed money. He said no angrily and got in the shower.

Things were worse at the office. A divorcing couple had arrived in separate cars to finish the negotiations for their property settlement. The assets they were fighting over were of no consequence to anyone else – pots, pans, a toaster – but since they had nothing, they had to fight over something. The fights are nastiest when the stakes are smallest.

Their lawyer was an hour late, and they had used the time to simmer and boil until finally Jan had separated them. The wife was parked in Trevor's office when he stumbled in from the back door.

'Where the hell you been?' she demanded loud enough for husband to hear up front. Husband charged down the hall, past Jan, who did not give chase, and burst into Trevor's small office.

'We've been waiting for an hour!' he announced.

'Shut up, both of you!' Trevor screamed, and Jan left the building. His clients were stunned at the volume.

'Sit down!' he screamed again, and they fell into the only empty chairs. 'You people pay five hundred bucks for a lousy divorce and you think you own the place!'

They looked at his red eyes and red face and decided this was not a man to mess with. The phone started ringing and no one answered it. Nausea hit again, and Trevor bolted out of his office and across the hall to the bathroom, where he puked, as quietly as possible. The toilet failed to flush, the little metal chain clinking harmlessly inside the tank.

The phone was still ringing. He staggered down the hall to fire Jan, and when he couldn't find her he left the building too. He walked to the beach, took off his shoes and socks, and splashed his feet in the cool salt water.

Two hours later, Trevor sat motionless at his desk, door locked to keep out clients, bare feet on the desk, with sand still wedged between the toes. He needed a nap and he needed a drink, and he stared at the ceiling trying to organize his priorities. The phone rang, this time duly answered by Jan, who was still employed but secretly checking want ads.

It was Brayshears, in the Bahamas. 'We have a wire, sir,' he said.

Trevor was instantly on his feet. 'How much?'

'A hundred thousand, sir.'

Trevor glanced at his watch. He had about an hour to catch a flight. 'Can you see me at three-thirty?' he asked.

'Certainly, sir.'

He hung up and yelled toward the front, 'Cancel my appointments for today and tomorrow. I'm leaving.'

'You don't have any appointments,' Jan yelled back. 'You're losing money faster than ever.'

He wouldn't bicker. He slammed the back door and drove away.

The flight to Nassau stopped first in Fort Lauderdale, though Trevor hardly knew it. After two quick beers he was sound asleep. Two more over the Atlantic, and a flight attendant had to wake him when the plane was empty.

The wire was from Curtis in Dallas, as expected. It was remitted by a Texas bank, payable to Boomer Realty, care of Geneva Trust Bank, Nassau. Trevor raked his one third off the top, again hiding $25,000 in his own secret account, and taking $8,000 in cash. He thanked Mr. Brayshears, said he hoped to see him soon, and staggered out of the building.

The thought of going home had not crossed his mind. He headed for the shopping district, where packs of heavy American tourists choked the sidewalks. He needed shorts and a straw hat and a bottle of sunscreen.

Trevor eventually made it to the beach, where he found a room in a nice hotel, $200 a night but what did he care? He lathered himself in oil and stretched out by the pool, close enough to the bar. A waitress in a thong fetched him drinks.

He woke up after dark, sufficiently cooked but not burned. A security guard escorted him to his room, where he fell on the bed and returned to his coma. The sun was up again before he moved.

After such a long period of rest, he awoke surprisingly clear-headed, and very hungry. He ate some fruit and went looking for sailboats, not exactly shopping for one, but paying close attention to the details. A thirty-footer would be sufficient, just large enough to live on yet manageable by a crew of one. There would be no passengers; just the lonely skipper hopping from island to island. The cheapest one he found was $90,000 and it needed some work.

Noon found him back at the pool with a cell phone trying to placate a client or two, but his heart wasn't in it. The same waitress brought another drink. Off the phone, he hid behind dark sunshades and tried to crunch the numbers. But things were wonderfully dull between his ears.

In the past month he'd earned about $80,000 in tax-free graft. Could the pace continue? If so, he'd have his million bucks in a year, and he could abandon his office and what was left of his career, and he could buy his little boat and hit the sea.

For the first time ever, the dream almost seemed real. He could see himself at the wheel, shirtless, shoeless, cold beer at the ready, gliding across the water from St. Barts to St. Kitts, from Nevis to St. Lucia, from one island to a thousand others, wind popping his mainsail, not a damned thing in the world to worry about. He closed his eyes and longed even harder for an escape.

His snoring woke him. The thong was nearby. He ordered some rum and checked his watch.

Two days later Trevor finally made it back to Trumble. He arrived with mixed feelings. First, he was quite anxious to pick up the mail and facilitate the scam, anxious to keep the extortion going and the money rolling in. On the other hand, he was tardy and Judge Spicer would not be happy.

'Where the hell you been?' Spicer growled at him as soon as the guard left the attorney-conference room. It seemed to be the standard question these days. 'I've missed three games because of you, and I picked nothing but winners.'

'The Bahamas. We got a hundred thousand from Curtis in Dallas.'

Spicer's mood changed dramatically. 'It took three days to check on a wire in the Bahamas?' he asked.

'I needed a little rest. Didn't know I was supposed to visit this place every day.'

Spicer was mellowing by the second. He'd just picked up another $22,000. It was safely tucked away with his other loot, in a place no one could find, and as he handed the lawyer yet another stack of pretty envelopes he was thinking of ways to spend the money.

'Aren't we busy,' Trevor said, taking the letters.

'Any complaints? You're making more than we are.'

'I have more to lose than you do.'

Spicer handed over a sheet of paper. 'I've picked ten games here. Five hundred bucks on each.'

Great, thought Trevor. Another long weekend at Pete's, watching one game after another. Oh well, there could be worse things. They played blackjack at a dollar a hand until the guard broke up the meeting.

Trevor's increased visits had been discussed by the warden and the higher-ups at the Bureau of Prisons in Washington. Paperwork had been created on the subject. Restrictions had been contemplated, but then abandoned. The visits were useless, and besides, the warden didn't want to alienate the Brethren. Why pick a fight?

The lawyer was harmless. After a few phone

calls around Jacksonville they decided that Trevor was basically unknown and probably had nothing better to do than hang out in the attorney-conference room of a prison.

The money gave new life to Beech and Yarber. Spending it would necessarily entail getting to it, and that would require they one day walk away as free men, free to do whatever they wanted with their growing fortunes.

With $50,000 or so now in the bank, Yarber was busy plotting an investment portfolio. No sense letting it sit there at 5 percent per annum, even if it was tax-free. One day very soon he'd roll it over into aggressive growth funds, with emphasis on the Far East. Asia would boom again, and his little pile of dirty money would be there to share in the wealth. He had five years to go, and if he earned between 12 and 15 percent on his money until then the $50,000 would grow to roughly $100,000 by the time he left Trumble. Not a bad start for a man who would be sixty-five, and hopefully still in good health.

But if he (and Percy and Ricky) could keep adding to the principal, he might indeed be rich when they turned him loose. Five lousy years – months and weeks he'd been dreading. Now he was suddenly wondering if he had enough time to extort all he needed. As Percy, he was writing letters to over twenty pen pals across North America. No two were in the same town. It was Spicer's job to keep the victims separated. Maps were being used in the law library to make certain

160

neither Percy nor Ricky was corresponding with men who appeared to live near one another.

When he wasn't writing letters, Yarber caught himself thinking about the money. Thankfully, the divorce papers from his wife had come and gone. He'd be officially single in a few months, and by the time he was paroled she'd have long since forgotten about him. Nothing would be shared. He'd be free to walk away without a single string attached.

Five years, and he had so much work to do. He'd cut out the sugar and walk an extra mile each day.

In the darkness of his top bunk, during sleepless nights, Hatlee Beech had done the same math as his colleagues. Fifty thousand dollars in hand, a healthy rate of return somewhere, add to the principal by squeezing from as many victims as they could catch, and one day there'd be a fortune. Beech had nine years, a marathon that once seemed endless. Now there was a flicker of hope. The death sentence they'd handed him was slowly becoming a time of harvest. Conservatively, if the scam netted him only $100,000 a year for the next nine years, plus a healthy rate of return, then he'd be a multimillionaire when he danced through the gates, also at the age of sixty-five.

Two, three, four million was not out of the question.

He knew exactly what he'd do. Since he loved Texas, he'd go to Galveston and buy one of those ancient Victorians near the sea, and he'd invite old friends to stop by and see how rich he was. Forget the law, he'd put in twelve-hour days working the money, nothing but work, nothing but money, so that by the time he was seventy he'd have more than his ex-wife.

For the first time in years, Hatlee Beech thought he might live to see sixty-five, maybe seventy.

He, too, gave up sugar, and butter, and he cut his cigarettes in half with the goal of going cold turkey real soon. He vowed to stay away from the infirmary and stop taking pills. He began walking a mile every day, in the sun, like his colleague from California. And he wrote his letters, he and Ricky.

And Justice Spicer, already equipped with sufficient motivation, was finding it difficult to sleep. He wasn't plagued by guilt or loneliness or humiliation, nor was he depressed by the indignity of prison. He was simply counting money, and juggling rates of return, and analyzing point spreads. With twenty-one months to go, he could see the end.

His lovely wife Rita had passed through the week before, and they'd spent four hours together over two days. She'd cut her hair, stopped drinking, and lost eighteen pounds, and she promised to be even skinnier when she picked him up at the front gate in less than two years. After four hours with her, Joe Roy was convinced the $90,000 was still buried behind the toolshed.

They'd move to Vegas, buy a new condo, and say to hell with the rest of the world.

With the Percy-and-Ricky scam working so well, Spicer had found a new worry. He'd leave Trumble first, happily, gladly, without looking back. But what about the money to be made after he was gone? If the scam was still printing money, what would happen to his share of the future earnings, money he was clearly entitled to? It had been, after all, his idea, one he'd borrowed from the prison in Louisiana. Beech and Yarber had been reluctant conspirators at first.

He had time to devise an exit strategy, just as he had time to contrive a way to get rid of the lawyer. But it would cost him some sleep.

The letter from Quince Garbe in Iowa was read by Beech: "'Dear Ricky (or whoever the hell you are): I don't have any more money. The first $100,000 was borrowed from a bank using a bogus financial statement. I'm not sure how I'll pay it back. My father owns our bank and all its money. Why don't you write him some letters, you thug! I can possibly scrape together $10,000 if we can agree that the extortion will stop there. I'm on the verge of suicide, so don't push. You're scum, you know that. I hope you get caught. Sincerely, Quince Garbe.'"

'Sounds pretty desperate,' Yarber said, looking up from his own pile of mail.

Spicer said, toothpick hanging from his bottom lip, 'Tell him we'll take twenty-five thousand.'

'I'll write him and tell him to wire it,' Beech said, opening another envelope addressed to Ricky.

FIFTEEN

During lunch, when experience had shown that traffic picked up somewhat at Mailbox America, an agent nonchalantly entered the place behind two other customers, and for the second time that day placed a key in Box 455. Lying on top of three pieces of junk mail – one from a pizza carryout, one from a car wash, one from the U.S. Postal Service – he noticed something new. It was an envelope, light orange in color, five by eight. With a pair of tweezers he kept on his key ring, he clamped the end of the envelope, slid it quickly from the box, and dropped it in a small leather briefcase. The junk mail was left undisturbed.

At Langley, it was carefully opened by experts. Two handwritten pages were removed, and copied.

An hour later, Deville entered Teddy's bunker, holding a file. Deville was in charge of what was commonly referred to, deep inside Langley, as the 'Lake mess.' He gave copies of the letter to Teddy and York, then scanned it to a large screen, where Teddy and York at first just stared at it. The printing was bold, in block form, easily readable, as if the author had labored over each word. It read:

Dear Al:

Where you been? Did you get my last letter? I wrote three weeks ago and I haven't heard a word. I guess you're busy, but please don't forget about me. I get very lonely here, and your letters have always inspired me to keep going. They give me strength and hope because I know somebody out there cares. Please don't give up on me, Al.

My counselor says that I might be released in two months. There's a halfway house in Baltimore, actually a few miles from where I grew up, and the people here are trying to get me a spot there. It would be for ninety days, enough time for me to find a job, some friends, etc., you know, get used to society again. It's a lockdown place at night, but I'd be free during the day.

There aren't many good memories, Al. Every person who ever loved me is now dead, and my uncle, the guy who's paying for this rehab, is very rich but very cruel.

I need friends so desperately, Al.

By the way, I've lost another five pounds, and my waist is now a thirty-two. The photo I sent you is getting outdated. I've never liked the way my face looks in it – too much flesh on the cheeks.

I'm much leaner now, and tanned. They let us tan for up to two hours a day here, weather permitting. It's Florida, but some

165

days are too cool. I'll send you another photo, maybe one from the chest up. I'm lifting weights like crazy. I think you'll like the next photo.

You said you would send me one of you. I'm still waiting. Please don't forget me, Al. I need one of your letters.

Love, Ricky

Since York had had the responsibility of investigating every aspect of Lake's life, he felt compelled to try and speak first. But he could think of nothing to say. They read the letter in silence again, and again.

Finally, Deville broke the ice by saying, 'Here's the envelope.' He flashed it on the wall. It was addressed to Mr. Al Konyers, at Mailbox America. The return address was: Ricky, Aladdin North, P.O. Box 44683, Neptune Beach, FL 32233.

'It's a front,' Deville said. 'There's no such place as Aladdin North. There's a telephone number, and you get an answering service. We've called ten times with questions, but the operators know nothing. We've called every rehab and treatment clinic in North Florida, and no one's heard of this place.'

Teddy was silent, still staring at the wall.

'Where's Neptune Beach?' York grunted.

'Jacksonville.'

Deville was excused, but told to stand by. Teddy began making notes on a green legal pad. 'There are other letters, and at least one photo,' he said, as if the problem were just part of the routine. Panic was a state unknown to Teddy Maynard.

'We have to find them,' he said.

'We've done two thorough searches of his home,' York said.

'Then do a third. I doubt if he would keep such stuff at his office.'

'How soon – '

'Do it now. Lake is in California looking for votes. We have no time on this, York. There may be other secret boxes, other men writing letters and bragging about their tans and waistlines.'

'Do you confront him?'

'Not yet.'

Since they had no sample of Mr. Konyers' handwriting, Deville made a suggestion that Teddy eventually liked. They would use the ruse of a new laptop, one with a built-in printer. The first draft was composed by Deville and York, and after an hour or so the fourth draft read as follows:

Dear Ricky:

I got your letter of the twenty-second; forgive me for not writing sooner. I've been on the road a lot lately, and I'm behind on everything. In fact, I'm writing this letter at thirty-five thousand feet, somewhere over the Gulf, en route to Tampa. And I'm using a new laptop, one so small it almost fits in my pocket. Amazing technology. The printer leaves something to be desired. I hope you can read it okay.

Wonderful news about your release, and the halfway house in Baltimore. I have some business interests there, and I'm sure I can help you find a job.

Keep your head up, only two months to go. You're a much stronger person now, and you're ready to live life to its fullest. Don't be discouraged.

I'll help in any way possible. When you get to Baltimore, I'll be happy to spend some time with you, show you around, you know.

I promise I'll write sooner. I can't wait to hear from you.

Love, Al

They decided Al was in a hurry and forgot to sign his name. The letter was marked up, revised, redrafted, pored over with more care than a treaty. The final version was printed on a piece of stationery from the Royal Sonesta Hotel in New Orleans, and placed in a thick, plain brown envelope with optic wiring hidden along the bottom edge. In the lower right-hand corner, in a spot that looked as if it had been slightly damaged and knotted in transit, a tiny transmitter the size of a pinhead was installed. When activated, it would send a signal a hundred yards for up to three days.

Since Al was traveling to Tampa, the envelope was stamped with a Tampa postmark, dated that day. This was done in less than half an hour by a team of very strange people down in Documents on the second floor.

At 4 P.M., a green van with many miles on it stopped at the curb in front of Aaron Lake's townhouse, near one of the many shade trees on Thirty-fourth, in a lovely section of Georgetown.

Its door advertised a plumbing company in the District. Four plumbers got out and began removing tools and equipment.

After a few minutes, the only neighbor who'd noticed grew bored and returned to her television. With Lake in California, the Secret Service was with him, and his home had yet to qualify for round-the-clock surveillance, at least by the Secret Service. That scrutiny would come quickly, though.

The ploy was a clogged sewer line in the small front lawn, something that could be done without entering the home. An outside job, one that would pacify the Secret Service in case they happened to drop by.

But two of the plumbers did indeed enter the home, with their own keys. Another van stopped by to check on progress, and to drop off a tool. Two plumbers from the second van mixed with those already there, and a regular unit began to form.

Inside the house, four of the agents began their tedious search for hidden files. They moved from room to room, inspecting the obvious, prying for the secrets.

The second van left, and a third one came from the other direction and parked with its tires on the sidewalk, as service vans often do. Four more plumbers joined the sewer cleaning, and two eventually drifted inside. After dark, a spotlight was rigged in the front yard, over the sewer cover, and directed into the home so the lights inside would not be noticed. The four men left outside sipped coffee and told jokes and tried to stay warm. Neighbors hurried by on foot.

After six hours the sewer was clean, as was the home. Nothing unusual was found, certainly no hidden file with correspondence from one Ricky in rehab. No sign of a photo. The plumbers turned off their lights, packed their tools, and disappeared without a trace.

At eight-thirty the next morning, when the doors opened at the Neptune Beach post office, an agent named Barr walked hurriedly in as if he were late for something. Barr was an expert on locks and keys, and he'd spent five hours the previous afternoon at Langley studying various boxes used by the Postal Service. He had four master keys, one of which he was certain would open number 44683. If not, he'd be forced to key it, which might take sixty seconds or so and could possibly draw attention. The third key worked, and Barr placed the brown envelope, postmarked the day before from Tampa, addressed to Ricky with no last name, care of Aladdin North, inside the box. There were two other letters already there. For good measure, he removed a piece of junk mail, then closed the door to the box, wadded up the mail, and threw it in the wastebasket.

Barr and two others waited patiently in a van in the parking lot, sipping coffee and videoing every postal customer. They were seventy yards away from the box. Their handheld receiver beeped with the faint signal from the envelope. A diverse group came and went with the flow – a black female in a short brown dress, a white male with a beard and leather jacket, a white female in a jogging suit, a black male in jeans – all agents of the CIA, all watching the box without a clue about who wrote the letter or where it was going. Their job was simply to find the person who'd rented the box.

They found him after lunch.

Trevor drank his lunch at Pete's, but only two beers. Cold drafts with salty peanuts from the community bowl, consumed while losing fifty bucks on a dogsled race in Calgary. Back at the office, he napped for an hour, snoring so loudly his long-suffering secretary finally had to close his door. She slammed it actually, but not loud enough to wake him.

Dreaming of sailboats, he made his trek to the post office, this time choosing to walk because the day was beautiful, he had nothing better to do, and his head needed clearing. He was delighted to find four of the little treasures angled neatly in Aladdin North's box. He placed them carefully in the pocket of his well-worn seersucker jacket, straightened his bow tie, and ambled forth, certain that another payday was fast approaching.

He'd never been tempted to read the letters. Let the Brethren do the dirty work. He could keep his hands clean, shuttle the mail, rake his third off the top. And besides, Spicer would kill him if he delivered mail that had been tampered with.

Seven agents watched him stroll back to his office.

Teddy was napping in his wheelchair when Deville

entered. York had gone home; it was after 10 P.M. York had a wife, Teddy did not.

Deville delivered his narrative while referring to pages of scribbled notes: 'The letter was removed from the box at one-fifty P.M. by a local lawyer named Trevor Carson. We followed him to his office in Neptune Beach, where he stayed for eighty minutes. It's a small one-man office, one secretary, not a lot of clients. Carson is a small-timer along the beaches, does divorces, real estate, two-bit stuff. He's forty-eight, divorced at least twice, native of Pennsylvania, college at Furman, law school at Florida State, got his license suspended eleven years ago for commingling client funds, then got it back.'

'All right, all right,' Teddy said.

'At three-thirty, he left his office, drove an hour to the federal prison at Trumble, Florida. Took the letters with him. We followed but lost the signal when he entered the prison. Since then, we've gathered some information about Trumble. It's a minimum-security prison, commonly referred to as a camp. No walls or fences, very low risk inmates. A thousand of them at Trumble. According to a source within the Bureau of Prisons here in Washington, Carson visits all the time. No other lawyer, no other person visits as much as Carson. Up until a month ago he went once a week, now it's at least three times a week. Sometimes four. All visits are official attorney-client conferences.'

'Who is his client?'

'It's not Ricky. He is the attorney of record for three judges.'

'Three judges?'

172

'Yes.'

'Three judges in prison?'

'That's right. They call themselves the Brethren.'

Teddy closed his eyes and rubbed his temples. Deville let things sink in for a moment, then continued: 'Carson was in the prison for fifty-four minutes, and when he exited we could not pick up the signal from the envelope. By this time, we were parked next to his car. He walked within five feet of our receiver, and we're certain he did not have the letter. We followed him back to Jacksonville, back to the beaches. He parked near a place called Pete's Bar and Grill, where he stayed for three hours. We searched his car, found his briefcase, and inside there were eight letters addressed to various men all over the country. All letters were outbound from the prison, none were inbound. Evidently, Carson shuttles mail back and forth to his clients. As of thirty minutes ago, he was still in the bar, quite drunk, betting on college basketball games.'

'A loser.'

'Very much so.'

The loser staggered out of Pete's after the second overtime of a game on the West Coast. Spicer had picked three out of four winners. Trevor had dutifully followed suit, and was up a thousand bucks for the night.

Drunk as he was, he was smart enough not to drive. His DUI three years earlier was still a painful memory, and besides the damned cops were all over the place. The restaurants and bars around the Sea Turtle Inn attracted the young and restless, thus the cops.

Walking was a challenge, though. He made it well enough to his office, a straight shot south, past the quiet little summer rentals and retirement cottages, all dark and tucked in for the night. He carried his briefcase with the letters from Trumble.

He pressed onward, searching for his house. He crossed the street for no reason, and half a block later recrossed it. There was no traffic. When he began to circle back, he came within twenty yards of an agent who'd ducked behind a parked car. The silent army watched him, suddenly fearful that the drunken fool might stumble into one of them.

At some point he gave up, and managed to find his office again. He rattled keys on the front steps, dropped his briefcase and forgot about it, and less than a minute after opening the door he was at his desk, sprawled in his swivel rocker, fast asleep, the front door half open.

The back door had been unlocked throughout the night. Following orders from Langley, Barr and company had entered the office and wired everything. There was no alarm system, no locks on the windows, nothing of value to attract thievery in the first place. Tapping the phones and bugging the walls had been an easy task, made so by the obvious fact that no one on the outside observed anything inside the offices of L. Trevor Carson, Attorney and Counselor-at-Law.

The briefcase was emptied, its contents cataloged at Langley's instructions. Langley wanted a precise record of the letters the lawyer had taken from Trumble. When everything had been inspected and photographed, the briefcase was placed in the hallway near his office. The snoring was impressive, and uninterrupted.

Shortly before 2, Barr managed to start the Beetle parked near Pete's. He drove it down the empty street and left it innocently on the curb in front of the law office, so that the drunk would rub his eyes in a few hours and pat himself on the back for such a nice job of driving. Or maybe he would shrink in horror at the thought of having driven while intoxicated once again. Either way, they'd be listening.

SIXTEEN

Thirty-seven hours before the polls opened in Virginia and Washington, the President appeared live on national television to announce that he had ordered an air attack in and around the Tunisian city of Talah. The Yidal terrorist unit was believed to train there, in a well-stocked compound on the edge of town.

And so the country became glued to yet another mini-war, one of pushbuttons and smart bombs and retired generals on CNN prattling on about this strategy or that. It was dark in Tunisia, thus no footage. The retired generals and their clueless interviewers did a lot of guessing. And waiting. Waiting for sunlight so the smoke and rubble could be broadcast to a jaded nation.

But Yidal had its sources, most likely the Israelis. The compound was empty when the smart bombs dropped in from nowhere. They hit their targets, shook the desert, destroyed the compound, but killed not a single terrorist. A couple strayed, however, one venturing into the center of Talah, where it hit a hospital. Another hit a small house where a family of seven was fast asleep. Fortunately, they never knew what happened.

Tunisian television was quick to cover the burning hospital, and at daybreak on the East Coast the country learned that the smart bombs weren't so smart after all. At least fifty bodies had been recovered, all very innocent civilians.

At some point during the early morning, the President developed a sudden uncharacteristic aversion to reporters, and could not be reached for comment. The Vice President, a man who'd said plenty when the attack started, was in seclusion with his staff somewhere in Washington.

The bodies piled up, the cameras kept rolling, and by midmorning world reaction was swift, brutal, and unanimous. The Chinese were threatening war. The French seemed inclined to join them. Even the Brits said the United States was trigger-happy.

Since the dead were nothing more than Tunisian peasants, certainly not Americans, the politicians were quick to politicize the debacle. The usual finger-pointing and grandstanding and calls for investigations happened before noon in Washington. And on the campaign circuit, those still in the race took a few moments to reflect on just how ill-fated the mission had been. None of them would have engaged in such desperate retaliation without better intelligence. None but the Vice President, who was still in seclusion. As the bodies were being counted, not a single candidate thought the raid was worthy of the risks. All condemned the President.

But it was Aaron Lake who attracted the most

attention. He found it difficult to move without tripping over cameramen. In a carefully worded statement, he said, without notes, 'We are inept. We are helpless. We are feeble. We should be ashamed of our inability to wipe out a ragtag little army of less than fifty cowards. You cannot simply push buttons and run for cover. It takes guts to fight wars on the ground. I have the guts. When I am President, no terrorist with American blood on his hands will be safe. That is my solemn promise.'

In the fury and chaos of the morning, Lake's words found their mark. Here was a man who meant what he said, who knew precisely what he would do. We wouldn't slaughter innocent peasants if a man with guts were making the decisions. Lake was the man.

In the bunker, Teddy weathered another storm. Bad intelligence was blamed for every disaster. When the raids were successful, the pilots and the brave boys on the ground and their commanders and the politicians who sent them into battle got the credit. But when the raids went wrong, as they usually did, the CIA got the blame.

He had advised against the attack. The Israelis had a tenuous and very secret agreement with Yidal – don't kill us, and we won't kill you. As long as the targets were Americans and an occasional European, then the Israelis would not get involved. Teddy knew this, but it was information he had not shared. Twenty-four hours before the attack, he had advised the President, in writing, that he doubted the terrorists would be in the compound when the bombs arrived. And, because of the target's proximity to Talah, there was an excellent chance of collateral damage.

Hatlee Beech opened the brown envelope without noticing that the right lower corner was somewhat wadded and slightly damaged. He was opening so many personal envelopes these days, he looked only at the return address to see who and where they came from. Nor did he notice the Tampa postmark.

He hadn't heard from Al Konyers in several weeks. He read the letter through without stopping, and found little if no interest in the fact that Al was using a new laptop. It was perfectly believable that Ricky's pen pal had taken a sheet of stationery from the Royal Sonesta in New Orleans, and was pecking out the letter at thirty-five thousand feet.

Wonder if he was flying first class? he asked himself. Probably so. They wouldn't have computer hookups back in coach, would they? Al had been in New Orleans on business, stayed at a very nice hotel, then flew first class to his next destination. The Brethren were interested in the financial conditions of all their pen pals. Nothing else mattered.

After he read the letter, he handed it to Finn Yarber, who was in the process of writing another one as poor Percy. They were working in the small conference room in the corner of the law library, their table littered with files and mail and a pretty assortment of soft pastel correspondence cards. Spicer was outside, at his table, guarding the door and studying point spreads.

179

'Who's Konyers?' Finn asked.

Beech was flipping through some files. They kept a neat folder on every pen pal, complete with the letters they received and copies of all letters they'd sent.

'Don't know much,' Beech said. 'Lives in the D.C. area, fake name, I'm sure. Uses one of those mailbox services. That's his third letter, I think.'

From the Konyers file Beech pulled out the first two letters. The one from December 11 read:

Dear Ricky:

Hello. My name is Al Konyers. I'm in my fifties. I like jazz, old movies, Humphrey Bogart, and I like to read biographies. I don't smoke and don't like people who do. Fun is Chinese take-out, a little wine, a black-and-white western with a good friend. Drop me a line.

Al Konyers

It was typewritten on plain white paper, the way most of them were at first. Fear was stamped between every line – fear of getting caught, fear of starting a long-distance relationship with a complete stranger. Every letter of every word was typewritten. He didn't even sign his name.

Ricky's first response was the standard letter Beech had written a hundred times now: Ricky's twenty-eight, in rehab, bad family, rich uncle, etc. And dozens of the same enthusiastic questions: What kind of work do you do? How about your family? Do you like to travel? If Ricky could bare his soul, then he needed something in return. Two pages of the same crap Beech had been writing for five months. He wanted so desperately to simply Xerox the damned thing. But he couldn't. He was forced to personalize each one, on nice pretty paper. And he sent Al the same handsome photo he'd sent to the others. The picture was the bait that hooked almost all of them.

Three weeks passed. On January 9, Trevor had delivered a second letter from Al Konyers. It was as clean and sterile as the first, probably typed with rubber gloves.

Dear Ricky:

I enjoyed your letter. I have to admit I felt sorry for you at first, but you seem to have adjusted well to rehab and know where you're going. I've never had problems with drugs and alcohol, so it's difficult for me to understand. It sounds as though you're getting the best treatment money can buy. You shouldn't be so harsh on your uncle. Think of where you might be if not for him.

You ask many questions about me. I'm not ready to discuss a lot of personal matters, but I understand your curiosity. I was married for thirty years, but not anymore. I live in D.C., and work for the government. My job is challenging and fulfilling.

I live alone. I have few close friends and prefer it that way. When I travel, it's usually to Asia. I adore Tokyo.

I'll keep you in my thoughts in the days to come.

Al Konyers

181

Just above the typewritten name, he'd scribbled the name 'Al,' with a black-felt pen, fine point.

The letter was most unimpressive for three reasons. First, Konyers did not have a wife, or at least he said he didn't. A wife was crucial for extortion. Threaten to tell the wife, to send her copies of all the letters from the gay pen pal, and the money rolled in.

Second, Al worked for the government, so he probably didn't have a lot of money.

Third, Al was much too scared to waste time with. Getting information was like pulling teeth. The Quince Garbes and Curtis Cateses were much more fun because they'd spent their lives in the closet and were now anxious to escape. Their letters were long and windy and filled with all the damning little facts an extortionist might need. Not Al. Al was boring. Al wasn't sure what he wanted.

So Ricky raised the stakes with his second letter, another piece of boilerplate Beech had perfected with practice. Ricky had just learned that he would be released in a few months! And he was from Baltimore. What a coincidence! And he might need some help getting a job. His rich uncle was refusing to help anymore, he was afraid of life on the outside without the help of friends, and he really couldn't trust his old friends because they were still on drugs, etc., etc.

The letter went unanswered, and Beech assumed that Al Konyers was frightened by it. Ricky was on his way to Baltimore, just an hour from Washington, and that was too close for Al.

While waiting for an answer from Al, the Quince

182

Garbe money landed, followed by the wire from Curtis in Dallas, and the Brethren found renewed energy in their scam. Ricky wrote Al the letter that was intercepted and analyzed at Langley.

Now, suddenly, Al's third letter had a very different tone. Finn Yarber read it twice, then reread the second letter from Al. 'Sounds like a different person, doesn't it?' he said.

'Yes, it does,' Beech said, looking at both letters. 'I think the old boy is finally excited about meeting Ricky.'

'I thought he worked for the government.'

'Says he does.'

'Then what's this about having business interests in Baltimore?'

'We worked for the government, didn't we?'

'Sure.'

'What was your highest salary on the bench?'

'When I was chief justice I made a hundred and fifty thousand.'

'I made a hundred and forty. Some of those professional bureaucrats make more than that. Plus, he's not married.'

'That's a problem.'

'Yeah, but let's keep pushing. He's got a big job, which means he's got a big boss, lots of colleagues, typical Washington hotshot. We'll find a pressure point somewhere.'

'What the hell,' Finn said.

What the hell, indeed. What was there to lose? So what if they pushed a little too hard, and Mr. Al got scared or got mad and decided to throw the letters away? You can't lose what you don't have.

Serious money was being made here. It was not

a time to be timid. Their aggressive tactics were producing spectacular results. The mail was growing each week, as was their offshore account. Their scam was foolproof because their pen pals lived double lives. Their victims had no one to complain to.

Negotiations were quick because the market was ripe. It was still winter in Jacksonville, and because the nights were chilly and the ocean was too cool to swim in, the busy season was a month away. There were hundreds of small rentals available along Neptune Beach and Atlantic Beach, including one almost directly across the street from Trevor. A man from Boston offered $600 cash for two months, and the real estate agent snatched it. The place was furnished with odds and ends no flea market would handle. The old shag carpet was well worn and emitted a permanent musty smell. It was perfect.

The renter's first chore was to cover the windows. Three of them faced the street and looked across to Trevor's, and during the first few hours of surveillance it became obvious how few clients came and went. There was so little business over there! When work surfaced it was usually done by the secretary, Jan, who also read a lot of magazines.

Others quietly moved into the rental, men and women with old suitcases and large duffel bags filled with electronic wizardry. The fragile furnishings were shoved to the rear of the cottage, and the front rooms were quickly filled with screens and monitors and listening devices of a dozen varieties.

Trevor himself would make an interesting case study for third-year law students. He arrived around 9 A.M., and spent the first hour reading newspapers. His morning client seemed to always arrive at ten-thirty, and after an exhaustive half-hour conference he was ready for lunch, always at Pete's Bar and Grill. He carried a phone with him, to prove his importance to the bartenders there, and he usually made two or three unnecessary calls to other lawyers. He called his bookie a lot.

Then he walked back to his office, past the rental where the CIA monitored every step, back to his desk where it was time for a nap. He came to life around three, and hit it hard for two hours. By then he needed another longneck from Pete's.

The second time they followed him to Trumble, he left the prison after an hour and returned to his office about 6 P.M. While he was having dinner in an oyster bar on Atlantic Boulevard, alone, an agent entered his office and found his old brief-case. In it were five letters from Percy and Ricky.

The commander of the silent army in and around Neptune Beach was a man named Klock-ner, the best Teddy had in the field of domestic street spying. Klockner had been instructed to intercept all mail flowing through the law office.

When Trevor went straight home after leaving the oyster bar, the five letters were taken across the street to the rental, where they were opened, copied, then resealed and replaced in Trevor's briefcase. None of the five was for Al Konyers.

At Langley, Deville read the five letters as they came off the fax. They were examined by two handwriting experts who agreed that Percy and

Ricky were not the same people. Using samples taken from their court files, it was determined, without much effort, that Percy was really former Justice Finn Yarber, and that Ricky was former U.S. District Judge Hatlee Beech.

Ricky's address was the Aladdin North box at the Neptune Beach post office. Percy, to their surprise, used a postal box in Atlantic Beach, one rented to an outfit called Laurel Ridge.

SEVENTEEN

For his next visit to Langley, the first in three weeks, the candidate arrived in a caravan of shiny black vans, all going too fast but who would complain. They were cleared and waved onward, deeper into the complex, until they roared to a collective stop near a very convenient door where all sorts of grim-faced, thick-necked young men were waiting. Lake rode the wave into the building, losing escorts as he went until finally he arrived not at the usual bunker but in Mr. Maynard's formal office, with a view of a small forest. Everyone else was left at the door. Alone, the two great men shook hands warmly and actually appeared happy to see one another.

Important things first. 'Congratulations on Virginia,' Teddy said.

Lake shrugged as if he wasn't sure. 'Thank you, in more ways than one.'

'It's a very impressive win, Mr. Lake,' Teddy said. 'Governor Tarry worked hard there for a year. Two months ago he had commitments from every precinct captain in the state. He looked unbeatable. Now, I think he's fading fast. It's often a disadvantage to be the front-runner early in the race.'

'Momentum is a strange animal in politics,' Lake observed wisely.

'Cash is even stranger. Right now, Governor Tarry can't find a dime because you've got it all. Money follows momentum.'

'I'm sure I'll say this many times, Mr. Maynard, but, well, thanks. You've given me an opportunity I'd hardly dreamed of.'

'Are you having any fun?'

'Not yet. If we win, the fun will come later.'

'The fun starts next Tuesday, Mr. Lake, with big Super Tuesday. New York, California, Massachusetts, Ohio, Georgia, Missouri, Maryland, Maine, Connecticut, all in one day. Almost six hundred delegates!' Teddy's eyes were dancing as if he could almost count the votes. 'And you're ahead in every state, Mr. Lake. Can you believe it?'

'No, I cannot.'

'It's true. You're neck and neck in Maine, for some damned reason, and it's close in California, but you're going to win big next Tuesday.'

'If you believe the polls,' Lake said, as if he didn't trust them himself. Fact was, like every candidate, Lake was addicted to the polls. He was actually gaining in California, a state with 140,000 defense workers.

'Oh, I believe them. And I believe that a landslide is coming on little Super Tuesday. They love you down South, Mr. Lake. They love guns and tough talk and such, and right now they're falling in love with Aaron Lake. Next Tuesday will be fun, but the following Tuesday will be a romp.'

Teddy Maynard was predicting a romp, and Lake couldn't help but smile. His polls showed the same trends, but it just sounded better coming from Teddy. He lifted a sheet of paper and read the latest polling data from around the country. Lake was ahead by at least five points in every state.

They reveled in their momentum for a few minutes, then Teddy turned serious. 'There's something you should know,' he said, and the smile was gone. He flipped a page and glanced at some notes. 'Two nights ago, in the Khyber Pass in the mountains of Afghanistan, a Russian long-range missile with nuclear warheads was moved by truck into Pakistan. It is now en route to Iran, where it will be used for God knows what. The missile has a range of three thousand miles, and the capability of delivering four nuclear bombs. The price was about thirty million dollars U.S., cash up front paid by the Iranians through a bank in Luxembourg. It's still there, in an account believed to be controlled by Natty Chenkov's people.'

'I thought he was stockpiling, not selling.'

'He needs cash, and he's getting it. In fact, he's probably the only man we know who's collecting it faster than you.'

Teddy didn't do humor well, but Lake laughed out of politeness anyway.

'Is the missile operational?' Lake asked.

'We think so. It originated from a collection of silos near Kiev, and we believe it's of a recent make and model. With so many lying around, why would the Iranians buy an old one? Yes, it's safe to assume it's fully operational.'

'Is it the first?'

'There've been some spare parts and plutonium, to Iran and Iraq and India and others, but I think this is the first fully assembled, ready-to-shoot missile.'

'Are they anxious to use it?'

'We don't think so. It appears as if the transaction was instigated by Chenkov. He needs the money to buy other kinds of weapons. He's shopping his wares, things he doesn't need.'

'Do the Israelis know it?'

'No. Not yet. You have to be careful with them. Everything is give and take. Someday, if we need something from them, then we might tell them about this transaction.'

For a moment, Lake longed to be President, and immediately. He wanted to know everything Teddy knew, then he realized he probably never would. There was, after all, a sitting President right then, at that moment, albeit a lame duck, and Teddy wasn't chatting with him about Chenkov and his missiles.

'What do the Russians think about my campaign?' he asked.

'At first, they weren't concerned. Now they're watching closely. But you have to remember, there is no such thing as a Russian voice anymore. The free marketers speak favorably of you because they fear the Communists. The hard-liners are scared of you. It's very complex.'

'And Chenkov?'

'I'm ashamed to say we're not that close to him,

yet. But we're working on it. We should have some ears in the vicinity soon.'

Teddy tossed his papers onto his desk, and rolled himself closer to Lake. The many wrinkles in his forehead pinched closer together, downward. His bushy eyebrows fell hard on his sad eyes. 'Listen to me, Mr. Lake,' he said, his voice much more somber. 'You have this thing won. There will be a bump or two in the road, things we cannot foresee, and even if we could we'd be powerless to prevent them. We'll ride them out together. The damage will be slight. You're something brand new and the people like you. You're doing a marvelous job and communicating. Keep the message simple – our security is at risk, the world is not as safe as it looks. I'll take care of the money, and I'll certainly keep the country frightened. That missile in the Khyber Pass, we could've detonated it. Five thousand people would've been killed, five thousand Pakistanis. Nuclear bombs exploding in the mountains. You think we'd wake up and worry about the stock market? Not a chance. I'll take care of the fear, Mr. Lake. You keep your nose clean and run hard.'

'I'm running as hard as I can.'

'Run harder, and no surprises, okay?'

'Certainly not.'

Lake wasn't sure what he meant by surprises, but he let it pass. Just a bit of grandfatherly wisdom, perhaps.

Teddy rolled away again. He found his buttons and a screen dropped from the ceiling. They spent twenty minutes viewing rough cuts of the next series of Lake ads, then said their goodbyes.

191

Lake sped away from Langley, two vans in front and one behind, all racing to Reagan National Airport, where the jet was waiting. He wanted a quiet night in Georgetown, at home where the world was held at bay, where he could read a book in solitude, with no one watching or listening. He longed for the anonymity of the streets, the nameless faces, the Arab baker on M Street who made a perfect bagel, the used-book dealer on Wisconsin, the coffeehouse where they roasted beans from Africa. Would he ever be able to walk the streets again, like a normal person, doing whatever he pleased? Something told him no, that those days were gone, probably forever.

When Lake was airborne, Deville entered the bunker and announced to Teddy that Lake had come and gone without trying to check the mailbox. It was time for the daily briefing on the Lake mess. Teddy was spending more time than he'd planned worrying about what his candidate might do next.

The five letters Klockner and his group intercepted from Trevor had been thoroughly researched. Two had been written by Yarber as Percy; the other three by Beech as Ricky. The five pen pals were in different states. Four were using fictitious names; one was bold enough not to hide behind an alias. The letters were basically the same: Percy and Ricky were troubled young men in rehab, trying desperately to pull their lives together, both talented and still able to dream big dreams, but in need of moral and physical support from new friends because the old ones were dangerous. They freely divulged their sins and foibles, their weaknesses and heartaches. They rambled about their lives after rehab, their hopes and dreams of all the things they wanted to do. They were proud of their tans and their muscles, and seemed anxious to show their new hardened bodies to their pen pals.

Only one letter asked for money. Ricky wanted a loan of $1,000 from a correspondent named Peter in Spokane, Washington. He said the money was needed to cover some expenses his uncle was refusing to pay.

Teddy had read the letters more than once. The request for money was important because it began to shed light on the Brethren's little game. Perhaps it was just a two-bit enterprise someone taught them, some other con who'd finished his time at Trumble and was now roaming at large stealing anew.

But the size of the stakes was not the issue. It was a flesh game – thinner waists and bronze skin and firm biceps – and their candidate was in the middle of it.

There were still questions, but Teddy was patient. They would watch the mail. The pieces would fall into place.

With Spicer guarding the door to the conference room, and daring anyone to use the law library, Beech and Yarber labored away with their mail. To Al Konyers, Beech wrote:

Dear Al:
    Thanks for your last letter. It means so much to me to hear from you. I feel like I've

193

been living in a cage for months, and I'm slowly seeing daylight. Your letters help to open the door. Please don't stop writing.

I'm sorry if I've bored you with too much personal stuff. I respect your privacy and hope I haven't asked too many questions. You seem like a very sensitive man who enjoys solitude and the finer things of life. I thought about you last night when I watched *Key Largo*, the old Bogart and Bacall film. I could almost taste the Chinese carry-out. The food here is pretty good, I guess, but they simply can't do Chinese.

I have a great idea. In two months when I get out of here, let's rent *Casablanca and African Queen*, get the carry-out, get a bottle of nonalcoholic wine, and spend a quiet evening on the sofa. God, I get excited just thinking about life on the outside and doing real things again.

Forgive me if I'm going too fast, Al. It's just that I've done without a lot of things here, and not just booze and good food. Know what I mean?

The halfway house in Baltimore is willing to take me if I can find a part-time job of some type. You said you had some interests there. I know I'm asking a lot because you don't know me, but can you arrange this? I will be forever grateful.

Please write me soon, Al. Your letters, and the hopes and dreams of leaving here in two months with a job on the outside, sustain me in my darkest hours.

Thanks, friend.

Love, Ricky

The one to Quince Garbe had a very different tone. Beech and Yarber had kicked it around for several days. The final draft read:

Dear Quince:
Your father owns a bank, yet you say you can only raise another $10,000. I think you're lying, Quince, and it really ticks me off. I'm tempted to send the file to your father and wife anyway.

I'll settle for $25,000, immediately, same wiring instructions.

And don't threaten suicide. I really don't care what you do. We'll never meet, and I think you're a sicko anyway.

Wire the damned money, Quince, and now!

Love, Ricky

Klockner worried that Trevor might visit Trumble one day before noon, then drop off the mail at some point along the way before returning to his office or his home. There was no way to intercept it while en route. It was imperative that he haul it back, and leave it overnight so they could get their hands on it.

He worried, but at the same time Trevor was proving to be a late starter. He showed few signs of life until after his two o'clock nap.

So when he informed his secretary that he was about to leave for Trumble at 11 A.M., the rental across the street sprang into action. A call was immediately placed to Trevor's office by a middle-aged woman claiming to be a Mrs. Beltrone, who explained to Jan that she and her rich husband were in dire need of a quick divorce. The secretary put her on hold, and yelled down the hallway for Trevor to wait a second. Trevor was gathering papers from his desk and placing them in his briefcase. The camera in the ceiling above him caught his look of displeasure at having been interrupted by a new client.

'She says she's rich!' Jan yelled, and Trevor's frown disappeared. He sat down and waited.

Mrs. Beltrone unloaded on the secretary. She was wife number three, the husband was much older, they had a home in Jacksonville but spent most of their time at their home in Bermuda. Also had a home in Vail. They'd been planning the divorce for some time, everything had been agreed upon, no fighting at all, very amicable, just needed a good lawyer to handle the paperwork. Mr. Carson had come highly recommended, but they had to act fast for some undisclosed reason.

Trevor took over and listened to the same story. Mrs. Beltrone was sitting across the street in the rental, working from a script the team had put together just for this occasion.

'I really need to see you,' she said after fifteen minutes of baring her soul.

'Well, I'm awfully busy,' Trevor said, as if he were flipping pages in half a dozen daily appointment books. Mrs. Beltrone was watching him on the monitor. His feet were on the desk, his eyes closed, his bow tie crooked. The life of an awfully busy lawyer.

'Please,' she begged. 'We need to get this over with. I must see you today.'

'Where's your husband?'

'He's in France, but he'll be here tomorrow.'

'Well, uh, let's see,' Trevor mumbled, playing with his bow tie.

'What's your fee?' she asked, and his eyes flew open.

'Well, this is obviously more complicated than your simple no-fault. I'd have to charge a fee of ten thousand dollars.' He grimaced when he said it, holding his breath for the response.

'I'll bring it today,' she said. 'Can I see you at one?'

He was on his feet, hovering over the phone. 'How about one-thirty?' he managed to say.

'I'll be there.'

'Do you know where my office is?'

'My driver can find it. Thanks, Mr. Carson.'

Just call me Trevor, he almost said. But she was gone.

They watched as he wrung his hands together, then pumped his fists, gritted his teeth, said, 'Yes!' He'd hooked a big one.

Jan appeared from the hall and said, 'Well?'

'She'll be here at one-thirty. Get this place cleaned up a little.'

'I'm not a maid. Can you get some money up front? I need to pay bills.'

'I'll get the damned money.'

Trevor attacked his bookshelves, straightening volumes he hadn't touched in years, dusting the planks with a paper towel, stuffing files in drawers.

When he charged his desk, Jan finally felt a twinge of guilt and began vacuuming the reception area.

They labored through lunch, their bitching and straining making for great amusement across the street.

No sign of Mrs. Beltrone at one-thirty.

'Where the hell is she?' Trevor barked down the hall just after two.

'Maybe she checked around, got some more references,' Jan said.

'What did you say?' he yelled.

'Nothing, boss.'

'Call her,' he demanded at two-thirty.

'She didn't leave a number.'

'You didn't get a number?'

'That's not what I said. I said she didn't leave a number.'

At three-thirty, Trevor stormed out of his office, still trying desperately to uphold his end of a raging argument with a woman he'd fired at least ten times in the past eight years.

They followed him straight to Trumble. He was in the prison for fifty-three minutes, and when he left it was after five, too late to drop off mail in either Neptune Beach or Atlantic Beach. He returned to his office and left his briefcase on his desk. Then, predictably, he went to Pete's for drinks and dinner.

EIGHTEEN

The unit from Langley flew to Des Moines, where the agents rented two cars and a van, then drove forty minutes to Bakers, Iowa. They arrived in the quiet, snowbound little town two days before the letter. By the time Quince picked it up at the post office, they knew the names of the postmaster, the mayor, the chief of police, and the short-order cook at the pancake house next to the hardware store. But no one in Bakers knew them.

They watched Quince hurry to the bank after leaving the post office. Thirty minutes later, two agents known only as Chap and Wes found the corner of the bank where Mr. Garbe, Jr., did business, and they presented themselves to his secretary as inspectors from the Federal Reserve. They certainly looked official – dark suits, black shoes, short hair, long overcoats, clipped speech, efficient manners.

Quince was locked inside, and at first seemed unwilling to come out. They impressed upon his secretary the urgency of their visit, and after almost forty minutes the door opened slightly. Mr. Garbe looked as though he'd been crying. He was pale, shaken, unhappy with the prospect of entertaining anyone. But he showed them in anyway, too unnerved to ask for identification. He didn't even catch their names.

He sat across the massive desk, and looked at the twins facing him. 'What can we do for you?' he asked, with a very faint smile.

'Is the door locked?' Chap asked.

'Why yes, it is.' The twins got the impression that most of Mr. Garbe's day was spent behind locked doors.

'Can anyone hear us?' Wes asked.

'No.' Quince was even more rattled now.

'We're not reserve officials,' Chap said. 'We lied.'

Quince wasn't sure if he should be angry or relieved or even more frightened, so he just sat there for a second, mouth open, frozen, waiting to be shot.

'It's a long story,' Wes said.

'You've got five minutes.'

'Actually, we have as long as we want.'

'This is my office. Get out.'

'Not so fast. We know some things.'

'I'll call security.'

'No you won't.'

'We've seen the letter,' Chap said. 'The one you just got from the post office.'

'I picked up several.'

'But only one from Ricky.'

Quince's shoulders sagged, his eyes closed slowly. Then they opened again and looked at the tormentors in total, absolute defeat. 'Who are you?' he mumbled.

'We're not enemies.'

'You're working for him, aren't you?'

'Him?'

'Ricky, or whoever the hell he is.'

'No,' Wes said. 'He's our enemy too. Let's just say that we have a client who's in the same boat you're in, more or less. We've been hired to protect him.'

Chap pulled a thick envelope from his coat pocket and tossed it on the desk. 'There's twenty-five thousand cash. Send it to Ricky.'

Quince stared at the envelope, his mouth open wide. His poor brain was choked with so many thoughts he was dizzy. So he closed his eyes again, and squinted fiercely in a vain effort to organize things. Forget the question of who they were. How did they read the letter? Why were they offering him money? How much did they know?

He sure as hell couldn't trust them.

'The money's yours,' Wes said. 'In return, we need some information.'

'Who is Ricky?' Quince asked, his eyes barely open.

'What do you know about him?' Chap asked.

'His name's not Ricky.'

'True.'

'He's in prison.'

'True,' Chap said again.

'Says he has a wife and children.'

'Partially true. The wife is now an ex-wife. The children are still his.'

'Says they're destitute, and that's why he's scamming people.'

'Not exactly. His wife is quite wealthy, and his

children have followed the money. We're not sure why he's scamming people.'

'But we'd like to stop him,' Chap added. 'We need your help.'

Quince suddenly realized that for the first time in his life, in all of his fifty-one years, he was sitting in the presence of two living, breathing people who knew he was a homosexual. The knowledge terrified him. For a second he wanted to deny it, to concoct some story of how he came to know Ricky, but invention failed him. He was too scared to be inspired.

Then he realized that these two, whoever they were, could ruin him. They knew his little secret, and they had the power to wreck his life.

And they were offering $25,000 cash?

Poor Quince covered his eyes with his knuckles and said, 'What do you want?'

Chap and Wes thought he was about to cry. They didn't particularly care, but there was no need for it. 'Here's the deal, Mr. Garbe,' said Chap. 'You take the money lying there on your desk, and you tell us everything about Ricky. Show us your letters. Show us everything. If you have a file or a box or some secret place where you've hidden everything, we'd like to see it. Once we've gathered all we need, then we'll leave. We'll disappear as quickly as we've come, and you'll never know who we are or who we're protecting.'

'And you'll keep the secrets?'

'Absolutely.'

'There's no reason for us to tell anyone about you,' Wes added.

'Can you make him stop?' Quince asked, staring at them.

Chap and Wes paused and glanced at each other. Their responses had been perfect so far, but this question had no clear answer. 'We can't promise, Mr. Garbe,' Wes said. 'But we'll try our best to put this Ricky character out of business. As we said, he's upsetting our client too.'

'You've got to protect me on this.'

'We'll do all we can.'

Suddenly Quince stood and leaned forward with his palms flat on the desk. 'Then I have no choice,' he announced. He didn't touch the money, but walked a few steps to an ancient glass bookcase filled with weathered and peeling volumes. With one key he unlocked the case, and with another he opened a small, hidden safe on the second shelf from the floor. Carefully, he withdrew a thin, letter-sized folder, which he delicately placed next to the envelope filled with cash.

Just as he opened the file, an offensive, high-pitched voice squawked through the intercom, 'Mr. Garbe, your father would like to see you immediately.'

Quince bolted upright in horror, his cheeks instantly pale, his face contorted in panic. 'Uh, tell him I'm in a meeting,' he said, trying to sound reassuring but coming off as a hopeless liar.

'You tell him,' she said, and the intercom clicked.

'Excuse me,' he said, actually trying to smile. He picked up the receiver, punched three numbers, and turned his back on Wes and Chap so that maybe they wouldn't hear.

'Dad, it's me. What's up?' he said, head low.

A long pause as the old man filled his ear.

Then, 'No, no, they're not from the Federal Reserve. They're, uh, they're lawyers from Des Moines. They represent the family of an old college buddy of mine. That's all.'

A shorter pause.

'Uh, Franklin Delaney, you wouldn't remember him. He died four months ago, without a will, a big mess. No, Dad, uh, it has nothing to do with the bank.'

He hung up. Not a bad piece of lying. The door was locked. That's all that mattered.

Wes and Chap stood and moved in tandem to the edge of the desk, where they leaned forward together as Quince opened the file. The first thing they noticed was the photo, paper-clipped to the inside flap. Wes gently removed it, and said, 'Is this supposed to be Ricky?'

'That's him,' Quince said, ashamed but determined to get through it.

'A nice-looking young man,' Chap said, as if they were staring at a *Playboy* centerfold. All three were immediately uncomfortable.

'You know who Ricky is, don't you?' Quince asked.

'Yes.'

'Then tell me.'

'No, it's not part of the deal.'

'Why can't you tell me? I'm giving you everything you want.'

'That's not what we agreed on.'

'I want to kill the bastard.'

'Relax, Mr. Garbe. We have a deal. You get the money, we get the file, nobody gets hurt.'

'Let's go back to the beginning,' Chap said, looking down at the fragile and suffering little man in the oversized chair. 'How did it all start?'

Quince moved some papers around in the file and produced a thin magazine. 'I bought this at a bookstore in Chicago,' he said, sliding it around so they could read it. The title was *Out and About*, and it described itself as a publication for mature men with alternative lifestyles. He let them take in the cover, then flipped to the back pages. Wes and Chap didn't try to touch it, but their eyes took in as much as possible. Very few pictures, lots of small print. It wasn't pornography by any means.

On page forty-six was a small section of personals. One was circled with a red pen. It read:

> SWM in 20s looking for kind and
> discreet gentleman in 40s or 50s
> to pen pal with.

Wes and Chap leaned lower to read it, then came back up together. 'So you answered this ad?' Chap said.

'I did. I sent a little note, and about two weeks later I heard from Ricky.'

'Do you have a copy of your note?'

'No. I didn't copy my letters. Nothing left this office. I was afraid to make copies around here.'

Wes and Chap frowned in disbelief, then great disappointment. What kind of dumb ass were they dealing with here?

'Sorry,' Quince said, tempted to grab the cash before they changed their minds.

Moving things along, he removed the first letter from Ricky and thrust it at them. 'Just lay it down,' Wes said, and they leaned in again, inspecting without touching. They were very slow readers, Quince noticed, and they read with incredible concentration. His mind was beginning to clear, and a glimmer of hope emerged. How sweet it was to have the money and not have to worry about another crooked loan, another pack of lies to cover his trail. And now he had allies, Wes and Chap here, and God knows who else working against Ricky. His heart slowed a little and his breathing was not as labored.

'The next letter please,' Chap said.

Quince laid them out in sequence, one beside the other, three lavender in color, one a soft blue, one yellow, all written in the tedious block handwriting of a person with plenty of time. When they finished one page, Chap would carefully arrange the next one with a pair of tweezers. Their fingers touched nothing.

The odd thing about the letters, as Chap and Wes would whisper to each other much later, was that they were so thoroughly believable. Ricky was wounded and tortured and in dire need of someone to talk to. He was pitiful and sympathetic. And there was hope because the worst was over for him and he would soon be free to pursue new friendships. The writing was superb!

After a deafening silence, Quince said, 'I need to make a phone call.'

'To whom?'

'It's business.'

Wes and Chap looked at each other with uncertainty, then nodded. Quince walked with the phone to his credenza and watched Main Street below while talking to another banker.

At some point, Wes began making notes, no doubt in preparation for the cross-examination to come. Quince loitered by the bookcase, trying to read a newspaper, trying to ignore the note-taking. He was calm now, thinking as clearly as possible, plotting his next move, the one after these goons left him.

'Did you send a check for a hundred thousand dollars?' Chap asked.

'I did.'

Wes, the grimmer-faced of the two, glared at him with contempt, as if to say, 'What a fool.'

They read some more, took a few notes, whispered and mumbled between themselves.

'How much money has your client sent?' Quince asked, just for the hell of it.

Wes got even grimmer and said, 'We can't say.'

No surprise to Quince. The boys had no sense of humor.

They sat down after an hour, and Quince took his seat in his banker's chair.

'Just a couple of questions,' Chap said, and Quince knew they'd be talking for another hour.

'How'd you book the gay cruise?'

'It's in the letter there. This thug gave me the name and number of a travel agency in New York. I called, then sent a money order. It was easy.'

'Easy? Have you done it before?'

'Are we here to talk about my sex life?'

'No.'

'So let's stick to the issues,' Quince said like a real ass, and he felt good again. The banker in him boiled for a moment. Then he thought of something he simply couldn't resist. With a straight face, he said, 'The cruise is still paid for. You guys wanna go?'

Fortunately, they laughed. It was a quick flash of humor, then back to business. Chap said, 'Did you consider using a pseudonym?'

'Yes, of course. It was stupid not to. But I'd never done this before. I thought the guy was legitimate. He's in Florida, I'm in Podunk, Iowa. It never crossed my mind the guy was a fraud.'

'We'll need copies of all this,' Wes said.

'That could be a problem.'

'Why?'

'Where would you copy it?'

'The bank doesn't have a copier?'

'It does, but you're not copying that file in this bank.'

'Then we'll take it to a quick print somewhere.'

'This is Bakers. We don't have a quick print.'

'Do you have an office supply store?'

'Yes, and the owner owes my bank eighty thousand dollars. He sits next to me at the Rotary Club. You're not copying it there. I'm not going to be seen with that file.'

Chap and Wes looked at each other, then at Quince. Wes said, 'Okay, look. I'll stay here with you. Chap will take the file and find a copier.'

'Where?'

'The drugstore,' Wes said.

'You've found the drugstore?'

'Sure, we needed some tweezers.'

'That copier's twenty years old.'

'No, they have a new one.'

'You must be careful, okay? The pharmacist is my secretary's second cousin. This is a very small town.'

Chap took the file and walked to the door. It clicked loudly when he unlocked it, and when he stepped through he was immediately under scrutiny. The secretary's desk was crowded with older women, all busy doing nothing until Chap emerged and they froze and gawked. Old Mr. Garbe was not far away, holding a ledger, pretending to be busy but himself consumed with curiosity. Chap nodded to them all and eased away, passing as he went virtually every employee of the bank.

The door clicked loudly again as Quince locked the damned thing before anyone could barge in. He and Wes chatted awkwardly about this and that for a few minutes, the conversation almost dying at times for lack of common ground. Forbidden sex had brought them together, and they certainly had to avoid that subject. Life in Bakers was of little interest. Quince could ask nothing about Wes' background.

Finally, he said, 'What should I say in my letter to Ricky?'

Wes warmed to the idea immediately. 'Well, I would wait, first of all. Wait a month. Let him sweat. If you hurry back with a response, and with the money, he might think it's too easy.'

'What if he gets mad?'

'He won't. He has plenty of time, and he wants the money.'

'Do you see all his mail?'

'We think we have access to most of it.'

Quince was overcome with curiosity. Sitting with a man who now knew his deepest secret, he felt as though he could prod. 'How will you stop him?'

And Wes, for no reason he would ever understand, said simply, 'We'll probably just kill him.'

A radiant peace broke out around the eyes of Quince Garbe, a warm calming glow that spread through his tortured countenance. His wrinkles softened. His lips spread into a tiny smile. His inheritance would be safe after all, and when the old man was gone and the money was his he'd flee this life and live as he pleased.

'How nice,' he said softly. 'How very nice.'

Chap took the file to a motel room where a leased color copier was waiting with other members of the unit. Three sets were made, and thirty minutes later he was back at the bank. Quince inspected his originals; everything was in order. He carefully relocked the file, then said to his guests, 'I think it's time for you to go.'

They left without shaking hands or the usual good-byes. What was there to say?

A private jet was waiting at the local airport, whose runway was barely long enough. Three hours after leaving Quince, Chap and Wes reported to Langley. Their mission was a resounding success.

★

210

A summary of the account in the Geneva Trust Bank was procured with a bribe of $40,000 to a Bahamian banking official, a man they'd used before. Boomer Realty had a balance of $189,000. Its lawyer had about $68,000 in his account. The summary listed all the transactions – money wired in, money taken out. Deville's people were trying desperately to track down the originators of the wires. They knew about Mr. Garbe's remitting bank in Des Moines, and they knew that another wire of $100,000 had been sent from a bank in Dallas. They could not, however, find out who'd originated that wire.

They were scrambling on many fronts when Teddy summoned Deville to the bunker. York was with him. The table was covered with copies of Garbe's file and copies of the bank summaries.

Deville had never seen his boss so dejected. York too had little to say. York was bearing the brunt of the Lake screwup, though Teddy was blaming himself.

'The latest,' Teddy said softly.

Deville never sat while in the bunker. 'We're still tracking the money. We've made contact with the magazine *Out and About*. It's published in New Haven, a very small outfit, and I'm not sure if we'll be able to penetrate. Our contact in the Bahamas is on retainer and we'll know if and when any wires are received. We have a unit ready to search Lake's offices on Capitol Hill, but that's a long shot. I'm not optimistic. We have twenty people on the ground in Jacksonville.'

'How many of our people are shadowing Lake?'

'We've just gone from thirty to fifty.'

'He must be watched. We cannot turn our backs. He is not the person we thought he was, and if we lose sight of him for one hour he might mail a letter, or buy another magazine.'

'We know. We're doing the best we can.'

'This is our highest domestic priority.'

'I know.'

'What about planting someone inside the prison?' Teddy asked. It was a new idea, one hatched by York within the past hour.

Deville rubbed his eyes and chewed his nails for a moment, then said, 'I'll go to work on it. We'll have to pull strings we've never pulled before.'

'How many prisoners are in the federal system?' York asked.

'One hundred thirty-five thousand, give or take,' Deville said.

'Surely we could slip in another, couldn't we?'

'I'll give it a look.'

'Do we have contacts at the Bureau of Prisons?'

'It's new territory, but we're working on it. We're using an old friend at Justice. I'm optimistic.'

Deville left them for a while. He'd get called back in an hour or so. York and Teddy would have another checklist of questions and thoughts and errands for him to tend to.

'I don't like the idea of searching his office on Capitol Hill,' York said. 'It's too risky. And besides, it would take a week. Those guys have a million files.'

'I don't like it either,' Teddy said softly.

'Let's get our guys in Documents to write a

letter from Ricky to Lake. We'll wire the envelope, track it, maybe it will lead us to his file.'

'That's an excellent idea. Tell Deville.'

York made a note on a pad filled with many other notes, most of which had been scratched through. He scribbled to pass the time, then asked the question he'd been saving. 'Will you confront him?'

'Not yet.'

'When?'

'Maybe never. Let's gather the intelligence, learn all we can. He seems to be very quiet about his other life, perhaps it came about after his wife died. Who knows? Maybe he can keep it quiet.'

'But he has to know that you know. Otherwise, he might take another chance. If he knows we're always watching, he'll behave himself. Maybe.'

'Meanwhile the world's going to hell. Nuclear arms are bought and sold and sneaked across borders. We're tracking seven small wars with three more on the brink. A dozen new terrorist groups last month alone. Maniacs in the Middle East building armies and hoarding oil. And we sit here hour after hour plotting against three felonious judges who are at this very moment probably playing gin rummy.'

'They're not stupid,' York said.

'No, but they're clumsy. Their nets have snared the wrong person.'

'I guess we picked the wrong person.'

'No, they did.'

213

NINETEEN

The memo arrived by fax from the Regional Supervisor, Bureau of Prisons, Washington. It was directed to M. Emmitt Broon, the warden of Trumble. In terse but standard language the supervisor said he'd reviewed the logs from Trumble and was bothered by the number of visits by one Trevor Carson, attorney for three of the inmates. Lawyer Carson had reached the point of logging in almost every day.

While every inmate certainly had a constitutional right to meet with his attorney, the prison likewise had the power to regulate the traffic. Beginning immediately, attorney-client visits would be restricted to Tuesdays, Thursdays, and Saturdays, between the hours of 3 and 6 P.M. Exceptions would be granted liberally for good cause shown.

The new policy would be utilized for a period of ninety days, after which time it would be reviewed.

Fine with the warden. He too had grown suspicious of Trevor's almost daily appearances. He'd questioned the front desk and the guards in a vain effort to determine what, exactly, was the nature of all this legal work. Link, the guard who usually escorted Trevor to the conference room, and who usually pocketed a couple of twenties on each visit, told the warden that the lawyer and Mr. Spicer talked about cases and appeals and such. 'Just a bunch of law crap,' Link said.

'And you always search his briefcase?' the warden had asked.

'Always,' Link had replied.

Out of courtesy, the warden dialed the number of Mr. Trevor Carson in Neptune Beach. The phone was answered by a woman who said rudely, 'Law office.'

'Mr. Trevor Carson, please.'

'Who's calling?'

'This is Emmitt Broon.'

'Well, Mr. Broon, he's taking a nap right now.'

'I see. Could you possibly wake him? I'm the warden at the federal prison at Trumble, and I need to speak with him.'

'Just a minute.'

He waited for a long time, and when she returned she said, 'I'm sorry. I couldn't wake him up. Could I have him return your call?'

'No, thank you. I'll just fax him a note.'

The idea of a reverse scam was hatched by York, while playing golf on a Sunday, and as his game progressed, occasionally on the fairways but more often in the sand and trees, the scheme grew and grew and became brilliant. He abandoned his pals after fourteen holes and called Teddy.

They would learn the tactics of their adversaries.

And they could divert attention away from Al Konyers. There was nothing to lose.

The letter was created by York, and assigned to one of the top forgers in Documents. The pen pal was christened Brant White, and the first note was handwritten on a plain, white, but expensive correspondence card.

Dear Ricky:

    Saw your ad, liked it. I'm fifty-five, in great shape, and looking for more than a pen pal. My wife and I just bought a home in Palm Valley, not far from Neptune Beach. We'll be down in three weeks, with plans to stay for two months.

    If interested, send photo. If I like what I see, then I'll give more details.

Brant

The return address was from Brant, P.O. Box 88645, Upper Darby, PA 19082.

To save two or three days, a Philadelphia postmark was applied in Documents, and the letter was flown to Jacksonville where agent Klockner himself delivered it to Aladdin North's little box in the Neptune Beach post office. It was a Monday.

After his nap the following day, Trevor picked up the mail and headed west, out of Jacksonville, along the familiar route to Trumble. He was greeted by the same guards, Mackey and Vince, at the front door, and he signed the same logbook Rufus shoved in front of him. He followed Link into the visitors' area and to a corner where Spicer was waiting in one of the small attorney-conference rooms.

'I'm catchin some heat,' Link said as they stepped into the room. Spicer did not look up. Trevor handed two twenties to Link, who took them in a flash.

'From who?' Trevor asked, opening his brief-case. Spicer was reading a newspaper.

'The warden.'

'Hell, he's cut back on my visits. What else does he want?'

'Don't you understand?' Spicer said, without lowering the newspaper. 'Link here is upset because he's not collecting as much. Right, Link?'

'You got that right. I don't know what kinda funny business you boys are runnin here, but if I tightened up on my inspections you'd be in trouble, wouldn't you?'

'You're being paid well,' Trevor said.

'That's what you think.'

'How much do you want?' Spicer said, staring at him now.

'A thousand a month, cash,' he said, looking at Trevor. 'I'll pick it up at your office.'

'A thousand bucks and the mail doesn't get checked,' Spicer said.

'Yep.'

'And not a word to anybody.'

'Yep.'

'It's a deal. Now get outta here.'

Link smiled at both of them and left the room. He positioned himself outside the door, and for the benefit of the closed-circuit cameras looked through the window occasionally.

Inside, the routine varied little. The exchange of mail happened first and took only a second. From a worn manila folder, the same one every time, Joe Roy Spicer removed the outgoing letters and handed them to Trevor, who took the incoming mail from his briefcase and gave it to his client.

There were six letters to be mailed. Some days there were as many as ten, seldom less than five. Though Trevor didn't keep records, or copies, or documents in a file that would serve as proof that he had anything whatsoever to do with the Brethren's little scam, he knew there had to be twenty or thirty potential victims currently being set up. He recognized some of the names and addresses.

Twenty-one to be exact, according to Spicer's precise records. Twenty-one serious prospects, with another eighteen who were marginal. Almost forty pen pals currently hiding in their various closets, some terrified of their shadows, others getting bolder by the week, still others on the verge of kicking down the door and dashing off to meet Ricky or Percy.

The difficult part was being patient. The scam was working, money was changing hands, the temptation was to squeeze them too quickly. Beech and Yarber were proving to be workhorses, laboring over their letters for hours at a time while Spicer directed operations. It took discipline to hook a new pen pal, one with money, then ply him with enough pretty words to earn his trust.

'Aren't we due for a bust?' Trevor said.

Spicer was flipping through the new letters. 'Don't tell me you're broke,' he said. 'You're making more than we are.'

'My money's tucked away just like yours. I'd just like to have some more of it.'

'So would I.' Spicer looked at the envelope from Brant in Upper Darby, Pa. 'Ah, a new one,' he mumbled to himself, then opened it. He read it quickly, and was surprised by its tone. No fear, no wasted words, no peeking around corners. This man was ready for action.

'Where's Palm Valley?' he asked.

'Ten miles south of the beaches. Why?'

'What kinda place is it?'

'It's one of the gated golf communities for rich retirees, almost all from up North.'

'How much are the houses?'

'Well, I've never been there, okay. They keep the damned gate locked, guards everywhere like somebody might break in and steal their golf carts, but –'

'How much are the houses?'

'Nothing less than a million. I've seen a couple advertised for three million.'

'Wait here,' Spicer said, gathering his file and walking to the door.

'Where you going?' Trevor asked.

'To the library. I'll be back in half an hour.'

'I got things to do.'

'No you don't. Read the newspaper.'

Spicer said something to Link, who escorted him through the visitors' area and out of the administration building. He walked quickly along the manicured grounds. The sun was warm, and the gardeners were earning their fifty cents an hour.

So were the keepers of the law library. Beech

and Yarber were hiding in their little conference room, taking a break from their writings with a game of chess, when Spicer entered in a rush, with an uncharacteristic smile. 'Boys, we've finally hooked the big one,' he said, and tossed Brant's letter on the table. Beech read it aloud.

'Palm Valley is one of the golf communities for rich folks,' Spicer explained proudly. 'Houses go for about three million. The boy's got plenty of dough and he ain't much for letters.'

'He does seem anxious,' Yarber observed.

'We need to move fast,' Spicer said. 'He wants to come down in three weeks.'

'What's the upside potential?' Beech asked. He loved the jargon of those who invested millions.

'At least a half a million,' Spicer said. 'Let's do the letter now. Trevor is waiting.'

Beech opened one of his many files and displayed his wares; sheets of paper in soft pastels. 'I think I'll try the peach,' he said.

'Oh definitely,' Spicer said. 'Gotta do peach.'

Ricky wrote a scaled-down version of the initial contact letter. Twenty-eight years old, college graduate, locked down in rehab but on the verge of release, probably in ten days, very lonely, looking for a mature man to start a relationship. How convenient that Brant would be living nearby, because Ricky had a sister in Jacksonville and he'd be staying with her. There were no obstacles, no hurdles to cross. He'd be ready for Brant when he came South. But he'd like a photo first. Was Brant really married? Would his wife be living at Palm Valley too? Or would she stay up there in Pennsylvania? Wouldn't it be great if she did?

They enclosed the same color photo they'd used a hundred times. It had proved to be irresistible.

The peach envelope was taken by Spicer back to the attorney-conference room where Trevor was napping. 'Mail this immediately,' Spicer barked at him.

They spent ten minutes on their basketball bets, then said goodbye without a handshake.

Driving back to Jacksonville, Trevor called his bookie, a new one, a bigger bookie, now that he was a player. The digital line was indeed more secure, but the phone wasn't. Agent Klockner and his band of operatives were listening as usual, and tracking Trevor's bets. He wasn't doing badly, up $4,500 in the past two weeks. By contrast, his law firm had put $800 on the books during the same period.

In addition to the phone, there were four mikes in the Beetle, most of them of little value but operational nonetheless. And under each bumper was a transmitter, both wired to the car's electrical system and checked every other night when Trevor was either drinking or sleeping. A powerful receiver in the rental across the street tracked the Beetle wherever it went. As Trevor puttered down the highway, talking on his phone like a big shot, tossing money around like a Vegas high roller, sipping scalded coffee from a quick-stop grocery, he was emitting more signals than most private jets.

March 7. Big Super Tuesday. Aaron Lake bounced triumphantly across the stage in a large

221

banquet room of a Manhattan hotel, while thousands cheered and music roared and balloons fell from above. He'd taken New York with 43 percent of the vote. Governor Tarry had a rather weak 29 percent, and the other also-rans got the rest. Lake hugged people he'd never seen before and waved to people he'd never see again, and he delivered without notes a stirring victory speech.

Then he was off, on his way to L.A. for another victory celebration. For four hours, in his new Boeing jet that would hold a hundred and leased for $1 million a month and flew at a speed of five hundred miles per hour, thirty-eight thousand feet above the country, he and his staff monitored the returns from the twelve states participating in big Super Tuesday. Along the East Coast, where the polls had already closed, Lake barely won in Maine and Connecticut, but put up big margins in New York, Massachusetts, Maryland, and Georgia. He lost Rhode Island by eight hundred votes, and won Vermont by a thousand. As he was flying over Missouri, CNN declared him the winner of that state by four percentage points over Governor Tarry. Ohio was just as close.

By the time Lake reached California, the rout was over. Of the 591 delegates at stake, he'd captured 390. He'd also solidified the momentum. And most important, Aaron Lake now had the money. Governor Tarry was falling hard and fast, and all bets were on Lake.

TWENTY

Six hours after claiming victory in California, Lake awoke to a frenzied morning of live interviews. He suffered through eighteen in two hours, then flew to Washington.

He went straight to his new campaign headquarters, on the ground floor of a large office building on H Street, a stone's throw from the White House. He thanked his workers, almost none of whom were volunteers. He worked his crowd, shook their hands, all the while asking himself, 'Where did these people come from?'

We're gonna win, he said over and over, and everybody believed it. Why not?

He met for an hour with his top people. He had $65 million, no debt. Tarry had less than $1 million on hand and he was still trying to count the money he owed. In fact, the Tarry campaign had missed a federal filing deadline because its books were in such a mess. All cash had vanished. Contributions had stopped. Lake was getting all the money.

The names of three potential Vice Presidents were debated with great enthusiasm. It was an

223

exhilarating exercise because it meant the nomination was in the bag. Lake's first choice, Senator Nance from Michigan, was drawing fire because he'd had some shady business deals in another life. His partners had been of Italian extraction, from Detroit, and Lake could close his eyes and see the press peeling skin off Nance. A committee was appointed to explore the issue further.

And a committee was appointed to begin planning Lake's presence at the convention in Denver. Lake wanted a new speech-writer, now, and he wanted him working on the acceptance speech.

Lake secretly marveled at his own overhead. His campaign chairman was getting $150,000 for the year, not for twelve months, but until Christmas. There was a chairman of finance, of policy, of media relations, of operations, and of strategic planning, and all had contracts for $120,000 for about ten months of work. Each chairman had two or three immediate underlings, people Lake hardly knew, and they earned $90,000 apiece. Then there were the campaign assistants, or CAs, not the volunteers that most candidates attracted, but real employees who earned $50,000 each and kept the offices in a frenzy. There were dozens of them. And dozens of clerks and secretaries and, hell, nobody made less than $40,000.

And on top of all this waste, Lake kept telling himself, if I make it to the White House then I'll have to find jobs for them there. Every damned one of them. Kids now running around with Lake buttons on every lapel will expect to have West Wing clearances and jobs paying $80,000 a year.

It's a drop in the bucket, he kept reminding

224

himself. Don't get hung up on the small stuff when so much more is at stake.

Negatives were pushed to the end of the meeting and given short shrift. A reporter for the *Post* had been digging into Lake's early business career. Without too much effort he'd stumbled upon the GreenTree mess, a failed land development, twenty-two years in the past. Lake and a partner had bankrupted GreenTree, legally shafting creditors out of $800,000. The partner had been indicted for bankruptcy fraud, but a jury let him walk. No one laid a glove on Lake, and seven times after that the people of Arizona elected him to Congress.

'I'll answer any question about GreenTree,' Lake said. 'It was just a bad business deal.'

'The press is about to shift gears,' said the chairman of media relations. 'You're new and you haven't been subjected to enough scrutiny. It's time for them to get nasty.'

'It's already started,' Lake said. 'I have no skeletons.'

For an early dinner he was whisked away to Mortimer's, the current power place to be seen, just down Pennsylvania, where he met Elaine Tyner, the lawyer running D-PAC. Over fruit and cottage cheese she laid out the current financials of the newest PAC on the block. Cash in hand of $29 million, no significant debt, money being churned around the clock, coming in from all directions, from everywhere in the world.

Spending it was the challenge. Since it was considered 'soft money,' or money that couldn't go directly to the Lake campaign, it had to be used elsewhere. Tyner had several targets. The first was a series of generic ads similar to the doomsday ads Teddy had put together. D-PAC was already buying prime-time spots for the fall. The second, and by far the most enjoyable, were the Senate and congressional races. 'They're lining up like ants,' she said with great amusement. 'It's amazing what a few million bucks can do.'

She told the story of a House race in a district in Northern California where the incumbent, a twenty-year veteran Lake knew and despised, started the year with a forty-point lead against an unknown challenger. The unknown found his way to D-PAC and surrendered his soul to Aaron Lake. 'We've basically taken over his campaign,' she said. 'We're writing speeches, polling, doing all his print and TV ads, we even hired a new staff for him. So far we've spent one-point-five million, and our boy has cut the lead to ten points. And we have seven months to go.'

In all, Tyner and D-PAC were meddling in thirty House races and ten in the Senate. She expected to raise a total of $60 million, and spend every dime of it by November.

Her third area of 'focus' was taking the pulse of the country. D-PAC was polling nonstop, every day, fifteen hours a day. If labor in western Pennsylvania was bothered by an issue, D-PAC would know it. If the Hispanics in Houston were pleased with a new welfare policy, D-PAC would know it. If the women in greater Chicago liked or disliked a Lake ad, D-PAC knew yes or no and by what percentage. 'We know everything,' she boasted. 'We're like Big Brother, always watching.'

226

The polling cost $60,000 a day, a bargain. No one could touch it. For the important matters, Lake was nine points ahead of Tarry in Texas, even in Florida, a state Lake had yet to visit, and very close in Indiana, Tarry's home state.

'Tarry's tired,' she said. 'Morale is low because he won in New Hampshire and the money was rolling in. Then you came from nowhere, a fresh face, no baggage, new message, you start winning, and suddenly the money finds you. Tarry can't raise fifty bucks at a church bake sale. He's losing key people because he can't pay them, and because they smell another winner.'

Lake chewed a piece of pineapple and savored the words. They weren't new; he'd heard them from his own people. But coming from a seasoned insider like Tyner, they were even more reassuring.

'What are the Vice President's numbers?' Lake asked. He had his own set, but for some reason trusted her more.

'He'll squeak out the nomination,' she said, offering nothing new. 'But the convention will be bloody. Right now, you're only a few points behind him on the big question: Who will you vote for in November?'

'November is far away.'

'It is and it isn't.'

'A lot can change,' Lake said, thinking of Teddy, and wondering what sort of crisis he'd create to terrify the American people.

The dinner was more of a snack, and from Mortimer's Lake he was driven to a small dining room at the Hay-Adams Hotel. It was a long, late dinner with friends, two dozen of his colleagues from the House. Few of them had rushed to endorse him when he'd entered the race, but now they were all wildly enthusiastic about their man. Most had their own pollsters. The bandwagon was rolling down the mountain.

Lake had never seen his old pals so happy to be around him.

The letter was prepared in Documents by a woman named Bruce, one of the agency's three best counterfeiters. Tacked to the corkboard just above the worktable in her small lab were letters written by Ricky. Excellent samples, much more than she needed. She had no idea who Ricky was, but there was no doubt his handwriting was contrived. It was fairly consistent, with the more recent samples clearly showing an ease that came only with practice. His vocabulary was not remarkable, but then she suspected he was trying to downplay it. His sentence structure showed few mistakes. Bruce guessed him to be between the ages of forty and sixty, with at least a college education.

But it wasn't her job to make such inferences, at least not in this case. With the same pen and paper as Ricky, she wrote a nice little note to Al. The text had been prepared by someone else, she did not know who. Nor did she care.

It was, 'Hey, Al, where have you been? Why haven't you written? Don't forget about me.' That kind of letter, but with a nice little surprise. Since Ricky couldn't use the phone, he was sending Al a cassette tape with a brief message from deep inside rehab.

Bruce fit the letter onto one page, then worked

for an hour on the envelope. The postmark she applied was from Neptune Beach, Florida.

She didn't seal the envelope. Her little project was inspected, then taken to another lab. The tape was recorded by a young agent who'd studied drama at Northwestern. In a soft, accentless voice he said, 'Hey, Al, this is Ricky. Hope you're surprised to hear my voice. They won't let us use the phones around here, I don't know why, but for some reason we can send tapes back and forth. I can't wait to get out of this place.' Then he rambled for five minutes about his rehab and how much he hated his uncle and the people who ran Aladdin North. But he did concede that they had rid him of his addictions. He was certain he would look back and not judge the place too harshly.

His entire narrative was nothing but babble. No plans were discussed for his release, no hint of where he might go or what he might do, only a vague reference about seeing Al one day.

They were not yet ready to bait Al Konyers. The sole purpose of the tape was to hide within its casing a transmitter strong enough to lead them to Lake's hidden file. A tiny bug in the envelope was too risky. Al might be smart enough to find it.

At Mailbox America in Chevy Chase, the CIA now controlled eight boxes, duly rented for one year by eight different people, each of whom had the same twenty-four-hour access that Mr. Konyers had. They came and went at all hours, checking their little boxes, picking up mail they'd sent themselves, occasionally taking a peek at Al's box if no one was looking.

Since they knew his schedule better than he

229

knew it himself, they waited patiently until he'd made his rounds. They felt certain he'd sneak out as before, dressed like a jogger, so they held the envelope with the tape until almost ten one night. Then they placed it in his box.

Four hours later, with a dozen agents watching every move, Lake the jogger jumped from a cab in front of Mailbox America, darted inside, his face hidden by the long bill of a running cap, went to his box, pulled out the mail, and hurried back into the cab.

Six hours later he left Georgetown for a prayer breakfast at the Hilton, and they waited. He addressed an association of police chiefs at nine, and a thousand high school principals at eleven. He lunched with the Speaker of the House. He taped a stressful Q&A session with some talking heads at three, then returned home to pack. His itinerary called for him to depart Reagan National at eight and fly to Dallas.

They followed him to the airport, watched the Boeing 707 take off, then called Langley. When the two Secret Service agents arrived to check the perimeter of Lake's townhouse, the CIA was already inside.

The search ended in the kitchen ten minutes after it began. A handheld receptor caught the signal from the cassette tape. They found it in the wastebasket, along with an empty half-gallon milk jug, two torn packages of oatmeal, some soiled paper towels, and that morning's edition of the *Washington Post*. A maid came twice a week. Lake had simply left the garbage for her to take care of.

They couldn't find Lake's file because he didn't have one. Smart man, he tossed away the evidence.

Teddy was almost relieved when he got word. The team was still in the townhouse, hiding and waiting for the Secret Service to leave. Whatever Lake did in his secret life, he worked hard not to leave a trail.

The tape unnerved Aaron Lake. Reading Ricky's letters and looking at his handsome face had given him a nervous thrill. The young man was far away and odds were they'd never meet. They could be pen pals and play tag at a distance and move slowly, at least that's what Lake had contemplated initially.

But hearing Ricky's voice had brought him much closer, and Lake was rattled. What had begun a few months earlier as a curious little game now held horrible possibilities. It was much too risky. Lake trembled at the thought of getting caught.

It still seemed impossible, though. He was well hidden behind the mask of Al Konyers. Ricky had not a clue. It was 'Al this' and 'Al that' on the tape. The post office box was his shield.

But he had to end it. At least for now.

The Boeing was packed with Lake's well-paid people. They didn't make an airplane big enough to haul his entire entourage. If he leased a 747, within two days it would be filled with CAs and advisers and consultants and pollsters, not to mention his own growing army of bodyguards from the Secret Service.

The more primaries he won, the heavier his

plane became. It might be wise to lose a couple of states so he could jettison some of the baggage.

In the darkness of the plane, Lake sipped tomato juice and decided to write a final letter to Ricky. Al would wish him the best, and simply terminate the correspondence. What could the boy do?

He was tempted to write the note right then, sitting in his deep recliner, his feet in the air. But at any moment an assistant of some variety would emerge with another breathless report that the candidate had to hear immediately. He had no privacy. He had no time to think or loaf or daydream. Every pleasant thought was interrupted by a new poll or a late-breaking story or an urgent need to make a decision.

Surely he'd be able to hide in the White House. Loners had lived there before.

TWENTY-ONE

The case of the stolen cell phone had fascinated the inmates at Trumble for the past month. Mr. T-Bone, a wiry street kid from Miami serving twenty for drugs, had taken original possession of the phone by means that were still unclear. Cell phones were strictly prohibited at Trumble, and the method by which he got one had created more rumors than T. Karl's sex life. The few who'd actually seen it had described it, not in court, but around the camp, as being no larger than a stopwatch. Mr. T-Bone had been seen lurking in the shadows, hunched at the waist, chin to his chest, back to the world, mumbling into the phone. No doubt he was still directing street operations in Miami.

Then it disappeared. Mr. T-Bone let it be known that he might kill whoever took it, and when the threats of violence didn't work he offered a reward of $1,000 cash. Suspicion soon fell upon another young drug dealer, Zorro, from a section of Atlanta just as rough as Mr. T-Bone's. A killing seemed likely, so the guards and the suits up front intervened and convinced the two that they'd be shipped away if things got out of hand. Violence was not tolerated at Trumble. The punishment was a trip to a medium-security pen with inmates who understood violence.

Someone told Mr. T-Bone about the weekly dockets the Brethren held, and in due course he found T. Karl and filed suit. He wanted his phone back, plus a million bucks in punitive damages.

When it was first set for trial, an assistant warden appeared in the cafeteria to observe the proceedings, and the matter was quickly postponed by the Brethren. The same thing happened just before the second trial. Allegations of who did or did not have possession of an outlawed cell phone could not be heard by anyone in administration. The guards who watched the weekly shows wouldn't repeat a word.

Justice Spicer finally convinced a prison counselor that the boys had a private matter to reconcile, without interference from the front. 'We're trying to settle a little matter,' he whispered. 'And we need to do it in private.'

The request worked its way upward, and at the third trial date the cafeteria was packed with spectators, most of whom were hoping to see bloodshed. The only prison official in the room was a solitary guard, sitting in the back, half asleep.

Neither of the litigants was a stranger to courtrooms, so it was no surprise that Mr. T-Bone and Zorro acted as their own attorneys. Justice Beech spent most of the first hour trying to keep the language out of the gutter. He finally gave up. Wild accusations spewed forth from the plaintiff, charges that couldn't have been proved with the aid of a thousand FBI agents. The denials were just as loud and preposterous from the defense. Mr. T-Bone scored heavy blows with two affidavits, signed by inmates whose names were revealed only to the Brethren, which contained eyewitness accounts of seeing Zorro trying to hide while talking on a tiny phone.

Zorro's angry response described the affidavits in language the Brethren had never before encountered.

The knockout punch came from nowhere. Mr. T-Bone, in a move that even the slickest lawyer would admire, produced documentation. His phone records had been smuggled in, and he showed the court in black and white that exactly fifty-four calls had been made to numbers in southeast Atlanta. His supporters, by far the majority but whose loyalty could vanish in an instant, whooped and hollered until T. Karl slammed his plastic gavel and got them quiet.

Zorro had trouble regrouping, and his hesitation killed him. He was ordered to immediately turn over the phone to the Brethren within twenty-four hours, and to reimburse Mr. T-Bone $450 for long-distance charges. If twenty-four hours passed with no phone, the matter would be referred to the warden, along with a finding of fact from the Brethren that Zorro did indeed possess an illegal cell phone.

The Brethren further ordered the two to maintain a distance of at least fifty feet from one another at all times, even when eating.

T. Karl rapped a gavel and the crowd began a

noisy exit. He called the next case, another petty gambling dispute, and waited for the spectators to leave. 'Quiet!' he shouted, and the racket only grew louder. The Brethren went back to their newspapers and magazines.

'Quiet!' he barked again, slamming his gavel.

'Shut up,' Spicer yelled at T. Karl. 'You're making more noise than they are.'

'It's my job,' T. Karl snapped back, the curls of his wig bouncing in all directions.

When the cafeteria was empty, only one inmate remained. T. Karl looked around and finally asked him, 'Are you Mr. Hooten?'

'No sir,' the young man said.

'Are you Mr. Jenkins?'

'No sir.'

'I didn't think so. The case of Hooten versus Jenkins is hereby dismissed for failure to show,' T. Karl said, and made a dramatic entry into his docket book.

'Who are you?' Spicer asked the young man, who was sitting alone and glancing around as if he wasn't sure he was welcome. The three men in the pale green robes were now looking at him, as was the clown with the gray wig and the old maroon pajamas and the lavender shower shoes, no socks. Who were these people!

He slowly got to his feet and moved forward with great apprehension until he stood before the three. 'I'm looking for some help,' he said, almost afraid to speak.

'Do you have business before the court?' T. Karl growled from the side.

'No sir.'

236

'Then you'll have to –'

'Shut up!' Spicer said. 'Court's adjourned. Leave.'

T.Karl slammed his docket book, kicked back his folding chair, and stormed out of the room, his shower shoes sliding on the tile, his wig bouncing behind him.

The young man appeared ready to cry. 'What can we do for you?' Yarber asked.

He was holding a small cardboard box, and the Brethren knew from experience that it was filled with the papers that had brought him to Trumble. 'I need some help,' he said again. 'I got here last week, and my roommate said you guys could help with my appeals.'

'Don't you have a lawyer?' Beech asked.

'I did. He wasn't very good. He's one reason I'm here.'

'Why are you here?' asked Spicer.

'I don't know. I really don't know.'

'Did you have a trial?'

'Yes. A long one.'

'And you were found guilty by a jury?'

'Yes. Me and a bunch of others. They said we were part of a conspiracy.'

'A conspiracy to do what?'

'Import cocaine.'

Another druggie. They were suddenly anxious to get back to their letter writing. 'How long is your sentence?' asked Yarber.

'Forty-eight years.'

'Forty-eight years! How old are you?'

'Twenty-three.'

The letter writing was momentarily forgotten.

237

They looked at his sad young face and tried to picture it fifty years later. Released at the age of seventy-one; it was impossible to imagine. Each of the Brethren would leave Trumble a younger man than this kid.

'Pull up a chair,' Yarber said, and the kid grabbed the nearest one and placed it in front of their table. Even Spicer felt a little sympathy for him.

'What's your name?' Yarber asked.

'I go by Buster.'

'Okay, Buster, what'd you do to get yourself forty-eight years?'

The story came in torrents. Balancing his box on his knees, and staring at the floor, he began by saying he'd never been in trouble with the law, nor had his father. They owned a small boat dock together in Pensacola. They fished and sailed and loved the sea, and running the dock was the perfect life for them. They sold a used fishing boat, a fifty-footer, to a man from Fort Lauderdale, an American who paid them in cash – $95,000. The money went in the bank, or at least Buster thought it did. A few months later the man was back for another boat, a thirty-eight-footer for which he paid $80,000. Cash for boats was not unusual in Florida. A third and fourth boat followed. Buster and his dad knew where to find good used fishing boats, which they overhauled and renovated. They enjoyed doing the work themselves. After the fifth boat, the narcs came calling. They asked questions, made vague threats, wanted to see the books and records. Buster's dad refused initially, then they hired a lawyer who advised them not to cooperate. Nothing happened for months.

Buster and his father were arrested at 3 A.M. on a Sunday morning by a pack of goons wearing vests and enough guns to hold Pensacola hostage. They were dragged half-dressed from their small home near the bay, lights flashing all over the place. The indictment was an inch thick, 160 pages, eighty-one counts of conspiracy to smuggle cocaine. He had a copy of it in his box. Buster and his dad were barely mentioned in the 160 pages, but they were nonetheless named as defendants and lumped together with the man they'd sold the boats to, along with twenty-five other people they'd never heard of. Eleven were Colombians. Three were lawyers. Everybody else was from South Florida.

The U.S. Attorney offered them a deal – two years each in return for guilty pleas and coopera-tion against the other codefendants. Pleading guilty to what? They'd done nothing wrong. They knew exactly one of their twenty-six coconspira-tors. They'd never seen cocaine.

Buster's father remortgaged their home to raise $20,000 for a lawyer, and they made a bad selection. At trial, they were alarmed to find themselves sitting at the same table with the Colombians and the real drug traffickers. They were on one side of the courtroom, all the coconspirators, sitting together as if they'd once been a well-oiled drug machine. On the other side, near the jury, were the government lawyers, groups of pompous little bastards in dark suits, taking notes, glaring at them as if they were child molesters. The jury glared at them too.

239

During seven weeks of trial, Buster and his father were practically ignored. Three times their names were mentioned. The government's principal charge against them was that they had conspired to procure and rebuild fishing boats with souped-up engines to transport drugs from Mexico to various drop-offs along the Florida panhandle. Their lawyer, who complained that he wasn't getting paid enough to handle a seven-week trial, proved ineffective at rebutting these loose charges. Still, the government lawyers did little damage and were much more concerned with nailing the Colombians.

But they didn't have to prove much. They had done a superior job of picking the jury. After eight days of deliberation, the jurors, obviously tired and frustrated, found every conspirator guilty of all charges. A month after they were sentenced, Buster's father killed himself.

As the narrative wound down, the kid looked as if he might cry. But he stuck out his jaw, gritted his teeth, and said, 'I did nothing wrong.'

He certainly wasn't the first inmate at Trumble to declare his innocence. Beech watched and listened and remembered a young man he'd sentenced once to forty years for drug trafficking back in Texas. The defendant had a rotten childhood, no education, a long record as a juvenile offender, not much of a chance in life. Beech had lectured him from the bench, high and lordly from above, and had felt good about himself for handing down such a brutal sentence. Gotta get these damned drug dealers off the streets!

A liberal is a conservative who's been arrested.

240

After three years on the inside of a prison Hatlee Beech agonized over many of the people he'd thrown the book at. People far guiltier than Buster here. Kids who just needed a break.

Finn Yarber watched and listened and felt immense pity for the young man. Everybody at Trumble had a sad story, and after a month or so of hearing them he'd learned to believe almost nothing. But Buster was believable. For the next forty-eight years he would wither and decline, all at taxpayer expense. Three meals a day. A warm bed at night – $31,000 a year was the latest guess of what a federal inmate cost the government. Such a waste. Half the inmates at Trumble had no business being there. They were non-violent men who should've been punished with stiff fines and community service.

Joe Roy Spicer listened to Buster's compelling story, and he sized the boy up for future use. There were two possibilities. First, in Spicer's opinion, the telephones were not being properly utilized in the Angola scam. The Brethren were old men writing letters as if they were young. It would be too risky to call Quince Garbe in Iowa, for example, and pretend to be Ricky, a robust twenty-eight-year-old. But with a kid like Buster working for them, they could convince any potential victim. There were plenty of young guys at Trumble, and Spicer had considered several of them. But they were criminals, and he didn't trust them. Buster was fresh off the streets, seemingly innocent, and he was coming to them for help. The boy could be manipulated.

The second possibility was an offshoot of the

first. If Buster joined their conspiracy, he would be in place when Joe Roy was released. The scam was proving too profitable to simply walk away from. Beech and Yarber were splendid at writing the letters, but they had no business sense. Perhaps Spicer could train young Buster here to fill his shoes, and to divert his share to the outside.

Just a thought.

'Do you have any money?' Spicer asked.

'No sir. We lost everything.'

'No family, no uncles, aunts, cousins, friends who could help you with your legal fees?'

'No sir. What kinda legal fees?'

'We usually charge for reviewing cases and helping with the appeals.'

'I'm dead broke, sir.'

'I think we can help,' Beech said. Spicer didn't work on the appeals anyway. The man never finished high school.

'Sort of a pro bono case, wouldn't you say?' Yarber said to Beech.

'A pro what?' Spicer asked.

'Pro bono.'

'What's that?'

'Free legal work,' Beech said.

'Free legal work. Done by whom?'

'By lawyers,' Yarber explained. 'Every lawyer is expected to donate a few hours of his time to help people who can't afford to hire him.'

'It's part of the Old English common law,' Beech added, further clouding the issue.

'It never caught on over here, did it?' Spicer said.

'We'll review your case,' Yarber said to Buster. 'But please do not be optimistic.'

'Thank you.'

They left the cafeteria in a group, three ex-judges in green choir robes followed by a scared young inmate. Frightened, but also quite curious.

TWENTY-TWO

Brant's reply from Upper Darby, Pa., had an urgent tone to it:

Dear Ricky:
Wow! What a photo! I'm coming down even sooner. I'll be there on April 20. Are you available? If so, we'll have the house to ourselves because my wife will stay here for another two weeks. Poor woman. We've been married for twenty-two years and she doesn't have a clue.
Here's a picture of me. That's my Learjet in the background, one of my favorite toys. We'll buzz around in it if you want.
Write me immediately, please.

Sincerely, Brant

There was still no last name, not that that was a problem. They would dig for it soon enough.
Spicer inspected the postmark, and for a passing moment thought about how quickly the mail was running between Jacksonville and Philadelphia. But the photo kept his attention. It was a four-by-

six candid shot, very similar to an ad for a get-rich-quick scheme where the huckster is pictured with a proud smile, flanked by his jet, his Rolls, and possibly his latest wife. Brant was standing beside a plane, smiling, dressed neatly in tennis shorts and a sweater, with no Rolls in sight but with an attractive middle-aged woman next to him.

It was the first photo, in their growing collection, in which one of their pen pals had included his wife. Odd, thought Spicer, but then Brant had mentioned her in both letters. Nothing surprised him anymore. The scam would work forever because there was an endless supply of potential victims willing to ignore the risks.

Brant himself was fit and tanned, short dark hair with shades of gray, and a mustache. He was not particularly handsome, but what did Spicer care?

Why would a man with so much be so careless? Because he'd always taken chances and never been caught. Because it was a way of life. And after they squeezed him and took his money, Brant would slow down for a while. He'd avoid the personal ads, and the anonymous lovers. But an aggressive type like Brant would soon return to his old ways.

Spicer figured the thrill of finding random partners overshadowed the risks. He was still bothered by the fact that he, of all people, spent time each day trying to think like a homosexual.

Beech and Yarber read the letter and studied the photo. The small cramped room was completely silent. Could this be the big one?

'Reckon how much that jet cost,' Spicer said, and all three laughed. It was nervous laughter, as if they weren't sure they could believe it.

'A couple of million,' Beech said. Since he was from Texas, and had been married to a rich woman, the other two assumed he knew more about jets than they. 'It's a small Lear.'

Spicer would settle for a small Cessna, anything that would lift him off the ground and take him away. Yarber didn't want a plane. He wanted tickets, in first class where they brought you champagne and two menus and you had your choice of movies. First class over the ocean, far away from this country.

'Let's bust him,' Yarber said.

'How much?' asked Beech, still staring at the photo.

'At least a half a million,' Spicer said. 'And if we get that, we'll go back for more.'

They sat in silence, each playing with his portion of half a million dollars. Trevor's third was suddenly getting in the way. He'd take $167,000 off the top, leaving each of them $111,000. Not bad for prisoners, but it should be a helluva lot more. Why was the lawyer making so much?

'We're going to cut Trevor's fee,' Spicer announced. 'I've been thinking about this for some time. Beginning now, the money will be split four ways. He takes an equal share.'

'He won't do it,' Yarber said.

'He has no choice.'

'It's only fair,' Beech said. 'We're doing the work, and he's getting more than each of us. I say we cut it.'

'I'll do it Thursday.'

Two days later, Trevor arrived at Trumble just

after four with a particularly bad hangover, one deadened by neither the two-hour lunch nor the one-hour nap.

Joe Roy seemed particularly edgy. He passed across the outgoing mail, but held a large, red, oversized envelope. 'We're getting ready to bust this guy,' he said, tapping it on the table.

'Who is he?'

'Brant somebody, near Philadelphia. He's hiding behind the post office, so you need to flush him out.'

'How much?'

'A half a million bucks.'

Trevor's red eyes narrowed and his dry lips fell open. He did the math – $167,000 in his pocket. His sailing career was suddenly drawing closer. Perhaps he didn't need a full million bucks before he slammed his office door and left for the Caribbean. Maybe half that would do it. And he was getting so close.

'You're kidding,' he said, knowing that Spicer was not. Spicer had no sense of humor, and he certainly took his money seriously.

'No. And we're changing your percentage.'

'I'll be damned if we are. A deal's a deal.'

'Deals can always be changed. From now on you get the same piece we do. One fourth.'

'No way.'

'Then you're fired.'

'You can't fire me.'

'I just did. What, you think we can't find another crooked lawyer to run mail for us?'

'I know too much,' Trevor said, his cheeks flashing pink and his tongue suddenly parched.

'Don't overestimate yourself. You're not that valuable.'

'Yes I am. I know everything that's going on here.'

'And so do we, hotshot. Difference is, we're already in jail. You're the one with the most to lose. You play hardball with me and you'll be sittin on this side of the table.'

Bolts of pain shot through Trevor's forehead and he closed his eyes. He was in no condition to argue. Why had he stayed at Pete's so late last night? He had to be sharp when he met with Spicer. Instead, he was tired and half-drunk.

His head spun and he thought he might be sick again. He did the math. They were arguing over the difference between $167,000 and $125,000. Frankly, both sounded good to Trevor. He couldn't run the risk of being fired because he'd managed to alienate what few clients he had. He spent less time in the office; he wouldn't return their calls. He'd found a far richer source of income, so to hell with the small-time foot traffic along the beaches.

And he was no match for Spicer. The man had no conscience. He was mean and conniving and desperate to stash away as much money as possible.

'Are Beech and Yarber in favor of this?' he asked, knowing damned well they were, and knowing that even if they weren't he'd never know the difference.

'Sure. They're doing all the work. Why should you make more than them?'

It did seem a little unfair. 'Okay, okay,' Trevor said, still in pain. 'There's a good reason you're in prison.'

'Are you drinking too much?'

'No! Why do you ask?'

'I've known drunks. Lots of them. You look like hell.'

'Thanks. You take care of your business, I'll take care of mine.'

'It's a deal. But nobody wants a drunk for a lawyer. You're handling all our money, in an enterprise that's very illegal. A little loose talk in a bar and somebody starts asking questions.'

'I can handle myself.'

'Good. Watch your back too. We're squeezing people, making them hurt. If I were on the other end of our little sting, I'd be tempted to come down and try to get some answers before I coughed up the money.'

'They're too scared.'

'Keep your eyes open anyway. It's important for you to stay sober and alert.'

'Thank you very much. Anything else?'

'Yeah, I got some games for you.' On to the important stuff. Spicer opened a newspaper and they began making their bets.

Trevor bought a quart of beer at a country store on the edge of Trumble, and sipped it slowly as he puttered back to Jacksonville. He tried his best not to think of their money, but his thoughts were out of control. Between his account and their account, there was just over $250,000 sitting offshore, money he could take anytime he wanted. Add a half a million bucks to it, and, well, he just couldn't stop adding – $750,000!

He'd never get caught stealing dirty money; that was the beauty of it. The victims of the Brethren weren't complaining now because they were too ashamed. They weren't breaking any laws. They were just scared. The Brethren, on the other hand, were committing crimes. So who would they run to if their money disappeared?

He had to stop thinking such thoughts.

But how could they, the Brethren, catch him? He'd be on a sailboat drifting between islands they'd never heard of. And when they were finally released, would they have the energy and money and willpower to track him down? Of course not. They were old men. Beech would probably die at Trumble.

'Stop it,' he yelled at himself.

He walked to Beach Java for a triple-shot latte, and returned to his office determined to do something productive. He went online and found the names of several private investigators in Philadelphia. It was almost six when he began calling. The first two went to answering machines.

The third, to the offices of Ed Pagnozzi, was answered by the investigator himself. Trevor explained that he was a lawyer in Florida and needed a quick job in Upper Darby.

'Okay. What kinda job?'

'I'm trying to track some mail here,' Trevor said glibly. He'd done this enough to have it well rehearsed. 'Pretty big divorce case. I got the wife, and I think the husband's hiding money. Anyway,

I need somebody up there to find out who's renting a certain post office box.'

'You gotta be kiddin.'

'Well, no, I'm pretty serious about this.'

'You want me to go snoopin around a post office?'

'It's just basic detective work.'

'Look, pal, I'm very busy. Call somebody else.' Pagnozzi was gone, off to more important matters. Trevor cursed him under his breath and punched the next number. He tried two more, and hung up on both when the machines answered. He'd try again tomorrow.

Across the street, Klockner listened to the brief chat with Pagnozzi one more time, then called Langley. The final piece of the puzzle had just fallen into place, and Mr. Deville would want to know it immediately.

While dependent on fancy words and smooth talk and compelling photos, the scam was basic in its operation. It preyed on human desire and it paid off by sheer terror. Its mechanics had been solved by Mr. Garbe's file, and by the Brant White reverse scam, and by the other letters they'd intercepted.

Only one question had gone unanswered: When aliases were used to rent post office boxes, how did the Brethren find the real names of their victims? The phone calls to Philadelphia had just given them their answer. Trevor simply hired a local private detective, evidently one with less business than Mr. Pagnozzi.

It was almost ten when Deville was finally

cleared to see Teddy. The North Koreans had shot another American soldier in the DMZ, and Teddy had been dealing with the fallout since noon. He was eating cheese and crackers and sipping a Diet Coke when Deville entered the bunker.

After a quick briefing, Teddy said, 'That's what I thought.'

His instincts were uncanny, especially with hindsight.

'This means, of course, that the lawyer could hire a local here to somehow uncover the real identity of Al Konyers,' Deville said.

'But how?'

'We can think of several ways. First is surveillance, the same way we caught Lake sneaking to his box. Watch the post office. That's somewhat risky because there's a good chance you'll get noticed. Second is bribery. Five hundred bucks cash to a postal clerk will work in a lot of places. Third is computer records. This is not highly classified material. One of our guys just hacked his way into the central post office in Evansville, Indiana, and got the list of all box leases. It was a random test, took him about an hour. That's high tech. Low tech is to simply break into the post office at night and have a look around.'

'How much does he pay for this?'

'Don't know, but we'll find out soon when he hires an investigator.'

'He has to be neutralized.'

'Eliminated?'

'Not yet. I'd rather buy him first. He is our window. If he's working for us, then we know everything and we keep him away from Konyers. Put together a plan.'

'And for his removal?'

'Go ahead and plan it, but we're in no hurry. Not yet anyway.'

TWENTY-THREE

The South did indeed like Aaron Lake, with his love of guns and bombs and tough talk and military readiness. He flooded Florida, Mississippi, Tennessee, Oklahoma, and Texas with ads that were even bolder than his first ones. And Teddy's people flooded the same states with more cash than had ever changed hands the night before an election.

The result was another rout, with Lake getting 260 of the 312 delegates at stake on little Super Tuesday. After the votes were counted on March 14, 1,301 of the 2,066 total delegates had been decided. Lake held a commanding lead over Governor Tarry – 801 to 390.

The race was over, barring an unforeseen catastrophe.

Buster's first job at Trumble was running a Weed Eater, for which he earned a starting wage of twenty cents an hour. It was either that or mopping floors in the cafeteria. He chose the weed eating because he liked the sun and vowed that his skin would not turn as pale as some of the bleached-out inmates he'd seen. Nor would he get fat like some of them. This is prison, he kept telling himself, how can they be so fat?

He worked hard in the bright sun, kept his tan, vowed to keep his flat stomach, and tried gamely to go through the motions. But after ten days Buster knew he would not last for forty-eight years.

Forty-eight years! He couldn't begin to comprehend such time. Who could?

He'd cried for the first forty-eight hours.

Thirteen months earlier he and his father were running their dock, working on boats, fishing twice a week in the Gulf.

He worked slowly around the concrete edge of the basketball court where a rowdy game was in progress. Then to the big sandbox where they sometimes played volleyball. In the distance, a solitary figure was walking around the track, an old-looking man with his long gray hair in a ponytail and with no shirt. He looked vaguely familiar. Buster worked both edges of a sidewalk, making his way to the track.

The lone walker was Finn Yarber, one of the judges who was trying to help him. He moved around the oval at a steady pace, head level, back and shoulders stiff and erect, not a picture of athleticism but not bad for a sixty-year-old man. He was barefoot and barebacked, sweat rolling off his leathery skin.

Buster turned off the Weed Eater and placed it on the ground. When Yarber drew near, he saw the kid and said, 'Hello, Buster. How's it goin?'

'I'm still here,' the kid said. 'Mind if I walk with you?'

'Not at all,' Finn said without breaking stride.

They did an eighth of a mile before Buster could find the courage to say, 'So how about my appeals?'

'Judge Beech is lookin at it. The sentencing appears to be in order, which is not good news. A lot of guys get here with flaws in their sentencing, and we can usually file a couple of motions and knock off a few years. Not so with you. I'm sorry.'

'That's okay. What's a few when you have forty-eight? Twenty-eight, thirty-eight, forty-eight, what does it matter?'

'You still have your appeals. There's a chance the decision can be overturned.'

'A slim chance.'

'You can't give up hope, Buster,' Yarber said, without the slightest trace of conviction. Keeping some measure of hope meant keeping some faith in the system. Yarber certainly had none. He'd been framed and railroaded by the same law he'd once defended.

But at least Yarber had enemies, and he could almost understand why they came after him.

This poor boy had done nothing wrong. Yarber had read enough of his file to believe Buster was completely innocent, another victim of an over-zealous prosecutor.

It appeared, at least from the record, that the kid's father may have been hiding some cash, but nothing serious. Nothing to warrant a 160-page conspiracy indictment.

Hope. He felt like a hypocrite for even thinking the word. The appeals courts were now packed with right-wing law and order types, and it was a rare drug case that got reversed. They'd slamdunk the kid's appeal with a rubber stamp, and tell themselves they were making the streets safer.

The biggest coward had been the trial judge. Prosecutors are expected to indict the world, but the judges are supposed to weed out the fringe defendants. Buster and his father should've been separated from the Colombians and their cohorts, and sent home before the trial began.

Now one was dead. The other was ruined. And nobody in the federal criminal system gave a damn. It was just another drug conspiracy.

At the first curve of the oval, Yarber slowed, then stopped. He looked off in the distance, beyond a grassy field to the edge of a treeline. Buster looked too. For ten days he'd been looking at the perimeter of Trumble, and seeing what wasn't there – fences, razor wire, guard towers.

'Last guy who left here,' Yarber said, gazing at nothing, 'left through those trees. They're thick for a few miles, then you come to a country road.'

'Who was he?'

'A guy named Tommy Adkins. He was a banker in North Carolina, got caught with his hand in the cookie jar.'

'What happened to him?'

'He went crazy and walked away one day. He was gone six hours before anybody knew it. A month later they found him in a motel room in Cocoa Beach, not the cops but the maids. He was curled in the fetal position on the floor, naked, suckin his thumb, his mind completely gone. They put him in some mental joint.'

'Six hours, huh?'

'Yeah, it happens about once a year. Somebody just walks away. They notify the cops in your hometown, put your name in the national computers, the usual drill.'

'How many get caught?'

'Almost all.'

'Almost.'

'Yeah, but they get caught because they do dumb things. Get drunk in bars. Drive cars with no taillights. Go see their girlfriends.'

'So if you had a brain you could pull it off?'

'Sure. Careful planning, a little cash, it would be easy.'

They began walking again, a bit slower. 'Tell me something, Mr. Yarber,' Buster said. 'If you were facing forty-eight years, would you take a walk?'

'Yes.'

'But I don't have a dime.'

'I do.'

'Then you'll help me.'

'We'll see. Give it some time. Settle in here. They're watchin you a bit closer because you're new, but with time they'll forget about you.'

Buster actually smiled. His sentence had just been reduced dramatically.

'You know what happens if you get caught?' Yarber said.

'Yeah, they add some more years. Big deal. Maybe I'll get fifty-eight. No sir, if I get caught, I blow my brains out.'

'That's what I'd do. You have to be prepared to leave the country.'

'And go where?'

'Go someplace where you look like the locals, and where they don't extradite to the U.S.'

'Anyplace in particular?'

'Argentina or Chile. You speak any Spanish?'

'No.'

'Start learnin. We have Spanish lessons here, you know. Some of the Miami boys teach them.'

They walked a lap in silence as Buster reconsidered his future. His feet were lighter, his shoulders straighter, and he couldn't keep a grin off his face.

'Why are you helping me?' he asked.

'Because you're twenty-three years old. Too young and too innocent. You've been screwed by the system, Buster. You have the right to fight back any way you can. Do you have a girlfriend?'

'Sort of.'

'Forget about her. She'll only get you in trouble. Besides, you think she'll wait forty-eight years?'

'She said she would.'

'She's lyin. She's already playin the field. Forget about her, unless you want to get caught.'

Yeah, he's probably right, thought Buster. He'd yet to get a letter from her, and though she lived only four hours away she hadn't made it to Trumble. They'd talked twice on the phone, and all she seemed to care about was whether he'd been attacked.

'Any kids?' asked Yarber.

'No. Not that I know of.'

'What about your mother?'

'She died when I was very young. My dad raised me. It was just the two of us.'

'Then you're the perfect guy to walk away.'

'I'd like to leave now.'

259

'Be patient. Let's plan it carefully.'

Another lap, and Buster wanted to sprint. He couldn't think of a damned thing he'd miss in Pensacola. He'd made As and Bs in Spanish in high school, and while he couldn't remember any of it, he hadn't struggled with the material. He'd pick it up fast. He'd take the courses and hang out with the Latins.

The more he walked the more he wanted his conviction to be affirmed. And the quicker the better. If it got reversed, he'd be forced to have another trial, and he had no confidence in the next jury.

Buster wanted to run, starting over there in the grassy field, to the treeline, through the woods to the country road where he wasn't sure what to do next. But if an insane banker could walk away and make it to Cocoa Beach, so could he.

'Why haven't you walked away?' he asked Yarber.

'I've thought about it. But in five years they'll let me go. I can last that long. I'll be sixty-five, in good health, with a life expectancy of sixteen years. That's what I'm livin for, Buster, the last sixteen years. I don't wanna be lookin over my shoulder.'

'Where will you go?'

'Don't know yet. Maybe a little village in the Italian countryside. Maybe the mountains of Peru. I've got the whole world to choose from, and I spend hours every day just dreamin about it.'

'So you have plenty of money?'

'No, but I'm gettin there.'

That raised a number of questions, but Buster

260

let them pass. He was learning that in prison you kept most of your questions to yourself.

When Buster was tired of walking, he stopped near his Weed Eater. 'Thanks, Mr. Yarber,' he said.

'No problem. Just keep it between the two of us.'

'Sure. I'm ready whenever you are.'

Finn was off, pacing another lap, his shorts now soaked with sweat, his gray ponytail dripping with moisture. Buster watched him go, then for a second looked across the grassy field, into the trees.

At that moment, he could see all the way to South America.

261

TWENTY-FOUR

For two long, hard months Aaron Lake and Governor Tarry had gone head to head, toe to toe, coast to coast, in twenty-six states with almost 25 million votes cast. They'd pushed themselves with eighteen-hour days, brutal schedules, relentless travel, the typical madness of a presidential race.

Yet they'd worked just as hard to avoid a face-to-face debate. Tarry didn't want one in the early primaries because he was the front-runner. He had the organization, the cash, the favorable polls. Why legitimize the opposition? Lake didn't want one because he was a newcomer to the national scene, a novice at highstakes campaigning, and besides it was much easier to hide behind a script and a friendly camera and make ads whenever needed. The risks of a live debate were simply too high.

Teddy didn't like the thought of one either.

But campaigns change. Front-runners fade, small issues become big ones, the press can create a crisis simply out of boredom.

Tarry decided he needed a debate because he was broke, and losing one primary after another. 'Aaron Lake is trying to buy this election,' he said over and over. 'And I want to confront him, man to man.' It sounded good, and the press had beaten it to death.

'He's running from a debate,' Tarry declared, and the pack liked that too.

'The governor's been dodging a debate since Michigan' was Lake's standard response.

And so for three weeks they played the he's-running-from-me game until their people quietly worked out the details.

Lake was reluctant, but he also needed a forum. Though he was winning week after week, he was rolling over an opponent who'd been fading for a long time. His polls and D-PAC's polls showed a great deal of voter interest in him, but mainly because he was new and handsome and seemingly electable.

Unknown to outsiders, the polls also showed some very soft areas. The first was on the question of Lake's single-issue campaign. Defense spending can excite the voters for only so long, and there was great concern, in the polls, about where Lake stood on other issues.

Second, Lake was still five points behind the Vice President in their hypothetical November matchup. The voters were tired of the Vice President, but at least they knew who he was. Lake remained a mystery to many. Also, the two would debate several times prior to November. Lake, who had the nomination in hand, needed the experience.

Tarry didn't help matters with his constant query, 'Who is Aaron Lake?' With some of his few remaining funds, he authorized the printing of

bumper stickers with the now famous question –
Who is Aaron Lake?

(It was a question Teddy asked himself almost
every hour, but for a different reason.)

The setting of the debate was in Pennsylvania at
a small Lutheran college with a cozy auditorium,
good acoustics and light, a controllable crowd.
Even the smallest of details were haggled over by
the two camps, but because both sides now needed
a debate agreements were eventually reached. The
precise format had nearly caused fistfights, but
once ironed out it gave everybody something. The
media got three reporters on the stage to ask direct
questions during one segment. The spectators got
twenty minutes to ask about anything, with nothing screened. Tarry, a lawyer, wanted five minutes
for opening remarks and a ten-minute closing
statement. Lake wanted thirty minutes of one-on-
one debate with Tarry, no holds barred, no one to
referee, just the two of them slugging it out
without rules. This had terrified the Tarry camp,
and had almost broken the deal.

The moderator was a local public radio figure,
and when he said, 'Good evening, and welcome to
the first and only debate between Governor Wen-
dell Tarry and Congressman Aaron Lake,' an
estimated 18 million people were watching.

Tarry wore a navy suit his wife had selected,
with the standard blue shirt and the standard red
and blue tie. Lake wore a dashing light brown suit,
a white shirt with a spread collar, and a tie of red
and maroon and a half-dozen other colors. The
entire ensemble had been put together by a fashion
consultant, and was designed to complement the

264

colors of the set. Lake's hair had received a tinting. His teeth had been bleached. He'd spent four hours in a tanning bed. He looked thin and fresh, and anxious to be onstage.

Governor Tarry was himself a handsome man. Though he was only four years older than Lake, the campaign was taking a heavy toll. His eyes were tired and red. He'd gained a few pounds, especially in his face. When he began his opening remarks, beads of sweat popped up along his forehead and glistened in the lights.

Conventional wisdom held that Tarry had more to lose because he'd already lost so much. Early in January, he'd been declared, by prophets as prescient as *Time* magazine, to have the nomination within his grasp. He'd been running for three years. His campaign was built on grassroots support and shoe leather. Every precinct captain and poll worker in Iowa and New Hampshire had drunk coffee with him. His organization was impeccable.

Then came Lake with his slick ads and single-issue magic.

Tarry badly needed either a stunning performance by himself, or a major gaffe by Lake.

He got neither. By a flip of the coin, he was chosen to go first. He stumbled badly in his opening remarks as he moved stiffly around the stage, trying desperately to look at ease but forgetting what his notes said. Sure he'd once been a lawyer, but his specialty had been securities. As he forgot one point after another, he returned to his common theme – Mr. Lake here is trying to buy this election because he has nothing to say. A

265

nasty tone developed quickly. Lake smiled hand-somely; water off a duck's back.

Tarry's weak beginning emboldened Lake, gave him a shot of confidence, and convinced him to stay behind the podium where it was safe and where his notes were. He began by saying that he wasn't there to throw mud, that he had respect for Governor Tarry, but they had just listened to him speak for five minutes and eleven seconds and he'd said nothing positive.

He then ignored his opponent, and briefly covered three issues that needed to be discussed. Tax relief, welfare reform, and the trade deficit. Not a word about defense.

The first question from the panel of reporters was directed at Lake, and it dealt with the budget surplus. What should be done with the money? It was a soft pitch, lobbed by a friendly reporter, and Lake was all over it. Save Social Security, he answered, then in an impressive display of finan-cial straight talk he outlined precisely how the money should be used. He gave figures and percentages and projections, all from memory.

Governor Tarry's response was simply to cut taxes. Give the money back to the people who'd earned it.

Few points were scored during the questioning. Both candidates were well prepared. The surprise was that Lake, the man who wanted to own the Pentagon, was so well versed in all other issues.

The debate settled into the usual give and take. The questions from the spectators were thoroughly predictable. The fireworks began when the candi-dates were allowed to quiz one another. Tarry went first, and, as expected, asked Lake if he was trying to buy the election.

'You weren't concerned about money when you had more than everybody else,' Lake shot back, and the audience came to life.

'I didn't have fifty million dollars,' Tarry said.

'Neither do I,' Lake said. 'It's more like sixty million, and it's coming in faster than we can count it. It's coming from working people and middle-income folks. Eighty-one percent of our contributors are people earning less than forty thousand dollars a year. Something wrong with those people, Governor Tarry?'

'There should be a limit on how much a candidate should spend.'

'I agree. And I've voted for limits eight different times in Congress. You, on the other hand, never mentioned limits until you ran out of money.'

Governor Tarry looked Quayle-like at the camera, the frozen stare of a deer in headlights. A few of Lake's people in the audience laughed just loud enough to be heard.

The beads of sweat returned to the governor's forehead as he shuffled his oversized notecards. He wasn't actually a sitting governor, but he still preferred the title. In fact, it had been nine years since the voters of Indiana sent him packing, after only one term. Lake saved this ammo for a few minutes.

Tarry then asked why Lake had voted for fifty-four new taxes during his fourteen years in Congress.

'I don't recall fifty-four taxes,' Lake said. 'But a lot of them were on tobacco and alcohol and gambling. I also voted against increases in personal income taxes, corporate income taxes, federal withholding taxes, and Social Security taxes. I'm not ashamed of that record. And speaking of taxes, Governor, during your four years in Indiana, how do you explain the fact that individual tax rates increased by an average of six percent?'

No quick response was forthcoming, so Lake plowed ahead. 'You want to cut federal spending, yet in your four years in Indiana state spending increased eighteen percent. You want to cut corporate income taxes, yet during your four years in Indiana, corporate income taxes went up three percent. You want to end welfare, yet when you were governor forty thousand people were added to the welfare rolls in Indiana. How do you explain this?'

Each blow from Indiana drew blood, and Tarry was on the ropes. 'I disagree with your figures, sir,' he managed to say. 'We created jobs in Indiana.'

'Is that so?' Lake said sardonically. He pulled up a sheet of paper from his podium as if it were a federal indictment against Governor Tarry. 'Maybe you did, but during your four years almost sixty thousand ex-workers signed up for unemployment,' he announced without looking at the paper.

Sure Tarry had had a bad four years as governor, but the economy had gone south on him. He had explained all this before and he'd love to do it again, but, gosh, he had only a few short minutes on national television. Surely he shouldn't waste it splitting hairs about the past. 'This race is not about Indiana,' he said, managing a smile. 'It's about all fifty states. It's about working people everywhere who'll be expected to pay more taxes to finance your gold-plated defense projects, Mr. Lake. You can't be serious about doubling the Pentagon's budget.'

Lake looked hard at his opponent. 'I'm very serious about it. And if you wanted a strong military, you'd be serious too.' He then rattled off a string of statistics that went on and on, each building on the other. It was conclusive proof of our military unreadiness, and when he finally finished our armed forces would've been hard-pressed to invade Bermuda.

But Tarry had a study to the contrary, a thick glossy manuscript produced by a think tank run by ex-admirals. He waved it for the cameras and argued such a buildup was unnecessary. The world was at peace, with the exception of a few civil and regional wars, disputes in which we had no national interest, and the United States was by far the only superpower left standing. The cold war was history. The Chinese were decades away from achieving anything remotely resembling parity. Why burden the taxpayers with tens of billions in new hardware?

They argued for a while about how to pay for it, and Tarry scored minor points. But they were on Lake's turf, and as the issue dragged on it became evident that Lake knew far more than the governor.

Lake saved his best for last. During his ten-minute recap, he returned to Indiana and continued the miserable list of Tarry's failures there during his sole term. The theme was simple, and very effective: If he can't run Indiana, how can he run the entire nation?

'I'm not knocking the people of Indiana,' Lake said at one point. 'In fact, they had the wisdom to return Mr. Tarry to private life after only one term. They knew he was doing a terrible job. That's why only thirty-eight percent of them voted for him when he asked for four more years.Thirty-eight percent! We should trust the people of Indiana. They know this man. They've seen him govern. They made a mistake, and they got rid of him. It would be sad if the rest of the country now made the same mistake.'

The instant polls gave a solid win to Lake. D-PAC called a thousand voters immediately after the debate. Almost 70 percent thought Lake was the better of the two.

On a late flight from Pittsburgh to Wichita, several bottles of champagne were opened on Air Lake and a small party began. The debate poll results were flowing in, each better than the last, and the mood was victorious.

Lake hadn't banned alcohol on his Boeing, but he had discouraged it. If and when a member of his staff took a drink, it was always a quick one, and always on the sly. But some moments called for a little celebration. He enjoyed two glasses of champagne himself. Only his closest people were present. He thanked them and congratulated them, and just for fun they watched the highlights of the debate while another bottle was opened. They paused the video each time Governor Tarry looked particularly puzzled, and the laughs grew louder.

But the party was brief; fatigue hit hard. These were people who'd been sleeping five hours a night for weeks. Most had slept even less the night before the debate. Lake himself was exhausted. He finished a third glass, the first time in many years he'd drunk that much, and settled into his massive leather recliner with a heavy quilt. Bodies sprawled everywhere in the darkness of the cabin.

He couldn't sleep; he seldom did on airplanes. There were too many things to think and worry about. It was impossible not to savor the victory in the debate, and as he kicked around under the quilt Lake repeated his best lines of the night. He had been brilliant, something he'd never admit to anyone else.

The nomination was his. He would be show-cased at the convention, then for four months he and the Vice President would slug it out in the grandest of American traditions.

He turned on the small overhead reading light. Someone else was reading down the aisle, near the flight deck. Another insomniac, with the only other light on in the cabin. People were actually snoring under their blankets, the sleep of hurried young people running on fumes.

Lake opened his briefcase and pulled out a small leather folder filled with his personal correspondence cards. They were four by six, heavy stock, off-white in color, and in light black Old English print had the name of 'Aaron Lake' printed at the top. With a thick, antique Mont Blanc pen, Lake scribbled a brief word to his college roommate, now a professor of Latin at a small college in Texas. He wrote a thank-you to the moderator of the debate, and one to his Oregon coordinator. Lake loved Clancy novels. He'd just finished the latest one, the thickest yet, and he wrote the author a complimentary note.

Sometimes his notes ran long, and for this reason he had plain cards, same size and color but without his name. He looked around to make sure everyone was sound asleep, and he quickly wrote:

Dear Ricky:
    I think it's best if we end our correspondence. I wish you well with your rehab.

                                    Sincerely, Al

He addressed an unmarked envelope. The address of Aladdin North came from memory. Then he returned to his personalized cards and wrote a series of thank-you notes to serious contributors. He wrote twenty of them before fatigue finally settled in. With the cards still in front of him, and his reading light still on, he yielded to exhaustion and within minutes was napping.

He'd slept less than an hour when panicked voices awakened him. Lights were on, people were moving, and there was smoke in the cabin. A buzzer of some sort was ringing loudly from the cockpit, and once he got his bearings Lake realized the nose of the Boeing was pointed downward. Total panic set in quickly as the air masks dropped from above. After years of half-watching flight attendants give their routine demonstrations before takeoff, the damned masks were actually going to be used. Lake snapped his into place and inhaled mightily.

The pilot announced they were making an emergency landing in St. Louis. The lights flickered, and someone actually screamed. Lake wanted to move about the cabin and reassure everyone, but the mask wouldn't move with him. In the section behind him were two dozen reporters and about that many Secret Service people.

Maybe the air masks didn't drop back there, he thought, then felt guilty.

The smoke got thicker, and the lights faded. After the onset of panic, Lake managed a rational thought or two, if only for a brief second. He quickly gathered the correspondence cards and envelopes. The one to Ricky got his attention just long enough to place it in the envelope to Aladdin North. He sealed it, and stuffed the folder back into his briefcase. The lights flickered again, then went out for good.

The smoke burned their eyes and warmed their faces. The plane was descending at a rapid pace. Warning bells and sirens shrieked from the flight deck.

This can't be happening, Lake told himself as he gripped his armrests. I'm about to be elected President of the United States. He thought of Rocky Marciano, Buddy Holly, Otis Redding, Thurman Munson, Senator Tower of Texas, Mickey Leland from Houston, a friend of his. And JFK, Jr., and Ron Brown.

The air suddenly turned cold and the smoke

dissipated rapidly. They were below ten thousand feet, and the pilot had somehow managed to vent the cabin. The plane leveled and from the windows they could see lights on the ground.

'Please continue to use the oxygen masks,' the pilot said in the darkness. 'We'll be on the ground in a few minutes. The landing should be uneventful.'

Uneventful? He must be kidding, thought Lake. He needed to find the nearest toilet.

Relief settled uneasily through the plane. Just before it touched down, Lake saw the flashing lights of a hundred emergency vehicles. They bounced a little, a typical landing, and when they stopped at the end of the runway the emergency doors flew open.

A controlled stampede occurred, and within minutes they were grabbed by rescue personnel and rushed to ambulances. The fire, in the luggage area of the Boeing, was still spreading when they landed. As Lake jogged away from the plane, firemen rushed toward it. Smoke boiled from under the wings.

Just a few more minutes, Lake said to himself, and we would be dead.

'That was a close one, sir,' a paramedic said as they raced away. Lake clutched his briefcase, with his little letters inside, and for the first time went rigid with horror.

The near miss, and the obligatory nonstop media barrage after it, probably did little to boost Lake's popularity. But the publicity certainly didn't hurt. He was everywhere on the morning news, one moment talking about his decisive victory over Governor Tarry in the debate, and the next giving details of what could've been his last flight.

'I think I'll take the bus for a while,' he said with a laugh. He used as much humor as he could muster, and took the high road of aw-shucks-it-was-nothing. His staff members had different stories, of breathing oxygen in the dark while the smoke grew thicker and hotter. And the reporters on board were eager sources of information, providing detailed narratives of the terror.

Teddy Maynard watched it all from his bunker. Three of his men were on the plane, and one had called him from the hospital in St. Louis.

It was a perplexing event. On the one hand, he still believed in the importance of a Lake presidency. The security of the nation depended on it.

On the other hand, a crash wouldn't have been a catastrophe. Lake and his double life would be gone. A huge headache wiped out. Governor Tarry had learned firsthand the power of unlimited cash. Teddy could cut a deal with him in time to win in November.

But Lake was still standing, taller than ever now. His tanned face was on the front of every newspaper and close to every camera. His campaign had progressed far faster than Teddy had dreamed.

So why was there so much angst in the bunker? Why was Teddy not celebrating?

Because he had yet to solve the puzzle of the Brethren. And he couldn't simply start killing people.

TWENTY-FIVE

The team in Documents used the same laptop they'd used to write the last letter to Ricky. This letter was composed by Deville himself, and approved by Mr. Maynard. It read:

Dear Ricky:
  Good news about your release to the halfway house in Baltimore. Give me a few days and I think I'll have a full-time job lined up for you there. It's a clerical position, not a lot of money, but a pretty good place to start.
  I suggest we go a bit slower than you want. Maybe a nice lunch at first, then we'll see where things go. I'm not the type to rush in.
  Hope you're doing well. I'll write you next week with the details of the job. Hang in there.

Best Wishes, Al

Only the 'Al' was handwritten. A D.C. postmark was applied, and the letter was flown and hand-delivered to Klockner in Neptune Beach.

Trevor happened to be in Fort Lauderdale,

oddly enough tending to legitimate legal business, and so the letter sat in the Aladdin North box for two days. When he returned, exhausted, he stopped by his office just long enough to commence a nasty argument with Jan, then stormed out, got back in his car, and went straight to the post office. To his delight, the box was full. He sorted out the junk mail, then drove a half mile to the Atlantic Beach post office and checked the box for Laurel Ridge, Percy's fancy rehab spa.

Once all the mail was collected, and much to the dismay of Klockner, Trevor left for Trumble. He made one call en route, to his bookie. He'd lost $2,500 in three days on hockey, a sport Spicer knew nothing about and refused to bet on. Trevor was picking his own favorites, with predictable results.

Spicer didn't answer the page at the courtyard at Trumble, so Beech met with Trevor in the attorney-conference room. They did their mail swap – eight letters going out, fourteen coming in.

'What about Brant in Upper Darby?' Beech asked, flipping through the envelopes.

'What about him?'

'Who is he? We're ready to bust him.'

'I'm still searching. I've been out of town for a few days.'

'Get it done, okay. This guy could be the biggest fish yet.'

'I'll do it tomorrow.'

Beech had no Vegas lines to ponder and he didn't want to play cards. Trevor left after twenty minutes.

*

Long after they should've eaten dinner, and long after the library should've been closed, the Brethren remained locked in their little room, saying little, avoiding eye contact with one another, each staring at the walls, deep in thought.

On the table were three letters. One was from Al's laptop, postmarked two days earlier in D.C. One was Al's handwritten note ending his correspondence with Ricky, postmarked from St. Louis, three days earlier. These two conflicted sharply, and were obviously written by different people. Someone was tampering with their mail.

The third letter had stopped them cold. They'd read it over and over, one by one, collectively, in silence, in unison. They'd picked at its corners, held it up to the light, even smelled it. There was a very faint smoky odor, same as the envelope and the note from Al to Ricky.

Handwritten in ink, it was dated April 18, at 1:20 A.M., and addressed to a woman named Carol.

Dear Carol:
What a great night! The debate couldn't have gone better, thanks in part to you and the Pennsylvania volunteers. Many thanks! Let's push harder and win this thing. We're ahead in Pennsylvania, let's stay there. See you next week.

It was signed by Aaron Lake. The card had his name personalized across the top. The handwriting was identical to that on the terse note Al had sent Ricky.

The envelope was addressed to Ricky at Aladdin North, and when Beech opened it he did not notice the second card stuck behind the first. Then it fell on the table, and when he picked it up he saw the name 'Aaron' Lake engraved in black.

That had happened sometime around 4 P.M., not long after Trevor had left. For almost five hours they'd studied the mail, and they were now almost certain that (a) the laptop letter was a fake, with the name 'Al' signed by someone who was quite good at forging; (b) the forged 'Al' signature was virtually identical to the original 'Al,' so the forger at some point had gained access to Ricky's correspondence with Al; (c) the notes to Ricky and Carol were handwritten by Aaron Lake; and (d) the one to Carol had obviously been sent to them by mistake.

Above all, Al Konyers was really Aaron Lake.

Their little scam had snared the most famous politician in the country.

Other, less important pieces of evidence also pointed toward Lake. His front was a mailbox service in the D.C. area, a place where Congressman Lake spent almost all of his time. Being a high-profile elected official, subject to the whims of voters every so often, he would certainly hide behind an alias. And he'd use a machine with a printer to hide his handwriting. Al had not sent a photograph, another sign that he had a lot to conceal.

They'd checked recent newspapers in the library to get the dates straight. The handwritten notes had been mailed from St. Louis the day after the debate, when Lake was there because his airplane had caught fire.

The timing seemed perfect for Lake to call off the letters. He'd started the correspondence before he entered the race. In three months he'd taken the country by storm and become very famous. Now, he had so much to lose.

Slowly, with no concern for time, they built their case against Aaron Lake. And when it looked airtight, they tried to break it down. The most compelling counterpoint came from Finn Yarber.

Suppose, he said, someone on Lake's staff had access to his stationery? Not a bad question, and one they'd kicked around for an hour. Wouldn't Al Konyers do such a thing in order to hide himself? What if he lived in the D.C. area and worked for Lake? Suppose Lake, a very busy man, trusted this assistant to write personal notes for him. Yarber couldn't remember allowing an assistant such authority back when he was Chief Justice. Beech had never let anyone write his personal notes. Spicer had never fooled with such nonsense. That's what phones were for.

But Yarber and Beech had never known the stress and fury of anything remotely similar to a presidential campaign. They'd been busy men in their times, they reflected with sadness, but nothing like Lake.

Say it was an assistant to Lake. So far he had a perfect cover because he'd told them almost nothing. No photo. Only the vaguest details about career and family. He liked old movies and Chinese food, and that was about all they'd extracted. Konyers was on their list of pen pals to soon dispose of because he was too timid. Why, then, would he call off the relationship at this moment?

There was no ready answer.

And the argument was a long shot anyway. Beech and Yarber concluded that no man in Lake's position, someone with a good chance of becoming President of the United States, would allow anyone else to write and sign personal notes. Lake had a hundred staff members to type letters and memos, all of which could be signed by him at a rapid clip.

Spicer had posed a more serious question. Why would Lake run the risk of a handwritten note? His prior letters had been typed on plain white paper, and mailed in a plain white envelope. They could spot a coward by his choice of stationery, and Lake was as fainthearted as anyone who'd answered their ad. The campaign, rich as it was, had plenty of word processors and typewriters and laptops, no doubt the latest in technology.

To find the answer, they went back to the little evidence they had. The letter to Carol had been written at 1:20 A.M. According to a newspaper, the emergency landing happened around 2:15, less than an hour later.

'He wrote it on the plane,' Yarber said. 'It was late, the plane was filled with people, almost sixty according to the paper, these people were exhausted, and maybe he couldn't get his hands on a computer.'

'Then why not wait?' asked Spicer. He'd proved to be excellent at asking questions no one, especially him, could answer.

'He made a mistake. He thought he was being smart, and he probably was. Somehow the mail got mixed.'

'Look at the big picture,' Beech said. 'The nomination is in the bag. He's just wiped out his only opponent, before a national audience, and he's finally convinced that his name will be on the ballot in November. But he's got this secret. He's got Ricky, and he's been thinking for weeks about what to do with Ricky. The boy's going to be released, he wants to have a rendezvous, etc. Lake feels the pressure on both fronts – from Ricky, and from the realization that he might just be elected President. So he decides to stiff Ricky. He writes a note that has one chance in a billion of getting screwed up, then the plane catches on fire. He makes a small mistake, but it turns into a monster.'

'And he doesn't know it,' Yarber added. 'Yet.'

Beech's theory settled in. They absorbed it in the heavy stillness of their little room. The gravity of their discovery weighed down their words and thoughts. The hours passed, and it slowly sank in.

For the next great question they grappled with the baffling reality that someone was meddling with their mail. Who? And why would anyone want to? How had they intercepted the letters? The puzzle seemed hopeless.

Again, they argued the scenario that the culprit was someone very close to Lake, perhaps an assistant with access who'd stumbled across the letters. And maybe he was trying to protect Lake from Ricky by commandeering the correspond-ence, with the goal of somehow, someday ending the relationship.

But there were too many unknowns to build any evidence. They scratched their heads and bit their nails, and finally admitted they would have to sleep on it. They couldn't plot the next move because the situation before them had more riddles than answers.

They slept little, and they were red-eyed and unshaved when they reconvened just after 6 A.M. with black coffee steaming from Styrofoam cups. They locked the door, pulled out the letters, placed them exactly where they'd been the night before, and began thinking.

'I think we should scope out the box in Chevy Chase,' said Spicer. 'It's easy, safe, usually quick. Trevor's been able to do it almost everywhere. If we know who's renting it, then a lot of questions will be answered.'

'It's hard to believe a man like Aaron Lake would be renting a box so he could hide letters like these,' Beech said.

'It's not the same Aaron Lake,' Yarber said. 'When he rented the box and began writing to Ricky, he was just a simple congressman, one of four hundred and thirty-five. You'd never heard of him. Now, things have changed dramatically.'

'And that's exactly why he's trying to end the relationship,' Spicer said. 'Things are very different now. He has much more to lose.'

The first step would be to get Trevor to investigate the post office box in Chevy Chase.

The second step was not as clear. They were concerned that Lake, and they assumed that Lake was Al and Al was Lake, might realize his screwup

283

with the letters. He had tens of millions of dollars (a fact they had certainly not overlooked), and he could easily use some of it to track down Ricky. Given the enormity of the stakes, Lake, if he did realize his mistake, would do almost anything to neutralize Ricky.

So they debated whether to write him a note, in which Ricky would beg Al not to slam the door like this. Ricky needed his friendship, nothing more, etc. The purpose would be to give the impression that everything was fine, nothing out of the ordinary. They hoped Lake would read it and scratch his head and wonder to himself just where, exactly, did that damned card to Carol get off to.

Such a note was unwise, they decided, because someone else was also reading the letters. Until they knew who, they couldn't risk any more contact with Al.

They finished their coffee and walked to the cafeteria. They ate alone, cereal and fruit and yogurt, healthy stuff because they would now live again on the outside. They walked four smoke-free laps together, at a leisurely pace, then returned to their chamber to finish the morning deep in thought.

Poor Lake. He was scrambling from one state to the next with fifty people in tow, late for three engagements at once, a dozen aides whispering in both ears. He had no time to think for himself.

And the Brethren had all day, hours upon hours to sit with their thoughts and their schemes. It was not an equal match.

TWENTY-SIX

There were two types of phones at Trumble; secured and unsecured. In theory, all calls made on unsecured lines were taped and subject to review by little elves in a booth somewhere who did nothing but listen to a million hours of useless chatter. In reality, about half the calls were actually taped, at random, and only about 5 percent were ever heard by anybody working for the prison. Not even the federal government could hire enough elves to handle all the listening.

Drug dealers had been known to direct their gangs from unsecured lines. Mafia bosses had been known to order hits on their rivals. The odds were very high against getting caught.

The secured lines were fewer in number, and by law could not be wired for surveillance. The secured calls went only to lawyers, and always with a guard posted nearby.

When Spicer's turn finally came to make a secured call, the guard had drifted away.

'Law office,' came the rude hello from the free world.

'Yes, this is Joe Roy Spicer, calling from the Trumble prison, and I need to speak with Trevor.'

'He's asleep.'

It was 1:30 P.M. 'Then wake the sonofabitch up,' Spicer growled.

'Hang on.'

'Would you please hurry? I'm on a prison phone.'

Joe Roy glanced around and wondered, not for the first time, what kind of lawyer they'd crawled in bed with.

'Why are you calling?' were Trevor's first words.

'Never mind. Wake your ass up and get to work. We need something done quickly.'

By now, the rental across from Trevor's office was buzzing. This was the first call from Trumble.

'What is it?'

'We need a box checked out. Quickly. And we want you to go supervise it. Don't leave until it's finished.'

'Why me?'

'Just do it, dammit, okay? This could be the biggest one yet.'

'Where is it?'

'Chevy Chase, Maryland. Write this down. Al Konyers, Box 455, Mailbox America, 39380 Western Avenue, Chevy Chase. Be very careful because this guy could have some friends, and there's a good chance someone else is already watching the box. Take some cash and hire a couple of good investigators.'

'I'm pretty busy around here.'

'Yeah, sorry I woke you up. Do it now, Trevor.

Leave today. And don't come back until you know who rented the box.'

'All right, all right.'

Spicer hung up, and Trevor put his feet back on his desk and appeared to return to his nap. But he was just contemplating matters. A moment later he yelled for Jan to check the flights to Washington.

In fourteen years as a field supervisor, Klockner had never seen so many people watch one person do so little. He made a quick call to Deville at Langley, and the rental sprang into action. It was time for the Wes and Chap show.

Wes walked across the street and entered the creaking and peeling door of Mr. L. Trevor Carson, Attorney and Counselor-at-Law. Wes was dressed in khakis and a pullover knit, loafers, no socks, and when Jan offered him her customary sneer she couldn't tell if he was a native or a tourist. 'What can I do for you?' she asked.

'I really need to see Mr. Carson,' Wes said with an air of desperation.

'Do you have an appointment?' she asked, as if her boss was so busy she couldn't keep track of his meetings.

'Well, no, it's sort of an emergency.'

'He's very busy,' she said, and Wes could almost hear the laughter from the rental.

'Please, I've got to talk to him.'

She rolled her eyes and didn't budge. 'What kind of matter is it?'

'I've just buried my wife,' he said, on the verge of tears, and Jan finally cracked a bit. 'I'm very sorry,' she said. Poor guy.

'She was killed in a car wreck on I–95, just north of Jacksonville.'

Jan was standing now and wishing she'd made fresh coffee. 'I'm so sorry,' she said. 'When did this happen?'

'Twelve days ago. A friend recommended Mr. Carson.'

Not much of a friend, she wanted to say. 'Would you like some coffee?' she asked, putting the top on her nail polish. Twelve days ago, she thought. Like all good legal secretaries, she read the newspapers with a keen eye on the accidents. Who knows, one might walk in the door.

Never Trevor's door. Until now.

'No, thanks,' Wes said. 'She was hit by a Texaco truck. The driver was drunk.'

'Oh my god!' she exclaimed, hand over her mouth. Even Trevor could handle this one.

Serious money, big fees, right here in the reception area, and that fool back there snoring off his lunch.

'He's in a deposition,' she said. 'Let me see if I can disturb him. Please have a seat.' She wanted to lock the front door so he couldn't escape.

'The name's Yates. Yates Newman,' he said, trying to help her.

'Oh yes,' she said, racing down the hall. She knocked politely on Trevor's door, then stepped inside. 'Wake up, asshole!' she hissed through clenched teeth, loud enough for Wes to hear up front.

'What is it?' Trevor said, standing, ready for a fistfight. He wasn't sleeping after all. He'd been reading an old *People*.

288

'Surprise! You have a client.'

'Who is it?'

'A man whose wife got run over by a Texaco truck twelve days ago. He wants to see you right now.'

'He's here?'

'Yep. Hard to believe, isn't it? Three thousand lawyers in Jacksonville and this poor guy falls through the cracks. Said a friend recommended you.'

'What'd you tell him?'

'I told him he needed to find new friends.'

'No, really, what did you tell him?'

'That you're in a deposition.'

'I haven't had a deposition in eight years. Send him back.'

'Be cool. I'll make him some coffee. Act like you're finishing some important stuff back here. Why don't you straighten this place up?'

'You just make sure he can't get out.'

'The Texaco driver was drunk,' she said, opening the door. 'Don't screw this up.'

Trevor froze, slack-jawed, glassy-eyed, his deadened mind suddenly springing to life. One third of $2 million, $4 million, hell, $10 million if he was really drunk and punitive damages kicked in. He wanted to at least straighten his desk, but he couldn't move.

Wes stared out the front window, stared at the rental, where his buddies were staring at him. He kept his back to the ruckus down the hall because he was struggling to keep a straight face. Footsteps, then Jan said, 'Mr. Carson will see you in just a moment.'

'Thanks,' he said softly, without turning around.

Poor guy's still grieving, she thought, then walked to the dirty kitchen to make coffee.

The deposition was over in a flash, and the other participants miraculously vanished without a trace. Wes followed her down the hall to Mr. Carson's cluttered office. Introductions were made. She brought them fresh coffee, and when she was finally gone, Wes made an unusual request.

'Is there any place to get a strong latte around here?'

'Why, certainly, yes, of course,' Trevor said, the words jumping across the desk. 'There's a place called Beach Java just a few blocks away.'

'Could you send her to get me one?'

Absolutely. Anything!

'Yes, of course. Tall or grande?'

'Tall's fine.'

Trevor bounced out of his office, and a few seconds later Jan hit the front door and practically ran down the street. When she was out of sight, Chap left the rental and walked to Trevor's. The front door was locked, so he opened it with a key of his own. Inside, he latched the chain, so poor Jan would be stuck on the porch with a cup of scalding latte.

Chap eased down the hall and made a sudden entrance into the lawyer's office.

'Excuse me,' Trevor said.

'It's okay,' Wes said. 'He's with me.'

Chap closed and locked the door, then he yanked a 9-millimeter pistol from his jacket and almost pointed it at poor Trevor, whose eyes bulged and heart froze.

'What –' he managed to emit in a high-pitched painful voice.

'Just shut up, okay,' said Chap, handing the pistol to Wes, who was sitting. Trevor's wild eyes followed it from one to the other, then it disappeared. What have I done? Who are these thugs? All my gambling debts are paid.

He was very happy to shut up. Whatever they wanted.

Chap leaned on the wall, pretty damned close to Trevor, as if he might lunge at any moment. 'We have a client,' he began. 'A wealthy man, who has been snagged in the little scam run by you and Ricky.'

'Oh my god,' Trevor mumbled. His worst nightmare.

'It's a wonderful idea,' Wes said. 'Extorting from rich gay men who are still hiding in the closet. They can't complain. Ricky's already in prison, so what does he have to lose?'

'Almost perfect,' Chap said. 'Until you hook the wrong fish, which is exactly what you've done.'

'It's not my scam,' Trevor said, his voice still two octaves above normal, his eyes still searching for the pistol.

'Yes, but it wouldn't work without you, would it?' Wes asked. 'There has to be a crooked lawyer on the outside to shuttle mail. And Ricky needs someone to direct the money and do a little investigative work.'

'You're not cops, are you?' Trevor asked.

'No. We're private thugs,' Chap said.

'Because if you're cops then I'm not sure I wanna talk anymore.'

291

'We're not cops, okay.'

Trevor was breathing and thinking again, the breathing going much faster than the thinking, but his training kicked in. 'I think I'll record this,' he said. 'Just in case you're cops.'

'I said we're not cops.'

'I don't trust cops, especially the FBI. The fibbies would walk in here just like the two of you, wave a gun around, and swear that they weren't fibbies. I just don't like cops. I think I'll get this on tape.'

Don't worry, pal, they wanted to say. It was all being recorded, live and in high-density digital color from a tiny camera in the ceiling a few feet behind where they were sitting. And there were mikes planted all around Trevor's littered desk so that when he snored or burped or even cracked his knuckles somebody across the street heard it.

The pistol was back. Wes held it with both hands and examined it carefully.

'You're not recording anything,' Chap said. 'As I told you, we're private boys. And we're calling the shots right now.' He took a step closer along the wall. Trevor watched him with one eye, and with the other helped Wes examine the pistol.

'In fact, we come in peace,' Chap said.

'We have some money for you,' Wes said, and put the damned thing away again.

'Money for what?' Trevor asked.

'We want you on our side. We want to retain your services.'

'To do what?'

'To help us protect our client,' Chap said. 'Here's the way we see it. You're a conspirator in

292

an extortion scheme operating from inside a federal prison, and you've been discovered by us. We could go to the feds, get you and your client busted, you'd be sent away for thirty months, probably to Trumble, where you'd fit right in. You'd be automatically disbarred, which means you'd lose all this.' Chap casually waved his right hand, dismissing the clutter and dust and heaps of old files untouched in years.

Wes jumped right in. 'We're prepared to go to the feds right now, and we could probably stop the mail out of Trumble. Our client would probably be spared any embarrassment. But there's an element of risk our client is not willing to take. What if Ricky has another cohort, either inside or out of Trumble, somebody we haven't found yet, and he somehow manages to expose our client in retaliation?'

Chap was already shaking his head. 'It's too risky. We'd rather work with you, Trevor. We'd rather buy you off, and kill the scam from this office.'

'I cannot be bought,' Trevor said with only a trace of conviction.

'Then we'll lease you for a while, how about that?' Wes said. 'Aren't all lawyers leased by the hour anyway?'

'I suppose, but you're asking me to sell out a client.'

'Your client is a felon who's committing crimes every day from inside a federal prison. And you're just as guilty as he is. Let's not get too sanctimonious here.'

'When you become a criminal, Trevor,' Chap

293

said gravely, 'you lose the privilege of being self-righteous. Don't preach to us. We know it's just a question of how much money.'

Trevor forgot about the gun for a moment, and he forgot about his law license hanging on the wall behind him, slightly crooked. As he so often did these days when faced with yet another unpleasantry from the practice of law, he closed his eyes and dreamed of his forty-foot schooner, anchored in the warm, still waters of a secluded bay, topless girls on the beach a hundred yards away, and himself barely clad, sipping a beverage on the deck. He could smell the salt water, feel the gentle breeze, taste the rum, hear the girls.

He opened his eyes and tried to focus on Wes across the desk. 'Who is your client?' he asked.

'Not so fast,' Chap said. 'Let's cut the deal first.'

'What deal?'

'We give you some money, and you work as a double agent. We get access to everything. We wire you when you talk to Ricky. We see all the mail. You don't make a move until we discuss it.'

'Why don't you just pay the extortion money?' Trevor asked. 'It'd be a whole lot easier.'

'We've thought of that,' Wes said. 'But Ricky doesn't play fair. If we paid him, then he'd come back for more. And more.'

'No, he wouldn't.'

'Really? What about Quince Garbe in Bakers, Iowa?'

Oh my god, thought Trevor, and he almost said it aloud. How much do they know? All he could manage was a very weak 'Who's he?'

'Come on, Trevor,' Chap said. 'We know where

the money is hidden in the Bahamas. We know about Boomer Realty, and about your little account, currently with a balance of almost seventy thousand bucks.'

'We've dug as far as we can dig, Trevor,' Wes said, jumping in with perfect timing. Trevor was watching tennis, back and forth, back and forth. 'But we've finally hit a rock. That's why we need you.'

Truthfully, Trevor had never liked Spicer. He was a cold, ruthless, nasty little man who'd had the gall to cut Trevor's percentage. Beech and Yarber were okay, but what the hell. It wasn't as if Trevor had a lot of choices here. 'How much?' he asked.

'Our client is prepared to pay a hundred thousand dollars, cash,' Chap said.

'Of course it's cash,' Trevor replied. 'A hundred thousand is a joke. That would be Ricky's first installment. My self-respect is worth a helluva lot more than a hundred thousand.'

'Two hundred thousand,' Wes said.

'Let's do it this way,' Trevor said, trying to willfully suppress his racing heart. 'How much is it worth to your client to have his little secret buried?'

'And you're willing to bury it?' Wes asked.

'Yep.'

'Give me a second,' Chap said, yanking a tiny phone from his pocket. He punched numbers as he opened the door and stepped into the hallway, then mumbled several sentences Trevor could barely hear. Wes stared at a wall, the gun lying peacefully beside his chair. Trevor couldn't see it, though he tried.

Chap returned and stared hard at Wes, as if his

eyebrows and wrinkles could somehow deliver a crucial message. In the brief hesitation, Trevor rushed in. 'I think it's worth a million bucks,' he said. 'It could be my last case. You're asking me to divulge confidential client information, a rather egregious act for a lawyer. It would get me disbarred in an instant.'

Disbarment would be a step up for old Trevor, but Wes and Chap let it pass. Nothing good could come from an argument about how valuable his law license might be.

'Our client will pay a million dollars,' Chap said.

And Trevor laughed. He couldn't help it. He cackled as if he'd just heard the perfect punch line, and across the street in the rental they laughed because Trevor was laughing.

Trevor managed to control himself. He stopped chuckling but couldn't wipe off the smile. A million bucks. Cash. Tax-free. Hidden offshore, in another bank, of course, away from the clutches of the IRS and every other branch of the government.

Then he managed to arrange a lawyerly frown, a little embarrassed that he'd reacted so unprofessionally. He was about to say something important when three sharp raps on glass came from the front. 'Oh yes,' he said. 'That would be the coffee.'

'She's gotta go,' Chap said.

'I'll send her home,' Trevor said, standing for the first time, a little light-headed.

'No. Permanently. Get her out of the office.'

'How much does she know?' Wes asked.

'She's dumb as a rock,' Trevor said happily.

'It's part of the deal,' Chap said. 'She goes, and

now. We have a lot to discuss, and we don't want her around.'

The knocking grew louder. Jan had unlocked the door but was caught by the security chain. 'Trevor! It's me!' she shouted through the two-inch crack.

Trevor walked slowly down the hall, scratching his head, searching for words. He came face to face with her through the window of the front door, and he looked very confused.

'Open up,' she growled. 'This coffee is hot.'

'I want you to go home,' he said.

'Why?'

'Why?'

'Yes, why?'

'Because, well, uh –' Words failed him for a second, then he thought of the money. Her exit was part of the deal. 'Because you're fired,' he said.

'What?'

'I said you're fired!' he yelled, loud enough for his new pals in the back to hear.

'You can't fire me! You owe me too much money.'

'I don't owe you a damned thing!'

'How about a thousand bucks in back salary!'

The windows of the rental were crowded with faces hidden by one-way shading. The voices echoed down the quiet street.

'You're crazy!' Trevor screamed. 'I don't owe you a dime!'

'One thousand forty bucks, to be exact!'

'You're nuts.'

'You sonofabitch! I stick with you for eight years, making minimum wage, then you finally get the big case, and you fire me. Is that what you're doing, Trevor!?'

'Something like that! Now leave!'

'Open the door, you little coward!'

'Leave, Jan!'

'Not until I get my things!'

'Come back tomorrow. I'm meeting with Mr. Newman.' With that, Trevor took a step back. When she saw he wasn't opening the door, she lost it. 'You sonofabitch!' she screamed even louder, then hurled the tall latte at the door. The thin, rickety window shook but didn't break, and was instantly covered with creamy brown liquid.

Trevor, safe on the inside, flinched anyway and watched in horror as this woman he knew so well lost her mind. She stormed away, red-faced and cursing, and took a few steps until a rock caught her attention. It was a remnant of a long-forgotten, low-budget landscaping project he'd once okayed at her insistence. She grabbed it, gritted her teeth, cursed some more, then launched it toward the door.

Wes and Chap had done a masterful job of playing it straight, but when the rock crashed through the door window, they couldn't help but laugh. Trevor yelled, 'You crazy bitch!' They laughed again and looked away from each other, trying gamely to tighten up.

Silence followed. Peace had broken out in and around the reception area.

Trevor appeared in the doorway of his office, unscathed, no visible injuries. 'Sorry about that,' he said softly, and went to his chair.

'You okay?' Chap asked.

'Sure. No problem. How about plain coffee?' he asked Wes.

'Forget about it.'

The details were hammered out during lunch, which Trevor insisted they enjoy at Pete's. They found a table in the back, near the pinball machines. Wes and Chap were concerned with privacy, but they soon realized that nobody listened because nobody conducted business at Pete's.

Trevor knocked down three longnecks with his french fries. They had soft drinks and burgers.

Trevor wanted all the money in hand before he betrayed his client. They agreed to deliver a hundred thousand cash that afternoon, and immediately start a wire transfer for the balance. Trevor demanded a different bank, but they insisted on keeping Geneva Trust in Nassau. They assured him their access was limited only to observing the account; they could not tamper with the funds. Besides, the money would arrive there by late afternoon. If they changed banks, then it might take a day or two. Both sides were anxious to complete the deal. Wes and Chap wanted full, immediate protection for their client. Trevor wanted his fortune. After three beers he was already spending it.

Chap left early to fetch the money. Trevor ordered a longneck to go, and they got into Wes' car for a ride around town. The plan was to meet Chap at some spot and take possession of the cash. As they rode south on Highway A1A, along the beach, Trevor began talking.

'Isn't it amazing,' he said, his eyes hidden behind cheap sunglasses, his head back on the headrest.

'What's amazing?'

'The risks people are willing to take. Your client, for example. A rich man. He could hire all the young boys he wanted, yet he answers an ad in a gay magazine and starts writing letters to a complete stranger.'

'I don't understand it,' Wes said, and the two straight boys bonded for a second. 'It's not my job to ask questions.'

'I suppose the thrill is in the unknown,' Trevor said and took a small sip.

'Yeah, probably so. Who's Ricky?'

'I'll tell you when I get the money. Which one's your client?'

'Which one? How many victims are you working on right now?'

'Ricky's been busy lately. Probably twenty or so in the works.'

'How many have you extorted?'

'Two or three. It's a nasty business.'

'How'd you get involved?'

'I'm Ricky's lawyer. He's very bright, very bored, somehow he cooked up this scheme to put the squeeze on gays still in the closet. Against my better judgment, I signed on.'

'Is he gay?' Wes asked. Wes knew the names of Beech's grandchildren. He knew Yarber's blood type. He knew who Spicer's wife was dating back in Mississippi.

'No,' said Trevor.

'He's a sicko then.'

300

'No, he's a nice guy. So who's your client?'

'Al Konyers.'

Trevor nodded and tried to remember how many letters he'd handled between Ricky and Al. 'What a coincidence. I was making plans to go to Washington to do some background work on Mr. Konyers. Not his real name, of course.'

'Of course not.'

'Do you know his real name?'

'No. We were hired by some of his people.'

'How interesting. So none of us knows the real Al Konyers?'

'That's correct. And I'm sure it'll stay that way.'

Trevor pointed to a convenience store and said, 'Pull in there. I need a beer.'

Wes waited near the gas pumps. It had been determined that they would not say anything about his drinking until the money changed hands and he'd told them everything. They would build some trust, then gently try to nudge him closer to sobriety. The last thing they needed was Trevor at Pete's every night, drinking and talking too much.

Chap was waiting in a matching rental car, in front of a Laundromat five miles south of Ponte Vedra Beach. He handed Trevor a thin, cheap briefcase and said, 'It's all there. A hundred thousand. I'll meet you guys back at the office.'

Trevor didn't hear him. He opened the briefcase and began counting the money. Wes turned around and headed north. Ten stacks of $10,000, all in $100 bills.

Trevor closed it, and crossed over to the other side.

301

TWENTY-SEVEN

Chap's first task as Trevor's new paralegal was to organize the front desk and rid it of anything remotely female. He put Jan's things in a cardboard box, everything from lipstick tubes and nail files to peanut candy and several X-rated romance novels. There was an envelope with eighty dollars and change. The boss claimed it for himself, said it was petty cash.

Chap wrapped her photos in old newspapers and placed them carefully in another box, along with the breakable knickknacks you find on most front desks. He copied her appointment books so they would know who was scheduled to appear in the future. The traffic would be light, he saw with little surprise. Not a single court date anywhere on the horizon. Two office appointments this week, two the next, then nothing. As Chap studied the calendars, it was obvious that Trevor had shifted to a slower gear at about the time the money arrived from Quince Garbe.

They knew Trevor's gambling had picked up in recent weeks, and probably his drinking. Several times Jan had told friends on the phone that

Trevor was spending more time at Pete's than at the office.

As Chap busied himself in the front room, packing her junk, rearranging her desk, dusting and vacuuming and throwing away old magazines, the phone rang occasionally. His job description covered the phone, and he stayed close to it. Most of the calls were for Jan, and he politely explained that she no longer worked there. 'Good for her' seemed to be the general feeling.

An agent dressed as a carpenter arrived early to replace the front door. Trevor marveled at Chap's efficiency. 'How'd you find one so quick?' he asked.

'You just have to work the yellow pages,' Chap said.

Another agent posing as a locksmith followed the carpenter and changed every lock in the building.

Their agreement included the provision that Trevor would see no new clients for at least the next thirty days. He'd argued long and hard against this, as if he had a stellar reputation to protect. Think of all the people who might need him, he'd complained. But they knew how slow the last thirty days had been, and they pressed him until he conceded. They wanted the place to themselves. Chap called those clients with scheduled appointments and told them that Mr. Carson would be tied up in court on the day they were supposed to stop by. Rescheduling would be difficult, Chap explained, but he'd give them a call when there was a break in the action.

'I didn't think he went to court,' one of them said.

'Oh yes,' Chap said. 'It's a really big case.'

When the client list was pared to the core, only one case required an office visit. It was an ongoing child support matter, and Trevor had represented the woman for three years. He couldn't simply give her the boot.

Jan stopped by to cause trouble, and brought with her a boyfriend of sorts. He was a wiry young man with a goatee, polyester pants, white shirt, and tie, and Chap figured he probably sold used cars. No doubt he could have easily thrashed Trevor, but he wanted no part of Chap.

'I'd like to speak to Trevor,' Jan said, her eyes darting around her newly organized desk.

'Sorry. He's in a meeting.'

'And who the hell are you?'

'I'm a paralegal.'

'Yeah, well get your money up front.'

'Thank you. Your things are in those two boxes over there,' Chap said, pointing.

She noticed the magazine racks were purged and neat, the wastebasket was empty, the furniture had been polished. There was a smell of antiseptic, as if they'd fumigated the place where she'd once sat. She was no longer needed.

'Tell Trevor he owes me a thousand dollars in unpaid salary,' she said.

'I will,' Chap replied. 'Anything else?'

'Yeah, that new client yesterday, Yates Newman. Tell Trevor I checked the newspapers. In the past two weeks there's been no accident deaths on

I-95. No record of a female named Newman getting killed either. Something's up.'

'Thank you. I'll tell him.'

She looked around for the last time, and smirked again when she saw the new door. Her boyfriend glared at Chap as if he might just step over and break his neck anyway, but the glaring was done as he headed for the door. They left without breaking anything, both of them carrying a box as they lumbered down the sidewalk.

Chap watched them leave, then began preparing for the challenge of lunch.

Dinner the night before had been nearby, at a crowded new seafood place two blocks from the Sea Turtle Inn. Given the size of the portions, the prices were outrageous, and that was exactly why Trevor, the newest millionaire in Jacksonville, had insisted they eat there. Of course the evening was on him and he spared no expense. He was drunk after the first martini, and didn't remember what he ate. Wes and Chap had explained that their client did not allow them to drink. They sipped designer water and kept his wineglass full.

'I'd find me another client,' Trevor said, laughing at his own humor.

'Guess I'll have to drink for all three of us,' he said halfway through dinner, then proceeded to do just that.

Much to their relief, they learned that he was a docile drunk. They kept pouring, in an effort to see how far he would go. He got quieter and lower in his seat, and long after dessert he tipped the waiter

$300 in cash. They helped him to their car and drove him home.

He slept with the new briefcase across his chest. When Wes turned off his light, Trevor was lying on his bed in his rumpled pants and white cotton shirt, bow tie undone, shoes still on, snoring, and clutching the briefcase tightly with both arms.

The wire had arrived just before five. The money was in place. Klockner had told them to get him drunk, see how he behaved in that condition, then start working in the morning.

At 7:30 A.M. they returned to his house, unlocked the door with their key, and found him pretty much as they'd left him. One shoe was off, and he was curled on his side with the briefcase tucked away like a football.

'Let's go! Let's go!' Chap had yelled while Wes turned on lights and raised shades and made as much noise as possible. Trevor, to his credit, scrambled from bed, raced to the bathroom, took a quick shower, and twenty minutes later walked into his den with a fresh bow tie and not a wrinkle anywhere. His eyes were slightly swollen, but he was smiling and determined to tackle the day.

The million dollars helped. In fact, he'd never conquered a hangover as quickly.

They had a quick muffin and strong coffee at Beach Java, then attacked his little office with vigor. While Chap took care of the front, Wes kept Trevor in his office.

Some of the pieces had fallen into place over dinner. The names of the Brethren had finally been extracted from Trevor, and Wes and Chap had done a splendid job of being surprised.

306

'Three judges?' they'd both repeated, in apparent disbelief.

Trevor had smiled and nodded with great pride, as if he and he alone had been the architect of this masterful scheme. He wanted them to believe that he'd had the brains and skill to convince three former judges that they should spend their time writing letters to lonely gay men so he, Trevor, could rake off a third of their extortion. Hell, he was practically a genius.

Other pieces of the puzzle remained unclear, and Wes was determined to keep Trevor locked away until he had answers.

'Let's talk about Quince Garbe,' he said. 'His post office box was rented to a fake corporation. How'd you learn his true identity?'

'It was easy,' Trevor said, very proud of himself. Not only was he a genius now, but he was a very rich one. He had awakened yesterday morning with a headache, and had spent the first half hour in bed, worrying about his gambling losses, worrying about his dwindling law practice, worrying about his increasing reliance on the Brethren and their scam. Twenty-four hours later, he'd awakened with a worse headache, but one soothed with the balm of a million bucks.

He was euphoric, giddy, and anxious to finish the task at hand so he could get on with life.

'I found a private investigator in Des Moines,' he said, sipping coffee, his feet on his desk, where they belonged. 'Sent him a check for a thousand bucks. He spent two days in Bakers – you been to Bakers?'

'Yep.'

'I was afraid I'd have to go. The scam works best if you can snare some prominent guy with money. He'll pay anything to keep you quiet. Anyway, this investigator found a postal clerk who needed some money. She was a single mother, houseful of kids, old car, small apartment, you get the picture. He called her at night and said he'd give her five hundred dollars cash if she could tell him who was renting Box 788 in the name of CMT Investments. Next morning he called her at the post office. They met in a parking lot during her lunch break. She gave him a piece of paper with the name of Quince Garbe, and he gave her an envelope with five one-hundred-dollar bills. She never asked who he was.'

'Is that a typical method?'

'It worked with Garbe. Curtis Cates, the guy in Dallas, the second one we scammed, was a little more complicated. The investigator we hired there couldn't find anyone on the inside, so he had to watch the post office for three days. Cost eighteen hundred dollars, but he finally saw him and got his license number.'

'Who's next?'

'Probably this guy in Upper Darby, Pennsylvania. His alias is Brant White, and he appears to be a hot prospect.'

'Do you ever read the letters?'

'Never. I don't know what's being said back and forth; don't wanna know. When they're ready to bust somebody, they'll tell me to scope out the box and get a real name. That's if their pen pal is using a front, like your client Mr. Konyers. You'd be amazed how many men use their real names. Unbelievable.'

'Do you know when they send the extortion letters?'

'Oh yeah. They tell me so I can alert the bank in the Bahamas that a wire might be on the way. The bank calls me as soon as the money hits.'

'Tell me about this Brant White in Upper Darby,' Wes said. He was taking pages of notes, as if something might be missed. Every word was being recorded on four different machines across the street.

'They're ready to bust him, that's all I know. He seems hot to trot because they've just swapped a couple of letters. Some of these guys, it's like pulling teeth, judging by the number of letters.'

'But you don't keep track of the letters?'

'There are no records here. I was afraid the feds would show up one day with a search warrant, and I wanted no evidence of my involvement.'

'Smart, very smart.'

Trevor smiled and savored his shrewdness. 'Yeah, well, I've done a lot of criminal law. After a while, you start thinking like a criminal. Anyway, I've been unable to find the right investigator in the Philadelphia area. Still working on it though.'

Brant White was a Langley creation. Trevor could hire every investigator in the Northeast and they'd never find a real person behind the post office box.

'In fact,' he continued, 'I was preparing to go up there myself when I got the call from Spicer telling me to go to Washington and track down Al Konyers. Then you guys showed up, and, well, the rest is history.' His words trailed away as he once again thought of the money. Sure it was a coincidence that Wes and Chap entered his life just hours after he was supposed to go searching for their client. But he didn't care. He could hear the seagulls and feel the hot sand. He could hear the reggae from the island bands, and feel the wind pushing his little boat.

'Is there another contact on the outside?' Wes asked.

'Oh no,' he said vainly. 'I don't need any help. The fewer people involved, the easier the operation works.'

'Very smart,' Wes said.

Trevor leaned back even deeper in his chair. The ceiling above him was cracked and peeling and in need of a fresh coat of enamel. A couple of days ago that might have worried him. Now he knew it would never get painted, not if they expected him to foot the bill. He'd walk out of the place one day very soon, once Wes and Chap here had finished with the Brethren. He'd spend a day or two boxing up his files to store for what reason he was not certain, and he'd give away his outdated and unused law books. He'd find some broke rookie fresh out of law school and looking for a few crumbs around city court, and he'd sell him the furniture and computer for a very reasonable price. And when all the loose ends were covered, he, L. Trevor Carson, Attorney and Counselor-at-Law, would walk out of the office and never look back.

What a glorious day that would be.

Chap interrupted the brief daydream with a sack

of tacos and soft drinks. Lunch had not been discussed among the three, but Trevor had already been checking his watch in anticipation of another long meal at Pete's. He grudgingly took a taco and seethed for a moment. He needed a drink.

'I think it's a good idea to lay off the booze during lunch,' Chap said as they huddled around Trevor's desk and tried not to spill black beans and ground beef.

'Do as you please,' Trevor said.

'I was talking to you,' Chap said. 'At least for the next thirty days.'

'That wasn't part of our deal.'

'It is now. You need to be sober and alert.'

'Why, exactly?'

'Because our client wants you that way. And he's paying you a million dollars.'

'Does he want me to floss twice a day and eat my spinach?'

'I'll ask him.'

'Tell him to kiss my ass while you're at it.'

'Don't overreact, Trevor,' Wes said. 'Just cut back on the drinking for a few days. It'll be good for you.'

If the money had set him free, these two were beginning to choke him. They'd now spent twenty-four hours together, and they showed no signs of leaving. In fact, the opposite was happening. They were moving in.

Chap left early to collect the mail. They'd convinced Trevor that he'd been very sloppy in his habits, and that's how they'd tracked him so easily. Suppose other victims were lurking out there? Trevor'd had little trouble in finding the real names of their victims. Why couldn't the victims do the same to the person behind Aladdin North and Laurel Ridge? From now on, Wes and Chap would take turns collecting the mail. They'd mix things up, visit the post offices at different times, use disguises, real cloak-and-dagger stuff.

Trevor eventually agreed. They seemed to know what they were doing.

There were four letters for Ricky waiting in the Neptune Beach post office, and two for Percy in Atlantic Beach. Chap quickly made the rounds, with a team behind him, watching anyone who might be watching him. The letters were taken to the rental, where they were quickly opened, and copied, then put back together.

The copies were read and analyzed by agents anxious to have something to do. Klockner read them too. Of the six, they'd seen five of the names before. All were lonely middle-aged men trying to muster the nerve to take the next step with Ricky or Percy. None seemed particularly aggressive.

One wall in a converted bedroom of the rental had been painted white and a large map of the fifty states had been stenciled on it. Red pushpins were used to mark Ricky's pen pals. Green for Percy. The names and hometowns of the correspondents were printed in black under the pins.

The nets were getting wider. Ricky had twenty-three men actively writing him; Percy, eighteen. Thirty states were represented. The Brethren were fine-tuning their venture with each passing week. They were now running ads in three magazines, as far as Klockner could tell. They held firm to their profile, and by the third letter they usually knew if a new guy had any money. Or a wife.

It was a fascinating game to watch, and now that they had complete access to Trevor they wouldn't miss a letter.

The day's mail was summarized in two pages, then given to an agent who took off to Langley. Deville had it in hand by 7 P.M.

The first call of the afternoon, at three-ten, came when Chap was washing windows. Wes was still in Trevor's office, grilling him with one question after another. Trevor was weary. He'd missed his nap and he desperately needed a drink.

'Law office,' Chap answered.

'Is this Trevor's office?' the caller asked.

'It is. Who's calling?'

'Who are you?'

'I'm Chap, the new paralegal.'

'What happened to the girl?'

'She no longer works here. What can I do for you?'

'This is Joe Roy Spicer. I'm a client of Trevor's, and I'm calling from Trumble.'

'Calling from where?'

'Trumble. It's a federal prison. Is Trevor there?'

'No sir. He's in Washington, and he should be back here in a couple of hours.'

'Okay. Tell him I'll call back at five.'

'Yes sir.'

Chap hung up and took a deep breath, as did Klockner across the street. The CIA had just had its first live contact with one of the Brethren.

*

The second call came at exactly five. Chap answered the phone and recognized the voice. Trevor was waiting in his office. 'Hello.'

'Trevor, this is Joe Roy Spicer.'

'Hello, Judge.'

'What'd you find in Washington?'

'We're still working on it. It's gonna be a tough one, but we'll find him.'

There was a long pause, as if Spicer didn't like this news and was uncertain about how much to say. 'Are you comin tomorrow?'

'I'll be there at three.'

'Bring five thousand dollars cash.'

'Five thousand dollars?'

'That's what I said. Get the money and bring it here. All in twenties and fifties.'

'What are you gonna do –'

'Don't ask stupid questions, Trevor. Bring the damned money. Put it in an envelope with the other mail. You've done it before.'

'All right.'

Spicer hung up without another word. Then Trevor spent an hour discussing the economics of Trumble. Cash was prohibited. Every inmate had a job and his wages were credited to his account. Expenditures, such as long-distance calls, commissary charges, copying expenses, stamps, were all debited against his account.

But cash was present, though seldom seen. It was smuggled in and hidden, and it was used to pay gambling debts and bribe guards for small favors. Trevor was afraid of it. If he, as the attorney, got caught sneaking it in, his visiting privileges would be permanently eliminated. He'd

314

smuggled on two previous occasions, both times $500, in tens and twenties.

He couldn't imagine what they wanted with $5,000.

TWENTY-EIGHT

After three days of stepping over and around Wes and Chap, Trevor needed a break. They wanted breakfast, lunch, and dinner together. They wanted to drive him home and pick him up for work, very early in the morning. They were running what was left of his practice – Chap the paralegal, Wes the office manager, both of them drilling him with endless questions because there was precious little lawyering to be done.

So it was no surprise when they announced they would drive him to Trumble. He didn't need a driver, he explained. He'd made the trip many times, in his trusty little Beetle, and he'd go it alone. This upset them, and they threatened to call their client for guidance.

'Call the damned client, for all I care,' Trevor yelled at them, and they backed down. 'Your client is not running my life.'

But the client was, and they all knew it. Only the money mattered now. Trevor had already performed his Judas act.

He left Neptune Beach in his Beetle, alone, followed by Wes and Chap in their rental car, and behind them was a white van occupied by people Trevor would never see. Nor did he want to see them. Just for the hell of it, he made a sudden turn into a convenience store for a six-pack, and laughed when the rest of the caravan slammed on brakes and barely avoided a wreck. Once out of town, he drove painfully slow, sipping his beer, savoring his privacy, telling himself he could suffer through the next thirty days. He could suffer through anything for a million bucks.

As he neared the village of Trumble, he had the first pangs of guilt. Could he pull this off? He was about to face Spicer, a client who trusted him, a prisoner who needed him, a partner in crime. Could he keep a straight face and act as if things were fine, while every word was being captured by a high-frequency mike in his briefcase? Could he swap letters with Spicer as if nothing had changed, knowing that the mail was being monitored? Plus, he was throwing away his law career, something he'd worked hard to attain and had once been proud of.

He was selling his ethics, his standards, even his morals for money. Was his soul worth a million bucks? Too late now. The money was in the bank. He took a sip of beer and washed away the fading twinges of guilt.

Spicer was a crook, and so were Beech and Yarber, and he, Trevor Carson, was just as culpable. There's no honor among thieves, he kept repeating silently.

Link got a whiff of the beer wafting off Trevor as they walked down the hall and into the visitors' area. At the lawyers' room Trevor looked inside.

He saw Spicer, partially hidden by a newspaper, and was suddenly nervous. What kind of low-life lawyer carries an electronic listening device into a confidential meeting with a client? The guilt hit Trevor like a brick, but there was no turning back.

The mike was almost as big as a golf ball, and had been meticulously installed by Wes in the bottom of Trevor's beaten-up and scruffy black leather briefcase. It was extremely powerful, and would easily transmit everything to the faceless boys in the white van. Wes and Chap were there too, ready with their earphones, anxious to hear it all.

'Afternoon, Joe Roy,' Trevor said.

'Same to you,' Spicer said.

'Lemme see the briefcase,' Link said. He gave a cursory look, then said, 'It looks fine.' Trevor had warned Wes and Chap that Link sometimes took a peek into the briefcase. The mike was covered by a pile of papers.

'Here's the mail,' Trevor said.

'How many?' Link asked.

'Eight.'

'You got any?' Link asked Spicer.

'No. None today,' Spicer replied.

'I'll be outside,' Link said.

The door closed; feet shuffled, and suddenly there was silence. A very long silence. Nothing. Not a word between lawyer and client. They waited in the white van for an eternity, until it was obvious something had gone wrong.

As Link stepped from the small room, Trevor quickly and deftly set the briefcase outside the

318

door, on the floor, where it rested benignly during the remainder of the attorney-client conference. Link noticed it, and thought nothing about it.

'What'd you do that for?' Spicer asked.

'It's empty,' Trevor said, shrugging. 'Let the closed-circuit see it. We have nothing to hide.' Trevor had had one final, brief attack of ethics. Maybe he'd bug the next chat with his client, but not this one. He'd simply tell Wes and Chap that the guard took his briefcase, something that happened occasionally.

'Whatever,' Spicer said, riffling through the mail until he came to two envelopes that were slightly thicker. 'Is this the money?'

'It is. I had to use some hundreds.'

'Why? I plainly said twenties and fifties.'

'That's all I could find, okay. I didn't anticipate needing that much cash.'

Joe Roy studied the addresses on the other letters. Then he asked, rather caustically, 'So what happened in Washington?'

'It's a tough one. One of those rent-a-box outfits in the suburbs, open twenty-four hours, seven days a week, always somebody on duty, lots of traffic. Security is tight. We'll figure it out.'

'Who are you using?'

'Some outfit in Chevy Chase.'

'Gimme a name.'

'Whatta you mean, gimme a name?'

'Give me the name of the investigator in Chevy Chase.'

Trevor drew a blank; invention failed him. Spicer was on to something, his dark liquid eyes glowing with intensity. 'I can't remember,' Trevor said.

'Where'd you stay?'

'What is this, Joe Roy?'

'Give me the name of your hotel.'

'Why?'

'I have the right to know. I'm the client. I'm paying for your expenses. Where did you stay?'

'Ritz-Carlton.'

'Which one?'

'I don't know. The Ritz-Carlton.'

'There are two. Which one was it?'

'I don't know. Not downtown.'

'What flight did you take?'

'Come on, Joe Roy. What is this?'

'What airline?'

'Delta.'

'The flight number?'

'I don't remember.'

'You got back yesterday. Less than twenty-four hours ago. What was your flight number?'

'I don't recall.'

'Are you sure you went to Washington?'

'Of course I went,' Trevor said, but his voice broke a little from a lack of sincerity. He had not planned his lies, and they were breaking down as fast as he put them up.

'You don't know your flight number, which hotel you stayed in, or the name of the investigator you spent the last two days with. You must think I'm stupid.'

Trevor didn't answer. He could only think of the mike in the briefcase and how lucky he was to have it outside. Getting flogged like this was something he'd rather Wes and Chap not hear.

'You've been drinking, haven't you?' Spicer asked, on the attack.

'Yes,' Trevor said, a temporary pause in the lying. 'I stopped and bought a beer.'

'Or two.'

'Yes, two.'

Spicer leaned on his elbows, his face halfway across the table. 'I got some bad news for you, Trevor. You're fired.'

'What?'

'Terminated. Sacked. Gone for good.'

'You can't fire me.'

'I just did. Effective immediately. By unanimous vote of the Brethren. We're notifying the warden so your name will be removed from the list of attorneys. When you leave today, Trevor, don't come back.'

'Why?'

'Lying, drinking too much, sloppy habits, a general lack of trust on behalf of your clients.'

It sounded true enough, but Trevor nevertheless took it hard. It had never crossed his mind that they'd have the guts to fire him. He clenched his teeth and asked, 'What about our little enterprise?'

'It's a clean break. You keep your money, we'll keep ours.'

'Who'll run it on the outside?'

'We'll worry about that. You can pursue an honest living, if you're able.'

'What would you know about an honest living?'

'Why don't you just leave, Trevor? Get up, walk out, it's been lovely.'

'Sure,' he mumbled, his thoughts a blur but two coming to the forefront. First, Spicer had brought no letters, the first time that had happened in many weeks. Second, the cash. What did they need the five grand for? Probably to bribe their new lawyer. They'd planned their ambush well, which was always an advantage they held because they had so much time on their hands. Three very bright men, with lots of idle time. It wasn't fair.

Pride made him stand. He extended a hand and said, 'Sorry it had to happen.'

Spicer shook it reluctantly. Just get out of here, he wanted to say.

When they made eye contact for the last time, Trevor said, almost in a whisper, 'Konyers is the man. Very rich. Very powerful. He knows about you.'

Spicer leapt up like a cat. With their faces just inches apart, he said, also in a whisper, 'Is he watching you?'

Trevor nodded and winked. Then he grabbed the door. He picked up his briefcase without a word to Link. What was he supposed to say to the guard? Sorry, old boy, but the thousand bucks a month in cash you were getting under the table just got cut off. Sad about it? Then ask Judge Spicer here why it happened.

But he let it pass. He was reeling and almost dizzy, and the alcohol didn't help. What would he tell Wes and Chap? That was the question of the moment. They would hammer him as soon as they could catch him.

He said good-bye to Link, and Vince, Mackey,

and Rufus up front, same as always but now for the last time, and walked into the hot sun.

Wes and Chap were parked three cars down. They wanted to talk but played it safe. Trevor ignored them as he tossed his briefcase into the passenger's seat and got in the Beetle. The caravan followed him away from the prison, and slowly down the highway toward Jacksonville.

Their decision to dispose of Trevor had been reached with a maximum of judicial deliberation. They'd spent hours hiding in their little room, studying the Konyers file until every word of every letter was memorized. They'd walked miles around the track, just the three of them, playing one scenario against another. They ate together, played cards together, all the while whispering new theories of who might be watching their mail.

Trevor was the nearest culprit, and the only one they could control. If their victims got sloppy, they could do nothing about it. But if their lawyer had failed to watch his trail, then he had to be fired. He was not the type to evoke a lot of trust in the first place. How many good, busy lawyers would be willing to risk their careers in a gay extortion scheme?

The only hesitation in ridding themselves of Trevor was the fear of what he might do with their money. They expected him to steal it, frankly, and they couldn't stop him. But they were willing to run that risk in return for a bigger score with Mr. Aaron Lake. To get to Lake, they felt they had to eliminate Trevor.

Spicer gave them the details of their meeting,

word for word. Trevor's muted message at the end stunned them. Konyers was watching Trevor. Konyers knew about the Brethren. Did that mean Lake knew about the Brethren? Who was really Konyers now? Why did Trevor whisper this and why did he leave his briefcase outside the door?

With the scrutiny that only a team of bored judges could generate, the questions poured forth. And then the strategies.

Trevor was making coffee in his newly cleaned and shined kitchen when Wes and Chap made their quiet entry and came straight at him.

'What happened?' Wes asked. They were frowning and gave the impression they'd been fretting for some time.

'What do you mean?' Trevor asked, as if things were splendid.

'What happened to the mike?'

'Oh that. The guard took the briefcase and kept it outside.'

They frowned at each other some more. Trevor poured the water into his coffee machine. The fact that it was almost five and he was making coffee was duly noted by the agents.

'Why did he do that?'

'It's routine. About once a month the guard will keep the briefcase during the visit.'

'Did he search it?'

Trevor busied himself by watching the coffee drip. Absolutely nothing was wrong. 'He made his usual quick exam, which I think he does with his eyes closed. He removed the ingoing letters, then took it. The mike was safe.'

'Did he notice the thick envelopes?'

'Of course not. Relax.'

'And the meeting went well?'

'It was routine, except that Spicer had no outgoing mail, which is a bit unusual these days, but it happens. I'll go back in two days and he'll have a stack of letters, and the guard will not even touch the briefcase. You'll get to hear every word. Want some coffee?'

They relaxed in unison. 'Thanks, but we'd better go,' Chap said. There were reports to make, questions to answer. They started for the door, but Trevor stopped them.

'Look, fellas,' he said very politely. 'I'm perfectly capable of getting dressed by myself, and of having a quick bowl of cereal, alone, the way I've done it for many years. And I like to open my office here no earlier than nine. Since it's my office, we'll open at nine, and not a minute sooner. You're welcome to be here at that unholy hour, but not at eight fifty-nine. Stay away from my house, and stay away from this office until nine. Understood?'

'Sure,' one of them said, and they were gone. It didn't really matter to them. They had bugs crawling all over the office, the house, the car, even the briefcase now. They knew where he bought his toothpaste.

Trevor drank the entire pot of coffee and sobered up. Then he began his movements, all carefully planned. He'd started preparing the moment he left Trumble. He assumed they were watching, back there with the boys from the white van. They had the gadgets and the toys, the mikes and the bugs, and Wes and Chap certainly knew how to use them. Money was no object. He told himself to believe they knew everything, just let his imagination run wild and assume they heard every word, followed every turn, and knew exactly where he was at all times.

The more paranoid he was, the better his chances of escape.

He drove to a mall sixteen miles away near Orange Park, in the sprawl south of Jacksonville. He roamed and window-shopped and ate pizza in a near-empty food court. It was difficult not to dart behind a rack of clothes in a store and wait for the shadows to walk by. But he resisted. In a Radio Shack, he bought a small cell phone. One month of long distance with a local service came with the package, and Trevor had what he needed.

He returned home after nine, certain that they were watching. He turned the television on full volume, and made more coffee. In the bathroom he stuffed his cash into pockets.

At midnight, with the house dark and quiet and Trevor evidently asleep, he slipped out the back door and into the night. The air was brisk, the moon full, and he tried his best to look as though he was simply going for a walk on the beach. He wore baggy cargo pants with pockets from the waist down, two denim shirts, and an oversized windbreaker with money stuffed inside the liner. In all, Trevor had $80,000 hidden on himself as he wandered aimlessly south, along the edge of the water, just another beachcomber out for a midnight stroll.

After a mile his pace quickened. When he'd

gone three miles he was exhausted, but he was in a desperate hurry. Sleep and rest would have to wait.

He left the beach and walked into the grungy lobby of a rundown motel. There was no traffic along Highway A1A; nothing was open except for the motel and a convenience store in the distance.

The door rattled enough for the clerk to come to life. A television was on somewhere in the back. A chubby young man of no more than twenty emerged and said, 'Good evening. Need a room?'

'No sir,' Trevor said, as he slowly drew a hand from a pocket and produced a thick roll of bills. He began peeling them off and placing them in a neat row on the counter. 'I need a favor.'

The clerk stared at the money, then rolled his eyes. The beach attracted all kinds. 'These rooms ain't that expensive,' he said.

'What's your name?' Trevor asked.

'Oh, I don't know. Let's say it's Sammy Sosa.'

'All right, Sammy. There's a thousand bucks. It's yours if you'll drive me to Daytona Beach. Take you ninety minutes.'

'It'll take me three hours because I have to drive back.'

'Whatever. That's more than three hundred bucks an hour. When's the last time you made three hundred bucks an hour?'

'It's been a while. I can't do it. I run the night shift, you see. My job is to be on duty from ten until eight.'

'Who's the boss?'

'He's in Atlanta.'

'When's the last time he stopped by?'

'I've never met him.'

'Of course you haven't. If you owned a dump like this, would you stop by?'

'It's not that bad. We have free color TVs and most of the air-conditioning works.'

'It's a dump, Sammy. You can lock that door, drive away, and come back three hours later, and no one will ever know it.'

Sammy looked at the money again. 'You runnin from the law or something?'

'No. And I'm not armed. I'm just in a hurry.'

'So what's up?'

'A bad divorce, Sammy. I have a little money. My wife wants it all and she has some pretty nasty lawyers. I gotta get out of town.'

'You got money, but no car?'

'Look, Sammy. You want the deal or not? If you say no, then I'll walk down the street to the convenience store and find somebody smart enough to take my cash.'

'Two thousand.'

'You'll do it for two thousand?'

'Yep.'

The car was worse than Trevor had expected. It was an old Honda, uncleaned by Sammy or any of the previous five owners. But A1A was deserted, and the trip to Daytona Beach took exactly ninety-eight minutes.

At 3:20 A.M., the Honda stopped in front of an all-night waffle grill, and Trevor got out. He thanked Sammy, said good-bye, and watched him drive away. Inside, he drank coffee and chatted with the waitress long enough to persuade her to go fetch a local phone directory. He ordered pancakes and used his new Radio Shack cell phone to find his way around town.

The nearest airport was Daytona Beach International. A few minutes after four, his cab stopped at the general aviation terminal. Dozens of small planes sat in neat rows on the tarmac. He stared at them as the cab drove away. Surely, he told himself, one of them was available for a quick charter. He just needed one, preferably a twin-engine.

TWENTY-NINE

The back bedroom of the rental had been converted into the meeting room, with four folding tables pushed together to make one large one. It was covered with newspapers, magazines, and doughnut boxes. Every morning at seven-thirty Klockner and his team met over coffee and pastries to review the night and plan the day. Wes and Chap were always there, and six or seven others joined them, depending on who was in town from Langley. The technicians from the front room sometimes sat in, though Klockner did not require their attendance. Now that Trevor was on their side, they needed fewer people to track him.

Or so they thought. Surveillance detected no movement inside his home before seven-thirty, which was not altogether unusual for a man who often went to bed drunk and woke up late. At eight, while Klockner was still meeting in the back, a technician called the house under the ruse of a wrong number. After three rings, the recorder came on and Trevor announced he was not in, please leave a message. This happened occasionally when he was trying to sleep late, but it usually

330

worked well enough to roust him from bed.

Klockner was notified at eight-thirty that the house was completely still; no shower, no radio, no television, no stereo, not a sound from the normal routine.

It was entirely possible he'd gotten drunk at home, by himself, but they knew he had not spent last night at Pete's. He'd gone to a mall and arrived home apparently sober.

'He could be sleeping,' Klockner said, unconcerned. 'Where's his car?'

'In his driveway.'

At nine, Wes and Chap knocked on Trevor's door, then opened it when there was no answer. The rental sprang to life when they reported there was no sign of him, and that his car was still there. Without panic, Klockner sent people to the beach, to the coffee shops near the Sea Turtle, even to Pete's, which was not yet open. They canvassed the area around his house and office, by foot and by car, and saw nothing.

At ten, Klockner called Deville at Langley. The lawyer's missing, was the message.

Every flight to Nassau was checked; nothing turned up, no sign of a Trevor Carson. Deville's contact in Bahamian customs could not be located, nor could he find the banking supervisor they'd been bribing.

Teddy Maynard was in the middle of a briefing on North Korean troop movements when he was interrupted by an urgent message that Trevor Carson, their drunken lawyer in Neptune Beach, Florida, was missing.

331

'How can you lose a fool like him?' Teddy growled at Deville, in a rare display of anger.

'I don't know.'

'I don't believe this!'

'Sorry, Teddy.'

Teddy shifted his weight and grimaced from the pain. 'Find him, dammit!' he hissed.

The plane was a Beech Baron, a twin-engine owned by some doctors and chartered by Eddie, the pilot Trevor had coaxed out of bed at six in the morning with the promise of cash on the spot and more under the table. The official quote was $2,200 for a round-trip between Daytona Beach and Nassau – two hours each way, total of four at $400 an hour, plus some fees for landing and immigration and pilot downtime. Trevor kicked in another $2,000 for Eddie's pocket if the trip took place immediately.

The Geneva Trust Bank in downtown Nassau opened at 9 EST, and Trevor was waiting when the doors were unlocked. He barged into the office of Mr. Brayshears and demanded immediate assistance. He had almost a million dollars in his account – $900,000 from Mr. Al Konyers, through Wes and Chap; about $68,000 from his dealings with the Brethren.

With one eye on the door, he pressed Brayshears to help him move the money, and quickly. The money was owned by Trevor Carson, and no one else. Brayshears had no choice. There was a bank in Bermuda managed by a friend of his, which suited Trevor just fine. He didn't trust Brayshears, and he planned to keep moving the money until he felt safe.

For a moment, Trevor cast a lustful eye at the account of Boomer Realty, currently with a balance of $189,000 and change. It was within his power, during that fleeting moment, to snatch their money too. They were nothing but felons – Beech, Yarber, the odious Spicer, all crooks. And they'd had the arrogance to fire him. They had forced him to run. He tried to hate them enough to take their money, but as he wavered back and forth he felt a soft spot for them. Three old men wasting away in prison.

A million was enough. Besides, he was in a hurry. If Wes and Chap suddenly charged in with guns, it wouldn't have surprised him. He thanked Brayshears and ran from the building.

When the Beech Baron lifted off the runway at Nassau International, Trevor couldn't help but laugh. He laughed at the heist, at the getaway, at his luck, at Wes and Chap and their rich client now minus a million, at his shabby little law office now mercifully idle. He laughed at his past and at his glorious future.

At three thousand feet he gazed downward at the still blue waters of the Caribbean. A lonely sailboat rocked along, its captain at the wheel, a scantily clad lady nearby. That would be him down there in just a few short days.

He found a beer in a carry-on cooler. He drank it and fell sound asleep. They landed on the island of Eleuthera, a place Trevor had seen in a travel magazine he'd bought the night before. There were beaches and hotels and all the water sports.

He paid Eddie in cash, then waited an hour at the small airport for a taxi to happen by.

He bought clothes at a tourist shop in Governor's Harbour, then walked to a hotel on the beach. He was amused at how quickly he stopped watching the shadows. Sure Mr. Konyers had plenty of money, but no one could afford a secret army big enough to track someone through the Bahamas. His future would be one of sheer delight. He would not ruin it by looking over his shoulder.

He drank rum by the pool as fast as the bar maid could bring it. At the age of forty-eight, Trevor Carson welcomed his new life in pretty much the same condition he'd left his old one.

The law office of Trevor Carson opened on time and things proceeded as if nothing was amiss. Its owner had fled, but its paralegal and office manager were on duty to take care of any business that might unexpectedly develop. They listened in all the right places, and heard nothing. The phone rang twice before noon, two misguided inquiries from souls lost in the yellow pages. Not a single client needed Trevor. Not a single friend called to say hello. Wes and Chap busied themselves by going through the few drawers and files they had not yet inspected. Nothing of consequence was found.

Another crew combed every inch of Trevor's house, primarily looking for the cash he'd been paid. Not surprisingly, they didn't find it. The cheap briefcase was in a closet, empty. There was no trail. Trevor had just walked away, with his cash.

The Bahamian banking official was tracked to New York, where he was visiting on government business. He was reluctant to get involved from such a long distance, but he eventually made his calls. Around 1 P.M. it was confirmed that the money had been moved. Its owner had done so in person, and the official would divulge nothing else.

Where did the money go? It was moved by wire, and that's all he would tell Deville. His country's banking reputation depended upon secrecy, and he could reveal only so much. He was corrupt, but he did have his limits.

U.S. Customs cooperated after some initial reluctance. Trevor's passport had been scanned at Nassau International early that morning, and so far he had not left the Bahamas, at least not officially. His passport was red-listed. If he used it to enter another country, U.S. Customs would know it within two hours.

Deville delivered a quick update to Teddy and York, his fourth of the day, then hung around for further instructions.

'He'll make a mistake,' York said. 'He'll use his passport somewhere, and we'll catch him. He doesn't know who's chasing him.'

Teddy seethed but said nothing. His agency had toppled governments and killed kings, yet he was constantly amazed at how the little things often got botched. One bumbling and witless lawyer from Neptune Beach slipped through their net while a dozen people were supposed to be watching. He thought he was beyond surprises.

The lawyer was to be their link, their bridge to the inside of Trumble. For a million dollars they thought they could trust him. There'd been no contingency plan for his sudden flight. Now they were scrambling to develop one.

'We need someone inside the prison,' Teddy said.

'We're close,' Deville answered. 'We're working with Justice and the Bureau of Prisons.'

'How close?'

'Well, in light of what's happened today, I think we can have a man there, inside Trumble, within forty-eight hours.'

'Who is he?'

'His name is Argrow, eleven years with the agency, age thirty-nine, solid credentials.'

'His story?'

'He'll transfer into Trumble from a federal prison in the Virgin Islands. His paperwork will be cleared by the Bureau here in Washington so the warden down there won't ask any questions. He's just another federal prisoner who requested a transfer.'

'And he's ready to go?'

'Almost. Forty-eight hours.'

'Do it now.'

Deville left, again with the burden of a difficult task that suddenly had to be done overnight.

'We have to find out how much they know,' Teddy said, almost in a mumble.

'Yes, but we have no reason to believe they suspect anything,' York said. 'I've read all their mail. There's nothing to indicate they are particularly excited about Konyers. He's just one of their

336

potential victims. We bought the lawyer to stop him from snooping around behind Konyers' post office box. He's off in the Bahamas now, drunk with his money, so he's not a threat.'

'But we still dispose of him,' Teddy said. It was not a question.

'Of course.'

'I'll feel better when he's gone,' Teddy said.

A guard with a uniform but no gun entered the law library in mid-afternoon. He first encountered Joe Roy Spicer, who was by the door to the chamber.

'The warden would like to see you,' the guard said. 'You and Yarber and Beech.'

'What's this about?' Spicer asked. He was reading an old copy of *Field & Stream*.

'None of my business. He wants you now. Up front.'

'Tell him we're busy.'

'I ain't tellin him nothin. Let's go.'

They followed him to the administration building, picking up other guards along the way until a regular entourage emerged from the elevator and stood before the warden's secretary. She and she alone somehow managed to escort the Brethren into the big office where Emmitt Broon was waiting. When she was gone, he said abruptly, 'I have been notified by the FBI that your lawyer is missing.'

No visible response from the three, but each instantly thought about the money hidden offshore.

He continued, 'He disappeared this morning,

and there's some money missing. I don't have the details.'

Whose money? they wanted to ask. No one knew about their hidden funds. Had Trevor stolen from someone else?

'Why are you telling us?' Beech asked.

The real reason was that the Justice Department in Washington had asked Broon to inform the three of the latest news. But the reason he gave was 'Just thought you'd want to know in case you needed to call him.'

They'd fired Trevor the day before, and had not yet informed the administration that he was no longer their attorney of record.

'What're we gonna do for a lawyer?' Spicer asked, as if life couldn't go on.

'That's your problem. Frankly, I'd say you gentlemen have had enough legal counsel to last you many years.'

'What if he contacts us?' Yarber asked, knowing full well they'd never hear from Trevor again.

'You are to notify me immediately.'

They agreed to do so. Whatever the warden wanted. He excused them.

Buster's escape was less complicated than a trip to the grocery. They waited until the next morning, until breakfast was over and most of the inmates were busy with their menial jobs. Yarber and Beech were on the track, walking an eighth of a mile apart so that one was always watching the prison while the other watched the woods in the distance. Spicer loitered near the basketball court, on the lookout for guards.

With no fences or towers or pressing security concerns, guards were not that critical at Trumble. Spicer saw none.

Buster was lost in the whining noise of his Weed Eater, which he slowly worked toward the track. He took a break to wipe his face and look around. Spicer, from fifty yards away, heard the engine die. He turned and quickly gave a thumbs-up, the sign to do it quickly. Buster stepped onto the track, caught up with Yarber, and for a few steps they walked together.

'Are you sure you want to do this?' Yarber asked.

'Yes. I'm positive.' The kid appeared calm and ready.

'Then do it now. Pace yourself. Be cool.'

'Thanks, Finn.'

'Don't get caught, son.'

'No way.'

At the turn, Buster kept walking, off the track, across the freshly cut grass, a hundred yards to some brush, then he was gone. Beech and Yarber saw him go, then turned to watch the prison. Spicer was calmly walking toward them. There was no sign of alarm around the courtyards or dorms or any of the other buildings on the prison grounds. Not a guard in sight.

They walked three miles, twelve laps, at the leisurely pace of fifteen minutes per mile, and when they'd had enough they retired to the coolness of the chamber to relax and listen for news of the escape. It would be hours before they heard a word.

Buster's pace was much faster. Once into the

woods, he began to jog without looking back. Watching the sun, he moved due south for half an hour. The woods were not thick; the undergrowth was thin and did not slow him. He passed a deer stand twenty feet up in an oak tree, and soon found a trail that ran to the southwest.

In his left front pants pocket he had $2,000 cash, given to him by Finn Yarber. In his other front pocket he had a map Beech had drawn by hand. And in his rear pocket he had a yellow envelope addressed to a man named Al Konyers in Chevy Chase, Maryland. All three were important, but the envelope had received the most attention from the Brethren.

After an hour, he stopped to rest, and to listen. Highway 30 was his first landmark. It ran east and west and Beech figured he would find it within two hours. He heard nothing, and started running again.

He had to pace himself. There was a chance his absence would be noticed just after lunch, when the guards sometimes walked the grounds in a very casual inspection. If one of them thought to look for Buster, then other questions might follow. But after two weeks of watching the guards, neither Buster nor any of the Brethren thought this was a possibility.

So he had at least four hours. And probably a lot more because his workday ended at five when he turned in his Weed Eater. When he didn't show, they'd start looking around the prison. After two hours of that, they'd notify the surrounding police agencies that another one had walked away from Trumble. They were never armed and dangerous, and no one got too excited. No search parties. No bloodhounds. No helicopters hovering over the woods. The county sheriff and his deputies would patrol the main roads and warn the citizens to lock their doors.

The escapee's name went into a national computer. They watched his home and watched his girlfriend, and they waited for him to do something stupid.

After ninety minutes of freedom, Buster stopped for a moment and heard the whine of an eighteen-wheeler not far away. The woods stopped abruptly at a right-of-way ditch, and there was the highway. According to Beech's map, the nearest town was several miles to the west. The plan was to hike along the highway, dodging traffic by using ditches and bridges, until civilization in some form was found.

Buster wore the standard prison issue of khaki pants and an olive-colored short-sleeve shirt, both darkened with sweat. The locals knew what the prisoners wore, and if he were spotted walking down Highway 30 someone would call the sheriff. Get to town, Beech and Spicer had told him, and find different clothes. Then pay cash for a bus ticket, and never stop running.

It took him three hours of ducking behind trees and jumping over roadside ditches before he saw the first buildings. He moved away from the highway, and cut through a hay field. A dog growled at him as he stepped onto a street lined with house trailers. Behind one of them he noticed a clothesline with someone's laundry hanging in

341

the windless air. He took a red and white pullover and threw away his olive shirt.

Downtown was nothing more than two blocks of stores, a couple of gas stations, a bank, some sort of town hall, and a post office. He bought denim shorts, a tee shirt, and a pair of boots at a discount store, and changed in the employee restroom. He found the post office inside the town hall. He smiled and thanked his friends at Trumble as he dropped their precious envelope into the Out-of-Town slot.

Buster caught a bus to Gainesville, where he purchased, for $480, the right to ride a bus anywhere in the United States for sixty days. He headed west. He wanted to get lost in Mexico.

THIRTY

The Pennsylvania primary on April 25 was to be Governor Tarry's last mighty effort. Undaunted by his dismal showing in the debate there two weeks earlier, he campaigned with great enthusiasm, but with very little money. 'Lake has it all,' he proclaimed at every stop, feigning pride at being the pauper. He did not leave the state for eleven straight days. Reduced to traveling in a large Winnebago camper, he ate his meals in the homes of supporters, stayed in cheap motels, and worked himself ragged shaking hands and walking neighborhoods.

'Let's talk about the issues,' he pleaded. 'Not about money.'

Lake, too, worked very hard in Pennsylvania. His jet traveled ten times faster than Tarry's RV. Lake shook more hands, made more speeches, and he certainly spent more money.

The result was predictable. Lake received 71 percent of the vote, a landslide so embarrassing to Tarry that he openly talked about quitting. But he vowed to hang on for at least another week, until the Indiana primary. His staff had left him. He was

343

$11 million in debt. He'd been evicted from his campaign headquarters in Arlington.

Yet, he wanted the good people of Indiana to have the opportunity to see his name on the ballot.

And who knew, Lake's shiny new jet might catch on fire, just like the previous one.

Tarry licked his rather deep wounds, and the day after the primary he promised to fight on.

Lake almost felt sorry for him, and he sort of admired his determination to endure until the convention. But Lake, along with everybody else, could do the math. Lake needed just forty more delegates to lock up the nomination, and there were almost five hundred still out there. The race was over.

After Pennsylvania, newspapers across the country confirmed his nomination. His happy handsome face was everywhere, a political miracle. He was praised by many as a symbol of why the system works – an unknown with a message who came from nowhere and captured the attention of the people. Lake's campaign gave hope to every person who dreamed of running for President. It didn't take months of pounding the back roads of Iowa. Skip New Hampshire, it was such a small state anyway.

And he was condemned for buying his nomination. Before Pennsylvania, it was estimated he'd spent $40 million. A more precise number was difficult because the money was being burned on so many fronts. Another $20 million had been spent by D-PAC and half a dozen other high-powered lobbying groups, all working on Lake's behalf.

No other candidate in history had spent anything close.

The criticism stung Lake, and it dogged him day and night. But he'd rather have the money and the nomination than suffer the alternative.

Big money was hardly taboo. Online entrepreneurs were making billions. The federal government, of all bumbling entities, was showing a surplus! Nearly everybody had a job, and an affordable mortgage, and a couple of cars. Lake's nonstop polling led him to believe that the big money was not yet an issue with the voters. In a November matchup against the Vice President, Lake was now practically even.

He once again returned to Washington, from the wars of the West, as a triumphant hero. Aaron Lake, lowly congressman from Arizona, was now the man of the hour.

Over a quiet and very long breakfast, the Brethren read the Jacksonville morning paper, the only one allowed inside Trumble. They were very happy for Aaron Lake. In fact, they were thrilled with his nomination. They were now among his most ardent supporters. Run, Aaron, run.

The news of Buster's walk to freedom had created hardly a stir. Good for him, the inmates were saying. He was just a kid with a long sentence. Run, Buster, run.

The escape wasn't mentioned in the morning paper. They passed it around, reading every word but the want ads and the obituaries. They were waiting now. No more letters would be written; none would be brought in because they'd lost their courier. Their little scam was on hold until they heard from Mr. Lake.

Wilson Argrow arrived at Trumble in an unmarked green van, handcuffed, with two marshals pulling at his elbows. He'd flown with his escorts from Miami to Jacksonville, of course at the expense of the taxpayers.

According to his paperwork, he had served four months of a sixty-month sentence for bank fraud. He had requested a transfer for reasons that were not clear, but his reasons were of no concern to anyone at Trumble. He was just another low-security prisoner in the federal system. They moved around all the time.

He was thirty-nine years old, divorced, college-educated, and his home address, for prison records, was in Coral Gables, Florida. His real name was Kenny Sands, an eleven-year veteran of the CIA, and though he'd never seen the inside of a prison, he'd had much tougher assignments than Trumble. He'd be there a month or two, then request another transfer.

Argrow maintained the cool facade of an old prison hand as he was processed, but his stomach churned. He'd been assured that violence was not tolerated at Trumble, and he could certainly take care of himself. But prison was prison. He suffered through a one-hour orientation by an assistant warden, then was given a quick tour of the grounds. He began to relax when he saw Trumble for himself. The guards had no guns, and most of the inmates looked rather harmless.

His cell mate was an old man with a spotty white

beard, a career criminal who'd seen many prisons and loved Trumble. He told Argrow he planned to die there. The man took Argrow to lunch and explained the vagaries of the menu. He showed him the game room, where groups of thick men bunched around folding tables studying their cards, every one with a cigarette stuck to the lips. 'Gambling's illegal,' his cell mate said with a wink.

They walked to the lifting area outdoors where the younger men sweated in the sun, polishing their tans while their muscles expanded. He pointed to the track in the distance and said, 'You gotta love the federal government.'

He showed Argrow the library, a place he never visited, and he pointed to a corner and said, 'That's the law library.'

'Who uses it?' Argrow asked.

'We usually have some lawyers here. Right now we have some judges too.'

'Judges?'

'Three of 'em.'

The old man had no interest in the library. Argrow followed him to the chapel, then around the grounds again.

Argrow thanked him for the tour, then excused himself and returned to the library, which was empty except for an inmate mopping a floor. Argrow went to the corner, and opened a door to the law library.

Joe Roy Spicer glanced up from his magazine and saw a man he'd never seen before. 'Lookin for something?' he asked, with no effort at being helpful.

Argrow recognized the face from the file. An ex-

Justice of the Peace caught stealing bingo profits. What a low-life.

'I'm new,' he said, forcing a smile. 'Just got here. This is the law library?'

'It is.'

'I guess anybody can use it, huh?'

'I guess,' Spicer said. 'You a lawyer?'

'Nope, a banker.'

A few months earlier, Spicer would've hustled him for some legal work, under the table, of course. But not now. They no longer needed the nickel-and-dime stuff. Argrow looked around and did not see Beech and Yarber. He excused himself and returned to his room.

Contact was made.

Lake's plan to rid himself of any memories of Ricky and their ill-fated correspondence depended upon someone else. He, Lake, was simply too scared and too famous to sneak away again in the middle of the night, in a disguise, in the back of a taxi, dashing through the suburbs to an all-night mailbox. The risks were too great; plus he seriously doubted if he could shake the Secret Service anymore. He couldn't count the number of agents now assigned to protect him. Count, hell, he couldn't see them all.

The young lady's name was Jayne. She'd joined the campaign in Wisconsin and had quickly worked her way into the inner circle. A volunteer at first, she now earned $55,000 a year as a personal aide to Mr. Lake, who trusted her completely. She seldom left his side, and they'd already had two little chats about Jayne's future job in the White House.

At the right moment, Lake would give Jayne the key to the box rented by Mr. Al Konyers, and instruct her to get the mail, close out the rental, and leave no forwarding address. He would tell her it was a box he'd rented in an effort to monitor the sale of classified defense contracts, back when he was convinced the Iranians were buying data they should never see. Or some such tale. She would believe him because she wanted to believe him.

If he were incredibly lucky, there would be no letter from Ricky. The box would be forever closed. And if a letter was waiting for Jayne, and if she was the least bit curious, Lake would simply tell her he had no idea who the person was. She would ask nothing further. Blind allegiance was her strong suit.

He waited for the right moment. He waited too long.

THIRTY-ONE

It arrived safely with a million other letters, tons of paperwork shipped into the capital to sustain the government for one more day. It was sorted by zip code, then by street. Three days after Buster dropped it off, Ricky's last letter to Al Konyers made it to Chevy Chase. A routine check of Mailbox America by a surveillance team found it. The envelope was examined, then quickly taken to Langley.

Teddy was between briefings, alone for a moment in his office, when Deville rushed in, holding a thin file. 'We got this thirty minutes ago,' he said as he handed over three sheets of paper. 'It's a copy. The original is in the file.'

The Director adjusted his bifocals and looked at the copies before he began reading. There was the Florida postmark, same as always. The handwriting was too familiar. He knew it was serious trouble before he began reading.

Dear Al:
  In your last letter you tried to end our correspondence. Sorry, it won't be that easy.

I'll get right to the point. I'm not Ricky, and you're not Al. I'm in a prison, not some fancy drug rehab clinic.

I know who you are, Mr. Lake. I know you're having a great year, just wrapped up the nomination and all, and you have all that money pouring in. They give us newspapers here at Trumble, and we've been following your success with great pride.

Now that I know who Al Konyers really is, I'm sure you'd like for me to keep quiet about our little secret. I'll be happy to remain silent, but it will cost you dearly.

I need money, and I want out of prison. I can keep secrets and I know how to negotiate.

The money is the easy part, because you have so much of it. My release will be more complicated, but you're collecting all sorts of very powerful friends. I'm sure you'll think of something.

I have nothing to lose, and I'm willing to ruin you if you don't negotiate with me.

My name is Joe Roy Spicer. I'm an inmate at Trumble Federal Prison. You figure out a way to contact me, and do it quickly.

I will not go away.

Sincerely,
Joe Roy Spicer

The next briefing was canceled. Deville found York, and ten minutes later they were locked away in the bunker.

Killing them was the first option discussed.

Argrow could do it with the right tools; pills and poisons and such. Yarber could die in his sleep. Spicer could drop dead on the track. Beech the hypochondriac could get a bad prescription from the prison pharmacy. They were not particularly fit or healthy, and certainly no match for Argrow. A nasty fall, a broken neck. There were many ways to make it look natural or accidental.

It would have to be done quickly, while they were still waiting for a reply from Lake.

But it would be messy, and unduly complicated. Three dead bodies all at once, in a harmless little prison like Trumble. And the three were close friends who spent most of their time together, and they would each die in different ways within a very short period of time. It would create an avalanche of suspicion. What if Argrow became a suspect? His background was hidden to begin with.

And the Trevor factor frightened them. Wherever he was, there was the chance he would hear of their deaths. The news would scare him even more, but it might also make him unpredictable. There was a chance he knew more than they thought.

Deville would work on plans to take them out, but Teddy was very reluctant. He had no qualms about killing the three, but he was not convinced it would protect Lake.

What if the Brethren had told someone else?

There were too many unknowns. Make the plans, Deville was told, but they would be used only when every other option was gone.

All scenarios were on the table. York suggested, for the sake of argument, that the letter be returned to the box so Lake could find it. It was his screwup to begin with.

'He wouldn't know what to do,' Teddy said.

'Do we?'

'Not yet.'

The thought of Aaron Lake reacting to this ambush and somehow trying to silence the Brethren was almost amusing, but there was a strong element of justice to it. Lake had created this mess; let him handle it.

'Actually, we created this mess,' Teddy said, 'and we'll deal with it.'

They couldn't predict, and thus they couldn't control, what Lake would do. Somehow the fool had avoided their net long enough to drop something in the mail to Ricky. And he'd been so stupid that the Brethren now knew who he was.

Not to mention the obvious: Lake was the type of person who secretly swapped letters with a gay pen pal. He was living a double life, and didn't deserve a lot of confidence.

Confronting Lake was discussed for a moment. York had been advocating a showdown since the first letter from Trumble, but Teddy wasn't convinced. The sleep he'd lost fretting over Lake was always filled with thoughts and hopes of stopping the mail long before now. Quietly take care of the problem, then have a chat with the candidate.

Oh, how he'd love to confront Lake. He'd love to sit him in a chair over there and start flashing copies of all those damned letters up on a screen. And a copy of the ad from *Out and About*. He'd tell him about Mr. Quince Garbe in Bakers, Iowa, another idiot who fell for the scam, and Curtis

Vann Gates in Dallas. 'How could you be so stupid!?' he wanted to scream at Aaron Lake.

But Teddy kept his eye on the bigger picture. The problems with Lake were small when compared to the urgency of national defense. The Russians were coming, and when Natty Chenkov and the new regime seized power the world would change forever.

Teddy had neutralized men far more powerful than three felonious judges rotting away in a federal prison. Meticulous planning was his strong suit. Patient, tedious planning.

The meeting was interrupted by a message from Deville's office. Trevor Carson's passport had been scanned at a departure checkpoint at the airport in Hamilton, Bermuda. He left on a flight to San Juan, Puerto Rico, that was scheduled to land in about fifty minutes.

'Did we know he was in Bermuda?' York asked.

'No, we did not,' Deville answered. 'Evidently he entered without using his passport.'

'Maybe he's not as drunk as we thought.'

'Do we have someone in Puerto Rico?' Teddy asked, his voice only a shade more excited.

'Of course,' said York.

'Let's pick up the scent.'

'Have the plans changed for ole Trevor?' Deville asked.

'No, not at all,' Teddy said. 'Not at all.'

Deville left to deal with the latest Trevor crisis. Teddy called an assistant and ordered mint tea. York was reading the letter again. When they were alone, he asked, 'What if we separate them?'

'Yes, I was thinking of that. Do it quickly, before

they have time to confer. Send them to three prisons far apart, put them in isolation for a period of time, make sure they have no phone privileges, no mail. Then what? They still have their secret. Any one of them could conceivably ruin Lake.'

'I'm not sure we have the contacts within the Bureau of Prisons.'

'It can be done. If necessary, I'll have a chat with the Attorney General.'

'Since when did you become friends with the Attorney General?'

'It's a matter of national security.'

'Three crooked judges sitting in a federal prison in Florida can somehow affect national security? I'd like to hear that conversation.'

Teddy sipped his tea with his eyes closed, all ten fingers on the cup. 'It's too risky,' he whispered. 'We make them mad, they become even more erratic. We can't take chances here.'

'Suppose Argrow can find their records,' York said. 'Think about it – these are con men, convicted criminals. No one will believe their story about Lake unless they have proof. The proof is documentation, pieces of paper, originals and copies of the correspondence. The proof exists somewhere. We find it, take it from them, then who will listen?'

Another small sip with his eyes closed, another long pause. Teddy shifted slightly in his chair and grimaced from the pain. 'True,' he said softly. 'But I'm worried about somebody on the outside, somebody we know nothing about. These guys are a step ahead of us, and they always will be. We're trying to figure out what they've known for some time. I'm not sure we'll ever catch up. Maybe they've thought about losing their little files. I'm sure the prison has rules against maintaining such paperwork, so they're already hiding things. The Lake letters are much too valuable not to copy again and stash on the outside.'

'Trevor was their mailman. We've seen every letter he's carried out of Trumble for the past month.'

'We think we have. But we don't know for certain.'

'But who?'

'Spicer has a wife. She's been to see him. Yarber's getting a divorce, but who knows what they're doing. She's visited in the past three months. Or maybe they're bribing guards to run mail for them. These people are bored and they're smart and they're very creative. We can't just assume we know everything they're up to. And if we make a mistake here, if we assume too much, then Mr. Aaron Lake gets himself shoved out of the closet.'

'How? How would they do it?'

'Probably contact a reporter, feed him one letter at a time until he was convinced. It would work.'

'The press would go insane.'

'It can't happen, York. We simply cannot allow it to happen.'

Deville returned in a rush. U.S. Customs had been notified by the authorities in Bermuda ten minutes after the flight departed for San Juan. Trevor would be landing in eighteen minutes.

Trevor was just following his money. He had

quickly grasped the fundamentals of wire transfers, and was now perfecting the art. In Bermuda, he had sent half of it to a bank in Switzerland, and the other half to a bank in Grand Cayman. East or west? That had been the great question. The quickest flight out of Bermuda went to London, but the idea of sneaking through Heathrow scared him. He was not a wanted man, at least not by the government. No charges were filed or pending. But the Brits were so efficient at customs. He'd go west and take his chances in the Caribbean.

He landed in San Juan and went straight to a bar where he ordered a tall draft and studied the flights. No hurry, no pressure, a pocket full of cash. He could go anywhere, do anything, and take as long as he wanted. He had another draft and decided to spend a few days in Grand Cayman, with his money. He went to the Air Jamaica counter and bought a ticket, then back to the bar because it was almost five and he had thirty minutes before boarding.

Of course he flew first class. He boarded early so he could get another drink, and as he watched the other passengers file by he saw a face he'd seen before.

Where was it now? Just moments ago, some-where in the airport. A long thin face, with a salt-and-pepper goatee, and little narrow slits for eyes behind square glasses. The eyes glanced at him just long enough to meet Trevor's, then looked away, down the aisle, as if nothing had been seen.

It had been near the airline counter, as Trevor was turning to leave after buying his ticket. The face was watching him. The man was standing nearby, studying the departure notices.

When you're on the run, the stray glances and second looks and drifting eyes all seem more suspicious. See a face once, and you don't even know it. See it again a half hour later, and somebody is watching every move you make.

Stop drinking, Trevor ordered himself. He asked for coffee after takeoff, and drank it quickly. He was the first passenger off the plane in Kingston, and he walked quickly through the terminal, through immigration. No sign of the man behind him.

He grabbed his two small bags and raced for the taxi stand.

THIRTY-TWO

The Jacksonville paper arrived at Trumble each morning around seven. Four copies were taken to the game room where they were to be read and left behind for any of the inmates who cared about life on the outside. Most of the time Joe Roy Spicer was the only one waiting at seven, and he usually took one paper for himself because he needed to study the Vegas lines throughout the day. The scene rarely changed: Spicer with a tall Styrofoam cup of coffee, feet on a card table, waiting for Roderick the guard to bring the papers.

So Spicer saw the story first, at the bottom of the front page. Trevor Carson, a local lawyer who'd been missing for some vague reason, found dead outside a hotel in Kingston, Jamaica, shot twice in the head last night, just after dark. The story had no picture of Trevor, Spicer noticed. Why would the paper have one on file? Why would anyone care if Trevor died?

According to Jamaican officials, Carson was a tourist who'd apparently been robbed. An unidentified source close to the scene had tipped the police as to the identity of Mr. Carson, since his wallet was missing. The source seemed to know a lot.

The paragraph recapping Trevor's legal career was quite brief. A former secretary, Jan something or other, had no comment. The story had been thrown together, and placed on the front page only because the victim was a murdered lawyer.

Finn was at the far end of the track, rounding the turn, walking at a rapid clip in the damp early morning air, his shirt already off. Spicer waited at the homestretch, and handed him the paper without a word.

They found Beech waiting in line in the cafeteria, holding his plastic tray and staring forlornly at the crude piles of freshly scrambled eggs. They sat together in a corner, away from everyone else, picking at their food, talking in muted voices.

'If he was running, who the hell was he running from?'

'Maybe Lake was after him.'

'He didn't know it was Lake. He didn't have a clue, did he?'

'Okay, then he was running from Konyers. The last time he was here he said Konyers was the big one. He said Konyers knew about us, then he disappeared the next day.'

'Maybe he was just scared. Konyers confronted him, threatened to expose his role in our scam, and so Trevor, who wasn't the most stable guy to begin with, decided to steal all he could and disappear.'

'Whose money was missing, that's what I want to know.'

'Nobody knows about our money. How could it be missing?'

'Trevor probably stole from everybody he could, then vanished. Happens all the time. Lawyers get in trouble, crack up. They raid their clients' trust funds and bolt.'

'Really?' asked Spicer.

Beech could think of three examples, and Yarber added a couple more for good measure.

'So who killed him?'

'There's a good chance he was just in the wrong part of town.'

'Outside the Sheraton Hotel? I don't think so.'

'Okay, what if Konyers iced him?'

'That's possible. Konyers somehow smoked out Trevor, learned he was the outside contact for Ricky. He put pressure on Trevor, threatened to nail him or whatever, and Trevor ran off to the Caribbean. Trevor didn't know Konyers was Aaron Lake.'

'And Lake certainly has the money and power to track down a drunken lawyer.'

'What about us? By now, Lake knows Ricky ain't Ricky, that Joe Roy here is the man, and that he has friends with him in prison.'

'Question is, can he get to us?'

'I guess I'll find out first,' Spicer said with a nervous laugh.

'And there's always the chance that Trevor was down there in Jamaica hanging around in the wrong part of town, probably drunk and trying to pick up a woman, and he got himself shot.'

They all agreed on this, that Trevor was perfectly capable of getting himself killed.

May he rest in peace. But only if he didn't steal their money.

They scattered for an hour or so. Beech went to the track, to walk and think. Yarber was on the clock, twenty cents an hour trying to fix a computer in the chaplain's office. Spicer went to the library, where he found Mr. Argrow reading law books.

The law library was open, no appointments were necessary, but the unwritten rule was that you should at least ask one of the Brethren before using their books. Argrow was new, and obviously had not yet learned the rules. Spicer decided to give him a break.

They acknowledged each other with a nod, then Spicer got busy clearing tables and straightening books.

'Rumor has it you guys do legal work,' Argrow said from across the room. No one else was present.

'You hear a lot of rumors around here.'

'My case is on appeal.'

'What happened at trial?'

'Jury nailed me on three counts of bank fraud, hiding money offshore, in the Bahamas. The judge gave me sixty months. I've served four. I'm not sure I'm gonna last for fifty-six more. I need some help with my appeals.'

'What court?'

'Virgin Islands. I worked for a big bank in Miami. Lots of drug money.'

Argrow was glib and fast and very anxious to talk, and this irritated Spicer, but only slightly. The reference to the Bahamas had his attention.

'For some reason, I developed a fascination for money laundering. I dealt with tens of millions every day, and it was intoxicating. I could move dirty money quicker than any banker in South Florida. Still can. But I made some bad friends, and bad choices.'

'You admit you're guilty?'

'Sure.'

'That puts you in the distinct minority around here.'

'No, I was wrong, but I think the sentence was too harsh. Somebody said you guys can get some time knocked off.'

Spicer was no longer concerned with the untidy tables and disorganized books. He took a chair nearby and had time to talk. 'We can take a look at your papers,' he said, as if he'd handled a thousand appeals.

You idiot, Argrow wanted to say. You dropped out of high school in the tenth grade, and stole a car when you were nineteen. Your father pulled some strings and got the charges dropped. You got yourself elected Justice of the Peace by voting dead people and stuffing absentee ballots, and now you're stuck in a federal pen and trying to play the big shot.

And, Argrow conceded, you, Mr. Spicer, now have the power to bring down the next President of the United States.

'What will it cost?' Argrow asked.

'How much do you have?' Spicer asked, just like a real lawyer.

'Not much.'

'I thought you knew how to hide money off-shore.'

'Oh, I do, believe me. And at one point I had a nice bundle, but I let it get away.'

'So you can't pay anything?'

'Not much. Maybe a couple of thousand or so.'

'What about your lawyer?'

'He got me convicted. I don't have enough to hire a new one.'

Spicer pondered the situation for a moment. He realized he did indeed miss Trevor. Things had been much simpler when they had him on the outside collecting money. 'You still got contacts in the Bahamas?'

'I have contacts all over the Caribbean. Why?'

'Because you'll have to wire the money. Cash is forbidden around here.'

'You want me to wire two thousand dollars?'

'No. I want you to wire five thousand dollars. That's our minimum fee.'

'Where's your bank?'

'In the Bahamas.'

Argrow's eyes narrowed. His eyebrows pushed together, and while he was deep in thought so was Spicer. The minds were in the process of meeting.

'Why the Bahamas?' Argrow asked.

'Same reason you used the Bahamas.'

Thoughts rattled around in both heads. 'Lemme ask you something,' Spicer said. 'You said you could move dirty money quicker than anybody else.'

Argrow nodded and said, 'No problem.'

'Can you still do it?'

'You mean, from in here?'

'Yes. From here.'

Argrow laughed and shrugged as if nothing could be easier. 'Sure. I still have some friends.'

'Meet me here in an hour. I might have a deal for you.'

An hour later, Argrow returned to the law library and found the three judges already in position, behind a table with papers and law books scattered about as if the Supreme Court of Florida were in session. Spicer introduced him to Beech and Yarber, and he took a seat across the table. No one else was present.

They talked for a moment about his appeal, and he was sufficiently vague on the details. His file was en route from the other prison, and they couldn't do much without it.

The appeal was a preliminary topic of conversation, and both sides of the table knew it.

'Mr. Spicer tells us you're an expert on moving dirty money,' Beech said.

'I was until I got caught,' Argrow said modestly. 'I take it you have some.'

'We have a little account offshore, money we've earned doing legal work and a few other things we can't be too open about. As you know, we can't charge for legal work.'

'But we do anyway,' added Yarber. 'And we get paid for it.'

'How much is in the account?' Argrow asked, knowing yesterday's closing balance to the exact penny.

'Let's wait on that,' Spicer said. 'There's a good chance the money may have disappeared.'

Argrow let the words hang for a second, and managed to appear confused. 'I'm sorry?' he said.

'We had a lawyer,' Beech said slowly, each word measured. 'He disappeared and he may have taken the money.'

'I see. And this account is in a bank in the Bahamas?'

'It was. We're not sure if it still is.'

'We doubt the money is still there,' Yarber added.

'But we'd like to know for sure,' Beech added.

'Which bank?' Argrow asked.

'Geneva Trust, in Nassau,' Spicer answered, glancing at his colleagues.

Argrow nodded smugly, as if he knew dark little dirty secrets about the bank.

'You know the bank?' Beech asked.

'Sure,' he said, and let them hang for a long second.

'And?' Spicer said.

Argrow was overcome with smugness and insider knowledge, so he stood rather dramatically and walked around the small library for a moment, deep in thought, then moved closer to the table again. 'Look, what do you guys want me to do? Let's cut to the chase.'

The three looked at him, then at each other, and it was obvious they weren't sure of two things: (a) how much they trusted this man they'd just met, and (b) what they really wanted from him.

But they figured the money was gone anyway, so what was there to lose. Yarber said, 'We're not too sophisticated when it comes to moving dirty money. That was not our original calling, you understand. Forgive our lack of knowledge, but is there any way to verify if the money is still where it once was?'

'We're just not sure if the lawyer stole it,' Beech added.

'You want me to verify the balance of a secret account?' Argrow asked.

'Yes, that's it,' said Yarber.

'We figure that maybe you still have some friends in the business,' Spicer said, treading water. 'And we're just curious as to whether there's any way to do this.'

'You're lucky,' Argrow said, and allowed the words to settle.

'How's that?' Beech asked.

'You picked the Bahamas.'

'Actually, the lawyer picked the Bahamas,' Spicer said.

'Anyway, the banks are pretty loose there. Lots of secrets get told. Lots of officials get bribed. Most of the serious money launderers stay away from the Bahamas. Panama is the current hot spot, and, of course, Grand Cayman is still rock solid.'

Of course, of course, they all three nodded. Offshore was offshore, wasn't it? Just another example of trusting an idiot like Trevor.

Argrow watched them with their puzzled faces and thought how truly clueless they were. For three men with the ability to totally wreck the American electoral process, they seemed awfully naive.

'You haven't answered our question,' Spicer said.

'Anything's possible in the Bahamas.'

'So you can do it?'

'I can try. No guarantees.'

'Here's the deal,' Spicer said. 'You verify the account, and we'll do your appeals for free.'

'That's not a bad deal,' Argrow said.

'We didn't think so. Agreed?'

'Agreed.'

For an awkward second they just looked at one another, proud of their mutual agreement but not sure who moved next. Finally, Argrow said, 'I'll need to know something about the account.'

'Such as?' Beech asked.

'Such as a name or a number.'

'The account name is Boomer Realty, Ltd. The account number is 144-DXN-9593.'

Argrow scribbled some notes on a sheet of scrap paper.

'Just curious,' Spicer said as they watched him closely. 'How do you plan to communicate with your contacts outside?'

'Phone,' Argrow said without looking up.

'Not these phones,' Beech said.

'These phones are not secure,' Yarber said.

'You can't use these phones,' Spicer said with an edge.

Argrow smiled and acknowledged their concerns, then he glanced over his shoulder and removed from his pants pocket an instrument of some sort, not much larger than a pocketknife. He held it between his thumb and index finger, and said, 'This is a phone, gentlemen.'

They stared in disbelief, then watched as he quickly unfolded it from the top and the bottom and from one side so that when properly opened it still looked much too small for any meaningful conversation. 'It's digital,' he said. 'Very secure.'

'Who gets the monthly bill?' asked Beech.

'I have a brother in Boca Raton. The phone and the service were gifts from him.' He snapped it back smartly, and it vanished before their eyes. Then he pointed to the small conference room behind them, to their chamber. 'What's in there?' he asked.

'Just a conference room,' Spicer said.

'It has no windows, right?'

'None, except for that small one in the door.'

'All right. What if I go in there, get on the phone, and go to work. You three stay here and watch out for me. If anyone enters the library, come knock on the door.'

The Brethren readily agreed, though they did not believe Argrow could pull it off.

The call went to the white van, parked a mile and a half from Trumble, on a gravel road sometimes maintained by the county. The road was next to a hay field, farmed by a man they'd yet to meet. The property line for the acreage owned by the federal government was a quarter of a mile away, but from where the van was sitting there was no sign of a prison.

Only two technicians were in the van, one fully asleep in the front seat, the other half asleep in the back with a headset on. When Argrow pressed the Send button on his fancy little gadget, a receiver in the van was activated, and both men came to life.

'Hello,' he said. 'This is Argrow.'

'Yes, Argrow, Chevy One here, go ahead,' said the technician in the back.

'I'm near the three stooges, going through the motions, supposedly making calls to friends on the outside to verify the existence of their account offshore. So far things are progressing even faster than I'd hoped.'

'Sounds like it.'

'Roger. I'll check in later.' He pushed the End button, but kept the phone at his head and appeared to be deep in conversation. He sat on the edge of the table, then he walked around some, glancing occasionally at the Brethren and beyond.

Spicer couldn't help but sneak a look through the window of the door. 'He's making calls,' he said excitedly.

'What do you expect him to be doing?' asked Yarber, who was actually reading recent court decisions.

'Relax, Joe Roy,' Beech said. 'The money disappeared with Trevor.'

Twenty minutes passed, and things became dull as usual. While Argrow worked the phones, the judges killed time, waiting at first, then returning to more pressing business. It had been six days since Buster had left with their letter. No word from Buster meant he'd walked away clean, dropped off the note to Mr. Konyers, and was now somewhere far away. Give it three days to travel to Chevy Chase, and the way they had it figured Mr. Aaron Lake should now be scrambling with a plan to deal with them.

Prison had taught them patience. Only one deadline worried them. Lake had the nomination, which meant he would be vulnerable to their blackmail until November. If he won, they would have four years in which to torment him. But if he lost he would fade quickly away, like all the losers. 'Where's Dukakis now?' Beech had asked.

They had no plans to wait until November. Patience was one thing, release was another. Lake was their one fleeting opportunity to walk away with enough money to coast forever.

They intended to give it a week, then write another letter to Mr. Al Konyers in Chevy Chase. They weren't sure how to smuggle it out, but they would think of something. Link, the guard up front whom Trevor had been bribing for months, was their first prospect.

Argrow's phone presented an option. 'If he'll let us use it,' Spicer said, 'then we can call Lake, call his campaign office, his congressional office, call every damned number we can get from directory assistance. Leave the message that Ricky in rehab really needs to see Mr. Lake. That'll scare the hell out of him.'

'But Argrow will have a record of our calls, or at least his brother will,' Yarber said.

'So? We'll pay him for the calls, and so what if they know we're trying to call Aaron Lake. Right now, half the country is trying to call him. Argrow won't have a clue why we're doing it.'

A brilliant idea, one they pondered for a long time. Ricky in rehab could make the calls and leave the messages. Spicer in Trumble could do the same. Poor Lake would get hounded.

Poor Lake. The man had money pouring in so fast he couldn't count it.

After an hour, Argrow emerged from the chamber and announced he was making progress. 'I need to wait an hour, then make a few more calls,' he said. 'What about lunch?'

They were anxious to continue their discussion, and they did so over sloppy joes and coleslaw.

THIRTY-THREE

Pursuant to Mr. Lake's precise instructions, Jayne drove alone to Chevy Chase. She found the shopping center on Western Avenue, and parked in front of Mailbox America. With Mr. Lake's key, she opened the box, removed eight pieces of junk mail, and placed them in a folder. There were no personal letters. She walked to the counter and informed the clerk that she wished to close the box on behalf of her employer, Mr. Al Konyers.

The clerk pecked a few times on a keyboard. The records indicated that a man named Aaron L. Lake had rented the box in the name of Al Konyers about seven months earlier. The rental had been paid for twelve months, so nothing was owed.

'That guy running for President?' the clerk asked as she slid a form across the counter.

'Yes,' Jayne said, signing where indicated.

'No forwarding address?'

'No.'

She left with the folder and headed south, back into the city. She had not stopped to question Lake's story about renting the box in a clandestine effort to expose fraud at the Pentagon. It didn't matter to her, nor did she have time to ask a lot of questions. Lake had them sprinting eighteen hours a day, and she had far more important things to worry about.

He was waiting in his campaign office, alone for the moment. The offices and hallways around him were choked with assistants of a dozen varieties, all running back and forth as if war were imminent. But Lake was enjoying a lull in the action. She gave him the folder and left.

Lake counted eight pieces of junk mail – taco delivery, long-distance service, a car wash, coupons for this and for that. And nothing from Ricky. The box was closed, there was no forwarding address. The poor boy would have to find someone else to help him through his new life. Lake fed the junk mail and the cancellation agreement through a small shredder under his desk, then paused a moment to count his blessings. He carried little baggage in life, and he'd made few mistakes. Writing to Ricky had been a stupid thing to do, yet he was walking away unscathed. What a lucky man!

He smiled and almost giggled to himself, then he bounced from his chair, grabbed his jacket, and rounded up his entourage. The candidate had meetings to attend, then a lunch with defense contractors.

Oh what a lucky man!

Back in the corner of the law library, with his three new friends guarding the perimeter like sleepy sentries, Argrow fiddled with the phone long enough to convince them he'd pulled strings all through the dark and murky world of offshore banking. Two hours of pacing and mumbling and holding the phone to his head like a frantic stockbroker, and he finally came out of the room.

'Good news, gentlemen,' he said with a tired smile.

They huddled around, eager for the results.

'It's still there,' he said.

Then the great question, the one they'd been planning, the one that would verify whether Argrow was a fraud or a player.

'How much?' asked Spicer.

'A hundred and ninety thousand, and small change,' he said, and they exhaled in unison. Spicer smiled. Beech looked away. Yarber looked at Argrow with a quizzical frown, but a rather pleasant one.

According to their figures, the balance was $189,000, plus whatever paltry rate of interest the bank was paying.

'He didn't steal it,' Beech mumbled, and they shared a pleasant memory of their dead lawyer, who suddenly was not the devil they'd made him out to be.

'I wonder why not,' Spicer mused, almost to himself.

'Well, it's still there,' Argrow said. 'That's a lot of legal work.'

It certainly appeared to be, and since neither of the three could think of a quick fib, they just let it pass.

'I suggest you move it, if you don't mind my

saying so,' Argrow said. 'This bank is known for its leaks.'

'Move it where?' Beech asked.

'If the money were mine, I'd move it to Panama immediately.'

This was a new issue, a train of thought they had not pursued because they had been obsessed with Trevor and his certain theft. But they weighed it carefully anyway, as if the matter had been discussed many times.

'Why would you move it?' Beech asked. 'It's safe, isn't it?'

'I guess,' Argrow answered, quick with a response. He knew where he was going, they did not. 'But you see how loose the confidentiality can be. I wouldn't use banks in the Bahamas these days, especially this one.'

'And we don't know if Trevor told anyone about it,' Spicer said, always anxious to nail the lawyer.

'If you want the money protected, move it,' Argrow said. 'It takes less than a day and you won't have to worry about it. And put the money to work. This account is just sitting there, drawing a few pennies in interest. Put it with a fund manager and let it earn fifteen or twenty percent. You're not gonna be using it any time soon.'

That's what you think, pal, they thought. But he made perfect sense.

'And I assume you can move it?' Yarber said.

'Of course I can. Do you doubt me now?'

All three shook their heads. No sir, they did not doubt him.

'I have some nice contacts in Panama. Think about it.' Argrow glanced at his watch as if he had lost interest in their account and had a hundred pressing matters elsewhere. A punch line was coming, and he didn't want to push.

'We've thought about it,' Spicer said. 'Let's move it now.'

He looked at three sets of eyes, all looking back at him. 'There's a fee involved,' he said, like a seasoned money launderer.

'What kinda fee?' Spicer asked.

'Ten percent, for the transfer.'

'Who gets ten percent?'

'I do.'

'That's rather steep,' said Beech.

'It's a sliding scale. Anything under a million pays ten percent. Anything over a hundred million pays one percent. It's pretty common in the business, and it's exactly the reason I'm wearing an olive prison shirt and not a thousand-dollar suit.'

'That's pretty sleazy,' said Spicer, the man who'd skimmed bingo profits from a charity.

'Let's not preach, okay. We're talking about a small cut from money that's already tainted, both here and there. Take it or leave it.' His tone was aloof, an icy veteran who'd cut much larger deals.

It was only $19,000, and this from a stash they'd been certain was gone. After his 10 percent, they still had $170,000, roughly $60,000 each, and it would've been more if treacherous Trevor hadn't raked so much off the top. And, besides, they were confident of greener pastures just around the corner. The loot in the Bahamas was pocket change.

'It's a deal,' Spicer said as he looked at the other two for approval. They both nodded slowly. All three were thinking the same thing now. If the shakedown of Aaron Lake proceeded as they dreamed it would, then serious money was coming their way. They would need a place to hide it, and maybe someone to help them. They wanted to trust this new guy Argrow. Let's give him the chance.

'Plus, you do my appeals,' Argrow said.

'Yes, we'll do the appeals.'

Argrow smiled and said, 'Not a bad deal. Lemme make some more calls.'

'There's one thing you should know,' Beech said.

'Okay.'

'The lawyer's name was Trevor Carson. He set up the account, directed the deposits, did everything really. And he was murdered night before last in Kingston, Jamaica.'

Argrow searched their faces for more. Yarber handed him a copy of the newspaper, which he read very deliberately. 'Why was he missing?' he asked after a long silence.

'We don't know,' Beech said. 'He left town, and we got word through the FBI that he was missing. We just assumed that he'd stolen our money.'

Argrow handed the paper back to Yarber, and crossed his arms over his chest. He cocked his head, narrowed his eyes, and managed to look suspicious. Let them sweat.

'How dirty is this money?' he asked, as if he might not want to get involved with it after all.

'It's not drug money,' Spicer said quickly, on the defensive, as if all other money was clean.

'We really can't say,' Beech replied.

'You've got a deal,' Yarber said. 'Take it or leave it.'

Good move, old boy, Argrow said to himself. 'The FBI is involved?' he asked.

'Only with the lawyer's disappearance,' Beech said. 'The feds know nothing about the offshore account.'

'Let me get this straight. You got a dead lawyer, the FBI, an offshore account hiding dirty money, right? What've you boys been up to?'

'You don't wanna know,' Beech said.

'I think you're right.'

'No one's forcing you to get involved,' Yarber said.

So a decision had to be made. For Argrow, the red flags were up, the minefield was marked. If he went forward, then he did so armed with sufficient warnings that his three new friends could be dangerous. This, of course, meant nothing to Argrow. But to Beech, Spicer, and Yarber, the opening in their tight little partnership, however slight it might be, meant they were admitting another conspirator. They would never tell him about their scam, and certainly not about Aaron Lake, nor would he share in any more of their loot, unless he earned it with his wiring prowess. But he already knew more than he should. They had no choice.

Desperation played no small role in their decision. With Trevor, they'd had access to the outside, something they'd taken for granted. Now that he was gone, their world had shrunk considerably.

Though they had yet to admit it, firing him had

been a mistake. With perfect hindsight, they should've warned him, and told him everything about Lake and the tampered mail. He'd been far from perfect, but they needed all the help they could get.

Perhaps they would've hired him back a day or two later, but they never had the chance. Trevor bolted, and now he was gone forever.

Argrow had access. He had a phone and friends; he had guts and he knew how to get things done. Perhaps they might need him, but they would take it slowly.

He scratched his head and frowned as if a headache was coming. 'Don't tell me anything else,' he said. 'I don't wanna know.'

He returned to the conference room and closed the door behind him, then perched on the edge of the table and once again seemed to be firing calls all over the Caribbean.

They heard him laugh twice, probably a joke with an old friend surprised to hear his voice. They heard him swear once, but had no idea at whom or for what reason. His voice rose and fell, and try as they might to read court decisions and dust off old books and study Vegas odds, they couldn't ignore the noise from the room.

Argrow put on quite a show, and after an hour of useless chatter he came out and said, 'I think I can finish it tomorrow, but we need an affidavit signed by one of you stating that you are the sole owners of Boomer Realty.'

'Who sees the affidavit?' Beech asked.

'Only the bank in the Bahamas. They're getting a copy of the story about Mr. Carson, and they want verification about the ownership of the account.'

The idea of actually signing any type of document in which they admitted they had anything to do with the dirty money terrified them. But the request made sense.

'Is there a fax machine around here?' Argrow asked.

'No, not for us,' Beech replied.

'I'm sure the warden has one,' Spicer said. 'Just trot up there and tell him you need to send a document to your offshore bank.'

It was unnecessarily sarcastic. Argrow glared at him, then let it pass. 'Okay, tell me how to get the affidavit from here to the Bahamas. How does the mail run?'

'The lawyer was our mail runner,' Yarber said. 'Everything else is subject to inspection.'

'How close do they inspect the legal mail?'

'They glance at it,' Spicer said. 'But they can't open it.'

Argrow paced around a bit, deep in thought. Then, for the benefit of his audience he stepped between two racks of books, so that he could not be seen from outside the law library. He deftly unfolded his gadget, punched numbers, and stuck it to his ear. He said, 'Yes, Wilson Argrow here. Is Jack in? Yes, tell him it's important.' He waited.

'Who the hell's Jack?' Spicer asked from across the room. Beech and Yarber listened but watched for passersby.

'My brother in Boca,' Argrow said. 'He's a real estate lawyer. He's visiting me tomorrow.' Then, into the phone, he said, 'Hey, Jack, it's me. You comin tomorrow? Good, can you come in the morning? Good. Around ten. I'll have some mail going out. Good. How's Mom? Good. I'll see you in the morning.'

The prospect of the resumption of mail intrigued the Brethren. Argrow had a brother who was a lawyer. And he had a phone, and brains, and guts.

He slid the gadget back into his pocket and walked from the racks. 'I'll give the affidavit to my brother in the morning. He'll fax it to the bank. By noon the next day the money will be in Panama, safe and sound and earning fifteen percent. Piece of cake.'

'We're assuming we can trust your brother?' Yarber said.

'With your life,' Argrow said, almost offended by the question. He was walking to the door. 'I'll see you guys later. I need some fresh air.'

THIRTY-FOUR

Trevor's mother arrived from Scranton. She was with her sister, Trevor's aunt Helen. They were both in their seventies and in reasonably good health. They got lost four times between the airport and Neptune Beach, then meandered through the streets for an hour before stumbling on Trevor's house, a place his mother hadn't seen in six years. She hadn't seen Trevor in two years. Aunt Helen hadn't seen him in at least ten, not that she particularly missed him.

His mother parked the rental car behind his little Beetle, and had a good cry before getting out.

What a dump, Aunt Helen said to herself.

The front door was unlocked. The place had been abandoned, but long before its owner fled the dishes had collected in the sink, the garbage had gone unattended, the vacuum hadn't left the closet.

The odor drove Aunt Helen out first, and Trevor's mother soon followed. They had no clue what to do. His body was still in Jamaica, in a crowded morgue, and according to the unfriendly young man she'd talked to at the State Department it would cost $600 to ship him home. The airlines would cooperate, but the paperwork was tied up in Kingston.

It took a half hour of bad driving to find his office. By then, word was out. Chap the paralegal was waiting at the reception desk, trying to look sad and busy at the same time. Wes the office manager was in a back room, just to listen and observe. The phone had rung constantly the day the news broke, but after a round of condolences from fellow lawyers and a client or two it went silent again.

On the front door was a cheap wreath, paid for by the CIA. 'Ain't that nice,' his mother said as they waddled up the sidewalk.

Another dump, thought Aunt Helen.

Chap greeted them and introduced himself as Trevor's paralegal. He was in the process of trying to close the office, a most difficult task.

'Where's the girl?' his mother asked, her eyes red from grieving.

'She left some time back. Trevor caught her stealing.'

'Oh dear.'

'Would you like some coffee?' he asked.

'That would be nice, yes.' They sat on the dusty and uneven sofa, while Chap fetched three coffees from a pot that just happened to be fresh. He sat across from them in an unstable wicker chair. The mother was bewildered. The aunt was curious, her eyes darting around the office, looking for any sign of prosperity. They were not poor, but at their ages affluence would never be attained.

'I'm very sorry about Trevor,' Chap said.

'It's just awful,' Mrs. Carson said, her lip quivering. Her cup shook and coffee splashed onto her dress. She didn't notice it.

'Did he have a lot of clients?' Aunt Helen asked.

'Yes, he was very busy. A good lawyer. One of the best I've ever worked with.'

'And you're a secretary?' Mrs. Carson asked.

'No, I'm a paralegal. I go to law school at night.'

'Are you handling his affairs?' Aunt Helen asked.

'Well, not really,' Chap said. 'I was hoping that's why the two of you were here.'

'Oh, we're too old,' his mother said.

'How much money did he leave?' asked the aunt.

Chap stepped it up a notch. This old bitch was a bloodhound. 'I have no idea. I didn't handle his money.'

'Who did?'

'I guess his accountant.'

'Who's his accountant?'

'I don't know. Trevor was very private about most things.'

'He certainly was,' his mother said sadly. 'Even as a boy.' She splashed her coffee again, this time on the sofa.

'You pay the bills around here, don't you?' asked the aunt.

'No. Trevor took care of his money.'

'Well, listen, young man, they want six hundred dollars to fly him home from down in Jamaica.'

'Why was he down there?' his mother interrupted.

'It was a short vacation,' Chap said.

'And she doesn't have six hundred dollars,' Helen finished.

'Yes I do.'

'Oh, there's some cash here,' Chap said, and Aunt Helen looked satisfied.

'How much?' she asked.

'A little over nine hundred dollars. Trevor liked to keep plenty of petty cash.'

'Give it to me,' Aunt Helen demanded.

'Do you think we should?' asked his mother.

'You'd better take it,' Chap said gravely. 'If not, it will just go into his estate and the IRS will get it all.'

'What else will go into his estate?' asked the aunt.

'All this,' Chap said, waving his arms at the office while he walked to the desk. He removed a wrinkled envelope stuffed with bills of all denominations, money they'd just transferred from the rental across the street. He gave it to Helen, who snatched it and counted the money.

'Nine twenty, and some change,' Chap said.

'Which bank did he use?' Helen asked.

'I have no idea. Like I said, he was very private about his money.' And in one respect, Chap was telling the truth. Trevor had wired the $900,000 from the Bahamas to Bermuda, and from there the trail had disappeared. The money was now hidden in a bank somewhere, in a numbered account accessible only by Trevor Carson. They knew he was headed for Grand Cayman, but the bankers there were famous for their secrecy. Two days of intense digging had revealed nothing. The man

386

who shot him took his wallet and room key, and while the police were inspecting the crime scene the gunman searched the hotel room. There was about $8,000 in cash hidden in a drawer, and nothing else of any significance. Not a clue as to where Trevor had parked his money.

It was the collected wisdom at Langley that Trevor, for some reason, suspected he was being followed closely. The bulk of the cash was missing, though he could have deposited it in a bank in Bermuda. His hotel room had been secured without a reservation – he simply walked in from the street and paid cash for one night.

A person on the run, chasing $900,000 from one island to the next, would have, somewhere on his body or in his effects, evidence of banking activities. Trevor had none.

While Aunt Helen riffled through what would surely be the only cash they'd net from the estate, Wes thought about the fortune lost somewhere in the Caribbean.

'What do we do now?' Trevor's mother asked.

Chap shrugged and said, 'I guess you need to bury him.'

'Can you help us?'

'That's not really something I do. I –'

'Should we take him back to Scranton?' Helen asked.

'That's up to you.'

'How much would that cost?' Helen asked.

'I have no idea. I've never had to do anything like this.'

'But all his friends are here,' his mother said, touching her eyes with a tissue.

387

'He left Scranton a long time ago,' Helen said, her eyes cutting in all directions, as if there was a long story behind Trevor's leaving Scranton. No doubt, thought Chap.

'I'm sure his friends here will want a memorial service,' Mrs. Carson said.

'Actually, one is already planned,' Chap said.

'It is!' she said, thrilled.

'Yes, it's tomorrow at four o'clock.'

'Where?'

'A place called Pete's, just down the street a few blocks.'

'Pete's?' Helen said.

'It's, well, it's sort of a restaurant.'

'A restaurant. What about a church?'

'I don't think he went.'

'He did when he was a boy,' his mother said in defense.

In memory of Trevor, the five o'clock happy hour would begin at four, and run until midnight. Fifty-cent longnecks, Trevor's favorite.

'Should we go?' asked Helen, sensing trouble.

'I wouldn't think so.'

'Why not?' asked Mrs. Carson.

'It could be a rough crowd. A bunch of lawyers and judges, you know the scene.' He frowned at Helen, and she got the message.

They asked about funeral parlors and cemetery lots, and Chap felt himself getting dragged deeper and deeper into their problems. The CIA killed Trevor. Was it expected to send him off with a proper burial?

Klockner thought not.

After the ladies left, Wes and Chap finished the

388

removal of the cameras, wires, mikes, and phone taps. They tidied up the place, and when they locked the doors for the last time Trevor's office had never been so orderly.

Half of Klockner's team had already left town. The other half monitored Wilson Argrow inside Trumble. And they waited.

When the forgers at Langley finished with Argrow's court file it fit in a cardboard box, and was flown to Jacksonville on a small jet along with three agents. It contained, among many other things, a fifty-one-page indictment handed down by a grand jury in Dade County, a correspondence file filled with letters from Argrow's defense lawyer and the U.S. Attorney's office, a thick file of motions and other pretrial maneuverings, research memos, a list of witnesses and summaries of their testimonies, a trial brief, jury analysis, an abstract of the trial, presentencing reports, and the final sentence itself. It was reasonably well organized, though not too neat to arouse suspicion. Copies were smudged, and pages were missing, and staples were hanging off, little touches of reality carefully added by the good folks in Documents to create authenticity. Ninety percent of it would not be needed by Beech and Yarber, but its sheer heft made it impressive. Even the cardboard box had some age on it.

The box was delivered to Trumble by Jack Argrow, a semiretired real estate lawyer in Boca Raton, Florida, and brother of the inmate. Lawyer Argrow's state bar certification had been faxed to the proper bureaucrat at Trumble, and his name was on the approved list of attorneys.

Jack Argrow was Roger Lyter, a thirteen-year man with a law degree from Texas. He'd never met Kenny Sands, who was Wilson Argrow. The two shook hands and said hello while Link looked suspiciously at the cardboard box sitting on the table.

'What's in there?' he asked.

'It's my court records,' Wilson said.

'Just paperwork,' Jack said.

Link stuck a hand in the box and moved some files around, and in a few seconds the search was over and he stepped out of the room.

Wilson slid a paper across the desk, and said, 'This is the affidavit. Wire the money to the bank in Panama, then get me written verification so I'll have something to show them.'

'Less ten percent.'

'Yes, that's what they think.'

The Geneva Trust Bank in Nassau had not been contacted. To do so would've been futile and risky. No bank would release funds under the circumstances Argrow was creating. And questions would be raised if he tried.

The wire transfer going to Panama was new money.

'Langley is quite anxious,' the lawyer said.

'I'm ahead of schedule,' the banker replied.

The box was emptied on a table in the law library. Beech and Yarber began sifting through its contents while Argrow, their new client, watched with feigned interest. Spicer had better things to do. He was in the middle of his weekly poker game.

'Where's the sentencing report?' Beech asked, scratching through the pile.

'I want to see the indictment,' Yarber mumbled to himself.

They found what they wanted, and both settled into their chairs for a long afternoon of reading. Beech's choice was quite dull. Yarber's, however, was not.

The indictment read like a crime narrative. Argrow, along with seven other bankers, five accountants, five securities brokers, two lawyers, eleven men identified only as drug traffickers, and six gentlemen from Colombia, had organized and run an elaborate enterprise designed to take drug proceeds in the form of cash and turn them into respectable deposits. At least $400 million had been laundered before the ring was infiltrated, and it appeared as though their man Argrow was right in the thick of things. Yarber admired him. If half the allegations were true, then Argrow was a very smart and talented financier.

Argrow became bored with the silence, and left to stroll around the prison. When Yarber finished reading the indictment, he interrupted Beech and made him read it. Beech enjoyed it too. 'Surely,' he said, 'he's got some of the loot buried somewhere.'

'You know he does,' Yarber agreed. 'Four hundred million bucks, and that's just what they could find. What about his appeal?'

'Doesn't look good. The judge followed the guidelines. I see no error.'

'Poor guy.'

'Poor guy, my ass. He'll be out four years before me.'

'I don't think so, Mr. Beech. We've spent our last Christmas in prison.'

'Do you really believe that?' Hatlee asked.

'Indeed I do.'

Beech placed the indictment back on the table, then stood and stretched and paced around the room 'We should've heard something by now,' he said, very softly though no one else was there.

'Patience.'

'But the primaries are almost over. He's back in Washington most of the time. He's had the letter for a week.'

'He can't ignore it, Hatlee. He's trying to figure out what to do. That's all.'

The latest memo from the Bureau of Prisons in Washington baffled the warden. Who in hell's name up there had nothing better to do than to stare at a map of the federal prisons and decide which one to meddle with that day? He had a brother making $150,000 selling used cars, and there he was making half that much running a prison and reading idiotic memos from pencil-pushers making $100,000 and not doing a productive damned thing. He was so sick of it!

RE: Attorney Visitation, Trumble Federal Prison

Disregard prior order, said order restricting attorney visitation to Tuesdays, Thursdays, and Saturdays, from 3 to 6 P.M.

Attorneys are now permitted to visit seven days a week, from 9 to 7 P.M.

'It takes a dead lawyer to get the rules changed,' he mumbled to himself.

THIRTY-FIVE

Deep in a basement garage, they rolled Teddy Maynard into his van and locked the doors. York and Deville sat with him. A driver and a bodyguard handled the van, which had a television, a stereo, and a small bar with bottled water and sodas, all of which were ignored by Teddy. He was subdued, and dreading the next hour. He was tired – tired of his work, tired of the fight, tired of forcing himself through another day, then another. Fight it six more months, he kept telling himself, then give it up and let someone else worry about saving the world. He'd go quietly to his small farm in West Virginia where he'd sit by the pond, watch the leaves fall into the water, and wait for the end. He was so tired of the pain.

There was a black car in front of them and a gray one behind, and the little convoy made its way around the Beltway, then east across the Roosevelt Bridge and onto Constitution Avenue.

Teddy was silent, so therefore York and Deville were too. They knew how much he loathed what he was about to do.

He talked to the President once a week, usually

on Wednesday morning, always by phone if Teddy had his way. They last saw each other nine months earlier when Teddy was in the hospital and the President needed to be briefed.

The favors usually fell to an equal level, but Teddy hated to be on the same footing with any President. He'd get the favor he wanted, but it was the asking that humiliated him.

In thirty years he'd survived six Presidents, and his secret weapon had been the favors. Gather the intelligence, hoard it, rarely tell the President everything, and occasionally gift-wrap a small miracle and deliver it to the White House.

This President was still pouting over the humiliating defeat of a nuclear test ban treaty Teddy had helped sabotage. The day before the Senate killed it, the CIA leaked a classified report raising legitimate concerns about the treaty, and the President got flattened in the stampede. He was leaving office, a lame duck more concerned with his legacy than with the pressing matters of the country.

Teddy had dealt with lame ducks before, and they were impossible. Since they wouldn't face the voters again, they dwelt on the big picture. In their waning days, they liked to travel, with lots of their friends, to foreign lands where they held summits with other lame ducks. They worried about their presidential libraries. And their portraits. And their biographies, so they spent time with historians. As the clock ticked they became wiser and more philosophical, and their speeches became grander. They talked of the future, of the challenges and the way things ought to be, conveniently ignoring the fact that they'd had eight years to do all the things that needed to be done.

There was nothing worse than a lame duck. And Lake would be just as bad if and when he had the chance.

Lake. The very reason Teddy was trekking to the White House, hat in hand, to grovel for a while.

They were cleared through the West Wing, where Teddy suffered the indignity of having his wheelchair examined by a Secret Service agent. Then they rolled him to a small office next to the cabinet room. A busy appointment secretary explained with no apology that the President was running late. Teddy smiled and waved her off and mumbled something to the effect that this President had never been on time for anything. He'd suffered a dozen fussy secretaries just like her, in the same position she was now in, and the others were long gone. She led York and Deville and the others away, down to the dining room where they would eat by themselves.

Teddy waited, as he knew he would. He read a thick report as if time meant nothing. Ten minutes passed. They brought him coffee. Two years ago the President had visited Langley, and Teddy had made him wait for twenty-one minutes. He needed a favor then, the President did, needed a little matter kept quiet.

The only advantage to being crippled was that he didn't have to jump to his feet when the President entered the room. He finally arrived in a rush, with aides scrambling behind him, as if this would impress Teddy Maynard. They shook hands and made the required greetings as the aides got rid of themselves. A waiter appeared and placed small green salads before them.

'It's good to see you,' the President said with a soft voice and drippy smile. Save it for television, Teddy thought, and he couldn't bring himself to return the lie. 'You're looking well,' he said, only because it was partially true. The President had a new tint to his hair, and he looked younger. They ate their salads, and a quietness settled around them.

Neither wanted a long lunch. 'The French are selling toys to the North Koreans again,' Teddy said, offering a crumb.

'What kinds of toys?' the President asked, though he knew precisely about the trafficking. And Teddy knew he knew.

'It's their version of stealth radar, which is quite stupid because they haven't perfected it yet. But the North Koreans are even dumber because they're paying for it. They'll buy anything from France, especially if the French try to hide it. The French, of course, know this, so it's all cloak and dagger and the North Koreans pay top dollar.'

The President pushed a button and the waiter appeared to remove their plates. Another brought chicken and pasta.

'How's your health?' the President asked.

'About the same. I'll probably leave when you do.'

This pleased them both, the prospect of the other leaving. For no apparent reason, the President then launched into a windy narrative about his Vice President, and what a wonderful job he would do in the Oval Office. He ignored his lunch and became very earnest in his opinions of what a fine human being and brilliant thinker and capable leader the man was. Teddy played with his chicken.

'How do you see the race?' the President asked.

'I honestly don't care,' Teddy said, lying again. 'As I told you, I'm leaving Washington when you do, Mr. President. I'm retiring to my little farm where there's no television, no newspapers, nothing but a little fishing and a lot of rest. I'm tired, sir.'

'Aaron Lake scares me,' the President said.

You don't know the half of it, Teddy thought. 'Why?' he asked, taking a bite. Eat, and let him talk.

'A single issue. Nothing but defense. You give the Pentagon unlimited resources and they'll waste enough to feed the third world. And all this money worries me.'

It never worried you before. The last thing Teddy wanted was a long, useless conversation about politics. They were wasting time. The sooner he finished his business, the sooner he could return to the safety of Langley. 'I'm here to ask a favor,' he said slowly.

'Yes, I know. What can I do for you?' The President was smiling and chewing, enjoying both the chicken and the rare moment of having the upper hand.

'It's a little out of the ordinary. I'd like clemency for three federal prisoners.'

The chewing and smiling stopped, not out of shock but out of confusion. Clemency was usually a simple matter, unless it involved spies or terrorists or infamous politicians. 'Spies?' the President asked.

'No. Judges. One from California, one from Texas, one from Mississippi. They're serving their time together in a federal prison in Florida.'

'Judges?'

'Yes, Mr. President.'

'Do I know these people?'

'I doubt it. The one from California was once the Chief Justice of the Supreme Court out there. He got himself recalled, then had a little trouble with the IRS.'

'I think I remember that.'

'He was convicted of tax evasion and sentenced to seven years. He's served two. The one from Texas was a trial judge, a Reagan appointee. He got drunk and killed a couple of hikers in Yellowstone.'

'I do remember that, but vaguely.'

'It was several years ago. The one from Mississippi was a Justice of the Peace who got caught embezzling bingo profits.'

'I must've missed that one.'

There was a long pause as they considered the questions. The President was bewildered and not certain where to start. Teddy wasn't sure what was coming, so they finished eating in silence. Neither wanted dessert.

The request was an easy one, at least for the President. The felons were virtually unknown, as were their victims. Any fallout would be quick and painless, especially for a politician whose career was less than seven months from being over. He'd been pressured to grant far more difficult pardons. The Russians always had a few spies they lobbied to get back. There were two Mexican businessmen locked away in Idaho for drug trafficking, and every time a treaty of some sort was on the table their clemency became an issue. There was a Canadian Jew serving a life sentence for spying, and the Israelis were determined to get him out.

Three unknown judges? The President could sign his name three times and the matter would be over. Teddy would owe him.

It would be a simple matter, but that was no reason to make things easy for Teddy.

'I'm sure there's a good reason for this request,' he said.

'Of course.'

'A matter of grave national security?'

'Not really. Just a few favors for old friends.'

'Old friends? Do you know these men?'

'No. But I know their friends.'

The lie was so obvious the President almost jumped at it. How could Teddy know the friends of three judges who just happened to be serving time together?

Nothing would come from grilling Teddy Maynard, nothing but frustration. And the President would not stoop that low. He would not beg for information he'd never get. Whatever Teddy's motives were, he would take them to his grave.

'This is a bit confusing,' the President said with a shrug.

'I know. Let's leave it at that.'

'What's the fallout?'

'Not much. The families of the two kids who

were killed in Yellowstone might squawk, and I wouldn't blame them.'

'How long ago was it?'

'Three and a half years.'

'You want me to pardon a Republican federal judge?'

'He's not a Republican now, Mr. President. They have to swear off politics once they take the bench. Now that he's been convicted, he can't even vote. I'm sure if you granted clemency he'd become a big fan of yours.'

'I'm sure he would.'

'If it'll make matters easier, these gentlemen will agree to leave the country for at least two years.'

'Why?'

'It might look bad if they return home. Folks will know that they somehow got out early. This can be kept very quiet.'

'Did the judge from California pay the taxes he tried to evade?'

'He did.'

'And did the guy from Mississippi repay the money he stole?'

'Yes sir.'

All the questions were superficial. He had to ask something.

The last favor had dealt with nuclear spying. The CIA had a report documenting widespread infiltration of Chinese spies in and through virtually all levels of the U.S. nuclear arms program. The President learned of the report just days before he was scheduled to visit China for a highly touted summit. He asked Teddy to come have lunch, and over the same chicken and pasta he asked that the report be held for a few weeks. Teddy agreed. Later, he wanted the report modified to place more blame on prior administrations. Teddy rewrote it himself. When it was finally released, the President deflected most of the blame.

Chinese spying and national security, versus three obscure ex-judges. Teddy knew he would get the pardons.

'If they leave the country, where will they go?' the President asked.

'We're not sure yet.'

The waiter brought coffee. When he was gone, the President asked, 'Will this in any way hurt the Vice President?'

And with the same expressionless face, Teddy said, 'No. How could it?'

'You tell me. I have no clue what you're doing.'

'There's nothing to worry about, Mr. President. I'm asking for a small favor. With a little luck, this will not be reported anywhere.'

They sipped their coffee and both wanted to leave. The President had a full afternoon with more pleasant matters. Teddy needed a nap. The President was relieved it was such a benign request. Teddy was thinking, If you only knew.

'Give me a few days to do the background,' the President said. 'These requests are pouring in, as you might guess. Seems everybody wants something now that my days are numbered.'

'Your last month here will be your happiest,' Teddy said with a rare grin. 'I've seen enough Presidents to know.'

After forty minutes together, they shook hands and promised to talk in a few days.

There were five ex-lawyers at Trumble, and the newest one was using the library when Argrow entered. Poor guy was up to his elbows in briefs and legal pads, working feverishly, no doubt pursuing his last feeble appeal.

Spicer was rearranging law books and managing to look sufficiently busy. Beech was in the chamber, writing something. Yarber was absent.

Argrow removed a folded sheet of white paper from his pocket, and gave it to Spicer. 'I just saw my lawyer,' he whispered.

'What is it?' Spicer asked, holding the paper.

'It's a wire confirmation. Your money is now in Panama.'

Spicer looked at the lawyer across the room, but he was oblivious to everything except his legal pad. 'Thanks,' he whispered. Argrow left the room, and Spicer took the paper to Beech, who examined it carefully.

Their loot was now safely guarded by the First Coast Bank of Panama.

THIRTY-SIX

Joe Roy had dropped eight more pounds, was down to ten cigarettes a day and averaging twenty-five miles a week around the track. Argrow found him there, walking and pacing in the late afternoon heat.

'Mr. Spicer, we need to talk,' Argrow said.

'Two more laps,' Joe Roy said without breaking stride.

Argrow watched him for a few seconds, then jogged fifty yards until he caught up. 'Mind if I join?' he asked.

'Not at all.'

They went into the first turn, stride for stride. 'I just met with my lawyer again,' Argrow said.

'Your brother?' Spicer asked, breathing heavily. His paces were not nearly as graceful as Argrow's, a man twenty years younger.

'Yes. He's talked to Aaron Lake.'

Spicer stopped as if he'd hit a wall. He glared at Argrow, then looked at something in the distance.

'Like I said, we need to talk.'

'I suppose we do,' Spicer said.

'I'll meet you in the law library in half an hour,'

Argrow said, and walked away. Spicer watched him until he disappeared.

There was no Jack Argrow, Attorney-at-Law, in the Boca Raton yellow pages, and this initially caused concern. Finn Yarber frantically worked the unsecured phone, seeking directory assistance all over South Florida. When he asked for Pompano Beach, the operator said, 'One moment, please,' and Finn actually smiled. He scribbled down the number, then dialed it. A recorded voice said, 'You've reached the law offices of Jack Argrow. Mr. Argrow keeps hours by appointment only, so please leave your name and number and a brief description of the real estate you're interested in, and we'll get in touch with you.' Finn hung up and walked quickly across the lawn to the law library, where his colleagues were waiting. Argrow was already ten minutes late.

A moment before he arrived, the same ex-lawyer entered the room carrying a bulky file, evidently ready to spend hours trying to save himself. To ask him to leave would cause a fight and create suspicion, and besides he wasn't the type who respected judges anyway. One by one they retired to the small conference room, where Argrow joined them. The room was cramped when Beech and Yarber worked there, writing their letters. With Argrow as the fourth man in, and bringing no small amount of pressure, the room had never felt so crowded. They sat around the small table, each able to reach and touch the other three.

'I know only what I've been told,' Argrow began. 'My brother is a semiretired lawyer in Boca

Raton. He has some money, and for years he's been active in Republican politics in South Florida. Yesterday he was approached by some people who work for Aaron Lake. They had investigated matters and knew that I was his brother, and that I was here in Trumble along with Mr. Spicer. They made promises, swore him to secrecy, and now he's sworn me to secrecy. Now that everything is nice and confidential, I think you can connect the dots.'

Spicer had not showered. His shirt and face were still wet, but his breathing had slowed. Not the slightest sound from either Beech or Yarber. The Brethren were in a collective trance. Keep going, they said with their eyes.

Argrow looked at the three faces, and pushed onward. He reached into his pocket and removed a sheet of paper, which he unfolded and laid before them. It was a copy of their last letter to Al Konyers, the outing letter, the extortion demand, signed by Joe Roy Spicer, current address of Trumble Federal Prison. They had the words memorized, so there was no need to read it again. They recognized the handwriting, that of poor little Ricky, and they realized that it had now come full circle. From the Brethren to Mr. Lake, from Mr. Lake to Argrow's brother, from Argrow's brother back to Trumble, all in thirteen days.

Spicer finally picked it up, and glanced at the words. 'I guess you know everything, don't you?' he asked.

'I don't know how much I know.'

'Tell us what they've told you.'

'You're running a scam, the three of you. You

406

advertise in gay magazines, you develop relationships with older men, by mail, you somehow learn their true identities, then you extort money from them.'

'That's a pretty fair summary of the game,' Beech said.

'And Mr. Lake made the mistake of answering one of your ads. I don't know when he did this, and I don't know how you found out who he was. There are some gaps in the plot, as far as I'm concerned.'

'It's best to keep it that way,' Yarber said.

'Fair enough. I didn't volunteer for this job.'

'What will you get out of it?' Spicer asked.

'Early release. I'll spend a few more weeks around here, then they'll move me again. I'll walk by the end of the year, and if Mr. Lake gets elected then I'll get a full pardon. Not a bad deal. My brother gets a huge favor from the next President.'

'So you're the negotiator?' Beech said.

'No, I'm the messenger.'

'Then shall we begin?'

'The first move belongs to you.'

'You've got the letter. We want some money and we want out of this place.'

'How much money?'

'Two million each,' Spicer said, and it was obvious this had been discussed many times already. All six eyes watched Argrow, waiting for the twitch, the frown, the shock. But there was no reaction, just a pause as he returned their stares. 'I have no authority here, okay? I can't say yes or no to your demands. All I do is relay the details to my brother.'

'We read the newspaper every day,' Beech said. 'Mr. Lake has more money than he can spend right now. Six million is a drop in the bucket.'

'He has seventy-eight million on hand, with no debt,' Yarber added.

'Whatever,' Argrow said. 'I'm just the courier, the mail runner, sort of like Trevor.'

They froze again, with the mention of their dead lawyer. They glared at Argrow, whose fingernails had caught his attention, and they wondered if the Trevor comment had been laid across the table as some sort of warning. How deadly had their game become? They were giddy with thoughts of money and freedom, but how safe were they now? How safe would they be in the future?

They would always know Lake's secret.

'And the terms of the money?' Argrow asked.

'Very simple,' Spicer said. 'All of it up front, all of it wired to some delightful little place, probably Panama.'

'Okay. Now what about your release?' Argrow asked.

'What about it?' asked Beech.

'Any suggestions?'

'Not really. We thought Mr. Lake could take care of that. He has lots of friends these days.'

'Yes, but he's not the President yet. He can't lean on the right people yet.'

'We're not waiting until January when he's inaugurated,' Yarber said. 'In fact, we're not waiting until November to see if he wins.'

'So you want to be released now?'

'Pretty damned quick,' Spicer said.

'Does it matter how you're released?'

They thought for a moment, then Beech said, 'It has to be clean. We're not running for the rest of our lives. We're not looking over our shoulders.'

'Do you leave together?'

'Yes,' Yarber said. 'And we have some definite plans on how we want to do it. First, though, we need to agree on the important things – money, and exactly when we walk out of here.'

'Fair enough. From this side of the table, they'll want your files, all of the letters and notes and records from your scam. Obviously, Mr. Lake has to receive assurances that the secrets will be buried.'

'If we get what we want,' Beech said, 'he has nothing to worry about. We'll gladly forget we ever heard of Aaron Lake. But we must warn you, so you can warn Mr. Lake, that if anything happens to us, his story will be told anyway.'

'We have an outside contact,' Yarber said.

'It's a delayed reaction,' Spicer added, as if he were helping explain the unexplainable. 'Something happens to us, like, for instance, the same thing that happened to Trevor, and a few days later a little delay bomb goes off. Mr. Lake gets himself outed anyway.'

'That won't happen,' Argrow said.

'You're the messenger. You don't know what will or will not happen,' Beech said, lecturing. 'These are the same people who killed Trevor.'

'You're not sure of that.'

'No, but we have our opinions.'

'Let's not argue something we can't prove, gentlemen,' Argrow said, ending the session. 'I'll see my brother at nine in the morning. Let's meet here at ten.'

Argrow left the room, left them sitting trance-like, deep in thought, counting their money but afraid to start spending it. He headed for the track, but turned away when he saw a group of inmates jogging. He roamed the grounds until he found a secluded spot behind the cafeteria, then he called Klockner.

Within an hour, Teddy was briefed.

THIRTY-SEVEN

The 6 A.M. bell shrieked through Trumble, through the corridors of the dorms, across the lawns, around the buildings, into the surrounding woods. It lasted for exactly thirty-five seconds, most inmates could tell you, and by the time it quit no one was left asleep. It jolted them to life, as if important events were planned that day, and they had to hurry and get ready. But the only pressing matter was breakfast.

The bell startled Beech, Spicer, and Yarber, but it didn't wake them. Sleep had been elusive, the reasons obvious. They lived in different dorms, but not surprisingly they met in line for coffee, at ten minutes after six. With their tall cups, and without a word, they walked to the basketball court where they sat on a bench and sipped in the early dawn. They watched the prison grounds; the track was behind them.

How many more days would they wear their olive shirts and sit in the Florida heat, getting paid pennies by the hour for doing nothing, just waiting, dreaming, drinking endless cups of coffee? Would it be a month, or two? Were they talking

411

days now? The possibilities had robbed them of sleep.

'There are only two possible ways,' Beech was saying. He was the federal judge, and they listened carefully, though it was familiar ground. 'The first is to go back to the sentencing jurisdiction and file a motion for reduced time. Under very narrow circumstances, the trial judge has the authority to release an inmate. It's rarely done, though.'

'Did you ever do it?' Spicer asked.

'No.'

'Asshole.'

'For what reasons?' Yarber asked.

'Only when the prisoner has provided new information about old crimes. If the prisoner provides substantial assistance to the authorities, then he might get a few years off.'

'That's not encouraging,' Yarber said.

'What's number two?' Spicer asked.

'We're shipped out to a halfway house, a really nice one where they don't expect us to live by the rules. The Bureau of Prisons has sole authority in placing inmates. If the right pressure is applied by our new friends in Washington, then the Bureau could move us out and basically forget about us.'

'Don't you have to live in a halfway house?' Spicer asked.

'Yes, in most of them. But they're all different. Some are locked down at night, with strict rules. Others are very laid back. You can phone in once a day, or once a week. It's all up to the Bureau.'

'But we'll still be convicted felons,' Spicer said.

'Doesn't bother me,' Yarber said. 'I'll never vote again.'

412

'I have an idea,' Beech said. 'It came to me last night. As part of our negotiations, we make Lake agree to pardon us if he's elected.'

'I thought of that too,' Spicer said.

'So did I,' said Yarber. 'But who cares if we have a record? The only thing that matters is that we get out.'

'It won't hurt to ask,' Beech replied. They concentrated on their coffee for a few minutes.

'Argrow's making me nervous,' Finn finally said.

'How's that?'

'Well, he drops in here from nowhere, and suddenly becomes our best friend. He does a magic trick with our money, gets it wired to a safer bank. Now he's the point man for Aaron Lake. Keep in mind, somebody out there was reading our mail. And it wasn't Lake.'

'He doesn't bother me,' Spicer said. 'Lake had to find somebody to talk to us. He pulled some strings, did some research, found out that Argrow was here and that he had a brother they could talk to.'

'That's awfully convenient, don't you think?' Beech asked.

'You too, huh?'

'Maybe. Finn's got a point. We know for a fact that somebody else got involved.'

'Who?'

'That's the big question,' Finn said. 'That's why I haven't slept in a week. There's somebody else out there.'

'Do we really care?' Spicer asked. 'If Lake can get us outta here, fine. If somebody else can get us outta here, what's wrong with that?'

'Don't forget Trevor,' Beech said. 'Two bullets in the back of the head.'

'This place might be safer than we think.'

Spicer was not convinced. He finished a drink and said, 'Do you really think that Aaron Lake, a man about to be elected President of the United States, would order a hit on a worthless lawyer like Trevor?'.

'No,' replied Yarber. 'He would not. It's much too risky. And he wouldn't kill us. But the mystery man would. The guy who killed Trevor is the same guy who read our mail.'

'I'm not convinced.'

They were together where Argrow expected to find them, in the law library, and they seemed to be waiting. He entered in a rush, and when he was sure they were alone, he said, 'I just met with my brother again. Let's talk.'

They scurried into their little conference room, closed the door, and crowded around the table.

'Things are about to happen very fast,' Argrow said nervously. 'Lake will pay the money. It'll be wired anywhere you want it. I can help if you want; otherwise you can handle it any way you wish.'

Spicer cleared his throat. 'That's two million each?'

'That's what you asked for. I don't know Mr. Lake, but evidently he moves fast.' Argrow glanced at his watch, then looked over his shoulder at the door. 'There are some people from Washington here to meet with you. Big shots.' He yanked some papers from his pocket, unfolded them, and laid a single sheet before each of the three. 'These are presidential pardons, signed yesterday.'

With great reserve, they reached forward, took the papers, and tried to read them. The copies certainly looked official. They gawked at the bold letters across the top, the paragraphs of fussy prose, the compact signature of the President of the United States, and not a single word could be summoned. They were just stunned.

'We've been pardoned?' Yarber finally managed to ask, his voice dry.

'Yes. By the President of the United States.'

They kept reading. They fidgeted and chewed their lips and clenched their jaws, and tried to quietly hide their shock.

'They're gonna come get you, take you to the warden's office where the big shots from Washington will deliver the good news. Act surprised, okay?'

'No problem.'

'That should be easy.'

'How did you get these copies?' Yarber asked.

'They were given to my brother. I have no idea how. Lake has powerful friends. Anyway, here's the deal. You'll be released within the hour. A van will take you to Jacksonville, to a hotel where my brother will meet you. You will wait there until the wire transfers are confirmed, then you will hand over all of your dirty little files. Everything. Understood?'

They nodded in unison. For two million bucks, they could have it all.

'You will agree to leave the country immediately, and not to return for at least two years.'

'How can we leave the country?' Beech asked. 'We have no passports, no papers.'

'My brother will have all of that. You will be given new identities, with a complete set of papers, including credit cards. It's all waiting for you.'

'Two years?' Spicer asked, and Yarber looked at him as if he'd lost his mind.

'That's right. Two years. It's part of the deal. Agreed?'

'I don't know,' Spicer said, his voice shaking. Spicer had never left the United States.

'Don't be foolish,' Yarber snapped at him. 'A complete pardon, a million bucks a year for two years to live abroad. Hell, yes, we'll take the deal.'

A sudden knock on the door terrified them. Two guards were looking in. Argrow grabbed the copies of the pardons and stuffed them in his pocket. 'Do we have a deal, gentlemen?'

They nodded yes, and all three shook hands with him.

'Good,' he said. 'Remember, act surprised.'

They followed the guards to the warden's office where they were introduced to two very stern-faced men from Washington, one from Justice, one from the Bureau of Prisons. The warden completed the stiff introductions without getting any of the names confused, then he handed each of the three a legal-sized document. They were the originals of what Argrow had just shown them.

'Gentlemen,' the warden announced with as much drama as he could muster, 'you've just been pardoned by the President of the United States.' He smiled warmly as if he were responsible for this good news.

416

They stared at their pardons, still in shock, still dizzy with a thousand questions, the biggest of which was, How in the world did Argrow scoop the warden and show them the documents first?

'I don't know what to say,' Spicer managed to mumble, then the other two mumbled something else.

The man from Justice said, 'The President reviewed your cases, and he felt that you have served enough time. He feels very strongly that you have more to offer your country and your communities by once again becoming productive citizens.'

They stared blankly at him. This fool didn't know they were about to assume new names and flee their country and their communities for at least two years? Who was on which side here?

And why was the President granting them clemency when they had enough dirt to destroy Aaron Lake, the man who was primed to defeat the Vice President? It was Lake who wanted them silenced, not the President? Right?

How could Lake convince the President to pardon them?

How could Lake convince the President to do anything, at this stage of the campaign?

They clutched their pardons and sat speechless, their faces drawn tight as the questions hammered away inside.

The man from the Bureau said, 'You should feel honored. Clemency is very rare.'

Yarber managed to acknowledge him with a quick nod, but even then he was thinking, Who's waiting for us on the outside?

'I think we're in shock,' Beech said.

It was a first for Trumble, inmates so important that the President decided to pardon them. The warden was quite proud of the three, but uncertain as to how the moment should be commemorated. 'When would you like to leave?' he asked, as if they might want to stick around for a party.

'Immediately,' Spicer said.

'Very well. We'll drive you to Jacksonville.'

'No thanks. We'll have someone pick us up.'

'Okay, then, well, there's some paperwork.'

'Make it quick,' Spicer said.

They were each given a duffel bag to collect their things in. As they walked rather briskly across the grounds, all still very close together and in perfect step, with a guard trailing behind, Beech said, under his breath, 'So who got us the damned pardons?'

'It wasn't Lake,' Yarber said, just barely loud enough to be heard.

'Of course it wasn't Lake,' Beech said. 'The President wouldn't do a damned thing Aaron Lake asked him to.'

They walked faster.

'What difference does it make?' Spicer asked.

'It doesn't make any sense,' Yarber said.

'So what're you gonna do, Finn?' Spicer asked without looking. 'Stay here for a few days and ponder the situation? And then if you figure out who's responsible for the pardon, then maybe you won't accept it? Gimme a break.'

'Somebody else is behind this,' Beech said.

'Then I love this somebody else, okay?' Spicer said. 'I'm not sticking around to ask questions.'

They ransacked their rooms in a mad rush, never slowing to say good-bye to anyone. Most of their friends were scattered around the camp anyway.

They had to hurry before the dream was over, or before the President changed his mind.

At eleven-fifteen, they walked through the front door of the administration building, the same door they'd each entered years ago, and waited on the hot sidewalk for their ride. None of the three looked back.

The van was driven by Wes and Chap, though they gave other names. They used so many.

Joe Roy Spicer lay down on the backseat, and covered his eyes with a forearm, determined not to see anything until he was far away. He wanted to cry and he wanted to scream, but he was numb with euphoria – sheer, uncut, unabashed euphoria. He hid his eyes and smiled a goofy smile. He wanted a beer and he wanted a woman, preferably his wife. He'd call her soon. The van was rolling now.

The suddenness of the release had them rattled. Most inmates count the days, and in doing so know with some measure of accuracy when the moment will come. And they know where they're going, and who's waiting for them there.

But the Brethren knew so little. And the few things they knew, they didn't really believe. The pardons were a hoax. The money was nothing but bait. They were being taken away to be slaughtered, same as poor Trevor. The van would stop any minute, and the two goons up front would

419

search their bags, find their dirty files, then murder them in a roadside ditch.

Maybe. But, at the moment, they did not miss the safety of Trumble.

Finn Yarber sat behind the driver and watched the road ahead. He held his pardon, ready to present it to anyone who might stop them and tell them the dream was over. Next to him was Hatlee Beech, who after a few minutes on the road began to cry, not loud, but with his eyes tightly closed and his lips quivering.

Beech had reason to cry. With almost eight and a half years to go, clemency meant more to him than to his two colleagues combined.

Not a word was uttered between Trumble and Jacksonville. As they approached the city, and the roads became wider and the traffic heavier, the three watched the scenery with great curiosity. People were driving, moving about. Planes overhead. Boats on the rivers. Things were normal again.

They inched through the traffic on Atlantic Boulevard, thoroughly enjoying every moment of the congestion. The weather was hot, the tourists were out, ladies with long bronze legs. They saw the seafood restaurants and bars with signs advertising cold beer and cheap oysters. When the street ended, the beach began, and they pulled under the veranda of the Sea Turtle. They followed one of their escorts through the lobby, where they caught a look or two because they were still dressed alike. Up to the fifth floor, and off the elevator before Chap said, 'Your rooms are right here, these three.' He was pointing down the hall. 'Mr. Argrow would like to see you as soon as possible.'

'Where is he?' Spicer asked.

Chap pointed again. 'Over there, in the corner suite. He's waiting.'

'Let's go,' Spicer said, and they followed Chap into the corner, their duffel bags bouncing against one another.

Jack Argrow looked nothing like his brother. He was much shorter, and his hair was blond and wavy where his brother's was dark and thinning. It was just a casual observation, but the three noticed it and mentioned it later. He shook their hands quickly, but only to be polite. He was edgy and talked very fast. 'How's my brother?' he asked.

'He's doing well,' Beech said.

'We saw him this morning,' Yarber added.

'I want him out of prison,' Jack snapped, as if they'd put him there in the first place. 'That's what I'll get outta this deal, you know. I'll get my brother out of prison.'

They glanced at each other; nothing could be said.

'Have a seat,' Argrow said. 'Look, I don't know how or why I'm in the middle of this, you understand. It makes me very nervous. I'm here on behalf of Mr. Aaron Lake, a man I believe will be elected, and make a great President. I suppose I can then get my brother outta prison. But anyway, I've never met Mr. Lake. Some of his people approached me about a week ago, and asked me to get involved in a very secret and delicate matter. That's why I'm here. It's a favor, okay? I don't know everything, you understand?' The sentences

421

were clipped and rapid. He talked with his hands and his mouth, and he couldn't be still.

The Brethren offered no response, none was really expected.

Two hidden cameras captured the scene and sent it immediately to Langley, where Teddy, York, and Deville watched it on a wide screen in the bunker. The ex-judges, now ex-inmates, looked like freshly released POWs, dazed and subdued, still in uniform, still in disbelief. They sat close together, watching Agent Lyter give a splendid performance.

After trying to outthink and outmaneuver them for three months, it was fascinating to finally see them. Teddy studied their faces, and grudgingly admitted a little admiration. They'd been shrewd and lucky enough to hook the right victim; now they were free and about to be well compensated for their ingenuity.

'Okay, look, the first thing is the money,' Argrow barked. 'Two million each. Where do you want it?'

It was not the sort of question they'd had much experience with. 'What are the options?' asked Spicer.

'You have to wire it somewhere,' Argrow snapped back.

'How about London?' Yarber asked.

'London?'

'We'd like the money, all of it, all six million, to be wired at one time, to one account, to a bank in London,' Yarber said.

'We can wire it anywhere. Which bank?'

'Can you help us with the details?' Yarber asked.

422

'I'm told we can do anything you want. I'll have to make a few calls. Why don't you go to your rooms, take a shower, change clothes. Give me fifteen minutes.'

'We don't have any clothes,' Beech said.

'There are some things in your rooms.'

Chap led them down the hall and gave them their keys.

Spicer stretched out on his king-sized bed and stared at the ceiling. Beech stood in the window of his room and looked north, for miles along the beach, the blue water gently rolling onto the white sand. Children played near their mothers. Couples strolled hand in hand. A fishing boat inched along on the horizon. Free at last, he said to himself. Free at last.

Yarber took a long hot shower – complete privacy, no time limit, plenty of soap, thick towels. Someone had placed a selection of toiletries on the vanity – deodorant, shaving cream, razors, toothpaste, toothbrush, floss. He took his time, then changed into a pair of Bermuda shorts, sandals, and a white tee shirt. He'd be the first to leave, and he needed to find a clothing store.

Twenty minutes later they reconvened in Argrow's suite, and they brought with them their collection of files wrapped neatly in a pillowcase. Argrow was just as anxious as before. 'There's a large bank in London called Metropolitan Trust. We can send the money there, then you can do with it whatever you want.'

'That's fine,' Yarber said. 'The account will be in my name only.'

Argrow looked at Beech and Spicer, and they

423

nodded their approval. 'Very well. I assume you have a plan of some sort.'

'We do,' Spicer said. 'Mr. Yarber here will leave for London this afternoon, and when he gets there he'll go to the bank and take care of the money. If all goes well, then we'll leave soon afterward.'

'I assure you things will go well.'

'And we believe you. We're just being careful.'

Argrow handed two sheets of paper to Finn. 'I need your signature to start the wire and open the account.' Yarber scribbled his name.

'Have you had lunch?' he asked.

They shook their heads. Lunch was certainly on their minds, but they weren't sure how to proceed.

'You're free men now. There are some nice restaurants just a few blocks from here. Go enjoy yourselves. Give me an hour to start the wire. Let's meet here at two-thirty.'

Spicer was holding the pillowcase. He sort of waved it at Argrow and said, 'Here are the files.'

'Right. Just throw them on the sofa there.'

THIRTY-EIGHT

They left the hotel on foot, without escorts, without restrictions, but with their pardons in their pockets, just in case. And though the sun was warmer near the beach, the air was certainly lighter. The sky was clearer. The world was pretty again. Hope filled the air. They smiled and laughed at almost anything. They strolled along Atlantic Boulevard, and mixed easily with the tourists.

Lunch was steak and beer at a sidewalk café, under an umbrella, so they could watch the foot traffic. Little was said as they ate and drank. Everything was seen, though, especially the younger ladies in shorts and skimpy tops. Prison had turned them into old men. Now they felt the urge to party.

Especially Hatlee Beech. He'd had wealth and status and ambition, and as a federal judge he'd had what was all but impossible to lose – a lifetime appointment. He'd fallen hard, lost everything, and during his first two years at Trumble he'd existed in a state of depression. He had accepted the fact that he would die there, and he'd seriously considered suicide. Now, at the age of fifty-six, he was emerging from the darkness in a rather splendid fashion. He was fifteen pounds lighter, nicely tanned, in good health, divorced from a woman who had money but not much else to offer, and about to collect a fortune. Not a bad middle-aged rally, he told himself. He missed his children, but they'd followed the money and forgotten about him.

Hatlee Beech was ready for some fun.

Spicer was also looking for a party, preferably one at a casino. His wife had no passport, so it would be a few weeks before she could join him in London, or wherever he might land. Did they have casinos in Europe? Beech thought so. Yarber had no idea, and didn't care.

Finn was the most reserved of the three. He drank a soda instead of beer, and he wasn't as interested in the flesh passing by. Finn was already in Europe. He'd never leave, never return to his native land. He was sixty, very fit, now with lots of money, and was about to bum around Italy and Greece for the next ten years.

Across the street, they found a small bookstore and bought several travel books. In a shop specializing in beachwear, they found just the right sunglasses. Then it was time to see Jack Argrow again, and finish the deal.

Klockner and company watched them stroll back to the Sea Turtle. Klockner and company were weary of Neptune Beach and Pete's and the Sea Turtle and the crowded rental. Six agents, including Chap and Wes, were still there, all very anxious for another assignment. The unit had discovered the Brethren, plucked them from inside Trumble, brought them to the beach, and now they just wanted them to leave the country.

Jack Argrow had not touched the files, or at least they appeared untouched. They were still wrapped in the pillowcase, on the sofa, in the exact spot Spicer had left them.

'The wire is under way,' Argrow said as they settled into his suite.

Teddy was still watching from Langley. The three were now wearing all manner of beach garb. Yarber had a fishing cap with a six-inch bill. Spicer had a straw hat and a yellow tee shirt of some variety. Beech, the Republican, wore khaki shorts, a knit pullover, and a golf cap.

There were three large envelopes on the dining table. Argrow handed one to each of the Brethren. 'Inside, you'll find your new identities. Birth certificates, credit cards, Social Security cards.'

'What about passports?' asked Yarber.

'We have a camera set up in the next room. The passports and driver's licenses will need photos. It'll take thirty minutes. There's also five thousand dollars cash in those small envelopes there.'

'I'm Harvey Moss?' Spicer asked, looking at his birth certificate.

'Yes. You don't like Harvey?'

'I guess I do now.'

'You look like a Harvey,' Beech said.

'And who are you?'

'Well, I'm James Nunley.'

'Nice to meet you, James.'

Argrow never cracked a smile, never relaxed for

a second. 'I need to know your travel plans. The people in Washington really want you out of the country.'

'I need to check flights to London,' Yarber said.

'We've already done that. A flight to Atlanta leaves Jacksonville in two hours. At seven-ten tonight, there's a flight leaving Atlanta for London Heathrow that arrives early tomorrow morning.'

'Can you get me a seat?'

'It's already done. First class.'

Finn closed his eyes and smiled.

'And what about you?' Argrow asked, looking at the other two.'

'I kinda like it here,' Spicer said.

'Sorry. We have a deal.'

'We'll take the same flights tomorrow afternoon,' Beech said. 'Assuming all goes well with Mr. Yarber.'

'Do you want us to handle the reservations?'

'Yes, please.'

Chap eased into the room without making a sound, and took the pillowcase from the sofa. He left with the files.

'Let's do the photos,' Argrow said.

Finn Yarber, now traveling as a Mr. William McCoy of San Jose, California, flew to Atlanta without incident. For an hour he walked the concourses of the airport, rode the underground shuttles, and thoroughly enjoyed the frenzy and chaos of being in the midst of a million people in a hurry.

His first-class seat was a massive leather recliner. After two glasses of champagne, he began to drift, and to dream. He was afraid to sleep because he was afraid to wake up. He was certain he would be back on his top bunk, staring at the ceiling, counting off another day at Trumble.

From a pay phone next to Beach Java, Joe Roy finally caught his wife. At first, she thought the call was a hoax and refused to accept the collect charges. 'Who is this?' she asked.

'It's me, dear. I'm no longer in prison.'

'Joe Roy?'

'Yes, now listen. I'm out of prison, okay. Are you there?'

'I think so. Where are you?'

'I'm staying at a hotel near Jacksonville, Florida. I was released from prison this morning.'

'Released? But how –'

'Don't ask, okay. I'll explain everything later. I'm leaving tomorrow for London. I want you to go to the post office first thing in the morning, and get an application for a passport.'

'London? Did you say London?'

'Yes.'

'England?'

'That's it, yes. I have to go there for a while. It's part of the deal.'

'For how long?'

'A couple of years. Listen, I know it's hard to believe, but I'm free and we're gonna live abroad for a couple of years.'

'What kinda deal? Have you escaped, Joe Roy? You said it'd be easy to do.'

'No. I have been released.'

'But you got more than twenty months to go.'

'Not anymore. Listen, get the application for a passport and follow the instructions.'

'Why do I need a passport?'

'So we can meet in Europe.'

'For two years?'

'Yes, that's it.'

'But Mother's sick. I can't just run off and leave Mother.'

He thought of all the things he'd like to say about her mother, then let it pass. A deep breath, a glance down the street. 'I'm going away,' he said. 'I have no choice.'

'Just come home,' she said.

'I can't. I'll explain it later.'

'An explanation would be nice.'

'I'll call you tomorrow.'

Beech and Spicer ate seafood in a restaurant crowded with people much younger. They roamed the sidewalks and eventually found their way to Pete's Bar and Grill, where they watched the Braves and enjoyed the noise.

Finn was somewhere over the Atlantic, following their money.

The customs agent at Heathrow barely glanced at Finn's passport, which was a marvel of forgery. It was well used and had accompanied Mr. William McCoy around the world. Aaron Lake did indeed have powerful friends.

Finn took a taxi to the Basil Street Hotel in Knightsbridge, and paid cash for the smallest room available. He and Beech had selected the hotel at random from a travel guide. It was an old-fashioned place, filled with antiques, and it rambled from floor to floor. At the small restaurant upstairs, he had breakfast of coffee, eggs, and black sausage, then went for a walk. At ten, his taxi stopped in front of the Metropolitan Trust in the City. The receptionist didn't care for his attire – jeans and a pullover – but when she realized he was an American she shrugged and seemed to tolerate it.

They made him wait for an hour, but he didn't mind it at all. Finn was nervous, but didn't show it. He'd wait for days, weeks, months to get the money. He'd learned how to be patient. The Mr. MacGregor who was in charge of the wire finally came for him. The money had just arrived, sorry for the delay. All six million bucks had crossed the Atlantic safely, and was now on British soil.

But not for long. 'I'd like to wire it to Switzerland,' Finn said, with the proper dose of confidence and experience.

That afternoon, Beech and Spicer flew to Atlanta. Like Yarber, they roamed the airport with unrestrained freedom while waiting for their London flight. They sat together in first class, ate and drank for hours, watched movies, tried to sleep as they crossed the ocean.

Much to their surprise, Yarber was waiting when they cleared customs at Heathrow. He delivered the wonderful news that the money had come and gone. It was hidden in Switzerland. He surprised them again with the idea of leaving immediately.

'They know we're here,' he said over coffee in an airport bar. 'Let's shake them.'

'You think they're following us?' Beech asked.

431

'Let's assume they are.'

'But why?' Spicer asked.

They discussed it for half an hour, then began looking for flights. Alitalia to Rome caught their attention. First class, of course.

'Do they speak English in Rome?' Spicer asked as they were boarding.

'Actually, they speak Italian,' Yarber said.

'You think the Pope will see us?'

'He's probably busy.'

THIRTY-NINE

Buster zigzagged westward for days until he made his final bus stop in San Diego. The ocean attracted him, the first water he'd seen in months. He hung around the docks looking for odd jobs and chatting with the regulars. A charter boat captain hired him as a gopher, and he jumped ship in Los Cabos, Mexico, at the southern tip of the Baja. The harbor there was filled with expensive fishing boats, much nicer than the ones he and his father once traded. He met a few of the captains, and within two days had a job as a deckhand. The customers were wealthy Americans from Texas and California, and they spent more time drinking than fishing. He earned no wages or salary, but worked for tips, which invariably got larger the more the clients drank. A slow day would net him $200; a good day, $500, all cash. He lived in an inexpensive motel, and after a few days stopped looking over his shoulder. Los Cabos quickly became his home.

Wilson Argrow was suddenly transferred out of

Trumble and sent to a halfway house in Milwaukee, where he stayed exactly one night before walking away. Since he didn't exist he couldn't be found. Jack Argrow met him at the airport with tickets, and they flew together to D.C. Two days after leaving Florida, the Argrow brothers, Kenny Sands and Roger Lyter, reported to Langley for their next assignment.

Three days before he was scheduled to depart D.C. for the convention in Denver, Aaron Lake arrived at Langley for lunch with the Director. It was to be a joyful occasion, the conquering candidate once again thanking the genius who'd asked him to run. His acceptance speech had been written for a month, but Teddy had a few suggestions he wanted to discuss.

He was escorted to Teddy's office, where the old man was waiting under his quilt, as always. He looked so pale and tired, Lake thought. The aides vanished, the door was closed, and Lake noticed that no table had been prepared. They sat away from the desk, face to face, very close together.

Teddy liked the speech and made just a few comments. 'Your speeches are getting too long,' he said quietly. But Lake had so much to say these days.

'We're still editing,' he said.

'This election belongs to you, Mr. Lake,' Teddy said, quite feebly.

'I feel good, but it will be a brawl.'

'You'll win by fifteen points.'

Lake stopped smiling and listened hard. 'That's, uh, quite a margin.'

'You're up slightly in the polls. Next month the Vice President will be up. It will go back and forth until the middle of October. Then, there will be a nuclear situation that will terrify the world. And you, Mr. Lake, will become the messiah.'

The prospect frightened even the messiah. 'A war?' Lake asked quietly.

'No. There will be casualties, but they won't be Americans. Natty Chenkov will get the blame, and the good voters of this republic will flock to the polls. You could win by as much as twenty points.'

Lake breathed deeply. He wanted to ask more questions, even perhaps object to the bloodshed. But it would be futile. Whatever terror Teddy had planned for October was already in the works. There was nothing Lake could say or do to stop it.

'Keep beating the same drum, Mr. Lake. The same message. The world is about to become a lot crazier, and we have to be strong to protect our way of life.'

'The message has worked so far.'

'Your opponent will become desperate. He'll attack you for the single issue, and he'll whine about the money. He'll beat you up and score some points. Don't panic. The world will be turned upside down in October, trust me.'

'I do.'

'You've got this thing won, Mr. Lake. Keep preaching the same message.'

'Oh, I will.'

'Good,' Teddy said, and closed his eyes for a moment as if he needed a quick nap. Then he opened them and said, 'Now, on an entirely different topic, I'm a little curious about your plans once you get to the White House.'

Lake was puzzled, and his face showed it.

Teddy continued the ambush: 'You need a partner, Mr. Lake, a First Lady, someone to grace the White House with her presence. Someone to entertain and decorate, a pretty woman, one young enough to have children. It's been a long time since we had children in the White House, Mr. Lake.'

'You must be kidding.' Lake was flabbergasted.

'I like this Jayne Cordell on your staff. She's thirty-eight, smart, articulate, quite pretty though she needs to drop fifteen pounds. Her divorce was twelve years ago, and it's forgotten. I think she'd make a fine First Lady.'

Lake cocked his head to one side, and was suddenly angry. He wanted to lash out at Teddy, but for the moment words failed him. He managed to mumble, 'Have you lost your mind?'

'We know about Ricky,' Teddy said, very coolly, with his eyes penetrating Lake's.

The wind was sucked out of Lake's lungs, and as he exhaled he said, 'Oh my god.' He studied his feet for a moment, his entire body frozen in shock.

To make matters worse, Teddy handed over a sheet of paper. Lake took it, and instantly recognized it as a copy of his last note to Ricky.

Dear Ricky:
    I think it's best if we end our correspondence. I wish you well with your rehab.

Sincerely, Al

436

Lake almost said that he could explain things; they were not as they seemed. But he decided to say nothing, at least not for a while. The questions flooded his thoughts – How much do they know? How in hell did they intercept the mail? Who else knows?

Teddy let him suffer in silence. There was no hurry.

When his thoughts cleared somewhat, the politician in Lake came to the surface. Teddy was offering a way out. Teddy was saying, 'Just play ball with me, son, and things will be fine. Do it my way.'

And so Lake swallowed hard and said, 'I actually like her.'

'Of course you do. She's perfect for the job.'

'Yes. She's very loyal.'

'Are you sleeping with her?'

'No. Not yet.'

'Start soon. Hold hands with her during the convention. Let the gossip start, let nature take its course. A week before the election, announce a Christmas wedding.'

'Big or small?'

'Huge. The social event of the year in Washington.'

'I like that.'

'Get her pregnant quickly. Just before your inauguration, announce that the First Lady is expecting. It'll make a marvelous story. And it will be so nice to see young children in the White House again.'

Lake smiled and nodded and appeared to like

the thought, then he suddenly frowned. 'Will anyone ever know about Ricky?' he asked.

'No. He's been neutralized.'

'Neutralized?'

'He'll never write another letter, Mr. Lake. And you'll be so busy playing with all your little children that you won't have time to think about people like Ricky.'

'Ricky who?'

'Atta boy, Lake. Atta boy.'

'I'm very sorry, Mr. Maynard. Very sorry. It won't happen again.'

'Of course it won't. I've got the file, Mr. Lake. Always remember that.' Teddy began rolling himself backward, as if the meeting was over.

'It was an isolated moment of weakness,' Lake said.

'Never mind, Lake. Take care of Jayne. Get her a new wardrobe. She works too hard and she looks tired. Ease up on her. She's going to make a wonderful First Lady.'

'Yes sir.'

Teddy was at the door. 'No more surprises, Lake.'

'No sir.'

Teddy opened the door and rolled himself away.

By late November, they had settled in Monte Carlo, primarily because of its beauty and warm weather, but also because so much English was spoken there. And there were casinos, a must for Spicer. Neither Beech nor Yarber could tell if he was winning or losing, but he was certainly enjoying himself. His wife was still tending to her mother, who'd yet to die. Things were tense because Joe Roy wouldn't go home, and she wouldn't leave Mississippi.

They lived in the same small but handsome hotel on the edge of town, and they usually had breakfast together twice a week before scattering. As the months passed and they settled into their new lives, they saw less and less of each other. They had differing interests. Spicer wanted to gamble and drink and spend time with the ladies. Beech preferred the sea and enjoyed fishing. Yarber traveled and studied the history of southern France and northern Italy.

But each always knew where the others were. If one disappeared, the other two wanted to know it.

They'd read nothing about their pardons. Beech and Yarber had spent hours in a library in Rome, reading American newspapers just after they fled. Not a word about them. They'd had no contact with anyone from home. Spicer's wife claimed to have told no one that he was out of prison. She still thought he'd escaped.

On Thanksgiving Day, Finn Yarber was enjoying an espresso at a sidewalk café in downtown Monte Carlo. It was warm and sunny, and he was only vaguely aware that it was an important holiday back home. He didn't care because he would never go back. Beech was asleep in his hotel room. Spicer was in a casino three blocks away.

A vaguely familiar face appeared from nowhere. In a flash, the man sat across from Yarber and said, 'Hello, Finn. Remember me?'

Yarber calmly took a sip of coffee and studied the face. He'd last seen it at Trumble.

'Wilson Argrow, from prison,' the man said, and Yarber put down his cup before he dropped it.

'Good morning, Mr. Argrow,' Finn said slowly, calmly, though there were many other things he wanted to say.

'I guess you're surprised to see me.'

'Yes, as a matter of fact.'

'Wasn't that exciting news about Aaron Lake's landslide?'

'I suppose. What can I do for you?'

'I just want you to know that we're always close by, just in case you need us.'

Finn actually chuckled, then said, 'That doesn't seem likely.' It had been five months since their release. They had moved from country to country, from Greece to Sweden, from Poland to Portugal, slowly heading south as the weather changed. How on earth could Argrow track them down?

It was impossible.

Argrow pulled a magazine from inside his jacket. 'I ran across this last week,' he said, handing it over. The magazine was turned to a page in the back where a personal ad was circled with a red marker:

> SWM in 20s looking for kind and
> discreet American gentleman in
> 40s or 50s to pen pal with.

Yarber had certainly seen it before, but he shrugged as if he hadn't a clue.

'Looks familiar, doesn't it?' Argrow asked.

'They all look the same to me,' Finn said. He

tossed the magazine on the table. It was the European edition of *Out and About*.

'We traced the address to the post office here in Monte Carlo,' Argrow said. 'A brand-new box rental, with a fake name and everything. What a coincidence.'

'Look, I don't know who you work for, but I have a very strong hunch that we're not in your jurisdiction. We haven't broken a single law. Why don't you bug off?'

'Sure, Finn, but two million bucks isn't enough?'

Finn smiled and looked around the lovely café. He took a sip of coffee and said, 'You gotta keep busy.'

'I'll see you around,' Argrow said, then jumped to his feet and vanished.

Yarber finished his coffee as if nothing had happened. He watched the street and the traffic for a while, then left to gather his colleagues.

A PAINTED HOUSE

Chapter 1

The hill people and the Mexicans arrived on the same day. It was a Wednesday, early in September 1952. The Cardinals were five games behind the Dodgers with three weeks to go, and the season looked hopeless. The cotton, however, was waist-high to my father, over my head, and he and my grandfather could be heard before supper whispering words that were seldom heard. It could be a 'good crop'.

They were farmers, hardworking men who embraced pessimism only when discussing the weather and the crops. There was too much sun, or too much rain, or the threat of floods in the lowlands, or the rising prices of seed and fertilizer, or the uncertainties of the markets. On the most perfect of days, my mother would quietly say to me, 'Don't worry. The men will find something to worry about.'

Pappy, my grandfather, was worried about the price for labor when we went searching for the hill people. They were paid for every hundred pounds of cotton they picked. The previous year, according to him, it was $1.50 per hundred. He'd already

1

heard rumors that a farmer over in Lake City was offering $1.60.

This played heavily on his mind as we rode to town. He never talked when he drove, and this was because, according to my mother, not much of a driver herself, he was afraid of motorized vehicles. His truck was a 1939 Ford, and with the exception of our old John Deere tractor, it was our sole means of transportation. This was no particular problem except when we drove to church and my mother and grandmother were forced to sit snugly together up front in their Sunday best while my father and I rode in the back, engulfed in dust. Modern sedans were scarce in rural Arkansas.

Pappy drove thirty-seven miles per hour. His theory was that every automobile had a speed at which it ran most efficiently, and through some vaguely defined method he had determined that his old truck should go thirty-seven. My mother said (to me) that it was ridiculous. She also said he and my father had once fought over whether the truck should go faster. But my father rarely drove it, and if I happened to be riding with him, he would level off at thirty-seven, out of respect for Pappy. My mother said she suspected he drove much faster when he was alone.

We turned onto Highway 135, and, as always, I watched Pappy carefully shift the gears – pressing slowly on the clutch, delicately prodding the stick shift on the steering column – until the truck reached its perfect speed. Then I leaned over to check the speedometer: thirty-seven. He smiled at me as if we both agreed that the truck belonged at that speed.

Highway 135 ran straight and flat through the farm country of the Arkansas Delta. On both sides as far as I could see, the fields were white with cotton. It was time for the harvest, a wonderful season for me because they turned out school for two months. For my grandfather, though, it was a time of endless worry.

On the right, at the Jordan place, we saw a group of Mexicans working in the field near the road. They were stooped at the waist, their cotton sacks draped behind them, their hands moving deftly through the stalks, tearing off the bolls. Pappy grunted. He didn't like the Jordans because they were Methodists – and Cubs fans. Now that they already had workers in their fields, there was another reason to dislike them.

The distance from our farm to town was fewer than eight miles, but at thirty-seven miles an hour, the trip took twenty minutes. Always twenty minutes, even with little traffic. Pappy didn't believe in passing slower vehicles in front of him. Of course, he was usually the slow one. Near Black Oak, we caught up to a trailer filled to the top with snowy mounds of freshly picked cotton. A tarp covered the front half, and the Montgomery twins, who were my age, playfully bounced around in all that cotton until they saw us on the road below them. Then they stopped and waved. I waved back, but my grandfather did not. When he drove, he never waved or nodded at folks, and this was, my mother said, because he was afraid to take his hands from the wheel. She said people talked about him behind his back, saying he was rude and

3

arrogant. Personally, I don't think he cared how the gossip ran.

We followed the Montgomery trailer until it turned at the cotton gin. It was pulled by their old Massey Harris tractor, and driven by Frank, the eldest Montgomery boy, who had dropped out of school in the fifth grade and was considered by everyone at church to be headed for serious trouble.

Highway 135 became Main Street for the short stretch it took to negotiate Black Oak. We passed the Black Oak Baptist Church, one of the few times we'd pass without stopping for some type of service. Every store, shop, business, church, even the school, faced Main Street, and on Saturdays the traffic inched along, bumper to bumper, as the country folks flocked to town for their weekly shopping. But it was Wednesday, and when we got into town, we parked in front of Pop and Pearl Watson's grocery store on Main.

I waited on the sidewalk until my grandfather nodded in the direction of the store. That was my cue to go inside and purchase a Tootsie Roll, on credit. It only cost a penny, but it was not a foregone conclusion that I would get one every trip to town. Occasionally, he wouldn't nod, but I would enter the store anyway and loiter around the cash register long enough for Pearl to sneak me one, which always came with strict instructions not to tell my grandfather. She was afraid of him. Eli Chandler was a poor man, but he was intensely proud. He would starve to death before he took free food, which, on his list, included Tootsie Rolls. He would've beaten me with a stick if he

4

knew I had accepted a piece of candy, so Pearl Watson had no trouble swearing me to secrecy.

But this time I got the nod. As always, Pearl was dusting the counter when I entered and gave her a stiff hug. Then I grabbed a Tootsie Roll from the jar next to the cash register. I signed the charge slip with great flair, and Pearl inspected my penmanship. 'It's getting better, Luke,' she said.

'Not bad for a seven-year-old,' I said. Because of my mother, I had been practicing my name in cursive writing for two years. 'Where's Pop?' I asked. They were the only adults I knew who insisted I call them by their 'first' names, but only in the store when no one else was listening. If a customer walked in, then it was suddenly Mr. and Mrs. Watson. I told no one but my mother this, and she told me she was certain no other child held such privilege.

'In the back, putting up stock,' Pearl said. 'Where's your grandfather?'

It was Pearl's calling in life to monitor the movements of the town's population, so any question was usually answered with another.

'The Tea Shoppe, checking on the Mexicans. Can I go back there?' I was determined to outquestion her.

'Better not. Y'all using hill people, too?'

'If we can find them. Eli says they don't come down like they used to. He also thinks they're all half crazy. Where's Champ?' Champ was the store's ancient beagle, which never left Pop's side.

Pearl grinned whenever I called my grandfather by his first name. She was about to ask me a question when the small bell clanged as the door

5

opened and closed. A genuine Mexican walked in, alone and timid, as they all seemed to be at first. Pearl nodded politely at the new customer.

I shouted, *'Buenos días, señor!'*

The Mexican grinned and said sheepishly, *'Buenos días,'* before disappearing into the back of the store.

'They're good people,' Pearl said under her breath, as if the Mexican spoke English and might be offended by something nice she said. I bit into my Tootsie Roll and chewed it slowly while rewrapping and pocketing the other half.

'Eli's worried about payin' them too much,' I said. With a customer in the store, Pearl was suddenly busy again, dusting and straightening around the only cash register.

'Eli worries about everything,' she said.

'He's a farmer.'

'Are you going to be a farmer?'

'No ma'am. A baseball player.'

'For the Cardinals?'

'Of course.'

Pearl hummed for a bit while I waited for the Mexican. I had some more Spanish I was anxious to try.

The old wooden shelves were bursting with fresh groceries. I loved the store during picking season because Pop filled it from floor to ceiling. The crops were coming in, and money was changing hands.

Pappy opened the door just wide enough to stick his head in. 'Let's go,' he said; then, 'Howdy, Pearl.'

'Howdy, Eli,' she said as she patted my head and sent me away.

'Where are the Mexicans?' I asked Pappy when we were outside.

'Should be in later this afternoon.'

We got back in the truck and left town in the direction of Jonesboro, where my grandfather always found the hill people.

We parked on the shoulder of the highway, near the intersection of a gravel road. In Pappy's opinion, it was the best spot in the county to catch the hill people. I wasn't so sure. He'd been trying to hire some for a week with no results. We sat on the tailgate in the scorching sun in complete silence for half an hour before the first truck stopped. It was clean and had good tires. If we were lucky enough to find hill people, they would live with us for the next two months. We wanted folks who were neat, and the fact that this truck was much nicer than Pappy's was a good sign.

'Afternoon,' Pappy said when the engine was turned off.

'Howdy,' said the driver.

'Where y'all from?' asked Pappy.

'Up north of Hardy.'

With no traffic around, my grandfather stood on the pavement, a pleasant expression on his face, taking in the truck and its contents. The driver and his wife sat in the cab with a small girl between them. Three large teenaged boys were napping in the back. Everyone appeared to be healthy and well-dressed. I could tell Pappy wanted these people.

7

'Y'all lookin' for work?' he asked.

'Yep. Lookin' for Lloyd Crenshaw, somewhere west of Black Oak.' My grandfather pointed this way and that, and they drove off. We watched them until they were out of sight.

He could've offered them more than Mr. Crenshaw was promising. Hill people were notorious for negotiating their labor. Last year, in the middle of the first picking on our place, the Fulbrights from Calico Rock disappeared one Sunday night and went to work for a farmer ten miles away.

But Pappy was not dishonest, nor did he want to start a bidding war.

We tossed a baseball along the edge of a cotton field, stopping whenever a truck approached.

My glove was a Rawlings that Santa had delivered the Christmas before. I slept with it nightly and oiled it weekly, and nothing was as dear to my soul.

My grandfather, who had taught me how to throw and catch and hit, didn't need a glove. His large, callused hands absorbed my throws without the slightest sting.

Though he was a quiet man who never bragged, Eli Chandler had been a legendary baseball player. At the age of seventeen, he had signed a contract with the Cardinals to play professional baseball. But the First War called him, and not long after he came home, his father died. Pappy had no choice but to become a farmer.

Pop Watson loved to tell me stories of how great Eli Chandler had been – how far he could hit a baseball, how hard he could throw one. 'Probably

8

the greatest ever from Arkansas,' was Pop's assessment.

'Better than Dizzy Dean?' I would ask.

'Not even close,' Pop would say, sighing.

When I relayed these stories to my mother, she always smiled and said, 'Be careful. Pop tells tales.'

Pappy, who was rubbing the baseball in his mammoth hands, cocked his head at the sound of a vehicle. Coming from the west was a truck with a trailer behind it. From a quarter of a mile away we could tell they were hill people. We walked to the shoulder of the road and waited as the driver downshifted, gears crunching and whining as he brought the truck to a stop.

I counted seven heads, five in the truck, two in the trailer.

'Howdy,' the driver said slowly, sizing up my grandfather as we in turn quickly scrutinized them.

'Good afternoon,' Pappy said, taking a step closer but still keeping his distance.

Tobacco juice lined the lower lip of the driver. This was an ominous sign. My mother thought most hill people were prone to bad hygiene and bad habits. Tobacco and alcohol were forbidden in our home. We were Baptists.

'Name's Spruill,' he said.

'Eli Chandler. Nice to meet you. Y'all lookin' for work?'

'Yep.'

'Where you from?'

'Eureka Springs.'

The truck was almost as old as Pappy's, with slick tires and a cracked windshield and rusted fenders and what looked like faded blue paint under a layer of dust. A tier had been constructed above the bed, and it was crammed with cardboard boxes and burlap bags filled with supplies. Under it, on the floor of the bed, a mattress was wedged next to the cab. Two large boys stood on it, both staring blankly at me. Sitting on the tailgate, barefoot and shirtless, was a heavy young man with massive shoulders and a neck as thick as a stump. He spat tobacco juice between the truck and the trailer and seemed oblivious to Pappy and me. He swung his feet slowly, then spat again, never looking away from the asphalt beneath him.

'I'm lookin' for field hands,' Pappy said.

'How much you payin'?' Mr. Spruill asked.

'One-sixty a hundred,' Pappy said.

Mr. Spruill frowned and looked at the woman beside him. They mumbled something.

It was at this point in the ritual that quick decisions had to be made. We had to decide whether we wanted these people living with us. And they had to accept or reject our price.

'What kinda cotton?' Mr. Spruill asked.

'Stoneville,' my grandfather said. 'The bolls are ready. It'll be easy to pick.' Mr. Spruill could look around him and see the bolls bursting. The sun and soil and rains had cooperated so far. Pappy, of course, had been fretting over some dire rainfall prediction in the *Farmers' Almanac*.

'We got one-sixty last year,' Mr. Spruill said.

I didn't care for money talk, so I ambled along the center line to inspect the trailer. The tires on the trailer were even balder than those on the truck. One was half flat from the load. It was a good thing that their journey was almost over.

10

Rising in one corner of the trailer, with her elbows resting on the plank siding, was a very pretty girl. She had dark hair pulled tightly behind her head and big brown eyes. She was younger than my mother, but certainly a lot older than I was, and I couldn't help but stare.

'What's your name?' she said.

'Luke,' I said, kicking a rock. My cheeks were immediately warm. 'What's yours?'

'Tally. How old are you?'

'Seven. How old are you?'

'Seventeen.'

'How long you been ridin' in that trailer?'

'Day and a half.'

She was barefoot, and her dress was dirty and very tight – tight all the way to her knees. This was the first time I remember really examining a girl. She watched me with a knowing smile. A kid sat on a crate next to her with his back to me, and he slowly turned around and looked at me as if I weren't there. He had green eyes and a long forehead covered with sticky black hair. His left arm appeared to be useless.

'This is Trot,' she said. 'He ain't right.'

'Nice to meet you, Trot,' I said, but his eyes looked away. He acted as if he hadn't heard me.

'How old is he?' I asked her.

'Twelve. He's a cripple.'

Trot turned abruptly to face a corner, his bad arm flopping lifelessly. My friend Dewayne said that hill people married their cousins and that's why there were so many defects in their families.

Tally appeared to be perfect, though. She gazed

11

thoughtfully across the cotton fields, and I admired her dirty dress once again.

I knew my grandfather and Mr. Spruill had come to terms because Mr. Spruill started his truck. I walked past the trailer, past the man on the tailgate who was briefly awake but still staring at the pavement, and stood beside Pappy. 'Nine miles that way, take a left by a burned-out barn, then six more miles to the St. Francis River. We're the first farm past the river on your left.'

'Bottomland?' Mr. Spruill asked, as if he were being sent into a swamp.

'Some of it is, but it's good land.'

Mr. Spruill glanced at his wife again, then looked back at us. 'Where do we set up?'

'You'll see a shady spot in the back, next to the silo. That's the best place.'

We watched them drive away, the gears rattling, the tires wobbling, crates and boxes and pots bouncing along.

'You don't like them, do you?' I asked.

'They're good folks. They're just different.'

'I guess we're lucky to have them, aren't we?'

'Yes, we are.'

More field hands meant less cotton for me to pick. For the next month I would go to the fields at sunrise, drape a nine-foot cotton sack over my shoulder, and stare for a moment at an endless row of cotton, the stalks taller than I was, then plunge into them, lost as far as anyone could tell. And I would pick cotton, tearing the fluffy bolls from the stalks at a steady pace, stuffing them into the heavy sack, afraid to look down the row and be reminded of how endless it was, afraid to slow down because someone would notice. My fingers would bleed, my neck would burn, my back would hurt.

Yes, I wanted lots of help in the fields. Lots of hill people, lots of Mexicans.

13

Chapter 2

With the cotton waiting, my grandfather was not a patient man. Though he still drove the truck at its requisite speed, he was restless because the other fields along the road were getting picked, and ours were not. Our Mexicans were two days late. We parked again near Pop and Pearl's, and I followed him to the Tea Shoppe, where he argued with the man in charge of farm labor.

'Relax, Eli,' the man said. 'They'll be here any minute.'

He couldn't relax. We walked to the Black Oak gin on the edge of town, a long walk – but Pappy did not believe in wasting gasoline. Between six and eleven that morning, he'd picked two hundred pounds of cotton, yet he still walked so fast I had to jog to keep up.

The gravel lot of the gin was crowded with cotton trailers, some empty, others waiting for their harvest to be ginned. I waved again at the Montgomery twins as they were leaving, their trailer empty, headed home for another load.

The gin roared with the chorus of heavy machines at work. They were incredibly loud and dangerous. During each picking season, at least one worker would fall victim to some gruesome injury inside the cotton gin. I was scared of the machines, and when Pappy told me to wait outside, I was happy to do so. He walked by a group of field hands waiting for their trailers without so much as a nod. He had things on his mind.

I found a safe spot near the dock, where they wheeled out the finished bales and loaded them onto trailers headed for the Carolinas. At one end of the gin the freshly picked cotton was sucked from the trailers through a long pipe, twelve inches around; then it disappeared into the building where the machines worked on it. It emerged at the other end in neat square bales covered in burlap and strapped tightly with one-inch steel bands. A good gin produced perfect bales, ones that could be stacked like bricks.

A bale of cotton was worth a hundred and seventy-five dollars, give or take, depending on the markets. A good crop could produce a bale an acre. We rented eighty acres. Most farm kids could do the math.

In fact, the math was so easy you wondered why anyone would want to be a farmer. My mother made sure I understood the numbers. The two of us had already made a secret pact that I would never, under any circumstances, stay on the farm. I would finish all twelve grades and go play for the Cardinals.

Pappy and my father had borrowed fourteen thousand dollars in March from the owner of the gin. That was their crop loan, and the money was spent on seed, fertilizer, labor, and other expenses. So far we'd been lucky – the weather had been nearly perfect, and the crops looked good. If our luck continued through the picking, and the fields yielded a bale an acre, then the Chandler farming operation would break even. That was our goal.

But, like most farmers, Pappy and my father carried debt from the previous year. They owed the owner of the gin two thousand dollars from 1951, which had seen an average crop. They also owed money to the John Deere dealer in Jonesboro for parts, to Lance Brothers for fuel, to the Co-op for seed and supplies, and to Pop and Pearl Watson for groceries.

I certainly wasn't supposed to know about their crop loans and debts. But in the summertime my parents often sat on the front steps late into the night, waiting for the air to cool so they could sleep without sweating, and they talked. My bed was near a window by the porch. They thought I was sleeping, but I heard more than I should have.

Though I wasn't sure, I strongly suspected Pappy needed to borrow more money to pay the Mexicans and the hill people. I couldn't tell if he got the money or not. He was frowning when we walked to the gin, and he was frowning when we left it.

The hill people had been migrating from the Ozarks for decades to pick cotton. Many of them owned their own homes and land, and quite often they had nicer vehicles than the farmers who hired them for the harvest. They worked very hard, saved their money, and appeared to be as poor as we were.

By 1950 the migration had slowed. The postwar boom had finally trickled down to Arkansas, at least to some portions of the state, and the younger hill people didn't need the extra money as badly as their parents. They simply stayed at home. Picking cotton was not something anyone would volunteer to do. The farmers faced a labor shortage that gradually grew worse; then somebody discovered the Mexicans.

The first truckload arrived in Black Oak in 1951. We got six of them, including Juan, my buddy, who gave me my first tortilla. Juan and forty others had traveled three days in the back of a long trailer, packed in tightly together, with little food, no shade from the sun or shelter from the rain. They were weary and disoriented when they hit Main Street. Pappy said the trailer smelled worse than a cattle truck. Those who saw it told others, and before long the ladies at the Baptist and Methodist churches were openly complaining about the primitive manner in which the Mexicans had been transported.

My mother had been vocal, at least to my father. I heard them discuss it many times after the crops were in and the Mexicans had been shipped back. She wanted my father to talk to the other farmers and receive assurances from the man in charge of labor that those who collected the Mexicans and sent them to us would treat them better. She felt it was our duty as farmers to protect the laborers, a notion my father shared somewhat, though he seemed unenthusiastic about leading the charge.

17

Pappy didn't give a damn. Nor did the Mexicans; they just wanted to work.

The Mexicans finally arrived just after four o'clock. There had been rumors that they would be riding in a bus, and I certainly hoped this was true. I didn't want my parents straining at the issue for another winter. Nor did I want the Mexicans to be treated so poorly.

But they were in a trailer again, an old one with planks for sides and nothing over the top to protect them. It was true that cattle had it better.

They carefully hopped down out of the trailer bed and onto the street, three or four at a time, in one wave after another. They spilled forth, emptying in front of the Co-op, and gathered on the sidewalk in small bewildered groups. They stretched and bent and looked around as if they had landed on another planet. I counted sixty-two of them. To my great disappointment, Juan was not there.

They were several inches shorter than Pappy, very thin, and they all had black hair and brown skin. Each carried a little bag of clothing and supplies.

Pearl Watson stood on the sidewalk in front of her store, hands on hips, glaring. They were her customers, and she certainly didn't want them mistreated. I knew that before church on Sunday the ladies would be in an uproar again. And I knew my mother would quiz me as soon as we arrived home with our gang.

Harsh words erupted between the man in charge of labor and the driver of the truck. Somebody down in Texas had, in fact, promised that the

Mexicans would be shipped in a bus. This was the second load to arrive in a dirty trailer. Pappy never shied away from a fight, and I could tell he wanted to jump into the fray and finish off the truck driver. But he was also angry with the labor man, and I guess he saw no point in whipping both of them. We sat on the tailgate of our truck and waited for the dust to clear.

When the yelling stopped, the paperwork began. The Mexicans clung together on the sidewalk in front of the Co-op. Occasionally, they would glance at us and the other farmers who were gathering along Main Street. Word was out – the new batch had arrived.

Pappy got the first ten. The leader was Miguel. He appeared to be the oldest and, as I noticed from my initial inspection, he had the only cloth bag. The rest of them carried their belongings in paper sacks.

Miguel's English was passable, but not nearly as good as Juan's had been. I chatted him up while Pappy finished the paperwork. Miguel introduced me to the group. There was a Rico, a Roberto, a José, a Luis, a Pablo, and several I couldn't understand. I remembered from a year earlier that it would take a week to distinguish among them.

Although they were clearly exhausted, each of them seemed to make some effort to smile – except for one who sneered at me when I looked at him. He wore a western-style hat, which Miguel pointed to and said, 'He thinks he's a cowboy. So that's what we call him.' Cowboy was very young, and tall for a Mexican. His eyes were narrow and mean. He had a thin mustache that only added to the fierceness. He frightened me so badly that I gave a passing thought to telling Pappy. I certainly didn't want the man living on our farm for the weeks to come. But instead I just backed away.

Our group of Mexicans followed Pappy down the sidewalk to Pop and Pearl's. I trailed along, careful not to step close to Cowboy. Inside the store, I assumed my position near the cash register, where Pearl was waiting for someone to whisper to.

'They treat them like animals,' she said.

'Eli says they're just happy to be here,' I whispered back. My grandfather was waiting by the door, arms folded across his chest, watching the Mexicans gather what few items they needed. Miguel was rattling instructions to the rest of them.

Pearl was not about to criticize Eli Chandler. But she shot him a dirty look, though he didn't see it. Pappy wasn't concerned with either me or Pearl. He was fretting because the cotton wasn't getting picked.

'It's just awful,' she said. I could tell Pearl couldn't wait for us to clear out so she could find her church friends and again stir up the issue. Pearl was a Methodist.

As the Mexicans, holding their goods, drifted to the cash register, Miguel gave each name to Pearl, who in turn opened a charge account. She rang up the total, entered the amount in a ledger by the worker's name, then showed the entry to both Miguel and the customer. Instant credit, American style.

They bought flour and shortening to make

tortillas, lots of beans in both cans and bags, and rice. Nothing extra – no sugar or sweets, no vegetables. They ate as little as possible, because food cost money. Their goal was to save every cent they could and take it back home.

Of course, these poor fellas had no idea where they were going. They did not know that my mother was a devoted gardener who spent more time tending her vegetables than she did the cotton. They were quite lucky, because my mother believed that no one living within walking distance of our farm would ever go without food.

Cowboy was last in line, and when Pearl smiled at him, I thought he was going to spit on her. Miguel stayed close. He'd just spent three days in the back of a trailer with the boy and probably knew all about him.

I said good-bye to Pearl for the second time that day, which was odd because I usually saw her only once a week.

Pappy led the Mexicans to the truck. They got into the bed and sat shoulder to shoulder, feet and legs intertwined. They were silent and stared blankly ahead as if they had no idea where their journey would end.

The old truck strained with the load but eventually leveled out at thirty-seven, and Pappy almost smiled. It was late in the afternoon, and the weather was hot and dry, perfect for picking. Between the Spruills and the Mexicans we finally had enough hands to harvest our crop. I reached into my pocket, and pulled out the other half of my Tootsie Roll.

Long before we arrived at our house, we saw

smoke and then a tent. We lived on a dirt road that was very dusty for most of the year, and Pappy was just puttering along so the Mexicans wouldn't get choked.

'What's that?' I asked.

'Looks like a tent of some sort,' Pappy said.

It was situated near the road, at the far end of our front yard, under a pin oak that was a hundred years old, very near the spot where home plate belonged. We slowed even more as we approached our mailbox. The Spruills had taken control of half our front yard. The large tent was dirty white with a pointed roof and was erected with a mismatched collection of hand-whittled sticks and metal poles. Two sides of the tent were open, and I could see boxes and blankets lying on the ground under the roof. I could also see Tally napping inside.

Their truck was parked beside it, and another canvas of some sort had been rigged over its bed. It was anchored with baling rope staked to the ground so that the truck couldn't move without first getting unhitched. Their old trailer had been partially unloaded, its boxes and burlap bags scattered on the grass as if a storm had hit.

Mrs. Spruill was tending a fire, hence the smoke. For some reason, she had chosen a slightly bare spot near the end of the yard. It was the exact spot where Pappy or my father squatted almost every afternoon and caught my fastballs and my curves. I wanted to cry. I would never forgive Mrs. Spruill for this.

'I thought you told them to set up out behind the silo,' I said.

'I did,' Pappy answered. He slowed the truck

22

almost to a stop, then turned into our place. The silo was out back, near the barn, a sufficient distance from our house. We'd had hill people camping back there before – never in the front yard.

He parked under another pin oak that was only seventy years old, according to my grandmother. It was the smallest of the three that shaded our house and yard. We rolled to a stop near the house, in the same dry ruts Pappy'd parked in for decades. Both my mother and grandmother were waiting at the kitchen steps.

Ruth, my grandmother, did not like the fact that the hill people had laid claim to our front yard. Pappy and I knew this before we got out of the truck. She had her hands on her hips.

My mother was eager to examine the Mexicans and ask me about their traveling conditions. She watched them pile out of the truck as she walked to me and squeezed my shoulder.

'Ten of them,' she said.

'Yes ma'am.'

Gran met Pappy at the front of the truck and said, quietly but sternly, 'Why are those people in our front yard?'

'I asked them to set up by the silo,' Pappy said, never one to back down, not even from his wife. 'I don't know why they picked that spot.'

'Can you ask them to move?'

'I cannot. If they pack up, they'll leave. You know how hill people are.'

And that was the end of Gran's questions. They were not about to argue in front of me and ten new Mexicans. She walked away, toward the house, shaking her head in disapproval. Pappy honestly didn't care where the hill people camped. They appeared to be able-bodied and willing to work, and nothing else mattered to him.

I suspected Gran was not that concerned either. The picking was so crucial that we would've taken in a chain gang if they could've averaged three hundred pounds of cotton a day.

The Mexicans followed Pappy off to the barn, which was 352 feet from the back porch steps. Past the chicken coop, the water pump, the clothes-lines, and the toolshed, past a sugar maple that would turn bright red in October. My father had helped me measure the exact distance one day last January. It seemed like a mile to me. From home plate to the left field wall in Sportsman's Park, where the Cardinals played, was 350 feet, and every time Stan Musial hit a home run I would sit on the steps the next day and marvel at the distance. In mid-July he'd hit a ball 400 feet against the Braves. Pappy had said, 'He hit it over the barn, Luke.'

For two days afterward, I'd sat on the steps and dreamed of hitting 'em over the barn.

When the Mexicans were past the toolshed, my mother said, 'They look very tired.'

'They rode in a trailer, sixty-two of them,' I said, eager, for some reason, to help stir things up.

'I was afraid of that.'

'An old trailer. Old and dirty. Pearl's already mad about it.'

'It won't happen again,' she said, and I knew that my father was about to get an earful. 'Run along and help your grandfather.'

I'd spent most of the previous two weeks in the barn, alone with my mother, sweeping and cleaning the loft, trying to make a home for the Mexicans. Most of the farmers put them in abandoned tenant houses or barns. There'd been a rumor that Ned Shackleford three miles south had made his live with the chickens.

Not so on the Chandler farm. For lack of another shelter, the Mexicans would be forced to live in the loft of our barn, but there wouldn't be a speck of dirt anywhere to be found. And it would have a pleasant smell. For a year my mother had gathered old blankets and quilts for them to sleep on.

I slipped into the barn, but stayed below, next to Isabel's stall. She was our milk cow. Pappy claimed his life had been saved in the First War by a young French girl named Isabel, and to honor the memory, he named our Jersey cow after her. My grandmother never believed that story.

I could hear them up in the loft, moving around, settling in. Pappy was talking to Miguel, who was impressed with how nice and clean the loft was. Pappy took the compliments as if he and he alone had done the scrubbing.

In fact, he and Gran had been skeptical of my mother's efforts to provide a decent place for the laborers to sleep. My mother had been raised on a small farm at the very edge of Black Oak, so she was almost a town girl. She actually grew up with kids who were too good to pick cotton. She never walked to school – her father drove her. She'd been to Memphis three times before she married my father. She'd been raised in a painted house.

Chapter 3

We Chandlers rented our land from Mr. Vogel of Jonesboro, a man I'd never seen. His name was rarely mentioned, but when it did slip into a conversation, it was uttered with respect and awe. I thought he was the richest man in the world.

Pappy and Gran had been renting the land since before the Great Depression, which arrived early and stayed late in rural Arkansas. After thirty years of backbreaking labor, they had managed to purchase from Mr. Vogel the house and the three acres around it. They also owned the John Deere tractor, two disks, a seed planter, a cotton trailer, a flatbed trailer, two mules, a wagon, and the truck. My father had a vague agreement that gave him an ownership interest in some of these assets. The land deed was in the names of Eli and Ruth Chandler.

The only farmers who made money were those who owned their land. The renters, like us, tried to break even. The sharecroppers had it the worst and were doomed to eternal poverty.

My father's goal was to own forty acres of land, free and clear. My mother's dreams were tucked

26

away, only to be shared with me as I grew older. But I already knew she longed to leave the rural life and was determined that I would not farm. By the time I was seven, she had made a believer out of me.

When she was satisfied that the Mexicans were being properly situated, she sent me to find my father. It was late, the sun was falling beyond the trees that lined the St. Francis River, and it was time for him to weigh his cotton sack for the final time and call it a day.

I walked barefoot along a dirt path between two fields, looking for him. The soil was dark and rich, good Delta farmland that produced enough to keep you tied to it. Ahead, I saw the cotton trailer, and I knew he was working his way toward it.

Jesse Chandler was the elder son of Pappy and Gran. His younger brother, Ricky, was nineteen and fighting somewhere in Korea. There were two sisters who'd fled the farm as soon as they'd finished high school.

My father didn't flee. He was determined to be a farmer like his father and grandfather, except he'd be the first Chandler to own his land. I didn't know if he had dreams of a life away from the fields. Like my grandfather, he had been an excellent baseball player, and I'm sure at one point he'd dreamed of major league glory. But he took a German bullet through his thigh in Anzio in 1944, and his baseball career came to an end.

He walked with a very slight limp, but then so did most people who toiled in the cotton patch.

I stopped at the trailer, which was almost empty. It sat on a narrow cotton road, waiting to be filled.

27

I climbed up on it. Around me, on all sides, neat rows of green and brown stalks stretched to the tree lines that bordered our land. At the top of the stalks, puffy bolls of cotton were popping forth. The cotton was coming to life by the minute, so when I stepped on the back of the trailer and surveyed the fields, I saw an ocean of white. The fields were silent – no voices, no tractor engines, no cars on the road. For a moment, hanging on to the trailer, I could almost understand why my father wanted to be a farmer.

I could barely see his old straw hat in the distance as he moved between rows. I jumped down and hurried to meet him. With dusk approaching, the gaps between the rows were even darker. Because the sun and rain had cooperated, the leaves were full and thick and weaving together so that they brushed against me as I walked quickly toward my father.

'Is that you, Luke?' he called, knowing full well that no one else would be coming to find him.

'Yes sir!' I answered, moving to the voice. 'Mom says it's time to quit!'

'Oh she does?'

'Yes sir.' I missed him by one row. I cut through the stalks, and there he was, bent at the waist, both hands moving through the leaves, adroitly plucking the cotton and stuffing it into the nearly full sack draped over his shoulder. He'd been in the fields since sunrise, breaking only for lunch.

'Did y'all find some help?' he asked without looking at me.

'Yes sir,' I said proudly. 'Mexicans and hill people.'

'How many Mexicans?'

'Ten,' I said, as if I'd personally rounded them up.

'That's good. Who are the hill people?'

'The Spruills. I forgot where they're from.'

'How many?' He finished a stalk and crept forward, with his heavy sack inching along behind him.

'A whole truckload. It's hard to tell. Gran's mad because they've set up camp in the front yard, even got a fire goin' where home plate is. Pappy told 'em to set up by the silo. I heard him. I don't think they're real smart.'

'Don't be sayin' that.'

'Yes sir. Anyway, Gran's not too pleased.'

'She'll be all right. We need the hill people.'

'Yes sir. That's what Pappy said. But I hate they've messed up home plate.'

'Pickin' is more important than baseball these days.'

'I guess.' Maybe in his opinion.

'How are the Mexicans?'

'Not too good. They stuffed 'em in a trailer again, and Mom's not too happy about it.'

His hands stopped for a second as he considered another winter of squabbles. 'They're just happy to be here,' he said, his hands moving again.

I took a few steps toward the trailer in the distance, then turned to watch him again. 'Tell that to Mom.'

He gave me a look before saying, 'Did Juan make it?'

'No sir.'

'Sorry to hear that.'

29

I'd talked about Juan for a year. He had promised me last fall that he'd be back. 'That's okay,' I said. 'The new guy is Miguel. He's real nice.'

I told him about the trip to town, how we found the Spruills, about Tally and Trot and the large young man on the tailgate, then back to town where Pappy argued with the man in charge of labor, then the trip to the gin, then about the Mexicans. I did all the talking because my day had certainly been more eventful than his.

At the trailer, he lifted the straps of his cotton sack and hung them over the hook at the bottom of the scales. The needle settled on fifty-eight pounds. He scribbled this in a ragged old ledger wired to the trailer.

'How much?' I asked when he closed the book.

'Four-seventy.'

'A triple,' I said.

He shrugged and said, 'Not bad.'

Five hundred pounds equaled a home run, something he accomplished every other day. He squatted and said, 'Hop on.'

I jumped on his back, and we started for the house. His shirt and overalls were soaked with sweat, and had been all day, but his arms were like steel. Pop Watson told me that Jesse Chandler once hit a baseball that landed in the center of Main Street. Pop and Mr. Snake Wilcox, the barber, measured it the next day and began telling people that it had traveled, on the fly, 440 feet. But a hostile opinion quickly emerged from the Tea Shoppe, where Mr. Junior Barnhart claimed, rather loudly, that the ball had bounced at least once before hitting Main Street.

Pop and Junior went weeks without speaking to each other. My mother verified the argument, but not the home run.

She was waiting for us by the water pump. My father sat on a bench and removed his boots and socks. Then he unsnapped his overalls and took off his shirt.

One of my chores at dawn was to fill a washtub with water and leave it in the sun all day so there'd be warm water for my father every afternoon. My mother dipped a hand towel in the tub and gently rubbed his neck with it.

She had grown up in a house full of girls, and had been raised in part by a couple of prissy old aunts. I think they bathed more than farm people, and her passion for cleanliness had rubbed off on my father. I got a complete scrubbing every Saturday afternoon, whether I needed it or not.

When he was washed up and dried off, she handed him a fresh shirt. It was time to welcome our guests. In a large basket, my mother had assembled a collection of her finest vegetables, all handpicked, of course, and washed within the past two hours. Indian tomatoes, Vidalia onions, red-skin potatoes, green and red bell peppers, ears of corn. We carried it to the back of the barn, where the Mexicans were resting and talking and waiting for their small fire to burn low so they could make their tortillas. I introduced my father to Miguel, who in turn presented some of his gang.

Cowboy sat alone, his back to the barn, making no move to acknowledge us. I could see him watching my mother from under the brim of his hat. It frightened me for a second; then I realized Jesse Chandler would snap Cowboy's skinny little neck if he made one wrong move.

We had learned a lot from the Mexicans the year before. They did not eat butter beans, snap beans, squash, eggplant, or turnips, but preferred tomatoes, onions, potatoes, peppers, and corn. And they would never ask for food from our garden. It had to be offered.

My mother explained to Miguel and the other men that our garden was full and that she would bring them vegetables every other day. They were not expected to pay for the food. It was part of the package.

We took another basket to the front of the house, where Camp Spruill seemed to be expanding by the hour. They had crept even farther across the yard, and there were more cardboard boxes and burlap sacks strewn about. They'd laid three planks across a box on one end and a barrel on the other to make a table, and they were crowded around it eating dinner when we approached them. Mr. Spruill got to his feet and shook my father's hand.

'Leon Spruill,' he said with food on his lip. 'Nice to meet you.'

'Happy to have you folks here,' my father said pleasantly.

'Thank you,' Mr. Spruill said, pulling up his pants. 'This here is my wife, Lucy.' She smiled and kept chewing slowly.

'This is my daughter, Tally,' he said, pointing.

When she looked at me, I could feel my cheeks burning.

'And these are my nephews, Bo and Dale,' he said, nodding to the two boys who'd been resting on the mattress when they had stopped on the highway. They were teenagers, probably fifteen or so. And sitting next to them was the giant I'd first seen on the tailgate, half-asleep.

'This is my son Hank,' Mr. Spruill said. Hank was at least twenty and was certainly old enough to stand up and shake hands. But he kept eating. Both jaws were ballooned with what appeared to be corn bread. 'He eats a lot,' Mr. Spruill said, and we tried to laugh.

'And this here is Trot,' he said. Trot never looked up. His limp left arm hung by his side. He clutched a spoon with his right hand. His standing in the family was left undeclared.

My mother presented the large basket of vegetables, and for a second, Hank stopped his chomping and looked up at the fresh supply. Then he returned to his beans. 'The tomatoes and corn are especially good this year,' my mother was saying. 'And there's plenty. Just let me know what you like.'

Tally chewed slowly and stared at me. I studied my feet.

'That's mighty nice of you, ma'am,' Mr. Spruill said, and Mrs. Spruill added a quick thanks. There was no danger of the Spruills going without food, not that they had missed any meals. Hank was burly with a thick chest that narrowed only slightly where it met his neck. Mr. and Mrs. Spruill were both stocky and appeared strong. Bo and Dale were lean but not thin. Tally, of course, was perfectly proportioned. Only Trot was gaunt and skinny.

'Didn't mean to interrupt dinner,' my father said, and we began backing away.

'Thanks again,' Mr. Spruill said.

I knew from experience that within a short time we would know more than we wanted about the Spruills. They would share our land, our water, our outhouse. We would take them vegetables from the garden, milk from Isabel, eggs from the coop. We would invite them to town on Saturday and to church on Sunday. We would work beside them in the fields from sunrise until almost dark. And when the picking was over, they would leave and return to the hills. The trees would turn, winter would come, and we would spend many cold nights huddled around the fire telling stories about the Spruills.

Dinner was potatoes, sliced thin and fried, boiled okra, corn on the cob, and hot corn bread – but no meats because it was almost fall, and because we'd had a roast the day before. Gran fried chicken twice a week, but never on Wednesdays. My mother's garden was producing enough tomatoes and onions to feed all of Black Oak, so she sliced a platter of them for every meal.

The kitchen was small and hot. A round oscillating fan rattled away on top of the refrigerator and tried to keep the air circulating as my mother and grandmother prepared dinner. Their movements were slow but steady. They were tired, and it was too hot to hurry up.

34

They were not particularly fond of each other, but both were determined to exist in peace. I never heard them argue, never heard my mother say anything bad about her mother-in-law. They lived in the same house, cooked the same meals, did the same laundry, picked the same cotton. With so much work to do, who had time to bicker?

But Gran had been born and bred deep in the cotton patch. She knew she would be buried in the soil she worked. My mother longed for an escape.

Through daily ritual, they had silently negotiated a method to their kitchen work. Gran hovered near the stove, checking the corn bread, stirring the potatoes, okra, and corn. My mother kept to the sink, where she peeled tomatoes and stacked the dirty dishes. I studied this from the kitchen table, where I sat every night and peeled cucumbers with a paring knife. They both loved music, and occasionally one would hum while the other sang softly. The music kept the tension buried.

But not tonight. They were too preoccupied to sing and hum. My mother was stewing over the fact that the Mexicans had been hauled in like cattle. My grandmother was pouting because the Spruills had invaded our front yard.

At exactly six o'clock, Gran removed her apron and sat across from me. The end of the table was flush against the wall and served as a large shelf that accumulated things. In the center was an RCA radio in a walnut casing. She turned on the switch and smiled at me.

The CBS news was delivered to us by Edward R. Murrow, live from New York. For a week there'd been heavy fighting in Pyonggang, near the Sea of Japan, and from an old map that Gran kept on her night table, we knew that Ricky's infantry division was in the area. His last letter had arrived two weeks earlier. It was a quickly written note, but between the lines it gave the impression that he was in the thick of things.

When Mr. Murrow got past his lead story about a spat with the Russians, he started on Korea, and Gran closed her eyes. She folded her hands together, put both index fingers to her lips, and waited.

I wasn't sure what she was waiting for. Mr. Murrow was not going to announce to the nation that Ricky Chandler was dead or alive.

My mother listened, too. She stood with her back to the sink, wiping her hands with a towel, staring blankly at the table. This happened almost every night in the summer and fall of 1952.

Peace efforts had been started, then abandoned. The Chinese withdrew, then attacked again. Through Mr. Murrow's reports and Ricky's letters, we lived the war.

Pappy and my father would not listen to the news. They busied themselves outside, at the toolshed or the water pump, doing small chores that could've waited, talking about the crops, searching for something to worry about besides Ricky. Both had fought in wars. They didn't need Mr. Murrow in New York to read some correspondent's cable from Korea and tell the nation what was occurring in one battle or the next. They knew.

In any case, it was a short report that night about Korea, and this was taken in our little farmhouse as something good. Mr. Murrow moved along to other matters, and Gran finally smiled at me. 'Ricky's okay,' she said, rubbing my hand. 'He'll be home before you know it.'

She'd earned the right to believe this. She had waited for Pappy during the First War, and she had prayed long distance for my father and his wounds during the Second. Her boys always came home, and Ricky would not let us down.

She turned the radio off. The potatoes and okra needed her attention. She and my mother returned to cooking, and we waited for Pappy to walk through the back screen door.

I think Pappy expected the worst from the war. The Chandlers had been lucky so far in the century. He wouldn't listen to the news, but he wanted to know if things looked good or bad. When he heard the radio go off, he usually made his way into the kitchen. That evening he stopped at the table and tousled my hair. Gran looked at him. She smiled and said, 'No bad news.'

My mother told me that Gran and Pappy often slept less than an hour or two before waking and worrying about their younger son. Gran was convinced Ricky was coming home. Pappy was not.

At six-thirty, we sat around the table, held hands, and gave thanks for all the food and all the blessings. Pappy led the praying, at least over dinner. He thanked God for the Mexicans and for the Spruills, and for the fine crops around us. I prayed quietly, and only for Ricky. I was grateful for the food, but it didn't seem nearly as important as he did.

The adults ate slowly and talked about nothing but cotton. I was not expected to add much to the conversation. Gran in particular was of the opinion that children should be seen and not heard.

I wanted to go to the barn and check out the Mexicans. And I wanted to sneak around front and maybe catch a glimpse of Tally. My mother suspected something, and when we finished eating, she told me to help her with the dishes. I would've preferred a whipping, but I had no choice.

We drifted to the front porch for our nightly sitting. It seemed like a simple enough ritual, but it wasn't. First we would let the meal settle, then we'd tend to baseball. We would turn on the radio and Harry Caray at KMOX in St. Louis would deliver the play-by-play of our beloved Cardinals. My mother and grandmother would shell peas or butter beans. Any loose ends of dinner gossip would be wrapped up. Of course, the crops were fretted over.

But that night it was raining two hundred miles away in St. Louis, and the game had been canceled. I sat on the steps, holding my Rawlings glove, squeezing my baseball inside it, watching the shadows of the Spruills in the distance and wondering how anyone could be so thoughtless as to build a fire on home plate.

The outside radio was a small General Electric that my father had bought in Boston when he left the hospital during the war. Its sole purpose was to bring the Cardinals into our lives. We seldom missed a game. It sat on a wooden crate near the creaking swing where the men rested. My mother and grandmother sat in padded wooden chairs not far away, on the other side of the porch, shelling peas. I was in the middle, on the front steps.

Before the Mexicans arrived, we'd had a portable fan we put near the screen door. Each night it would hum away quietly and manage to push the heavy air around just enough to make things bearable. But, thanks to my mother, it was now in the loft of our barn. This had caused friction, though most of it had been kept away from me.

And so the night was very quiet – no ball game, no fan – just the slow talk of weary farm people waiting for the temperature to drop a few more degrees.

The rain in St. Louis inspired the men to worry about the weather. The rivers and creeks in the Arkansas Delta flooded with frustrating regularity. Every four or five years they left their banks and washed away the crops. I couldn't remember a flood, but I'd heard so much about them I felt like a veteran. We would pray for weeks for a good rain. One would come, and as soon as the ground was soaked, Pappy and my father would start watching the clouds and telling flood stories.

The Spruills were winding down. Their voices were fading. I could see their shadows moving around the tents. Their fire flickered low, then died.

All was quiet on the Chandler farm. We had hill people. We had Mexicans. The cotton was waiting.

Chapter 4

At some point in the vast darkness of the night, Pappy, our human alarm clock, awoke, put on his boots, and began stomping around the kitchen making the first pot of coffee. The house was not large – three bedrooms, a kitchen, a living room – and it was so old the plank floors sagged in places. If one person chose to wake up the rest, he or she could certainly do so.

I was allowed to stay in bed until my father came after me. It was difficult to sleep, though, with all those people on the farm and all that cotton to pick. I was already awake when he shook me and said it was time to go. I dressed quickly and met him on the back porch.

There was no hint of sunrise as we walked across the backyard, the dew soaking our boots. We stopped at the chicken coop, where he bent low and slipped inside. I was told to wait in front of it, since last month while gathering eggs in the darkness, I'd stepped on a huge rat snake and cried for two days. At first my father had not been sympathetic; rat snakes are harmless and just a part

40

of life on the farm. My mother, however, intervened with a fury, and for the time being, I was not permitted to collect eggs alone.

My father filled a straw bowl with a dozen eggs and handed it to me. We headed to the barn, where Isabel was waiting. Now that we'd roused the chickens, the roosters began crowing.

The only light came from a pale bulb hanging from the hayloft. The Mexicans were awake. A fire had been lit behind the barn, and they were huddled near it as if they were cold. I was already warm from the humidity.

I could milk the cow, and on most mornings that chore belonged to me. But the rat snake still had me frightened, plus we were in a hurry because we had to be in the fields by sunrise. My father rapidly milked two gallons, which would've taken me half the morning. We delivered the food to the kitchen, where the women were in charge. The ham was already in the skillet, its rich aroma thick in the air.

Breakfast was fresh eggs, milk, salt-cured ham, and hot biscuits, with sorghum optional. As they cooked, I settled into my chair, ran my fingers across the damp, checkered oilcloth, and waited for my cup of coffee. It was the one vice my mother allowed me.

Gran placed the cup and saucer before me, then the sugar bowl and the fresh cream. I doctored the coffee until it was as sweet as a malt, then sipped it slowly.

At breakfast, conversation in the kitchen was held to a minimum. It was exciting to have so many strangers on our farm for the harvest, but the

41

enthusiasm was dampened by the reality that we would spend most of the next twelve hours unshielded in the sun, bent over, picking until our fingers bled.

We ate quickly, the roosters making a ruckus in the side yard. My grandmother's biscuits were heavy and perfectly round, and so warm that when I carefully placed a slice of butter in the center of one, it melted instantly. I watched the yellow cream soak into the biscuit, then took a bite. My mother conceded that Ruth Chandler made the best biscuits she'd ever tasted. I wanted so badly to eat two or three, like my father, but I simply couldn't hold them. My mother ate one, same as Gran. Pappy had two, my father three. Several hours later, in the middle of the morning, we would stop for a moment under the shade of a tree or beside the cotton trailer to eat the leftover biscuits.

Breakfast was slow in the winter because there was little else to do. The pace was somewhat faster in the spring when we were planting, and in the summer when we were chopping. But during the fall harvest, with the sun about to catch us, we ate with a purpose.

There was some chatter about the weather. The rain in St. Louis that had canceled last night's Cardinals game was weighing on Pappy's mind. St. Louis was so far away that no one at the table, except for Pappy, had ever been there, yet the city's weather was now a crucial element in the harvest of our crops. My mother listened patiently. I didn't say a word.

My father had been reading the almanac and

offered the opinion that the weather would cooperate throughout the month of September. But mid-October looked ominous. Bad weather was on the way. It was imperative that for the next six weeks we work until we dropped. The harder we worked, the harder the Mexicans and the Spruills would work. This was my father's version of a pep talk.

The subject of day laborers came up. These were locals who went from farm to farm looking for the best deal. Most were town people we knew. During the previous fall, Miss Sophie Turner, who taught fifth and sixth grades, had bestowed a great honor on us when she had chosen our fields to pick in.

We needed all the day laborers we could get, but they generally picked wherever they wanted.

When Pappy finished his last bite, he thanked his wife and my mother for the good food and left them to clean up the mess. I strutted onto the back porch with the men.

Our house faced south, the barn and crops were to the north and west, and to the east I saw the first hint of orange peeking over the flat farmland of the Arkansas Delta. The sun was coming, undaunted by clouds. My shirt was already sticking to my back.

A flatbed trailer was hitched to the John Deere, and the Mexicans had already gotten on. My dad went up to speak to Miguel. 'Good morning. How did you sleep? Are you ready to work?' Pappy went to fetch the Spruills.

I had a spot, a nook between the fender and the seat of the John Deere, and I had spent hours there firmly grasping the metal pole holding the umbrella that would cover the driver, either Pappy or my father, when we chugged through the fields plowing or planting or spreading fertilizer. I took my place and looked down at the crowded trailer, Mexicans on one side, Spruills on the other. At that moment I felt very privileged because I got to ride on the tractor, and the tractor belonged to us. My haughtiness, however, would vanish shortly, because all things were level among the cotton stalks.

I'd been curious as to whether poor Trot would go to the fields. Picking required two good arms. Trot had only one, as far as I'd been able to determine. But there he was, sitting at the edge of the trailer, his back to everyone else, feet hanging over the side, alone in his own world. And there was Tally, who didn't acknowledge me, but just looked into the distance.

Without a word, Pappy popped the clutch, and the tractor and trailer lurched forward. I checked to make sure no one fell off. Through the kitchen window I could see my mother's face, watching us as she cleaned the dishes. She would finish her chores, spend an hour in her garden, then join us for a hard day in the fields. Same for Gran. No one rested when the cotton was ready.

We puttered past the barn, the diesel thumping, the trailer creaking, and turned south toward the lower forty, a tract next to Siler's Creek. We always picked the lower forty first because the floods would start there.

We had the lower forty and the back forty. Eighty acres was no small farming operation.

In a few minutes we arrived at the cotton trailer,

and Pappy stopped the tractor. Before I jumped down, I looked to the east and saw the lights of our house, less than a mile away. Behind it, the sky was coming to life with streaks of orange and yellow. There wasn't a cloud to be seen, and this meant no floods in the near future. It also meant no shelter from the scorching sun.

Tally said, 'Good morning, Luke,' as she walked by.

I managed to return her greeting. She smiled at me as if she knew some secret that she would never tell.

Pappy didn't give an orientation, and none was needed. Choose a row in either direction, and start picking. No chitchat, no stretching of the muscles, no predictions about the weather. Without a word the Mexicans draped their long cotton sacks over their shoulders, lined up, and went south. The Arkansans went north.

For a second, I stood there in the semidarkness of an already hot September morning, staring down a very long, straight row of cotton, a row that had somehow been assigned to me. I thought, I'll never get to the end of it, and I was suddenly tired.

I had cousins in Memphis, sons and daughters of my father's two sisters, and they had never picked cotton. City kids, in the suburbs, in nice little homes with indoor plumbing. They returned to Arkansas for funerals – sometimes for Thanksgiving. As I stared at my endless row of cotton, I thought of those cousins.

Two things motivated me to work. First, and most important, I had my father on one side and my grandfather on the other. Neither tolerated

45

laziness. They had worked the fields when they were children, and I would certainly do the same. Second, I got paid for picking, same as the other field hands. A dollar-sixty for a hundred pounds. And I had big plans for the money.

'Let's go,' my father said firmly in my direction. Pappy was already settled among the stalks, ten feet into his row. I could see his outline and his straw hat. I could hear the Spruills a few rows over chatting among themselves. Hill people sang a lot, and it was not uncommon to hear them crooning some low, mournful tune as they picked. Tally laughed about something, her luxurious voice echoing across the fields.

She was only ten years older than I was.

Pappy's father had fought in the Civil War. His name was Jeremiah Chandler, and according to family lore, he'd almost single-handedly won the Battle of Shiloh. When Jeremiah's second wife died, he took a third, a local maiden thirty years his junior. A few years later she gave birth to Pappy.

A thirty-year gap for Jeremiah and his bride. Ten for Tally and me. It could work.

With solemn resolve, I flung my nine-foot cotton sack across my back, the strap over my right shoulder, and attacked the first boll of cotton. It was damp from the dew, and that was one reason we started so early. For the first hour or so, before the sun got too high and baked everything, the cotton was soft and gentle to our hands. Later, after it was dumped into the trailer, it would dry and could be easily ginned. Cotton soaked with rainwater could not be ginned, something every farmer had learned the hard way.

I picked as fast as possible, with both hands, and stuffed the cotton into the sack. I had to be careful, though. Either Pappy or my father, or possibly both of them, would inspect my row at some point during the morning. If I left too much cotton in the bolls, then I would be reprimanded. The severity of the scolding would be determined by how close my mother was to me at that particular moment.

As deftly as I could, I worked my small hands through the maze of stalks, grabbing the bolls, avoiding if possible the burrs because they were pointed and could draw blood. I bobbed and weaved and inched along, falling farther behind my father and Pappy.

Our cotton was so thick that the stalks from each row intertwined. They brushed against my face. After the incident with the rat snake, I watched every step around our farm, especially in the fields, since there were cottonmouths near the river. I'd seen plenty of them from the back of the John Deere when we were plowing and planting.

Before long I was all alone, a child left behind by those with quicker hands and stronger backs. The sun was a bright orange ball, rising fast into position to sear the land for another day. When my father and Pappy were out of sight, I decided to take my first break. Tally was the nearest person. She was five rows over and fifty feet in front of me. I could barely see her faded denim bonnet above the cotton.

Under the shade of the stalks, I stretched out on my cotton sack, which after an hour was depressingly flat. There were a few soft lumps, but nothing

47

significant. The year before, I'd been expected to pick fifty pounds a day, and my fear was that this quota was about to be increased.

Lying on my back, I watched through the stalks the perfectly clear sky, hoped for clouds, and dreamed of money. Every August we received by mail the latest edition of the Sears, Roebuck catalog, and few events were more momentous, at least in my life. It came in a brown wrapper, all the way from Chicago, and was required by Gran to be kept at the end of the kitchen table, next to the radio and the family Bible. The women studied the clothes and the home furnishings. The men scrutinized the tools and auto supplies. But I dwelt on the important sections – toys and sporting goods. I made secret Christmas lists in my mind. I was afraid to write down all the things I dreamed of. Someone might find such a list and think I was either hopelessly greedy or mentally ill.

On page 308 of the current catalog was an incredible ad for baseball warm-up jackets. There was one for almost every professional team. What made the ad so amazing was that the young man doing the modeling was wearing a Cardinals jacket, and it was in color. A bright Cardinal red, in some type of shiny fabric, white buttons down the front. Of all the teams, someone with uncanny wisdom at Sears, Roebuck had picked the Cardinals to display.

It cost $7.50, plus shipping. And it came in children's sizes, which presented another quandary because I was bound to grow and I wanted to wear the jacket for the rest of my life.

Ten days of hard labor, and I'd have enough

money to purchase the jacket. I was certain nothing like it had ever been seen in Black Oak, Arkansas. My mother said it was a bit gaudy, whatever that meant. My father said I needed boots. Pappy thought it was a waste of money, but I could tell he secretly admired it.

At the first hint of cool weather I would wear the jacket to school every day, and to church on Sundays. I would wear it to town on Saturdays, a bolt of bright red amid the drearily clad throngs loitering on the sidewalks. I would wear it everywhere, and I'd be the envy of every kid in Black Oak (and a lot of adults, too).

They would never have the chance to play for the Cardinals. I, on the other hand, would become famous in St. Louis. It was important to start looking the part.

'Lucas!' a stern voice shot through the stillness of the fields. Stalks were snapping nearby.

'Yes sir,' I said, jumping to my feet, keeping low, thrusting my hands at the nearest bolls of cotton.

My father was suddenly standing over me. 'What are you doing?' he asked.

'I had to pee,' I said, without stopping my hands.'

'It took a long time,' he said, unconvinced.

'Yes sir. It's all that coffee.' I looked up at him. He knew the truth.

'Try to keep up,' he said, turning around and walking away.

'Yes sir,' I said to his back, knowing I could never keep up with him.

A twelve-foot sack like the adults used held about sixty pounds of cotton, so by eight-thirty or nine o'clock the men were ready to weigh. Pappy and my father were in charge of the scales, which hung from the end of the trailer. The sacks were hoisted upward to one of them. The straps were looped over the hooks at the bottom of the scales. The needle sprang around like the long hand of a large clock. Everyone could see how much each person picked.

Pappy recorded the data in a small book near the scales. Then the cotton sack was shoved even higher and emptied into the trailer. No time for a rest. You caught the empty sack when it was tossed down. You selected another row and disappeared for another two hours.

I was in the middle of an endless row of cotton, sweating, boiling in the sun, bending at the shoulders, trying to be fast with my hands, and stopping occasionally to monitor the movements of Pappy and my father so that maybe I could arrange another nap. But there was never an opportunity to drop my sack. Instead, I plowed ahead, working hard, waiting for the sack to get heavy, and wondering for the first time if I really needed the Cardinals jacket.

After an eternity alone in the fields, I heard the John Deere fire up, and I knew it was time for lunch. Though I had not completed my first row, I didn't really care about my lack of progress. We met at the tractor, and I saw Trot curled in a knot on the flat deck trailer. Mrs. Spruill and Tally were patting him. At first I thought he might be dead, then he moved a little. 'The heat got him,' my father whispered to me, as he took my sack and whirled it around over his shoulder as if it were empty.

50

I followed him to the scales, where Pappy quickly weighed it. All that back-numbing labor for thirty-one pounds of cotton.

When the Mexicans and Spruills were accounted for, we all headed for the house. Lunch was at noon sharp. My mother and Gran had left the fields an hour earlier to prepare it.

From my perch on the John Deere, I clutched the umbrella stand with my scratched and sore left hand and watched the field workers bounce along. Mr. and Mrs. Spruill were holding Trot, who was still lifeless and pale. Tally sat nearby, her long legs stretched across the deck of the trailer. Bo, Dale, and Hank seemed unconcerned about poor Trot. Like everyone else, they were hot and tired and ready for a break.

On the other side, the Mexicans sat in a row, shoulder to shoulder, feet hanging off the side and almost dragging the ground. A couple of them wore no shoes or boots.

When we were nearly at the barn, I saw something that at first I couldn't believe. Cowboy, sitting at the very end of the short trailer, turned quickly, and glanced at Tally. She seemed to have been waiting for him to look, because she gave him one of her pretty little smiles, similar to the ones I'd been getting. Though he didn't return the smile, it was obvious he was pleased.

It happened in a flash, and nobody saw it but me.

Chapter 5

According to Gran and my mother, conspiring together, the early afternoon nap was crucial to the proper growth of a child. I believed this only when we were picking cotton. For the rest of the year, I fought a nap with as much vigor as I put into planning my baseball career.

But during the harvest, everybody rested after lunch. The Mexicans ate quickly and sprawled under a maple tree near the barn. The Spruills ate leftover ham and biscuits and likewise found shade.

I wasn't allowed to use my bed because I was dirty from the fields, so I slept on the floor in my bedroom. I was tired and stiff from my labors. I dreaded the afternoon session because it always seemed longer, and it was certainly hotter. I drifted away immediately and was even stiffer when I awoke a half hour later.

Trot was causing concern in the front yard. Gran, who fancied herself as some sort of country medicine woman, had gone to check on him, no doubt with the intention of whipping up one of her dreadful concoctions to force down his throat.

They had him on an old mattress under a tree with a wet cloth on his forehead. It was obvious he couldn't go back to the fields, and Mr. and Mrs. Spruill were reluctant to leave him alone.

They, of course, had to pick cotton to earn money to live on. I did not. A plan had been devised in my absence to require me to sit with Trot while everybody else worked in the heat for the rest of the afternoon. If Trot somehow took a turn for the worse, I was supposed to sprint to the lower forty and fetch the nearest Spruill. I tried to appear unhappy with this arrangement when my mother explained it to me.

'What about my Cardinals jacket?' I asked her with as much concern as I could muster.

'There's plenty of cotton left for you,' she said. 'Just sit with him this afternoon. He should be better tomorrow.'

There were, of course, eighty acres of cotton, all of which had to be picked twice during the next two months or so. If I lost my Cardinals jacket, it wouldn't be because of Trot.

I watched the trailer leave again, this time with my mother and Gran sitting with the field hands. It squeaked and rattled away from the house, past the barn, down the field road, and was finally lost among the rows of cotton. I couldn't help but wonder whether Tally and Cowboy were making eyes at each other. If I found the courage, I would ask my mother about this.

When I walked to the mattress, Trot was lying perfectly still with his eyes closed. He didn't appear to be breathing.

'Trot,' I said loudly, suddenly terrified that he had died on my watch.

He opened his eyes, and very slowly sat up and looked at me. Then he glanced around, as if to make certain we were alone. His withered left arm wasn't much thicker than a broom handle, and it hung from his shoulder without moving much. His black hair shot out in all directions.

'Are you okay?' I asked. I'd yet to hear him speak, and I was curious to know if he could do so.

'I guess,' he grunted, his voice thick and his words blurred. I couldn't tell if he had a speech impediment or if he was just tired and dazed. He kept looking around to make sure everyone else was gone, and it occurred to me that perhaps Trot had been faking a bit. I began to admire him.

'Does Tally like baseball?' I asked, one of a hundred questions I wanted to drill him with. I thought it was a simple question, but he was overcome by it and immediately closed his eyes and rolled to one side, then curled his knees to his chest and began another nap.

A breeze rustled the top of the pin oak. I found a thick, grassy spot in the shade near his mattress, and stretched out. Watching the leaves and branches high above, I considered my good fortune. The rest of them were sweating in the sun as time crept along. For a moment I tried to feel guilty, but it didn't work. My luck was only temporary, so I decided to enjoy it.

As did Trot. While he slept like a baby, I watched the sky. Soon, though, boredom hit. I went to the house to get a ball and my baseball glove. I threw myself pop flies near the front porch, something I could do for hours. At one point I caught seventeen in a row.

Throughout the afternoon, Trot never left the mattress. He would sleep, then sit up and look around, then watch me for a moment. If I tried to strike up a conversation, he usually rolled over and continued his nap. At least he wasn't dying.

The next casualty from the cotton patch was Hank. He ambled in late in the day, walking slowly and complaining about the heat. Said he needed to check on Trot.

'I picked three hundred pounds,' he said, as if this would impress me. 'Then the heat got me.' His face was red with sunburn. He wore no hat, which said a lot about his intelligence. Every head was covered in the fields.

He looked Trot over for a second, then went to the back of the truck and began rummaging through their boxes and sacks like a starving bear. He crammed a cold biscuit into his huge mouth, then stretched out under the tree.

'Fetch me some water, boy,' he growled abruptly in my direction.

I was too surprised to move. I'd never heard a hill person give an order to one of us. I wasn't sure what to do. But he was grown, and I was just a kid.

'Sir?' I said.

'Fetch me some water!' he repeated, his voice rising.

I was certain they had water stored somewhere among their things. I took a very awkward step toward their truck. This upset him.

'Cold water, boy! From the house. And hurry! I been workin' all day. You ain't.'

I rushed into the house, to the kitchen, where Gran kept a gallon jug of water in the refrigerator. My hands shook as I poured the water into a glass. I knew that when I reported this, it would cause trouble. My father would have words with Leon Spruill.

I handed Hank the glass. He drained it quickly, smacked his lips, then said, 'Gimme another glass.'

Trot was sitting and watching this. I ran back to the house and refilled it. When Hank finished the second, he spat near my feet. 'You're a good boy,' he said, and tossed me the glass.

'Thanks,' I said, catching it.

'Now leave us alone,' he said as he lay down on the grass. I retreated to the house and waited for my mother.

You could quit picking at five if you wanted. That was when Pappy pulled the trailer back to the house. Or you could stay in the fields until dark, like the Mexicans. Their stamina was amazing. They would pick until they couldn't see the bolls anymore, then walk a half mile with their heavy sacks to the barn, where they would build a small fire and eat a few tortillas before sleeping hard.

The other Spruills gathered around Trot, who managed to look even sicker for the short minute or so they examined him. Once it was determined that he was alive and somewhat alert, they hurriedly turned their attention to dinner. Mrs. Spruill built a fire.

Next, Gran hovered over Trot. She appeared to be deeply concerned, and I think the Spruills appreciated this. I knew, however, that she merely wanted to conduct experiments on the poor boy with one of her vile remedies. Since I was the smallest victim around, I was usually the guinea pig for any new brew she discovered. I knew from experience that she could whip up a concoction so curative that Trot would bolt from the mattress and run like a scalded dog. After a few minutes. Trot got suspicious and began watching her closely. He now seemed more aware of things, and Gran took this as a sign that he didn't need any medicine, at least not immediately. But she placed him under surveillance, and she'd make her rounds again tomorrow.

My worst chore of the late afternoon was in the garden. I thought it was cruel to force me, or any other seven-year-old kid for that matter, to awake before sunrise, work in the fields all day, and then pull garden duty before supper. But I knew we were lucky to have such a beautiful garden.

At some point before I was born, the women had sectioned off little areas of turf, both inside the house and out, and laid claim to them. I don't know how my mother got the entire garden, but there was no doubt it belonged to her.

It was on the east side of our house, the quiet side, away from the kitchen door and the barnyard and the chicken coop. Away from Pappy's pickup and the small dirt drive where the rare visitor parked. It was enclosed in a wire fence four feet tall, built by my father under my mother's direction, and designed to keep out deer and varmints.

Corn was planted around the fence so that once you closed the rickety gate with the leather latch, you stepped into a secret world hidden by the stalks.

My job was to take a straw basket and follow my mother around as she gathered whatever she deemed ripe. She had a basket, too, and she slowly filled it with tomatoes, cucumbers, squash, peppers, onions, and eggplant. She talked quietly, not necessarily to me, but to the garden in general.

'Look at the corn, would you? We'll eat those next week.'

'Yes ma'am.'

'The pumpkins should be just right for Halloween.'

'Yes ma'am.'

She was constantly searching for weeds, little trespassers that survived only momentarily in our garden. She stopped, pointed, and said, 'Pull those weeds there, Luke, by the watermelons.'

I set the basket on the dirt trail and pulled with a vengeance.

The garden work was not as rough in the late summer as it was in the spring, when the ground had to be tilled and the weeds grew faster than the vegetables.

A long green snake froze us for a second, then it disappeared into the butter bean vines. The garden was full of snakes, all harmless, but snakes nonetheless. My mother was not deathly afraid of them, but we gave them plenty of room. I lived in fear of reaching for a cucumber and feeling fangs sink into the back of my hand.

My mother loved this little plot of soil because it was hers – no one else really wanted it. She treated it like a sanctuary. When the house got crowded, I could always find her in the garden, talking to her vegetables. Harsh words were rare in our family.

When they happened, I knew my mother would disappear into her refuge.

I could hardly carry my basket by the time she'd finished her selections.

The rain had stopped in St. Louis. At exactly eight o'clock, Pappy turned on the radio, fiddled with the knobs and the antenna, and there was colorful Harry Caray, the raspy voice of the Cardinals. There were about twenty games remaining in the season. The Dodgers were in front, and the Giants were in second place. The Cards were in third. It was more than we could stand. Cardinal fans naturally hated the Yankees, and trailing behind two other New York teams in our own league was unbearable.

Pappy was of the opinion that the manager, Eddie Stanky, should've been fired months earlier. When the Cardinals won, it was because of Stan Musial. When they lost, with the same players on the field, it was always the fault of the manager.

Pappy and my father sat side by side on the swing, its rusted chains squeaking as they rocked gently. Gran and my mother shelled butter beans and peas on the other side of the small porch. I was lounging on the top step, within earshot of the radio, watching the Spruill show wind down, waiting with the adults for the heat to finally relent. I missed the steady hum of the old fan, but I knew better than to bring up the subject.

Conversation arose softly from the women as they talked about church stuff – the fall revival and the upcoming dinner-on-the-grounds. A Black Oak girl was getting married in Jonesboro, in a big

59

church, supposedly to a boy with money, and this had to be discussed every night in some fashion. I could not imagine why the women were drawn back to the subject, night after night.

The men had virtually nothing to say, at least nothing unrelated to baseball. Pappy was capable of long stretches of silence, and my father wasn't much better. No doubt, they were worrying about the weather or cotton prices, but they were too tired to fret aloud.

I was content simply to listen, to close my eyes and try to picture Sportsman's Park in St. Louis, a magnificent stadium where thirty thousand people could gather to watch Stan Musial and the Cardinals. Pappy had been there, and during the season I made him describe the place to me at least once a week. He said when you saw the field it seemed to expand. There was grass so green and smooth you could roll marbles across it. The dirt on the infield was actually raked until it was perfect. The scoreboard in left-center was bigger than our house. And all those people, those unbelievably lucky people of St. Louis who got to see the Cardinals and didn't have to pick cotton.

Dizzy Dean and Enos 'Country' Slaughter and Red Schoendienst, all the great Cardinals, all the fabled Gashouse Gang, had played there. And because my father and grandfather and uncle could play the game, there was not the slightest doubt in my mind that I would one day rule Sportsman's Park. I would glide across the perfect outfield grass in front of thirty thousand fans and personally grind the Yankees into the dirt.

The greatest Cardinal of all time was Stan

Musial, and when he came to the plate in the second inning with a runner at first, I saw Hank Spruill ease through the darkness and sit in the shadows, just close enough to hear the radio.

'Is Stan up?' my mother asked.

'Yes ma'am,' I said. She pretended to take an interest in baseball because she knew nothing about it. And if she acted interested in Stan Musial, then she could survive any conversation on the subject around Black Oak.

The soft snap and crunch of the butter beans and peas stopped. The swing was still. I squeezed my baseball glove. My father held the opinion that Harry Caray's voice took on an edge when Musial stepped in, but Pappy was not convinced.

The first pitch by the Pirates pitcher was a fastball low and away. Few pitchers challenged Musial with fastballs on the first pitch. The year before, he'd led the National League with a .355 batting average, and in 1952, he was running neck and neck with the Cubs' Frankie Baumholtz for the lead. He had power and speed, a great glove, and he played hard every day.

I had a Stan Musial baseball card hidden in a cigar box in my drawer, and if the house ever caught on fire, I would grab it before I grabbed anything else.

The second pitch was a high curveball, and with the count of two balls, you could almost hear the fans get out of their seats. A baseball was about to get ripped into some remote section of Sportsman's Park. No pitcher fell behind Stan Musial and survived the moment. The third pitch was a fastball, and Harry Caray hesitated just long

61

enough for us to hear the crack of the bat. The crowd exploded. I held my breath, waiting in that split second for old Harry to tell us where the ball was going. It bounced off the wall in right field, and the crowd roared even louder. The front porch got excited, too. I jumped to my feet, as if by standing I could somehow see St. Louis. Pappy and my father both leaned forward as Harry Caray yelled through the radio. My mother managed some form of exclamation.

Musial was battling his teammate Schoendienst for the National League lead in doubles. The year before, he'd had twelve triples, tops in the majors. As he rounded second, I could barely hear Caray above the crowd. The runner from first scored easily, and Stan slid into third, in the dirt, his feet touching the base, the hapless third baseman taking the late throw and tossing it back to the pitcher. I could see him get to his feet as the crowd went nuts. Then with both hands he slapped the dirt off his white uniform with the bright red trim.

The game had to go on, but for us Chandlers, at least the men, the day was now complete. Musial had hit a bomb, and because we had little hope that the Cardinals would win the pennant, we gladly took our victories where we could get them. The crowd settled down, Harry's voice lowered, and I sank back onto the porch, still watching Stan at third.

If those damned Spruills hadn't been out there, I would've eased into the darkness and taken my position at home plate. I would wait for the fastball, hit it just like my hero, then race around the bases and slide majestically into third base, over by the shadows where the monster Hank was loitering.

'Who's winnin'?' Mr. Spruill asked from somewhere in the darkness.

'Cardinals. One to nothin'. Bottom of the second. Musial just hit a triple,' Hank answered. If they were such baseball fans, why had they built their fire on home plate and pitched their ragged tents around my infield? Any fool could look at our front yard, the trees notwithstanding, and see that it was meant for baseball.

If not for Tally, I would have dismissed the entire bunch. And Trot. I did feel sympathy for the poor kid.

I had decided not to bring up the issue of Hank and the cold water. I knew that if I reported it to my father, or to Pappy, then a serious discussion would take place with Mr. Spruill. The Mexicans knew their place, and the hill people were expected to know theirs. They did not ask for things from our house, and they did not give orders to me or anyone else.

Hank had a neck thicker than any I'd ever seen. His arms and hands were also massive, but what scared me were his eyes. I thought they were blank and stupid most of the time, but when he barked at me to fetch him the cold water, they narrowed and glowed with evil.

I didn't want Hank mad at me, nor did I want my father to confront him. My father could whip anybody, except for maybe Pappy, who was older but, when necessary, much meaner. I decided to set aside the incident for the time being. If it

63

happened again, then I would have no choice but to tell my mother.

The Pirates scored two in the fourth, primarily because, according to Pappy, Eddie Stanky didn't change pitchers when he should have. Then they scored three in the fifth, and Pappy got so mad he went to bed.

In the seventh inning, the heat broke just enough to convince us we could get some sleep. The peas and butter beans had been shelled. The Spruills were all tucked away. We were exhausted, and the Cardinals were going nowhere. It wasn't difficult to leave the game.

After my mother tucked me in and we said our prayers, I kicked the sheets off so I could breathe. I listened to the crickets sing their screeching chorus, calling to each other across the fields. They serenaded us every night in the summer, unless it was raining. I heard a voice in the distance – a Spruill was rambling about, probably Hank rummaging for one last biscuit.

In the living room we had a box fan, a large window unit, which in theory was supposed to suck the hot air through the house and blow it out across the barnyard. It worked about half the time. One door inadvertently closed or blown shut would disrupt the movements of air, and you'd lie in your own sweat until you fell asleep. Wind from the outside would somehow confuse the box fan, and the hot air would gather in the living room, then creep through the house, smothering us. The fan broke down often – but it was one of Pappy's proudest possessions, and we knew of only two other farm families at church who owned such a luxury.

That night it happened to be working.

Lying in Ricky's bed, listening to the crickets, enjoying the slight draft over my body as the sticky summer air was pulled toward the living room, I let my thoughts drift to Korea, a place I never wanted to see. My father would tell me nothing about war. Not a hint. There were a few glorious adventures of Pappy's father and his victories in the Civil War, but when it came to the wars of this century, he offered little. I wanted to know how many people he'd shot. How many battles he'd won. I wanted to see his scars. There were a thousand questions I wanted to ask him.

'Don't talk about war,' my mother had cautioned me many times. 'It's too awful.'

And now Ricky was in Korea. It had been snowing when he left us in February, three days after his nineteenth birthday. It was cold in Korea, too. I knew that much from a story on the radio. I was safe and warm in his bed while he was lying in a trench shooting and getting shot at.

What if he didn't come home?

It was a question I tortured myself with every night. I thought about him dying until I cried. I didn't want his bed. I didn't want his room. I wanted Ricky home, so we could run the bases in the front yard and throw baseballs against the barn and fish in the St. Francis. He was really more of a big brother than an uncle.

Boys were getting killed over there, lots of them. We prayed for them at church. We talked about the war at school. At the moment, Ricky was the only boy from Black Oak in Korea, which bestowed upon us Chandlers some odd distinction I cared nothing about.

'Have you heard from Ricky?' was the great question that confronted us every time we went to town.

Yes or no, it didn't matter. Our neighbors were just trying to be thoughtful. Pappy wouldn't answer them. My father would give a polite response. Gran and my mother would chat quietly for a few minutes about his last letter.

I always said, 'Yeah. He's coming home soon.'

Chapter 6

Shortly after breakfast, I followed Gran down the front steps and through the middle of the front yard. She was a woman on a mission: Dr. Gran making her early morning rounds, thrilled that a bona-fide sick person was present within her jurisdiction.

The Spruills were hunched over their makeshift table, eating quickly. Trot's lazy eyes came to life when Gran said, 'Good mornin',' and went straight toward him.

'How's Trot?' she said.

'Much better,' said Mrs. Spruill.

'He's fine,' said Mr. Spruill.

Gran touched the boy's forehead. 'Any fever?' she demanded. Trot shook his head with a vengeance. There'd been no fever the day before. Why would there be one this morning?

'Are you light-headed?'

Trot wasn't sure what that meant, nor were the rest of the Spruills. I figured the boy went through life in a perpetual state of light-headedness.

Mr. Spruill took charge, wiping a drip of sorghum from the corner of his mouth with a

67

forearm. 'We figure we'll take him to the fields and let him sit under the trailer, out of the sun.'

'If a cloud comes up, then he can pick,' added Mrs. Spruill. It was evident the Spruills had already made plans for Trot.

Dammit, I thought.

Ricky had taught me a few cuss words. I usually practiced them in the woods by the river, then prayed for forgiveness as soon as I was done.

I had envisioned another lazy day under the shade trees in the front yard, guarding Trot while playing baseball and taking it easy.

'I suppose,' said Gran as she took her thumb and index finger and pried one of his eyes wide open. Trot shot a frightened look with his other eye.

'I'll stay close by,' Gran said, clearly disappointed. Over breakfast I'd heard her tell my mother that she'd decided the proper remedy would be a strong dose of castor oil, lemon, and some black herb she grew in a window box. I'd stopped eating when I heard this. It was her old standby, one she'd used on me several times. It was more powerful than surgery. My ailments were instantly cured as the dosage burned from my tongue to my toes, and kept burning.

She once mixed a surefire remedy for Pappy because he was constipated. He'd spent two days in the outhouse, unable to farm, begging for water, which I hauled back and forth in a milk jug. I thought she'd killed him. When he emerged – pale, gaunt, somewhat thinner – he walked with a purpose to the house, angrier than anyone had ever seen him. My parents threw me in the pickup, and we went for a long drive.

Gran again promised Trot she'd watch him during the day. He said nothing. He'd stopped eating and was staring blankly across the table, in the general direction of Tally, who was pretending I didn't exist.

We left and returned to the house. I sat on the front steps, waiting for a glimpse of Tally, silently cussing Trot for being so stupid. Maybe he'd collapse again. Surely when the sun was overhead he'd succumb, and they'd need me to watch him on the mattress.

When we gathered at the trailer, I greeted Miguel as his gang emerged from the barn and took their places on one side of the trailer. The Spruills took the other side. My father sat in the middle, crowded between the two groups. Pappy drove the tractor, and I observed them from my prized perch next to his seat. Of particular interest this morning was any activity between the loathsome Cowboy and my beloved Tally. I didn't notice any. Everyone was in a daze, eyes half-open and downcast, dreading another day of sun and drudgery.

The trailer rocked and swayed as we slowly made our way into the white fields. As I gazed at the fields of cotton, I couldn't think of my shiny red Cardinals baseball jacket. I tried mightily to pull up images of the great Musial and his muscled teammates running across the manicured green grass of Sportsman's Park. I tried to imagine all of them clad in their red and white uniforms with some no doubt wearing baseball jackets just like the one in the Sears, Roebuck catalog. I tried to picture these scenes because they never failed to inspire me, but the tractor stopped, and all I could see was the looming cotton, just standing there, row after row, waiting.

Last year, Juan had revealed to me the pleasures of Mexican food, especially tortillas. The workers ate them three times a day, so I figured they must be good. I'd eaten lunch one day with Juan and his group, after I'd eaten in our house. He'd fixed me two tortillas, and I'd devoured them. Three hours later I was on hands and knees under the cotton trailer, as sick as a dog. I was scolded by every Chandler present, my mother leading the pack.

'You can't eat their food!' she said with as much scorn as I'd ever heard.

'Why not?' I asked.

'Because it's not clean.'

I was expressly forbidden to eat anything cooked by the Mexicans. And this, of course, made the tortillas taste even better. I got caught again when Pappy made a surprise appearance at the barn to check on Isabel. My father took me behind the toolshed and whipped me with his belt. I laid off the tortillas for as long as I could.

But a new chef was with us, and I was eager to measure Miguel's food against Juan's. After lunch, when I was certain everyone was asleep, I sneaked out the kitchen door and walked nonchalantly toward the barn. It was a dangerous little excursion because Pappy and Gran did not nap well, even when they were exhausted from the fields.

The Mexicans were sprawled in the shade of the

north end of the barn, most of them sleeping on the grass. Miguel knew I was coming because we'd talked for a moment earlier in the morning when we met to get our cotton weighed. His haul was seventy pounds, mine was fifteen.

He knelt over the coals of a small fire and warmed a tortilla in a skillet. He flipped it, and when it was brown on one side, he added a thin layer of salsa — finely chopped tomatoes and onions and peppers, all from our garden. It also contained jalapeños and chopped red peppers that had never been grown in the state of Arkansas. These the Mexicans imported themselves in their little bags.

A couple of the Mexicans were interested in the fact that I wanted a tortilla. The rest of them were working hard at their siestas. Cowboy was nowhere to be seen. Standing at the corner of the barn, with a full view of the house and any Chandler who might come looking, I ate a tortilla. It was hot and spicy and messy. I couldn't tell any difference between Juan's and Miguel's. They were both delicious. Miguel asked if I wanted another, and I could easily have eaten one. But I didn't want to take their food. They were all small and skinny and dirt-poor, and last year when I got caught and the adults took turns scolding me and heaping untold measures of shame upon me, Gran had been creative enough to invent the sin of taking food from the less fortunate. As Baptists, we were never short on sins to haunt us.

I thanked him and crept back to the house and onto the front porch without waking a single Spruill. I curled into the swing as if I'd been napping all along. No one was stirring, but I couldn't sleep. A breeze came from nowhere, and I daydreamed of a lazy afternoon on the porch, no cotton to be picked, nothing to do but maybe fish in the St. Francis and catch pop flies in the front yard.

The work almost killed me during the afternoon. Late in the day, I limped toward the cotton trailer, lugging my harvest behind me, hot and thirsty, soaked with sweat, my fingers swollen from the tiny shallow punctures inflicted by the burrs. I already had forty-one pounds for the day. My quota was still fifty, and I was certain I had at least ten pounds in my sack. I was hoping my mother would be somewhere near the scales because she would insist that I be allowed to quit and go to the house. Both Pappy and my father would send me back for more, quota or not.

Only those two were allowed to weigh the cotton, and if they happened to be deep in a row somewhere, then you got a break while they worked their way back to the trailer. I saw neither of them, and the idea of a nap flashed before me.

The Spruills had gathered at the east end of the trailer, in the shade. They were sitting on their bulky cotton sacks, resting and looking at Trot, who, as far as I could tell, hadn't moved more than ten feet during the entire day.

I freed myself from the shoulder strap of my cotton sack and walked to the end of the trailer. 'Howdy,' one of the Spruills said.

'How's Trot?' I asked.

'Reckon he'll be all right,' Mr. Spruill said. They were eating crackers and Vienna sausages, a favorite pick-me-up in the fields. Sitting next to Trot was Tally, who completely ignored me.

'You got anything to eat, boy?' Hank suddenly demanded, his liquid eyes flashing at me. For a second I was too surprised to say anything. Mrs. Spruill shook her head and studied the ground.

'Do you?' he demanded, shifting his weight so that he faced me squarely.

'Uh, no,' I managed to say.

'You mean "No sir," don't you, boy?' he said angrily.

'Come on, Hank,' Tally said. The rest of the family seemed to withdraw. All heads were lowered.

'No sir,' I said.

'No sir what?' His voice was sharper. It was obvious Hank enjoyed picking fights. They'd probably been through this many times.

'No sir,' I said again.

'You farm people are right uppity, you know that? You think you're better than us hill folk 'cause you have this land and 'cause you pay us to work it. Ain't that right, boy?'

'That's enough, Hank,' Mr. Spruill said, but he lacked conviction. I suddenly hoped Pappy or my father would appear. I was ready for these people to leave our farm.

My throat constricted, and my lower lip began to shake. I was hurt and embarrassed and didn't know what to say.

Hank wasn't about to be quiet. He reclined on an elbow, and with a nasty smile said, 'We're just one notch above them wetbacks, ain't we, boy? Just hired labor. Just a bunch of hillbillies who

73

drink moonshine and marry our sisters. Ain't that right, boy?'

He paused for a split second as if he really wanted me to respond. I was tempted to run away, but I just stared at my boots. The rest of the Spruills may have felt sorry for me, but none of them came to my rescue.

'We got a house nicer than yours, boy. You believe that? A lot nicer.'

'Quiet down, Hank,' Mrs. Spruill said.

'It's bigger, got a long front porch, got a tin roof without tar patches, and you know what else it's got? You ain't gonna believe this, boy, but our house's got paint on it. White paint. You ever see paint, boy?'

With that, Bo and Dale, the two teenagers who rarely made a sound, began chuckling to themselves, as if they wanted to appease Hank while not offending Mrs. Spruill.

'Make him stop, Momma,' Tally said, and my humiliation was interrupted, if only for a second.

I looked at Trot, and to my surprise he was resting on his elbows, his eyes as wide as I'd ever seen them, absorbing this one-sided little confrontation. He seemed to be enjoying it.

Hank gave a goofy grin to Bo and Dale, and they laughed even louder. Mr. Spruill also looked amused now. Perhaps he'd been called a hillbilly once too often.

'Why don't you sodbusters paint your houses?' Hank boomed in my direction.

The word 'sodbusters' hit their nerves. Bo and Dale shook with laughter. Hank bellowed at his own punch line. The entire bunch seemed on the verge of knee-slapping when Trot said, with as much volume as he could muster, 'Stop it, Hank!'

His words were slurred slightly so that 'Hank' came out 'Hane', but he was clearly understood by the rest of them. They were startled, and their little joke came to an abrupt end. Everyone looked at Trot, who was glaring at Hank with as much disgust as possible.

I was on the verge of tears, so I turned and ran past the trailer and along the field road until I was safely out of their sight. Then I ducked into the cotton and waited for friendly voices. I sat on the hot ground, surrounded by stalks four feet tall, and I cried, something I really hated to do.

The trailers from the better farms had tarps to hold the cotton and keep it from blowing onto the roads leading to the gin. Our old tarp was tied firmly in place, securing the fruits of our labor, ninety pounds of which had been picked by me over the past two days. No Chandler had ever taken a load to the gin with bolls flying out like snow and littering the road. Lots of other folks did, though, and part of the picking season was watching the weeds and ditches along Highway 135 slowly grow white as the farmers hurried to the gin with their harvest.

With the loaded cotton trailer dwarfing our pickup, Pappy drove less than twenty miles an hour on the way to town. And he didn't say anything. We were both digesting our dinner. I was thinking about Hank and trying to decide what to do. I'm sure Pappy was worrying about the weather.

75

If I told him about Hank, I knew exactly what would happen. He'd march me down the front yard to Spruillville, and we'd have an ugly confrontation. Because Hank was younger and bigger, Pappy would have in his hand a stick of some sort, and he'd be very happy to use it. He'd demand that Hank apologize, and when he refused, Pappy would start the threats and insults. Hank would misjudge his opponent, and before long the stick would come into play. Hank wouldn't have a prayer. My father would be forced to cover the Chandler flanks with his twelve-gauge. The women would be safe on the porch, but my mother would once again be humiliated by Pappy's penchant for violence.

The Spruills would lick their wounds and pack up their ragged belongings. They'd move down the road to another farm where they were needed and appreciated, and we'd be left short-handed.

I'd be expected to pick even more cotton.

So I didn't say a word.

We drove slowly along Highway 135, stirring up the cotton on the right shoulder of the road, watching the fields where an occasional gang of Mexicans was still working, racing against the dark.

I decided I would simply avoid Hank and the rest of the Spruills until the picking was over and they went back to the hills, back to their wonderfully painted houses and their moonshine and sister-marrying. And at some point late in the winter when we sat around the fire in the living room and told stories about the harvest, I would finally serve up all of Hank's misdeeds. I'd have plenty of time to work on my stories, and would embellish where I deemed appropriate. It was a Chandler tradition.

I had to be careful, though, when telling the painted house story.

As we neared Black Oak, we passed the Clench farm, home of Foy and Laverl Clench and their eight children, all of whom, I was certain, were still in the fields. No one, not even the Mexicans, worked harder than the Clenches. The parents were notorious slave drivers, but the children seemed to enjoy picking cotton and pursuing even the most mundane chores around the farm. The hedge rows around the front yard were perfectly manicured. Their fences were straight and needed no repair. Their garden was huge and its yield legendary. Even their old truck was clean. One of the kids washed it every Saturday.

And their house was painted, the first one on the highway into town. White was the color, with gray trim around the edges and corners. The porch and front steps were dark green.

Soon all the houses were painted.

Our house had been built before the First War, back when indoor plumbing and electricity were unheard of. Its exterior was one-by-six clapboards made of oak, probably cut from the land we now farmed. With time and weather the boards had faded into a pale brown, pretty much the same color as the other farmhouses around Black Oak. Paint was unnecessary. The boards were kept clean and in good repair, and besides paint cost money.

But shortly after my parents were married, my

mother decided the house needed an upgrade. She went to work on my father, who was anxious to please his young wife. His parents, though, were not. Pappy and Gran, with all the stubbornness that came from the soil, flatly refused to even consider painting the house. The cost was the official reason. This was relayed to my mother through my father. No fight occurred – no words. Just a tense period one winter when four adults lived in a small unpainted house and tried to be cordial.

My mother vowed to herself that she would not raise her children on a farm. She would one day have a house in a town or in a city, a house with indoor plumbing and shrubs around the porch, and with paint on the boards, maybe even bricks.

'Paint' was a sensitive word around the Chandler farm.

I counted eleven trailers ahead of us when we arrived at the gin. Another twenty or so were empty and parked to one side. Those were owned by farmers with enough money to have two. They could leave one to be ginned at night while the other stayed in the fields. My father desperately wanted a second trailer.

Pappy parked and walked to a group of farmers huddled by a trailer. I could tell by the way they were standing that they were worried about something.

For nine months the gin sat idle. It was a tall, long, box-like structure, the biggest building in the county. In early September it came to life when the harvest began. At the height of the picking season

78

it ran all day and all night, stopping only on Saturday evening and Sunday morning. Its compresses and mills roared with a noisy precision that could be heard throughout Black Oak.

I saw the Montgomery twins throwing rocks at the weeds beside the gin, and I joined them. We compared stories about Mexicans and told lies about how much cotton we'd personally picked. It was dark, and the line of trailers moved slowly.

'My pop says cotton prices are goin' down,' Dan Montgomery said as he tossed a rock into the darkness. 'Says the cotton traders in Memphis are pushin' down prices 'cause there's so much cotton.'

'It's a big crop,' I said. The Montgomery twins wanted to be farmers when they grew up. I felt sorry for them.

When the rains flooded the land and wiped out the crops, the prices went up because the traders in Memphis couldn't get enough cotton. But the farmers, of course, had nothing to sell. And when the rains cooperated and the crops were huge, the prices went down because the traders in Memphis had too much cotton. The poor people who labored in the fields didn't make enough to pay their crop loans.

Good crops or bad crops, it didn't make any difference.

We talked baseball for a while. The Montgomerys did not own a radio, so their knowledge of the Cardinals was limited. Again, I felt sorry for them.

When we left the gin. Pappy had nothing to say. The wrinkles in his forehead were closer together, and his chin was jutting out a bit, so I knew he'd heard bad news. I assumed it had something to do with the price of cotton.

I said nothing as we left Black Oak. When the lights were behind us, I laid my head on the window opening so the wind would hit my face. The air was hot and still, and I wanted Pappy to drive faster so we could cool off.

I would listen more closely for the next few days. I'd give the adults time to whisper among themselves, then I'd ask my mother what was going on.

If it involved bad news about farming, she would eventually tell me.

Chapter 7

Saturday morning. At sunrise, with Mexicans on one side and the Spruills on the other, we were in the trailer moving toward the fields. I kept close to my father, for fear that the monster Hank might come after me again. I hated all the Spruills that morning, perhaps with the exception of Trot, my lone defender. They ignored me. I hoped they were ashamed of themselves.

I tried not to think about the Spruills as we moved through the fields. It was Saturday. A magical day for all the poor souls who toiled the land. On the Chandler farm, we'd work half a day, then head for town to join all the other farmers and their families who went there to buy food and supplies, to mix and mingle along Main Street, to catch the gossip, to escape for a few hours the drudgery of the cotton patch. The Mexicans and the hill people went, too. The men would gather in groups in front of the Tea Shoppe and the Co-op and compare crops and tell stories about floods. The women would pack into Pop and Pearl's and take forever buying a few groceries. The kids were allowed to roam the sidewalks on Main Street and its neighboring alleys until four o'clock, that wonderful hour when the Dixie opened for the matinee.

When the trailer stopped, we hopped off and found our cotton sacks. I was half asleep, not paying attention to anything in particular, when the sweetest voice said, 'Good mornin', Luke.' It was Tally, just standing there smiling at me. It was her way of saying she was sorry for yesterday.

Because I was a Chandler, I was capable of deep stubbornness. I turned my back to her and walked away. I told myself I hated all Spruills. I attacked the first row of cotton as if I might just wipe out forty acres before lunch. After a few minutes, though, I was tired. I was lost in the stalks, in the dark, and I could still hear her voice and see her smile.

She was only ten years older than I was.

The Saturday bath was a ritual I hated more than all others. It took place after lunch, under the stern supervision of my mother. The tub, hardly big enough for me, was used later in the day by each member of the family. It was kept in a remote corner of the back porch, shielded from view by an old bedsheet.

First, I had to haul the water from the pump to the back porch, where I filled the tub about a third full. This took eight trips with a bucket, and I was exhausted before the bath began. Then I pulled the bedsheet across the porch and stripped naked with remarkable speed. The water was very cold.

With a bar of store-bought soap and a wash-cloth, I worked furiously to remove dirt and make bubbles and otherwise cloud the water so my mother couldn't see my privates when she came to direct matters. She appeared first to collect my dirty clothes, then to bring me a clean change. Then she went straight for the ears and neck. In her hands the washcloth became a weapon. She scraped my tender skin as if the soil I collected working in the fields offended her. Throughout the process, she continued to marvel at how dirty I could get.

When my neck was raw, she attacked my hair as if it were filled with lice and gnats. She poured cold water from the bucket over my head to rinse off the soap. My humiliation was complete when she finished scouring my arms and feet – mercifully, she left the midsection for me.

The water was muddy when I hopped out – a week's worth of dirt collected from the Arkansas Delta. I pulled the plug and watched it seep through the cracks of the porch as I toweled off and stepped into my clean overalls. I felt fresh and clean and five pounds lighter, and I was ready for town.

Pappy decided that his truck would make only one run to Black Oak. That meant that Gran and my mother would ride in the front with him and my father and I would ride in the back with all ten Mexicans. Getting packed into a box didn't bother the Mexicans at all, but it sure irritated me.

As we drove away, I watched the Spruills as they knocked down poles and unhitched ropes and hurried about the business of freeing their old truck so they could get to town. Everyone was busy but Hank, who was eating something in the shade.

To prevent the dust from boiling over the fenders and choking us in the back, Pappy drove less than five miles per hour down our road. While it was thoughtful of him, it didn't help matters much. We were hot and suffocating. The Saturday bath was a ritual in rural Arkansas. In Mexico, apparently, it was not.

On Saturday, some farm families arrived in town by noon. Pappy thought it was sinful to spend too much time enjoying Saturday, so we took our time getting there. During the winter, he even threatened to avoid town, except for church on Sunday. My mother said he once went a month without leaving the farm, and this included a boycott of church because the preacher had somehow offended him. It didn't take much to offend Pappy. But we were lucky. A lot of sharecroppers never left the farm. They didn't have money for groceries and didn't have a car to get to town. And there were some renters like us and landowners who seldom went to town. Mr. Clovis Beckly from Caraway hadn't been to town in fourteen years, according to Gran. And he hadn't been to church since before the First War. I'd heard folks openly praying for him during revivals.

I loved the traffic and the crowded sidewalks and the uncertainty of whom you might see next. I liked the groups of Mexicans camped under shade trees, eating ice cream and greeting their countrymen from other farms in excited bursts of Spanish. I liked the crowds of strangers, hill people who would be gone before long. Pappy told me once that when he was in St. Louis before the First War, there were half a million other people there and that he got lost just walking down a street.

That would never happen to me. When I walked down the streets in St. Louis, everybody would know me.

I followed my mother and Gran to Pop and Pearl Watson's. The men went to the Co-op because that's where all the farmers went on Saturday afternoon. I could never determine exactly what they did there, besides gripe about the price of cotton and fret over the weather.

Pearl was busy at the cash register. 'Hi, Mrs. Watson,' I said when I could get close enough. The store was packed with women and Mexicans.

'Well, hello, Luke,' she said as she winked at me. 'How's the cotton?' she asked. It was the same question you heard over and over.

'Pickin' well,' I said, as if I'd hauled in a ton.

It took Gran and my mother an hour to buy five pounds of flour, two pounds of sugar, two pounds of coffee, a bottle of vinegar, a pound of table salt, and two bars of soap. The aisles were crowded with women more concerned with saying hello than with buying food. They talked about their gardens and the weather and church the next day, and about who was definitely having a baby and who might be. They prattled on about a funeral here, a revival there, an upcoming wedding.

Not one word about the Cardinals.

My only chore in town was to haul the groceries back to the truck. When this was accomplished, I was free to roam Main Street and its alleys without being supervised. I moved with the languid foot traffic toward the north end of Black Oak, past the

Co-op, past the drugstore and the hardware store and the Tea Shoppe. Along the sidewalk, packs of people stood gossiping, with no intention of moving. Telephones were scarce, and there were only a few televisions in the county, so Saturday was meant for catching up on the latest news and events.

I found my friend Dewayne Pinter trying to convince his mother that he should be free to roam. Dewayne was a year older than I was but still in the second grade. His father let him drive their tractor around the farm, and this elevated his status among all second graders at the Black Oak School. The Pinters were Baptists and Cardinals fans, but for some unknown reason, Pappy still didn't like them.

'Good afternoon, Luke,' Mrs. Pinter said to me.

'Hello, Mrs. Pinter.'

'Where's your mother?' she asked, looking behind me.

'I think she's still at the drugstore. I'm not sure.'

With that, Dewayne was able to tear himself away. If I could be trusted to walk the streets alone, then so could he. As we walked off, Mrs. Pinter was still barking instructions. We went to the Dixie, where the older kids were hanging out and waiting for four o'clock. In my pocket I had a few coins – five cents for the matinee, five cents for a Coca-Cola, three cents for popcorn. My mother had given me the money as an advance against what I would earn picking cotton. I was supposed to pay it back one day, but she and I both knew it would never happen. If Pappy tried to collect it, he would have to step around Mom.

Evidently Dewayne had had a better week with the cotton than I had. He had a pocket full of dimes and couldn't wait to show them off. His family also rented land, and they owned twenty acres outright, a lot more than the Chandlers.

A freckle-faced girl named Brenda lingered near us, trying to start a conversation with Dewayne. She'd told all of her friends that she wanted to marry him. She was making his life unbearable by following him around at church, shadowing him every Saturday up and down Main Street, and always asking if he would sit by her at the movies.

Dewayne despised her. When a pack of Mexicans walked by, we got lost in the middle of them.

A fight erupted behind the Co-op, a popular spot for the older boys to gather and trade punches. It happened every Saturday, and nothing electrified Black Oak like a good fight. The crowd pushed its way through a wide alley next to the Co-op, and in the rush I heard someone say, 'I'll bet it's a Sisco.'

My mother had warned me against watching fights behind the Co-op, but it wasn't a strict prohibition because I knew she wouldn't be there. No proper female would dare to be caught watching a fight. Dewayne and I snaked our way through the mob, anxious to see some violence.

The Siscos were dirt-poor sharecroppers who lived less than a mile from town. They were always around on Saturday. No one was sure how many kids were in the family, but they could all fight. Their father was a drunk who beat them, and their mother had once whipped a fully armed deputy who was trying to arrest her husband. Broke his

87

arm and his nose. The deputy left town in disgrace. The oldest Sisco was in prison for killing a man in Jonesboro.

The Sisco kids didn't go to school or church, so I managed to avoid them. Sure enough, when we got close and peeked through the spectators, there was Jerry Sisco punching a stranger in the face.

'Who's that?' I asked Dewayne. The crowd was yelling for each fighter to hurry up and maim the other.

'Don't know,' Dewayne said. 'Probably a hillbilly.'

That made sense. With the county full of hill people picking cotton, it was only logical that the Siscos would start a fight with someone who didn't know them. The locals knew better. The stranger's face was puffy, and there was blood dripping from his nose. Jerry Sisco ripped a sharp right to his teeth and knocked the man down.

A whole gang of Siscos and their ilk were in one corner, laughing, and probably drinking. They were shaggy and dirty with ragged clothes and only a few had shoes. Their toughness was legendary. They were lean and hungry and fought with every dirty trick in the book. The year before, Billy Sisco had almost killed a Mexican in a fight behind the gin.

On the other side of the makeshift arena was a group of hill people, all yelling for their man – 'Doyle', it turned out – to get up and do something. Doyle was rubbing his chin when he jumped up and made a charge. He managed to ram his head into Jerry Sisco's stomach, sending both of them to the ground. This brought a cheer from the

88

hill people. The rest of us wanted to cheer, too, but we didn't want to upset the Siscos. This was their game, and they'd come after anybody.

The two fighters clutched and clawed and rolled around in the dirt like wild animals as the yelling got louder. Doyle suddenly cocked his right hand and landed a perfect punch in the middle of Jerry Sisco's face, sending blood everywhere. Jerry was still for a split second, and we were all secretly hoping that perhaps a Sisco had met his match. Doyle was about to land another punch when Billy Sisco abruptly charged from the pack and kicked Doyle square in the back. Doyle shrieked like a wounded dog and rolled to the ground, where both Siscos were immediately on him, kicking and pounding him.

Doyle was about to be slaughtered. Though there was nothing fair about it, it was simply the risk you ran if you fought a Sisco. The hill people were silent, and the locals watched without taking a step forward.

Then the two Siscos dragged Doyle to his feet, and with all the patience of an executioner. Jerry kicked him in the groin. Doyle screamed and dropped to the ground. The Siscos were delirious with laughter.

The Siscos were in the process of picking him up again when Mr. Hank Spruill, he of the tree-trunk neck, stepped out from the crowd and hit Jerry hard, causing him to fall. Quick as a cat, Billy Sisco threw a left jab that popped Hank in the jaw, but a curious thing happened. The jab didn't phase Hank Spruill. He turned around and grabbed Billy by his hair and without any apparent effort spun him around and flung him into the grouping of Siscos in the crowd. From the strewn pack came a new Sisco, Bobby, aged no more than sixteen, but just as mean as his brothers.

Three Siscos against Hank Spruill.

As Jerry was getting to his feet, Hank, with unbelievable speed, kicked him in the ribs so hard that we heard cracking. Then Hank turned and slapped Bobby with the back of his hand, knocking him down, and kicked him in the teeth. By this time Billy was making another lunge, and Hank, like a circus strongman, lifted the much skinnier boy into the air and flipped him into the side of the Co-op, where he crashed loudly, rattling the boards and windows, before falling to the pavement on his head. I couldn't have tossed a baseball any easier.

When Billy hit the ground, Hank took him by the throat and dragged him back into the center of the arena, where Bobby was on all fours, struggling to get to his feet. Jerry was crumpled to one side, clutching his ribs and whimpering.

Hank kicked Bobby between the legs. When the boy yelped, Hank let out a hideous laugh.

He then clutched Billy by the throat and began lashing his face with the back of his right hand. Blood was spurting everywhere; it covered Billy's face and was pouring down his chest.

Finally, Hank released Billy and turned to the rest of the Siscos. 'Anybody want some more!' he shouted. 'Come on! Get you some!'

The other Siscos cowered behind one another while their three heroes floundered in the dirt.

The fight should've been over, but Hank had

other plans. With delight and deliberation, he kicked each of the three in their faces and heads until they stopped moving and groaning. The crowd began to disperse.

'Let's go,' a man said from behind me. 'You kids don't need to see this.' But I couldn't move.

Then Hank found a broken piece of an old two-by-four. For a moment the crowd stopped its exit to watch with morbid curiosity.

When Hank hit Jerry across the nose, someone in the crowd said, 'Oh my God.'

Another voice in the mob said something about finding the sheriff.

'Let's get outta here,' an old farmer said, and the crowd began leaving again, this time a little quicker.

Hank still wasn't finished. His face was red with anger; his eyes flashed like a demon's. He kept pounding them until the old two-by-four began to shatter into small pieces.

I didn't see any of the other Spruills in the crowd. As the beating became a butchering, everyone fled. No one in Black Oak wanted to tangle with the Siscos. And now nobody wanted to face this madman from the hills.

When we were back on the sidewalk, those of us who'd seen the fight were silent. It was still happening. I wondered if Hank would beat them until they were dead.

Neither Dewayne nor I said a word as we darted through the crowd and ran toward the movie house.

The Saturday afternoon movie was a special time for all of us farm kids. We didn't have televisions, and entertainment was considered sinful. For two hours we were transported from the harshness of life in the cotton patch to a fantasy land where the good guys always won. Through the movies we learned how criminals operated, how cops caught them, how wars were fought and won, how history was made in the Wild West. It was even through a movie that I learned the sad truth that the South had, in fact, not won the Civil War, contrary to what I'd been told both at home and at school.

But this Saturday the Gene Autry western bored Dewayne and me. Every time there was a fistfight on the screen, I thought of Hank Spruill and could see him still out there behind the Co-op hammering the Siscos. Autry's scuffles were tame compared to the real-life carnage we'd just witnessed. The movie was almost over before I mustered the courage to tell Dewayne.

'That big hillbilly we saw beat the Siscos?' I whispered. 'He's working on our farm.'

'You know him?' he whispered back, disbelieving.

'Yep. Know him real well.'

Dewayne was impressed and wanted to ask more questions, but the place was packed and Mr. Starnes, the manager, enjoyed patrolling the aisles with his flashlight, just looking for trouble. Any kid caught talking would be yanked up by the ear and ejected. Also, Brenda with the freckles had managed to get the seat directly behind Dewayne, making us both uncomfortable.

There were a few adults sprinkled throughout the audience, but they were mostly town people.

Mr. Starnes made the Mexicans sit in the balcony, but it didn't seem to bother them. Only a handful would waste money on a picture show.

We rushed out at the end, and within minutes we were behind the Co-op again, half-expecting to see the bloody corpses of the Sisco boys. But no one was there. There was no evidence of any fight – no blood, no limbs, no shattered two-by-four.

Pappy held the opinion that people with self-respect should leave town on Saturday before dark. Bad things happened on Saturday night. Other than the fights, though, I'd never witnessed any true evil. I'd heard there were drinking and dice games behind the gin, and even more fights, but all that was kept out of sight and was engaged in by very few people. Still, Pappy was afraid we'd somehow be contaminated.

Ricky was the hell-raiser of the Chandler family, and my mother told me that he had the reputation of staying in town too long on Saturday. There was an arrest somewhere in the recent family history, but I could never get the details. She said that Pappy and Ricky had fought for years over what time they should leave. I could remember several occasions when we left without him. I'd cry because I was sure I'd never see him again, then Sunday morning he would be sitting in the kitchen drinking coffee as if nothing had happened. Ricky always came home.

We met at the truck, which was now surrounded by dozens of other vehicles parked haphazardly around the Baptist church because the farmers were still rolling in. The crowd was thicker along Main Street and seemed to be congregating near the school, where fiddlers and banjo pickers sometimes broke out into bluegrass sessions. I didn't want to leave, and in my opinion there was no hurry to get home.

Gran and my mother had some last-minute business inside the church, where most of the women found something to do on the day before the Sabbath. From the other side of the truck, I overheard my dad and Pappy talking about a fight. Then I heard the name Sisco, and I became very still. Miguel and some of the Mexicans arrived and wouldn't stop chattering in Spanish, so I missed any further gossip.

A few minutes later, Stick Powers, one of Black Oak's two deputies, walked over from the street and said hello to Pappy and my father. Stick was supposed to have been a POW in the war, and he walked with a limp, which he claimed was the result of abuse in a German camp. Pappy said he'd never left Craighead County, never heard a shot fired in anger.

'One of them Sisco boys is near 'bout dead,' I heard him say as I moved in closer. It was almost dark now, and no one was watching me.

'Nothing wrong with that,' Pappy said.

'They say that hillbilly is working out at your place.'

'I didn't see the fight, Stick,' Pappy said, his quick temper already rising. 'You got a name?'

'Hank something or other.'

'We got lots of somethings and others.'

'Mind if I ride out tomorrow and look around?' Stick asked.

'I can't stop you.'

'No, you can't.' Stick wheeled on his good leg and gave the Mexicans a look as if they were guilty as sin.

I eased around to the other side of the truck and said, 'What was that all about?'

As usual, when it was something I was not supposed to know or hear, they simply ignored me.

We rode home in the dark, the lights of Black Oak fading behind us, the cool wind from the road blowing our hair. At first, I wanted to tell my father about the fight, but I couldn't do it in front of the Mexicans. Then I decided not to be a witness. I wouldn't tell anybody since there was no way to win. Any involvement with the Siscos would make my life dangerous, and I didn't want the Spruills to get mad and leave. The picking had hardly begun, and I was already tired of it. And most important, I didn't want Hank Spruill angry with me or my father or Pappy.

Their old truck was not in our front yard when we arrived home. They were still in town, probably visiting with other hill people.

After supper, we took our places on the porch as Pappy fiddled with his radio. The Cardinals were at Philadelphia, playing under the lights. Musial came to bat in the top of the second, and I began to dream.

Chapter 8

We awoke at dawn Sunday to the crack of lightning and the rumble of low thunder. A storm blew from the southwest, delaying sunrise, and as I lay in the darkness of Ricky's room, I again asked the great question of why it rained on Sundays. Why not during the week, so I wouldn't be forced to pick cotton? Sunday was already a day of rest.

My grandmother came for me and told me to sit on the porch so we could watch the rain together. She fixed my coffee, mixing it with plenty of milk and sugar, and we rocked gently in the swing as the wind howled. The Spruills were scurrying about, throwing things in boxes, trying to find shelter away from their leaking tents.

The rain fell in waves, as if trying to make up for two weeks of dry weather. A mist swirled around the porch like a fog, and above us the tin roof sang under the torrents.

Gran carefully picked her moments to speak. There were times, usually once a week, when she would take me for a walk, or meet me on the porch, just the two of us. Because she'd been married to Pappy for thirty-five years, she'd learned the art of silence. She could walk or swing for long periods of time while saying little.

'How's the coffee?' she asked, barely audible above the storm.

'It's fine, Gran,' I said.

'What would you like for breakfast?'

'Biscuits.'

'Then I'll make us some biscuits.'

The Sunday routine was a little more relaxed. We generally slept later, though the rain had awakened us early today. And for breakfast we skipped the usual eggs and ham and somehow managed to survive on biscuits and molasses. The kitchen work was a little lighter. It was, after all, a day of rest.

The swing moved slowly back and forth, going nowhere, its rusty chains squeaking softly above us. Lightning popped across the road, somewhere on the Jeter property.

'I had a dream about Ricky last night,' she said.

'A good dream?'

'Yes, very good. I dreamed the war suddenly ended, but they forgot to tell us. And one night we were sitting here on the porch, listening to the radio, and out there on the road we saw a man running toward us. It was Ricky. He was in his army uniform, and he started yelling about the war being over.'

'I wish I could have a dream like that,' I said.

'I think the Lord's telling us something.'

'Ricky's coming home?'

'Yes. Maybe not right away, but the war'll be over soon. We'll look up one day and see him walking across the yard there.'

I looked at the yard. Puddles and streams were beginning to form and run down toward the Spruills. The grass was almost gone, and the wind was blowing the first of the dead leaves from our oaks.

'I pray for Ricky every night, Gran,' I said, quite proud.

'I pray for him every hour,' she said, with a hint of mist in her eyes.

We rocked and watched the rain. My thoughts about Ricky were rarely of a soldier in uniform, with a gun, under fire, hopping from one safe place to another. Rather, my memories were of my best friend, my uncle who was more like a brother, a buddy with a fishing pole or a baseball glove. He was only nineteen, an age that seemed both old and young to me.

Before long my mother came to the door. The Saturday bath was followed by the Sunday scrubbing, a quick but brutal ritual in which my neck and ears were scraped by a woman possessed. 'We need to get ready,' she said. I could already feel the pain.

I followed Gran to the kitchen for more coffee. Pappy was at the kitchen table, reading the Bible and preparing his Sunday school lesson. My father was on the back porch, watching the storm and gazing into the distance at the river, no doubt beginning to worry that floodwaters were coming.

The rains stopped long before we left for church. The roads were muddy, and Pappy drove even slower than usual. We puttered along, sometimes sliding in the ruts and puddles of the old dirt road.

My father and I were in the back, holding tightly to the sides of the bed, and my mother and Gran rode up front, everybody dressed in their best. The sky had cleared, and now the sun was overhead, already baking the wet ground so that you could see the humidity drifting lazily above the cotton stalks.

'It's gonna be a hot one,' my father said, issuing the same forecast he uttered every day from May through September.

When we reached the highway, we stood and leaned on the cab so the wind was in our faces. It was much cooler that way. The fields were vacant; not even the Mexicans were allowed to work on the Sabbath. Every harvest season brought the same rumors of heathen farmers sneaking around and picking cotton on Sunday, but I personally had never witnessed such sinful behavior.

Most things were sinful in rural Arkansas, especially if you were a Baptist. And a great part of our Sunday worship ritual was to be preached at by the Reverend Akers, a loud and angry man who spent too much of his time conjuring up new sins. Of course, I didn't care for the preaching – most kids didn't – but there was more to Sunday church than worship. It was a time for visiting, and spreading news and gossip. It was a festive gathering, with everyone in good spirits, or at least pretending to be. Whatever the worries of the world – the coming floods, the war in Korea, the fluctuating price of cotton – they were all put aside during church.

The Lord didn't intend for His people to worry, Gran always said, especially when we were in His house. This forever struck me as odd, because she worried almost as much as Pappy.

Other than the family and the farm, nothing was as important to us as the Black Oak Baptist Church. I knew every single person in our church, and they of course knew me. It was a family, for better or worse. Everybody loved one another, or at least professed to, and if one of our members was the slightest bit ill, then all manner of prayer and Christian caring poured forth. A funeral was a week-long, almost holy event. The fall and spring revivals were planned for months and greatly anticipated. At least once a month we had some form of dinner-on-the-grounds – a potluck picnic under the trees behind the church – and these often lasted until late afternoon. Weddings were important, especially for the ladies, but they lacked the high drama of funerals and burials.

The church's gravel parking lot was almost full when we arrived. Most of the vehicles were old farmers' trucks like ours, all covered with a fresh coat of mud. There were a few sedans, and these were driven either by town folk or by farmers who owned their land. Down the street at the Methodist church, there were fewer trucks and more cars. As a general rule, the merchants and schoolteachers worshiped there. The Methodists thought they were slightly superior, but as Baptists, we knew we had the inside track to God.

I jumped from the truck and ran to find my friends. Three of the older boys were tossing a baseball behind the church, near the cemetery, and I headed in their direction.

'Luke,' someone whispered. It was Dewayne,

hiding in the shade of an elm tree and looking scared. 'Over here.'

I walked to the tree.

'Have you heard?' he said. 'Jerry Sisco died early this mornin'.'

I felt as if I'd done something wrong, and I couldn't think of anything to say. Dewayne just stared at me. Finally, I managed to respond. 'So?'

'So they're tryin' to find people who saw what happened.'

'Lot of folks saw it.'

'Yeah, but nobody wants to say anything. Everybody's scared of the Siscos, and everybody's scared of your hillbilly.'

'Ain't my hillbilly,' I said.

'Well, I'm scared of him anyway. Ain't you?'

'Yep.'

'What're we gonna do?'

'Nothin'. We ain't sayin' a word, not now anyhow.'

We agreed that we would indeed do nothing. If we were confronted, we would lie. And if we lied, we would say an extra prayer.

The prayers were long and windy that Sunday morning. So were the rumors and gossip of what had happened to Jerry Sisco. News spread quickly before Sunday school began. Dewayne and I heard details about the fight that we couldn't believe were being reported. Hank grew larger by the moment. 'Hands as big as a country ham,' somebody said. 'Shoulders like a Brahma bull,' said somebody else. 'Had to weigh three hundred pounds.'

The men and older boys grouped near the front

of the church, and Dewayne and I milled around, just listening. I heard it described as a murder, then a killing, and I wasn't clear about the difference until I heard Mr. Snake Wilcox say, 'Ain't no murder. Good folks get murdered. White trash like the Siscos get killed.'

The killing was the first in Black Oak since 1947, when some sharecroppers east of town got drunk and had a family war. A teenage boy found himself on the wrong end of a shotgun, but no charges were filed. They fled during the night, never to be heard from again. No one could remember the last 'real' murder.

I was mesmerized by the gossip. We sat on the front steps of the church, looking down the sidewalk toward Main Street, and heard men arguing and spouting off about what should or shouldn't be done.

Down the street, I could see the front of the Co-op, and for a moment I thought I could see Jerry Sisco again, his face a mess, as Hank Spruill clubbed him to death.

I had watched a man get killed. Suddenly, I felt the urge to sneak back into the sanctuary and start praying. I knew I was guilty of something.

We drifted into the church, where the girls and women were also huddled and whispering their versions of the tragedy. Among them, Jerry's stature was rising. Brenda, the freckled girl with a crush on Dewayne, lived only a quarter of a mile from the Siscos, and since they were practically neighbors, she was receiving more than her share of attention. The women were definitely more sympathetic than the men.

Dewayne and I found the cookies in the fellow-ship hall, then went to our little classrooms, listening every step of the way.

Our Sunday school teacher, Miss Beverly Dill Cooley, who taught at the high school in Monette, started things off with a lengthy, and quite gener-ous, obituary for Jerry Sisco, a poor boy from a poor family, a young man who never had a chance. Then she made us hold hands and close our eyes while she lifted her voice to heaven and for a very long time asked God to receive poor Jerry into His warm and eternal embrace. She made Jerry sound like a Christian, and an innocent victim.

I glanced at Dewayne, who had one eye on me. There was something odd about this. As Bap-tists, we'd been taught from the cradle that the only way you made it to heaven was by believing in Jesus and trying to follow His example in living a clean and moral Christian life. It was a simple message, one that was preached from the pulpit every Sunday morning and every Sunday night, and every revival preacher who passed through Black Oak repeated the message loud and clear. We heard it at Sunday school, at Wednesday night prayer service, and at Vacation Bible School. It was in our music, our devotionals, our literature. It was straightforward, unwavering, and without loopholes, compromise, or wiggle room.

And anyone who did not accept Jesus and live a Christian life simply went to hell. That's where Jerry Sisco was, and we all knew it.

But Miss Cooley prayed on. She prayed for all the Siscos in this time of grief and loss, and she prayed for our little town as it reached out to help this family.

I couldn't think of a single soul in Black Oak who would reach out to the Siscos.

It was a strange prayer, and when she finally said 'amen', I was completely bewildered. Jerry Sisco had never been near a church, but Miss Cooley prayed as if he were with God at that very moment. If outlaws like the Siscos could make it to heaven, the pressure was off the rest of us.

Then she started on Jonah and the whale again, and for a while we forgot about the killing.

An hour later, during worship, I sat in my usual spot, in the same pew where the Chandlers always sat, halfway back on the left side, between Gran and my mother. The pews were not marked or reserved, but everyone knew where everybody else was supposed to sit. In three more years, when I was ten, my parents said I would be allowed to sit with my friends, providing of course that I could do so without misbehaving. This promise had been extracted by me from both parents. It might as well have been twenty years.

The windows were up, but the heavy air was not moving. The ladies fanned themselves while the men sat still and sweated. By the time Brother Akers rose to preach, my shirt was stuck to my back.

He was angry, as usual, and he began shouting almost immediately. He attacked sin right off the bat; sin had brought tragedy to Black Oak. Sin had brought death and destruction, as it always had and always would. We sinners drank and gambled and cursed and lied and fought and killed and committed adultery because we allowed ourselves to be separated from God, and that's why a young man from our town had lost his life. God didn't intend for us to kill one another.

I was confused again. I thought Jerry Sisco got himself killed because he'd finally met his match. It had nothing to do with gambling and adultery and most of the other sins Brother Akers was so worked up over. And why was he yelling at us? We were the good folks. We were in church!

I seldom understood what Brother Akers was preaching about, and occasionally I'd hear Gran mumble over Sunday dinner that she'd also been hopelessly confused during one of his sermons. Ricky had once told me he thought the old man was half crazy.

The sins grew, one piling on top of the other until my shoulders began to sag. I had yet to lie about watching the fight, but I was already beginning to feel the heat.

Then Brother Akers traced the history of murder, beginning with Cain slaying Abel, and he walked us through the bloody path of biblical carnage. Gran closed her eyes, and I knew she was praying – she always was. Pappy was staring at a wall, probably thinking about how a dead Sisco might affect his cotton crop. My mother seemed to be paying attention, and mercifully I began to nod off.

When I awoke, my head was in Gran's lap, but she didn't care. When she was worried about Ricky, she wanted me near her. The piano was now playing, and the choir was standing. It was time for the invitation. We stood and sang five stanzas of 'Just As I Am,' and then the Reverend dismissed us.

Outside, the men gathered under a shade tree and started a long discussion about something or other. Pappy was in the middle of things, talking in a hushed voice, waving his hands in an urgent manner. I knew better than to get close.

The women grouped in small clusters and gossiped along the front lawn, where the children also played and the old folks said their farewells. There was never any hurry to leave church on Sundays. There was little to do at home except eat lunch, take a nap, and get ready for another week of picking cotton.

Slowly, we made our way to the parking lot. We said good-bye to our friends again, then waved as we pulled away. Alone in the back of the truck with my father, I tried to muster the courage to tell him about watching the fight. The men at church had talked of nothing else. I wasn't sure how I figured into the plot, but my instincts told me to confess it all to my father and then hide behind him. But Dewayne and I had promised to keep quiet until confronted, then we'd start squirming. I said nothing as we drove home.

About a mile from our farm, where the gravel thinned and eventually surrendered to dirt, the road met the St. Francis River, where a one-lane wooden bridge crossed over. The bridge had been built in the thirties as a WPA project, so it was sturdy enough to withstand the weight of tractors and loaded cotton trailers. But the thick planks popped and creaked every time we drove over, and if you looked at the brown water directly below, you'd swear the bridge was swaying.

We crept across, and on the other side we saw the Spruills. Bo and Dale were in the river, shirtless, their pants rolled up to their knees, skipping rocks. Trot was sitting on a thick branch of driftwood, his feet dangling in the water. Mr. and Mrs. Spruill were hiding under a shade tree, where food was spread on a blanket.

Tally was also in the water, her legs bare up to her thighs, her long hair loose and falling onto her shoulders. My heart pounded as I watched her kick the water, alone in her own world.

Downriver, in a spot where few fish had ever been caught, was Hank with a small cane pole. His shirt was off, and his skin was already pink from the sun. I wondered if he knew that Jerry Sisco was dead. Probably not. He would find out soon enough, though.

We waved slowly at them. They froze as if they had been caught trespassing, then they smiled and nodded. But Tally never looked up. Neither did Hank.

Chapter 9

Sunday lunch was always fried chicken, biscuits, and gravy, and though the women cooked as fast as they could, it still took an hour to prepare. We were famished by the time we sat down to eat. I often thought, to myself of course, that if Brother Akers didn't bark and ramble so long, we wouldn't be nearly as hungry.

Pappy gave thanks. The food was passed around, and we were just beginning to eat when a car door slammed close to the house. We stopped eating and looked at one another. Pappy stood silently and walked to the kitchen window. 'It's Stick Powers,' he said, looking out, and my appetite vanished. The law had arrived, and nothing good was about to happen.

Pappy met him at the back porch. We could hear every word.

'Good afternoon, Eli.'

'Stick. What can I do for you?'

'I guess you heard that Sisco boy died.'

'I heard,' Pappy said without the slightest hint of sadness.

'I need to talk to one of your hands.'

'It was just a fight, Stick. The usual Saturday foolishness that the Siscos have been doin' for years. You never stopped 'em. Now one of 'em bit off more'n he could chew.'

'I still gotta investigate.'

'You'll have to wait till after lunch. We just sat down. Some folks go to church.'

My mother cringed when Pappy said this. Gran slowly shook her head.

'I been on duty,' Stick said.

According to the gossip, Stick had a bout with the Spirit every four years, when it was election time. Then for three and a half years he didn't feel the need to worship. In Black Oak, if you didn't go to church, folks knew it. We had to have somebody to pray for during revivals.

'You're welcome to sit on the porch,' Pappy said, then returned to the kitchen table. When he took his seat, the others began eating again. I now had a knot in my throat the size of a baseball, and the fried chicken simply wouldn't go down.

'Has he had lunch?' Gran whispered across the table.

Pappy shrugged as if he couldn't have cared less. It was almost two-thirty. If Stick hadn't found something to eat by then, why should we worry?

But Gran cared. She stood and pulled a plate from the cabinet. As we watched, she covered it with potatoes and gravy, sliced tomatoes and cucumbers, two biscuits that she carefully buttered, and a thigh and a breast. Then she filled a tall glass with iced tea and took it to the back porch. Again, we heard every word.

'Here, Stick,' she said. 'Nobody misses a meal around here.'

'Thanks, Miss Ruth, but I've already ate.'

'Then eat again.'

'I really shouldn't.'

We knew that by then Stick's fleshy nostrils had caught a whiff of the chicken and the biscuits.

'Thank you, Miss Ruth. This is mighty kind.'

We were not surprised when she returned empty-handed. Pappy was angry but managed to hold his tongue. Stick was there to cause trouble, to interfere with our farmhands, which meant he was threatening our cotton. Why feed him?

We ate in silence, which allowed me a few moments to collect my thoughts. Since I didn't want to act suspiciously, I forced the food into my mouth and chewed as slowly as possible.

I wasn't sure what the truth was, nor could I distinguish right from wrong. The Siscos were ganging up on the poor hillbilly when Hank went to his rescue. There were three Siscos, and Hank was alone. He had quickly stopped them, and the fight should've been over. Why did he pick up that piece of wood? It was easy to assume the Siscos were always wrong, but Hank had won the fight long before he began clubbing them.

I thought about Dewayne and our secret pact. Silence and ignorance were still the best strategies, I decided.

We didn't want Stick to hear us, so we said nothing throughout the entire meal. Pappy ate slower than usual, because he wanted Stick to sit and wait and stew, and maybe get mad and leave. I doubted if the delay bothered Stick. I could almost hear him licking his plate.

My father gazed at the table as he chewed, his mind seemingly off on the other side of the world, probably Korea. Both my mother and Gran looked very sad, which was not unusual after the verbal beating we received each week from Brother Akers. That's another reason I always tried to sleep during his sermons.

The women had much more sympathy for Jerry Sisco. As the hours passed, his death became sadder. His meanness and other undesirable qualities were slowly forgotten. He was, after all, a local boy, someone we knew, if only in passing, and he'd met a terrible end.

And his killer slept in our front yard.

We heard noises. The Spruills were back from the river.

The inquest took place under our tallest pin oak, about halfway between the front porch and Camp Spruill. The men gathered first, Pappy and my father stretching and rubbing their stomachs, and Stick looking particularly well fed. He carried a sizable belly, which pulled his brown shirt at the buttons, and it was obvious that Stick did not spend his days in the cotton fields. Pappy said he was lazy as hell and slept most of the time in his patrol car, under a shade tree near Gurdy Stone's hot dog stand on the edge of town.

From the other end of the yard came the Spruills, all of them, with Mr. Spruill leading the pack and Trot bringing up the rear, twisting and shuffling along in his now familiar gait. I walked behind Gran and my mother, peeking between them and trying to keep my distance. Only the Mexicans were absent.

A loose huddle formed around Stick; the Spruills loitering on one side, the Chandlers hanging around the other, though when it came down to it, we were all on the same side. I was not pleased to be allied with Hank Spruill, but the cotton was more important than anything else.

Pappy introduced Stick to Mr. Spruill, who awkwardly shook Stick's hand and then took a few steps back. It looked like the Spruills were expecting the worst, and I tried to remember if any of them had witnessed the fight. There'd been a large crowd and things had happened so fast. Dewayne and I had been mesmerized by the bloodletting. I couldn't recall really noticing the faces of the other spectators.

Stick worked a blade of grass that was protruding from one corner of his mouth, and with both thumbs hung in his pants pockets, he studied our hill people. Hank leaned against the pin oak, sneering at anybody who dared to look at him.

'Had a big fight in town yesterday behind the Co-op,' Stick announced in the direction of the Spruills. Mr. Spruill nodded but said nothing. 'Some local boys got into it with a fella from the hills. One of 'em, Jerry Sisco, died this mornin' in the hospital in Jonesboro. Fractured skull.'

Every Spruill began fidgeting, except Hank, who didn't move. They obviously had not heard the latest on Jerry Sisco.

Stick spat and shifted his weight, and he seemed to enjoy being the man in the middle, the voice of authority with a badge and a gun. 'And so I'm lookin' around, askin' questions, just tryin' to find out who was involved.'

'Ain't none of us,' Mr. Spruill said. 'We're peaceful folks.'

'Is that so?'

'Yes sir.'

'Did y'all go to town yesterday?'

'We did.'

Now that the lying had started, I pecked from between the two women for a better look at the Spruills. They were clearly frightened. Bo and Dale stood close together, their eyes darting around. Tally studied the dirt at her bare feet, unwilling to look at us. Mr. and Mrs. Spruill seemed to be looking for friendly faces. Trot, of course, was in another world.

'You got a boy named Hank?' Stick asked.

'Maybe,' Mr. Spruill said.

'Don't play games with me,' Stick growled with sudden anger. 'I ask you a question, you give me a straight answer. We got a jail over in Jonesboro with lots of room. I can take the whole family in for questions. You understand?'

'I'm Hank Spruill!' came a thunderous voice. Hank strutted through the huddle and stood within striking distance of Stick, who was much smaller but managed to maintain his cockiness.

Stick studied him for a second, then asked, 'Did you go to town yesterday?'

'I did.'

'Did you get in a fight behind the Co-op?'

'Nope. I stopped a fight.'

'Did you beat up the Sisco boys?'

113

'I don't know their names. There was two of 'em beatin' up a boy from the hills. I stopped it.'

Hank's face was smug. He showed no fear, and I grudgingly admired him for the way he confronted the law.

The deputy looked around the crowd, and his eyes stopped with Pappy. Stick was hot on the trail and quite proud of himself. With his tongue he moved the blade of grass to the other corner of his mouth, then looked up at Hank again.

'Did you use a stick of wood?'

'Didn't need to.'

'Answer the question. Did you use a stick of wood?'

Without hesitating, Hank said, 'Nope. They had a two-by-four.'

This, of course, conflicted with what someone else had reported to Stick. 'I guess I better take you in,' Stick said, but made no move for the handcuffs dangling from his belt.

Mr. Spruill took a step forward and said to Pappy, 'If he leaves, we leave, too. Right now.'

Pappy was prepared for this. Hill people were noted for their ability to break camp and disappear quickly, and none of us doubted Mr. Spruill meant what he said. They would be gone in an hour, back to Eureka Springs, back to their mountains and their moonshine. It would be virtually impossible to harvest eighty acres of cotton with just the Mexicans to help us. Every pound was crucial. Every hand.

'Slow down, Stick,' Pappy said. 'Let's talk about this. You and I both know the Siscos are good for

114

nothin'. They fight often, and they fight dirty. Seems to me they picked on the wrong fella.'

'I got a dead body, Eli. You understand?'

'Two against one sounds like self-defense to me. Nothin' fair about two against one.'

'But look how big he is.'

'Like I said, the Siscos picked on the wrong fella. You and I both know they had it comin'. Let the boy tell his story.'

'I ain't no boy!' Hank snapped.

'Tell what happened,' Pappy said, stalling for time. Drag it out, and maybe Stick would find some reason to leave and come back in a few days.

'Go ahead,' Stick said. 'Let's hear your story. God knows ain't nobody else talkin'.'

Hank shrugged and said, 'I walked up to the fight, saw these two little sodbusters beatin' up on Doyle, and so I broke it up.'

'Who's Doyle?' Stick asked.

'Boy from Hardy.'

'You know him?'

'Nope.'

'Then how do you know where he's from?'

'Just do.'

'Damn it!' Stick said, then spat near Hank. 'Nobody knows nothin'. Nobody saw nothin'. Half the town was behind the Co-op, but nobody knows a damned thing.'

'Sounds like two against one,' Pappy said again. 'And watch your language. You're on my property, and there're ladies present.'

'Sorry,' Stick said, touching his hat and nodding in the direction of Mother and Gran.

'He was just breakin' up a fight,' my father said, his first words.

'There's more to it, Jesse. I've heard that after the fight was over, he picked up a piece of wood and beat the boys. I figure that's when the skull was fractured. Two against one ain't fair, and I know it's the Siscos, but I ain't sure one of 'em had to get killed.'

'I didn't kill nobody,' Hank said. 'I broke up a fight. And there was three of 'em, not two.'

It was about time Hank set the record straight. It seemed odd to me that Stick didn't know that three of the Siscos had been maimed. All he had to do was count the battered faces. But they had probably been hauled off by their kin and hidden back home.

'Three?' Stick repeated in disbelief. The entire gathering seemed to freeze.

Pappy seized the moment. 'Three against one, and there's no way you can take him in for murder. No jury in this county'll ever convict if it's three against one.'

For a moment Stick seemed to agree, but he wasn't about to concede. 'That's if he's tellin' the truth. He'll need witnesses, and right now they're few and far between.' Stick turned to face Hank again and said, 'Who were the three?'

'I didn't ask their names, sir,' Hank said with perfect sarcasm. 'We didn't have a chance to say howdy. Three against one takes up a lotta time, especially if you're the one.'

Laughter would've upset Stick, and nobody wanted to run that risk. So we just lowered our heads and grinned.

116

'Don't get smart with me, boy!' Stick said, trying to reassert himself. 'Don't suppose you got any witnesses, do you?'

The humor vanished into a long period of silence. I was hoping that maybe Bo or Dale would step forward and claim to be a witness. Since the Spruills had just proved that they would lie under pressure, it seemed sensible to me that one of them would quickly verify Hank's version. But nobody moved, nobody spoke. I slipped over a few inches and was directly behind my mother.

Then I heard words that would change my life. With the air perfectly still, Hank said, 'Little Chandler saw it.'

Little Chandler almost wet his pants.

When I opened my eyes, everyone was staring at me, of course. Gran and my mother looked particularly horrified. I felt guilty and looked guilty, and I knew in an instant that every person there believed Hank. I was a witness! I'd seen the fight.

'Come here, Luke,' Pappy said, and I walked as slowly as humanly possible to a spot in the center. I glanced up at Hank, and his eyes were glowing. He wore his usual smirk, and his face told me that he knew I was caught. The crowd inched in as if surrounding me.

'Did you see the fight?' Pappy asked.

I'd been taught in Sunday school from the day I could walk that lying would send you straight to hell. No detours. No second chances. Straight into the fiery pit, where Satan was waiting with the likes of Hitler and Judas Iscariot and General Grant. Thou shalt not bear false witness, which, of course, didn't sound exactly like a strict prohibition against lying, but that was the way the Baptists interpreted it. And I'd been whipped a couple of times for telling little fibs. 'Just tell the truth and get it over with' was one of Gran's favorite sayings.

I said, 'Yes sir.'

'What were you doin' there?'

'I heard there was a fight, so I took off and watched it.' I wasn't about to include Dewayne, at least not until I had to.

Stick dropped to one knee so that his chubby face was eye-level with mine. 'Tell me what you saw,' he said. 'And tell the truth.'

I glanced at my father, who was hovering over my shoulder. And I looked at Pappy, who, oddly, didn't seem at all angry with me.

I sucked in air until my lungs were full, and I looked at Tally, who was watching me very closely. Then I looked at Stick's flat nose and his black, puffy eyes, and I said, 'Jerry Sisco was fightin' some man from the hills. Then Billy Sisco jumped on him, too. They were beatin' him up pretty bad when Mr. Hank stepped in to help the man from the hills.'

'Right then, was it two against one, or two against two?' Stick asked.

'Two against one.'

'What happened to the first hill boy?'

'I don't know. He just left. I think he was hurt pretty bad.'

'All right. Keep goin'. And tell the truth.'

'He's tellin' the truth!' Pappy snarled.

'Go on.'

I glanced around again to make sure Tally was

118

still watching. Not only was she studying me closely, but now she had a pleasant little smile. 'Then, all of a sudden, Bobby Sisco charged from the crowd and attacked Mr. Hank. It was three against one, just like Mr. Hank said.'

Hank's face did not relax. If anything, he looked at me with even more viciousness. He was thinking ahead, and he wasn't finished with me.

'I guess that settles it,' Pappy said. 'I ain't no lawyer, but I could sway a jury if it's three against one.'

Stick ignored him and leaned even closer to me. 'Who had the two-by-four?' he asked, his eyes narrowing as if this were the most important question of all.

Hank suddenly exploded. 'Tell him the truth, boy!' he shouted. 'One of them Siscos picked up that stick of wood, didn't he?'

I could feel the stares of Gran and my mother behind me. And I knew Pappy wanted to reach over and shake me by the neck and somehow make the right words come out.

In front of me, not too far away, Tally was pleading with her eyes. Bo and Dale, and even Trot, were looking at me.

'Didn't he, boy!' Hank barked again.

I met Stick's gaze and began nodding, slowly at first, a timid little lie delivered without a word. And I kept nodding, and kept lying, and in doing so, did more to harvest our cotton than six months of good weather.

I was skirting around the edges of the fiery depths. Satan was waiting, and I could feel the heat. I'd run to the woods and pray for forgiveness

119

as soon as I could. I'd ask God to go easy on me. He'd given us the cotton; it was up to us to protect it and gather the crops.

Stick slowly stood, but he kept staring at me, our eyes locked together, because both of us knew I was lying. Stick didn't want to arrest Hank Spruill, not then anyway. First, he'd have to put the handcuffs on him, a task that could turn ugly. Second, he'd upset all the farmers.

My father grabbed me by the shoulder and shoved me back toward the women. 'You've scared him to death, Stick,' he said with an awkward laugh, trying to break the tension and get me out of there before I said something wrong.

'Is he a good boy?' Stick asked.

'He tells the truth,' my father said.

'Of course he tells the truth,' Pappy said with a good dose of anger.

The truth had just been rewritten.

'I'm gonna keep askin' around,' Stick said and began walking toward his car. 'I might be back later.'

He slammed the door of his old patrol car and left our yard. We watched him drive away until he was out of sight.

Chapter 10

Since we didn't work on Sunday, the house became smaller as my parents and grandparents busied themselves with the few light chores that were permitted. Naps were attempted, then abandoned because of the heat. Occasionally, when the moods were edgy, my parents tossed me in the back of the pickup, and we went for a long drive. There was nothing to see – all the land was flat and covered with cotton. The views were the same as those from our front porch. But it was important to get away.

Not long after Stick left, I was marched into the garden and ordered to haul food. A road trip was in the making. Two cardboard boxes were filled with vegetables. They were so heavy that my father had to place them in the back of the truck. As we drove off, the Spruills were scattered across the front yard in various stages of rest. I didn't want to look at them.

I sat in the back between the boxes of vegetables and watched the dust boil from behind the truck, forming gray clouds that rose quickly and hung over the road in the heavy air before slowly dissipating from the lack of wind. The rain and the mud from the early morning were long forgotten. Everything was hot again: the wooden planks of the truck bed, its rusted and unpainted frame, even the corn and potatoes and tomatoes my mother had just washed. It snowed twice a year in our part of Arkansas, and I longed for a thick, cold blanket of white across our winter fields, cottonless and barren.

The dust finally stopped at the edge of the river, and we crept across the bridge. I stood to see the water below, the thick brown stream barely moving along the banks. There were two cane poles in the back of the truck, and my father had promised we'd fish for a while after the food was delivered.

The Latchers were sharecroppers who lived no more than a mile from our house, but they might as well have been in another county. Their run-down shack was in a bend of the river, with elms and willows touching the roof and cotton growing almost to the front porch. There was no grass around the house, just a ring of dirt where a horde of little Latchers played. I was secretly happy that they lived on the other side of the river. Otherwise, I might have been expected to play with them.

They farmed thirty acres and split the crop with the owner of the land. Half of a little left nothing, and the Latchers were dirt-poor. They had no electricity, no car or truck. Occasionally, Mr. Latcher would walk to our house and ask Pappy for a ride on the next trip to Black Oak.

The trail to their house was barely wide enough for our truck, and when we rolled to a stop, the porch was already filled with dirty little faces. I had once counted seven Latcher kids, but an accurate total was impossible. It was hard to tell the boys from the girls; all had shaggy hair, narrow faces with the same pale blue eyes, and they all wore raggedy clothes.

Mrs. Latcher emerged from the decrepit porch, wiping her hands on her apron. She managed to smile at my mother. 'Hello, Mrs. Chandler,' she said in a soft voice. She was barefoot, and her legs were as skinny as twigs.

'Nice to see you, Darla,' my mother said. My father busied himself at the back of the truck, fiddling with the boxes, killing time while the ladies handled the chitchat. We did not expect to see Mr. Latcher. Pride would prevent him from coming forward and accepting food. Let the women take care of it.

As they talked about the harvest and how hot it was, I moved away from the truck, under the watchful eyes of all those kids. I walked to the side of the house, where the tallest boy was loafing in the shade, trying to ignore us. His name was Percy, and he claimed to be twelve, though I had my doubts. He didn't look big enough to be twelve, but since the Latchers didn't go to school, it was impossible to lump him together with boys his own age. He was shirtless and barefoot, his skin a dark bronze from hours in the sun.

'Hi, Percy,' I said, but he did not respond. Sharecroppers were funny like that. Sometimes they would speak, other times they just gave you a blank look, as if they wanted you to leave them alone.

I studied their house, a square little box, and

wondered once more how so many people could live in such a tiny place. Our toolshed was almost as large. The windows were open, and the torn remains of curtains hung still. There were no screens to keep the flies and mosquitoes out, and certainly no fans to push the air around.

I felt very sorry for them. Gran was fond of quoting the Scriptures: 'Blessed are the poor in spirit, for theirs is the kingdom of heaven,' and 'The poor will always be with you.' But it seemed cruel for anyone to live in such conditions. They had no shoes. Their clothes were so old and worn, they were embarrassed to go to town. And because they had no electricity, they couldn't listen to the Cardinals.

Percy had never owned a ball or a glove or a bat, had never played catch with his dad, had never dreamed of beating the Yankees. In fact, he'd probably never dreamed of leaving the cotton patch. That thought was almost overwhelming.

My father produced the first box of vegetables while my mother called out its contents, and the Latcher kids moved onto the front steps, eagerly looking on but still keeping their distance. Percy didn't move; he stared at something in the fields, something neither he nor I could see.

There was a girl in the house. Her name was Libby, age fifteen, the oldest of the brood, and according to the latest rumors in Black Oak, she was pregnant. The father had yet to be named; in fact, the gossip currently held that she was refusing to reveal to anyone, including her parents, the name of the boy who'd gotten her pregnant.

Such gossip was more than Black Oak could

stand. War news, a fist-fight, a case of cancer, a car wreck, a new baby on the way from two people lawfully wed – all these events kept the talk flying. A death followed by a good funeral, and the town buzzed for days. An arrest of even the lowliest of citizens was an event to be dissected for weeks. But a fifteen-year-old girl, even a sharecropper's daughter, having an illegitimate baby was something so extraordinary that the town was beside itself. Problem was, the pregnancy had not been confirmed. Only rumored. Since the Latchers never left the farm, it was proving to be quite difficult to nail down the evidence. And since we lived closest to them, it had apparently fallen upon my mother to investigate.

She had enlisted me to help with the verifying. She'd shared some of the gossip with me, and because I'd been watching farm animals breed and reproduce all my life, I knew the basics. But I was still reluctant to get involved. Nor was I completely certain why we had to confirm the pregnancy. It had been talked about so much that the entire town already believed the poor girl was expecting. The big mystery was the identity of the father. 'They ain't gonna pin it on me,' I'd heard Pappy say at the Co-op, and all the old men roared with laughter.

'How's the cotton?' I asked Percy. Just a couple of real farmers.

'Still out there,' he said, nodding at the fields, which began just a few feet away. I turned and stared at their cotton, which looked the same as ours. I was paid $1.60 for every hundred pounds I picked. Sharecropper children were paid nothing.

Then I looked at the house again, at the windows and the curtains and the sagging boards, and I stared into the backyard, where their wash hung on the clothesline. I studied the stretch of dirt that led past their out-house to the river, and there was no sign of Libby Latcher. They probably had her locked in a room, with Mr. Latcher guarding the door with a shotgun. One day she'd have the baby, and no one would know it. Just another Latcher running around naked.

'My sister ain't here,' he said, still lost in the distance. 'That's what you're lookin' for.'

My mouth fell open, and my cheeks got very hot. All I could say was, 'What?'

'She ain't here. Now get back to your truck.'

My father hauled the rest of the food onto the porch, and I walked away from Percy.

'Did you see her?' my mother whispered as we were leaving. I shook my head.

As we drove away, the Latchers were crawling over and around the two boxes as if they hadn't eaten in a week.

We'd return in a few days with another load of produce in a second attempt to confirm the rumors. As long as they kept Libby hidden, the Latchers would be well-fed.

The St. Francis River was fifty feet deep, according to my father, and around the bottom of the bridge pier there were channel catfish that weighed sixty pounds and ate everything that floated within reach. They were large, dirty fish – scavengers that moved only when food was nearby. Some lived for twenty years. According to family legend, Ricky

126

caught one of the monsters when he was thirteen. It weighed forty-four pounds, and when he slit its belly with a cleaning knife, all sorts of debris spilled onto the tailgate of Pappy's truck: a spark plug, a marble, lots of half-eaten minnows and small fish, two pennies, and some suspicious matter that was eventually determined to be human waste.

Gran never fried another catfish. Pappy gave up river food altogether.

With red worms as bait, I fished the shallow backwaters around a sandbar for bream and crappie, two small species that were plentiful and easy to catch. I waded barefoot through the warm, swirling waters and occasionally heard my mother yell, 'That's far enough, Luke!' The bank was lined with oaks and willows, and the sun was behind them. My parents sat in the shade, on one of the many quilts the ladies at the church made during the winter, and shared a cantaloupe from our garden.

They talked softly, almost in whispers, and I didn't try to listen, because it was one of the few moments during the picking season when they could be alone. At night, after a day in the fields, sleep came fast and hard, and I rarely heard them talk in bed. They sometimes sat on the porch in the darkness, waiting for the heat to pass, but they weren't really alone.

The river scared me enough to keep me safe. I had not yet learned to swim – I was waiting for Ricky to come home. He had promised to teach me the next summer, when I would be eight. I stayed close to the bank, where the water barely covered my feet.

Drownings were not uncommon, and all my life I'd heard colorful tales of grown men caught in shifting sandbanks and being swept away while entire families watched in horror. Calm waters could somehow turn violent, though I'd never witnessed this myself. The mother of all drownings supposedly took place in the St. Francis, though the exact location varied according to the narrator. A small child was sitting innocently on a sandbar when suddenly it shifted, and the child was surrounded by water and sinking fast. An older sibling saw it happen and dashed into the swirling waters, only to be met with a fierce current that carried him away, too. Next, an even older sibling heard the cries of the first two, and she charged into the river and was waist-deep before she remembered she couldn't swim. Undaunted, she bravely thrashed onward, yelling at the younger two to hold steady, she'd get there somehow. But the sandbar collapsed entirely, sort of like an earthquake, and new currents went in all directions.

The three children were drifting farther and farther away from shore. The mother, who may or may not have been pregnant, and who may or may not have been able to swim, was fixing lunch under a shade tree when she heard the screams of her children. She flung herself into the river, whereupon she, too, was soon in trouble.

The father was fishing off a bridge when he heard the commotion, and rather than waste time running to the shore and entering from that venue, he simply jumped headlong into the St. Francis and broke his neck.

The entire family perished. Some of the bodies were found. Some were not. Some were eaten by the channel cats, and the others were swept out to sea, wherever the sea was. There was no shortage of theories as to what finally happened to the bodies of this poor family, which, oddly, had remained nameless through the decades.

This story was repeated so that kids like myself would appreciate the dangers of the river. Ricky loved to scare me with it, but often got his versions confused. My mother said it was all fiction.

Even Brother Akers managed to weave it through a sermon to illustrate how Satan was always at work spreading misery and heartache around the world. I was awake and listening very closely, and when he left out the part about the broken neck, I figured he was exaggerating, too.

But I was determined not to drown. The fish were biting, small bream that I hooked and threw back. I found a seat on a stump near a lagoon and caught one fish after another. It was almost as much fun as playing baseball. The afternoon passed slowly by, and I was thankful for the solitude. Our farm was crowded with strangers. The fields were waiting with the promise of backbreaking labor. I'd seen a man get killed, and I had somehow gotten myself in the middle of it.

The gentle rushing sound of the shallow water was soothing. Why couldn't I just fish all day? Sit by the river in the shade? Anything but pick cotton. I wasn't going to be a farmer. I didn't need the practice.

'Luke,' came my father's voice from down the

bank. I pulled in the hook and worm, and walked to where they were sitting.

'Yes sir,' I said.

'Sit down,' he said. 'Let's talk.'

I sat at the very edge of the quilt, as far from them as possible. They didn't appear to be angry; in fact, my mother's face was pleasant.

But my father's voice was stern enough to worry me. 'Why didn't you tell us about the fight?' he asked.

The fight that wouldn't go away.

I wasn't really surprised to hear the question. 'I was scared, I guess.'

'Scared of what?'

'Scared of gettin' caught behind the Co-op watchin' a fight.'

'Because I told you not to, right?' asked my mother.

'Yes ma'am. And I'm sorry.'

Watching a fight was not a major act of disobedience, and all three of us knew it. What were boys supposed to do on Saturday afternoon when the town was packed and excitement was high? She smiled because I said I was sorry. I was trying to look as pitiful as possible.

'I'm not too worried about you watchin' a fight,' my father said. 'But secrets can get you in trouble. You shoulda told me what you saw.'

'I saw a fight. I didn't know Jerry Sisco was gonna die.'

My logic stopped him for a moment. Then he said, 'Did you tell Stick Powers the truth?'

'Yes sir.'

'Did one of the Siscos pick up the piece of wood first? Or was it Hank Spruill?'

If I told the truth, then I would be admitting that I had lied in my earlier version. Tell the truth or tell a lie, that was the question that always remained. I decided to try to blur things a bit. 'Well, to be honest, Dad, things happened so fast. There were bodies fallin' and flyin' everywhere. Hank was just throwin' those boys around like little toys. And the crowd was movin' and hollerin'. Then I saw a stick of wood.'

Surprisingly, this satisfied him. After all, I was only seven years old, and had been caught up in a mob of spectators, all watching a horrible brawl unfold behind the Co-op. Who could blame me if I wasn't sure about what happened?

'Don't talk to anyone about this, all right? Not a soul.'

'Yes sir.'

'Little boys who keep secrets from their parents get into big trouble,' my mother said. 'You can always tell us.'

'Yes ma'am.'

'Now go fish some more,' my father said, and I ran back to my spot.

Chapter 11

The week began in the semidarkness of Monday morning. We met at the trailer for the ride into the fields, a ride that grew shorter each day as the picking slowly moved away from the river back toward the house.

Not a word was spoken. Before us were five endless days of overwhelming labor and heat, followed by Saturday, which on Monday seemed as far away as Christmas.

I looked down from my perch on the tractor and prayed for the day when the Spruills would leave our farm. They were grouped together, as dazed and sleepy as I was. Trot was not with them, nor would he be joining us in the fields. Late Sunday, Mr. Spruill had asked Pappy if it would be all right if Trot hung around the front yard all day. 'The boy can't take the heat,' Mr. Spruill said. Pappy didn't care what happened to Trot. He wasn't worth a nickel in the fields.

When the tractor stopped, we took our sacks and disappeared into the rows of cotton. Not a word from anyone. An hour later, the sun was baking us. I thought of Trot, wasting the day under the shade tree, napping when he felt like it, no doubt happy about the work he was missing. He might have been a little off in the head, but right then he was the smartest of all the Spruills.

Time stopped when we were picking cotton. The days dragged on, each yielding ever so slowly to the next.

Over supper on Thursday, Pappy announced, 'We won't be goin' to town Saturday.'

I felt like crying. It was harsh enough to labor in the fields all week, but to do so without the reward of popcorn and a movie was downright cruel. What about my weekly Coca-Cola?

A long silence followed. My mother watched me carefully. She did not seem surprised, and I got the impression that the adults had already had this discussion. Now they were just going through the motions for my benefit.

I thought, What is there to lose? So I gritted my teeth and said, 'Why not?'

'Because I said so,' Pappy fired back at me, and I knew I was in dangerous territory.

I looked at my mother. There was a curious grin on her face.

'You're not scared of the Siscos, are you?' I asked, and I half-expected one of the men to make a grab for me.

There was a moment of deathly silence. My father cleared his throat and said, 'It's best if the Spruills stay out of town for a while. We've discussed it with Mr. Spruill, and we've agreed that we'll all stay put Saturday. Even the Mexicans.'

'I ain't afraid of nobody, son,' Pappy growled down the table. I refused to look at him. 'And don't sass me,' he threw in for good measure.

My mother's grin was still firmly in place, and her eyes were twinkling. She was proud of me.

'I'll need a couple of things from the store,' Gran said. 'Some flour and sugar.'

'I'll run in,' Pappy said. 'I'm sure the Mexicans'll need some things, too.'

Later, they moved to the front porch for our ritual of sitting, but I was too wounded to join them. I lay on the floor of Ricky's room, in the darkness, listening to the Cardinals through the open window and trying to ignore the soft, slow talk of the adults. I tried to think of new ways to hate the Spruills, but I was soon overwhelmed by the sheer volume of their misdeeds. At some point in the early evening, I grew too still, and fell asleep on the floor.

Lunch on Saturday was usually a happy time. The work week was over. We were going to town. If I could survive the Saturday scrubbing on the back porch, then life was indeed wonderful, if only for a few hours.

But on this Saturday there was no excitement. 'We'll work till four,' Pappy said, as if he was doing us a real favor. Big deal. We'd knock off an hour early. I wanted to ask him if we were going to work on Sunday, too, but I'd said enough on Thursday night. He was ignoring me and I was ignoring him. This type of pouting could go on for days.

So we went back to the fields instead of going to Black Oak. Even the Mexicans seemed irritated by

134

this. When the trailer stopped, we took our sacks and slowly disappeared into the cotton. I picked a little and stalled a lot, and when things were safe, I found a spot and went down for a nap. They could banish me from town, they could force me into the fields, but they couldn't make me work hard. I think there were a lot of naps that Saturday afternoon.

My mother found me, and we walked to the house, just the two of us. She was not feeling well, and she also knew the injustice that was being inflicted upon me. We gathered some vegetables from the garden, but only a few things. I suffered through and survived the dreaded bath. And when I was clean, I ventured into the front yard, where Trot was spending his days guarding Camp Spruill. We had no idea what he did all day; no one really cared. We were too busy and too tired to worry about Trot. I found him sitting behind the wheel of their truck, pretending he was driving, making a strange sound with his lips. He glanced at me and returned to his driving and sputtering.

When I heard the tractor coming, I went into the house, where I found my mother lying on her bed, something she never did during the day. There were voices around, tired voices in the front, where the Spruills were unwinding, and in the rear, where the Mexicans were dragging themselves to the barn. I hid in Ricky's room for a while, a baseball in one hand, a glove on the other, and I thought of Dewayne and the Montgomery twins and the rest of my friends all sitting in the Dixie watching the Saturday feature and eating popcorn.

The door opened and Pappy appeared. 'I'm

135

goin' to Pop and Pearl's for a few things. You wanna go?'

I shook my head no, without looking at him.

'I'll buy you a Coca-Cola,' he said.

'No thanks,' I said, still staring at the floor.

Eli Chandler wouldn't beg for mercy in front of a firing squad, and he wasn't about to plead with a seven-year-old. The door closed, and seconds later the truck engine started.

Wary of the front yard, I headed for the back. Near the silo, where the Spruills were supposed to be camping, there was a grassy area where baseball could be played. It wasn't as long and wide as my field in the front, but it was open enough and ran to the edge of the cotton. I tossed pop flies as high as I could, and I stopped only after I'd caught ten in a row.

Miguel appeared from nowhere. He watched me for a minute, and under the pressure of an audience, I dropped three in a row. I tossed him the ball, gently, because he had no glove. He caught it effortlessly and snapped it back to me. I bobbled it, dropped it, kicked it, then grabbed it and threw it back to him, this time a little harder.

I had learned the previous year that a lot of Mexicans played baseball, and it was obvious that Miguel knew the game. His hands were quick and soft, his throws sharper than mine. We tossed the ball for a few minutes, then Rico and Pepe and Luis joined us.

'You have a bat?' Miguel asked.

'Sure,' I said, and ran to the house to get it.

When I returned, Roberto and Pablo had joined the others, and the group was flinging my baseball

136

in all directions. 'You bat,' Miguel said, and he took charge. He put a piece of an old plank on the ground, ten feet in front of the silo, and said, 'Home plate.' The others scattered throughout the infield. Pablo, in shallow center, was at the edge of the cotton. Rico squatted behind me, and I took my position on the right side of the plate. Miguel performed a fierce windup, scared me for a second, then tossed a soft one that I swung at mightily but missed.

I also missed the next three, then ripped a couple. The Mexicans cheered and laughed when I made contact, but said nothing when I didn't. After a few minutes of batting practice, I gave the bat to Miguel and we swapped places. I started him with fastballs, and he didn't appear to be intimidated. He hit line drives and hot grounders, some of which were fielded cleanly by the Mexicans, while others were simply retrieved. Most of them had played before, but a couple had never even thrown a baseball.

The other four at the barn heard the commotion and they wandered over. Cowboy was shirtless, and his pants were rolled up to his knees. He seemed to be a foot taller than the rest.

Luis hit next. He wasn't as experienced as Miguel, and I had no trouble fooling him with my change-up. Much to my delight, I noticed Tally and Trot sitting under an elm, watching the fun.

Then my father strolled over.

The longer we played, the more animated the Mexicans became. They hollered and laughed at one another's miscues. God only knew what they were saying about my pitching.

137

'Let's play a game,' my father said. Bo and Dale had arrived, also shirtless and shoeless. Miguel was consulted, and after a few minutes of plotting, it was decided that the Mexicans would play the Arkansans. Rico would catch for both teams, and again I was sent to the house, this time to fetch my father's old catcher's mitt and my other ball.

When I returned the second time, Hank had appeared and was ready to play. I was not happy about being on the same team with him, but I certainly couldn't say anything. Nor was I certain where Trot would fit in. And Tally was a girl. What a disgrace: a girl for a teammate. Still, the Mexicans had us outnumbered.

Another round of plotting, and it was somehow determined that we would bat first. 'You have little guys,' Miguel said with a smile. More planks were laid around as bases. My father and Miguel established the ground rules, which were quite creative for such a misshapen field. The Mexicans scattered around the bases, and we were ready to play.

To my surprise, Cowboy walked out to the mound and began warming up. He was lean but strong, and when he threw the ball, the muscles in his chest and shoulders bulged and creased. The sweat made his dark skin shine. 'He's good,' my father said softly. His windup was smooth, his delivery seamless, his release almost nonchalant, but the baseball shot from his fingers and popped into Rico's mitt. He threw harder and harder. 'He's very good,' my father said, shaking his head. 'That boy's played a lot of baseball.'

'Girls first,' somebody said. Tally picked up the

138

bat and walked to the plate. She was shoeless, and wearing tight pants rolled up to her knees and a loose shirt with its tail tied in a knot. You could see her stomach. At first, she didn't look at Cowboy, but he was certainly staring at her. He moved a few feet toward the plate and tossed the first pitch underhanded. She swung and missed, but it was an impressive swing, at least for a girl.

Then their eyes met briefly. Cowboy was rubbing the baseball, Tally was swinging the bat, nine Mexicans were chattering like locusts.

The second pitch was even slower, and Tally made contact. The ball rolled by Pepe at third, and we had our first base runner. 'Bat, Luke,' my father said. I strolled to the plate with all the confidence of Stan Musial, hoping that Cowboy wouldn't throw the hard stuff at me. He let Tally hit one, surely he'd do the same for me. I stood in the box, listening as thousands of rabid Cardinal fans chanted my name. A packed house, Harry Caray yelling into the microphone – then I looked at Cowboy thirty feet away, and my heart stopped. He wasn't smiling, nothing close. He held the baseball with both hands and looked at me as if he could saw my head off with a fastball.

What would Musial do? Swing the damned bat!

The first pitch was also underhanded, so I started breathing again. It was high, and I didn't swing, and the Mexican chorus had a lot to say about that. The second pitch was down the middle, and I swung for the fence, for the left field wall, 350 feet away. I closed my eyes and swung for the thirty thousand lucky souls in Sportsman's Park. I also swung for Tally.

'Strike one!' my father yelled, a little too loud, I thought. 'You're tryin' to kill it, Luke,' he said.

Of course I was. I tried to kill the third pitch, too, and when Rico threw it back, I was faced with the horror of being down two strikes. A strikeout was unthinkable. Tally had just hit the ball nicely. She was on first base, anxious for me to put the ball in play so she could advance. We were playing on my field, with my ball and bat. All of those people were watching.

I stepped away from the plate and was stricken with the terror of striking out. The bat was suddenly heavier. My heart was pounding, my mouth was dry. I looked at my father for help, and he said, 'Let's go, Luke. Hit the ball.' I looked at Cowboy, and his nasty smile was even nastier. I did not know if I was ready for what he was going to throw.

I stutter-stepped back to the plate, gritted my teeth, and tried to think of Musial, but my only thoughts were of defeat, and I swung at a very slow pitch. When I missed for the third time, there was total silence. I dropped the bat, picked it up, and heard nothing as I walked back to my team, my lip quivering, already daring myself not to cry. I couldn't look at Tally, and I sure couldn't look at my father.

I wanted to run into the house and lock the doors.

Trot was next, and he held the bat with his right hand just under the label. His left arm hung limp, as always, and we were a little embarrassed at the sight of this poor kid trying to swing. But he was smiling and happy to be playing, and that was

140

more important than anything else at the moment. He hacked at the first two, and I began to think the Mexicans would beat us by twenty runs. Somehow, though, he hit the third pitch, a gentle looping fly that landed behind second base, where at least four Mexicans managed to miss it. Tally flew around second and made it to third, while Trot shuffled down to first.

My humiliation, already enormous, grew even greater. Trot on first, Tally on third, only one out.

Bo was next, and because he was a large teenager with no visible handicaps, Cowboy stepped back and threw from a full windup. His first pitch was not too fast, but poor Bo was already shaking by the time the ball crossed home plate. He swung after Rico caught it, and Hank roared with laughter. Bo told him to shut up; Hank made some response, and I thought we might have a Spruill family brawl in the top of the first inning.

The second pitch was a little faster. Bo's swing was a little slower. 'Make him throw it underhand!' Bo yelled at us, trying to laugh it off.

'What a sissy,' Hank said. Mr. and Mrs. Spruill had joined the spectators, and Bo glanced at them.

I expected the third pitch to be even faster; so did Bo. Cowboy instead threw a change-up, and Bo swung long before the ball arrived.

'He's mighty good,' my father said of Cowboy.

'I'm hittin' next,' Hank announced, stepping in front of Dale, who didn't argue. 'I'll show you boys how it's done.'

The bat looked like a toothpick as Hank hacked and chopped with his practice swings, as if he might hit the ball across the river. Cowboy's first

141

pitch was a fastball away, and Hank didn't swing. It popped into Rico's glove, and the Mexicans erupted in another burst of Spanish jeering.

'Throw the ball over the plate!' Hank yelled as he looked at us for approval. I was hoping Cowboy would drill a fastball into his ear.

The second pitch was much harder. Hank swung and missed. Cowboy caught the ball from Rico, and glanced over at third, where Tally was waiting and watching.

Then Cowboy threw a curve, a pitch that went straight for Hank's head, but as he ducked and dropped the bat, the baseball broke and fell magically through the strike zone. The Mexicans roared with laughter. 'Strike!' Miguel yelled from second base.

'Ain't no strike!' Hank yelled, his face red.

'No umpires,' my father said. 'It's not a strike unless he swings at it.'

Fine with Cowboy. He had another curve in his arsenal. It at first appeared quite harmless, a slow fat pitch headed toward the center of the plate. Hank reached back for a massive swing. The ball, however, broke down and away and bounced before Rico blocked it. Hank hit nothing but air. He lost his balance and fell across the plate, and when the Spanish chorus exploded again, I thought he might attack all of them. He stood up, squinted at Cowboy and mumbled something, then resumed his position at the plate.

Two outs, two strikes, two on. Cowboy finished him off with a fast-ball. Hank speared the bat into the ground when he finishing flailing at the pitch.

'Don't throw the bat!' my father said loudly. 'If

you can't be a sport, then don't play.' We were walking onto the field as the Mexicans hurried off.

Hank gave my father a look of disgust, but he said nothing. For some reason it was determined that I would pitch. 'Throw the first inning, Luke,' my father said. I didn't want to. I was no match for Cowboy. We were about to be embarrassed at our own game.

Hank was at first, Bo at second, Dale at third. Tally was in left-center, hands on hips, and Trot was in right field looking for four-leaf clovers. What a defense! With my pitching we needed to put all of our fielders as far away from home plate as possible.

Miguel sent Roberto to the plate first, and I was sure this was deliberate, because the poor guy had never seen a baseball. He hit a lazy pop-up that my father caught at shortstop. Pepe hit a fly ball that my father caught behind second base. Two up, two outs, I was on a roll, but my luck was about to run out. The serious sticks lined up, one after the other, and hit baseballs all over our farm. I tried fastballs, curveballs, change-ups, it didn't matter. They scored runs by the truckload, and had a delightful time doing it. I was miserable because I was getting shelled, but it was also amusing to watch the Mexicans dance and celebrate as the rout hit full stride.

My mother and Gran were sitting under a tree, watching the spectacle with Mr. and Mrs. Spruill. Everyone was accounted for except Pappy, who was still in town.

When they'd scored about ten runs, my father

called time and walked to the mound. 'You had enough?' he asked.

What a ridiculous question. 'I suppose,' I said. 'Take a break,' he said.

'I can pitch,' Hank yelled from first base. My father hesitated for a second, then tossed him the ball. I wanted to go to right field, out with Trot, where there wasn't much happening, but my coach said, 'Go to first.'

I knew from experience that Hank Spruill had remarkable quickness. He had taken down the three Siscos in a matter of seconds. So it was no great surprise to see him throw a baseball as if he'd been throwing one for years. He looked confident taking his windup and catching the ball from Rico. He threw three nice fastballs by Luis, and the first inning massacre was over. Miguel informed my father that they had scored eleven runs. It seemed like fifty.

Cowboy returned to the mound and took up where he left off. Dale went down on strikes, and my father stepped to the plate. He anticipated a fastball, got one, and ripped it hard, a long fly ball that curved foul and landed deep in the cotton patch. Pablo went to search for it while we used my other ball. Under no circumstances would we leave the game until both baseballs were accounted for.

The second pitch was a hard curve, and my father's knees buckled before he read the pitch. 'That was a strike,' he said, shaking his head in wonder. 'It was also a major league curveball,' he said just loud enough to be heard but to no one in particular.

He flied to shallow center, where Miguel cradled the ball with both hands, and the team from Arkansas was about to get shut out again. Tally strolled to the plate. Cowboy stopped his scowling and walked halfway in. He tossed a couple underhanded, trying to hit her bat, and she finally hit a slow roller to second, where two Mexicans fought over it long enough for the runner to be safe.

I was next. 'Choke up a little,' my father said, and I did. I would've done anything. Cowboy tossed one even slower, a lazy looping pitch that I smacked to center field. The Mexicans went wild. Everyone cheered. I was a little embarrassed by all the fuss, but it sure beat striking out. The pressure was off; my future as a Cardinal was back on track.

Trot swung at the first three and missed them all by at least a foot. 'Four strikes,' Miguel said, and the rules were changed again. When you're leading by eleven runs in the second inning, you can afford to be generous. Trot chopped at the pitch, and the ball rolled back to Cowboy, who just for the fun of it threw to third in a vain effort to catch Tally. She was safe; the bases were loaded. The Mexicans were trying to give us runs. Bo walked to the plate, but Cowboy did not retreat to the mound. He lobbed one underhanded, and Bo hit a scorching ground ball to short, where Pablo lunged to avoid it. Tally scored, and I moved to third.

Hank picked up the bat and ripped a few practice swings. With the bases loaded, he was thinking of only one thing – a grand slam. Cowboy had other plans. He stepped back and stopped smiling. Hank hovered over the plate, staring down the pitcher, daring him to throw something he could hit.

The infield noise died for a moment; the Mexicans crept forward, on their toes, anxious to take part in this encounter. The first pitch was a blistering fastball that crossed the plate a fraction of a second after Cowboy released it. Hank never thought about swinging; he never had the chance. He backed away from the plate and seemed to concede that he was overmatched. I glanced at my father, who was shaking his head. How hard could Cowboy throw?

Then he threw a fat curve, one that looked tempting but broke out of the strike zone. Hank ripped but never got close. Then a hard curve, one that went straight at his head and, at the last second, dipped across the plate. Hank's face was blood-red.

Another fastball that Hank lunged at. Two strikes, bases loaded, two outs. Without the slightest hint of a smile, Cowboy decided to play a little. He threw a slow curve that broke outside, then a harder one that made Hank duck. Then another slow one that he almost chopped at. I got the impression that Cowboy could wrap a baseball around Hank's head if he wanted. The defense was chattering again, at full volume.

Strike three was a knuckleball that floated up to the plate and looked slow enough for me to hit. But it wobbled and dipped. Hank took a mighty swing, missed by a foot, and again landed in the dirt. He screamed a nasty word and threw the bat near my father.

'Watch your language,' my father said, picking up the bat.

Hank mumbled something else and dusted himself off. Our half of the inning was over.

Miguel walked to the plate in the bottom of the second. Hank's first pitch went straight for his head, almost hitting it. The ball bounced off the silo and rolled to a stop near third base. The Mexicans were silent. The second pitch was even harder, and two feet inside. Again, Miguel hit the dirt, and his teammates began mumbling.

'Stop the foolishness!' my father said loudly from shortstop. 'Just throw strikes.'

Hank offered him his customary sneer. He threw the ball over the plate, and Miguel slapped it to right field, where Trot was playing defense with his back to home plate, staring at the distant tree line of the St. Francis River. Tally raced after the ball and stopped when she reached the edge of the cotton. A ground rule triple.

The next pitch was the last of the game. Cowboy was the batter. Hank reached back for all the juice he could find, and he hurled a fastball directly at Cowboy. He ducked but didn't move back fast enough, and the ball hit him square in the ribs with the sickening sound of a melon landing on bricks. Cowboy emitted a quick scream, but just as quickly he threw my bat like a tomahawk, end over end with all the speed he could muster. It didn't land where it should have – between Hank's eyes. Instead, it bounced at his feet and ricocheted off his shins. He screamed an obscenity and instantly charged like a crazed bull.

Others charged, too. My father from shortstop.

147

Mr. Spruill from beside the silo. Some of the Mexicans. Me, I didn't move. I held my ground at first base, too horrified to take a step. Everyone seemed to be yelling and running toward home plate.

Cowboy retreated not a step. He stood perfectly still for a second, his brown skin wet, his long arms taut and ready, and his teeth showing. When the bull was a few feet away, Cowboy's hands moved quickly around his pockets and a knife appeared. He jerked it, and a very long switchblade popped free – shiny, glistening steel, no doubt very sharp. It snapped when it sprang open, a sharp click that I would hear for years to come.

He held it high for all to see, and Hank skidded to a stop.

'Put it down!' he yelled from five feet away.

With his left hand, Cowboy made a slight, beckoning motion, as if to say, Come on, big boy. Come and get it.

The knife shocked everyone, and for a few seconds there was silence. No one moved. The only sound was heavy breathing. Hank was staring at the blade, which seemed to grow. There was no doubt in anyone's mind that Cowboy had used it before, knew how to use it well, and would happily behead Hank if he took another step closer.

Then my father, holding the bat, stepped between the two, and Miguel appeared beside Cowboy.

'Put it down,' Hank said again. 'Fight like a man.'

'Shut up!' my father said, waving the bat around at both of them. 'Ain't nobody fightin'.'

Mr. Spruill grabbed Hank's arm and said, 'Let's go, Hank.'

My father looked at Miguel and said, 'Get him back to the barn.'

Slowly, the other Mexicans grouped around Cowboy and sort of shoved him away. He finally turned and began walking, the switchblade still very much in view. Hank, of course, wouldn't budge. He stood and watched the Mexicans leave, as if by doing so he was claiming victory.

'I'm gonna kill that boy,' he said.

'You've killed enough,' my father said. 'Now leave. And stay away from the barn.'

'Let's go,' Mr. Spruill said again, and the others – Trot, Tally, Bo, and Dale – began to drift toward the front yard. When the Mexicans were out of sight, Hank stomped away. 'I'm gonna kill him,' he mumbled, just loud enough for my father to hear.

I collected the baseballs, the gloves, and the bat, and hurried after my parents and Gran.

Chapter 12

Later that afternoon, Tally found me in the back-yard. It was the first time I'd seen her walk around the farm, though as the days passed, the Spruills showed more interest in exploring the area.

She was carrying a small bag. She was barefoot but had changed into the same tight dress she'd been wearing the first time I'd seen her.

'Will you do me a favor, Luke?' she asked ever so sweetly. My cheeks turned red. I had no idea what favor she wanted, but there was no doubt she'd get it from me.

'What?' I asked, trying to be difficult.

'Your grandma told my mom that there's a creek close by where we can bathe. Do you know where it is?'

'Yeah. Siler's Creek. 'Bout a half a mile that way,' I said, pointing to the north.

'Are there any snakes?'

I laughed like snakes shouldn't bother anyone. 'Maybe just a little water snake or two. No cottonmouths.'

'And the water's clear, not muddy?'

'Should be clear. It hasn't rained since Sunday.'

She looked around to make sure no one was listening, then she said, 'Will you go with me?'

My heart stopped, and my mouth was suddenly dry. 'Why?' I managed to ask.

She grinned again and rolled her eyes away.

'I don't know,' she cooed. 'To make sure nobody sees me.'

She could've said, 'Because I don't know where the creek is,' or 'To make sure there are no snakes.' Or something, anything that had nothing to do with seeing her bathe.

But she didn't.

'Are you scared?' I asked.

'Maybe a little.'

We took the field road until the house and barn were out of sight, then turned onto a narrow path we used for spring planting. Once we were alone, she began to talk. I had no idea what to say, and I was relieved that she knew how to handle the situation.

'I'm real sorry 'bout Hank,' she said. 'He's always causin' trouble.'

'Did you see the fight?' I asked.

'Which one?'

'The one in town.'

'No. Was it awful?'

'Yeah, pretty bad. He beat those boys so bad. He beat 'em long after the fight was over.'

She stopped, then I stopped, too. She walked close to me, both of us breathing heavily. 'Tell me the truth, Luke. Did he pick up that stick first?'

Looking at her beautiful brown eyes, I almost said, 'Yes.' But in a flash something caught me. I

151

thought I'd better play it safe. He was, after all, her brother, and in the midst of one of the many Spruill fights, she might tell him everything I said. Blood's thicker than water, Ricky always said. I didn't want Hank coming after me.

'It happened real fast,' I said, and started walking off. She caught up immediately and said nothing for a few minutes.

'Do you think they'll arrest him?' she asked.

'I don't know.'

'What does your grandpa think?'

'Hell if I know.' I thought I might impress her by using some of Ricky's words.

'Luke, your language!' she said, quite unimpressed.

'Sorry.' We walked on. 'Has he ever killed anybody before?' I asked.

'Not that I know of,' she said.

'He went up North once,' she continued as we approached the creek. 'And there was some trouble. But we never knew what happened.'

I was certain there was trouble wherever Hank went.

Siler's Creek ran along the northern boundary of our farm, where it snaked its way into the St Francis, at a point you could almost see from the bridge. Heavy trees lined both sides, so in the summer it was usually a cool place to swim and bathe. It would dry up, though, and quickly, and more often than not, there wasn't much water.

I led her down the bank to a gravel bar, where the water was deepest. 'This is the best spot,' I said.

'How deep is it?' she asked, looking around.

The water was clear. ''Bout here,' I said, touching a spot not far below my chin.

'There's nobody around here, right?' She seemed a bit nervous.

'No. Everybody's back at the farm.'

'You go back up by the trail and look out for me, okay?'

'Okay,' I said, without moving.

'Go on, Luke,' she said, placing her bag on the bank.

'Okay,' I said, and started away.

'And, Luke, no peeking, okay?'

I felt as if I'd just been caught. I waved her off as if the thought hadn't crossed my mind. 'Of course not,' I said.

I crawled up the bank and found a spot a few feet above the ground, on the limb of an elm. Perched there, I could almost see the top of our barn.

'Luke!' she called.

'Yes!'

'Is everything clear?'

'Yep!'

I heard water splash but kept my eyes to the south. After a minute or two, I slowly turned around and looked down the creek. I couldn't see her, and I was somewhat relieved. The gravel bar was just around a slight bend, and the trees and limbs were thick.

Another minute passed, and I began to feel useless. No one knew we were here, so no one would be trying to sneak up on her. How often would I have the chance to see a pretty girl bathing? I could recall no specific prohibition from the church or

153

the Scriptures, though I knew it was wrong. But maybe it wasn't terribly sinful.

Because it involved mischief, I thought of Ricky. What would he do in a situation like this?

I climbed down from the elm and sneaked through weeds and brush until I was above the gravel bar, then I slowly crawled through the bushes.

Her dress and underclothes were hung over a branch. Tally was deep in the water, her head covered with white lather as she gently washed her hair. I was sweating, but not breathing. Lying on my stomach in the grass, peering through two big limbs, I was invisible to her. The trees were moving more than I was.

She was humming, just a pretty girl bathing in a creek, enjoying the cool water. She wasn't looking around in fear; she trusted me.

She dipped her head under the water, rinsing out the shampoo, sending the lather away in the slight current. Then she stood and reached for a bar of soap. Her back was to me, and I saw her rear end, all of it. She was wearing nothing, which was exactly what I wore during my weekly baths, and it was what I expected. But confirming it sent a shudder throughout my body. Instinctively, I raised my head, I guess for a closer look, then ducked again when I regained my senses.

If she caught me, she'd tell her father, who'd tell my father, who'd beat me until I couldn't walk. My mother would scold me for a week. Gran wouldn't speak to me, she'd be so hurt. Pappy would give me a tongue-lashing, but only for the benefit of the others. I'd be ruined.

In water up to her waist, she bathed her arms and chest, which I could see from the side. I had never seen a woman's breasts before, and I doubted if any seven-year-old boy in Craighead County had. Maybe some kid had stumbled upon his mother, but I was certain no boy my age had ever had this view.

For some reason, I thought of Ricky again, and a wicked idea came from nowhere. Having seen most of her privates, I now wanted to see everything. If I yelled 'Snake!' at the top of my voice, she would scream in horror. She would forget the soap and the washcloth and the nudity and all that, and she would scamper for dry land. She would go for her clothes, but for a few glorious seconds I would see it all.

I swallowed hard, tried to clear my throat, but realized how dry my mouth was. With my heart racing away, I hesitated, and in doing so learned a valuable lesson in patience.

To wash her legs, Tally stepped closer to the bank. She rose from the creek until the water covered nothing but her feet. Slowly, with the soap and cloth she bent and stretched and caressed her legs and buttocks and stomach. My heart pounded at the ground.

She rinsed by splashing water over her body. And when she was finished, and still standing in ankle-deep water, wonderfully naked, Tally turned and stared directly at the spot where I happened to be hiding.

I dropped my head and burrowed even deeper into the weeds. I waited for her to yell something, but she did not. This sin was unforgivable, I was now certain.

I inched backward, very slowly, not making a sound, until I was near the edge of the cotton. Then I crawled furiously along the tree line and resumed my position near the trail, as if nothing had happened. I tried to look bored when I heard her coming.

Her hair was wet; she'd changed dresses. 'Thanks, Luke,' she said.

'Uh, sure,' I managed to say.

'I feel so much better.'

So do I, I thought.

We walked slowly back toward the house. Nothing was said at first, but when we were halfway home she asked, 'You saw me, didn't you, Luke?' Her voice was light and playful, and I didn't want to lie.

'Yes,' I said.

'That's okay. I'm not mad.'

'You're not?'

'No. I guess it's only natural, you know, for boys to look at girls.'

It certainly seemed natural. I could think of nothing to say.

She continued, 'If you'll go with me to the creek the next time, and be my lookout, then you can do it again.'

'Do what again?'

'Watch me.'

'Okay,' I said, a little too quickly.

'But you can't tell anybody.'

'I won't.'

Over supper, I picked at my food and tried to behave as if nothing had happened. It was difficult eating, though, with my stomach still turning flips. I could see Tally just as clearly as if we were still at the creek.

I'd done a terrible thing. And I couldn't wait to do it again.

'What're you thinkin' 'bout, Luke?' Gran asked.

'Nothin' much,' I said, jolted back into reality.

'Come on,' Pappy said. 'Something's on your mind.'

Inspiration hit fast. 'That switchblade,' I said.

All four adults shook their heads in disapproval.

'Think pleasant thoughts,' Gran said.

Don't worry, I thought to myself. Don't worry.

Chapter 13

For the second Sunday in a row, death dominated our worship. Mrs. Letha Haley Dockery was a large, loud woman whose husband had left her many years earlier and fled to California. Not surprisingly, there were a few rumors of what he did once he arrived there, and the favorite, which I'd heard a few times, was that he had taken up with a younger woman of another race – possibly Chinese, though, like a lot of gossip around Black Oak, it couldn't be confirmed. Who'd ever been to California?

Mrs. Dockery had raised two sons, neither of whom had received much distinction but who had the good sense to leave the cotton patch. One was in Memphis; the other out West, wherever, exactly, that was.

She had other family scattered around northeastern Arkansas, and in particular there was a distant cousin who lived in Paragould, twenty miles away. Very distant, according to Pappy, who didn't like Mrs. Dockery at all. This cousin in Paragould had a son who was also fighting in Korea.

When Ricky was mentioned in prayer in our church, an uncomfortable event that happened all the time, Mrs. Dockery was quick to jump forward and remind the congregation that she, too, had family in the war. She'd corner Gran and would whisper gravely about the burden of waiting for news from the front. Pappy talked to no one about the war, and he had rebuked Mrs. Dockery after one of her early attempts to commiserate with him. As a family, we simply tried to ignore what was happening in Korea, at least in public.

Months earlier, during one of her frequent plays for sympathy, someone had asked Mrs. Dockery if she had a photo of her nephew. As a church, we'd been praying for him so much, somebody wanted to see him. She'd been humiliated when she couldn't produce one.

When he was first shipped off, his name had been Jimmy Nance, and he was a nephew of her fourth cousin – her 'very close cousin.' As the war progressed, he became Timmy Nance, and he also became not just a nephew, but a genuine cousin himself, something of the second or third degree. We couldn't keep it straight. Though she preferred the name Timmy, occasionally Jimmy would sneak back into the conversation.

Whatever his real name, he'd been killed. We heard the news in church that Sunday before we could get out of the truck.

They had her in the fellowship hall, surrounded by ladies from her Sunday school class, all of them bawling and carrying on. I watched from a distance while Gran and my mother waited in line to comfort her, and I truly felt sorry for Mrs.

Dockery. However thick or thin the kinship, the woman was in great agony.

Details were discussed in whispers: He'd been driving a jeep for his commander when they hit a land mine. The body wouldn't be home for two months, or maybe never. He was twenty years old and had a young wife at home, up in Kennett, Missouri.

While all this conversation was going on, the Reverend Akers entered the room and sat beside Mrs. Dockery. He held her hand, and they prayed long and hard and silently. The entire church was there, watching her, waiting to offer sympathies.

After a few minutes, I saw Pappy ease out of the door.

So this is what it will look like, I thought, if our worst fears come true: From the other side of the world, they will send the news that he's dead. Then friends will gather around us, and everybody will cry.

My throat suddenly ached and my eyes were beginning to moisten. I said to myself, 'This cannot happen to us. Ricky doesn't drive a jeep over there, and if he did, he'd have better sense than to run over a land mine. Surely, he's coming home.'

I wasn't about to get caught crying, so I sneaked out of the building just in time to see Pappy get in his truck, where I joined him. We sat and stared through the windshield for a long time; then without a word, he started the engine, and we left.

We drove past the gin. Though it was silent on Sunday mornings, every farmer secretly wanted it

160

roaring at full throttle. It operated for only three months out of the year.

We left town with no particular destination in mind, at least I couldn't determine one. We stayed on the back roads, graveled and dusty with the rows of cotton just a few feet off the shoulders.

His first words were, 'That's where the Siscos live.' He nodded to his left, unwilling to take a hand off the wheel. In the distance, just barely visible over the acres of cotton stalks, was a typical sharecropper's house. The rusted tin roof sagged, the porch sloped, the yard was dirt, and the cotton grew almost to the clothesline. I didn't see anyone moving around, and that was a relief. Knowing Pappy, he might get the sudden urge to pull up in the front yard and start a brawl.

We kept going slowly through the endlessly flat cotton fields. I was skipping Sunday school, an almost unbelievable treat. My mother wouldn't like it, but she wouldn't argue with Pappy. It was my mother who had told me that he and Gran reached out for me when they were most worried about Ricky.

He spotted something, and we slowed almost to a stop. 'That's the Embry place,' he said, nodding again. 'You see them Mexicans?' I stretched and strained and finally saw them, four or five straw hats deep in the sea of white, bending low as if they had heard us and were hiding.

'They're pickin' on Sunday?' I said.

'Yep.'

We gained speed, and finally, they were out of sight. 'What're you gonna do?' I asked, as if the law were being broken.

161

'Nothin'. That's Embry's business.'

Mr. Embry was a member of our church. I couldn't imagine him allowing his fields to be worked on the Sabbath. 'Reckon he knows about it?' I asked.

'Maybe he doesn't. I guess it'd be easy for the Mexicans to sneak out there after he left for church.' Pappy said this without much conviction.

'But they can't weigh their own cotton,' I said, and Pappy actually smiled.

'No, I guess not,' he said. So it was determined that Mr. Embry allowed his Mexicans to pick on Sunday. There were rumors of this every fall, but I couldn't imagine a fine deacon like Mr. Embry taking part in such a low sin. I was shocked; Pappy was not.

Those poor Mexicans. Haul 'em like cattle, work 'em like dogs, and their one day of rest was taken away while the owner hid in church.

'Let's keep quiet about this,' Pappy said, smug that he'd confirmed a rumor.

More secrets.

We heard the congregation singing as we walked toward the church. I'd never been on the outside when I wasn't supposed to be. 'Ten minutes late,' Pappy mumbled to himself as he opened the door. They were standing and singing, and we were able to slide into our seats without much commotion. I glanced at my parents, but they were ignoring me. When the song was over, we sat down, and I found myself sitting snugly between my grandparents. Ricky might be in danger, but I would certainly be protected.

162

The Reverend Akers knew better than to touch on the subjects of war and death. He began by delivering the solemn news about Timmy Nance, news everyone had already heard. Mrs. Dockery had been taken home to recover. Meals were being planned by her Sunday school class. It was time, he said, for the church to close ranks and comfort one of its own.

It would be Mrs. Dockery's finest hour, and we all knew it.

If he dwelt on war, he'd have to deal with Pappy when the service was over, so he stuck to his prepared message. We Baptists took great pride in sending missionaries all over the world, and the entire denomination was in the middle of a great campaign to raise money for their support. That's what Brother Akers talked about – giving more money so we could send more of our people to places like India, Korea, Africa, and China. Jesus taught that we should love all people, regardless of their differences. And it was up to us as Baptists to convert the rest of the world.

I decided I wouldn't give an extra dime.

I'd been taught to tithe one tenth of my earnings, and I did so grudgingly. It was there in the Scriptures, though, and hard to argue with. But Brother Akers was asking for something above and beyond, something optional, and he was flat out of luck as far as I was concerned. None of my money was going to Korea. I'm sure the rest of the Chandlers felt the same way. Probably the entire church.

He was subdued that morning. He was preaching on love and charity, not sin and death, and I

163

don't think his heart was in it. With things quieter than usual, I began to nod off.

After the service, we were in no mood for small talk. The adults went straight to the truck, and we left in a hurry. On the edge of town, my father asked, 'Where did you and Pappy go?'

'Just drivin' around,' I said.

'Where to?'

I pointed to the east and said, 'Over there. Nowhere, really. I think he just wanted to get away from church.'

He nodded as if he wished he'd gone with us.

As we were finishing Sunday dinner, there was a slight knock at the back door. My father was the closest to it, so he stepped onto the back porch and found Miguel and Cowboy.

'Mother, you're needed,' he said, and Gran hurried out of the kitchen. The rest of us followed.

Cowboy's shirt was off; the left side of his chest was swollen and looked awful. He could barely raise his left arm, and when Gran made him do it, he grimaced. I felt sorry for him. There was a small flesh wound where the baseball had struck. 'I can count the seams,' Gran said.

My mother brought a pan of water and a cloth. After a few minutes, Pappy and my father grew bored and left. I'm sure they were worrying about how an injured Mexican might affect production.

Gran was happiest when she was playing doctor, and Cowboy got the full treatment. After she dressed the wound, she made him lie on the back porch, his head on a pillow from our sofa.

'He's got to be still,' she said to Miguel.

'How much pain?' she asked.

'Not much,' Cowboy said, shaking his head. His English surprised us.

'I wonder if I should give him a painkiller,' she mused in the direction of my mother.

Gran's painkillers were worse than any broken bone, and I gave Cowboy a horrified look. He read me perfectly and said, 'No, no medicine.' She put ice from the kitchen into a small burlap bag and gently placed it on his swollen ribs. 'Hold it there,' she said, putting his left arm over the bag. When the ice touched him, his entire body went rigid, but he relaxed as the numbness set in. Within seconds, water was running down his skin and dripping onto the porch. He closed his eyes and breathed deeply.

'Thank you,' Miguel said.

'*Gracias,*' I said, and Miguel smiled at me.

We left them there, and gathered on the front porch for a glass of iced tea.

'His ribs are broken,' Gran said to Pappy, who was on the porch swing, digesting his dinner. He really didn't want to say anything, but after a few seconds of silence he grunted and said, 'That's too bad.'

'He needs to see a doctor.'

'What's a doctor gonna do?'

'Maybe there's internal bleeding.'

'Maybe there ain't.'

'It could be dangerous.'

'If he was bleedin' inside, he'd be dead by now, wouldn't he?'

'Sure he would,' my father added.

Two things were happening here. First and

foremost, the men were terrified of having to pay a doctor. Second, and almost as significant, both had fought in the trenches. They had seen stray body parts, mangled corpses, men with limbs missing, and they had no patience with the small stuff. Routine cuts and breaks were hazards of life. Tough it out.

Gran knew she would not prevail. 'If he dies, it'll be our fault.'

'He ain't gonna die, Ruth,' Pappy said. 'And even if he does, it won't be our fault. Hank's the one who broke his ribs.'

My mother left and went inside. She was not feeling well again, and I was beginning to worry about her. Talk shifted to the cotton, and I left the porch.

I crept around back, where Miguel was sitting not far from Cowboy. Both appeared to be sleeping. I sneaked into the house and went to check on my mother. She was lying on her bed, her eyes open. 'Are you okay, Mom?' I asked.

'Yes, of course, Luke. Don't worry about me.'

She would've said that no matter how bad she felt. I leaned on the edge of her bed for a few moments, and when I was ready to leave, I said, 'You're sure you're okay?'

She patted my arm and said, 'I'm fine, Luke.'

I went to Ricky's room to get my glove and baseball. Miguel was gone when I walked quietly out of the kitchen. Cowboy was sitting on the edge of the porch, his feet hanging off the boards, his left arm pressing the ice to his wounds. He still scared me, but in his present condition I doubted if he would do any harm.

I swallowed hard and held out my baseball, the same one that had broken his ribs. 'How do you throw that curve?' I asked him. His unkind face relaxed, then he almost smiled. 'Here,' he said, and pointed to the grass next to the porch. I hopped down, and stood next to his knees.

Cowboy gripped the baseball with his first two fingers directly on the seams. 'Like this,' he said. It was the same way Pappy had taught me.

'And then you snap,' he said, twisting his wrist so that his fingers were under the ball when it was released. It was nothing new. I took the ball and did exactly as he said.

He watched me without a word. That hint of a smile was gone, and I got the impression he was in a lot of pain.

'Thanks,' I said. He barely nodded.

Then my eyes caught the tip of his switchblade protruding from a hole in the right front pocket of his work pants. I couldn't help but stare at it. I looked at him, and then we both looked down at the weapon. Slowly, he removed it. The handle was dark green and smooth, with carvings on it. He held it up for me to see, then he pressed the switch, and the blade sprang forth. It snapped, and I jerked back.

'Where'd you get that?' I asked. A dumb question, to which he offered no answer.

'Do it again,' I said.

In a flash, he pressed the blade against his leg, folding it back into the handle, then waved it near my face as he snapped the blade out again.

'Can I do it?' I asked.

No, he shook his head firmly.

167

'You ever stuck anybody with it?'

He drew it closer to himself and gave me a nasty look. 'Many men,' he said.

I'd seen enough. I backed away, then trotted past the silo, where I could be alone. I threw pop flies to myself for an hour, hoping desperately that Tally would happen by on her way to the creek again.

Chapter 14

We gathered in silence at the tractor early Monday morning. I wanted so badly to sneak back into the house and into Ricky's bed and sleep for days. No cotton, no Hank Spruill, nothing to make life unpleasant. 'We can rest in the winter,' Gran was fond of saying, and it was true. Once the cotton was picked and the fields plowed under, our little farm hibernated through the cold months.

But in the middle of September, cold weather was a distant dream. Pappy and Mr. Spruill and Miguel huddled near the tractor and spoke earnestly while the rest of us tried to listen. The Mexicans were waiting in a group not far away. A plan was devised whereby they would start with the cotton near the barn, so they could simply walk to the fields. We Arkansans would work a little farther away, and the cotton trailer would act as a dividing line between the two groups. Distance was needed between Hank and Cowboy, otherwise there would be another killing.

'I don't want any more trouble,' I heard Pappy say. Everyone knew the switchblade would never leave Cowboy's pocket, and we doubted that

Hank, dumb as he was, would be stupid enough to attack him again. Over breakfast that morning Pappy had ventured the guess that Cowboy wasn't the only armed Mexican. One reckless move by Hank, and there might be switchblades flying everywhere. This had been shared with Mr. Spruill, who had assured Pappy that there would be no more trouble. But by then no one believed that Mr. Spruill, or anybody else, could control Hank.

It had rained late last night, but there was no trace of it in the fields; the cotton was dry, the soil almost dusty. But the rain had been seen by Pappy and my father as an ominous warning of the inevitable flooding, and there was an anxiousness about the two that was contagious.

Our crops were nearly perfect, and we had just a few more weeks to gather them before the skies opened. When the tractor stopped near the cotton trailer, we quickly grabbed our sacks and disappeared among the stalks. There was no laughing or singing from the Spruills, not a sound from the Mexicans in the distance. And no napping on my part. I picked as fast as I could.

The sun rose quickly and cooked the dew from the bolls of cotton. The thick air clung to my skin and soaked my overalls, and sweat dripped from my chin. One slight advantage in being so small was that most of the stalks were taller than me; I was partially shaded.

Two days of heavy picking, and the cotton trailer was full. Pappy took it to town; always Pappy, never my father. Like my mother and the garden, it was one of those chores that had been designated long before I came along. I was expected to ride with him, something I always enjoyed because it meant a trip to town, if only to the gin.

After a quick dinner, we took the truck to the field and hitched up the cotton trailer. Then we climbed along its edges and secured the tarp so that no bolls would blow away. It seemed a crime to waste a single ounce of something we'd worked so hard to gather.

As we drove back to the house, I saw the Mexicans behind the barn, grouped tightly, slowly eating their tortillas. My father was at the toolshed, patching an inner tube for a front tire on the John Deere. The women were washing dishes. Pappy abruptly stopped the truck. 'Stay here,' he said to me. 'I'll be right back.' He'd forgotten something.

When he returned from the house, he was carrying his twelve-gauge shotgun, which he slid under the seat without a word.

'We goin' huntin'?' I asked, knowing full well that I would not get an answer.

The Sisco affair had not been discussed over dinner or on the front porch. I think the adults had agreed to leave the subject alone, at least in my presence. But the shotgun suggested an abundance of possibilities.

I immediately thought of a gunfight, Gene Autry style, at the gin. The good guys, the farmers, of course, on one side, blasting away while ducking behind and between their cotton trailers; the bad guys, the Siscos and their friends, on the other side returning fire. Freshly picked cotton flying through the air as the trailers took one hit after another.

171

Windows crashing. Trucks exploding. By the time we crossed the river, there were casualties all over the gin lot.

'You gonna shoot somebody?' I asked, in an effort to force Pappy to say something.

'Tend to your own business,' he said gruffly as he shifted gears.

Perhaps he had a score to settle with some offending soul. This brought to mind one of the favorite Chandler stories. When Pappy was much younger, he, like all farmers, worked the fields with a team of mules. This was long before tractors, and all farming was done by man and animal. A ne'er-do-well neighbor named Woolbright saw Pappy in the fields one day, and evidently Pappy was having a bad day with the mules. According to Woolbright, Pappy was beating the poor beasts about their heads with a large stick. As Woolbright later told the story at the Tea Shoppe, he'd said, 'If I'd had a wet burlap sack, I'd've taught Eli Chandler a thing or two.' Word filtered back, and Pappy heard what Woolbright said. A few days later, after a long hot day in the fields, Pappy took a burlap sack, put it in a bucket of water, and skipping dinner, walked three miles to Woolbright's house. Or five miles or ten miles, depending on who happened to be telling the story.

Once there, he called on Woolbright to come out and settle things. Woolbright was just finishing dinner, and he may or may not have had a houseful of kids. Anyway, Woolbright walked to the screen door, looked out into his front yard, and decided things were safer inside.

Pappy yelled at him repeatedly to come on out.

'Here's your burlap sack, Woolbright!' he yelled. 'Now come on out and finish the job.'

Woolbright retreated deeper into his house, and when it was evident he wasn't coming out, Pappy threw the wet burlap sack through the screen door. Then he walked three or five or ten miles back home and went to bed, without dinner.

I'd heard the story enough to believe it was true. Even my mother believed it. Eli Chandler had been a hot-tempered brawler in his younger days, and at the age of sixty he still had a short fuse.

But he wouldn't kill anybody, unless it was in self-defense. And he preferred to use his fists or less menacing weapons like burlap sacks. The gun was traveling with us just in case. The Siscos were crazy people.

The gin was roaring when we arrived. A long line of trailers waited ahead of us, and I knew we'd be there for hours. It was dark when Pappy turned off the engine and tapped his fingers on the wheel. The Cardinals were playing, and I was anxious to get home.

Before getting out of the truck, Pappy surveyed the trailers and the trucks and tractors, and he watched the farmhands and gin workers go about their business. He was looking for trouble, and seeing none, he finally said, 'I'll go check in. You wait here.'

I watched him shuffle across the gravel and stop at a group of men outside the office. He stayed there awhile, talking and listening. Another group was congregated near a trailer in the line ahead of us, young men smoking and talking and waiting.

173

Though the gin was the center of activity, things moved slowly.

I caught a glimpse of a figure as it appeared from somewhere behind our truck. 'Howdy, Luke,' the voice said, giving me a start. When I jerked around, I saw the friendly face of Jackie Moon, an older boy from north of town.

'Hi, Jackie,' I said, very relieved. For a split second I thought one of the Siscos had started the ambush. He leaned on the front fender with his back to the gin, and produced a cigarette, one that he'd already rolled. 'Y'all heard from Ricky?' he asked.

I watched the cigarette. 'Not lately,' I said. 'We got a letter a couple of weeks ago.'

'How's he doin'?'

'Fine, I guess.'

He scraped a match on the side of our truck and lit the cigarette. He was tall and skinny and had been a basketball star at Monette High School for as long as I could remember. He and Ricky had played together, until Ricky got caught smoking behind the school. The coach, a veteran who'd lost a leg in the war, bounced Ricky from the team. Pappy had stomped around the Chandler farm for a week threatening to kill his younger son. Ricky told me privately that he was tired of basketball anyway. He wanted to play football, but Monette couldn't have a team because of cotton picking.

'I might be goin' over there,' Jackie said.

'To Korea?'

'Yep.'

I wanted to ask why he thought he was needed in Korea. As much as I hated picking cotton, I

174

would much rather do it than get shot at. 'What about basketball?' I asked. There was a rumor that Arkansas State was recruiting Jackie.

'I'm quittin' school,' he said, and blew a cloud into the air.

'Why?'

'I'm tired of it. Been goin' for twelve years already, on and off. That's more 'an anybody else in my family. I figure I've learned enough.'

Kids quit school all the time in our county. Ricky tried several times, and Pappy had become indifferent. Gran, on the other hand, laid down the law, and he finally graduated.

'Lot of boys gettin' shot over there,' he said, staring into the distance.

That was not something I wanted to hear, so I said nothing. He finished his cigarette and thrust his hands deep into his pockets. 'They're tellin' that you saw that Sisco fight,' he said, again without looking at me.

I figured that somehow the fight would get discussed during this trip to town. I remembered my father's stern warning not to discuss the incident with anyone.

But I could trust Jackie. He and Ricky had grown up together.

'Lots of folks saw it,' I said.

'Yeah, but ain't nobody talkin'. Hillbillies ain't sayin' a word 'cause it's one of their own. Locals ain't talkin' 'cause Eli's told everybody to shut up. That's what they're tellin', anyway.'

I believed him. I didn't doubt for a second that Eli Chandler had used the Baptist brethren to circle the wagons, at least until the cotton was in.

175

'What about the Siscos?' I asked.

'Ain't nobody seen 'em. They're layin' low. Had the funeral last Friday. Siscos dug the grave themselves; buried him out behind the Bethel church. Stick's watchin' 'em real close.'

There was another long gap in the conversation as the gin howled behind us. He rolled another cigarette, lit it, and finally said, 'I saw you there, at the fight.'

I felt like I'd been caught committing a crime. All I could think to say was, 'So.'

'I saw you with the little Pinter boy. And when that hillbilly picked up that piece of wood, I looked at the two of you and thought to myself, "Those boys don't need to see this." And I was right.'

'I wish I hadn't seen it.'

'I wish I hadn't, either,' he said, and discharged a neat circle of smoke.

I looked toward the gin to make sure Pappy wasn't close. He was still inside somewhere, in the small office where the gin owner kept the paperwork. Other trailers had arrived and were parked behind us. 'Have you talked to Stick?' I asked.

'Nope. Don't plan to. You?'

'Yeah, he came out to the house.'

'Did he talk to the hillbilly?'

'Yeah.'

'So Stick knows his name?'

'I guess.'

'Why didn't he arrest him?'

'I'm not sure. I told him it was three against one.'

He grunted and spat into the weeds. 'It was three against one all right, but nobody had to get killed. I don't like the Siscos, nobody does, but he didn't have to beat 'em like that.'

I didn't say anything. He drew on the cigarette and began talking, the smoke pouring out of his mouth and nose.

'His face was blood-red and his eyes were glowin', and all 'a sudden he stopped and just looked down at 'em, as if a ghost grabbed him and made him quit. Then he backed away and straightened up, and looked at 'em again as if somebody else had done it. Then he walked away, back onto Main Street, and all the other Siscos and their people ran up and got the boys. They borrowed Roe Duncan's pickup and hauled 'em home. Jerry never woke up. Roe hisself drove Jerry to the hospital in the middle of the night, but Roe said he was already dead. Fractured skull. Lucky the other two didn't die. He beat 'em just as bad as he beat Jerry. Ain't never seen nothin' like it.'

'Me neither.'

'I'd skip the fights for a while if I was you. You're too young.'

'Don't worry.' I looked at the gin and saw Pappy. 'Here comes Pappy,' I said.

He dropped the cigarette and stepped on it. 'Don't tell anybody what I said, all right?'

'Sure.'

'I don't want to get involved with that hillbilly.'

'I won't say a word.'

'Tell Ricky I said hello. Tell him to hold 'em off till I get there.'

'I will, Jackie.' He disappeared as quietly as he had come.

More secrets to keep.

Pappy unhitched the trailer and got behind the wheel. 'We ain't waitin' three hours,' he mumbled, and started the engine. He drove away from the gin and left town. At some point late in the night, a gin worker would hitch a small tractor to our trailer and pull it forward. The cotton would be sucked into the gin, and an hour later two perfect bales would emerge. They would be weighed, and then samples would be cut from each and set aside for the cotton buyer to evaluate. After breakfast, Pappy would return to the gin to get our trailer. He would examine the bales and the samples, and he would find something else to worry about.

The next day a letter arrived from Ricky. Gran had it lying on the kitchen table when we came through the back door, our feet dragging and our backs aching. I'd picked seventy-eight pounds of cotton that day, an all-time record for a seven-year-old, though records were impossible to monitor because so much lying went on. Especially among kids. Both Pappy and my father were now picking five hundred pounds every day.

Gran was humming and smiling, so we knew the letter had good news. She snatched it up and read it aloud to us. By then she had it memorized.

Dear Mom and Dad and Jesse and Kathleen and Luke:
   I hope all is well at home. I never thought I'd miss the cotton picking, but I sure wish I was home right now. I miss everything – the farm, the fried chicken, the Cardinals. Can you believe

*the Dodgers will take the pennant? Makes me
sick.*

*Anyway, I'm doing fine over here. Things are
quiet. We're not on the front anymore. My unit
is about five miles back, and we're catching up
on some sleep. We're warm and rested and eating
good, and right now nobody is shooting at us and
we're not shooting at anybody.*

*I really think I'll be home soon. It seems like
things are slowing down a little. We hear some
rumors about peace talks and such, so we've got
our fingers crossed.*

*I got your last batch of letters, and they mean
a lot to me. So keep writing. Luke, your letter
was a tad short, so write me a longer one.*

> *Gotta run. Love to all,*
> *Ricky*

We passed it around and read it again and again,
then Gran placed it in a cigar box next to the radio.
All of Ricky's letters were there, and it was not
uncommon to walk through the kitchen at night
and catch Pappy or Gran rereading them.

The new letter made us forget about our stiff
muscles and burned skin, and we all ate in a hurry
so we could sit around the table and write to
Ricky.

Using my Big Chief writing tablet and a pencil, I
told him all about Jerry Sisco and Hank Spruill,
and I spared no detail. Blood, splintered wood,
Stick Powers, everything. I didn't know how to
spell a lot of the words, so I simply guessed. If
anyone would forgive me for misspelling, it was
Ricky. Since I didn't want them to know that I

was spreading gossip all the way to Korea, I covered my tablet as best I could.

Five letters were written at the same time, and I'm sure five versions of the same events were described to Ricky. The adults told funny stories as we wrote. It was a happy moment in the midst of the harvest. Pappy turned on the radio, and we got the Cardinals as our letters grew longer and longer.

Sitting around the kitchen table, laughing and writing and listening to the game, there was not a single doubt that Ricky would soon be home.

He said he would be.

Chapter 15

Thursday afternoon, my mother found me in the fields and said that I was needed in the garden. I happily unstrapped my picking sack and left the other laborers lost in the cotton. We walked to the house, both of us relieved that the workday was over.

'We need to visit the Latchers,' she said along the way. 'I worry about them so. They might be hungry, you know.'

The Latchers had a garden, though not much of one. I doubted if anyone was going hungry. They certainly didn't have a crumb to spare, but starvation was unheard of in Craighead County. Even the poorest of the sharecroppers managed to grow tomatoes and cucumbers. Every farm family had a few chickens laying eggs.

But my mother was determined to see Libby so that the rumors could be confirmed or denied.

As we entered our garden, I realized what my mother was doing. If we hurried, and made it to the Latchers' before quitting time, then the parents and all those kids would be in the fields. Libby, if she was in fact pregnant, would be hanging around the house, most likely alone. She would have no choice but to come out and accept our vegetables. We could blindside her, nail her with Christian goodness while her protectors were away. It was a brilliant plan.

Under the strict supervision of my mother, I began picking tomatoes, cucumbers, peas, butter beans, corn – almost everything in the garden. 'Get that small red tomato there, Luke, to your right,' she said. 'No, no, those peas can wait.' And, 'No, that cucumber isn't quite ready.'

Though she often gathered the produce herself, she preferred to oversee matters. A balance to the garden could be maintained if she could keep her distance, survey the entire plot, and with the eye of an artist, direct my efforts, or my father's, in removing the food from the vines.

I hated the garden, but at that moment I hated the fields even more. Anything was better than picking cotton.

As I reached for an ear of corn, I saw something between the stalks that stopped me cold. Beyond the garden was a small, shaded strip of grass, too narrow to play catch on, and thus good for nothing. Next to it was the east wall of our house, the side away from any traffic. On the west side was the kitchen door, the parking place for our truck, the footpaths that led to the barn, the outbuildings, and the fields. Everything happened on the west side; nothing on the east.

At the corner, facing the garden and out of view of everyone, someone had painted a portion of the bottom board. Painted it white. The rest of the house was the same pale brown it had always been, the same drab color of old, sturdy oak planks.

'What is it, Luke?' my mother asked. She was never in a hurry in the garden, because it was her sanctuary, but today she was planning an ambush, and time was crucial.

'I don't know,' I said, still frozen.

She stepped beside me and peered through the cornstalks that bordered and secluded her garden, and when her eyes settled upon the painted board, she, too, stood still.

The paint was thick at the corner, but thinned as the board ran toward the rear of the house. It was obviously a work in progress. Someone was painting our house.

'It's Trot,' she said softly, a smile forming at the corners of her mouth.

I hadn't thought of him, hadn't yet had time to consider a culprit, but it immediately became clear that he was the painter. Who else could it be? Who else loitered around the front yard all day with nothing to do while the rest of us slaved in the fields? Who else would work at such a pitiful pace? Who else would be dense enough to paint another man's house without permission?

And it had been Trot who'd yelled at Hank to stop torturing me about our little unpainted, sodbuster house. Trot had come to my rescue.

But where would Trot get the money to buy paint? And why would he do it in the first place? Oh, there were dozens of questions.

She took a step back, then left the garden. I followed her to the corner of the house, where we examined the paint. We could smell it there, and it appeared to be sticky. She surveyed the front yard. Trot was nowhere to be seen.

'What're we gonna do?' I asked.

'Nothing, at least not now.'

'You gonna tell anybody?'

'I'll talk to your father about it. In the meantime, let's keep it a secret.'

'You told me secrets were bad for boys.'

'They're bad when you keep them from your parents.'

We filled two straw baskets with vegetables and loaded them into the truck. My mother drove about once a month. She could certainly handle Pappy's truck, but she could not relax behind the wheel. She gripped it fiercely, pumped the clutch and brakes, then turned the key. We jerked and lurched in reverse, and even laughed as the old truck slowly got turned around. As we left, I saw Trot lying under the Spruill truck, watching us from behind a rear tire.

The frolicking stopped minutes later when we got to the river. 'Hang on, Luke,' she said as she shifted into low and leaned over the wheel, her eyes wild with fear. Hang on to what? It was a one-lane bridge with no guardrails. If she drove off, then we'd both drown.

'You can do it, Mom,' I said without much conviction.

'Of course I can,' she said. I'd crossed the bridge with her before, and it was always an adventure. We crept over it, both afraid to look down. We didn't breathe until we hit dirt on the other side.

'Good job, Mom,' I said.

'Nothin' to it,' she said, finally exhaling.

At first I couldn't see any Latchers in the fields, but as we approached the house, I saw a cluster of straw hats deep in the cotton, at the far end of their crop. I couldn't tell if they heard us, but they did not stop picking. We parked close to the front porch as the dust settled around the truck. Before we could get out, Mrs. Latcher was coming down the front steps, wiping her hands nervously on a rag of some sort. She seemed to be talking to herself and appeared very worried.

'Hello, Mrs. Chandler,' she said, looking off. I never knew why she didn't use my mother's first name. She was older and had at least six more children.

'Hello, Darla. We've brought some vegetables.'

The two women were facing each other. 'I'm so glad you're here,' Mrs. Latcher said, her voice very anxious.

'What's the matter?'

Mrs. Latcher glanced at me, but only for a second. 'I need your help. It's Libby. I think she's about to have a baby.'

'A baby?' my mother said, as if she hadn't a clue.

'Yes. I think she's in labor.'

'Then let's call the doctor.'

'Oh no. We can't do that. No one can know about this. No one. It has to be kept quiet.'

I had moved to the rear of the truck, and I was crouching down a bit so Mrs. Latcher couldn't see me. That way, I figured she'd talk more. Something big was about to happen, and I didn't want to miss any of it.

'We're so ashamed,' she said, her voice cracking.

185

'She won't tell us who the father is, and right now I don't care. I just want the baby to get here.'

'But you need a doctor.'

'No ma'am. Nobody can know about this. If the doctor comes, then the whole county'll know. You gotta keep it quiet, Mrs. Chandler. Can you promise me?'

The poor woman was practically crying. She was desperate to keep a secret that had been the talk of Black Oak for months.

'Let me see her,' my mother said without answering the question, and the women started for the house. 'Luke, you stay here at the truck,' she said over her shoulder.

As soon as they disappeared inside, I walked around the house and peeked into the first window I saw. It was a tiny living room with old, dirty mattresses on the floor. At the next window, I heard their voices. I froze and listened. The fields were behind me.

'Libby, this is Mrs. Chandler,' Mrs. Latcher was saying. 'She's here to help you.'

Libby whimpered something I couldn't understand. She seemed to be in great pain. Then I heard her say, 'I'm so sorry.'

'It's gonna be okay,' my mother said. 'When did the labor start?'

'About an hour ago,' Mrs. Latcher replied.

'I'm so scared, Mama,' Libby said, much louder. Her voice was pure terror. Both ladies tried to calm her.

Now that I was no longer a novice on the subject of female anatomy, I was quite anxious to have a look at a pregnant girl. But she sounded too close to the window, and if I got caught peeking in, my father would beat me for a week. An unauthorized view of a woman in labor was undoubtedly a sin of the greatest magnitude. I might even be stricken blind on the spot.

But I couldn't help myself. I crouched and slinked just under the windowsill. I removed my straw hat and was easing upward when a heavy clod of dirt landed less than two feet from my head. It crashed onto the side of the house with a boom, rattling the rickety boards and scaring the women to the point of making them yell. Bits of dirt splattered and hit the side of my face. I hit the ground and rolled away from the window. Then I scrambled to my feet and looked at the fields.

Percy Latcher was not far away, standing between two rows of cotton, holding another clod of dirt with one hand, and pointing at me with another.

'It's your boy,' a voice said.

I looked at the window and got a glimpse of Mrs. Latcher's head. One more look at Percy, and I raced like a scalded dog back to the pickup. I jumped into the front seat, rolled up the window, and waited for my mother.

Percy disappeared into the fields. It would be quitting time soon, and I wanted to leave before the rest of the Latchers drifted in.

A couple of toddlers appeared on the porch, both of them naked, a boy and a girl, and I wondered what they thought of their big sister having yet another one. They just stared at me.

My mother came out in a hurry, Mrs. Latcher on her heels, talking rapidly as they walked to the truck.

'I'll get Ruth,' my mother said, meaning Gran.

'Please do, and hurry,' Mrs. Latcher said.

'Ruth's done this many times.'

'Please get her. And please don't tell anyone. Can we trust you, Mrs. Chandler?'

My mother was opening the door, trying to get inside. 'Of course you can.'

'We're so ashamed,' Mrs. Latcher said, wiping tears. 'Please don't tell anyone.'

'It's goin' to be all right, Darla,' my mother said, turning the key. 'I'll be back in half an hour.'

We lunged into reverse, and after a few bolts and stops, we were turned around and leaving the Latcher place. She was driving much faster, and this kept her attention, mostly.

'Did you see Libby Latcher?' she finally asked.

'No ma'am,' I said quickly and firmly. I knew the question was coming, and I was ready with the truth.

'Are you sure?'

'Yes ma'am.'

'What were you doin' beside the house?'

'I was just walkin' around when Percy threw a dirt clod at me. That's what hit the house. It wasn't my fault, it was Percy's.' My words were fast and sure, and I know she wanted to believe me. More important matters were on her mind.

We stopped at the bridge. She shifted into low, held her breath, and again said, 'Hang on, Luke.'

Gran was in the backyard, at the pump drying her face and hands and about to start supper. I had to run to keep up with my mother.

188

'We have to go to the Latchers',' she said. 'That girl is in labor, and her mother wants you to deliver it.'

'Oh, dear,' Gran said, her weary eyes suddenly alive with adventure. 'So she's really pregnant.'

'Very much so. She's been in labor for over an hour.'

I was listening hard and thoroughly enjoying my involvement, when suddenly and for no apparent reason, both women turned and stared at me. 'Luke, go to the house,' my mother said rather sternly, and began pointing, as if I didn't know where the house was.

'What'd I do?' I asked, wounded.

'Just go,' she said, and I began to slink away. Arguing would get me nowhere. They resumed their conversation in hushed tones, and I was at the back porch when my mother called to me.

'Luke, run to the fields and get your father! We need him!'

'And hurry!' Gran said. She was thrilled with the prospect of doctoring on a real patient.

I didn't want to go back to the fields, and I would've argued but for the fact that Libby Latcher was having a baby at that very moment. I said, 'Yes ma'am,' and sprinted past them.

My father and Pappy were at the trailer, weighing cotton for the last time that day. It was almost five, and the Spruills had gathered with their heavy sacks. The Mexicans were nowhere to be seen.

I managed to pull my father aside and explain the situation. He said something to Pappy, and we

189

trotted back to the house. Gran was gathering supplies – rubbing alcohol, towels, painkillers, bottles of nasty remedies that would make Libby forget about childbirthing. She was arranging her arsenal on the kitchen table, and I had never seen her move so fast.

'Get cleaned up!' she said sharply to my father. 'You'll drive us there. It might take some time.' I could tell he was less than excited about getting dragged into this, but he wasn't about to argue with his mother.

'I'll get cleaned up, too,' I said.

'You're not going anywhere,' my mother said to me. She was at the kitchen sink, slicing a tomato. Pappy and I would get leftovers for supper, in addition to the usual platter of cucumbers and tomatoes.

They left in a rush, my father driving, my mother wedged between him and Gran, the three of them off to rescue Libby. I stood on the front porch and watched them speed away, a cloud of dust boiling behind the truck until it stopped at the river. I really wanted to go.

Supper would be beans and cold biscuits. Pappy hated leftovers. He thought the women should've prepared supper before tending to the Latchers, but then, he was opposed to sending them food in the first place.

'Don't know why both women had to go,' he mumbled as he sat down. 'They're as curious as cats, aren't they, Luke? They can't wait to get over there, and see that pregnant girl.'

'Yes sir,' I said.

He blessed the food with a quick prayer, and we ate in silence.

'Who are the Cardinals playin'?' he asked.

'Reds.'

'You wanna listen to it?'

'Sure.' We listened to the game every night. What else was there to do?

We cleared the table and placed our dirty dishes in the sink. Pappy would never consider washing them; that was work for the women. After dark, we sat on the porch in our usual positions and waited for Harry Caray and the Cardinals. The air was heavy and still dreadfully hot.

'How long does it take to have a baby?' I asked.

'Depends,' Pappy said from his swing. That was all he said, and after waiting long enough, I asked, 'Depends on what?'

'Oh, lots of things. Some babies pop right out, others take days.'

'How long did I take?'

He thought for a moment. 'Don't guess I remember. First babies usually take longer.'

'Were you around?'

'Nope. I was on a tractor.' The arrival of babies was not a subject Pappy cared to dwell on, and the conversation lagged.

I saw Tally ease away from the front yard and disappear into the darkness. The Spruills were settling in; their cooking fire was just about out.

The Reds scored four runs in the top of the first inning. Pappy got so upset he went to bed. I turned off the radio and sat on the porch, watching for Tally. Before long, I heard Pappy snoring.

Chapter 16

I was determined to sit on the front steps and wait for my parents and Gran to return from the Latchers'. I could almost see the scene over there; the women in the back room with Libby, the men sitting outside with all those children, as far away from the birthing as possible. Their house was just across the river, not far at all, and I was missing it.

Fatigue was hitting hard, and I almost fell asleep. Camp Spruill was still and dark, but I hadn't seen Tally come back yet.

I tiptoed through the house, heard Pappy in a deep sleep, and went to the back porch. I sat on the edge with my legs hanging off. The fields beyond the barn and the silo were a soft gray when the moon broke through the scattered clouds. Otherwise, they were hidden in black. I saw her walking alone on the main field road, just as moonlight swept the land for a second. She was in no hurry. Then everything was black again. There was not a sound for a long time, until she stepped on a twig near the house.

'Tally,' I whispered as loudly as I could.

After a long pause, she answered, 'Is that you, Luke?'

'Over here,' I said. 'On the porch.'

She was barefoot and made no sound when she walked. 'What're you doin' out here, Luke?' she said, standing in front of me.

'Where've you been?' I asked.

'Just takin' a walk.'

'Why are you takin' a walk?'

'I don't know. Sometimes I have to get away from my family.'

That certainly made sense to me. She sat beside me on the porch, pulled her skirt up past her knees, and began swinging her legs. 'Sometimes I want to just run away from them,' she said, very softly. 'You ever want to run away, Luke?'

'Not really. I'm only seven. But I'm not gonna live here for the rest of my life.'

'Where you gonna live?'

'St Louis.'

'Why St Louis?'

'That's where the Cardinals play.'

'And you're gonna be a Cardinal?'

'Sure am.'

'You're a smart boy, Luke. Only a fool would wanna pick cotton for the rest of his life. Me, I wanna go up North, too, up where it's cool and there's lots of snow.'

'Where?'

'I'm not sure. Montreal, maybe.'

'Where's that?'

'Canada.'

'Do they have baseball?'

'I don't think so.'

'Then forget it.'

'No, it's beautiful. We studied it in school, in history. It was settled by the French, and that's what everybody speaks.'

'Do you speak French?'

'No, but I can learn.'

'It's easy. I can already speak Spanish. Juan taught me last year.'

'Really?'

'*Si.*'

'Say something else.'

'*Buenos días. Por favor. Adios. Gracias. Señor. ¿Cómo está?*'

'Wow.'

'See, I told you it was easy. How far away is Montreal?'

'I'm not sure. A long way, I think. That's one reason I wanna go there.'

A light suddenly came on in Pappy's bedroom. It fell across the far end of the porch and startled us. 'Be quiet,' I whispered.

'Who is it?' she whispered back, ducking as if bullets were about to come our way.

'That's just Pappy getting some water. He's up and down all night long.' Pappy went to the kitchen and opened the refrigerator. I watched him through the screen door. He drank two glasses of water, then stomped back to his bedroom and turned off the light. When things were dark and silent again, she said, 'Why is he up all night?'

'He worries a lot. Ricky's fightin' in Korea.'

'Who's Ricky?'

'My uncle. He's nineteen.'

She pondered this for a moment, then said, 'Is he cute?'

'I don't know. Don't really think about that. He's my best buddy, and I wish he'd come home.'

We thought about Ricky for a moment as our feet dangled off the porch and the night passed.

'Say, Luke, the pickup left before dinner. Where'd it go?'

'Over to the Latchers'.'

'Who are they?'

'Some sharecroppers just across the river.'

'Why'd they go over there?'

'I can't tell you.'

'Why not?'

''Cause it's a secret.'

'What kinda secret?'

'Big one.'

'Come on, Luke. We already have secrets, don't we?'

'I guess.'

'I haven't told anybody that you watched me at the creek, have I?'

'I guess not.'

'And if I did, you'd get in big trouble, wouldn't you?'

'I reckon I would.'

'So there. I can keep a secret, you can keep a secret. Now what's goin' on over at the Latchers'?'

'You promise you won't tell.'

'I promise.'

The whole town already knew Libby was pregnant. What was the use in pretending it was a secret anyway? 'Well, there's this girl, Libby Latcher, and she's havin' a baby. Right now.'

195

'How old is she?'

'Fifteen.'

'Gosh.'

'And they're tryin' to keep it quiet. They wouldn't call a real doctor 'cause then everybody would know about it. So they asked Gran to come over and birth the baby.'

'Why are they keepin' it quiet?'

''Cause she ain't married.'

'No kiddin'. Who's the daddy?'

'She ain't sayin'.'

'Nobody knows?'

'Nobody but Libby.'

'Do you know her?'

'I've seen her before, but there's a bunch of Latchers. I know her brother Percy. He says he's twelve, but I'm not so sure. Hard to tell 'cause they don't go to school.'

'Do you know how girls get pregnant?'

'I reckon not.'

'Then I'd better not tell you.'

That was fine with me. Ricky had tried once to talk about girls, but it was sickening.

Her feet swung faster as she digested this wonderful gossip. 'The river ain't far,' she said.

''Bout a mile.'

'How far on the other side do they live?'

'Just a little ways down a dirt trail.'

'You ever see a baby birthed, Luke?'

'Nope. Seen cows and dogs but not a real baby.'

'Me neither.'

She dropped to her feet, grabbed my hand, and yanked me off the porch. Her strength was surprising. 'Let's go, Luke. Let's go see what we can see.' She was dragging me before I could think of anything to say.

'You're crazy, Tally,' I protested, trying to stop her.

'No, Luke,' she whispered. 'Its an adventure, just like down at the creek the other day. You liked that, didn't you?'

'Sure did.'

'Then trust me.'

'What if we get caught?'

'How we gonna get caught? Everybody's sound asleep around here. Your grandpa just woke up and didn't think about lookin' in on you. Come on, don't be a chicken.'

I suddenly realized I would've followed Tally anywhere.

We crept behind the trees, through the ruts where the truck should've been, along the short drive, staying as far away from the Spruills as possible. We could hear snoring and the heavy breathing of weary people asleep at last. We made it to the road without a sound. Tally was quick and agile, and she cut through the night. We turned toward the river, and the moon broke free and lit our path. The one-lane road was barely wide enough for two trucks to squeeze past each other, and cotton grew close to its edges. With no moon we had to watch our steps, but with the light we could look up and see ahead. We were both barefoot. There was just enough gravel in the road to keep our steps short and quick, but the soles of our feet were like the leather of my baseball glove.

I was scared but determined not to show it. She seemed to have no fear – no fear of getting caught,

197

no fear of the darkness, no fear of sneaking up on a house where a baby was being born. At times Tally was aloof, almost moody and dark, and seemed as old as my mother. Then she could be a kid who laughed when she played baseball, liked being looked at when she bathed, took long walks in the dark, and most important, enjoyed the company of a seven-year-old.

We stopped in the center of the bridge and carefully looked over its side at the water below. I told her about the channel catfish down there, about how big they were and the trash they fed on, and about the forty-four-pound one that Ricky had caught. She held my hand as we crossed to the other side, a gentle squeeze, one of affection and not safeguarding.

The trail to the Latchers' was much darker. We slowed considerably because we were trying to see the house while staying on the trail. Since they had no electricity, there were no lights, nothing but blackness in their bend of the river.

She heard something and stopped cold. Voices, off in the distance. We stepped to the edge of their cotton and waited patiently for the moon. I pointed here and there and gave her my best guess as to the location of their house. The voices were of children, no doubt the Latcher brood.

The moon finally cooperated, and we got a look at the landscape. The dark shadow of the house was the same distance as our barn was to our back porch, about 350 feet, same as home plate is from the outfield wall in Sportsman's Park. Most great distances in my life were measured by that wall. Pappy's truck was parked in the front.

'We'd better go around this way,' she said calmly, as if she'd led many such raids. We sank into the cotton and followed one row and then another as we silently moved in a great semicircle through their crops. In most places, their cotton was almost as tall as I was. When we came to a gap where the stalks were thin, we stopped and studied the terrain. There was a faint light in the back room of the house, the room where they kept Libby. When we were directly east of it, we began cutting across rows of cotton, very quietly moving toward the house.

The chances of someone seeing us were slim. We weren't expected, of course, and they were thinking of other matters. And the crops were thick and dark at night; a kid could crawl on hands and knees through the stalks without ever being seen.

My partner in crime moved deftly, as ably as any soldier I'd seen in the movies. She kept her eyes on the house and carefully brushed the stalks aside, always clearing a path for me. Not a word was spoken. We took our time, slowly advancing on the side of the house. The cotton grew close to the narrow dirt yard, and when we were ten rows away, we settled in a spot and surveyed the situation.

We could hear the Latcher kids gathered near our pickup, which was parked as far away from the front porch as possible. My father and Mr. Latcher sat on the tailgate, talking softly. The children were quiet, then they all talked at once. Everyone seemed to be waiting, and after a few minutes I got the impression they'd been waiting for a long time.

Before us was the window, and from our hiding

place we were closer to the action than the rest of the Latchers and my father. And we were wonderfully hidden from everything; a searchlight from the roof of the house could not have spotted us.

There was a candle on a table of some sort just inside the window. The women moved around, and judging from the shadows that rose and fell, I figured there were several candles in the room. The light was dim, the shadows heavy.

'Let's move forward,' Tally whispered. By then we'd been there for five minutes, and though I was frightened, I didn't think we would ever get caught.

We advanced ten feet, then nestled down in another safe place.

'This is close enough,' I said.

'Maybe.'

The light from the room fell to the ground outside. The window had no screen, no curtains. As we waited, my heart slowed, and my breathing returned to normal. My eyes focused on the surroundings, and I began to hear the sounds of the night – the crickets' chorus, the bullfrogs croaking down by the river, the murmuring of the deep voices of the men in the distance.

My mother and Gran and Mrs. Latcher also talked in very low voices. We could hear, but we couldn't understand.

When all was quiet and still, Libby screamed in agony, and I nearly jumped out of my skin. Her pained voice echoed through the fields, and I was sure she had died. Silence engulfed the pickup. Even the crickets seemed to stop for a second.

'What happened?' I asked.

'A labor contraction,' Tally said, without taking her eyes off the window.

'What's that?'

She shrugged. 'Just part of it. It'll get worse.'

'That poor girl.'

'She asked for it.'

'What do you mean?' I asked.

'Never mind,' she said.

Things were quiet for a few minutes, then we heard Libby crying. Her mother and Gran tried to console her. 'I'm so sorry,' Libby said over and over.

'It's gonna be all right,' her mother said.

'Nobody'll know about it,' Gran said. It was obviously a lie, but maybe it provided a little relief for Libby.

'You're gonna have a beautiful baby,' my mother said.

A stray Latcher wandered over, one of the mid-sized ones, and sneaked its way close to the window, the same way I'd crept upon it just a few hours earlier, just moments before Percy nearly maimed me with the dirt clod. He or she – I couldn't tell the difference – began snooping and was getting an eyeful when an older sibling barked at the end of the house, 'Lloyd, get away from that window.'

Lloyd immediately withdrew and scurried away in the darkness. His trespass was promptly reported to Mr. Latcher, and a vicious tail-whipping ensued somewhere nearby. Mr. Latcher used a stick of some variety. He kept saying, 'Next time I'll get me a bigger stick!' Lloyd thought the current one was more than enough. His screams probably could be heard at the bridge.

When the mauling was over, Mr. Latcher boomed, 'I told you kids to stay close, and to stay away from the house!'

We could not see this episode, nor did we have to, to get the full effect.

But I was more horrified thinking about the severity and duration of the beating I'd get if my father knew where I was at that moment. I suddenly wanted to leave.

'How long does it take to have a baby?' I whispered to Tally. If she was weary, she didn't show it. She rested on her knees, frozen, her eyes never leaving the window.

'Depends. First one always takes longer.'

'How long does the seventh one take?'

'I don't know. By then they just drop out, I guess. Who's had seven?'

'Libby's mom. Seven or eight. I think she drops one a year.'

I was about to doze off when the next contraction hit. Again it rattled the house and led first to weeping and then to soothing words inside the room. Then things leveled off once more, and I realized this might go on for a long time.

When I couldn't keep my eyes open any longer, I curled up on the warm soil between the two rows of cotton. 'Don't you think we oughta leave?' I whispered.

'No,' she said firmly, without moving.

'Wake me up if anything happens,' I said.

Tally readjusted herself. She sat on her rear and crossed her legs, and gently placed my head in her

202

lap. She rubbed my shoulder and my head. I didn't want to go to sleep, but I just couldn't help it.

When I awoke, I was at first lost in a strange world, lying in a field, in total blackness. I didn't move. The ground around me wasn't warm anymore, and my feet were cold. I opened my eyes and stared above, terrified until I realized there was cotton standing over me. I heard urgent voices nearby. Someone said, 'Libby,' and I was jolted back to reality. I reached for Tally, but she was gone.

I rose from the ground and peered through the cotton. The scene hadn't changed. The window was still open, the candles still burning, but my mother and Gran and Mrs. Latcher were very busy.

'Tally!' I whispered urgently, too loud, I thought, but I was more scared than ever.

'Shhhhh!' came the reply. 'Over here.'

I could barely see the back of her head, two rows in front and over to the right. She had, of course, angled for a better view. I knifed through the stalks and was soon at her side.

Home plate is sixty feet from the pitcher's mound. We were much closer to the window than that. Only two rows of cotton stood between us and the edge of their side yard. Ducking low and looking up through the stalks, I could finally see the shadowy sweating faces of my mother and grandmother and Mrs. Latcher. They were staring down, looking at Libby, of course, and we could not see her. I'm not sure I wanted to at this point, but my buddy certainly did.

The women were reaching and shoving and urging her to push and breathe and push and breathe, all the while assuring her that things were going to be fine. Things didn't sound fine. The poor girl was bawling and grunting, occasionally yelling – high piercing shrieks that were hardly muffled by the walls of the room. Her anguished voice carried deep through the still night, and I wondered what her little brothers and sisters thought of it all.

When Libby wasn't grunting and crying, she was saying, 'I'm sorry. I'm so sorry.' It went on and on, time after time, a mindless chant from a suffering girl.

'It's okay, sweetie,' her mother replied a thousand times.

'Can't they do something?' I whispered.

'Nope, not a thing. The baby comes when it wants to.'

I wanted to ask Tally just exactly how she knew so much about child-birthing, but I held my tongue. It was none of my business, and she would probably tell me so.

Suddenly, things were quiet and still inside the room. The Chandler women backed away, then Mrs. Latcher leaned down with a glass of water. Libby was silent.

'What's the matter?' I asked.

'Nothing.'

The break in the action gave me time to think of other things, namely getting caught. I'd seen enough. This adventure had run its course. Tally had likened it to the trip to Siler's Creek, but it paled in comparison with that little escapade.

We'd been gone for hours. What if Pappy stumbled into Ricky's room to check on me? What if one of the Spruills woke up and started looking for Tally? What if my father got bored with it all and went home?

The beating I'd get would hurt for days, if in fact I survived it. I was beginning to panic when Libby started heaving loudly again, while the women implored her to breathe and push.

'There it is!' my mother said, and a frenzy followed as the women hovered frantically over their patient.

'Keep pushin'!' Gran said loudly.

Libby groaned even more. She was exhausted, but at least the end was in sight.

'Don't give up, sweetie,' her mother said. 'Don't give up.'

Tally and I were perfectly still, mesmerized by the drama. She took my hand and squeezed it tightly. Her jaws were clenched, her eyes wide with wonder.

'It's comin'!' my mother said, and for a brief moment things were quiet. Then we heard the cry of a newborn, a quick gurgling protest, and a new Latcher had arrived.

'It's a boy,' Gran said, and she lifted up the tiny infant, still covered in blood and afterbirth.

'It's a boy,' Mrs. Latcher repeated.

There was no response from Libby.

I'd seen more than I bargained for. 'Let's go,' I said, trying to pull away, but Tally wasn't moving.

Gran and my mother continued working on Libby while Mrs. Latcher cleaned the baby, who was furious about something and crying loudly. I

205

couldn't help but think of how sad it would be to become a Latcher, to be born into that small, dirty house with a pack of other kids.

A few minutes passed, and Percy appeared at the window. 'Can we see the baby?' he asked, almost afraid to look in.

'In a minute,' Mrs. Latcher replied.

They gathered at the window, the entire collection of Latchers, including the father, who was now a grandfather, and waited to see the baby. They were just in front of us, halfway between home and the mound, it seemed, and I stopped breathing for fear they would hear us. But they weren't thinking about intruders. They were looking at the open window, all still with wonder.

Mrs. Latcher brought the infant over and leaned down so he could meet his family. He reminded me of my baseball glove; he was almost as dark, and wrapped in a towel. He was quiet for the moment and appeared unimpressed with the mob watching him.

'How's Libby?' one of them asked.

'She's fine,' Mrs. Latcher said.

'Can we see her?'

'No, not right now. She's very tired.' She withdrew the baby, and the other Latchers retreated slowly to the front of the house. I could not see my father, but I knew he was hiding somewhere near his truck. Hard cash could not entice him to look at an illegitimate newborn.

For a few minutes, the women seemed as busy as they'd been just before the birth, but then they slowly finished their work.

My trance wore off, and I realized that we were a

206

long way from home. 'We gotta go, Tally!' I whispered urgently. She was ready and I followed her as we backtracked, cutting our way through the stalks until we were away from the house, then turning south and running with the rows of cotton. We stopped to get our bearings. The light from the window could not be seen. The moon had disappeared. There were no shapes or shadows from the Latcher place. Total darkness.

We turned west, again stepping across the rows, cutting through the stalks, pushing them aside so they wouldn't scrape our faces. The rows ended, and we found the trail leading to the main road. My feet hurt, and my legs ached, but we couldn't waste time. We ran to the bridge. Tally wanted to watch the waters swirling below, but I made her keep going.

'Let's walk,' she said, on our side of the bridge, and for a moment we stopped running. We walked in silence, both of us trying to catch our breath. Fatigue was quickly gaining on us; the adventure had been worth it, but we were paying the price. We were approaching our farm when there was a rumbling behind us. Headlights! On the bridge! In terror, we bolted into high gear. Tally could easily outrun me, which would've been humiliating except that I didn't have time for shame, and she held back a step so she wouldn't lose me.

I knew my father would not drive fast, not at night, on our dirt road, with Gran and my mother with him, but the headlights were still gaining on us. When we were close to our house, we jumped the shallow ditch and ran along a field. The engine was getting louder.

'I'll wait here, Luke,' she said, stopping near the edge of our yard. The truck was almost upon us. 'You run to the back porch and sneak in. I'll wait till they go inside. Hurry.'

I kept running, and darted around the back corner of the house just as the truck pulled into the yard. I crept into the kitchen without a sound, then to Ricky's room, where I grabbed a pillow and curled up on the floor, next to the window. I was too dirty and wet to get into bed, and I prayed they'd be too tired to check on me.

They made little noise as they entered the kitchen. They whispered as they removed their shoes and boots. A ray of light slanted into my room. Their shadows moved through it, but no one looked in on little Luke. Within minutes they were in bed, and the house was quiet. I planned to wait a bit, then slip into the kitchen and wash my face and hands with a cloth. Afterward I'd crawl into the bed and sleep forever. If they heard me moving about, I'd simply say that they had awakened me when they got home.

Formulating this plan was the last thing I remember before falling fast asleep.

Chapter 17

I don't know how long I slept, but it felt like only minutes. Pappy was kneeling over me, asking me why I was on the floor. I tried to answer, but nothing worked. I was paralyzed from fatigue.

'It's just me and you,' he said. 'The rest of 'em's sleepin' in.' His voice was dripping with contempt.

Still unable to think or speak, I followed him to the kitchen, where the coffee was ready. We ate cold biscuits and sorghum in silence. Pappy, of course, was irritated because he expected a full breakfast. And he was furious because Gran and my parents were sleeping instead of preparing for the fields.

'That Latcher girl had a baby last night,' he said, wiping his mouth. That Latcher girl and her new baby were interfering with our cotton, and our breakfast, and Pappy could barely control his temper.

'She did?' I said, trying to appear surprised.

'Yeah, but they still ain't found the daddy.'

'They haven't?'

'No. They wanna keep it quiet, okay, so don't say anything about it.'

'Yes sir.'

'Hurry up. We gotta go.'

'What time did they get in?'

'Around three.'

He left and started the tractor. I placed the dishes in the sink and looked in on my parents. They were deathly still; the only sounds were of deep breathing. I wanted to shake off my boots, crawl into bed with them, and sleep for a week. Instead, I dragged myself outside. The sun was just breaking over the trees to the east. In the distance, I could see the silhouettes of the Mexicans walking into the fields.

The Spruills were trudging over from the front yard. Tally was nowhere to be seen. I asked Bo, and he said she was feeling bad. Maybe an upset stomach. Pappy heard this, and his frustration jumped up another notch. Another picker in bed instead of in the fields.

All I could think was: Why hadn't I thought of an upset stomach?

We rode a quarter of a mile to a spot where the half-full cotton trailer was parked, rising like a monument amid the flat fields and calling us back for another day of misery. We slowly took our sacks and began picking. I waited for Pappy to move down his row, then I moved far away from him, and far away from the Spruills.

I worked hard for an hour or so. The cotton was wet and soft to the touch, and the sun was not yet overhead. I was not motivated by money or fear; rather, I wanted a soft place to sleep. When I was so deep in the fields no one could find me, and there was enough cotton in my sack to make a nice little mattress, I hit the ground.

My father arrived mid-morning, and out of eighty acres of cotton, just happened to select the row next to mine. 'Luke!' he said angrily as he stumbled upon me. He was too startled to scold me, and by the time I came to my senses, I was complaining of an upset stomach, a headache, and for good measure I threw in the fact that I had not slept much the night before.

'Why not?' he asked, hovering over me.

'I was waitin' on y'all to get home.' There was an element of truth in this.

'And why were you waitin' on us?'

'I wanted to know about Libby.'

'Well, she had a baby. What else do you wanna know?'

'Pappy told me.' I slowly got to my feet and tried to appear as sick as possible.

'Go to the house,' he said, and I left without a word.

Chinese and North Korean troops ambushed an American convoy near Pyonggang, killing at least eighty and taking many prisoners. Mr. Edward R. Murrow opened his nightly news with the story, and Gran started praying. As always, she was seated across the kitchen table from me. My mother was leaning on the kitchen sink, and she, too, stopped everything and closed her eyes. I heard Pappy cough on the back porch. He was also listening.

Peace talks had been abandoned again, and the Chinese were moving more troops into Korea. Mr.

211

Murrow said that a truce, once so close, now seemed impossible. His words were a little heavier that night, or maybe we were just more exhausted than usual. He broke for a commercial, then returned with a story about an earthquake.

Gran and my mother were moving slowly around the kitchen when Pappy entered. He tousled my hair as if things were just fine. 'What's for supper?' he asked.

'Pork chops,' my mother answered.

Then my father drifted in, and we took our places. After Pappy blessed the food, all of us prayed for Ricky. There was practically no conversation; everyone was thinking about Korea, but nobody wanted to mention it.

My mother was talking about a project her Sunday school class was pondering, when I heard the faint squeaking of the screen door out on the back porch. No one heard the noise but me. There was no wind, nothing to shove the door one way or the other. I stopped eating.

'What is it, Luke?' Gran asked.

'I thought I heard somethin',' I said.

Everyone looked at the door. Nothing. They resumed eating.

Then Percy Latcher stepped into the kitchen, and we froze. He took two steps through the door and stopped, as if he were lost. He was barefoot, covered with dirt from head to foot, and his eyes were red, as if he'd been crying for hours. He looked at us; we looked at him. Pappy started to stand up and deal with the situation. I said, 'It's Percy Latcher.'

Pappy remained in his seat, holding a knife in his

right hand. Percy's eyes were glazed, and when he breathed, a low moaning sound came forth as if he were trying to suppress a rage. Or maybe he was wounded, or somebody across the river was hurt and he'd raced to our house for help.

'What is it, boy?' Pappy barked at him. 'It's common courtesy to knock before you come in.'

Percy fixed his unflinching eyes upon Pappy and said, 'Ricky done it.'

'Ricky done what?' Pappy asked, his voice suddenly softer, already in retreat.

'Ricky done it.'

'Ricky done what?' Pappy repeated.

'That baby's his,' Percy said. 'It's Ricky's.'

'Shut up, boy!' Pappy snapped at him and clutched the edge of the table as if he might bolt for the door to whip the poor kid.

'She didn't wanna do it, but he talked her into it,' Percy said, staring at me instead of Pappy. 'Then he went off to the war.'

'Is that what she's tellin'?' Pappy asked angrily.

'Don't yell, Eli,' Gran said. 'He's just a boy.' Gran took a deep breath, and seemed to be the first to at least consider the possibility that she had delivered her own grandchild.

'That's what she's tellin',' Percy said. 'And it's true.'

'Luke, go to your room and shut the door,' my father said, jolting me out of a trance.

'No,' my mother said before I could move. 'This affects all of us. He can stay.'

'He shouldn't hear this.'

'He's already heard it.'

'He should stay,' Gran said, siding with my

213

mother and settling the matter. They were assuming I wanted to stay. What I really wanted to do at that moment was to run outside, find Tally, and go for a long walk – away from her crazy family, away from Ricky and Korea, away from Percy Latcher. But I didn't move.

'Did your parents send you over here?' my mother asked.

'No ma'am. They don't know where I am. The baby cried all day. Libby's gone crazy, talkin' 'bout jumpin' off the bridge, killin' herself, stuff like that, and she told me what Ricky done to her.'

'Did she tell your parents?'

'Yes ma'am. Everybody knows now.'

'You mean everybody in your family knows.'

'Yes ma'am. We ain't told nobody else.'

'Don't,' Pappy grunted. He was settling back into his chair, his shoulders beginning to sag, defeat sinking in rapidly. If Libby Latcher claimed Ricky was the father, then everyone would believe her. He wasn't home to defend himself. And in a swearing contest, Libby would likely have more supporters than Ricky, given his reputation as a hell-raiser.

'Have you had supper, son?' Gran asked.

'No ma'am.'

'Are you hungry?'

'Yes ma'am.'

The table was covered with food that would not be touched. We Chandlers certainly had just lost our appetites. Pappy shoved back from the table and said, 'He can have mine.' He bounced to his feet, left the kitchen, and went to the front porch. My father followed him without a word.

'Sit here, son,' Gran said, indicating Pappy's chair.

They fixed him a plate of food and a glass of sweet tea. He sat down and ate slowly. Gran drifted to the front porch, leaving me and my mother to sit with Percy. He did not speak unless he was spoken to.

After a lengthy discussion on the front porch, a meeting Percy and I missed because we were banished to the back porch, Pappy and my father loaded the boy up and took him home. I sat in the swing with Gran as they drove away, just as it was getting dark. My mother was shelling butter beans.

'Will Pappy talk to Mr. Latcher?' I asked.

'I'm sure he will,' my mother said.

'What will they talk about?' I was full of questions because I assumed I now had the right to know everything.

'Oh, I'm sure they'll talk about the baby,' Gran said. 'And Ricky and Libby.'

'Will they fight?'

'No. They'll reach an agreement.'

'What kind of agreement?'

'Everybody'll agree not to talk about the baby, and to keep Ricky's name out of it.'

'That includes you, Luke,' my mother said. 'This is a dark secret.'

'I ain't tellin' nobody,' I said, with conviction. The thought of folks knowing that the Chandlers and the Latchers were somehow related horrified me.

'Did Ricky really do that?' I asked.

'Of course not,' Gran said. 'The Latchers are not

trustworthy people. They're not good Christians; that's how the girl got pregnant. They'll probably want some money out of the deal.'

'Money?'

'We don't know what they want,' my mother said.

'Do you think he did it, Mom?'

She hesitated for a second before saying, softly, 'No.'

'I don't think he did, either,' I said, making it unanimous. I would defend Ricky forever, and if anybody mentioned the Latcher baby, then I'd be ready to fight.

But Ricky was the likeliest suspect, and we all knew it. The Latchers rarely left their farm. There was a Jeter boy about two miles away, but I'd never seen him anywhere near the river. Nobody lived close to the Latchers but us. Ricky had been the nearest tomcat.

Church business suddenly became important, and the women talked about it nonstop. I had many more questions about the Latcher baby, but I couldn't sneak in a word. I finally gave up and went to the kitchen to listen to the Cardinals game.

I sorely wanted to be in the back of our pickup over at the Latchers', eavesdropping on the men as they handled the situation.

Long after I'd been sent to bed, I lay awake, fighting sleep because the air was alive with voices. When my grandparents talked in bed, I could hear their soft, low sounds creeping down the narrow hallway. I couldn't understand a word, and they tried their best to make sure no one heard them.

216

But at times, when they were worried or when they were thinking about Ricky, they were forced to talk late at night. Lying in his bed, listening to their muted utterances, I knew things were serious.

My parents retreated to the front porch, where they sat on the steps, waiting for a breeze and a break from the relentless heat. At first they whispered, but their burdens were too heavy, and their words could not be suppressed. Certain that I was asleep, they talked louder than they normally would have.

I slipped out of bed and slid across the floor like a snake. At the window, I glanced out and saw them in their familiar spot, backs to me, a few feet away.

I absorbed every sound. Things had not gone well at the Latchers'. Libby had been somewhere in the back of the house with the baby, who cried nonstop. All the Latchers seemed frayed and worn out by the crying. Mr. Latcher was angry with Percy for coming to our house, but he was even angrier when he talked about Libby. She was telling that she didn't want to fool around with Ricky, but he made her anyway. Pappy denied this was the case, but he had nothing to stand on. He denied everything, and said he doubted if Ricky had ever met Libby.

But they had witnesses. Mr. Latcher himself said that on two occasions, just after Christmas, Ricky pulled up in their front yard in Pappy's pickup and took Libby for a ride. They drove to Monette, where Ricky bought her a soda.

My father speculated that if that really did happen, then Ricky chose Monette because fewer

217

people would know him there. He'd never be seen in Black Oak with the daughter of a sharecropper.

'She's a beautiful girl,' my mother said.

The next witness was a boy of no more than ten. Mr. Latcher summoned him from the pack huddled around the front steps. His testimony was that he'd seen Pappy's truck parked at the end of a field row, next to a thicket. He sneaked up on the truck, and got close enough to see Ricky and Libby kissing. He kept it quiet because he was scared, and had come forth with the story only a few hours earlier.

The Chandlers, of course, had no witnesses. On our side of the river, there'd been no hint of a budding romance. Ricky certainly would not have told anyone. Pappy would've hit him.

Mr. Latcher said he suspected all along that Ricky was the father, but Libby had denied it. And in truth, there were a couple of other boys who'd shown an interest in her. But now she was telling everything – that Ricky had forced himself on her, that she didn't want the baby.

'Do they want us to take it?' my mother asked.

I almost groaned in pain.

'No, I don't think so,' my father said. 'What's another baby around their house?'

My mother thought the baby deserved a good home. My father said it was out of the question until Ricky said it was his child. Not likely, knowing Ricky.

'Did you see the baby?' my mother asked.

'No.'

'He's the spittin' image of Ricky,' she said.

My one recollection of the newest Latcher was

218

that of a small object that reminded me, at the time, of my baseball glove. He barely looked human. But my mother and Gran spent hours analyzing the faces of people to determine who favored whom, and where the eyes came from, and the nose and hair. They'd look at babies at church and say, 'Oh, he's definitely a Chisenhall.' Or, 'Look at those eyes, got 'em from his grand-mother.'

They all looked like little dolls to me.

'So you think he's a Chandler?' my father said.

'No doubt about it.'

Chapter 18

It was Saturday again, but Saturday without the usual excitement of going to town. I knew we were going because we had never skipped two Saturdays in a row. Gran needed groceries, especially flour and coffee, and my mother needed to go to the drugstore. My father hadn't been to the Co-op in two weeks. I didn't have a vote in the matter, but my mother knew how important the Saturday matinee was to the proper development of a child, especially a farm kid with little contact with the rest of the world. Yes, we were going to town, but without the usual enthusiasm.

A new horror was upon us, one that was far more frightening than all this business about Hank Spruill. What if somebody heard what the Latchers were telling? It took just one person, one whisper at one end of Main Street, and the gossip would roar through the town like a wildfire. The ladies in Pop and Pearl's would drop their baskets and cover their mouths in disbelief. The old farmers hanging around the Co-op would smirk and say, 'I'm not surprised.' The older kids from church would point at me as if I were somehow the guilty one. The town would seize the rumor as if it were the gospel truth, and Chandler blood would be forever tainted.

So I didn't want to go to town. I wanted to stay home and play baseball and maybe go for a walk with Tally.

Little was said over breakfast. We were still very subdued, and I think this was because we all knew the truth. Ricky had left behind a little memory. I wondered to myself if he knew about Libby and the baby, but I wasn't about to bring up the subject. I'd ask my mother later.

'Carnival's in town,' Pappy said. Suddenly the day was better. My fork froze in midair.

'What time are we goin'?' I asked.

'The same. Just after lunch,' Pappy said.

'How late can we stay?'

'We'll see about that,' he said.

The carnival was a wandering band of gypsies with funny accents who lived in Florida during the winter and hit the small farming towns in the fall, when the harvest was in full swing and folks had money in their pockets. They usually arrived abruptly on a Thursday and then set up on the baseball field without permission, and stayed through the weekend. Nothing excited Black Oak like the carnival.

A different one came to town each year. One had an elephant and a giant loggerhead turtle. One had no animals at all but specialized in odd humans – tumbling midgets, the girl with six fingers, the man with an extra leg. But all carnivals had a Ferris wheel, a merry-go-round, and two or three other rides that squeaked and rattled and generally terrified all the mothers. The Slinger had been such a ride, a circle of swings on chains that went faster and faster until the riders were flying parallel to the ground and screaming and begging to stop. A couple of years earlier in Monette, a chain had snapped, and a little girl had been flung across the midway and into the side of a trailer. The next week the Slinger was in Black Oak, with new chains, and folks lined up to ride it.

There were booths where you threw rings and darts and shot pellet pistols to win prizes. Some carnivals had fortune-tellers, others had photo booths, still others had magicians. They were all loud and colorful and filled with excitement. Word would spread quickly through the county, and people would flock in, and in a few hours Black Oak would be packed. I was desperate to go.

Perhaps, I thought, the excitement of the carnival would suppress any curiosity about Libby Latcher. I choked down my biscuits and ran outside.

'The carnival's in town,' I whispered to Tally when we met at the tractor for the ride to the fields.

'Y'all goin'?' she asked.

'Of course. Nobody misses the carnival.'

'I know a secret,' she whispered, her eyes darting around.

'What is it?'

'Somethin' I heard last night.'

'Where'd you hear it?'

'By the front porch.'

I didn't like the way she was stringing me along. 'What is it?'

She leaned even closer. ''Bout Ricky and that Latcher girl. Guess you got a new cousin.' Her words were cruel, and her eyes looked mean. This was not the Tally I knew.

'What were you doin' out there?' I asked.

'None of your business.'

Pappy came from the house and walked to the tractor. 'You'd better not tell,' I said through clenched teeth.

'We keep our secrets, remember?' she said, moving away

'Yeah.'

I ate lunch quickly, then hurried about the task of getting myself scrubbed and bathed. My mother knew I was anxious to get to town, so she wasted no time with her scouring.

All ten Mexicans piled into the back of the truck with me and my father, and we pulled away from our farm. Cowboy had picked cotton all week with broken ribs, a fact that had not gone unnoticed by Pappy and my father. They admired him greatly. 'They're tough people,' Pappy had said.

The Spruills were scurrying about, trying to catch us. Tally had spread the word about the carnival, and even Trot seemed to be moving with a purpose.

When we crossed the river, I looked long and hard down the field road that led to the Latchers' place, but their little shack was not visible. I glanced at my father. He was looking, too, his eyes hard, almost angry. How could those people have intruded into our lives?

We crept along the gravel road, and soon the

Latcher fields were behind us. By the time we stopped at the highway, I was once again dreaming of the carnival.

Our driver, of course, would never get in a hurry. With the truck so loaded with people, I doubted if it would do thirty-seven, and Pappy certainly didn't push it. It took an hour, it seemed.

Stick's patrol car was parked by the Baptist church. Traffic on Main was already slow, the sidewalks brimming with activity. We parked, and the Mexicans scattered. Stick appeared from under a shade tree and walked straight for us. Gran and my mother headed for the stores. I hung back with the men, certain that serious matters were about to be discussed.

'Howdy, Eli. Jesse,' Stick said, his hat tilted to one side, a blade of grass in the corner of his mouth.

'Afternoon, Stick,' Pappy said. My father just nodded. They had not come to town to spend time with Stick, and their irritation was just under the surface.

'I'm thinkin' 'bout arrestin' that Spruill boy,' he said.

'I don't care what you do,' Pappy shot back, his anger rising fast. 'Just wait till the cotton's in.'

'Surely you can wait a month,' my father said.

Stick chewed on the grass, spat, and said, 'I suppose so.'

'He's a good worker,' my father said. 'And there's plenty of cotton. You take him now, and we'll lose six field hands. You know how those people are.'

'I suppose I could wait,' Stick said again. He

seemed anxious to reach a compromise. 'I been talkin' to a lot of people, and I ain't so sure your boy here is tellin' the truth.' He gave me a long look as he said this, and I kicked gravel.

'Leave him out of it, Stick,' my father said. 'He's just a kid.'

'He's seven years old!' Pappy snapped. 'Why don't you find you some real witnesses.'

Stick's shoulders drew back as if he'd been hit.

'Here's the deal,' Pappy said. 'You leave Hank alone until the cotton's in, then I'll drive to town and let you know we're finished with him. At that point, I don't care what you do with him.'

'That'll work,' Stick said.

'But I still think you ain't got a case. It was three against one, Stick, and no jury will convict.'

'We'll see,' Stick said smugly. He walked away, thumbs in his pockets, with just enough of a swagger to annoy us.

'Can I go to the carnival?' I asked.

'Of course you can,' Pappy said.

'How much money do you have?' my father asked.

'Four dollars.'

'How much you gonna spend?'

'Four dollars.'

'I think two's enough.'

'How 'bout three?'

'Make it two-fifty, okay?'

'Yes sir.' I ran from the church, along the sidewalk, darting between people, and was soon at the baseball field, which was across the street from the Co-op, the Dixie theater, and the pool hall. The carnival covered it all, from the backstop

225

to the outfield fence. The Ferris wheel stood in the middle, surrounded by the smaller rides, the booths, and the midway. Shrill music rattled from the loudspeakers on the merry-go-round and the carousel. Long lines of people were already waiting. I could smell popcorn and corn dogs and something frying in grease.

I found the trailer with the cotton candy. It cost a dime, but I would've paid much more for it. Dewayne saw me at the midway as I was watching some older boys shoot air guns at little ducks that swam in a pool. They never hit them, and this was because, according to Pappy, the gunsights were crooked.

Candied apples were also a dime. We bought one apiece and took our time inspecting the carnival. There was a witch in a long black dress, black hair, black everything, and for twenty-five cents she could tell your future. A dark-eyed old lady could do the same thing, for the same price, with tarot cards. A flamboyant man with a microphone could guess your age or your weight for a dime. If he didn't get within three years or ten pounds you won a prize. The midway had the usual collection of games – softballs thrown at milk jugs, basketballs aimed at rims that were too small, darts at balloons, hoops over bottlenecks.

We strolled through the carnival, savoring the noise and excitement. A crowd was gathering at the far end, near the backstop, and we drifted over. A large sign proclaimed the presence of 'Samson, the World's Greatest Wrestler, Direct from Egypt,' and under it was a square mat with padded poles in the corners and ropes around it. Samson was not in the ring, but his appearance was only moments away, according to Delilah, a tall, shapely woman with the microphone. Her costume revealed all of her legs and most of her chest, and I was certain that never before had so much skin been exposed in public in Black Oak. She explained, to a silent crowd mostly of men, that the rules were simple. Samson paid ten-to-one to any person who could stay in the ring with him for one minute. 'Only sixty seconds!' she yelled. 'And the money is yours!' Her accent was strange enough to convince us that they were indeed from another land. I'd never seen anybody from Egypt, though I knew from Sunday school that Moses had had some adventures there.

She paraded back and forth in front of the ring, all eyes following her every move. 'On his current tour, Samson has won three hundred matches in a row,' she said, tauntingly. 'In fact, the last time Samson lost was in Russia, when it took three men to beat him, and they had to cheat to do it.'

Music started blaring from a lone speaker hanging on the sign. 'And now, ladies and gentlemen!' she shouted above the music, 'I present to you, the one, the only, the greatest wrestler in the world, the incredible Samson!'

I held my breath.

He bounded from behind a curtain and jumped into the ring amid tepid applause. Why should we clap for him? He was there to whip us. His hair was the first thing I noticed. It was black and wavy and fell to his shoulders like a woman's. I'd seen illustrations of Old Testament stories where the men had such hair, but that was five thousand years ago. He was a giant of a man, with a thick body and ridges of muscles clumped around his shoulders and down his chest. His arms were covered with black hair and looked strong enough to lift buildings. So that we might get the full benefit of his physique, Samson wasn't wearing a shirt. Even after we'd spent months in the fields, his skin was much darker than ours, and now I was really convinced that he was from parts unknown. He had fought Russians!

He strutted around the ring in step with the music, curling his arms and flexing his mammoth muscles. He performed like this until we'd witnessed all he had, which was more than enough, in my opinion.

'Who's first?' Delilah yelled into the microphone as the music died. 'Two-dollar minimum!'

The crowd was suddenly still. Only a fool would crawl into that ring.

'I ain't scared,' somebody yelled, and we watched in disbelief as a young man I'd never seen before stepped forward and handed two dollars to Delilah. She took the money and said, 'Ten-to-one. Stay in the ring for sixty seconds, and you'll win twenty dollars.' She shoved the microphone at the young man and said, 'What's your name?'

'Farley.'

'Good luck, Farley.'

He climbed into the ring as if he had no fear of Samson, who'd been watching without the slightest hint of worry. Delilah took a mallet and struck a bell on the side of the ring. 'Sixty seconds!' she said.

Farley moved around a bit, then retreated to a

corner as Samson took a step in his direction. Both men studied each other, Samson looking down with contempt, Farley looking up with anticipation.

'Forty-five seconds!' she called out.

Samson moved closer, and Farley darted to the other side of the ring. Being much smaller, he was also much quicker, and apparently was using the strategy of flight. Samson stalked him; Farley kept darting.

'Thirty seconds!'

The ring was not big enough to run much, and Samson had caught his share of scared rabbits. He tripped Farley during one of his sprints, and when he picked him up, he wrapped an arm tightly around the boy's head and began a headlock.

'Oh, looks like the Guillotine!' Delilah gushed, with a little too much drama. 'Twenty seconds!'

Samson twisted his prey and grimaced with sadistic pleasure, while poor Farley flailed at his side.

'Ten seconds!'

Samson whirled and then flung Farley across the ring. Before Farley could get up, the World's Greatest Wrestler grabbed him by the foot, lifted him in the air, held him over the ropes, and with two seconds to go, dropped him to the ground for the victory.

'Wow, that was close, Samson!' Delilah said into the microphone.

Farley was in a daze, but he walked away in one piece and seemed to be proud of himself. He had proved his manhood, had shown no fear, and had come within two seconds of winning twenty bucks.

The next volunteer was likewise a stranger, a bulky young man named Claude, who paid three dollars for a chance to win thirty. He weighed twice as much as Farley but was much slower, and within ten seconds Samson had nailed him with a Flying Dropkick and wrapped him into a Pretzel. With ten seconds to go, he hoisted Claude over his head, and in a magnificent display of strength, walked to the edge of the ring and tossed him.

Claude, too, walked away proudly. It was apparent that Samson, despite his theatrics and menacing demeanor, was a good sport and would not harm anyone. And since most young men wanted to have some contact with Delilah, a line soon formed at her side.

It was quite a spectacle, and Dewayne and I sat for a long time watching Samson dispose of one victim after another with all the moves in his repertoire. The Boston Crab, the Scissors, the Piledriver, the Jackhammer, the Body Slam. Delilah merely had to mention one of the maneuvers in her microphone and Samson would quickly demonstrate it.

After an hour, Samson was soaked with sweat and needed a break, so Dewayne and I scooted off to ride the Ferris wheel twice. We were debating whether to get another helping of cotton candy when we heard some young men talking about the girlie show.

'She takes off everything!' one of them said as he walked by, and we forgot about the cotton candy. We followed them to the end of the midway, where the gypsies' trailers were parked. Behind the trailers was a small tent that had obviously been erected so that no one would see it. A few men smoked and waited, and they all had a guilty look about them. There was music coming from the tent.

Some carnivals had girlie shows. Ricky, not surprisingly, had been seen leaving one the year before, and this had caused quite an uproar in our house. He wouldn't have been caught if Mr. Ross Lee Hart had not also been caught. Mr. Hart was a steward in the Methodist church, a farmer who owned his land, an upright citizen who was married to a woman with a big mouth. She went searching for him late on a Saturday night, in the midst of the carnival, and happened to see him leaving the forbidden tent. She wailed at the sight of her wayward husband; he ducked behind the trailers. She gave chase, yelling and threatening, and Black Oak had a new story.

Mrs. Hart, for some reason, told everyone what her husband had done, and the poor man was an outcast for many months. She also let it be known that leaving the tent right behind him was Ricky Chandler. We suffered in silence. Never go to a girlie show in your hometown was the unwritten rule. Drive to Monette or Lake City or Caraway, but don't do it in Black Oak.

Dewayne and I didn't recognize any of the men hanging around the girlie tent. We circled through the trailers and flanked in from the opposite side, but a large dog had been chained to the ground, guarding against Peeping Toms like us. We retreated and decided to wait for darkness.

As four o'clock approached, we had to make a painful decision – go to the matinee, or stay at the carnival. We were leaning toward the picture show when Delilah appeared at the wrestling ring. She had changed costumes, and was now wearing a two-piece red outfit that revealed even more. The crowd flocked to her, and before long Samson was once again hurling farm boys and hillbillies and even an occasional Mexican out of the ring.

His only challenge came at dark. Mr. Horsefly Walker had a deaf and dumb son who weighed three hundred pounds. We called him Grunt, not out of disrespect or cruelty – he'd just always been called that. Horsefly put up five dollars, and Grunt slowly climbed into the ring.

'He's a big one, Samson,' Delilah purred into the mike.

Samson knew it might take a bit longer to shove three hundred pounds out of the ring, so he attacked immediately. He went in low with a Chinese Take-Down, a move designed to slap both ankles together and cause the opponent to collapse. Grunt fell all right, but he fell on Samson, who couldn't help but groan in pain. Some of the crowd yelled, too, and began cheering on Grunt, who, of course, couldn't hear a thing. Both men rolled and kicked around the ring until Grunt pinned Samson for a second.

'Forty seconds!' Delilah said, the clock running much slower with Samson flat on his back. He kicked a few times, to no avail, then employed the Jersey Flip, a quick move in which his feet swung up and caught Grunt by the ears, then rolled him backward. Samson sprang to his feet as Delilah narrated the moves. A Flying Dropkick stunned Grunt.

'Fifteen seconds!' she said, the clock once again moving quickly. Grunt charged like a mad bull, and both men went down again. The crowd cheered again. Horsefly was hopping around the outside of the ring, delirious. They grappled for a while, then Delilah said, 'Ten seconds.'

There were some boos directed at the time-keeper. Samson twisted and yanked Grunt's arm behind his back, grabbed a foot, and slid the poor boy across the ring and through the ropes. He landed at his father's feet. Horsefly yelled, 'You cheatin' sonofabitch!'

Samson took offense to this language and motioned for Horsefly to enter the ring himself. Horsefly took a step forward and Samson spread the ropes. Delilah, who'd obviously seen such threats many times, said, 'I wouldn't do that if I were you. He hurts people when he's angry.'

By then Horsefly was looking for a reason to hold his ground. Samson looked ten feet tall standing at the edge of the ring, sneering down. Horsefly bent down to check on Grunt, who was rubbing his shoulder and appeared to be on the verge of tears. Samson laughed at them as they walked away, then to taunt us, began flexing his biceps as he strolled around the ring. A few in the crowd hissed at him, and that was exactly what he wanted.

He handled a few more challengers, then Delilah announced that her man had to eat dinner. They'd be back in an hour for their final exhibition.

It was now dark. The air was filled with the sounds of the carnival; the excited screams of kids on the rides, the whoops and hollers of the winners

233

at the booths on the midway, the music shrieking forth from a dozen assorted speakers, all playing different tunes, the constant jabbering of the barkers as they enticed folks to part with their money to view the world's largest turtle or to win another prize, and, above all, the overwhelming electricity of the crowd. People were so thick you couldn't stir 'em with a stick, as Gran liked to say. Mobs crowded around the booths, watching and cheering. Long lines snaked around the rides. Packs of Mexicans moved slowly about, staring in amazement, but for the most part, hanging on to their money. I had never seen so many people in one place.

I found my parents near the street, drinking lemonade and watching the spectacle from a safe distance. Pappy and Gran were already at the truck, ready to leave but willing to wait. The carnival came only once a year.

'How much money you got?' my father asked.

''Bout a dollar,' I said.

'That Ferris wheel doesn't look safe, Luke,' my mother said.

'I've been on it twice. It's okay.'

'I'll give you another dollar if you won't ride it again.'

'It's a deal.'

She handed me a dollar bill. We agreed that I would check back in an hour or so. I found Dewayne again, and we decided it was time to investigate the girlie show. We darted through the throng along the midway and slowed near the gypsies' trailers. It was much darker back there. In

234

front of the tent were some men smoking cigarettes, and in the door was a young woman in a skimpy costume swinging her hips and dancing in a naughty way.

As Baptists, we knew that all manner of dancing was not only inherently evil but downright sinful. It was right up there with drinking and cussing on the list of major transgressions.

The dancer was not as attractive as Delilah, nor did she reveal as much or move as gracefully. Of course, Delilah had years of experience and had traveled the world.

We sneaked along the shadows, advancing slowly until a strange voice from nowhere said, 'That's far enough. You boys get outta here.' We froze and looked around, and about that time we heard a familiar voice yell from behind us, 'Repent, ye workers of iniquity! Repent!'

It was the Reverend Akers, standing tall with his Bible in one hand while a long, crooked finger pointed out from the fist of the other.

'You brood of vipers!' he yelled at the top of his lungs.

I don't know if the young lady stopped dancing or if the men scattered. I didn't bother to look. Dewayne and I hit the ground on all fours and crawled like hunted prey through the maze of trailers and trucks until we saw light between two of the booths on the midway. We emerged and got lost in the crowd.

'You think he saw us?' Dewayne asked when we were safe.

'I don't know. I doubt it.'

We circled around and wandered back to a safe

spot near the gypsies' trailers. Brother Akers was in fine form. He'd moved to within thirty feet of the tent and was casting out demons at the top of his voice. And he was having success. The dancer was gone, as were the men who'd been hanging around smoking. He'd killed the show, although I suspected they were all inside, hunkering down and waiting him out.

But Delilah was back, wearing yet another costume. It was made of leopard skin and barely covered the essentials, and I knew Brother Akers would have something to say about it the next morning. He loved the carnival because it gave him so much material for the pulpit.

A regular mob crowded around the wrestling ring, gawking at Delilah and waiting for Samson. Again, she introduced him with the lines we'd already heard. He finally jumped into the ring, and he, too, had chosen leopard skin. Tight shorts, no shirt, shiny black leather boots. He strutted and posed and tried to get us to boo him.

My friend Jackie Moon crawled into the ring first, and like most victims, engaged the strategy of dodging. He darted around effectively for twenty seconds until Samson had had enough. A Guillotine, then a Turkish Roll-Down, as Delilah explained, and Jackie was on the grass not far from where I was standing. He laughed. 'That wasn't so bad.'

Samson wasn't about to hurt anybody; it would harm his business. But as his final exhibition wore on, he became much cockier and yelled at us constantly, 'Is there a man among you?' His accent was of some exotic variety; his voice was deep and frightening. 'Are there no warriors in Black Oak, Arkansas?'

I wished I were seven feet tall. Then I'd hop up there and attack ol' Samson while the crowd went wild. I'd whip him good, send him flying, and become the biggest hero in Black Oak. But, for now, I could only boo him.

Hank Spruill entered the picture. He walked along the edge of the ring between bouts, and stopped long enough to get Samson's attention. The crowd was silent as the two glared at each other. Samson walked to the edge of the ring and said, 'Come on in, little one.'

Hank, of course, just sneered. Then he walked over to Delilah and took money from his pocket.

'Ooh la la, Samson,' she said, taking his cash. 'Twenty-five dollars!'

Everyone seemed to be mumbling in disbelief. 'Twenty-five bucks!' said a man from behind. 'That's a week's work.'

'Yeah, but he might win two hundred fifty,' said another man.

As the crowd squeezed together, Dewayne and I moved to the front so we could see through the grown-ups.

'What's your name?' Delilah asked, shoving the microphone up.

'Hank Spruill,' he growled. 'You still payin' ten-to-one?'

'That's the deal, big boy. Are you sure you want to bet twenty-five dollars?'

'Yep. And all I gotta do is stay in the ring for one minute?'

'Yes, sixty seconds. You know Samson hasn't

lost a fight in five years. Last time he lost was in Russia, and they cheated him.'

'Don't care 'bout Russia,' Hank said, taking off his shirt. 'Any other rules?'

'No.' She turned to the crowd, and with as much drama as she could muster, she yelled, 'Ladies and gentlemen. The great Samson has been challenged to his biggest fight of all time. Mr. Hank Spruill has put up twenty-five dollars for a ten-to-one fight. Never before in history has someone made so large a challenge.'

Samson was posturing around the ring, shaking his sizable locks and looking forward to the skirmish with great anticipation.

'Lemme see the money,' Hank growled at Delilah.

'Here it is,' she said, using the microphone.

'No, I wanna see the two-fifty.'

'We won't be needing it,' she said with a laugh, a chuckle with just a trace of nervousness. But she lowered the microphone, and they haggled over the details. Bo and Dale appeared from the crowd, and Hank made them stand next to the small table where Delilah kept the money. When he was convinced the money was in place, he stepped into the ring, where the great Samson stood with his massive arms folded over his chest.

'Ain't he the one who killed that Sisco boy?' someone asked from behind us.

'That's him,' was the reply.

'He's almost as big as Samson.'

He was a few inches shorter, and not as thick in the chest, but Hank seemed oblivious to any danger. Samson started dancing around on one side of the ring while Hank watched him and stretched his arms.

'Are you ready?' Delilah wailed into the microphone, and the crowd pressed forward. She hit the bell. Both fighters eyed each other fiercely. Hank stayed in his corner, though. The clock was on his side. After a few seconds, Samson, whom I suspected knew he had his hands full, waded in, dancing and juking and bobbing like a real wrestler is supposed to do. Hank was still.

'Come on out, boy!' Samson boomed from five feet away, but Hank kept to his corner.

'Forty-five seconds,' Delilah said.

Samson's mistake was to assume that it was a wrestling match, instead of a brawl. He came in low, in an effort to apply one of his many grips or holds, and for a split second left his face open. Hank struck like a rattler. His right hand shot forward with a punch that was almost too quick to be seen, and it landed flush on the mighty Samson's jaw.

Samson's head jerked sharply, his handsome hair slung in all directions. The impact caused a cracking sound. Stan Musial could not have hit a baseball any harder.

Samson's eyes rolled back in his gigantic head. Because of its size, it took Samson's body a second to realize that its head had been crippled. One leg went woozy and bent at the knee. Then the other leg collapsed, and the World's Greatest Wrestler, Direct from Egypt, landed on his back with a thud. The small ring bounced and its ropes shook. Samson appeared to be dead.

Hank relaxed in his corner by placing his arms

239

on the top ropes. He was in no hurry. Poor Delilah was speechless. She tried to say something to assure us that this was just part of the exhibition, but at the same time she wanted to jump into the ring and tend to Samson. The crowd was stunned.

In the center of the ring, Samson began groaning and trying to get to his feet. He made it to his hands and knees, and rocked back and forth a few times before he managed to pull a foot forward. With one great lurch he tried to stand, but his feet weren't with him. He lunged toward the ropes and managed to catch them to break his fall. He was looking directly at us, but the poor guy saw nothing. His eyes were red and wild, and he seemed to have no idea where he was. He hung on the ropes, tottering, trying to regain his senses, still searching for his feet.

Mr. Horsefly Walker ran up to the ring and yelled to Hank, 'Kill the sonofabitch! Go ahead, finish him off!'

But Hank didn't move. Instead, he just yelled, 'Time!' but Delilah had forgotten about the clock.

There were a few cheers and jeers from the crowd, but for the most part, it was subdued. The spectators were shocked at the sight of Samson floundering, his senses knocked out of him.

Samson turned and tried to focus his eyes on Hank. Clutching the ropes for support, he stumbled a couple of steps, then made one last, desperate lunge. Hank simply ducked out of the way, and Samson landed hard on the corner pole. The ropes strained with his weight and the other three poles seemed ready to break. Samson was groaning and thrashing about like a bear who'd been shot. He pulled his feet under him and steadied himself enough to turn around. He should've stayed on the mat. Hank darted in and threw an overhand right, a punch that began in the center of the ring and landed exactly where the first one did. Since his target was defenseless, he reloaded and landed a third and final blow. Samson went down in a heap. Delilah screamed and scrambled into the ring. Hank relaxed in his corner, arms on the top ropes, grinning, no concern whatsoever for his opponent.

I wasn't sure what to do, and most of the other spectators were quiet, too. On the one hand, it was good to see an Arkansas boy so thoroughly crush this Egyptian giant. But on the other hand, it was Hank Spruill, and he'd used his fists. His victory was tainted, not that it mattered to him. All of us would've felt better if a local boy had battled Samson evenly.

When Hank was certain that time had expired, he stepped through the ropes and jumped to the ground. Bo and Dale had the money, and the three of them disappeared.

'He done killed Samson,' someone behind me said. The World's Greatest Wrestler was flat on his back, arms and legs spread wide, his woman crouched over him, trying to wake him. I felt sorry for them. They were wonderfully colorful, an act we wouldn't see again for a long time, if ever. In fact, I doubted if Samson and Delilah would ever return to Black Oak, Arkansas.

When he sat up, we relaxed. A handful of good folks clapped softly for him, then the crowd began to break up.

Why couldn't Hank join the carnival? He could get paid for beating up people, and it would get him off our farm. I decided to mention it to Tally.

Poor Samson had worked hard all day in the heat, and in a split second had lost the day's wages. What a way to make a living. I'd finally seen a worse job than picking cotton.

Chapter 19

In the spring and winter, Sunday afternoons were often used as a time for visiting. We'd finish lunch and take our naps, then load into the pickup and drive to Lake City or Paragould and drop in completely unannounced on some relatives or old friends, who'd always be delighted to see us. Or perhaps they'd drop in on us. 'Y'all come see us' was the common phrase, and folks took it literally. No arrangements or forewarnings were necessary, or even possible. We didn't have a telephone and neither did our relatives or friends.

But visiting was not a priority in the late summer and fall because the work was heavier and the afternoons were so hot. We forgot about aunts and uncles for a time, but we knew we'd catch up later.

I was sitting on the front porch, listening to the Cardinals and watching my mother and Gran shell peas and butter beans, when I saw a cloud of dust coming from the bridge. 'Car's comin',' I said, and they looked in that direction.

Traffic on our road was rare. It was almost always one of the Jeters from across the way or one of the Tollivers east of us. Occasionally a strange

243

car or truck would pass, and we'd watch it without a word until the dust had settled, then we'd talk about it over dinner and speculate as to who it was and what they were doing in our part of Craighead County. Pappy and my father would mention it at the Co-op, and my mother and Gran would tell all the ladies before Sunday school, and sooner or later they'd find someone else who'd seen the strange vehicle. Usually the mystery was solved, but occasionally one passed through and we never found out where it came from.

This car moved slowly. I saw a hint of red that grew bigger and brighter, and before too long a shiny two-door sedan was turning into our driveway. The three of us were now standing on the porch, too surprised to move. The driver parked behind our pickup. From the front yard the Spruills were gawking, too.

The driver opened his door and got out. Gran said, 'Well, it's Jimmy Dale.'

'It certainly is,' my mother said, losing some of her anticipation.

'Luke, run and get Pappy and your father,' Gran said. I sprinted through the house yelling for the men, but they'd heard the door slam and were coming from the backyard.

We all met in front of the car, which was new and clean and undoubtedly the most beautiful vehicle I'd ever seen. Everybody hugged and shook hands and exchanged greetings, then Jimmy Dale introduced his new wife, a thin little thing who looked younger than Tally. Her name was Stacy. She was from Michigan, and when she spoke her words came through her nose. She clipped them quickly and efficiently, and within seconds she made my skin crawl.

'Why does she talk like that?' I whispered to my mother as the group moved to the porch.

'She's a Yankee' was the simple explanation.

Jimmy Dale's father was Ernest Chandler, Pappy's older brother. Ernest had farmed in Leachville until a heart attack killed him a few years earlier. I did not personally remember Ernest, or Jimmy Dale, though I'd heard plenty of stories about them. I knew that Jimmy Dale had fled the farm and migrated to Michigan, where he found a job in a Buick factory making three dollars an hour, an unbelievable wage by Black Oak standards. He'd helped other local boys get good jobs up there. Two years earlier, after another bad crop, my father had spent a miserable winter in Flint, putting windshields into new Buicks. He'd brought home a thousand dollars and had spent it all on outstanding farm debts.

'That's some car,' my father said as they sat on the front steps. Gran was in the kitchen making iced tea. My mother had the unpleasant task of chatting up Stacy, a misfit from the moment she stepped out of the car.

'Brand new,' Jimmy Dale said proudly. 'Got it last week, just in time to drive home. Me and Stacy here got married a month ago, and that's our wedding present.'

'Stacy and I got married, not me and Stacy,' said the new wife, cutting in from across the porch. There was a slight pause in the conversation as the rest of us absorbed the fact that Stacy had just corrected her husband's grammar in the presence of others. I'd never heard this before in my life.

'Is it a fifty-two?' Pappy asked.

'No, it's a fifty-three, newest thing on the road. Built it myself.'

'You don't say.'

'Yep. Buick lets us custom order our own cars, then we get to watch when they come down the line. I put the dashboard in that one.'

'How much did it cost?' I asked, and I thought my mother would come for my throat.

'Luke!' she shouted. My father and Pappy cast hard looks at me, and I was about to say something when Jimmy Dale blurted out, 'Twenty-seven hundred dollars. It's no secret. Every dealer in the country knows how much they cost.'

By now the Spruills had drifted over and were inspecting the car – every Spruill but Tally, who was nowhere to be seen. It was Sunday afternoon and time, in my way of thinking, for a cool bath at Siler's Creek. I had been hanging around the porch waiting for her to appear.

Trot waddled around the car while Bo and Dale circled it, too. Hank was peering inside, probably looking for the keys. Mr. and Mrs. Spruill were admiring it from a distance.

Jimmy Dale watched them carefully. 'Hill people?'

'Yeah, they're from Eureka Springs.'

'Nice folks?'

'For the most part,' Pappy said.

'What's that big one doin'?'

'You never know.'

We'd heard at church that morning that Samson

had eventually gotten to his feet and walked from the ring, so Hank had not added another casualty to his list. Brother Akers had preached for an hour on the sinfulness of the carnival – wagering, fighting, lewdness, vulgar costumes, mingling with gypsies, all sorts of filth. Dewayne and I listened to every word, but our names were never mentioned.

'Why do they live like that?' Stacy asked, looking at Camp Spruill. Her crisp words knifed through the air.

'How else could they live?' Pappy asked. He, too, had already made the decision that he did not like the new Mrs. Jimmy Dale Chandler. She sat perched like a little bird on the edge of a rocker, looking down on everything around her.

'Can't you provide housing for them?' she asked.

I could tell that Pappy was starting to burn.

'Anyway, Buick'll let us finance the cars for twenty-four months,' Jimmy Dale said.

'Is that so?' said my father, still staring at it. 'I think that's 'bout the finest car I've ever seen.'

Gran brought a tray to the porch and served tall glasses of iced tea with sugar. Stacy declined. 'Tea with ice,' she said. 'Not for me. Do you have any hot tea?'

Hot tea? Who'd ever heard of such foolishness?

'No, we don't drink hot tea around here,' Pappy said from his swing as he glared at Stacy.

'Well, up in Michigan we don't drink it with ice,' she said.

'This ain't Michigan,' Pappy shot back.

'Would you like to see my garden?' my mother said abruptly.

'Yeah, that's a great idea,' Jimmy Dale said. 'Go on, sweetheart, Kathleen has the prettiest garden in Arkansas.'

'I'll go with you,' Gran said in an effort to shove the girl off the porch and away from controversy. The three women disappeared, and Pappy waited just long enough to say, 'Where in God's name did you find her, Jimmy Dale?'

'She's a sweet girl, Uncle Eli,' he answered without much conviction.

'She's a damned Yankee.'

'Yankees ain't so bad. They were smart enough to avoid cotton. They live in nice houses with indoor plumbing and telephones and televisions. They make good money and they build good schools. Stacy's had two years of college. Her family's had a television for three years. Just last week I watched the Indians and Tigers on it. Can you believe that, Luke? Watching baseball on television.'

'No sir.'

'Well, I did. Bob Lemon pitched for the Indians. Tigers ain't much; they're in last place again.'

'I don't much care for the American League,' I said, repeating words I'd heard my father and grandfather say since the day I started remembering.

'What a surprise,' Jimmy Dale said with a laugh. 'Spoken like a true Cardinal fan. I was the same way till I went up North. I've been to eleven games this year in Tiger Stadium, and the American League kinda grows on you. Yankees were in town two weeks ago; place was sold out. They got this new guy, Mickey Mantle, 'bout as smooth as I've

248

seen. Good power, great speed, strikes out a lot, but when he hits it, it's gone. He'll be a great one. And they got Berra and Rizzuto.'

'I still hate 'em,' I said, and Jimmy Dale laughed again.

'You still gonna play for the Cardinals?' he asked.

'Yes sir.'

'You ain't gonna farm?'

'No sir.'

'Smart boy.'

I'd heard the grown-ups talk about Jimmy Dale. He was quite smug that he'd managed to flee the cotton patch and make a better living up North. He liked to talk about his money. He'd found the better life and was quick with his advice to other farm boys around the county.

Pappy thought that farming was the only honorable way a man should work, with the possible exception of playing professional baseball.

We sipped our tea for a while, then Jimmy Dale said, 'So how's the cotton?'

'So far so good,' Pappy said. 'The first pickin' went well.'

'Now we'll go through it again,' my father added. 'Probably be done in a month or so.'

Tally emerged from the depths of Camp Spruill, holding a towel or some type of cloth. She circled wide around the red car, where her family still stood entranced; they didn't notice her. She looked at me from the distance but made no sign. I was suddenly bored with baseball and cotton and cars and such, but I couldn't just race off. It would be rude to leave company in such a manner, and my father would suspect something. So I sat there and watched Tally disappear past the house.

'How's Luther?' my father asked.

'Doin' well,' Jimmy Dale said. 'I got 'im on at the plant. He's makin' three dollars an hour, forty hours a week. Luther ain't never seen so much money.'

Luther was another cousin, another Chandler from a distant strain. I'd met him once, at a funeral.

'So he ain't comin' home?' Pappy said.

'I doubt it.'

'Is he gonna marry a Yankee?'

'I ain't asked him. I reckon he'll do whatever he wants to do.'

There was a pause, and the tension seemed to fade for a moment. Then Jimmy Dale said, 'You can't blame him for stayin' up there. I mean, hell, they lost their farm. He was pickin' cotton around here for other people, makin' a thousand bucks a year, didn't have two dimes to rub together. Now he'll make more than six thousand a year, plus a bonus and retirement.'

'Did he join the union?' my father asked.

'Damned right he did. I got all the boys from here in the union.'

'What's a union?' I asked.

'Luke, go check on your mother,' Pappy said. 'Go on.'

Once again I had asked an innocent question, and because of it, I was banished from the conversation. I left the porch, then raced to the back of the house in hopes of seeing Tally. But she was gone, no doubt down at the creek bathing without her faithful lookout.

Gran was at the garden gate, resting on the fence, watching my mother and Stacy go from plant to plant. I stood beside her, and she tousled my hair. 'Pappy said she's a damned Yankee,' I said softly.

'Don't swear.'

'I'm not swearin'. I'm just repeatin'.'

'They're good people, they're just different.' Gran's mind was somewhere else. At times that summer she would talk to me without seeing me. Her tired eyes would drift away as her thoughts left our farm.

'Why does she talk like that?' I asked.

'She thinks we talk funny.'

'She does?'

'Of course.'

I couldn't understand this.

A green snake less than a foot long poked its head from the cucumber patch, then raced down a dirt trail directly at my mother and Stacy. They saw it at about the same instant. My mother pointed and calmly said, 'There's a little green snake.'

Stacy reacted in a different manner. Her mouth flew open, but she was so horrified that it took a second or two for any sound to come forth. Then she let loose with a scream that the Latchers could've heard, a blood-curdling shriek that was far more terrifying than even the deadliest of snakes.

'A snake!' she screamed again as she jumped behind my mother. 'Jimmy Dale! Jimmy Dale!'

The snake had stopped dead on the trail and appeared to be looking up at her. It was just a harmless little green snake. How could anybody be afraid of it? I darted through the garden and picked him up, thinking I was helping matters. But the sight of a little boy holding such a lethal creature was more than Stacy could stand. She fainted and fell into the butter beans as the men came running from the front porch.

Jimmy Dale scooped her up as we tried to explain what had happened. The poor snake was limp; I thought he'd fainted, too. Pappy could not suppress a grin as we followed Jimmy Dale and his wife to the back porch, where he laid her on a bench while Gran went to get remedies.

Stacy came to eventually, her face pale, her skin clammy. Gran hovered over her with wet cloths and smelling salts.

'Don't they have snakes up in Michigan?' I whispered to my father.

'Reckon not.'

'It was just a little green one,' I said.

'Thank God she didn't see a rat snake. She'd be dead,' my father said.

My mother boiled water and poured it into a cup with a tea bag. Stacy sat up and drank it, and for the first time in history hot tea was consumed on our farm. She wanted to be alone, so we returned to the front porch while she rested.

Before long, the men were into the Buick. They had the hood up and were poking their heads around the engine. When no one was paying attention to me, I moved away from the porch and headed for the rear of the house, looking for Tally.

I hid by the silo, in a favorite spot where I couldn't be seen. I heard an engine start, a smooth powerful sound, and knew it wasn't our old truck. They were going for a ride, and I heard my father call my name. But when I didn't respond, they left.

I gave up on Tally and walked back to the house. Stacy was sitting on a stool under a tree, looking forlornly across our fields, arms crossed as if she were very unhappy. The Buick was gone.

'You didn't go for a ride?' she asked me.

'No ma'am.'

'Why not?'

'Just didn't.'

'Have you ever ridden in a car?' Her tone was mocking, so I started to lie.

'No ma'am.'

'How old are you?'

'Seven.'

'You're seven years old, and you've never ridden in a car?'

'No ma'am.'

'Have you ever seen a television?'

'No ma'am.'

'Have you ever used a telephone?'

'No ma'am.'

'Unbelievable.' She shook her head in disgust, and I wished I'd stayed by the silo. 'Do you go to school?'

'Yes ma'am.'

'Thank God for that. Can you read?'

'Yes ma'am. I can write, too.'

'Are you going to finish high school?'

'Sure am.'

'Did your father?'

'He did.'

'And your grandfather?'

'No ma'am.'

'I didn't think so. Does anybody go to college around here?'

'Not yet.'

'What does that mean?'

'My mother says I'm goin' to college.'

'I doubt it. How can you afford college?'

'My mother says I'm goin'.'

'You'll grow up to be just another poor cotton farmer, like your father and grandfather.'

'You don't know that,' I said. She shook her head in total frustration.

'I've had two years of college,' she said very proudly.

It didn't make you any smarter, I wanted to say. There was a long pause. I wanted to leave but wasn't sure how to properly remove myself from the conversation. She sat perched on the stool, gazing into the distance, gathering more venom.

'I just can't believe how backward you people are,' she said.

I studied my feet. With the exception of Hank Spruill, I had never met a person whom I disliked as much as Stacy. What would Ricky do? He'd probably cuss her, and since I couldn't get by with that, I just decided to walk away.

The Buick was returning, with my father at the wheel. He parked it, and all the adults got out. Jimmy Dale yelled for the Spruills to come over. He loaded up Bo, Dale, and Trot in the backseat, Hank in the front, and away they went, flying down our dirt road, headed for the river.

It was late in the afternoon before Jimmy Dale made any mention of leaving. We were ready for them to go, and I was particularly worried that they might hang around long enough for supper. I couldn't imagine sitting around the dinner table trying to eat while Stacy commented on our food and habits. So far she had despised everything else about our lives, why should she relent over supper?

We moved slowly to the Buick, our languid good-byes taking forever, as usual.

No one was ever in a hurry when it was time to go. The announcement was made that the hour was late, then repeated, and then someone made the first move to the car or truck amid the first wave of farewells. Hands were shaken, hugs given, promises exchanged. Progress was made until the group got to the vehicle, at which time the entire procession came to a halt as someone remembered yet another quick story. More hugs, more promises to come back soon. After considerable effort, the departing ones were safely tucked away inside the vehicle, then those sending them off would stick their heads in for another round of good-byes. Maybe another quick story. A few protests would finally get the engine started, and the car or truck would slowly back up, everyone still waving.

When the house was out of sight, someone other than the driver would say, 'What was the hurry?'

And someone standing in the front yard, still waving, would say, 'Wonder why they had to rush off?'

When we made it to the car, Stacy whispered something to Jimmy Dale. He then turned to my mother and said softly, 'She needs to go to the bathroom.'

My mother looked worried. We didn't have bathrooms. You relieved yourself in the outhouse, a small wooden closet sitting on a deep hole, hidden out behind the toolshed, halfway between the back porch and the barn.

'Come with me,' my mother said to her, and they left. Jimmy Dale suddenly remembered another story, one about a local boy who went to Flint and got arrested for public drunkenness outside a bar. I eased away and walked through the house. Then I sneaked off the back porch and ran between two chicken coops to a point where I could see my mother leading Stacy to the outhouse. She stopped and looked at it and seemed very reluctant to enter. But she had no choice.

My mother left her and retreated to the front yard.

I struck quickly. As soon as my mother was out of range, I knocked on the door of the outhouse. I heard a faint shriek, then a desperate, 'Who is it?'

'Miss Stacy, it's me, Luke.'

'I'm in here!' she said, her usually clear words now hurried and muffled in the stifling humidity of the outhouse. It was dark in there, the only light coming from the tiny cracks between the planks.

'Don't come out right now!' I said with as much panic as I could fake.

'What?'

'There's a big black snake out here!'

'Oh my God!' she gasped. She would've fainted again, but she was already sitting down.

256

'Be quiet!' I said. 'Otherwise, he'll know you're in there.'

'Holy Jesus!' she said, her voice breaking. 'Do something!'

'I can't. He's big, and he bites.'

'What does he want?' she begged, as if she were on the verge of tears.

'I don't know. He's a shitsnake, he hangs around here all the time.'

'Get Jimmy Dale!'

'Okay, but don't come out. He's right by the door. I think he knows you're in there.'

'Oh my God,' she said again, and started crying. I ducked back between the chicken coops, then looped around the garden on the east side of the house. I moved slowly and quietly along the hedges that were our property line until I came to a point in a thicket where I could hide and watch the front yard. Jimmy Dale was leaning on his car, telling a story, waiting for his young bride to finish her business.

Time dragged on. My parents and Pappy and Gran listened and chuckled as one story led to another. Occasionally one of them would glance toward the backyard.

My mother finally became concerned and left the group to check on Stacy. A minute later there were voices, and Jimmy Dale bolted toward the outhouse. I buried myself deeper in the thicket.

It was almost dark when I entered the house. I'd been watching from a distance, from beyond the silo, and I knew my mother and Gran were preparing supper. I was in enough trouble – being

257

late for a meal would have only compounded the situation.

They were seated, and Pappy was about to bless the food when I walked through the door from the back porch and quietly took my seat. They looked at me, but I chose instead to stare at my plate. Pappy said a quick prayer, and the food was passed around. After a silence sufficiently long enough to build tension, my father said, 'Where you been, Luke?'

'Down by the creek,' I said.

'Doin' what?'

'Nothin'. Just lookin' around.'

This sounded suspicious enough, but they let it pass. When all was quiet, Pappy, with perfect timing and with the devil in his voice, said, 'You see any shitsnakes at the creek?'

He barely got the words out before he cracked up.

I looked around the table. Gran's jaws were clenched as if she were determined not to smile. My mother covered her mouth with her napkin, but her eyes betrayed her; she wanted to laugh, too. My father had a large bite of something in his mouth, and he managed to chew it while keeping a straight face.

But Pappy was determined to howl. He roared at the end of the table while the rest of them fought to maintain their composure. 'That was a good one, Luke!' he managed to say while catching his breath. 'Served her right.'

I finally laughed, too, but not at my own actions. The sight of Pappy laughing so hard while the other three so gamely tried not to struck me as funny.

'That's enough, Eli,' Gran said, finally moving her jaws.

I took a large bite of peas and stared at my plate. Things grew quiet again, and we ate for a while with nothing said.

After dinner, my father took me for a walk to the toolshed. On its door he kept a wooden hickory stick, one that he'd cut himself and polished to a shine. It was reserved for me.

I'd been taught to take my punishment like a man. Crying was forbidden, at least openly. In these awful moments, Ricky always inspired me. I'd heard horror stories of the beatings Pappy had given him, and never, according to his parents and mine, had he been brought to tears. When Ricky was a kid, a whipping was a challenge.

'That was a mean thing you did to Stacy,' my father began. 'She was a guest on our farm, and she's married to your cousin.'

'Yes sir.'

'Why'd you do it?'

''Cause she said we were stupid and backward.' A little embellishment here wouldn't hurt.

'She did?'

'Yes sir. I didn't like her, neither did you or anybody else.'

'That may be true, but you still have to respect your elders. How many licks you think that's worth?' The crime and the punishment were always discussed beforehand. When I bent over, I knew exactly how many licks I'd receive.

'One,' I said. That was my usual assessment.

'I think two,' he said. 'Now what about the bad language?'

'I don't think it was that bad,' I said.

'You used a word that was unacceptable.'

'Yes sir.'

'How many licks for that?'

'One.'

'Can we agree on three, total?' he asked. He never whipped me when he was angry, so there was usually a little room for negotiation. Three sounded fair, but I always pushed a little. After all, I was on the receiving end. Why not haggle?

'Two's more fair,' I said.

'It's three. Now bend over.'

I swallowed hard, gritted my teeth, turned around, bent over, and grabbed my ankles. He smacked my rear three times with the hickory stick. It stung like hell, but his heart wasn't in it. I'd received far worse.

'Go to bed, right now,' he said, and I ran to the house.

Chapter 20

Now that Hank had $250 of Samson's money in his pocket, he was even less enthusiastic about picking cotton. 'Where's Hank?' Pappy asked Mr. Spruill as we took the sacks and began our work on Monday morning. 'Sleepin', I reckon' was the abrupt response, and nothing else was said at that moment.

He arrived in the fields sometime in the middle of the morning. I didn't know exactly when because I was at the far end of a row of cotton, but soon I heard voices and knew that the Spruills were once again at war.

An hour or so before lunch, the sky began to darken, and a slight breeze came from the west. When the sun disappeared, I stopped picking and studied the clouds. A hundred yards away I saw Pappy do the same thing – hands on hips, straw hat cocked to one side, face frowning upward. The wind grew stronger and the sky darker, and before long the heat was gone. All of our storms came from Jonesboro, which was known as Tornado Alley.

Hail hit first, hard tiny specks the size of pea

gravel, and I headed for the tractor. The sky to the southwest was dark blue, almost black, and the low clouds were bearing down on us. The Spruills were moving quickly down their rows, all heading for the trailer. The Mexicans were running toward the barn.

I began to run, too. The hail stung the back of my neck and prompted me to run even faster. The wind was howling through the trees along the river and pushing the cotton stalks to their sides. Lightning cracked somewhere behind me, and I heard one of the Spruills, Bo, probably, give a yell.

'We don't need to get near the cotton trailer,' Pappy was saying as I arrived. 'Not with that lightnin'.'

'Better get to the house,' my father said.

We loaded onto the flatbed trailer, all of us scrambling in a great hurry, and just as Pappy turned the tractor around, the rain hit with a fury. It was cold and sharp and falling sideways in the fierce wind. We were instantly soaked; I wouldn't have been wetter if I'd jumped in the creek.

The Spruills huddled together with Tally in the center. Just a few feet away, my father clutched me to his chest, as if the wind might take me away. My mother and Gran had left the fields not long before the storm hit.

The rain beat us in waves. It was so thick I could barely see the rows of cotton just a few feet in front of me. 'Hurry up, Pappy!' I kept saying. The storm was so loud I couldn't hear the familiar knock of the tractor engine. Lightning cracked again, this time much closer, so close that my ears hurt. I thought we were going to die.

It took forever to get to the house, but when we did, the rain suddenly stopped. The sky was even darker, black in every direction. 'It's a funnel!' Mr. Spruill said loudly as we were just getting off the trailer. To the west, far beyond the river and high above the tree line, a slim funnel cloud dipped downward. It was light gray, almost white against the black sky, and it grew larger and louder as it made its way very slowly toward the ground. It was several miles away, and because of the distance it didn't seem too dangerous.

Tornadoes were common in our part of Arkansas, and I'd heard stories about them all of my life. Decades earlier Gran's father had supposedly survived a horrible twister, one that had run in circles and struck the same small farm more than once. It was a tall tale, one that Gran told without much conviction. Twisters were a way of life, but I'd not seen one until now.

'Kathleen!' my father yelled toward the house. He didn't want my mother to miss such a spectacle. I glanced at the barn, where the Mexicans were as still and as amazed as we were. A couple of them were pointing.

We watched the funnel in muted fascination, without fear or terror, because it was nowhere near our farm and going away, to the north and east. It moved slowly, as if it were searching for the perfect place to touch down. Its tail was clearly visible above the horizon, way above the land, and it skipped along in midair, dancing at times while it decided where and when to strike. The bulk of the funnel spun tightly, a perfect upside-down cone whirling in a fierce spiral.

The screen door slammed behind us. My mother and Gran were on the steps, both of them wiping their hands with dish towels.

'It's headed for town,' Pappy said with great authority, as if he could predict where tornadoes would hit.

'I think so,' my father added, suddenly another expert weatherman.

The twister's tail sank lower and stopped skipping. It appeared as if it had indeed touched down somewhere far away, because we could no longer see the end of it.

The church, the gin, the movie theater, Pop and Pearl's grocery – I was tallying the damage when suddenly the twister lifted itself up and seemed to disappear completely.

There was another roar behind us. Across the road, deep into the Jeter property, another tornado had arrived. It had crept up on us while we were watching the first one. It was a mile or two away and seemed headed straight for our house. We watched in horror, unable to move for a second or two.

'Let's get in the barn!' Pappy shouted. Some of the Spruills were already running toward their camp, as if they'd be safe inside a tent.

'Over here!' Mr. Spruill shouted and pointed to the barn. Suddenly everyone was yelling and pointing and scurrying about. My father grabbed my hand, and we began running. The ground was shaking and the wind was screaming. The Mexicans were scattering in all directions; some thought it best to hide in the fields, others were headed toward our house until they saw us running to the barn. Hank flew past me with Trot on his back. Tally outran us, too.

Before we made it to the barn, the twister left the ground and rose quickly into the sky. Pappy stopped and watched, and then so did everybody else. The funnel went slightly to the east of our farm, and instead of a frontal assault, it left behind only a sprinkling of thick brown rainwater and specks of mud. We watched it jump along in midair, looking for another site to drop down in, just like the first one.

For a few minutes we were too stunned and too frightened to say much.

I studied the clouds in all directions, determined not to be blindsided again. I wasn't the only one cutting my eyes around.

Then it started raining once more, and we went to the house.

The storm raged for two hours and threw almost everything in nature's arsenal at us: gale-force winds and blinding rains, twisters, hail, and lightning so quick and so close that we hid under our beds at times. The Spruills took refuge in our living room, while we cowered throughout the rest of the house. My mother kept me close. She was deathly afraid of storms and that made the entire ordeal even worse.

I wasn't exactly sure how we would die – blown away by the wind or seared by a lightning bolt or swept away by the water – but it was obvious to me that the end had come. My father slept through most of it, though, and his indifference was a great comfort. He'd lived in foxholes and been shot at by the Germans, so nothing frightened him. The three of us lay on the floor of their bedroom – my father snoring, my mother praying, and me in the middle listening to the sounds of the storm. I thought of Noah and his forty days of rain, and I waited for our little house to simply lift up and begin floating.

When the rain and wind finally passed, we went outside to survey the destruction. Other than wet cotton, there was surprisingly little damage – several scattered tree branches, the usual washed-out gullies, and some ripped-up tomato plants in the garden. The cotton would be dry by the next morning, and we'd be back in business.

During a late lunch Pappy said, 'I reckon I better go check on the gin.' We were anxious to get to town. What if it had been leveled by the twister?

'I'd like to see the church,' Gran said.

'Me, too,' I said.

'Why do you wanna see the church?' my father asked.

'To see if the twister got it.'

'Let's go,' Pappy said, and we jumped from our chairs. The dishes were piled into the sink and left unwashed, something I'd never seen before.

Our road was nothing but mud, and in places large sections had been washed away. We slipped and slid for a quarter of a mile until we came to a crater. Pappy rammed it in low and tried to plow through the ditch on the left side, next to the Jeters' cotton. The truck stopped and settled, and we were hopelessly stuck. My father hiked back to the house to get the John Deere while we waited.

As usual, I was in the back of the truck, and so I had plenty of room to move around. My mother was packed in the front with Pappy and Gran. I think it was Gran who said something to the effect that perhaps it wasn't such a good idea to go to town after all. Pappy just stewed.

When my father returned, he hooked a twenty-foot log chain to the front bumper and slowly pulled us out of the ditch. The men had decided it was best for the tractor to drag us all the way to the bridge. When we got there, Pappy unhitched the chain, and my father rode over on the tractor. Then we crossed in the truck. The road on the other side was even worse, according to the men, so they rehitched the chain, and the tractor pulled the truck for two miles until we came to a gravel road. We left the John Deere there and headed for town, if, in fact, it was still there. God only knew what carnage awaited us. I could barely conceal my excitement.

We finally made it to the highway, and when we turned toward Black Oak, we left a long trail of mud on the asphalt. Why couldn't all roads be paved? I asked myself.

Things appeared normal as we drove along. No flattened trees or crops, no debris slung for miles, no gaping holes through the landscape. All the houses seemed to be in order. The fields were empty because the cotton was wet, but other than that, life had not been disturbed.

Standing in the back of the truck, looking over the cab with my father, I strained my eyes for the first glimpse of town. It arrived soon enough. The gin was roaring as usual. God had protected the church. The stores along Main Street were intact. 'Thank God,' my father said. I was not unhappy to see the buildings untouched, but things could've been more interesting.

We weren't the only curious ones. Traffic was heavy on Main Street, and people crowded the sidewalks. This was unheard of for a Monday. We parked at the church, and once we determined that it had not been hit, I scampered down to Pop and Pearl's, where the foot traffic appeared to be particularly thick. Mr. Red Fletcher had a group going, and I got there just in time.

According to Mr. Red, who lived west of town, he had known a twister was about to appear because his old beagle was hiding under the kitchen table, a most ominous sign. Taking his cue from his dog, Mr. Red began studying the sky, and before long was not surprised to see it turn black. He heard the twister before he saw it. It dipped down from nowhere, came straight for his farm, and stayed on the ground long enough to flatten two chicken coops and peel the roof off his house. A piece of glass struck his wife and drew blood, so we had a bona fide casualty. Behind me I heard folks whisper excitedly about driving out to the Fletcher place to inspect the destruction.

'What'd it look like?' somebody asked.

'Black as coal,' Mr. Red said. 'Sounded like a freight train.'

This was even more exciting because our twisters had been a light gray in color, almost white. His had been black. Apparently, all manner of tornadoes had ravaged our county.

Mrs. Fletcher appeared at his side, her arm

heavily bandaged and in a sling, and we couldn't help but stare. She looked as though she might just pass out on the sidewalk. She displayed her wound and received plenty of attention until Mr. Red realized he'd lost the audience, so he stepped forward and resumed his narrative. He said his tornado left the ground and began hopping about. He jumped in his truck and tried to follow it. He gave it a good chase through a driving hailstorm and almost caught up with it as it circled back.

Mr. Red's truck was older than Pappy's. Some of those in the crowd began looking around in disbelief. I wanted one of the adults to ask, 'What were you gonna do if you caught it, Red?' Anyway, he said he soon gave up the chase and returned home to see about Mrs. Fletcher. When he had seen it last, his tornado was headed straight for town.

Pappy told me later that Mr. Red Fletcher would tell a lie when the truth sounded better.

There was a lot of lying that afternoon in Black Oak, or perhaps just a lot of exaggerating. Twister stories were told and retold from one end of Main Street to the other. In front of the Co-op, Pappy described what we'd seen, and for the most part he stuck to the facts. The double-twister story carried the moment and had everyone's attention until Mr. Dutch Lamb stepped forward and claimed to have seen three! His wife verified it, and Pappy went to the truck.

By the time we left town, it was a miracle that hundreds hadn't been killed.

The last of the clouds were gone by dark, but the heat did not return. We sat on the porch after supper and waited for the Cardinals. The air was clear and light – the first hint of autumn.

Six games were left, three against the Reds and three against the Cubs, all to be played at home at Sportsman's Park, but with the Dodgers seven games in first place, the season was over. Stan the Man Musial was leading the league in batting and slugging, and he also had more hits and doubles than anybody else. The Cardinals would not win the pennant, but we still had the greatest player in the game. At home after a road trip to Chicago, the boys were happy to be back in St Louis, according to Harry Caray, who often passed along greetings and gossip as if all the players lived in his house.

Musial hit a single and a triple, and the score was tied at three after nine innings. It was late, but we weren't tired. The storm had chased us from the fields, and the cool weather was something to be savored. The Spruills were sitting around a fire, talking softly and enjoying a moment without Hank. He often disappeared after supper.

In the bottom of the tenth, Red Schoendienst singled, and when Stan Musial came to the plate, the fans went wild, according to Harry Caray, who, as Pappy said, often watched one game and described another. The attendance was fewer than ten thousand; we could tell the crowd was slim. But Harry was making enough noise for the other twenty thousand. After 148 games, he was just as excited as he'd been on opening day. Musial ripped a double, his third hit of the game, scoring Schoendienst and winning it four to three.

A month earlier we would have celebrated, along with Harry, on the front porch. I would have sprinted around the bases in the yard, sliding into second, just like Stan the Man. Such a dramatic victory would have sent us all to bed happy, though Pappy would still want to fire the manager.

But things were different now. The win meant little; the season was ending with the Cardinals in third place. The front yard had been overwhelmed by the Spruills. Summer was gone.

Pappy turned off the radio with Harry winding down. 'There's no way Baumholtz can catch him,' Pappy said. Frankie Baumholtz of the Cubs was six points behind Musial in the race for the hitting title.

My father grunted his agreement. The men had been quieter than usual during the game. The storms and cool weather had struck them like an illness. The seasons were changing, yet nearly one third of the cotton was still out there. We'd had near perfect weather for seven months; surely it was time for a change.

Chapter 21

Autumn lasted less than twenty-four hours. By noon the next day the heat was back, the cotton was dry, the ground was hard, and all those pleasant thoughts about cool days and blowing leaves were forgotten. We had returned to the edge of the river for the second picking. A third one might materialize later in the fall, a 'Christmas picking,' as it was known, in which the last remnants of cotton were gathered. By then the hill people and the Mexicans would be long gone.

I stayed close to Tally for most of the day and worked hard to keep up with her. She had become aloof for some reason, and I was desperate to learn why. The Spruills were a tense bunch, no more singing or laughing in the fields, very few words spoken among them. Hank came to work mid-morning and began picking at a leisurely pace. The rest of the Spruills seemed to avoid him.

Late in the afternoon I dragged myself back to the trailer – for the final time, I hoped. It was an hour before quitting time, and I was looking for my mother. Instead I saw Hank with Bo and Dale at the opposite end of the trailer, waiting in the shade for either Pappy or my father to weigh their cotton. I ducked low in the stalks so they wouldn't see me and waited for friendlier voices.

Hank was talking loudly, as usual. 'I'm tired of pickin' cotton,' he said. 'Damned tired of it! So I been thinkin' about a new job, and I done figured a new way to make money. Lots of it. I'm gonna follow that carnival around, go from town to town, sorta hide in the shadows while ol' Samson and his woman rake in the cash. I'll wait till the money piles up; I'll watch him fling them little sodbusters outta the ring, and then late at night, when he's good and tired, I'll jump up outta nowhere, lay down fifty bucks, whip his ass again, and walk away with all his money. If I do it once a week, that's two thousand dollars a month, twenty-four thousand bucks a year. All cash. Hell, I'll get rich.'

There was mischief in his voice, and Bo and Dale were laughing by the time he finished. Even I had to admit it was funny.

'What if Samson gets tired of it?' Bo asked.

'Are you kiddin'? He's the world's greatest wrestler, straight from Egypt. Samson fears no man. Hell, I might take his woman, too. She looked pretty good, didn't she?'

'You'll have to let him win every now and then,' Bo said. 'Otherwise he won't fight you.'

'I like the part about takin' his woman,' Dale said. 'I really liked her legs.'

'Rest of her wasn't bad,' Hank said. 'Wait – I got it! I'll run 'im off and become the new Samson! I'll grow my hair down to my ass, dye it black, get me some little leopard-skin shorts, talk real funny, and these ignorant rednecks 'round here'll think I'm

273

from Egypt, too. Delilah won't be able to keep her hands off me.'

They laughed hard and long, and their amusement was contagious. I chuckled to myself at the notion of Hank strutting around the ring in tight shorts, trying to convince people he was from Egypt. But he was too stupid to be a showman. He would hurt people and scare away his challengers.

Pappy arrived at the trailer and started weighing the cotton. My mother drifted in, too, and whispered to me that she was ready to go to the house. So was I. We made the long walk together, in silence, both happy that the day was almost over.

The house painting had resumed. We noticed it from the garden, and upon closer inspection saw where our painter – Trot, we still presumed – had worked his way up to the fifth board from the bottom and had applied the first coat to an area about the size of a small window. My mother touched it gently; the paint stuck to her finger.

'It's fresh,' she said, glancing toward the front yard, where, as usual, there was no sign of Trot.

'You still think it's him?' I asked.

'Yes, I do.'

'Where does he get the paint?'

'Tally buys it for him, out of her pickin' money.'

'Who told you?'

'I asked Mrs. Foley at the hardware store. She said a crippled boy from the hills and his sister bought two quarts of white enamel house paint and a small brush. She thought it was strange – hill people buyin' house paint.'

'How much will two quarts paint?'

'Not very much.'

'You gonna tell Pappy?'

'I am.'

We made a quick pass through the garden, gathering just the essentials – tomatoes, cucumbers, and two red peppers that caught her eye. The rest of the picking crew would be in from the fields in a short while, and I was anxious for the fireworks to start once Pappy learned that his house was getting painted.

In a few minutes, there were whispers and brief conversations outside. I was forced to slice cucumbers in the kitchen, a tactic to keep me away from the controversy. Gran listened to the news on the radio while my mother cooked. At some point, my father and Pappy walked to the east side of the house and inspected Trot's work in progress.

Then they came to the kitchen, where we sat and blessed the food and began eating without a word about anything but the weather. If Pappy was angry about the house painting, he certainly didn't show it. Maybe he was just too tired.

The next day my mother kept me behind and puttered around the house for as long as she could. She did the breakfast dishes and some laundry, and together we watched the front yard. Gran left and headed for the cotton, but my mother and I stayed back, doing chores and keeping busy.

Trot was not to be seen. He'd vanished from the front yard. Hank stumbled from a tent around eight and knocked over cans and jugs until he found the leftover biscuits. He ate until there was nothing left, then he belched and looked at our house as if he might raid it for food. Eventually he lumbered past the silo on his way to the cotton trailer.

We waited, peeking through the front windows. Still no sign of Trot. We finally gave up and walked to the fields. When my mother returned three hours later to prepare lunch, there was a small area of fresh paint on some boards under the window of my room. Trot was painting slowly toward the rear of the house, his work limited by his reach and by his desire for privacy. At the current rate of progress, he'd finish about half the east side before it was time for the Spruills to pack up and head for the hills.

After three days of peace and hard work, it was time for more conflict. Miguel met Pappy at the tractor after breakfast, and they walked in the direction of the barn, where some of the other Mexicans were waiting. In the semidarkness of the dawn I tagged along, just close enough to hear but not get noticed. Luis was sitting on a stump, his head low as if he were sick. Pappy examined him closely. He had suffered some type of injury.

The story, as Miguel explained it in rapid, broken English, was that during the night someone had thrown clods of dirt at the barn. The first one landed against the side of the hayloft just after the Mexicans had bedded down. It sounded like a gunshot – planks rattled, and the whole barn seemed to shake. A few minutes passed, and then another one landed. Then another. About ten minutes went by, and they thought perhaps it was over, but yet another one hit, this one on the tin roof just above their heads. They were angry and scared, and sleep became impossible. Through the cracks in the wall, they watched the cotton field behind the barn. Their tormentor was out there somewhere, deep in the cotton, invisible in the blackness of the night, hiding like a coward.

Luis had slowly opened the loft door for a better look, and when he did a missile landed squarely in his face. It was a rock from the road in front of our house. Whoever threw it had saved it for such an occasion, a direct shot at one of the Mexicans. Dirt clods were fine for making noise, but the rock was used to maim.

Luis's nose was cut, broken, and swollen to twice its normal size. Pappy yelled for my father to fetch Gran.

Miguel continued the story. Once they tended to Luis and got him somewhat comfortable, the shelling resumed. Every ten minutes or so, just as they were settling down again, another volley would crash in from the darkness. They watched carefully through the cracks but saw no movements in the field. It was just too dark to see anything. Finally their assailant grew tired of his fun and games and stopped the assault. For most of them, sleep had been fitful.

Gran arrived and took over. Pappy stomped away, cursing under his breath. I was torn between the two dramas: Did I want to watch Gran doctor on Luis, or did I want to listen as Pappy blew off steam?

I followed Pappy back to the tractor, where he growled at my father in words I could not understand. Then he charged the flatbed trailer where the Spruills were waiting, still half-asleep.

'Where's Hank?' he snarled at Mr. Spruill.

'Sleepin', I reckon.'

'Is he gonna work today?' Pappy's words were sharp.

'Go ask him,' Mr. Spruill said, getting to his feet to address Pappy face-to-face.

Pappy took a step closer. 'The Mexicans couldn't sleep last night 'cause somebody's throwin' dirt clods against the barn. Any idea who it was?'

My father, with a much cooler head, stepped between the two.

'Nope. You accusin' somebody?' Mr. Spruill asked.

'I don't know,' Pappy said. 'Ever'body else's workin' hard, sleepin' hard, dead tired at night. Ever'body but Hank. Seems to me, he's the only one with plenty of time on his hands. And it's the sorta stupid thing Hank would do.'

I didn't like this open conflict with the Spruills. They were as tired of Hank as we were, but they were still his family. And they were hill people, too – make them mad and they'd simply leave. Pappy was on the verge of saying too much.

'I'll speak to him,' Mr. Spruill said, somewhat softer, as if he knew Hank was the likely culprit. His chin dropped an inch or two, and he looked at Mrs. Spruill. The family was in turmoil because of Hank, and they were not ready to defend him.

'Let's get to work,' my father said. They were anxious for the confrontation to end. I glanced at Tally, but she was looking away, lost in her thoughts, ignoring me and everybody else. Pappy climbed onto the tractor, and we left to pick cotton.

Luis lay on the back porch all morning with an ice pack on his face. Gran buzzed around and tried repeatedly to force her remedies upon him, but Luis held firm. By noon he'd had enough of this American style of doctoring and was anxious to return to the fields, broken nose or not.

Hank's cotton production had fallen from about four hundred pounds a day to less than two hundred. Pappy was livid about this. As the days dragged on, the situation festered, and there were more whispers among the adults. Pappy had never owned $250 free and clear.

'How much did he pick today?' he asked my father over supper. We had just finished the blessing and were passing around the food.

'Hundred and ninety pounds.'

My mother closed her eyes in frustration. Supper was supposed to be a pleasant time for families to visit and reflect. She hated controversy during our meals. Idle gossip – chitchat about the goings-on of people we knew or perhaps didn't know – was okay, but she didn't like conflict. Food was not properly digested unless your body was relaxed.

'I've a good mind to drive to town tomorrow, find Stick Powers, and tell him I'm finished with the boy,' Pappy said, waving a fork at the air.

There was no way he would do this, and we knew it. He knew it, too. If Stick somehow managed to get Hank Spruill handcuffed and shoved into the back of his patrol car, which was a showdown I would've loved to witness, the rest of the Spruills would be packed and gone in a matter of minutes. Pappy wasn't about to risk a crop over an idiot like Hank. We'd grit our teeth and just try to survive his presence on our farm. We'd hope and pray he wouldn't kill anyone else and that no one killed him, and in a few short weeks the harvest would be completed, and he'd be gone.

'You're not sure it's him,' Gran said. 'No one saw him throwin' at the barn.'

'Some things you ain't gotta see,' Pappy fired back. 'We ain't seen Trot with a paintbrush, but we're perfectly happy to believe he's doin' the paintin'. Right?'

My mother, with perfect timing, said, 'Luke, who are the Cardinals playin'?' It was her standard line, a not-too-subtle way of letting the others know that she wanted to eat in peace.

'The Cubs,' I said.

'How many more games?' she asked.

'Just three.'

'How far ahead is Musial?'

'Six points. He's at three-thirty-six. Baumholtz is at three-thirty. He can't catch him.'

At this point my father was always expected to come to the aid of his wife and keep the conversation away from heavier matters. He cleared his throat and said, 'I bumped into Lou Jeffcoat last Saturday – I forgot to tell you. He said the Methodists have a new pitcher for Sunday's game.'

Pappy had cooled off enough to say, 'He's lyin'. That's what they say every year.'

'Why would they need a new pitcher?' Gran

asked with a faint smile, and I thought my mother was going to laugh.

Sunday was the Fall Picnic, a glorious event that engulfed Black Oak. After worship, usually a very long worship, at least for us Baptists, we would meet at the school, where the Methodists would be gathering. Under the shade trees the ladies would set up enough food to feed the entire state, and after a long lunch the men would play a baseball game.

It was no ordinary game, because bragging rights were at stake. The winners ribbed the losers for an entire year. In the dead of winter I had heard men at the Tea Shoppe ride each other about The Game.

The Methodists had won it for the last four years, yet they always started rumors about having a new pitcher.

'Who's pitchin' for us?' my father asked. Pappy coached the Baptist team every year, though after four straight losses, folks were beginning to grumble.

'Ridley, I guess,' Pappy said without hesitation. He'd been thinking about the game for a year.

'I can hit Ridley!' I said.

'You got a better idea?' Pappy shot at me.

'Yes sir.'

'Well, I can't wait to hear it.'

'Pitch Cowboy,' I said, and everybody smiled. What a wonderful idea.

But the Mexicans couldn't play in The Game, nor could the hill people. Each roster was made up of certified church members only – no farm laborers, no relatives from Jonesboro, no ringers of any variety. There were so many rules that if they'd been put down in writing, the rule book would've been thicker than the Bible. The umpires were brought in from Monette and were paid five dollars a game plus all the lunch they could eat. Supposedly, no one knew the umpires, but after last year's loss there were rumors, at least around our church, that they were either Methodists or married to Methodists.

'That would be nice, wouldn't it?' my father said, dreaming of Cowboy mowing down our rivals. One strikeout after another. Curveballs dropping in from all directions.

With the conversation back in pleasant territory, the women took over. Baseball was pushed aside as they talked about the picnic, the food, what the Methodist women would be wearing, and so on. Supper came to the usual quiet close, and we headed for the porch.

I had decided that I would write Ricky a letter and tell him about Libby Latcher. I was certain that none of the adults would do so; they were too busy burying the secret. But Ricky needed to know what Libby had accused him of. He needed to respond in some way. If he knew what was happening, then maybe he could get himself sent home to deal with the situation. And the sooner the better. The Latchers were staying to themselves, telling no one, as far as we knew, but secrets were hard to keep around Black Oak.

Before Ricky left for Korea, he'd told us the story of a friend of his, a guy from Texas he'd met in boot camp. This guy was only eighteen, but he was already married, and his wife was pregnant. The army sent him to California to shuffle papers for a few months so he wouldn't get shot. It was a hardship case of some variety, and the guy would be back in Texas before his wife gave birth.

Ricky now had a hardship; he just didn't know it. I would be the one to tell him. I excused myself from the porch under the pretense of fatigue and went to Ricky's room, where I kept my Big Chief writing tablet. I took it to the kitchen table – the light was better there – and began writing slowly in large printed letters.

I dwelt briefly on baseball, the pennant race, then the carnival and Samson, and I wrote a couple of sentences about the twisters earlier in the week. I had neither the time nor the stomach to talk about Hank, so I got to the meat of the story. I told him that Libby Latcher had had a baby, though I did not confess that I had actually been nearby when the thing arrived.

My mother wandered in from the porch and asked what I was doing. 'Writin' Ricky,' I said.

'How nice,' she said. 'You need to go to bed.'

'Yes ma'am.' I had written a full page and was quite proud of myself. Tomorrow I would write another page. Then maybe another. I was determined that it would be the longest letter Ricky had so far received.

Chapter 22

I was nearing the end of a long row of cotton, close to the thicket that bordered Siler's Creek, when I heard voices. The stalks were especially tall, and I was lost amid the dense foliage. My sack was half-full, and I was dreaming of the afternoon in town, of a movie at the Dixie with a Coca-Cola and popcorn. The sun was almost overhead; it had to be approaching noon. I planned to make the turn and then head back to the trailer, working hard and finishing the day with a flourish.

When I heard people talking, I dropped to one knee, and then I slowly sat on the ground without making another sound. For a long time I heard nothing at all, and I was beginning to think that maybe I had been wrong, when the voice of a girl barely made it through the stalks to where I was hiding. She was somewhere to my right; I couldn't tell how far away.

I slowly stood and peeked through the cotton but saw nothing. Then I crouched again and began creeping down the row toward the end, my cotton sack abandoned for the moment. Silently, I crawled and stopped, crawled and stopped, until I heard her again. She was several rows over, hiding, I thought, in the cotton. I froze for a few minutes until I heard her laugh, a soft laugh that was muffled by the cotton, and I knew it was Tally.

For a long time I rocked gently on all fours and tried to imagine what she was doing hiding in the fields, as far away from the cotton trailer as possible. Then I heard another voice, that of a man. I decided to move in closer.

I found the widest gap between two stalks and cut through the first row without a sound. There was no wind to rustle the leaves and bolls, so I had to be perfectly still. And patient. Then I made it through the second row and waited for the voices.

They were quiet for a long time, and I began to worry that maybe they'd heard me. Then there was giggling, both voices working at once, and low, hushed conversation that I could barely hear. I stretched out flat on my stomach and surveyed the situation from the ground, down where the stalks were thickest and there were no bolls and leaves. I could almost see something several rows away, maybe the darkness of Tally's hair, maybe not. I decided I was close enough.

There was no one nearby. The others – the Spruills and the Chandlers – were working their way back to the trailer. The Mexicans were far away, nothing visible but their straw hats.

Though shaded, I was sweating profusely. My heart was racing, my mouth dry. Tally was hiding deep in the cotton with a man, doing something bad, or if not, then why was she hiding? I wanted to do something to stop them, but I had no right. I was just a little kid, a spy who was trespassing on their business. I thought about retreating, but the voices held me.

The snake was a water moccasin, a cotton-mouth, one of many in our part of Arkansas. They lived around the creeks and rivers and occasionally ventured inland to sun or to feed. Each spring when we planted, it was common to see them ground up behind our disks and plows. They were short, black, thick, aggressive, and filled with venom. Their bites were rarely fatal, but I'd heard many tall tales of horrible deaths.

If you saw one, you simply killed it with a stick or a hoe or anything you could grab. They weren't as quick as rattlers, nor did they have the striking range, but they were mean and nasty.

This one was crawling down the row directly at me, less than five feet away. We were eyeball-to-eyeball. I'd been so occupied with Tally and whatever she was doing that I'd forgotten everything else. I uttered something in horror and bolted upright, then I ran through a row of cotton, then another.

A man said something in a louder voice, but for the moment I was more concerned with the snake. I hit the ground near my cotton sack, strapped it over my shoulder, and began crawling toward the trailer. When I was certain the cottonmouth was far away, I stopped and listened. Nothing. Complete silence. No one was chasing me.

Slowly, I stood and peeked through the cotton. To my right, several rows away and already with her back to me, was Tally, her cotton sack strapped over her shoulder and her straw hat cocked to one side, steadily making her way along as if nothing had happened.

And to my left, cutting low through the cotton and escaping like a thief, was Cowboy.

On most Saturday afternoons Pappy could find some reason to delay our trip to town. We'd finish lunch, and I'd suffer the indignity of the bath, then he'd find something to do because he was determined to make us wait. The tractor had some ailment that suddenly needed his attention. He'd crawl around with his old wrenches, making a fuss about how it had to be repaired right then so he could buy the necessary parts in town. Or the truck wasn't running just right, and Saturday after lunch was the perfect time to poke around the engine. Or the water pump needed his attention. Sometimes he sat at the kitchen table and attended to the small amount of paperwork it took to run the farming operation.

Finally, when everyone was good and mad, he'd take a long bath, and then we'd head to town.

My mother was anxious to see the newest member of Craighead County, even though he was a Latcher, so while Pappy piddled in the tool-shed, we loaded four boxes of vegetables and headed across the river. My father somehow avoided the trip. The baby's alleged father was his brother, and that, of course, made my father the baby's alleged uncle, and that was something my father simply wasn't ready to accept. And I was sure he had no interest in another encounter with Mr. Latcher.

My mother drove, and I prayed, and we somehow made it safely over the bridge. We rolled to a stop on the other side of the river. The truck stalled, and the engine died. As she was taking a deep breath, I decided to say, 'Mom, there's somethin' I need to tell you.'

'Can it wait?' she asked, reaching for the ignition.

'No.'

We were sitting in a hot truck, just off the bridge, on a one-lane dirt road without a house or another vehicle in sight. It struck me as the perfect place and time for an important conversation.

'What is it?' she said, folding her arms across her chest as if she'd already decided I'd done something terrible.

There were so many secrets. Hank and the Sisco beating. Tally at the creek. The birth of Libby's baby. But those had been tucked away for a while. I'd become adept at keeping them private. The current one, though, had to be shared with my mother.

'I think Tally and Cowboy like each other,' I said, and immediately I felt lighter.

'Is that so?' she said with a smile, as if I didn't know much because I was just a kid. Then the smile slowly vanished as she considered this. I wondered if she, too, knew something about the secret romance.

'Yes ma'am.'

'And what makes you think this?'

'I caught them in the cotton patch this mornin'.'

'What were they doing?' she asked, seeming a little frightened that maybe I'd seen something I shouldn't have.

'I don't know, but they were together.'

288

'Did you see them?'

I told her the story, beginning with the voices, then the cottonmouth, then their escape. I omitted no details, and, amazingly, I did not exaggerate anything. Maybe the size of the snake, but for the most part I clung to the truth.

She absorbed it and seemed genuinely astounded.

'What were they doin', Mom?' I asked.

'I don't know. You didn't see anything, did you?'

'No ma'am. Do you think they were kissin'?'

'Probably,' she said quickly.

She reached for the ignition again and said, 'Oh well, I'll talk to your father about it.'

We drove away in a hurry. After a moment or two I really couldn't tell if I felt any better. She'd told me many times that little boys shouldn't keep secrets from their mothers. But every time I confessed one, she was quick to shrug it off and tell my father what I'd told her. I'm not sure how I benefited from being so candid. But it was all I could do. Now the adults knew about Tally and Cowboy. Let them worry about the problem.

The Latchers were picking near their house, so by the time we rolled to a stop, we had an audience. Mrs. Latcher emerged from the house and managed a smile, then she helped us haul the food to the front porch.

'I guess you wanna see the baby,' she said softly to my mother.

I wanted to see it also, but I knew my chances were slim. The women went into the house. I found a spot under a tree near our truck, and

289

I planned to loiter, alone, just minding my own business while I waited for my mother. I didn't want to see any of the Latchers. The fact that we were now probably related by blood made me ill.

Three of them suddenly appeared from around the truck – three boys, with Percy leading the group. The other two were younger and smaller but just as lean and wiry as Percy. They approached me without a word.

'Howdy, Percy,' I said, trying to at least be polite.

'What're you doin' here?' he growled. He had a brother on each side, all three of them lined up against me.

'My mother made me come,' I said.

'You ain't got no business here.' He was practically hissing through his teeth, and I wanted to back up. In fact, I wanted to tuck tail and run.

'I'm waitin' for my mother,' I said.

'We're gonna whup your ass,' Percy said, and all three of them clenched their fists.

'Why?' I managed to say.

''Cause you're a Chandler, and your Ricky did that to Libby.'

'Wasn't my fault,' I said.

'Don't matter.' The smallest one looked particularly fierce. He was squinting and twisting his mouth up at the corners, sort of snarling at me, and I figured the first punch would come from him.

'Three on one ain't fair,' I said.

'Wasn't fair what happened to Libby,' Percy said and then, quick as a cat, he punched me in the stomach. A horse could not have kicked any harder, and I went down with a shriek.

I'd had a few scuffles at school – playground push-and-shoves that were broken up by the teachers before serious blows were landed. Mrs. Emma Enos, the third-grade teacher, gave me three licks for trying to fight Joey Stallcup, and Pappy could not have been prouder. And Ricky used to be rough with me, wrestling and boxing and such. I was no stranger to violence. Pappy loved to fight, and when I hit the ground, I thought of him. Somebody kicked me; I grabbed a foot, and instantly there was a pile of little warriors, all kicking and clawing and cussing in the dirt. I grabbed the hair of the midsized one while the other two pounded my back. I was determined to yank his head off when Percy landed a nasty shot to my nose. I went blind for a second, and they, squealing like wild animals, piled on again.

I heard the women yell from the porch. It's about time! I thought. Mrs. Latcher arrived first and began pulling boys from the heap, scolding them loudly as she flung them around. Since I was on the bottom, I got up last. My mother looked at me in horror. My clean clothes were covered with dirt. My nose was oozing warm blood.

'Luke, are you all right?' she said, grabbing my shoulders.

My eyes were watery, and I was beginning to ache. I nodded my head yes, no problem.

'Cut me a switch!' Mrs. Latcher yelled at Percy. She was growling and still flinging the two smaller ones around. 'Whatta you mean beatin' up that little boy like that? He ain't done nothin'.'

The blood was really flowing now, dripping off my chin and staining my shirt. My mother made me lie down and tilt my head back to stop the bleeding, and while we were doing this, Percy produced a stick.

'I want you to watch this,' Mrs. Latcher said in my direction.

'No, Darla,' my mother said. 'We're leaving.'

'No, I want your boy to see this,' she said. 'Now bend over, Percy.'

'I ain't gonna do it, Ma,' Percy said, obviously scared.

'Bend over, or I'll get your father. I'll teach you some manners. Beatin' up that little boy, a visitor to our place.'

'No,' Percy said, and she hit him in the head with the stick. He screamed, and she whacked him across the ear.

She made him bend over and grab his ankles. 'You let go and I'll beat you for a week,' she threatened him. He was already crying when she started flogging away. Both my mother and I were stunned by her anger and brutality. After eight or ten very hard licks, Percy started yelping.

'Shut up!' she shouted.

Her arms and legs were as thin as the stick, but what she lacked in size she made up for in quickness. Her blows landed like machine-gun fire, fast and crisp, popping like a bullwhip. Ten, twenty, thirty shots, and Percy was bawling, 'Please stop it, Ma! I'm sorry!'

The beating went on and on, far past the point of punishment. When her arm was tired, she shoved him to the ground, and Percy curled into a tight ball and wept. By then the other two were already in tears. She grabbed the middle one by the hair. She called him Rayford and said, 'Bend over.' Rayford slowly clutched his ankles and somehow withstood the assault that followed.

'Let's go,' my mother whispered to me. 'You can lie down in the back.'

She helped me up to the bed of the truck, and by then Mrs. Latcher was pulling on the other boy, yanking him by the hair. Percy and Rayford were lying in the dirt, victims of the battle they'd started. My mother turned the truck around, and as we drove off, Mrs. Latcher was battering the youngest one. There were loud voices, and I sat up just enough to see Mr. Latcher running around the house with a trail of children behind him. He yelled at his wife; she ignored him and kept hammering away. When he reached her, he grabbed her. Kids were swarming everywhere; everyone seemed to be either screaming or crying.

The dust boiled behind us, and I lost sight of them. As I lay down again and tried to get comfortable, I prayed that I would never again set foot on their farm. I never wanted to see any of those people for the rest of my life. And I prayed long and hard that no one would ever hear the rumor that the Chandlers and the Latchers were related.

My return home was triumphant. The Spruills were cleaned up and ready for town. They were sitting under a tree, drinking iced tea with Pappy and Gran and my father, when we rolled to a stop less than twenty feet away. As dramatically as I could, I stood in the back of the truck, and with great satisfaction watched them react in shock at the sight of me. There I was – beaten, bloodied, dirty, clothes ripped, but still standing.

I climbed down, and everyone gathered around me. My mother stormed forward and very angrily said, 'You're not gonna believe what happened! Three of them jumped Luke! Percy and two others caught him when I was in the house. The little criminals! We're takin' food over, and they pull a stunt like this.'

Tally was concerned, too, and I think she wanted to reach out and touch me, to make sure I was all right.

'Three of 'em?' Pappy repeated, his eyes dancing.

'Yes, and they were all bigger than Luke,' my mother said, and the legend began to grow. The size of my three attackers would increase as the days and months went by.

Gran was in my face, staring at my nose, which had a small cut on it. 'Might be broken,' she said, and though I was thrilled to hear it, I was not looking forward to her treatment.

'You didn't run, did you?' Pappy asked. He, too, was moving in closer.

'No sir,' I said proudly. I'd still be running if given half a chance.

'He did not,' my mother said sternly. 'He was kickin' and clawin' just as hard as they were.'

Pappy beamed, and my father smiled.

'We'll go back tomorrow and finish 'em off,' Pappy said.

'You'll do no such thing,' my mother said. She was irritated because Pappy loved a brawl. But then, she came from a house full of girls. She did not understand fighting.

'Did you land a good punch?' Pappy asked.

'They were all cryin' when I left,' I said.

My mother rolled her eyes.

Hank shoved his way through the group and bent down to inspect the damage. 'Say there was three of 'em, huh?' he growled at me.

'Yes sir,' I said, nodding.

'Good for you, boy. It'll make you tough.'

'Yes sir,' I said.

'If you want me to, I'll show you some tricks on how to handle a three-on-one situation,' he said with a smile.

'Let's get cleaned up,' my mother said.

'I think it's broken,' Gran said.

'You okay, Luke?' Tally asked.

'Yep,' I said, as tough as I could.

They led me away in a victory march.

Chapter 23

The Fall Picnic was always held on the last Sunday in September, though no one knew exactly why. It was simply a tradition in Black Oak, a ritual as ingrained as the carnival and the spring revival. It was supposed to somehow link the coming of a new season, the beginning of the end of the harvest, and the end of baseball. It wasn't clear if all this was accomplished with one picnic, but at least the effort was made.

We shared the day with the Methodists, our friends and friendly rivals. Black Oak was too small to be divided. There were no ethnic groups, no blacks or Jews or Asians, no permanent outsiders of any variety. We were all of Anglo-Irish stock, maybe a strain or two of German blood, and everybody farmed or sold to the farmers. Everybody was a Christian or claimed to be. Disagreements flared up when a Cubs fan said too much at the Tea Shoppe, or when some idiot declared John Deere to be inferior to another brand of tractor, but for the most part life was peaceful. The older boys and younger men liked to fight behind the Co-op on Saturdays, but it was more sport than

296

anything else. A beating like the one Hank gave the Siscos was so rare that the town was still talking about it.

Individual grudges lasted a lifetime; Pappy carried more than his share. But there were no serious enemies. There was a clear social order, with the sharecroppers at the bottom and the merchants at the top, and everyone was expected to know his place. But folks got along.

The line between Baptists and Methodists was never straight and true. Their worship was slightly different, with the ritual of sprinkling little babies being their most flagrant deviation from the Scriptures, as we saw things. And they didn't meet as often, which, of course, meant that they were not as serious about their faith. Nobody met as much as us Baptists. We took great pride in constant worship. Pearl Watson, my favorite Methodist, said she'd like to be a Baptist, but that she just wasn't physically able.

Ricky told me once in private that when he left the farm he might become a Catholic because they only met once a week. I didn't know what a Catholic was, and so he tried to explain things, but Ricky on theology was a shaky discussion at best.

My mother and Gran spent more time than usual ironing our clothes that Sunday morning. And I certainly got scrubbed with more purpose. Much to my disappointment, my nose had not been broken, there was no swelling, and the cut was barely noticeable.

We had to look our very best because the Methodist ladies had slightly nicer dresses. In spite of all the fuss, I was excited and couldn't wait to get to town.

We had invited the Spruills. This was done out of a sense of friendliness and Christian concern, though I wanted to pick and choose. Tally would be welcome; the rest could stay in the front yard for all I cared. But when I surveyed their camp after breakfast, I saw little movement. Their truck had not been disconnected from the myriad of wires and ropes that held their shelters upright. 'They ain't comin',' I reported to Pappy, who was studying his Sunday school lesson.

'Good,' he said quietly.

The prospect of Hank milling about the picnic, grazing from table to table, gorging himself on food and looking for a fight, was not appealing.

The Mexicans really had no choice. My mother had extended an invitation to Miguel early in the week, then followed it up with a couple of gentle reminders as Sunday grew near. My father had explained to him that a special worship service would be held in Spanish, then there would be plenty of good food. They had little else to do on Sunday afternoons.

Nine of them piled into the back of our truck; only Cowboy was absent. This set my imagination on fire. Where was he and what was he doing? Where was Tally? I didn't see her in the front yard as we drove away. My heart sank as I thought of them back in the fields, hiding and doing whatever they wanted to do. Instead of going to church with us, Tally was probably sneaking around again, doing bad things. What if she now used Cowboy as her lookout while she bathed in Siler's Creek? I couldn't stand that thought, and I worried about her all the way to town.

Brother Akers, with a rare smile on his face, took the pulpit. The sanctuary was packed, and people were sitting in the aisles and standing along the back wall. The windows were open, and on the north side of the church, under a tall oak, the Mexicans were grouped together, hats off, dark heads making a sea of brown.

He welcomed our guests, our visitors from the hills, and also the Mexicans. There were a few hill people, but not many. As always, he asked them to stand and identify themselves. They were from places like Hardy, Mountain Home, and Calico Rock, and they were as spruced up as we were.

A loudspeaker had been placed in a window, so Brother Akers's words were broadcast out of the sanctuary and into the general direction of the Mexicans, where Mr. Carl Durbin picked up the words and translated them into Spanish. Mr. Durbin was a retired missionary from Jonesboro. He'd worked in Peru for thirty years among some real Indians up in the mountains, and every so often he'd come and talk to us during missions week and show us photos and slides of the strange land he'd left behind. In addition to Spanish, he also spoke an Indian dialect, and this forever fascinated me.

Mr. Durbin stood under the shade tree with Mexicans seated on the grass all around him. He wore a white suit and a white straw hat, and his voice carried back to the church with almost as much volume as old Brother Akers's did with the loudspeaker. Ricky'd once said that Mr. Durbin had a lot more sense than Brother Akers, and he'd offered this opinion over Sunday dinner and created trouble yet again. It was a sin to criticize your preacher, at least out loud.

I sat at the end of the pew, next to the window, so I could watch and listen to Mr. Durbin. I couldn't understand a word he was saying, but I knew his Spanish was slower than the Mexicans'. They talked so fast that I often wondered how they understood each other. His sentences were smooth and deliberate and laden with a heavy Arkansas accent. Though I had not a clue as to what he was saying, he was still more captivating than Brother Akers.

Not surprisingly, with such a large crowd, the morning's sermon took on a life of its own and became a marathon. Small crowd, shorter sermon. Big crowd, like Easter and Mother's Day and the Fall Picnic, and Brother Akers felt the need to perform. At some point, in the midst of his ramblings, Mr. Durbin seemed to get bored with it all. He ignored the message being broadcast from inside the sanctuary and began to deliver his own sermon. When Brother Akers paused to catch his breath, Mr. Durbin kept right on preaching. And when Brother Akers's hellfire and brimstone was at its fever pitch, Mr. Durbin was resting with a glass of water. He took a seat on the ground with the Mexicans and waited for the shouting to stop inside the sanctuary.

I waited, too. I passed the time by dreaming of the food that we'd soon have – heaping plates of fried chicken and gallons of homemade ice cream.

The Mexicans began glancing at the church windows. I'm sure they thought Brother Akers had gone crazy. 'Relax,' I wanted to tell them, 'it happens all the time.'

We sang five stanzas of 'Just As I Am' for the benediction. No one walked down the aisle, and Brother Akers reluctantly dismissed us. I met Dewayne at the front door, and we raced down the street to the baseball field to see if the Methodists were there. Of course they were; they never worshiped as long as we did.

Behind the backstop, under three elm trees that had caught a million foul balls, the food was being arranged on picnic tables covered with red-and-white checkerboard cloths. The Methodists were swarming around, the men and children hauling food while the ladies organized the dishes. I found Pearl Watson and chatted her up. 'Brother Akers still goin'?' she asked with a grin.

'He just turned us loose,' I said. She gave Dewayne and me two chocolate cookies. I ate mine in two bites.

Finally, the Baptists started arriving, amid a chorus of 'Hello' and 'Where you been?' and 'What took so long?' Cars and trucks were pulled close, and soon were parked bumper to bumper along the fences around the field. At least one and maybe two would get hit with foul balls. Two years earlier, Mr. Wilber Shifflett's brand-new Chrysler sedan lost a windshield when Ricky hit a home run over the left-field fence. The explosion had been terrific – a loud thud, then the racket of glass bursting. But Mr. Shifflett had money, so no one got too worried. He knew the risks when he parked there. The Methodists beat us that year, too, seven to five, and Ricky was of the opinion that the manager, Pappy, should've changed pitchers in the third inning.

They didn't speak to each other for some time.

The tables were soon covered with large bowls of vegetables, platters heaped with fried chicken, and baskets filled with corn bread, rolls, and other breads. Under the direction of the Methodist minister's wife, Mrs. Orr, dishes were moved here and there until a certain order took shape. One table had nothing but raw vegetables – tomatoes of a dozen varieties, cucumbers, white and yellow onions in vinegar. Next to it were the beans – black-eyed peas, crowder peas, green beans cooked with ham, and butter beans. Every picnic had potato salad, and every chef had a different recipe. Dewayne and I counted eleven large bowls of the dish, and no two looked the same. Deviled eggs were almost as popular, and there were plates of them that covered half a table. Last, and most important, was the fried chicken. There was enough to feed the town for a month.

The ladies scurried about, fussing over the food while the men talked and laughed and greeted each other, but always with one eye on the chicken. Kids were everywhere, and Dewayne and I drifted to one tree in particular, where some ladies were arranging the desserts. I counted sixteen coolers of homemade ice cream, all covered tightly with towels and packed with ice.

Once the preparations had met the approval of Mrs. Orr, her husband, the Reverend Vernon Orr, stood in the center of the tables with Brother

Akers, and the crowd grew still and quiet. The year before, Brother Akers had thanked God for His blessings; this year the honor went to the Methodists. The picnic had an unspoken pattern to it. We bowed our heads and listened as the Reverend Orr thanked God for His goodness, for all the wonderful food, for the weather, the cotton, and on and on. He left out nothing; Black Oak was indeed grateful for everything.

I could smell the chicken. I could taste the brownies and ice cream. Dewayne kicked me, and I wanted to lay him out. I didn't, though, because I'd get whipped for fighting during a prayer.

When the Reverend Orr finally finished, the men corralled the Mexicans and lined them up to be served. This was a tradition; Mexicans first, hill people second, children third, then the adults. Stick Powers appeared from nowhere, in uniform, of course, and managed to cut in line between the Mexicans and the hill folks. I heard him explain that he was on duty and didn't have much time. He carried away two plates – one covered with chicken and one covered with everything else he could pile on. We knew he'd eat until he was stuffed, then find a tree on the edge of town and sleep off his lunch.

Several of the Methodists asked me about Ricky – how was he doing, had we heard from him. I tried to be nice and answer their questions, but as a family we Chandlers did not enjoy this attention. And now that we were horrified over the Latcher secret, any mention of Ricky in public scared us.

'Tell him we're thinkin' about him,' they said.

303

They always said this, as if we owned a phone and called him every night.

'We're prayin' for him,' they said.

'Thank you,' I always replied.

A perfectly wonderful moment like the Fall Picnic could be ruined with an unexpected question about Ricky. He was in Korea, in the trenches, in the thick of the war, dodging bullets and killing people, not knowing if he would ever come home to go to church with us, to picnic with the town, to play against the Methodists again. In the midst of the excitement I suddenly felt very alone, and very frightened.

'Get tough,' Pappy would say. The food helped immensely. Dewayne and I took our plates and sat behind the first-base dugout, where there was a small sliver of shade. Quilts were being placed all around the outfield, and families were sitting together in the sun. Umbrellas were popping up; the ladies were fanning their faces, their small children, and their plates. The Mexicans were squeezed under one tree, down the right-field foul line, away from the rest of us. Juan had confessed to me the year before that they weren't sure if they liked fried chicken. I'd never heard such nonsense. It was a heck of a lot better than tortillas, I'd thought at the time.

My parents and grandparents ate together on a quilt near third base. After much haggling and negotiating, I'd been granted permission to eat with my buddies, a huge step for a seven-year-old.

The line never stopped. By the time the men reached the last table, the teenaged boys were back for more. One plate was enough for me. I wanted to save room for the ice cream. Before long we wandered over to the dessert table, where Mrs. Irene Flanagan was standing guard, preventing vandalism from the likes of us.

'How many chocolates you got?' I asked, looking at the collection of ice cream coolers just waiting in the shade.

She smiled and said, 'Oh, I don't know. Several.'

'Did Mrs. Cooper bring her peanut butter ice cream?' Dewayne asked.

'She did,' Mrs. Flanagan said and pointed to a cooler in the middle of the pack. Mrs. Cooper somehow mixed chocolate and peanut butter in her ice cream, and the results were incredible. Folks clamored for it all year round. The year before, two teenaged boys, one a Baptist and one a Methodist, almost came to blows over who would get the next serving. While peace was being restored by the Reverend Orr, Dewayne managed to grab two bowls of the stuff. He charged down the street with them and hid behind a shed, where he devoured every drop. He talked of little else for a month.

Mrs. Cooper was a widow. She lived in a pretty little house two blocks behind Pop and Pearl's store, and when she needed yard work done she'd simply make a cooler of peanut butter ice cream. Teenagers would materialize from nowhere, and she had the neatest yard in town. Even grown men had been known to stop by and pull a few weeds.

'You'll have to wait,' Mrs. Flanagan said.

'Till when?' I asked.

'Till everyone is finished.'

305

We waited forever. Some of the older boys and the younger men began stretching their muscles and tossing baseballs in the outfield. The adults talked and visited and talked and visited, and I was certain the ice cream was melting. The two umpires arrived from Monette, and this sent a ripple of excitement through the crowd. They, of course, had to be fed first, and for a while they were more concerned with fried chicken than with baseball. Slowly, the quilts and umbrellas were taken from the outfield. The picnic was ending. It was almost time for the game.

The ladies gathered around the dessert table and began serving us. Finally Dewayne got his peanut butter ice cream. I opted for two scoops of chocolate over one of Mrs. Lou Kiner's fudge brownies. For twenty minutes there was a near-riot around the dessert table, but order was maintained. Both preachers stood in the midst of the pack, both eating as much ice cream as anybody else. The umpires declined, citing the heat as the reason that they should finally stop eating.

Someone shouted, 'Play ball!' and the crowd moved toward the backstop. The Methodists were coached by Mr. Duffy Lewis, a farmer out west of town and, according to Pappy, a man of limited baseball intelligence. But after four losses in a row, Pappy's low opinion of Mr. Lewis had become almost muted. The umpires called the two coaches to a meeting behind home plate, and for a long time they discussed Black Oak's version of the rules of baseball. They pointed to fences and poles and limbs over-hanging the field – each had its own rules and its own history. Pappy disagreed

306

with most of what the umpires said, and the haggling went on and on.

The Baptists had been the home team the year before, so we hit first. The Methodist pitcher was Buck Prescott, son of Mr. Sap Prescott, one of the largest landowners in Craighead County. Buck was in his early twenties and had attended Arkansas State for two years, something that was quite rare. He had tried to pitch in college, but there had been some problems with the coach. He was left-handed, threw nothing but curveballs, and had beaten us the year before, nine to two. When he walked out to the mound, I knew we were in for a long day. His first pitch was a slow, looping curveball that was high and outside but called a strike anyway, and Pappy was already yapping at the umpire. Buck walked the first two batters, struck out the next two, then retired my father on a fly ball to center field.

Our pitcher was Duke Ridley, a young farmer with seven kids and a fastball even I could hit. He claimed he once pitched in Alaska during the war, but this had not been verified. Pappy thought it was a lie, and after watching him get shelled the year before, I had serious doubts, too. He walked the first three batters while throwing only one strike, and I thought Pappy might charge the mound and maim him. Their cleanup batter popped up to the catcher. The next guy flied out to shallow left. We got lucky when their number-six batter, Mr. Lester Hurdle, at age fifty-two the oldest player on either roster, hit a long fly ball to right, where our fielder, Bennie Jenkins, gloveless and shoeless, caught it with his bare hands.

The game settled into a pitcher's duel, not necessarily because the pitching was sharp, but more because neither team could hit. We drifted back to the ice cream, where the last melting remnants were being dished out. By the third inning the ladies of both denominations had grouped into small clusters of conversation and, for them, the game was of lesser importance. Somewhere not far away, a car radio was on, and I could hear Harry Caray. The Cardinals were playing the Cubs in the final game of the season.

As Dewayne and I retreated from the dessert table with our last cups of ice cream, we walked behind a quilt where half a dozen young women were resting and talking. 'Well, how old is Libby?' I heard one of them say.

I stopped, took a bite, and looked beyond them at the game as if I weren't the least bit interested in what they were saying.

'She's just fifteen,' another said.

'She's a Latcher. She'll have another one soon.'

'Is it a boy or a girl?'

'Boy's what I heard.'

'And the daddy?'

'Not a clue. She won't tell anybody.'

'Come on,' Dewayne said, hitting me with his elbow. We moved away and walked to the first-base dugout. I wasn't sure if I was relieved or scared. Word was out that the Latcher baby had arrived, but its father had not been identified.

It wouldn't be long, I thought. And we'd be ruined. I'd have a cousin who was a Latcher, and everybody would know it.

The tight pitching duel ended in the fifth inning

when both teams erupted for six runs. For thirty minutes baseballs were flying everywhere – line drives, wild throws, balls in the outfield gaps. We changed pitchers twice, and I knew we were in trouble when Pappy went to the mound and pointed at my father. He was not a pitcher, but at that point there was no one left. He kept his pitches low, though, and we were soon out of the inning.

'Musial's pitching!' someone yelled. It was either a joke or a mistake. Stan Musial was a lot of things, but he'd never pitched before. We ran behind the bleachers to where the cars were parked. A small crowd was closing in on a '48 Dodge owned by Mr. Rafe Henry. Its radio was at full volume, and Harry Caray was wild – Stan the Man was indeed on the mound, pitching against the Cubs, against Frankie Baumholtz, the man he'd battled all year for the hitting title. The crowd at Sportsman's Park was delirious. Harry was yelling into the microphone. We were shocked at the thought of Musial on the mound.

Baumholtz hit a ground ball to third, and they sent Musial back to center field. I ran to the first-base dugout and told Pappy that Stan the Man had actually pitched, but he didn't believe me. I told my father, and he looked suspicious, too. The Methodists were up eight to six, in the bottom of the seventh, and the Baptist dugout was tense. A good flood would have caused less concern, at least at that moment.

It was at least ninety-five degrees. The players were soaked with sweat, their clean overalls and white Sunday shirts stuck to their skin. They were moving slower – paying the price for all that fried chicken and potato salad – and not hustling enough to suit Pappy.

Dewayne's father wasn't playing, so they left after a couple of hours. A few others drifted away. The Mexicans were still under their tree by the right-field foul pole, but they were sprawled out now and appeared to be sleeping. The ladies were even more involved with their shade-tree gossip; they could not have cared less who won the game.

I sat alone in the bleachers and watched the Methodists score three more in the eighth. I dreamed of the day when I'd be out there, hitting home runs and making incredible plays in center field. Those wretched Methodists wouldn't have a chance when I got big enough.

They won eleven to eight, and for the fifth year in a row Pappy had led the Baptists to defeat. The players shook hands and laughed when the game was over, then headed to the shade, where iced tea was waiting. Pappy didn't smile or laugh, nor did he shake hands with anybody. He disappeared for a while, and I knew he would pout for a week.

The Cardinals lost, too, three to zero. They finished the season four games behind the Giants and eight games behind the Brooklyn Dodgers, who would face the Yankees in an all – New York World Series.

The leftovers were gathered and hauled back to the cars and trucks. The tables were cleaned, and the litter was picked up. I helped Mr. Duffy Lewis rake the mound and home plate, and when we finished, the field looked as good as ever. It took an hour to say good-bye to everyone. There were the

310

usual threats from the losing team about what would happen next year, and the usual taunts from the winners. As far as I could tell, no one was upset but Pappy.

As we left town I thought about the end of the season. Baseball began in the spring, when we planted and when hopes were high. It sustained us through the summer, often our only diversion from the drudgery of the fields. We listened to each game, then talked about the plays and the players and the strategies until we listened to the next one. It was very much a part of our daily lives for six months, then it was gone. Just like the cotton.

I was sad by the time we arrived home. No games to listen to on the front porch. Six months without the voice of Harry Caray. Six months with no Stan Musial. I got my glove and went for a long walk down a field road, tossing the ball in the air, wondering what I would do until April.

For the first time in my life, baseball broke my heart.

Chapter 24

The heat broke in the first few days of October. The nights became cool, and the rides to the fields in the early morning were chilly. The stifling humidity was gone, and the sun lost its glare. By midday it was hot again, but not August-hot, and by dark the air was light. We waited, but the heat did not return. The seasons were changing; the days grew shorter.

Since the sun didn't sap our strength as much, we worked harder and picked more. And, of course, the change in weather was all Pappy needed to embrace yet another level of concern. With winter just around the corner, he now remembered tales of staring at rows and rows of muddy, rotting, and unpicked cotton on Christmas Day.

After a month in the fields, I missed school. Classes would resume at the end of October, and I began thinking of how nice it would be to sit at a desk all day, surrounded by friends instead of cotton stalks, and with no Spruills to worry about. Now that baseball was over, I had to dream about something. It was a tribute to my desperation to be left with only school to long for.

My return to school would be glorious because I would be wearing my shiny new Cardinals baseball jacket. Hidden inside my cigar box in the top drawer of my bureau was the grand sum of $14.50, the result of hard work and frugal spending. I was reluctantly tithing money to the church and investing wisely in Saturday movies and popcorn, but for the most part my wages were being tucked safely away next to my Stan Musial baseball card and the pearl-handled pocketknife that Ricky gave me the day he left for Korea.

I wanted to order the jacket from Sears, Roebuck, but my mother insisted I wait until the harvest was over. We were still negotiating this. Shipping took two weeks, and I was determined to return to class decked out in Cardinal red.

Stick Powers was waiting for us late one afternoon. I was with Gran and my mother, and we had left the fields a few minutes ahead of the others. As always, Stick was sitting under a tree, the one next to Pappy's truck, and his sleepy eyes betrayed the fact that he'd been napping.

He tipped his hat to my mother and Gran and said, 'Afternoon, Ruth, Kathleen.'

'Hello, Stick,' Gran said. 'What can we do for you?'

'Lookin' for Eli or Jesse.'

'They'll be along shortly. Somethin' the matter?'

Stick chewed on the blade of grass protruding from his lips and took a long look at the fields as if he were burdened with heavy news that might or might not be suitable for women.

'What is it, Stick?' Gran asked. With a boy off in the war, every visit by a man in a uniform was frightening. In 1944 one of Stick's predecessors had delivered the news that my father had been wounded at Anzio.

Stick looked at the women and decided they could be trusted. He said, 'That eldest Sisco boy, Grady, the one in prison for killin' a man over in Jonesboro, well, he escaped last week. They say he's back in these parts.'

For a moment the women said nothing. Gran was relieved that the news wasn't about Ricky. My mother was bored with the whole Sisco mess.

'You'd better tell Eli,' Gran said. 'We need to fix supper.'

They excused themselves and went into the house. Stick watched them, no doubt thinking about supper.

'Who'd he kill?' I asked Stick as soon as the women were inside.

'I don't know.'

'How'd he kill him?'

'Beat 'im with a shovel's what I heard.'

'Wow, must've been some fight.'

'I guess.'

'You think he's comin' after Hank?'

'Look, I'd better go see Eli. Where exactly is he?'

I pointed to a spot deep in the fields. The cotton trailer was barely visible.

'That's a far piece,' Stick mumbled. 'Reckon I can drive down there?'

'Sure,' I said, already heading for the patrol car. We got in.

'Don't touch anything,' Stick said when we were settled into the front seat. I gawked at the switches and radio, and of course Stick had to make the most of the moment. 'This here's the radio,' he said, picking up the mike. 'This here flips on the siren, this the lights.' He grabbed a handle on the dash and said, 'This here's the spotlight.'

'Who do you talk to on the radio?' I asked.

'HQ mainly. That's headquarters.'

'Where's headquarters?'

'Over in Jonesboro.'

'Can you call 'em right now?'

Stick reluctantly grabbed the mike, stuck it to his mouth, cocked his head sideways, and, with a frown, said, 'Unit four to base. Come in.' His voice was lower, and his words were faster, with much more importance.

We waited. When HQ didn't respond, he cocked his head to the other side, pressed the button on the mike, and repeated, 'Unit four to base. Come in.'

'You're unit four?' I asked.

'That's me.'

'How many units are there?'

'Depends.'

I stared at the radio and waited for HQ to acknowledge Stick. It seemed impossible to me that a person sitting in Jonesboro could talk directly to him, and that Stick could talk back.

In theory that was how it was supposed to work, but evidently HQ wasn't too concerned with Stick's whereabouts. For the third time he said

315

into the mike, 'Unit four to base. Come in.' His words had a little more bite to them now.

And for the third time HQ ignored him. After a few long seconds, he slapped the mike back onto the radio and said, 'It's probably ol' Theodore, asleep again.'

'Who's Theodore?' I asked.

'One of the dispatchers. He sleeps half the time.'

So do you, I thought to myself. 'Can you turn on the siren?' I asked.

'Nope. It might scare your momma.'

'What about the lights?'

'Nope, they burn up the battery.' He reached for the ignition; the engine grunted and strained but wouldn't turn over.

He tried again, and just before the engine quit completely, it turned over and started, sputtering and kicking. HQ had obviously given Stick the worst leftover of the fleet. Black Oak was not exactly a hotbed of criminal activity.

Before he could put it into gear, I saw the tractor moving slowly down the field road. 'Here they come,' I said. He squinted and strained, then turned off the engine. We got out of the car and walked back to the tree.

'You think you wanna be a deputy?' Stick asked.

And drive a ragged patrol car, nap half the day, and deal with the likes of Hank Spruill and the Siscos? 'I'm gonna play baseball,' I said.

'Where?'

'St. Louis.'

'Oh, I see,' he said with one of those funny smiles adults give to little kids who are dreaming. 'Ever' little boy wants to be a Cardinal.'

316

I had many more questions for him, most of which dealt with his gun and the bullets that went into it. And I had always wanted to inspect his handcuffs, to see how they locked and unlocked. As he watched the trailer draw nearer, I studied his revolver and holster, eager to grill him.

But Stick had spent enough time with me. He wanted me to leave. I held my barrage of questions.

When the tractor stopped, the Spruills and some of the Mexicans crawled off the trailer. Pappy and my father came straight for us, and by the time they stopped under the tree there was already tension.

'What do you want, Stick?' Pappy snarled.

Pappy in particular was irritated with Stick and his nagging presence in our lives. We had a crop to harvest; little else mattered. Stick was shadowing us, in town and on our own property.

'What is it, Stick?' Pappy said. Contempt was evident in his tone. He had just spent ten hours picking five hundred pounds of cotton, and he knew our deputy hadn't broken a sweat in years.

'That oldest Sisco boy, Grady, the one in prison for murder, he escaped last week sometime, and I think he's back home.'

'Then go get him,' Pappy said.

'I'm lookin' for him. I've heard they might start some trouble.'

'Such as?'

'Who knows with the Siscos. But they might come after Hank.'

'Let 'em come,' Pappy said, anxious for a good fight.

317

'I've heard they've got guns.'

'I got guns, Stick. You get word to the Siscos that if I see one of 'em anywhere near this place, I'll blow his stupid head off.' Pappy was practically hissing at Stick by the time he finished. Even my father seemed to warm to the idea of protecting his property and family.

'It won't happen out here,' Stick said. 'Tell your boy to stay away from town.'

'You tell him,' Pappy shot back. 'He ain't my boy. I don't care what happens to 'im.'

Stick looked around at the front yard, where the Spruills were going about the business of preparing supper. He had no desire to venture over there.

He looked at Pappy and said, 'Tell him, Eli.' He turned and walked to his car.

It groaned and sputtered and finally started, and we watched him back into the road and drive away.

After supper I was watching my father patch an inner tube from our tractor when Tally appeared in the distance. It was late but not yet dark, and she seemed to cling to the long shadows as she moved toward the silo. I watched her carefully until she stopped and waved for me to follow. My father was mumbling, the patching was not going well, and I slipped away toward the house. Then I ran behind our truck, found the shadows, and within seconds we were walking along a field row in the general direction of Siler's Creek.

'Where you goin'?' I finally asked, after it became apparent she was not going to speak first.

'I don't know. Just walkin'.'

'You goin' to the creek?'

She laughed softly and said, 'You'd like that, wouldn't you, Luke? You wanna see me again, don't you?'

My cheeks burned, and I couldn't think of anything to say.

'Maybe later,' she said.

I wanted to ask her about Cowboy, but that subject seemed so ugly and private that I didn't have the nerve to go near it. And I wanted to ask her how she knew that Libby Latcher was telling that Ricky was the father of her baby, but again, it was something else I just couldn't bring up. Tally was always mysterious, always moody, and I adored her completely. Walking with her along the narrow path made me feel twenty years old.

'What did that deputy want?' she asked.

I told her everything. Stick had delivered no forbidden secrets. The Siscos were talking big, and they were crazy enough to try something. I relayed it all to Tally.

She thought about it as we walked, then asked, 'Is Stick gonna arrest Hank for killin' that boy?'

I had to be careful here. The Spruills were at war with each other, but any hint of an outside threat and they'd close ranks. 'Pappy's worried about y'all leavin',' I said.

'What's that gotta do with Hank?'

'If he gets arrested, then y'all might leave.'

'We ain't leavin', Luke. We need the money.'

We had stopped walking. She was looking at me, and I was studying my bare feet. 'I think Stick wants to wait till the cotton's in,' I said.

She absorbed this without a word, then turned

and started back toward the house. I tagged along, certain I'd said too much. She said good night at the silo and disappeared into the darkness.

Hours later, when I was supposed to be asleep, I listened through the open window as the Spruills growled and snapped at each other. Hank was in the middle of every fight. I could not always hear what they were saying or bickering about, but it seemed as though each new skirmish was caused by something Hank had said or done. They were tired; he was not. They woke before sunrise and spent at least ten hours in the fields; he slept as late as he wanted, then picked cotton at a languid pace.

And evidently he was roaming at night again. Miguel was waiting by the back steps when my father and I opened the kitchen door on our way to gather eggs and milk for breakfast. He pleaded for help. The shelling had resumed; someone had bombed the barn with heavy clods of dirt until after midnight. The Mexicans were exhausted and angry, and there was about to be a fight of some variety.

This was our sole topic of conversation over breakfast, and Pappy was so angry he could barely eat. It was decided that Hank had to go, and if the rest of the Spruills left with him, then we'd somehow manage. Ten well-rested and hardworking Mexicans were far more valuable than the Spruills.

Pappy started to leave the table and go straight to the front yard with his ultimatum, but my father calmed him. They decided that we would wait until quitting time, thereby getting a full day of labor out of the Spruills. Plus they'd be less likely to break camp with darkness upon them.

I just listened. I wanted to jump in and describe my conversation with Tally, especially the part about her family needing the money. In my opinion, they wouldn't leave at all, but would be delighted to get rid of Hank. My opinions, however, were never welcome during these tense family discussions. I chewed my biscuit and hung on every word.

'What about Stick?' Gran asked.

'What about him?' Pappy fired in her direction.

'You were gonna tell Stick when you were finished with Hank.'

Pappy took a bite of ham and thought about this.

Gran was a step ahead, but then she had the advantage of thinking without being angry. She sipped her coffee and said, 'Seems to me the thing to do is tell Mr. Spruill that Stick is comin' after Hank. Let the boy sneak away at night. He'll be gone, that's all that matters, and the Spruills'll be thankful you kept him from gettin' arrested.'

Gran's plan made perfect sense. My mother managed a slight grin. Once again the women had analyzed a situation more quickly than the men.

Pappy didn't say another word. My father quickly finished eating and went outside. The sun was barely above the distant trees, yet the day was already eventful.

After lunch Pappy said abruptly, 'Luke, we're goin' to town. The trailer's full.'

The trailer wasn't completely full, and we never

took it to the gin in the middle of the day. But I wasn't about to object. Something was up.

There were only four trailers ahead of us when we arrived at the gin. Usually, at this time of the harvest, there would be at least ten, but then we always came after supper, when the place was crawling with farmhands. 'Noon's a good time to gin,' Pappy said.

He left the keys in the truck, and as we were walking away he said, 'I need to go to the Co-op. Let's head to Main Street.' Sounded good to me.

The town of Black Oak had three hundred people, and virtually all of them lived within five minutes of Main Street. I often thought how wonderful it would be to have a neat little house on a shady street, just a stone's throw from Pop and Pearl's and the Dixie theater, with no cotton anywhere in sight.

Halfway to Main, we took an abrupt turn. 'Pearl wants to see you,' he said, pointing at the Watsons' house just to our right. I'd never been in Pop and Pearl's house, never had any reason to enter, but I'd seen it from the outside. It was one of the few houses in town with some bricks on it.

'What?' I asked, completely bewildered.

He said nothing, and I just followed.

Pearl was waiting at the door. When we entered I could smell the rich, sweet aroma of something baking, though I was too confused to realize she was preparing a treat for me. She gave me a pat on the head and winked at Pappy. In one corner of the room, Pop was bent at the waist, his back to us, fiddling with something. 'Come here, Luke,' he said, without turning around.

322

I'd heard that they owned a television. The first one in our county had been purchased a year earlier by Mr. Harvey Gleeson, the owner of the bank, but he was a recluse, and no one had yet seen his television, as far as we knew. Several church members had kinfolks in Jonesboro who owned televisions, and whenever they went there to visit they came back and talked nonstop about this wonderful new invention. Dewayne had seen one inside a store window in Blytheville, and he'd strutted around school for an insufferable period of time.

'Sit here,' Pop said, pointing to a spot on the floor, right in front of the set. He was still adjusting knobs. 'It's the World Series,' he said. 'Game three, Dodgers at Yankee Stadium.'

My heart froze; my mouth dropped open. I was too stunned to move. Three feet away was a small screen with lines dancing across it. It was in the center of a dark, wooden cabinet with the word Motorola scripted in chrome just under a row of knobs. Pop turned one of the knobs, and suddenly we heard the scratchy voice of an announcer describing a ground ball to the shortstop. Then Pop turned two knobs at once, and the picture became clear.

It was a baseball game. Live from Yankee Stadium, and we were watching it in Black Oak, Arkansas!

Chairs moved behind me, and I could feel Pappy inching closer. Pearl wasn't much of a fan. She busied herself in the kitchen for a few minutes, then emerged with a plate of chocolate cookies and a glass of milk. I took them and thanked her. They

323

were fresh from the oven and smelled delicious. But I couldn't eat, not right then.

Ed Lopat was pitching for the Yankees, Preacher Roe for the Dodgers. Mickey Mantle, Yogi Berra, Phil Rizzuto, Hank Bauer, Billy Martin with the Yankees, and Pee Wee Reese, Duke Snider, Roy Campanella, Jackie Robinson, and Gil Hodges with the Dodgers. They were all there in Pop and Pearl's living room, playing before sixty thousand fans in Yankee Stadium. I was mesmerized to the point of being mute. I simply stared at the television, watching but not believing.

'Eat the cookies, Luke,' Pearl said as she passed through the room. It was more of a command than an invitation, and I took a bite of one.

'Who are you pullin' for?' asked Pop.

'I don't know,' I mumbled, and I really didn't. I had been taught to hate both teams. And it had been easy hating them when they were away in New York, in another world. But now they were in Black Oak, playing the game I loved, live from Yankee Stadium. My hatred vanished. 'Dodgers, I guess,' I said.

'Always pull for the National League,' Pappy said behind me.

'I suppose,' Pop said reluctantly. 'But it's mighty hard to pull for the Dodgers.'

The game was broadcast into our world by Channel 5 out of Memphis, an affiliate of the National Broadcasting Company, whatever that meant. There were commercials for Lucky Strike cigarettes, Cadillac, Coca-Cola, and Texaco. Between innings the game would vanish and there would be a commercial, and when it was over, the screen would change again, and we'd be back inside Yankee Stadium. It was a dizzying experience, one that captivated me completely. For an hour I was transported to another world.

Pappy had business and at some point left the house and walked to Main Street. I did not hear him leave, but during a commercial I realized he was gone.

Yogi Berra hit a home run, and as I watched him circle the bases in front of sixty thousand fanatics, I knew I would never again be able to properly hate the Yankees. They were legends, the greatest players on the greatest team the game had known. I softened up considerably but vowed to keep my new feelings to myself. Pappy would not allow Yankee sympathizers in his house.

In the top of the ninth, Berra let a pitch get past him. The Dodgers scored two runs and won the game. Pearl wrapped the cookies in foil and sent them with me. I thanked Pop for allowing me to share this unbelievable adventure, and I asked him if I could come back when the Cardinals were playing.

'Sure,' he said, 'but it might be a long time.'

Walking back to the gin, I asked Pappy a few questions about the basics of television broadcasting. He talked about the signals and towers in very vague and confusing terms and finally admitted that he knew little about it, being as how it was such a new invention. I asked when we might get one. 'One of these days,' he said, as if it would never happen. I felt ashamed for asking.

We pulled our empty trailer back to the farm, and I picked cotton until quitting time. During supper the adults gave me the floor. I talked nonstop about the game and the commercials and everything I'd seen on Pop and Pearl's television.

Modern America was slowly invading rural Arkansas.

Chapter 25

Just before dark my father and Mr. Leon Spruill went for a short walk past the silo. My father explained that Stick Powers was preparing to arrest Hank for the murder of Jerry Sisco. Since Hank was causing so much trouble anyway, it might be the perfect time for him to ease away into the night and return to the hills. Evidently Mr. Spruill took it well and made no threats to leave. Tally was right; they needed the money. And they were sick of Hank. It appeared as though they would stay and finish the harvest.

We sat on the front porch and watched and listened. There were no sharp words, no signs of breaking camp. Nor was there any evidence that Hank might be leaving. Through the shadows we could see him every now and then, moving around their camp, sitting by the fire, rummaging for more leftovers. One by one the Spruills went to bed. So did we.

I finished my prayers and was lying in Ricky's bed, wide awake, thinking about the Yankees and Dodgers, when an argument started in the distance. I slid across the floor and peeked through

327

the window. All was dark and still, and for a moment I couldn't see anyone. The shadows shifted, and next to the road I could see Mr. Spruill and Hank standing face-to-face, both talking at once. I couldn't understand what they were saying, but they were obviously angry.

This was too good to miss. I crawled into the hallway and stopped long enough to make sure all the adults were asleep. Then I crept across the living room, through the front screen door, onto the porch, down the steps, and scooted to the hedgerow on the east side of our property. There was a half-moon and scattered clouds, and after a few minutes of silent stalking I was close to the road. Mrs. Spruill had joined the discussion. They were arguing about the Sisco beating. Hank was adamant about his innocence. His parents didn't want him arrested.

'I'll kill that fat deputy,' he growled.

'Just go back home, son, let things cool down,' Mrs. Spruill kept saying.

'The Chandlers want you to leave,' Mr. Spruill said at one point.

'I got more money in my pocket than these sodbusters'll ever have,' Hank snarled.

The argument was spinning in several directions. Hank said harsh things about us, the Mexicans, Stick Powers, the Siscos, the general population of Black Oak, and he even had a few choice words for his parents and Bo and Dale. Only Tally and Trot went unscathed. His language grew worse and his voice louder, but Mr. and Mrs. Spruill did not retreat.

'All right, I'll leave,' he finally said, and he

stormed toward a tent to fetch something. I sneaked to the edge of the road, then scampered across it and fell into the depths of the Jeter cotton on the other side. I had a perfect view of our front yard. Hank was stuffing an old canvas bag with food and clothes. My guess was that he would walk to the highway and start hitchhiking. I cut through the rows and crept along the side of the shallow ditch, in the direction of the river. I wanted to see Hank when he walked by.

They had more words, then Mrs. Spruill said, 'We'll be home in a few weeks.' The talking stopped, and Hank stomped by me, in the center of the road, a bag slung over his shoulder. I inched my way to the end of the row and watched as he headed for the bridge.

I couldn't help but smile. Peace would be restored to our farm. I squatted there for a long time, long after Hank had disappeared, and thanked the stars above that he was finally gone.

I was about to begin my backtracking when something suddenly moved directly across the road from me. The cotton stalks rustled just slightly, and a man rose and stepped forward. He was low and quick, obviously trying to avoid being seen. He glanced back down the road, in the direction of our house, and for an instant the moonlight hit his face. It was Cowboy.

For a few seconds I was too scared to move. It was safe on the Jeter side of the road, hidden by their cotton. I wanted to retrace my steps, hurry to the house, crawl into Ricky's bed.

And I also wanted to see what Cowboy was up to.

Cowboy stayed in the knee-deep ditch and moved quickly, without a sound. He would advance, then stop and listen. Move forward, then halt. I was a hundred feet behind him, still on Jeter property, moving as fast as I dared. If he heard me, then I would duck into the thick cotton.

Before long I could see the hulking figure of Hank, still in the center of the road, going home in no particular hurry. Cowboy slowed his chase, and I, too, slowed my pursuit.

I was barefoot, and if I stepped on a cottonmouth I would die a horrible death. Go home, something told me. Get out of there.

If Cowboy wanted to fight, why was he waiting? Our farm was now out of sight and sound. But the river was just ahead, and maybe that's what Cowboy wanted.

As Hank neared the bridge, Cowboy quickened his pace and started walking in the center of the road. I stayed at the edge of the cotton, sweating and out of breath and wondering why I was being so foolish.

Hank got to the river and started over the bridge. Cowboy began running. When Hank was about halfway over, Cowboy stopped long enough to cock his arm and throw a rock. It landed on the boards near Hank, who stopped and whirled around. 'Come on, you little wetback,' he growled.

Cowboy never stopped walking. He was on the bridge, heading up the slight incline, showing no fear whatsoever as Hank waited and cursed him. Hank looked twice as big as Cowboy. They would meet in the middle of the bridge, and there was no doubt that one of them was about to get wet.

330

When they were close, Cowboy suddenly cocked his arm again and threw another rock, almost at point-blank range. Hank ducked, and somehow it missed him. Then he charged at Cowboy. The switchblade snapped open, and in a flash it was introduced into the fray. Cowboy held it high. Hank caught himself long enough to swing wildly with his bag. It brushed Cowboy and knocked off his hat. The two circled each other on the narrow bridge, both looking for an advantage. Hank growled and cursed and kept his eye on the knife, then he reached into the bag and removed a small jar of something. He gripped it like a baseball and got ready to hurl it. Cowboy kept low, bending at the knees and waist, waiting for the perfect moment. As they circled slowly, each came within inches of the edge of the bridge.

Hank gave a mighty grunt and threw the jar as hard as he could at Cowboy, who was less than ten feet away. It hit him somewhere in the neck or throat, I couldn't tell exactly, and for a second Cowboy wobbled as if he might fall. Hank threw the bag at him and charged in. But with amazing quickness Cowboy switched hands with the knife, pulled a rock from his right pants pocket, and threw it harder than any baseball he'd ever pitched. It hit Hank somewhere in the face. I couldn't see it, but I certainly heard it. Hank screamed and clutched his face, and by the time he could recover it was too late.

Cowboy ducked and hooked low and drove the blade up through Hank's stomach and chest. Hank let loose with a painful squeal, one of horror and shock.

Then Cowboy yanked it out and thrust it in again and again. Hank dropped to one knee, then two. His mouth was open, but nothing came out. He just stared at Cowboy, his face frozen in terror.

With strokes that were quick and vicious, Cowboy slashed away and finished the job. When Hank was down and still, Cowboy quickly went through his pants pockets and robbed him. Then he dragged him to the side of the bridge and shoved him over. The corpse landed with a splash and immediately went under. Cowboy went through the bag, found nothing he wanted, and threw it over, too. He stood at the edge of the bridge and watched the water for a long time.

I had no desire to join Hank, so I burrowed between two rows of cotton and hid so low that I couldn't have found myself. My heart was pounding faster than ever before. I was shaking and sweating and crying and praying, too. I should've been in bed, safe and asleep with my parents next door and my grandparents just down the hall. But they seemed so far away. I was alone in a shallow foxhole, alone and frightened and in great danger. I'd just seen something that I still didn't believe.

I don't know how long Cowboy stood there on the bridge, watching the water, making sure Hank was gone. The clouds would move over the half-moon, and I could barely see him. They'd move again, and there he was, still standing, his dirty cowboy hat cocked to one side. After a long time, he walked off the bridge and stopped by the edge of the river to wash his knife. He watched the river some more, then turned and started walking down the road. When he passed me he was twenty feet away, and I felt like I was buried at least two feet in the ground.

I waited forever, until he was long out of sight, until there was no possible way he could hear me, then I crawled out of my little hole and began my journey home. I wasn't sure what I would do once I got there, but I'd be safe. I'd think of something.

I stayed low, moving through the tall Johnson grass along the edge of the field. As farmers we hated Johnson grass, but for the first time in my life I was thankful for it. I wanted to hurry, to sprint down the middle of the road and get home as fast as possible, but I was terrified, and my feet were heavy. Fatigue and fear gripped me, and I could hardly move at times. It took forever before I saw the outlines of our house and barn. I watched the road in front of me, certain that Cowboy was up there somewhere, watching his rear, watching his flanks. I tried not to think about Hank. I was too concerned with getting to the house.

When I stopped to catch my breath, I picked up the unmistakable smell of a Mexican. They seldom bathed, and after a few days of picking cotton they took on their own particular odor.

It passed quickly, and after a minute or two of heavy breathing I wondered if I was just imagining things. Not taking chances, I retreated once again to the depths of the Jeter cotton and slowly headed east, cutting through row after row without a sound. When I could see the white tents of Camp Spruill, I knew I was almost home.

What would I tell about Hank? The truth, nothing but. I was burdened with enough secrets; there was room for no more, especially one as heavy as this. I'd crawl into Ricky's room, try and get some sleep, and when my father woke me to collect eggs and milk I'd tell the whole story. Every step, every move, every cut of the knife – my father would hear it all. He and Pappy would head to town to report the killing to Stick Powers, and they'd have Cowboy in jail before lunch. They'd probably hang him before Christmas.

Hank was dead. Cowboy would be in jail. The Spruills would pack up and leave, but I didn't care. I never wanted to see another Spruill, not even Tally. I wanted everybody off our farm and out of our lives.

I wanted Ricky to come home and the Latchers to move away, then everything would be normal again.

When I was within sprinting distance of our front porch, I decided to make my move. My nerves were frayed, my patience gone. I'd been hiding for hours, and I was tired of it. I scooted to the very end of the cotton rows and stepped over the ditch into the road. I ducked low, listened for a second, then started to run. After two steps, maybe three, there was a sound from behind, then a hand slapped my feet together and down I went. Cowboy was on top of me, a knee in my chest, the switchblade an inch from my nose. His eyes were glowing. 'Silence!' he hissed.

We were both breathing hard and sweating profusely, and his odor hit me hard; no doubt the same one I'd smelled just minutes earlier. I stopped wiggling and gritted my teeth. His knee was crushing me.

'Been to the river?' he asked.

I shook my head no. Sweat from his chin dripped into my eyes and burned. He waved the blade a little, as if I couldn't see it already.

'Then where you been?' he asked.

I shook my head again; I couldn't speak. Then I realized my whole body was shaking, trembling in rigid fear.

When it was apparent I could not utter a word, he took the tip of the blade and tapped my forehead. 'You speak one word about tonight,' he said slowly, his eyes doing more talking than his mouth, 'and I will kill your mother. Understand?'

I nodded fiercely. He stood and walked away, quickly disappearing into the blackness and leaving me in the dust and dirt of our road. I started crying, and crawling, and I made it to our truck before I passed out.

They found me under their bed. In the confusion of the moment, with my parents yelling at me and quizzing me about everything – my dirty clothes, the bloody nicks on my arms, why exactly was I sleeping under their bed – I managed to conjure up the tale that I'd had a horrible dream. Hank had drowned! And I had gone to check on him.

'You were sleepwalkin'!' my mother said in disbelief, and I seized this immediately.

'I guess,' I said, nodding. Everything after that was a blur – I was dead tired and scared and not sure if what I'd seen at the river had really happened or had in fact been a dream. I was horrified at the thought of ever facing Cowboy again.

'Ricky used to do that,' Gran added from the hallway. 'Caught 'im one night out past the silo.'

This helped calm things somewhat. They led me to the kitchen and sat me at the table. My mother scrubbed me while Gran doctored the Johnson grass cuts on my arms. The men saw that matters were under control, so they left to gather eggs and milk.

A loud thunderstorm hit just as we were about to eat, and the sounds were a great relief to me. We wouldn't be going to the fields for a few hours. I wouldn't be near Cowboy.

They watched me as I picked at my food. 'I'm okay,' I said at one point.

The rain fell heavy and loud onto our tin roof, drowning out conversation so that we ate in silence, the men worrying about the cotton, the women worrying about me.

I had enough worries to crush us all.

'Could I finish later?' I asked, slightly shoving my plate away. 'I'm really sleepy.'

My mother decided that I would go back to bed and rest for as long as I needed to. As the women were clearing the table, I whispered to my mother and asked her if she would lie down with me. Of course she would.

She fell asleep before I did. We were in my parents' bed, in their semidark bedroom, still and cool and listening to the rain, with the men in the kitchen not far away, drinking coffee and waiting, and I felt safe.

I wanted it to rain forever. The Mexicans and the Spruills would leave. Cowboy would be shipped home, back to where he could cut and slash all he wanted, and I'd never know about it. And sometime next summer, when plans were made for the harvest, I'd make sure Miguel and his band of Mexicans were not hauled back to our county.

I wanted my mother next to me, with my father nearby. I wanted to sleep, but when I closed my eyes I saw Hank and Cowboy on the bridge. I was suddenly hopeful that Hank was still there, still in Camp Spruill rummaging for a biscuit, still throwing rocks at the barn at midnight. Then it would all be a dream.

Chapter 26

I clung to my mother throughout the day, after the storm passed, after lunch, after the rest of them went to the fields and we stayed around the house. There were whispers between my parents and a frown from my father, but she was adamant. There were times when little boys just needed to be with their mothers. I was afraid to let her out of my sight.

The very thought of telling what I saw on the bridge made me weak. I tried not to think about either the killing or the telling of it, but it was impossible to think of anything else.

We gathered vegetables from the garden. I followed her with the straw basket, my eyes cutting in all directions, ready for Cowboy to leap from nowhere and slaughter both of us. I could smell him, feel him, hear him. I could see his nasty liquid eyes watching every move we made. The weight of his switchblade on my forehead grew heavier.

I thought of nothing but him, and I stayed close to my mother.

'What's the matter, Luke?' she asked more than once. I was aware that I wasn't talking, but I

338

couldn't force words out. There was a faint ringing in my ears. The world was moving slower. I just wanted a place to hide.

'Nothin',' I said. Even my voice was different – low and scratchy.

'You still tired?'

'Yes ma'am.'

And I'd be tired for a month if it kept me out of the fields and away from Cowboy.

We stopped to examine Trot's house painting. Since we were there and not picking cotton. Trot was nowhere to be seen. If we left the house, then he would return to his project. The east wall now had a white strip about three feet high, running from the front almost to the rear. It was clean and neat, obviously the work of someone who wasn't burdened with time.

At his current pace there was no way Trot would finish the house before the Spruills left. What would happen after they left? We couldn't live in a house with a two-toned east wall.

I had more important things to worry about.

My mother decided she would 'put up,' or can, some tomatoes. She and Gran spent hours during the summer and early fall putting up vegetables from our garden – tomatoes, peas, beans, okra, mustard greens, corn. By the first of November the pantry shelves would be packed four-deep with quart jars of food, enough to get us through the winter and early spring. And, of course, they also put up enough for anyone who might need a little help. I was certain that we'd be hauling food to the Latchers in the months to come, now that we were kinfolk.

The very thought made me furious, but again, I wasn't worried about the Latchers anymore.

My job was to peel tomatoes. Once peeled they would be chopped and placed into large pots and cooked just enough to soften them, then packed into Kerr quart jars, with a tablespoon of salt, and secured with new lids. We used the same jars from year to year, but we always bought new lids. A slight leak around the seal and a jar would spoil, and it was always a bad moment during the winter when Gran or my mother opened a jar and its contents couldn't be eaten. It didn't happen often.

Once properly packed and sealed, the jars were placed in a row inside a large pressure cooker half-filled with water. There they would boil for half an hour, under pressure, to remove any remaining air and to further seal the lid. Gran and my mother were very fussy about their canning. It was a source of pride among the women, and I often heard the ladies around the church boast of putting up so many jars of butter beans or of this and that.

The canning began as soon as the garden started producing. I was forced to help with it occasionally and always hated it. Today was different. Today I was quite happy to be in the kitchen with my mother, with Cowboy out in the fields far away.

I stood at the kitchen sink with a sharp paring knife, and when I cut the first tomato I thought of Hank on the bridge. The blood, the switchblade, the painful cry with the first cut, then the silent look of horror as other cuts followed. In that first instant, I think Hank knew he was about to be

340

carved up by someone who'd done it before. He knew he was dead.

My head hit the leg of a kitchen chair. When I awoke on the sofa, my mother was holding ice on a knot above my right ear. She smiled and said, 'You fainted, Luke.'

I tried to say something but my mouth was too dry. She gave me a sip of water and told me I wasn't going anywhere for a while. 'Are you tired?' she asked.

I nodded and closed my eyes.

Twice a year the county sent a few loads of gravel to our road. The trucks dumped it, and right behind them a road grader came along and leveled things out. The grader was operated by an old man who lived near Caraway. He had a black patch over one eye, and the left side of his face was scarred and disfigured to the point of making me cringe when I saw it. He'd been injured in the First War, according to Pappy, who claimed to know more about the old man than he was willing to tell. Otis was his name.

Otis had two monkeys that helped him grade the roads around Black Oak. They were little black things with long tails, and they ran along the frame of the grader, sometimes hopping down on the blade itself, just inches above the dirt and gravel. Sometimes they sat on his shoulder, or on the back of his seat, or on the long rod that ran from the steering wheel to the front end. As Otis motored up and down the road, working the levers, changing the angle and pitch of the blade, spitting tobacco juice, the monkeys jumped and swung without fear and seemed to have a delightful time.

If, for some dreadful reason, we kids didn't make it to the Cardinals, many of us wanted to be road grader operators. It was a big, powerful machine under the control of one man, and all those levers had to be worked with such precision – hands and feet moving with great coordination. Plus, level roads were crucial to the farmers of rural Arkansas. Few jobs were more important, at least in our opinion.

We had no idea what it paid, but we were certain it was more profitable than farming.

When I heard the diesel engine, I knew Otis was back. I walked hand in hand with my mother to the edge of the road, and sure enough, between our house and the bridge were three mounds of new gravel. Otis was spreading it, slowly working his way toward us. We stepped back under a tree and waited.

My head was clear, and I felt strong. My mother kept tugging at my shoulder, as if she thought I might faint again. As Otis drew near, I stepped closer to the road. The engine roared; the blade churned up dirt and gravel. We were getting our road fixed, a most important event.

Sometimes Otis waved, sometimes he did not. I saw his scars and his black eye patch. Oh, the questions I had for that man!

And I saw only one monkey. He was sitting on the main frame, just beyond the steering wheel, and he looked very sad. I scanned the grader for his little partner, but there were no other monkeys.

We waved at Otis, who glanced at us but did not

wave back. This was a terrible sign of rudeness in our world, but then Otis was different. Because of his war wounds, he had no wife, no children, nothing but isolation.

Suddenly the grader stopped. Otis turned and looked down at me with his good eye, then motioned for me to climb aboard. I instantly moved toward him, and my mother rushed forward to say no. Otis yelled, 'It's okay! He'll be fine.' It didn't matter: I was already climbing up.

He yanked my hand and pulled me up to the platform where he sat. 'Stand here,' he said gruffly, pointing to a little spot next to him. 'Hold on here,' he growled, and I clutched a handle next to an important-looking lever that I was terrified to touch. I looked down at my mother, who had her hands on her hips. She was shaking her head as if she could choke me, but then I saw a hint of a smile.

He hit the throttle, and the engine behind us roared to life. He pushed the clutch with his foot, moved a gearshift, and we were off. I could've walked faster, but with the noise from the diesel it seemed as if we were racing along.

I was on Otis's left side, very close to his face, and I tried not to look at his scars. After a couple of minutes, he seemed oblivious to my presence. The monkey, however, was quite curious. He watched me as if I were an intruder, then he slinked along on all fours, slowly, prepared to lunge at me at any moment. He jumped onto Otis's right shoulder, walked around the back of his neck, and settled onto his left shoulder, staring at me.

343

I was staring at him. He was no bigger than a baby squirrel, with fine black fur and little black eyes barely separated by the bridge of his nose. His long tail fell down the front of Otis's shirt. Otis was working the levers, moving the gravel, mumbling to himself, seemingly unaware of the monkey on his shoulder.

When it was apparent that the monkey was content just to study me, I turned my attention to the workings of the road grader. Otis had the blade down in the shallow ditch, tilted at a steep angle so that mud and grass and weeds were being dug out and shoved into the road. I knew from previous observations that he would go up and down several times, cleaning the ditches, grading the center, spreading the gravel. Pappy was of the opinion that Otis and the county should fix our road more often, but most farmers felt that way.

He turned the grader around, ran the blade into the other ditch, and headed back toward our house. The monkey hadn't moved.

'Where's the other monkey?' I said loudly, not far from Otis's ear.

He pointed down at the blade and said, 'Fell off.'

It took a second for this to register, and then I was horrified at the thought of that poor little monkey falling over the blade and meeting such an awful death. It didn't seem to bother Otis, but the surviving monkey was undoubtedly mourning the loss of his buddy. He just sat there, sometimes looking at me, sometimes gazing away, very much alone. And he certainly stayed away from the blade.

344

My mother hadn't moved. I waved at her, and she waved at me, and again Otis took no part in any of it. He spat every so often, a long stream of brown tobacco juice that hit the ground in front of the rear wheels. He wiped his mouth with a dirty sleeve, both right and left, depending on which hand happened to be engaged with a lever. Pappy said that Otis was very levelheaded – tobacco juice ran out of both corners of his mouth.

Past our house I could see, from my lofty position, the cotton trailer in the middle of a field and a few straw hats scattered about. I searched until I found the Mexicans, in the same general area as usual, and I thought of Cowboy out there, switchblade in his pocket, no doubt quite proud of his latest killing. I wondered if he'd told his pals about it. Probably not.

For a moment I was frightened because my mother was back behind us, alone. This didn't make any sense, and I knew it, but most of my thoughts were irrational.

When I saw the tree line along the river, a new fear gripped me. I was suddenly afraid to see the bridge, the scene of the crime. Surely there were bloodstains, evidence that something awful had happened. Did the rain wash them away? Days often went by without a car or truck passing over the bridge. Had anyone seen Hank's blood? There was a good chance the evidence would be gone.

Had there really been bloodshed? Or was it all a bad dream?

Nor did I want to see the river. The water moved slowly this time of the year, and Hank was such a large victim. Could he be ashore by now?

Washed up on a gravel bar like a beached whale? I certainly didn't want to be the one to find him.

Hank had been cut to pieces. Cowboy had the nearest switchblade and plenty of motive. It was a crime that even Stick Powers could solve.

I was the only eyewitness, but I'd already decided I would take it to my grave.

Otis shifted gears and turned around, no small feat with a road grader, as I was learning. I caught a glimpse of the bridge, but we were too far away to see much. The monkey grew weary of staring at me and shifted shoulders. He peeked at me around Otis's head for a minute or so, then just sat there, perched like an owl, studying the road.

Oh, if Dewayne could see me now! He'd burn with envy. He'd be humiliated. He'd be so overcome with defeat that he wouldn't speak to me for a long time. I couldn't wait for Saturday. I'd spread the word along Main Street that I'd spent the day with Otis on the road grader – Otis and his monkey. Just one monkey, though, and I'd be forced to tell what happened to the other. And all those levers and controls that, from the ground, looked so thoroughly intimidating but in reality were no problem for me at all. I'd learned how to operate them! It would be one of my finest moments.

Otis stopped in front of our house. I climbed down and yelled, 'Thank you!' but he was off without a nod or word of any sort.

I suddenly thought about the dead monkey, and I started crying. I didn't want to cry, and I tried not to, but the tears were pouring out, and I couldn't control myself. My mother came running from the house, asking what was wrong. I didn't know what was wrong; I was just crying. I was scared and tired, almost faint again, and I just wanted everything to be normal, with the Mexicans and the Spruills out of our lives, with Ricky home, with the Latchers gone, with the nightmare of Hank erased from my memory. I was tired of secrets, tired of seeing things I was not supposed to see.

And so I just cried.

My mother held me tightly. When I realized she was frightened, I managed to tell her about the dead monkey.

'Did you see it?' she asked in horror.

I shook my head and kept explaining. We walked back to the porch and sat for a long time.

Hank's departure was confirmed at some point during the day. Over supper my father said that Mr. Spruill had told him that Hank had left during the night. He was hitchhiking back to their home in Eureka Springs.

Hank was floating at the bottom of the St. Francis River, and when I thought about him down there with the channel catfish, I lost my appetite. The adults were watching me closer than usual. During the past twenty-four hours I'd fainted, had nightmares, cried several times, and, as far as they knew, gone for a long walk in my sleep. Something was wrong with me, and they were concerned.

'Wonder if he'll make it home,' Gran said. This launched a round of stories about folks who'd disappeared. Pappy had a cousin who had been

347

migrating with his family from Mississippi to Arkansas. They were traveling in two old trucks. They came to a railroad crossing. The first truck, the one driven by the cousin in question, crossed first. A train came roaring by, and the second truck waited for it to pass. It was a long train, and when it finally cleared, there was no sign of the first truck on the other side. The second truck crossed and came to a fork in the road. The cousin was never seen again, and that had been thirty years ago. No sign of him or the truck.

I'd heard this story many times. I knew Gran would go next, and sure enough, she told the tale about her mother's father, a man who'd sired six kids then hopped on a train and fled to Texas. Someone in the family stumbled across him twenty years later. He had another wife and six more kids.

'You okay, Luke?' Pappy said when the eating was over. All of his gruffness was gone. They were telling stories for my benefit, trying to amuse me because I had them worried.

'Just tired, Pappy,' I said.

'You want to go to bed early?' my mother asked, and I nodded.

I went to Ricky's room while they washed the dishes. My letter to him was now two pages long, a monumental effort. It was still in my writing tablet, hidden under the mattress, and it covered most of the Latcher conflict. I read it again and was quite pleased with myself. I toyed with the idea of telling Ricky about Cowboy and Hank, but decided to wait until he came home. By then the Mexicans would be gone, things would be safe again, and Ricky would know what to do.

I decided that the letter was ready to be mailed, then started worrying about how I might accomplish mailing it. We always sent our letters at the same time, often in the same large manila envelope. I decided that I'd consult with Mr. Lynch Thornton at the post office on Main Street.

My mother read me the story of Daniel in the lions' den, one of my favorites. Once the weather broke and the nights became cool, we spent less time on the porch and more time reading before bed. My mother and I read, the others did not. She preferred Bible stories, and this suited me fine. She would read awhile, then explain things. Then read some more. There was a lesson in every story, and she made sure I understood each one. Nothing irritated me more than for Brother Akers to screw up the details in one of his long-winded sermons.

When I was ready for bed, I asked her if she would stay there, in Ricky's bed with me, until I fell asleep.

'Of course I will,' she said.

Chapter 27

After a day of rest, there was no way my father would tolerate further absence from the fields. He pulled me out of bed at five, and we went about our routine chores of gathering eggs and milk.

I knew I couldn't continue to hide in the house with my mother, so I bravely went through the motions of getting ready to pick cotton. I'd have to face Cowboy at some point before he left. It was best to get it over with and to do it with plenty of folks around.

The Mexicans were walking to the fields, skipping the morning ride on the flatbed trailer. They could start picking a few minutes earlier, plus it kept them away from the Spruills. We left the house just before dawn. I held firm to Pappy's seat on the tractor and watched my mother's face slowly disappear in the kitchen window. I'd prayed long and hard the night before, and something told me she would be safe.

As we made our way along the field road, I studied the John Deere tractor. I'd spent hours on it, plowing, disking, planting, even hauling cotton to town with my father or Pappy, and its operation had always seemed sufficiently complex and challenging. Now, after thirty minutes on the road grader, with its puzzling array of levers and pedals, the tractor seemed quite simple. Pappy just sat there, hands on the wheel, feet still, half-asleep – while Otis had been a study in constant motion – another reason why I should grade roads and not farm if, of course, the baseball career did not work out, a most unlikely event.

The Mexicans were already half a row down, lost in the cotton and oblivious to our arrival. I knew Cowboy was with them, but in the early light I couldn't tell one Mexican from the other.

I avoided him until we broke for lunch. Evidently he'd seen me during the morning, and I guess he figured a little reminder would be appropriate. While the rest of his pals ate leftovers under the shade of the cotton trailer, Cowboy rode in with us. He sat alone on one side of the flatbed, and I ignored him until we were almost to the house.

When I finally mustered the courage to look at him, he was cleaning his fingernails with his switchblade, and he was waiting for me. He smiled – a wicked grin that conveyed a thousand words – and he gently waved the knife at me. No one else saw it, and I looked away immediately.

Our agreement had just been solidified even further.

By late afternoon the cotton trailer was full. After a quick dinner Pappy announced that he and I would haul it to town. We went to the fields and hooked it to the truck, then left the farm on our newly graded road. Otis was quite a craftsman. The road was smooth, even in Pappy's old truck.

As usual, Pappy said nothing as he drove, and this was fine with me because I also had nothing to say. Lots of secrets but no way to unload them. We crossed the bridge slowly, and I scanned the thick, slow waters below but saw nothing out of the ordinary – no sign of blood or of the crime I'd witnessed.

More than a full day had passed since the killing, a normal day of work and drudgery on the farm. I thought about the secret with every breath, but I was masking it well, I thought. My mother was safe, and that was all that mattered.

We passed the road to the Latchers', and Pappy glanced their way. For the moment, they were just a minor nuisance.

On the highway, farther away from the farm, I began to think that one day soon I might be able to unload my burden. I could tell Pappy, alone, just the two of us. Before long Cowboy would be back in Mexico, safe in that foreign world. The Spruills would return home, and Hank wouldn't be there. I could tell Pappy, and he would know what to do.

We entered Black Oak behind another trailer and followed it to the gin. When we parked I scrambled out and stuck close to Pappy's side. Some farmers were huddled just outside the gin office, and a serious discussion had been under way for a while. We walked up on them and listened.

The news was somber and threatening. The night before, heavy rains had hit Clay County, north of us. Some places reported six inches in ten hours. Clay County was upstream on the St. Francis. The creeks and streams were flooded up there and pouring into the river.

The water was rising.

There was a debate as to whether this would affect us. The minority opinion was that the storm would have little impact on the river near Black Oak. We were too far away and, absent more rains, a small rise in the St. Francis wouldn't flood anything. But the majority view was far more pessimistic, and since the bulk of them were professional worriers anyway, the news was accepted with great concern.

One farmer said his almanac called for heavy rains in mid-October.

Another said his cousin in Oklahoma was getting flooded, and since our weather came from the West, he felt it was a sure sign that the rains were inevitable.

Pappy mumbled something to the effect that the weather from Oklahoma traveled faster than any news.

There was much debate and lots of opinions, and the overall tone was one of gloom. We'd been beaten so many times by the weather, or by the markets, or by the price of seed and fertilizer, that we expected the worst.

'We ain't had a flood in October in twenty years,' declared Mr. Red Fletcher, and this set off a heated debate on the history of autumn floods. There were so many different versions and recollections that the issue was hopelessly confused.

Pappy didn't join the fray, and after half an hour of listening we backed away. He unhooked the trailer, and we headed home, in silence, of course. A couple of times I cut my eyes at him and found him just as I expected – mute, worried, driving with both hands, forehead wrinkled, his mind on nothing but the coming flood.

We parked at the bridge and walked through the mud to the edge of the St. Francis River. Pappy inspected it for a moment as if he might see it rise. I was terrified that Hank would suddenly float to the top and come ashore right in front of us. Without a word, Pappy picked up a stick of driftwood about an inch in diameter and three feet long. He knocked a small limb off it and drove it with a rock into the sandbar where the water was two inches deep. With his pocketknife, he notched it at water level. 'We'll check it in the mornin',' he said, his first words in a long time.

We studied our new gauge for a few moments, both certain that we would see the river rise. When it didn't happen, we returned to the truck.

The river scared me and not because it might flood. Hank was out there, cut and dead and bloated with river water, ready to wash ashore where someone would find him. We'd have a real murder on our hands, not a just a killing like the Sisco beating, but a genuine slaying.

The rains would get rid of Cowboy. And the rains would swell the river and move it faster. Hank, or what was left of him, would get swept downstream to another county or maybe even another state where someday someone would find him and not have the slightest clue as to who he was.

Before I fell asleep that night, I prayed for rain. I

prayed as hard as I possibly could. I asked God to send the biggest flood since Noah.

We were in the middle of breakfast on Saturday morning when Pappy stomped in from the back porch. One look at his face satisfied our curiosity. 'River's up four inches, Luke,' he said to me as he took his seat and began reaching for food. 'And there's lightnin' to the west.'

My father frowned but kept chewing. When it came to the weather, he was always pessimistic. If the weather was fine, then it was just a matter of time before it turned bad. If it was bad, then that's what he'd expected all along. Gran took the news with no expression at all. Her younger son was fighting in Korea, and that was far more important than the next rain. She had never left the soil, and she knew that some years were good, some bad, but life didn't stop. God gave us life and health and plenty of food, and that was more than most folks could say. Plus, Gran had little patience for all the fretting over the weather. 'Can't do anything about it,' she said over and over.

My mother didn't smile or frown, but she had a curious look of contentment. She was determined not to spend her life scratching a meager existence from the land. And she was even more determined that I would not farm. Her days on the farm were numbered, and another lost crop could only hasten our departure.

By the time we finished eating, we heard thunder. Gran and my mother cleared the dishes, then made another pot of coffee. We sat at the table, talking and listening, waiting to see how rough the storm would be. I thought my prayer was about to be answered, and I felt guilty for such a devious wish.

But the thunder and lightning moved to the north. No rain fell. By 7 A.M. we were in the fields, picking hard and longing for noon.

When we left for town, only Miguel hopped in the back of the truck. The rest of the Mexicans were working, he explained, and he needed to buy a few things for them. I was relieved beyond words. I wouldn't be forced to ride in with Cowboy crouched just a few feet away from me.

We hit rain at the edge of Black Oak, a cool drizzle instead of a fierce storm. The sidewalks were busy with folks moving slowly under the store canopies and balconies, trying, but failing, to stay dry.

The weather kept many farm families away from town. This was evident when the four o'clock matinee began at the Dixie theater. Half the seats were empty, a sure sign that it was not a normal Saturday. Halfway through the first show the aisle lights flickered, then the screen went blank. We sat in the darkness, ready to panic and bolt, and listened to the thunder.

'Power's out,' said an official voice in the rear. 'Please leave slowly.'

We huddled into the cramped lobby and watched the rain fall in sheets along Main Street. The sky was dark gray, and the few cars that passed by used their headlights.

Even as kids we knew that there was too much rain, too many storms, too many rumors of rising waters. Floods happened in the spring, rarely during the harvest. In a world where everyone either farmed or traded with farmers, a wet season in mid-October was quite depressing.

When it slacked off a little, we ran down the sidewalk to find our parents. Heavy rains meant muddy roads, and the town would soon be empty as the farm families left for home before dark. My father had mentioned buying a saw blade, so I ducked into the hardware store in hopes of finding him. It was crowded with people waiting and watching the weather outside. In little pockets of conversation, old men were telling stories of ancient floods. Women were talking about how much rain there'd been in other towns – Paragould, Lepanto, and Manila. The aisles were filled with people who were just talking, not buying or looking for merchandise.

I worked my way through the crowd, looking for my father. The hardware store was ancient, and toward the rear it became darker and cavern-like. The wooden floors were wet from the traffic and sagged from years of use. At the end of an aisle, I turned and came face-to-face with Tally and Trot. She was holding a gallon of white paint. Trot was holding a quart. They were loitering like everybody else, waiting for the storm to pass. Trot saw me and tried to hide behind Tally. 'Hello, Luke,' she said with a smile.

'Howdy,' I said, looking at the paint bucket. She set it on the floor beside her. 'What's the paint for?'

'Oh, it's nothin',' she said, smiling again. Once again I was reminded that Tally was the prettiest girl I'd ever met, and when she smiled at me my mind went blank. Once you've seen a pretty girl naked, you feel a certain attachment to her.

Trot wedged himself tightly behind her, like a toddler hiding behind his mother. She and I talked about the storm, and I relayed the exciting news about the power going out in the middle of the matinee. She listened with interest, and the more I talked the more I wanted to talk. I told her about the rumors of rising waters and about the gauge Pappy and I had set at the river. She asked about Ricky, and we talked about him for a long time.

Of course I forgot about the paint.

The lights flickered, and the power returned. It was still raining, though, and no one left the store.

'How's that Latcher girl?' she asked, her eyes darting around as if someone might hear her. It was one of our great secrets.

I was about to say something, when it suddenly hit me that Tally's brother was dead, and she knew nothing about it. The Spruills probably thought Hank was home by now, back in Eureka Springs, back in their nice little painted house. They'd see him in a few weeks, sooner if it kept raining. I looked at her and tried to speak, but all I could think about was how shocked she'd be if I said what I was thinking.

I adored Tally, in spite of her moods and her secrets, in spite of her funny business with Cowboy. I couldn't help but adore her, and I certainly didn't want to hurt her. The very thought of blurting out that Hank was dead made me weak in the knees.

I stuttered and stammered and looked at the floor. I was suddenly cold and scared. 'See you

358

later,' I managed to say, then turned and back-tracked to the front.

During a break in the rain, the stores emptied and folks scurried along the sidewalks, heading for the cars and trucks. The clouds were still dark, and we wanted to get home before the showers hit again.

Chapter 28

Sunday was gray and overcast, and my father didn't care for the notion of getting wet while riding in the back of the truck on the way to church. Plus, our truck was not exactly waterproof, and the women usually got dripped on while riding in the cab during a good shower. We rarely missed a Sunday worship, but the threat of rain occasionally kept us at home. We hadn't missed a service in months, and so when Gran suggested we eat a late breakfast and listen to the radio we quickly agreed. Bellevue Baptist was the largest church in Memphis, and its services were broadcast on station WHBQ. Pappy didn't like the preacher, said he was too liberal, but we enjoyed hearing him nonetheless. And the choir had a hundred voices, which was about eighty more than the one at the Black Oak Baptist Church.

Long after breakfast, we sat at the kitchen table, sipping coffee (myself included), listening to a sermon being delivered to a congregation of three thousand members, and worrying about the drastic change in the weather. The adults were worrying; I was only pretending.

360

Bellevue Baptist had an orchestra, of all things, and when it played the benediction, Memphis seemed a million miles away. An orchestra in a church. Gran's older daughter, my aunt Betty, lived in Memphis, and though she didn't worship at Bellevue she knew someone who did. All the men wore suits. All the families drove nice cars. It was indeed a different world.

Pappy and I drove to the river to check our gauge. The rains were taking a toll on Otis's recent grade work. The shallow ditches beside the road were full, gullies were forming from the runoff, and mud holes were holding water. We stopped in the middle of the bridge and studied the river on both sides. Even I could tell the water was up. The sandbars and gravel bars were covered. The water was thicker and a lighter shade of brown, evidence of drainage from the creeks that ran through the fields. The current swirled and was moving faster. Debris – driftwood and logs and even a green branch or two – floated atop the water.

Our gauge was still standing, but barely. Just a few inches remained above the water. Pappy had to get his boots wet to retrieve the stick. He pulled it up, examined it as if it had done something wrong, and said, almost to himself, 'Up 'bout ten inches in twenty-four hours.' He squatted and tapped the stick on a rock. Watching him, I became aware of the noise of the river. It wasn't loud, but the water was rushing by and streaming over the gravel bars and against the bridge piers. The current splashed through the thick shrubs hanging over the banks and pecked away at the roots of a nearby willow tree. It was a menacing noise. One I'd never heard.

Pappy was hearing it all too well. With the stick he pointed at the bend in the river, far to the right, and said, 'It'll get the Latchers first. They're on low ground.'

'When?' I asked.

'Depends on the rain. If it stops, then it might not flood at all. Keeps rainin' though, and it'll be over the banks in a week.'

'When's the last time it flooded?'

'Three years ago, but that was in the spring. Last fall flood was a long time ago.'

I had plenty of questions about floods, but it was not a subject Pappy liked to dwell on. We studied the river for a while, and listened to it, then we walked back to the truck and drove home.

'Let's go to Siler's Creek,' he said. The field roads were too muddy for the truck, so Pappy fired up the John Deere, and we pulled out of the farmyard with most of the Spruills and all of the Mexicans watching us with great curiosity. The tractor was never operated on Sunday. Surely Eli Chandler was not about to work on the Sabbath.

The creek had been transformed. Gone were the clear waters where Tally liked to bathe. Gone were the cool little rivulets running around rocks and logs. Instead the creek was much wider and filled with muddy water rushing to the St. Francis, half a mile away. We got off the tractor and walked to the bank. 'This is where our floods come from,' Pappy said. 'Not the St. Francis. The ground's lower here, and when the creek runs over, it heads straight for our fields.'

362

The water was at least ten feet below us, still safely contained in the ravine that had been cut through our farm decades earlier. It seemed impossible that the creek could ever rise high enough to escape.

'You think it'll flood, Pappy?' I asked.

He thought long and hard, or maybe he wasn't thinking at all. He watched the creek and finally said, with no conviction whatsoever, 'No. We'll be fine.'

There was thunder to the west.

I walked into the kitchen early Monday morning, and Pappy was at the table, drinking coffee, fiddling with the radio. He was trying to pick up a station in Little Rock to check on the weather. Gran was at the stove, frying bacon. The house was cold, but the heat and smell from the skillet warmed things considerably. My father handed me an old flannel coat, a hand-me-down from Ricky, and I reluctantly put it on.

'We pickin' today, Pappy?' I asked.

'We'll know directly,' he said, without taking his eyes off the radio.

'Did it rain last night?' I asked Gran, who had leaned over to kiss my forehead.

'All night long,' she said. 'Now go fetch some eggs.'

I followed my father out of the house, down the back steps, until I saw something that stopped me cold. The sun was barely up, but there was plenty of light. There was no mistake in what I was seeing.

I pointed and managed to say only, 'Look.'

My father was ten steps away, heading for the chicken coops. 'What is it, Luke?' he asked.

In the spot under the oak tree where Pappy had parked his truck every day of my life, the ruts were bare. The truck was gone.

'The truck,' I said.

My father walked slowly to my side, and for a long time we stared at the parking spot. The truck had always been there, forever, like one of the oaks or one of the sheds. We saw it every day, but we didn't notice it because it was always there.

Without a word, he turned and walked up the back steps, across the porch, and into the kitchen. 'Any reason why the truck would be gone?' he asked Pappy, who was trying desperately to hear a scratchy report from some faraway place. Gran froze and cocked her head sideways as if she needed the question repeated. Pappy turned the radio off. 'Say what?' he said.

'The truck's gone,' my father said.

Pappy looked at Gran, who looked at my father. They all looked at me as if I'd once again done something wrong. About this time my mother entered the kitchen, and the entire family marched single file out of the house and right up to the muddy ruts where the truck should've been.

We searched the farm, as if the truck could have somehow moved itself to another location.

'I left it right here,' Pappy said in disbelief. Of course he'd left it right there. The truck had never been left overnight anywhere else on the farm.

In the distance Mr. Spruill yelled, 'Tally!'

'Somebody took our truck,' Gran said, barely audible.

'Where was the key?' my father asked.

'By the radio, same as always,' Pappy said. There was a small pewter bowl at the end of the kitchen table, next to the radio, and the truck key was always left there. My father went to inspect the bowl. He returned promptly and said, 'The key's gone.'

'Tally!' Mr. Spruill yelled again, louder. There was a flurry of activity in and around the Spruills' camp. Mrs. Spruill emerged and began walking quickly toward our front porch. When she saw us standing beside the house, gawking at the empty parking space, she ran over and said, 'Tally's gone. We can't find her nowhere.'

The other Spruills were soon behind her, and before long the two families were looking at each other. My father explained that our truck was missing. Mr. Spruill explained that his daughter was missing.

'Can she drive a truck?' Pappy asked.

'No, she can't,' Mrs. Spruill said, and this complicated matters.

There was silence for a moment as everybody pondered the situation.

'You don't suppose Hank could've come back and got it, do you?' Pappy asked.

'Hank wouldn't steal your truck,' Mr. Spruill said with a mix of anger and confusion. At that moment almost anything seemed both likely and impossible.

'Hank's home by now,' Mrs. Spruill said. She was on the verge of tears.

I wanted to scream, 'Hank's dead!' and then run into the house and hide under a bed. Those poor

365

people didn't know their son would never make it home. This secret was becoming too heavy to carry alone. I took a step behind my mother.

She leaned close to my father and whispered, 'Better go check on Cowboy.' Because I had told her about Tally and Cowboy, my mother was ahead of the rest of them.

My father thought for a second, then looked in the direction of the barn. So did Pappy, Gran, and finally the rest of the group.

Miguel was slowly making his way to us, taking his time, leaving tracks in the wet grass. His dirty straw hat was in his hand, and he walked in such a way that made me think that he had no desire to do whatever he was about to do.

'Mornin', Miguel,' Pappy said, as if the day was off to the same old beginning.

'Señor,' he said, nodding.

'Is there a problem?' Pappy asked.

'Sí, señor. A little problem.'

'What is it?'

'Cowboy is gone. I think he sneaked away in the night.'

'Must be contagious,' Pappy mumbled, then spat into the grass. It took a few seconds for the Spruills to add things together. At first Tally's disappearance had nothing to do with Cowboy's, at least to them. Evidently they knew nothing about the couple's secret little romance. The Chandlers figured things out long before the Spruills, but then we had the benefit of my inside knowledge.

Reality slowly settled in.

'You think he took her?' Mr. Spruill said, almost

366

in panic. Mrs. Spruill was sniffling now, trying to hold back her tears.

'I don't know what to think,' Pappy said. He was much more concerned with his pickup than with the whereabouts of Tally and Cowboy.

'Did Cowboy take his things with him?' my father asked Miguel.

'Sí, señor.'

'Did Tally take her things with her?' my father asked Mr. Spruill.

He didn't answer, and the question hung in the air until Bo said, 'Yes sir. Her bag's gone.'

'What's in her bag?'

'Clothes and such. And her money jar.'

Mrs. Spruill cried harder. Then she wailed, 'Oh my baby!' I wanted to crawl under the house.

The Spruills were a beaten bunch. All heads were down, shoulders shrunk, eyes half-closed. Their beloved Tally had run away with someone they considered low-bred, a dark-skinned intruder from a godforsaken country. Their humiliation before us was complete, and very painful.

I was hurting, too. How could she have done such a terrible thing? She was my friend. She treated me like a confidant, and she protected me like a big sister. I loved Tally, and now she had run off with a vicious killer.

'He took her!' Mrs. Spruill bawled. Bo and Dale led her away, leaving only Trot and Mr. Spruill to tend to the matter. Trot's normally vacant look had been replaced with one of great confusion and sadness. Tally had been his protector, too. Now she was gone.

The men launched into a windy discussion of

what to do next. The top priority was to find Tally, and the truck, before she could get too far. There was no clue as to when the two left. They had obviously used the storm to cover their getaway. The Spruills had heard nothing during the night, nothing but thunder and rain, and the driveway passed within eighty feet of their tents.

They could've been gone for hours, certainly enough time to drive to Jonesboro or Memphis or even Little Rock.

But the men seemed optimistic that Tally and Cowboy could be found, and quickly. Mr. Spruill left to unhitch his truck from the tents and tables. I begged my father to let me go with them, but he said no. Then I went to my mother, and she held firm, too. 'It's not your place,' she said.

Pappy and my father squeezed into the front seat with Mr. Spruill, and off they went, sliding on our road, tires spinning, mud slinging behind them.

I went past the silo to the weedy remains of an old smoke shed and sat for an hour under the rotted tin roof, watching rain drip in front of me. I was relieved that Cowboy had left our farm, and for this I thanked God in a short but sincere prayer. But any relief in his departure was over-shadowed by my disappointment in Tally. I managed to hate her for what she had done. I cursed her, using words Ricky had taught me, and when I had spewed forth all the foul language I could remember, I asked God to forgive me.

And I asked Him to protect Tally.

It took the men two hours to find Stick Powers. He said he'd been en route from headquarters in

Jonesboro, but Pappy said he looked as if he'd been sleeping for a week. Stick was plainly thrilled to have such a high crime within his jurisdiction. Stealing the truck of a farmer was only a notch below murder in our code, and Stick kicked into high gear. He radioed every jurisdiction he could pick up on his old radio, and before long most of northeast Arkansas was buzzing with the news.

According to Pappy, Stick was not too worried about Tally's whereabouts. He guessed correctly that she had voluntarily run off with a Mexican, which was a low-class and disgraceful thing to do, but not exactly a felony, even though Mr. Spruill kept using the word 'kidnapping.'

It was doubtful that the two lovebirds would venture a long journey in our truck. They most certainly wanted to flee Arkansas, and Stick reasoned that their most likely means would be by bus. They would be too suspicious as hitchhikers; Arkansas drivers were not likely to pick up such a swarthy character as Cowboy, especially with a young white girl at his side. 'They're probably on a bus headed North,' Stick said.

When Pappy told us this, I remembered Tally's dream of living in Canada, a long way from the heat and humidity. She wanted lots of snow, and for some reason she had chosen Montreal as her place in the world.

The men discussed money. My father did the math and guessed that Cowboy had earned close to four hundred dollars picking cotton. No one knew, though, how much he'd sent home. Tally had earned about half that much and had probably saved most of it. We knew she'd been buying house paint for Trot, but we had no idea of her other expenditures.

It was at this point in Pappy's narrative that I wanted to bare my soul about Hank. Cowboy had robbed him after he killed him. There was no way of knowing how much picking money Hank had saved, but I knew for certain that there was $250 of Samson's money now in Cowboy's pocket. I almost blurted this out as we sat around the kitchen table, but I was simply too frightened. Cowboy was gone, but they might catch him somewhere.

Wait, I kept telling myself. Just wait. The moment will come when I can unload my burdens.

Whatever their finances, it was obvious that Tally and Cowboy had enough money to ride a bus for a long time.

And we were broke, as usual. There was a brief conversation about how to replace the truck in the event that it was never found, but the subject was too painful to pursue. Plus, I was listening.

We ate an early lunch, then sat on the back porch and watched the rain.

Chapter 29

Stick's old, loud patrol car came rolling into the front yard, with our stolen truck right behind it. Stick got out, full of importance because he'd solved the most urgent part of the crime. Black Oak's other deputy was driving the truck, which, as far as we could tell, had not changed at all. The Spruills ran over, anxious for some word about Tally.

'Found it at the bus station in Jonesboro,' Stick announced as the small crowd gathered around him. 'Just like I figured.'

'Where was the key?' asked Pappy.

'Under the seat. And the tank's full of gas. Don't know if it was full when they left here, but it's full now.'

'It was half empty,' Pappy said, astonished. We were all surprised, not only to see the truck again but to see it unchanged in any way. We'd spent the day worrying about a future with no truck, with no means of transportation. We'd be in the same boat as the Latchers, forced to bum rides to town from anybody passing by. I couldn't imagine such a plight, and I was now more determined than ever to someday live in a city where folks had cars.

'I guess they just borrowed it,' Mr. Spruill said, almost to himself.

'That's the way I see it,' Stick said. 'You still want to press charges?' he asked Pappy.

He and my father exchanged frowns. 'I guess not,' Pappy said.

'Did anybody see them?' Mrs. Spruill asked quietly.

'Yes ma'am. They bought two tickets for Chicago, then hung around the bus station for five hours. The clerk knew somethin' was up, but figured it wasn't his business. Runnin' off with a Mexican ain't the smartest thing in the world, but it ain't no crime. The clerk said he watched them through the night, and they tried to ignore each other as if nothin' was happenin'. They wouldn't sit together. But when the bus loaded they got on together.'

'What time did the bus leave?' Mr. Spruill asked.

'Six this mornin'.' Stick removed a folded envelope from his pocket and handed it to Mr. Spruill. 'Found this on the front seat. I think it's a note from Tally to y'all. I ain't read it.'

Mr. Spruill handed it to Mrs. Spruill, who quickly opened it and removed a sheet of paper. She started reading, and she began wiping her eyes. Everybody watched her, waiting without a sound. Even Trot, who was hiding behind Bo and Dale, leaned forward and watched the letter being read.

'Ain't none o' my business, ma'am,' Stick said,

372

'but if there's any useful information, then maybe I need to know.'

Mrs. Spruill kept reading, and when she finished, she looked at the ground and said, 'She says she ain't comin' home. She says she and Cowboy are gonna get married and live up North, where they can find good jobs and such.' The tears and sniffles had suddenly vanished. Mrs. Spruill was now more angry than anything else. Her daughter hadn't been kidnapped; she'd run off with a Mexican, and she was going to marry him.

'They gonna stay in Chicago?' Stick asked.

'Don't say. Just says up North.'

The Spruills began drifting away, backpedaling in retreat. My father thanked Stick and the other deputy for bringing our truck home.

'You're gettin' more rain than most folks,' Stick said as he opened the door to his patrol car.

'It's wet all over,' Pappy shot back.

'River's risin' to the north,' Stick said, as if he were an expert. 'More rain's on the way.'

'Thanks, Stick,' Pappy said.

Stick and the other deputy got into the patrol car, Stick settling himself behind the wheel. Just as he was about to close the door he jumped out and said, 'Say, Eli, I called the sheriff up at Eureka Springs. He ain't seen the big one, Hank. The boy shoulda been home by now, don't you think?'

'I reckon. He left a week ago.'

'Wonder where he is?'

'Ain't none of my concern,' Pappy said.

'I ain't through with him, you know. When I find him, I'm gonna put his big ass in the jail in Jonesboro, and we're gonna have us a trial.'

'You do that, Stick,' Pappy said, then turned around. 'You do that.'

Stick's bald tires slipped and spun in the mud, but he finally got to the road. My mother and Gran returned to the kitchen to start cooking.

Pappy got his tools and spread them on the tailgate of the truck. He opened the hood and began a thorough inspection of the engine. I sat on the fender, handing him wrenches, watching every move.

'Why would a nice girl like Tally want to marry a Mexican?' I asked.

Pappy was tightening a fan belt. There was little doubt that Cowboy hadn't bothered to stop, open the hood, and meddle with the engine while he was fleeing with Tally, but Pappy nonetheless was compelled to adjust and fix and tinker as if the vehicle had been sabotaged. 'Women,' he said.

'What do you mean?'

'Women do stupid things.'

I waited for clarification, but his answer was complete.

'I don't understand,' I finally said.

'Neither do I. Neither will you. You're not supposed to understand women.'

He removed the air filter and gazed with suspicion at the carburetor. For a moment it looked as if he'd found evidence of tampering, but then he turned a screw and seemed content.

'You think they'll ever find her?' I asked.

'They ain't lookin'. We got the truck back, so there's no crime, no police tryin' to find 'em. I doubt if the Spruills'll go look for 'em. Why bother? If they got lucky and found 'em, what're they gonna do?'

'Can't they make her come home?'

'No. Once she gets married, then she's an adult. You can't make a married woman do a damned thing.'

He cranked the engine and listened to it idle. It sounded the same to me, but Pappy thought he heard a new rattle. 'Let's take it for spin,' he said. Wasting gasoline was a sin in Pappy's book, but he seemed anxious to burn a little of the free stuff Tally and Cowboy had left behind.

We got in and backed onto the road. I was sitting where Tally had been, just hours earlier, when they'd sneaked away during the storm. I thought of nothing but her, and I was as bewildered as ever.

The road was too wet and muddy to allow Pappy to reach his perfect speed of thirty-seven miles an hour, but he still thought he could tell that something was wrong with the engine. We stopped at the bridge and looked at the river. The gravel bars and sandbars were gone; there was nothing but water between the banks – water and debris from upriver. It rushed by, faster than I had ever seen it. Pappy's stick, his flood gauge, was long gone, washed away by the swirling currents. We didn't need it to tell us that the St. Francis was about to flood.

Pappy seemed mesmerized by the water and its noise. I couldn't tell if he wanted to curse or cry. Neither would've helped, of course, and I think that Pappy, for perhaps the first time, realized he was about to lose another crop.

Whatever was wrong with the engine had fixed itself by the time we returned home. Pappy announced over supper that the truck was as good as ever, whereupon we launched into a long and creative discussion about Tally and Cowboy and where they might be and what they might be doing. My father had heard that there were a lot of Mexicans up in Chicago, and he guessed that Cowboy and his new bride would simply blend into that vast city and never be seen again.

I was so worried about Tally that I could barely force down my food.

Late the next morning, with the sun trying its best to peek through the clouds, we returned to the fields to pick cotton. We were tired of sitting around the house watching the skies. Even I wanted to go to the fields.

The Mexicans were especially anxious to work. They were, after all, two thousand miles from home and not getting paid.

But the cotton was too wet and the ground was too soft. Mud caked on my boots, and it stuck to my picking sack, so that after an hour I felt as if I were dragging a tree trunk. We quit after two hours and left for the house, a sad and dispirited group.

The Spruills had had enough. It came as no surprise to see them breaking camp. They did so slowly, as if they were only reluctantly admitting defeat. Mr. Spruill told Pappy that there was no use in their staying if they couldn't work. They were tired of the rains and we couldn't blame them. They'd been camping out for six weeks in our front yard. Their old tents and tarps were sagging under the weight of all the rain. The mattresses they slept on were half-exposed to the weather and splattered with mud. I would've left a long time before.

We sat on the porch and watched them gather their junk and pack it all haphazardly into the truck and trailer. There would be more room now with Hank and Tally gone.

I was suddenly frightened by their leaving. They would be home soon, and Hank wouldn't be there. They would wait, then search, then start asking questions. I wasn't sure if and how this might one day affect me, but I was scared just the same.

My mother forced me into the garden, where we gathered enough food for twenty people. We washed the corn, cucumbers, tomatoes, okra, and greens in the kitchen sink, then she carefully arranged it all in a cardboard box. Gran put together a dozen eggs, two pounds of country ham, a pound of butter, and two quart jars of strawberry preserves. The Spruills would not leave without food for the trip.

By mid-afternoon they had finished packing. Their truck and trailer were hopelessly overloaded – boxes and burlap sacks clung to the sides, loosely secured by baling wire and destined to fall off. When it was apparent they were about to leave, we walked as a family down the front steps and across the yard to say our farewells. Mr. and Mrs. Spruill met us and accepted our food. They apologized for leaving before the cotton was picked, but we all knew there was a good chance the crops were finished anyway. They tried to smile and be gracious, but their pain was obvious. Watching them, I couldn't help but think that they would always regret the day they decided to work on our farm. If they had picked another one, Tally wouldn't have met Cowboy. And Hank might still be alive, though given his lust for violence he was probably doomed to an early death. 'He who lives by the sword dies by the sword,' Gran was fond of quoting.

I felt guilty about all the evil thoughts I'd held against them. And I felt like a thief because I knew the truth about Hank, and they didn't.

I said good-bye to Bo and Dale, neither of whom had much to say. Trot was hiding behind the trailer. As the farewells were winding down, he shuffled toward me and mumbled something I did not understand. Then he stuck out his hand and offered me his paintbrush. I had no choice but to take it.

The exchange was witnessed by the adults, and for a moment nothing was said.

'Over here,' Trot grunted, and he pointed to their truck. Bo took the cue and reached for something just inside the tailgate. He pulled forward a gallon of white enamel, a clean unopened bucket with a bright Pittsburgh Paint logo across the front. He set it on the ground in front of me, then produced another one.

'It's for you,' Trot said.

I looked at the two gallons of paint, then I looked at Pappy and Gran. Though the house painting had not been discussed in days, we had known for some time that Trot would never finish the project. Now he was passing the job to me. I glanced at my mother and saw a curious smile on her lips.

'Tally bought it,' Dale said.

I tapped the brush on my leg and finally managed to say, 'Thanks.' Trot gave me a goofy grin, which made the rest of them smile. Once again they headed toward their truck, but this time they managed to get in. Trot was in the trailer, alone now. Tally had been with him when we first saw them. He looked sad and deserted.

Their truck started with great reluctance. The clutch whined and scraped, and when it finally released, the entire assemblage lurched forward. The Spruills were off, pots and pans rattling, boxes shaking from side to side, Bo and Dale bouncing on a mattress, and Trot curled into a corner of the trailer, bringing up the rear. We waved until they were out of sight.

There'd been no talk of next year. The Spruills were not coming back. We knew we'd never see them again.

What little grass was left in the front yard had been flattened, and when I surveyed the damage I was instantly glad they were gone. I kicked the ashes where they'd built their fires on home plate and once again marveled at how insensitive they'd been. There were ruts from their truck and holes from their tent poles. Next year I'd put up a fence to keep hill people off my baseball field.

My immediate project, however, was to finish what Trot had begun. I hauled the paint to the front porch, one gallon at a time, and was surprised by the weight. I was expecting Pappy to say something, but the situation drew no comment from him. My mother, however, gave some orders to my father, who quickly erected a scaffold on the east side of the house. It was a two-by-six oak plank, eight feet long, braced by a sawhorse on one end and an empty diesel drum on the other. It tilted slightly toward the drum, but not enough to unbalance the painter. My father opened the first gallon, stirred it with a stick, and helped me onto the scaffold. There were some brief instructions, but since he knew so little about house painting I was let loose to learn on my own. I figured if Trot could do it, so could I.

My mother watched me carefully and offered such wisdom as 'Don't let it drip' and 'Take your time.' On the east side of the house, Trot had painted the first six boards from the bottom, from the front of the house to the rear, and with my scaffold I was able to reach another three feet above his work. I wasn't sure how I would paint up to the roof, but I decided I would worry about it later.

The old boards soaked up the first layer of paint. The second one went on smooth and white. After a few minutes I was fascinated by my work because the results were immediate.

'How am I doin'?' I asked without looking down.

'It's beautiful, Luke,' my mother said. 'Just work slow, and take your time. And don't fall.'

'I'm not gonna fall.' Why did she always warn me against dangers that were so obvious?

My father moved the scaffold twice that afternoon, and by supper-time I had used an entire gallon of paint. I washed my hands with lye soap, but the paint was stuck to my fingernails. I didn't care. I was proud of my new craft. I was doing something no Chandler had ever done.

The house painting was not mentioned over supper. Weightier matters were at hand. Our hill people had packed up and left, and they had done so with a large amount of the cotton still unpicked. There had been no rumors of other workers leaving because of wet fields. Pappy didn't want folks to know we were yielding anything to the rains. The weather was about to change, he insisted. We'd never had so many storms this late in the year.

At dusk we moved to the front porch, which was now even quieter. The Cardinals were a distant memory, and we rarely listened to anything else after supper. Pappy didn't want to waste electricity so I sat on the steps and looked out at our front yard, still and empty. For six weeks it had been covered with all manner of shelter and storage. Now there was nothing.

A few leaves dropped and scattered across the yard. The night was cool and clear, and this prompted my father to predict that tomorrow would be a fine opportunity to pick cotton for twelve hours. All I wanted to do was paint.

Chapter 30

I glanced at the clock above the stove as we ate. It was ten minutes after four, the earliest breakfast I could remember. My father spoke only long enough to give his weather forecast – cool, clear, not a cloud anywhere, with the ground soft but firm enough to pick cotton.

The adults were anxious. Much of our crop was still unharvested, and if it remained so, our little farming operation would fall farther into debt. My mother and Gran finished the dishes in record time, and we left the house in a pack. The Mexicans rode with us to the fields. They huddled together on one side of the trailer and tried to stay warm.

Clear, dry days had become rare, and we attacked this one as if it might be the last. I was exhausted by sunrise, but complaining would only get me a harsh lecture. Another crop disaster was looming, and we needed to work until we dropped. The desire for a brief nap arose, but I knew my father would whip me with his belt if he caught me sleeping.

Lunch was cold biscuits and ham, eaten hurriedly in the shade of the cotton trailer. It was warm by midday, and a siesta would have been appropriate. Instead, we sat on our picking sacks, nibbled our biscuits, and watched the sky. Even when we talked, our eyes were looking up.

And, of course, a clear day meant that the storms were on the way, so after twenty minutes of lunch, my father and Pappy declared the break to be over. The women jumped up as quickly as the men, anxious to prove they could work just as hard. I was the only reluctant one.

It could've been worse: The Mexicans didn't even stop to eat.

I spent the tedious afternoon thinking about Tally, then Hank, then back to Tally. I also thought about the Spruills and envied them for escaping. I tried to imagine what they would do when they arrived home and Hank wasn't there waiting for them. I tried to tell myself that I didn't really care.

We had not received a letter from Ricky in several weeks. I had heard the adults whisper about this around the house. I had not yet sent my long narrative to him, primarily because I wasn't sure how to mail it without getting caught. And I was having second thoughts about burdening him with the Latcher news. He had enough on his mind. If Ricky were home, we'd go fishing and I'd tell him everything. I'd begin with the Sisco killing and spare no details – the Latcher baby, Hank and Cowboy, everything. Ricky would know what to do. I longed for him to come home.

I don't know how much cotton I picked that

day, but I'm sure it was a world record for a seven-year-old. When the sun fell behind the trees along the river, my mother found me, and we walked to the house. Gran stayed behind, picking as fast as the men.

'How long they gonna work?' I asked my mother. We were so tired that walking was a challenge.

'Till dark, I guess.'

It was almost dark when we got to the house. I wanted to collapse on the sofa and sleep for a week, but my mother asked me to wash my hands and help with supper. She made corn bread and warmed up leftovers while I peeled and sliced tomatoes. We listened to the radio – not a word about Korea.

In spite of a brutal day in the fields, Pappy and my father were in good spirits when we sat down to eat. Between them, they had picked eleven hundred pounds. The recent rains had driven up the price of cotton in the Memphis market, and if we could just get a few more days of dry weather, then we might survive another year. Gran listened from a distance. She listened but did not hear, and I knew she was off in Korea again. My mother was too tired to talk.

Pappy hated leftovers, but he still thanked the Lord for them. He also gave thanks for the dry weather and asked for more of it. We ate slowly; the day's exhaustion finally settled in. Conversation was soft and short.

I heard the thunder first. It was a low rumble, far away, and I glanced around the table to see if the adults had heard it, too. Pappy was talking about the cotton markets. A few minutes later the rumbling was much closer, and when lightning cracked in the distance, we stopped eating. The winds picked up, and the tin roof on the back porch began to gently rattle. We avoided eye contact.

Pappy folded his hands together and rested his elbows on the table as if he might pray again. He had just asked God for more good weather. Now we were about to get another drenching.

My father's shoulders dropped a few inches. He rubbed his forehead and gazed at a wall. The rain began pecking the roof, a little too loudly, and Gran said, 'It's hail.'

Hail meant high winds and fierce rain, and sure enough a storm roared across our farm. We sat at the table for a long time listening to the thunder and rain, ignoring the half-eaten supper before us, wondering how many inches would fall and how long it would be before we could pick again. The St. Francis couldn't hold much more, and when it spilled out, the crops would be finished.

The storm passed, but the rain continued, heavy at times. We finally left the kitchen. I walked to the front porch with Pappy and saw nothing but a pool of water between our house and the road. I felt sorry for him as he sat in the swing and gazed in disbelief at the waves of water God was sending us.

Later my mother read Bible stories to me, her voice barely audible above the rain on the roof. The tale of Noah and the flood was off-limits. I fell asleep before young David slew Goliath.

The next day my parents announced that they were driving into town. I was invited – it would've been too cruel to deny me the trip – but Pappy and Gran were not included. It was a little family outing. Ice cream was mentioned as a possibility. Thanks to Cowboy and Tally, we had some free gasoline, and there was nothing to do around the farm. Water was standing between the rows of cotton.

I sat in the front with them and paid close attention to the speedometer. Once we turned onto the main highway and headed north toward Black Oak, my father finished shifting and sped up to forty-five miles an hour. As far as I could tell, the truck ran the same as it did at thirty-seven, but I wasn't about to mention this to Pappy.

It was oddly comforting to see the other farms idled by the rain. No one was trudging through the fields, trying to pick. Not a single Mexican could be seen.

Our land was low, prone to early flooding, and we'd lost crops before when other farmers had not. Now it appeared as if everybody was getting soaked in equal measure.

It was midday with nothing to do but wait, and so families were gathered on porches, watching the traffic. The women were shelling peas. The men were talking and worrying. The children were either sitting on the steps or playing in the mud. We knew them all, every house. We waved, they waved back, and we could almost hear them say, 'Reckon why the Chandlers are headin' to town?'

Main Street was quiet. We parked in front of the hardware store. Three doors down at the Co-op, a group of farmers in overalls was engaged in serious conversation. My father felt obliged to report there first, or at least to listen to their thoughts and opinions on when the rain might end. I followed my mother to the drugstore, where they sold ice cream at a soda fountain in the rear. A pretty town girl named Cindy had worked there for as long as I could remember. Cindy had no other customers at the moment, and I received an especially generous helping of vanilla ice cream covered with cherries. It cost my mother a nickel. I perched myself on a stool. When it was clear that I had found my spot for the next thirty minutes, my mother left to buy a few things.

Cindy had an older brother who'd been killed in a gruesome car wreck, and every time I saw her I thought about the stories I'd heard. There'd been a fire, and they couldn't get her brother out of the wreckage. And there'd been a crowd, which, of course, meant there were many versions of just how awful it really was. She was pretty, but she had sad eyes, and I knew this was because of the tragedy. She didn't want to talk, and that was fine with me. I ate slowly, determined to make the ice cream last a long time, and watched her move around behind the counter.

I'd heard enough whispers between my parents to know that they were planning to make some sort of telephone call. Since we didn't own a phone, we'd have to borrow one. I was guessing it would be the phone at Pop and Pearl's store.

Most of the homes in town had phones, as did all the businesses. And the farmers who lived two or three miles from town had phones, too, since the lines ran that far. My mother once told me it would be years before they strung phone lines out to our place. Pappy didn't want one anyway. He said that if you had a phone then you had to talk to folks whenever it was convenient for them, not you. A television might be interesting, but forget a phone.

Jackie Moon came through the door and made his way back to the soda counter. 'Hey, little Chandler,' he said, then tousled my hair and sat down beside me. 'What brings you here?' he asked.

'Ice cream,' I said, and he laughed.

Cindy stepped in front of us and said, 'The usual?'

'Yes ma'am,' he said. 'And how are you?'

'I'm fine, Jackie,' she cooed. They studied each other carefully, and I got the impression that something was going on. She turned to prepare the usual, and Jackie examined her from head to toe.

'Y'all heard from Ricky?' he asked me, his eyes still on Cindy.

'Not lately,' I said, staring too.

'Ricky's a tough guy. He'll be all right.'

'I know,' I said.

He lit a cigarette and puffed on it for a moment. 'Y'all wet out there?' he asked.

'Soaked.'

Cindy placed a bowl of chocolate ice cream and a cup of black coffee in front of Jackie.

'They say it's supposed to rain for the next two weeks,' he said. 'I don't doubt it.'

'Rain, rain, rain,' Cindy said. 'That's all people talk about these days. Don't you get tired of talkin' about the weather?'

'Ain't nothin' else to talk about,' Jackie said. 'Not if you're farmin'.'

'Only a fool would farm,' she said, then tossed her hand towel on the counter and walked to the front register.

Jackie finished a bite of ice cream. 'She's probably right about that, you know.'

'Probably so.'

'Your daddy goin' up North?' he asked.

'Goin' where?'

'Up North, to Flint. I hear some of the boys are already makin' calls, tryin' to get on at the Buick plant. They say the jobs are tight this year, can't take as many as they used to, so folks are already scramblin' to get on. Cotton's shot to hell again. Another good rain and the river's over the banks. Most farmers'll be lucky to make half a crop. Kind of silly, ain't it? Farm like crazy for six months, lose everything, then run up North to work and bring back enough cash to pay off debts. Then plant another crop.'

'You goin' up North?' I asked.

'Thinkin' about it. I'm too young to get stuck on a farm for the rest of my life.'

'Yeah, me too.'

He sipped his coffee, and for a few moments we silently contemplated the foolishness of farming.

'I hear that big hillbilly took off,' Jackie finally said.

Fortunately I had a mouthful of ice cream, so I just nodded.

'I hope they catch him,' he said. 'I'd like to see him go to trial, get what's comin' to him. I already told Stick Powers that I'd be a witness. I saw the

389

whole thing. Other folks are comin' out now, tellin' Stick what really happened. The hillbilly didn't have to kill that Sisco boy.'

I shoveled in another scoop and kept nodding. I had learned to shut up and look stupid when the subject of Hank Spruill came up.

Cindy was back, shuffling behind the counter, wiping this and that and humming all the while. Jackie forgot about Hank. 'You 'bout finished?' he said, looking at my ice cream. I guess he and Cindy had something to discuss.

'Just about,' I said.

She hummed, and he stared until I finished. When I'd eaten the last bit, I said good-bye and went to Pop and Pearl's, where I hoped to learn more about the telephone call. Pearl was alone by the register, her reading glasses on the tip of her nose, her gaze meeting mine the second I walked in. It was said that she knew the sound of each truck that passed along Main Street and that she could not only identify the farmer driving it but also could tell how long it had been since he'd been to town. She missed nothing.

'Where's Eli?' she asked after we'd exchanged pleasantries.

'He stayed at home,' I said, looking at the bin of Tootsie Rolls. She pointed and said, 'Have one.'

'Thanks. Where's Pop?'

'In the back. Just you and your parents, huh?'

'Yes ma'am. You seen 'em?'

'No, not yet. They buyin' groceries?'

'Yes ma'am. And I think my dad needs to borrow a phone.' This stopped her cold as she thought of all the reasons why he needed to call someone. I unwrapped the Tootsie Roll.

'Who's he callin'?' she asked.

'Don't know.' Pity the poor soul who borrowed Pearl's phone and wanted to keep the details private. She'd know more than the person on the other end.

'Y'all wet out there?'

'Yes ma'am. Pretty wet.'

'That's such bad land anyway. Seems like y'all and the Latchers and the Jeters always get flooded first.' Her voice trailed off as she contemplated our misfortune. She glanced out the window, slowly shaking her head at the prospect of another bleak harvest.

I'd yet to see a flood – at least not one that I could remember – so I had nothing to say. The weather had dampened everyone's spirits, including Pearl's. With heavy clouds hanging over our part of the world, it was hard to be optimistic. Another gloomy winter was coming.

'I hear some people are goin' up North,' I said. I knew Pearl would have the details if the rumors were indeed true.

'I hear that, too,' she said. 'They're tryin' to line up jobs just in case the rains stay.'

'Who's goin'?'

'Hadn't heard,' she said, but I could tell from the tone of her voice that she had the latest gossip. The farmers had probably used her phone.

I thanked her for the Tootsie Roll and left the store. The sidewalks were empty. It was nice to have the town to myself. On Saturdays you could hardly walk for all the people. I caught a glimpse of my parents in the hardware store buying something, so I went to investigate.

They were buying paint, lots of it. Lined up perfectly on the counter, along with two brushes still in their plastic wrappers, were five one-gallon buckets of white Pittsburgh Paint. The clerk was totaling the charges when I walked up. My father was fumbling for something in his pocket. My mother stood close to his side, straight and proud. It was obvious to me that she had pushed the buying of the paint. She smiled down at me with great satisfaction.

'That's fourteen dollars and eighty cents,' the clerk said.

My father withdrew his cash and began counting bills.

'I can just put it on your account,' the clerk said.

'No, this doesn't go there,' my mother said. Pappy would have a heart attack if he got a monthly statement showing that much spent for paint.

We hauled it to the truck.

Chapter 31

The buckets of paint were lined along the back porch, like soldiers poised for an ambush. Under my mother's supervision, the scaffolding was moved by my father and rigged at the northeast corner of the house, enabling me to paint from the bottom almost to the roofline. I had turned the first corner. Trot would've been proud.

Another gallon was opened. I removed the wrapper from one of the new brushes and worked the bristles back and forth. It was five inches wide and much heavier than the one Trot had given me.

'We're gonna work in the garden,' my mother said. 'We'll be back directly.' And with that she left with my father in tow, carrying three of the largest baskets on the farm. Gran was in the kitchen making strawberry preserves. Pappy was off worrying somewhere. I was left alone.

The investment by my parents in this project added weight to my mission. The house would now be painted in its entirety, whether Pappy liked it or not. And the bulk of the labor would be supplied by me. There was, however, no hurry. If the floods came, I would paint when it wasn't raining. If we finished the crop, I'd have all winter to complete my masterpiece. The house had never been painted in its fifty years. Where was the urgency?

After thirty minutes I was tired. I could hear my parents talking in the garden. There were two more brushes – another new one and the one Trot had given me – just lying there on the porch beside the buckets of paint. Why couldn't my parents pick up the brushes and get to work? Surely they planned to help.

The paintbrush was really heavy. I kept my strokes short and slow and very neat. My mother had cautioned me against trying to apply too much at once. 'Don't let it drip.' 'Don't let it run.'

After an hour I needed a break. Lost in my own world, facing such a mammoth project, I began to think ill of Trot for dumping it on me. He'd painted about a third of one side of the house then fled. I was beginning to think that perhaps Pappy was right after all. The house didn't need painting.

Hank was the reason. Hank had laughed at me and insulted my family because our house was unpainted. Trot had risen to my defense. He and Tally had conspired to start this project, not knowing that the bulk of it would fall on my shoulders.

I heard voices close behind me. Miguel, Luis, and Rico had walked up and were eyeing me with curiosity. I smiled and we exchanged *buenas tardes*. They moved in closer, obviously puzzled as to why the smallest Chandler had been given such a large task. For a few minutes, I concentrated on my work and inched my way along. Miguel was at the porch inspecting the unopened gallons and the other brushes. 'Can we play?' he asked.

What an absolutely wonderful idea!

Two more gallons were opened. I gave Miguel my brush, and within seconds, Luis and Rico were sitting on the scaffold, their bare feet hanging down, painting as if they'd been doing it all their lives. Miguel started on the back porch. Before long the other six Mexicans were sitting on the grass in the shade watching us.

Gran heard the noise, and she stepped outside, wiping her hands with a dish towel. She looked at me and laughed, then went back to her strawberry preserves.

The Mexicans were delighted to have something to do. The rains had forced them to kill long hours in and around the barn. They had no truck to take them to town, no radio to listen to, no books to read. (We weren't even sure if they knew how to read.) They rolled dice occasionally, but they would stop the moment one of us drew near.

They attacked the unpainted house with a vengeance. The six non-painters offered endless advice and opinions to those with the brushes. Evidently some of their suggestions were hilarious because at times the painters laughed so hard they couldn't work. The Spanish grew faster and louder, all nine laughing and talking. The challenge was to convince one with a brush to relinquish it for a spell and allow the next one to improve on the work. Roberto emerged as the expert. With a dramatic flair, he instructed the novices, Pablo and Pepe especially, on proper technique. He walked behind the others as they worked, quick with advice or a joke or a rebuke. The brushes changed hands, and through the ridicule and abuse, a system of teamwork emerged.

I sat under the tree with the other Mexicans, watching the transformation of the back porch. Pappy returned on the tractor. He parked it by the toolshed and, from a distance, he watched for a moment. Then he circled wide to the front of the house. I couldn't tell if he approved or not, and I'm not sure that it mattered anymore. There was no spring in his step, no purpose to his movement. Pappy was just another beaten farmer in the midst of losing yet another cotton crop.

My parents returned from the garden with the baskets laden with produce. 'Well, if it isn't Tom Sawyer,' my mother said to me.

'Who's he?' I asked.

'I'll tell you the story tonight.'

They placed the baskets on the porch, careful to avoid the painting area, and went inside. All the adults were gathered in the kitchen, and I wondered if they were talking about me and the Mexicans. Gran appeared with a pitcher of iced tea and a tray of glasses. That was a good sign. The Mexicans took a break and enjoyed their tea. They thanked Gran, then immediately started bickering over who got the brushes.

The sun battled the clouds as the afternoon passed. There were moments when its light was clear and unbroken and the air was warm, almost summerlike. Inevitably, we would look up at the sky in hopes that the clouds were finally leaving Arkansas, never to return, or at least not until the

396

spring. Then the earth turned dark again, and cooler.

The clouds were winning, and we all knew it. The Mexicans would soon be leaving our farm, just as the Spruills had. We couldn't expect people to sit around for days, watching the sky, trying to stay dry, and not getting paid.

The paint was gone by late afternoon. The rear of our house, including the porch, was finished, and the difference was astounding. The brilliant, shiny boards contrasted sharply with the unpainted ones at the corner. Tomorrow we would attack the west side, assuming I could somehow negotiate more paint.

I thanked the Mexicans. They laughed all the way back to the barn. They would fix and eat their tortillas, go to bed early, and hope they could pick cotton tomorrow.

I sat in the cool grass, admiring their work, not wanting to go inside because the adults were not in good spirits. They would force a smile at me and try to say something amusing, but they were worried sick.

I wished I had a brother – younger or older, I didn't care. My parents wanted more children, but there were problems of some sort. I needed a friend, another kid to talk with, play with, conspire with. I was tired of being the only little person on the farm.

And I missed Tally. I tried valiantly to hate her, but it simply wasn't working.

Pappy walked around the corner of the house and inspected the new coat of paint. I couldn't tell if he was upset or not.

'Let's ride down to the creek,' he said, and without another word we walked to the tractor. He started it, and we followed the ruts in the field road. Water was standing where the tractor and cotton trailer had gone many times. The front tires splashed mud as we chugged along. The rear tires chewed up the ground and made the ruts deeper. We were slogging through a field that was fast becoming a marsh.

The cotton itself looked pitiful. The bolls sagged from the weight of the rainfall. The stalks were bent from the wind. A week of blazing sunshine might dry the ground and the cotton and allow us to finish picking, but such weather was long gone.

We turned north and crept along an even soggier trail, the same one Tally and I had walked a few times. The creek was just ahead.

I stood slightly behind Pappy, clutching the umbrella stand and the brace above the left rear tire, and I watched the side of his face. His jaws were clenched, his eyes were narrowed. Other than the occasional flare of temper, he was not one to show emotion. I'd never seen him cry or even come close. He worried because he was a farmer, but he did not complain. If the rains washed away our crops, then there was a reason for it. God would protect us and provide for us through good years and bad. As Baptists we believed God was in control of everything.

I was certain there was a reason the Cardinals lost the pennant, but I couldn't understand why God was behind it. Why would God allow two teams from New York to play in the World Series? It completely baffled me.

The water was suddenly deeper in front of us, six inches up the front tires. The trail was flooded, and for a moment I was puzzled by this. We were near the creek. Pappy stopped the tractor and pointed. 'It's over the banks,' he said matter-of-factly, but there was defeat in his voice. The water was coming through a thicket that once sat high above the creek bed. Somewhere down there Tally had bathed in a cool, clear stream that had disappeared.

'It's flooding,' he said. He turned off the tractor, and we listened to the sounds of the current as it came over the sides of Siler's Creek and ran onto the bottomland that was our lower forty acres. It got lost between the rows of cotton as it crept down the slight valley. It would stop somewhere in the middle of the field, about halfway to our house, at a point where the land began a gentle slope upward. There it would gather and gain depth before spreading east and west and covering most of our acreage.

I was finally seeing a flood. There had been others but I'd been too young to remember them. All of my young life I'd heard tall tales of rivers out of control and crops submerged, and now I was witnessing it for myself, as if for the first time. It was frightening because once it started no one knew when it would end. Nothing held the water; it ran wherever it wanted. Would it reach our house? Would the St. Francis spill over and wipe out everyone? Would it rain for forty days and forty nights and cause us to perish like the ones who'd laughed at Noah?

Probably not. There was something in that story

399

about the rainbow as God's promise to never again flood the earth.

It was certainly flooding now. The sight of a rainbow was almost a holy event in our lives, but we hadn't seen one in weeks. I didn't understand how God could allow such things to happen.

Pappy had been to the creek at least three times during the day, watching and waiting and probably praying.

'When did it start?' I asked.

'I reckon an hour ago. Don't know for sure.'

I wanted to ask when it would stop, but I already knew the answer.

'It's backwater,' he said. 'The St. Francis is too full, there's no place for it to go.'

We watched it for a long time. It poured forth and came toward us, rising a few inches on the front tires. After a while I was anxious to head back. Pappy, however, was not. His worries and fears were being confirmed, and he was mesmerized by what he was seeing.

In late March, he and my father had begun plowing the fields, turning over the soil, burying the stalks and roots and leaves from the previous crop. They were happy then, pleased to be outdoors after a long hibernation. They watched the weather and studied the almanac, and they had begun hanging around the Co-op to hear what the other farmers were saying. They planted in early May if the weather was right. May 15 was an absolute deadline for putting the cotton seeds in the ground. My contribution to the operation began in early June, when school was out and weeds began sprouting. They gave me a hoe, pointed me in the right direction, and for many hours a day I chopped cotton, a task almost as hard and mind-numbing as picking the stuff. All summer as the cotton and the weeds around it grew, we chopped. If the cotton bloomed by July 4, then it was going to be a bumper crop. By late August we were ready to pick. By early September we were searching for hill people and trying to line up some Mexicans.

And now, in mid-October, we were watching it get swept away. All the labor, the sweat and sore muscles, all the money invested in seed and fertilizer and fuel, all the hopes and plans, everything was now being lost to the backwaters of the St. Francis River.

We waited, but the flood did not stop. In fact the front tires of the tractor were half-covered with water when Pappy at last started the engine. There was barely enough light to see. The trail was covered with water, and at the rate the flood was spreading we'd lose the lower forty by sunrise.

I had never witnessed such silence over supper. Not even Gran could find anything pleasant to say. I played with my butter beans and tried to imagine what my parents were thinking. My father was probably worried about the crop loan, a debt that would now be impossible to repay. My mother was working on her escape from the cotton patch. She was not nearly as disappointed as the other three adults. A disastrous harvest, following such a promising spring and summer, gave her an arsenal of artillery to use against my father.

The flood kept my mind off heavier matters – Hank, Tally, Cowboy – and for this reason it was not an unpleasant subject to think about. But I said nothing.

School would reopen soon, and my mother decided I should begin a nightly routine of reading and writing. I was longing for the classroom, something I would never admit, and so I enjoyed the homework. She commented on how rusty my cursive writing had become and declared that I needed a lot of practice. My reading wasn't too smooth either.

'See what pickin' cotton'll do to you?' I said.

We were alone in Ricky's room, reading to each other before I went to bed. 'I have a secret for you,' she whispered. 'Can you keep a secret?'

If you only knew, I thought. 'Sure.'

'Promise?'

'Sure.'

'You can't tell anybody, not even Pappy and Gran.'

'Okay, what is it?'

She leaned even closer. 'Your father and I are thinkin' about goin' up North.'

'What about me?'

'You're goin', too.'

That was a relief. 'You mean to work like Jimmy Dale?'

'That's right. Your father has talked to Jimmy Dale, and he can get him a job at the Buick plant in Flint, Michigan. There's good money up there. We're not stayin' forever, but your father needs to find somethin' steady.'

'What about Pappy and Gran?'

'Oh, they'll never leave here.'

'Will they keep farmin'?'

'I suppose. Don't know what else they'd do.'

'How can they farm without us?'

'They'll manage. Listen, Luke, we can't sit here year after year losin' money while we borrow more. Your father and I are ready to try somethin' else.'

I had mixed emotions about this. I wanted my parents to be happy, and my mother would never be content on a farm, especially when forced to live with her in-laws. I certainly didn't want to be a farmer, but then my future was already secure with the Cardinals. But the thought of leaving the only place I'd ever lived was unsettling. And I couldn't imagine life without Pappy and Gran.

'It'll be excitin', Luke,' she said, her voice still a whisper. 'Trust me.'

'I guess so. Ain't it cold up there?'

'Isn't,' she corrected me. 'There's a lot of snow in the wintertime, but I think that'll be fun. We'll make a snowman and snow ice cream, and we'll have us a white Christmas.'

I remembered Jimmy Dale's stories about watching the Detroit Tigers play and how folks had good jobs and televisions and the schools were better. Then I remembered his wife, the rotten Stacy with her whiny nasal voice, and how I'd scared her in the outhouse.

'Don't they talk funny up there?' I asked.

'Yes, but we'll get used to it. It'll be an adventure, Luke, and if we don't like it, then we'll come home.'

'We'll come back here?'

'We'll come back to Arkansas, or somewhere in the South.'

'I don't want to see Stacy.'

'Neither do I. Look, you go to bed and think about it. Remember, it's our secret.'

'Yes ma'am.'

She tucked me in and turned off the light.

More news to file away.

Chapter 32

As soon as Pappy took his last bite of scrambled eggs, he wiped his mouth and looked through the window over the sink. There was enough light to see what we wanted. 'Let's take a look,' he said, and the rest of us followed him out of the kitchen, off the back porch, and across the rear yard in the direction of the barn. I was huddled under a sweater, trying to keep up with my father. The grass was wet, and after a few steps so were my boots. We stopped at the nearest field and stared at the dark tree line in the distance, at the edge of Siler's Creek, almost a mile away. There were forty acres of cotton in front of us, half our land. There were also floodwaters; we just didn't know how much.

Pappy began walking between two rows of cotton, and soon we could only see his shoulders and straw hat. He would stop when he found the creek's advance. If he walked for a while, then the creek had not done the damage we feared. Perhaps it was retreating, and maybe the sun would come out. Maybe we could salvage something.

At about sixty feet, the distance from the mound

to home plate, he stopped and looked down. We couldn't see the ground or what was covering it, but we knew. The creek was still moving toward us.

'It's already here,' he said over his shoulder. 'Two inches of it.'

The field was flooding faster than the men had predicted. And given their talent for pessimism, this was no small feat.

'This has never happened in October,' Gran said, wringing her hands on her apron.

Pappy watched the action around his feet. We kept our eyes on him. The sun was rising, but it was cloudy, and the shadows came and went. I heard a voice and looked to the right. The Mexicans had assembled in a quiet group, watching us. A funeral couldn't have been more somber.

We were all curious about the water. I'd personally witnessed it the day before, but I was anxious to see it creeping through our fields, inching its way toward our house, like some giant snake that couldn't be stopped. My father stepped forward and walked between two rows of cotton. He stopped near Pappy and put his hands on his hips, just like his father. Gran and my mother were next. I followed, and not far away, the Mexicans joined in as we fanned out through the field in search of the floodwaters. We stopped in a neat line, all of us staring at the thick, brown overflow from Siler's Creek.

I broke off a piece of stalk and stuck it in the ground at the edge of the advancing water. Within a minute, the stick was engulfed by the current.

We retreated slowly. My father and Pappy

talked to Miguel and the Mexicans. They were ready to leave, either to go home or to another farm where the cotton could be picked. Who could blame them? I hung around, just close enough to listen. It was decided that Pappy would go with them to the back forty, where the ground was slightly higher, and there they would try to pick for a while. The cotton was wet, but if the sun broke through, then maybe they could get a hundred pounds each.

My father would go to town, for the second day in a row, and check with the Co-op to see if there was another farm where our Mexicans might work. There was much better land in the northeastern part of the county, higher fields away from creeks and away from the St. Francis. And there had been rumors that the folks up near Monette had not received as much rain as those of us in the southern end of the county.

I was in the kitchen with the women when my father relayed the new plans for the day.

'That cotton's soakin' wet,' Gran said with disapproval. 'They won't pick fifty pounds. It's a waste of time.'

Pappy was still outside and didn't hear these comments. My father did, but he was in no mood to argue with his mother. 'We'll try and move them to another farm,' he said.

'Can I go to town?' I asked both parents. I was quite anxious to leave because the alternative might be a forced march with the Mexicans to the back forty, where I'd be expected to drag a picking sack through mud and water while trying to pluck off soaked cotton bolls.

My mother smiled and said, 'Yes, we need some paint.'

Gran gave another look of disapproval. Why were we spending money we didn't have on house paint when we were losing another crop? However, the house was about half and half – a striking contrast between new white and old pale brown. The project had to be finished.

Even my father seemed uneasy about the idea of parting with more cash, but he said to me, 'You can go.'

'I'll stay here,' my mother said. 'We need to put up some okra.'

Another trip to town. I was a happy boy. No pressure to pick cotton, nothing to do but ride down the highway and dream of somehow obtaining candy or ice cream once I arrived in Black Oak. I had to be careful, though, because I was the only happy Chandler.

The St. Francis seemed ready to burst when we stopped at the bridge. 'Reckon it's safe?' I asked my father.

'Sure hope so.' He shifted into first, and we crept over the river, both of us too afraid to look down. With the weight of our truck and the force of the river, the bridge shook when we reached the middle. We picked up speed and were soon on the other side. We both exhaled.

Losing the bridge would be a disaster. We'd be isolated. The waters would rise around our house, and we would have no place to go. Even the Latchers would be better off. They lived on the other side of the bridge, the same side as Black Oak and civilization.

We looked at the Latchers' land as we drove past. 'Their house is flooded,' my father said, though we couldn't see that far. Their crops were certainly gone.

Closer to town, there were Mexicans in the fields, though not as many as before. We parked by the Co-op and went inside. Some grim-faced farmers were sitting in the back, sipping coffee and talking about their problems. My father gave me a nickel for a Coca-Cola, then he joined the farmers.

'Y'all pickin' out there?' one asked him.

'Maybe a little.'

'How's that creek?'

'She came over last night. Moved more than half a mile before sunrise. The lower forty's gone.'

They observed a moment of silence for this terrible news, each of them staring at the floor and feeling pity for us Chandlers. I hated farming even more.

'I guess the river's holdin',' another man said.

'It is out our way,' my father said. 'But it won't be long.'

They all nodded and seemed to share this prediction. 'Anybody else got water over the banks?' my father asked.

'I hear the Tripletts lost twenty acres to Deer Creek, but I ain't seen it myself,' said one farmer.

'All the creeks are backin' up,' another said. 'Puttin' a lot of pressure on the St. Francis.'

More silence as they contemplated the creeks and the pressure.

'Anybody need some Mexicans?' my father finally asked. 'I got nine of 'em with nothin' to do. They're ready to head home.'

'Any word from number ten?'

'Nope. He's long gone, and we ain't had time to worry about him.'

'Riggs knows some farmers up north of Blytheville who'll take the Mexicans.'

'Where's Riggs?' my father asked.

'He'll be back directly.'

Hill people were leaving in droves, and the conversation settled on them and the Mexicans. The exodus of labor was further evidence that the crops were finished. The dreary mood in the rear of the Co-op grew even darker, so I left to check on Pearl and perhaps cajole a Tootsie Roll out of her.

Pop and Pearl's grocery store was closed, a first for me. A small sign gave its hours as nine to six, Monday through Friday, and nine to nine on Saturday. Closed on Sundays, but that went without saying. Mr. Sparky Dillon, the mechanic down at the Texaco place, came up behind me and said, 'Ain't open till nine, son.'

'What time is it?' I asked.

'Eight-twenty.'

I'd never been in Black Oak at such an early hour. I looked up and down Main Street, uncertain as to where I should shop next. I settled on the drugstore, with the soda fountain in the rear, and I was walking toward it when I heard traffic. Two trucks were approaching from the south, from our end of the county. They were obviously hill people, going home, with their belongings stacked high and strapped to the frames of the trucks. The family in the first truck could have passed for the

410

Spruills, with teenagers squatting on an old mattress and gazing sadly at the stores as they passed. The second truck was much nicer and cleaner. It, too, was loaded with wooden boxes and burlap bags, but they were packed neatly together. The husband drove, and the wife sat in the passenger's seat. From the woman's lap a small child waved at me as they passed. I waved back.

Gran always said that some of the hill people had nicer homes than we did. I could never understand why they packed up and came down from the Ozarks to pick cotton.

I saw my father go into the hardware store, so I followed him. He was in the back, near the paint, talking with the clerk. Four gallons of white Pittsburgh Paint were on the counter. I thought about the Pittsburgh Pirates. They had finished last again in the National League. Their only great player was Ralph Kiner, who'd hit thirty-seven home runs.

Someday I would play in Pittsburgh. I would proudly wear my Cardinal red and crush the lowly Pirates.

It had taken all the paint we had left to finish the rear of the house the day before. The Mexicans were about to leave. To me it made sense to buy more paint and take advantage of the free labor present on our farm. Otherwise they'd be gone, and I'd once again get stuck with the entire project.

'That's not enough paint,' I whispered to my father as the clerk added the bill.

'It'll do for now,' he said with a frown. The issue was money.

'Ten dollars plus tax of thirty-six cents,' the clerk said. My father reached into his pocket and pulled out a thin roll of bills. He slowly counted them out, as if he didn't want to let go.

He stopped at ten – ten one-dollar bills. When it was painfully clear he didn't have enough, he faked a laugh and said, 'Looks like I just brought ten bucks. I'll pay you the tax next time I'm in.'

'Sure, Mr. Chandler,' the clerk said.

They carried two gallons each and loaded the paint into the back of our truck. Mr. Riggs was back at the Co-op, so my father went to have their talk about our Mexicans. I returned to the hardware store and went straight to the clerk.

'How much is two gallons?' I asked.

'Two-fifty a gallon, total of five dollars.'

I reached into my pocket and pulled out my money. 'Here's five,' I said as I handed him the bills. At first he didn't want to take it.

'Did you pick cotton for that money?' he asked.

'Yes sir.'

'Does your daddy know you're buyin' paint?'

'Not yet.'

'What're y'all paintin' out there?'

'Our house.'

'Why you doin' that?'

''Cause it ain't never been painted.'

He reluctantly took my money. 'Plus eighteen cents for tax,' he said. I handed him a dollar bill and said, 'How much does my daddy owe for the tax?'

'Thirty-six cents.'

'Take it out of this.'

'Okay.' He gave me the change, then loaded two

412

more gallons into our truck. I stood on the sidewalk watching our paint as if someone might try to steal it.

Next to Pop and Pearl's I saw Mr. Lynch Thornton, the postmaster, unlock the door to the post office and step inside. I walked toward him, keeping a watchful eye on the truck. Mr. Thornton was usually a cranky sort, and many believed that this was because he was married to a woman who had a problem with whiskey. All forms of alcohol were frowned upon by almost everyone in Black Oak. The county was dry. The nearest liquor store was in Blytheville, though there were some bootleggers in the area who did quite well. I knew this because Ricky'd told me. He'd said he didn't like whiskey, but he had a beer every now and then. I'd heard so many sermons on the evils of alcohol that I was worried about Ricky's soul. And while it was sinful enough for men to sneak around and drink, for women to do so was scandalous.

I wanted to ask Mr. Thornton how I could go about mailing my letter to Ricky, and do so in a way that no one would know it. The letter was three pages long, and I was quite proud of my effort. But it had all the Latcher baby details, and I still wasn't sure I should send it to Korea.

'Howdy,' I said to Mr. Thornton, who was behind the counter adjusting his visor and settling in for the morning.

'You that Chandler boy?' he said, barely looking up.

'Yes sir.'

'Got somethin' for you.' He disappeared for a

413

second, then handed me two letters. One was from Ricky.

'That all?' he said.

'Yes sir. Thank you.'

'How's he doin'?'

'He's fine, I guess.'

I ran from the post office back to our truck, clutching the letters. The other was from the John Deere place in Jonesboro. I studied the one from Ricky. It was addressed to all of us: Eli Chandler and Family, Route 4, Black Oak, Arkansas. In the upper left corner was the return address, a confusing collection of letters and numbers with San Diego, California, on the last line.

Ricky was alive and writing letters; nothing else really mattered. My father was walking toward me. I ran to meet him with the letter, and we sat in the doorway of the dry goods store and read every word. Ricky was again in a hurry, and his letter was only one page. He wrote us that his unit had seen little action, and though he seemed frustrated by this, it was music to our ears. He also said that rumors of a ceasefire were everywhere, and that there was even talk of being home by Christmas.

The last paragraph was sad and frightening. One of his buddies, a kid from Texas, had been killed by a land mine. They were the same age and had gone through boot camp together. When Ricky got home, he planned to go to Fort Worth to see his friend's mother.

My father folded the letter and stuck it in his overalls. We got in the truck and left town.

Home by Christmas. I couldn't think of a finer gift.

414

We parked under the pin oak, and my father went to the back of the truck to collect the paint. He stopped, counted, then looked at me.

'How'd we end up with six gallons?'

'I bought two,' I said. 'And I paid the tax.'

He didn't seem sure what to say. 'You use your pickin' money?' he finally asked.

'Yes sir.'

'I wish you hadn't done that.'

'I want to help.'

He scratched his forehead and studied the issue for a minute or so, then said, 'I reckon that's fair enough.'

We hauled the paint to the back porch, and then he decided he would go to the back forty to check on Pappy and the Mexicans. If the cotton could be picked, then he'd stay there. I was given permission to start painting the west side of the house. I wanted to work alone. I wanted to seem outmatched and undermanned by the enormity of the job before me so that when the Mexicans returned, they'd feel sorry for me.

They arrived at noon, muddy and tired and with little to show for their morning. 'Cotton's too wet,' I heard Pappy say to Gran. We ate fried okra and biscuits, then I went back to my work.

I kept one eye on the barn, but for an eternity I labored with no relief in sight. What were they doing back there? Lunch was over, the tortillas long since put away. Surely their siestas were also complete. They knew the house was half-painted. Why wouldn't they come help?

The sky darkened in the west, but I didn't notice it until Pappy and Gran stepped onto the back

415

porch. 'Might rain, Luke,' Pappy said. 'Better stop paintin'.'

I cleaned my brush and put the paint under a bench on the back porch as if the storm might damage it. I sat above it, with Pappy on one side and Gran on the other, and we once again listened to the low rumblings in the southwest. We waited for more rain.

Chapter 33

Our new ritual was repeated the next day after a late breakfast. We walked across the rain-soaked grass between our house and our barn, and we stood at the edge of the cotton field and saw water, not rainfall that had collected during the night, but the same thick floodwater from the creek. It stood three inches deep, and seemed ready to swell beyond the field and begin its slow march toward the barn, the toolshed, the chicken coops, and, eventually, the house.

The stalks were slanted to the east, permanently bent by the wind that had laid siege to our farm last night. The bolls were sagging under the weight of the water.

'Will it flood our house, Pappy?' I asked.

He shook his head and put his arm around my shoulders. 'No, Luke, it's never got to the house. Come close a time or two, but the house is a good three feet above where we're standin' right now. Don't you worry about the house.'

'It got in the barn once,' my father said. 'The year after Luke was born, wasn't it?'

'Forty-six,' Gran said. She never missed a date.

417

'But it was in May,' she added. 'Two weeks after we'd planted.'

The morning was cool and windy with high, thin clouds and little chance of rain. A perfect day for painting, assuming, of course, that I could find some help. The Mexicans drifted close, but not close enough to speak.

They would be leaving soon, perhaps within hours. We'd haul them to the Co-op and wait for them to be picked up by a farmer with drier land. I heard the adults discussing this over coffee before sunrise, and I almost panicked. Nine Mexicans could paint the west side of our house in less than a day. It would take me a month. There was no time to be timid.

As we retreated, I headed for the Mexicans. '*Buenos días*,' I said to the group. '*¿Cómo está?*'

All nine answered in some fashion. They were going back to the barn after another wasted day. I walked along with them until I was far enough away that my parents couldn't hear. 'Y'all want to paint some?' I asked.

Miguel rattled the translation, and the entire group seemed to smile.

Ten minutes later three of the six paint buckets were open and there were Mexicans hanging all over the west side of our house. They fought over the three brushes. Another crew was rigging a scaffold. I was pointing here and there, giving instructions that no one seemed to hear. Miguel and Roberto were spitting forth their own commands and opinions in Spanish. Both languages were being ignored in equal measure.

My mother and Gran peeked at us through the

418

kitchen window as they washed the breakfast dishes. Pappy went to the toolshed to fiddle with the tractor. My father was off on a long walk, probably surveying the crop damage and wondering what to do next.

There was an urgency to the painting. The Mexicans joked and laughed and badgered one another, but they worked twice as fast as two days earlier. Not a second was wasted. The brushes changed hands every half hour or so. The reinforcements were kept fresh. By mid-morning they were halfway to the front porch. It was not a large house.

I was happy to retreat and stay out of the way. The Mexicans worked so fast it seemed downright inefficient for me to take up a brush and stall the momentum. Besides, the free labor was temporary. The hour was soon approaching when I'd be left alone to finish the job.

My mother brought iced tea and cookies, but the painting did not stop. Those under the shade tree with me ate first, then three of them changed places with the painters.

'Do you have enough paint?' my mother whispered to me.

'No ma'am.'

She returned to the kitchen.

Before lunch, the west side was finished, a thick, shiny coat sparkling in the intermittent sun. There was a gallon left. I took Miguel to the east side, where Trot had begun a month earlier, and pointed up to an unpainted strip that I'd been unable to reach. He barked some orders, and the crew moved to the opposite side of the house.

A new method was employed. Instead of make-shift scaffolding, Pepe and Luis, two of the smaller ones, balanced themselves on the shoulders of Pablo and Roberto, the two heaviest ones, and began painting just below the roofline. This, of course, drew an endless stream of comments and jokes from the others.

When the paint was gone, it was time to eat. I shook hands with all of them and thanked them profusely. They laughed and chattered all the way back to the barn. It was midday, the sun was out, and the temperature was rising. As I watched them walk away, I looked at the field beside the barn. The floodwaters were in sight. It seemed odd that the flood could advance when the sun was shining.

I turned and inspected the work. The back and both sides of our house looked almost new. Only the front remained unpainted, and since by now I was a veteran, I knew that I could complete the job without the Mexicans.

My mother stepped outside and said, 'Lunch-time, Luke.' I hesitated for a second, still admiring the accomplishment, so she walked to where I was standing, and together we looked at the house. 'It's a very good job, Luke,' she said.

'Thanks.'

'How much paint is left?'

'None. It's all gone.'

'How much do you need to paint the front?'

The front was not as long as the east or west side, but it had the added challenge of a porch, as did the rear. 'I reckon four or five gallons,' I said, as if I'd been house painting for decades.

420

'I don't want you to spend your money on paint,' she said.

'It's my money. Y'all said I could spend it on whatever I wanted.'

'True, but you shouldn't have to spend it on somethin' like this.'

'I don't mind. I want to help.'

'What about your jacket?'

I'd lost sleep worrying about my Cardinals jacket, but now it seemed unimportant. Plus, I'd been thinking about another way to get one. 'Maybe Santa Claus'll bring one.'

She smiled and said, 'Maybe so. Let's have lunch.'

Just after Pappy thanked the Lord for the food, saying nothing about the weather or the crops, my father grimly announced that the backwaters had begun trickling across the main field road into the back forty acres. This development was absorbed with little comment. We were numb to bad news.

The Mexicans gathered around the truck and waited for Pappy. They each had a small sack with their belongings, the same items they'd arrived with six weeks earlier. I shook hands with each one and said goodbye. As always, I was anxious for another ride to town, even though this little trip was not a pleasant one.

'Luke, go help your mother in the garden,' my father said as the Mexicans were loading up. Pappy was starting the engine.

'I thought I was goin' to town,' I said.

'Don't make me repeat myself,' he said sternly.

I watched them drive away, all nine of the

421

Mexicans waving sadly as they looked at our house and farm for the last time. According to my father, they were headed to a large farm north of Blytheville, two hours away, where they would work for three or four weeks, weather permitting, and then go back to Mexico. My mother had inquired as to how they would be shipped home, by cattle truck or bus, but she did not press the issue. We had no control over those details, and they seemed much less important with floodwaters creeping through our fields.

Food was important, though: food for a long winter, one that would follow a bad crop, one in which everything we ate would come from the garden. There was nothing unusual about this, except that there wouldn't be a spare dime to buy anything but flour, sugar, and coffee. A good crop meant there was a little money tucked away under a mattress, a few bills rolled up and saved and sometimes used for luxuries like Coca-Colas, ice cream, saltines, and white bread. A bad crop meant that if we didn't grow it, we didn't eat.

In the fall we gathered mustard greens, turnips, and peas, the late-producing vegetables that had been planted in May and June. There were a few tomatoes left, but not many.

The garden changed with each season, except for winter, when it was finally at rest, replenishing itself for the months to come.

Gran was in the kitchen boiling purple hull peas and canning them as fast as she could. My mother was in the garden waiting for me.

'I wanted to go to town,' I said.

'Sorry, Luke. We have to hurry. Much more rain

422

and the greens'll rot. And what if the water reaches the garden?'

'They gonna buy some paint?'

'I don't know.'

'I wanted to go buy some more paint.'

'Maybe tomorrow. Right now we have to get these turnips out of the ground.' Her dress was pulled up to her knees.

She was barefoot with mud up to her ankles. I'd never seen my mother so dirty. I fell to the ground and attacked the turnips. Within minutes I was covered in mud from head to foot.

I pulled and picked vegetables for two hours, then cleaned them in the washtub on the back porch. Gran carried them into the kitchen, where they got cooked and packed away in quart jars.

The farm was quiet – no thunder or wind, no Spruills in the front or Mexicans out by the barn. We were alone again, just us Chandlers, left to battle the elements and to try to stay above water. I kept telling myself that life would be better when Ricky came home because I'd have someone to play with and talk to.

My mother hauled another basket of greens to the porch. She was tired and sweating, and she began cleaning herself with a rag and a bucket of water. She couldn't stand to be dirty, a trait she had been trying to pass along to me.

'Let's go to the barn,' she said. I hadn't been in the loft in six weeks, since the Mexicans had arrived.

'Sure,' I said, and we headed that way.

We spoke to Isabel, the milk cow, then climbed the ladder to the hayloft. My mother had worked hard to prepare a clean place for the Mexicans to live. She had spent the winter collecting old blankets and pillows for them to sleep on. She had taken a fan, one that for years had found good use on the front porch, and placed it in the loft. She had coerced my father into running an electrical line from the house to the barn.

'They're humans, regardless of what some people around here think,' I'd heard her say more than once.

The loft was as clean and neat as the day they'd arrived. The pillows and blankets were stacked near the fan. The floor had been swept. Not a piece of trash or litter could be found. She was quite proud of the Mexicans. She had treated them with respect, and they had returned the favor.

We shoved open the loft door, the same one Luis had stuck his head through when Hank was bombing the Mexicans with rocks and dirt clods, and we sat on the ledge with our feet hanging down. Thirty feet up, we had the best view of any place on our farm. The tree line far to the west was the St. Francis, and straight ahead, across our back field, was the water from Siler's Creek.

In places the water was almost to the tops of the cotton stalks. From this view we could much better appreciate the advancing flood. We could see it between the perfect rows running directly toward the barn, and we could see it over the main field road, seeping into the back forty.

If the St. Francis River left its banks, our house would be in danger.

'I guess we're done pickin',' I said.

'Sure looks like it,' she said, just a little sad.

424

'Why does our land flood so quick?'

'Because it's low and close to the river. It's not very good land, Luke, never will be. That's one reason we're leavin' here. There's not much of a future.'

'Where we goin'?'

'North. That's where the jobs are.'

'How long –'

'Not long. We'll stay until we can save some money. Your father'll work in the Buick plant with Jimmy Dale. They're payin' three dollars an hour. We'll make do, tough it out, you'll be in a school up there, a good school.'

'I don't want to go to a new school.'

'It'll be fun, Luke. They have big, nice schools up North.'

It didn't sound like fun. My friends were in Black Oak. Other than Jimmy Dale and Stacy, I didn't know a soul up North. My mother put her hand on my knee and rubbed it, as if this would make me feel better.

'Change is always difficult, Luke, but it can also be excitin'. Think of it as an adventure. You wanna play baseball for the Cardinals, don't you?'

'Yes ma'am.'

'Well, you'll have to leave home and go up North, live in a new house, make new friends, go to a new church. That'll be fun, won't it?'

'I guess so.'

Our bare feet were dangling, gently swinging back and forth. The sun was behind a cloud, and a breeze shifted into our faces. The trees along the edge of our field were changing colors to yellow and crimson, and leaves were falling.

'We can't stay here, Luke,' she said softly, as if her mind were already up North.

'When we come back what're we gonna do?'

'We're not gonna farm. We'll find a job in Memphis or Little Rock, and we'll buy us a house with a television and a telephone. We'll have a nice car in the driveway, and you can play baseball on a team with real uniforms. How does that sound?'

'Sounds pretty good.'

'We'll always come back and visit Pappy and Gran and Ricky. It'll be a new life, Luke, one that's far better than this.' She nodded toward the field, toward the ruined cotton out there drowning.

I thought of my Memphis cousins, the children of my father's sisters. They rarely came to Black Oak, only for funerals and maybe for Thanksgiving, and this was fine with me because they were city kids with nicer clothes and quicker tongues. I didn't particularly like them, but I was envious at the same time. They weren't rude or snobbish, they were just different enough to make me ill at ease. I decided then and there that when I lived in Memphis or Little Rock I would not, under any circumstances, act like I was better than anybody else.

'I have a secret, Luke,' my mother said.

Not another one. My troubled mind could not hold another secret. 'What is it?'

'I'm goin' to have a baby,' she said and smiled at me.

I couldn't help but smile, too. I enjoyed being the only child, but, truth was, I wanted somebody to play with.

'You are?'

426

'Yes. Next summer.'

'Can it be a boy?'

'I'll try, but no promises.'

'If you gotta have one, I'd like a little brother.'

'Are you excited?'

'Yes ma'am. Does Daddy know about it?'

'Oh yes, he's in on the deal.'

'Is he happy, too?'

'Very much so.'

'That's good.' It took some time to digest this, but I knew right away that it was a fine thing. All of my friends had brothers and sisters.

An idea hit, one that I couldn't shake. Since we were on the subject of having babies, I was overcome with an urge to unload one of my secrets. It seemed like a harmless one now, and an old one, too. So much had happened since Tally and I sneaked off to the Latchers' house that the episode was now sort of funny.

'I know all about how babies are born,' I said, a little defensively.

'Oh you do?'

'Yes ma'am.'

'How's that?'

'Can you keep a secret, too?'

'I certainly can.'

I began the story, laying sufficient blame on Tally for everything that might get me in trouble. She'd planned it. She'd begged me to go. She'd dared me. She'd done this and that. Once my mother realized where the story was leading, her eyes began to dance, and she said every so often, 'Luke, you didn't!'

I had her. I embellished here and there, to help

427

move the story and build tension, but for the most part I stuck to the facts. She was hooked.

'You saw me in the window?' she asked in disbelief.

'Yes ma'am. Gran, too, and Mrs. Latcher.'

'Did you see Libby?'

'No ma'am, but we sure heard her. Does it always hurt like that?'

'Well, not always. Keep going.'

I spared no detail. As Tally and I raced back to the farm, the headlights in pursuit, my mother clutched my elbow almost hard enough to break it. 'We had no idea!' she said.

'Of course not. I barely beat y'all in the house. Pappy was still snorin', and I was afraid y'all would come check on me and see that I was covered with sweat and dirt.'

'We were too tired.'

'It was a good thing. I slept about two hours, then Pappy woke me up to go to the fields. I've never been so sleepy in my life.'

'Luke, I can't believe you did that.' She wanted to scold, but she was too caught up in the story.

'It was fun.'

'You shouldn't have.'

'Tally made me do it.'

'Don't blame Tally.'

'I wouldn't've done it without her.'

'I can't believe the two of you did it,' she said, but I could tell she was impressed with the story. She grinned and shook her head in amazement. 'How often did y'all go roamin' around at night?'

'I think that was it.'

'You liked Tally, didn't you?'

428

'Yes ma'am. She was my friend.'

'I hope she's happy.'

'Me too.'

I missed her, but I hated to admit it to myself. 'Mom, do you think we'll see Tally up North?'

She smiled and said, 'No, I don't think so. Those cities up there – St. Louis, Chicago, Cleveland, Cincinnati – have millions of people. We'll never see her.'

I thought about the Cardinals and the Cubs and the Reds. I thought about Stan Musial racing around the bases in front of thirty thousand fans at Sportsman's Park. Since the teams were up North, then that was where I was headed anyway. Why not leave a few years early?

'I guess I'll go,' I said.

'It'll be fun, Luke,' she said again.

When Pappy and my father returned from town, they looked as though they'd been whipped. I guess they had. Their labor was gone, their cotton was soaked. If the sun broke through and the floodwaters receded, they didn't have enough hands to work the fields. And they weren't sure if the cotton would dry out. This time, the sun was not to be seen, and the water was still rising.

After Pappy went into the house, my father unloaded two gallons of paint and set them on the front porch. He did this without saying a word, though I was watching his every move. When he was finished, he went to the barn.

Two gallons would not paint the front of the house. I was irritated by this, then I realized why my father had not bought more. He didn't have the money. He and Pappy had paid the Mexicans, and there was nothing left.

I suddenly felt rotten because I had kept the painting alive after Trot had gone. I had pushed the project along, and in doing so had forced my father to spend what little money he had.

I stared at the two buckets set side by side, and tears came to my eyes. I hadn't realized how broke we were.

My father had poured his guts into the soil for six months, and now he had nothing to show for it. When the rains came, I, for some reason, had decided that the house should be painted.

My intentions had been good, I thought. So why did I feel so awful?

I got my brush, opened a can, and began the final phase of the job. As I slowly made the short strokes with my right hand, I wiped tears with my left.

Chapter 34

The first frost would kill what was left of our garden. It usually came in the middle of October, though the almanac that my father read as devoutly as he read the Bible had already missed its predicted date twice. Undaunted, he kept checking the almanac every morning with his first cup of coffee. It provided endless opportunities for worry.

Since we couldn't pick cotton, the garden got our attention. All five of us marched to it just after breakfast. My mother was certain that the frost was coming that very night and, if not, then for sure the next night. And so on.

For a miserable hour I pulled black-eyed peas off vines. Pappy, who hated garden work more than I did, was nearby picking butter beans and doing so with commendable effort. Gran was helping my mother pick the last of the tomatoes. My father hauled baskets back and forth, under the supervision of my mother. When he walked by me, I said, 'I really want to go paint.'

'Ask your mother,' he said.

I did, and she said I could after I picked one

more basket of peas. The garden was getting harvested like never before. By noon there wouldn't be a stray bean anywhere.

I soon returned to the solitude of house painting. With the clear exception of operating a road grader, it was a job I preferred over all others. The difference between the two was that I couldn't actually operate a road grader, and it would be years before I'd be able to. But I could certainly paint. After watching the Mexicans, I'd learned even more and improved my technique. I applied the paint as thinly as possible, trying my best to stretch the two gallons.

By mid-morning one bucket was empty. My mother and Gran were now in the kitchen, washing and canning the vegetables.

I didn't hear the man walk up behind me. But when he coughed to get my attention, I jerked around and dropped my paintbrush.

It was Mr. Latcher, wet and muddy from the waist down. He was barefoot, and his shirt was torn. He'd obviously walked from their place to ours.

'Where's Mr. Chandler?' he asked.

I wasn't sure which Mr. Chandler he wanted. I picked up my brush and ran to the east side of the house. I yelled for my father, who poked his head through some vines. When he saw Mr. Latcher beside me, he stood up quickly. 'What is it?' he asked as he hurried toward us.

Gran heard voices and was suddenly on the front porch, my mother right behind her. A glance at Mr. Latcher told us something was very wrong.

'The water's up in the house,' he said, unable to look my father in the eye. 'We gotta get out.'

My father looked at me, then at the women on the porch. Their wheels were already spinning.

'Can you help us?' Mr. Latcher said. 'We ain't got no place to go.'

I thought he was going to cry, and I felt like it myself.

'Of course we'll help,' Gran said, instantly taking charge of the situation. From that point on, my father would do precisely what his mother told him. So would the rest of us.

She sent me to find Pappy. He was in the toolshed, trying to stay busy puttering with an old tractor battery. Everyone gathered by the truck to formulate a plan.

'Can we drive up to the house?' Pappy asked.

'No sir,' Mr. Latcher said. 'Water's waist-deep down our road. It's up on the porch now, six inches in the house.'

I couldn't imagine all those Latcher kids in a house with half a foot of floodwater.

'How's Libby and the baby?' Gran asked, unable to contain herself.

'Libby's fine. The baby's sick.'

'We'll need a boat,' my father said. 'Jeter keeps one up at the Cockleburr Slough.'

'He won't mind if we borrow it,' Pappy said.

For a few minutes the men discussed the rescue – how to get the boat, how far down the road the truck could go, how many trips it would take. What was not mentioned was just exactly where the Latchers would go once they had been rescued from their house.

433

Again Gran was very much in charge. 'You folks can stay here,' she said to Mr. Latcher. 'Our loft is clean – the Mexicans just left. You'll have a warm bed and plenty of food.'

I looked at her. Pappy looked at her. My father glanced over, then studied his feet. A horde of hungry Latchers living in our barn! A sick baby crying at all hours of the night. Our food being given away. I was horrified at the thought, and I was furious with Gran for making such an offer without first discussing it with the rest of us.

Then I looked at Mr. Latcher. His lips were trembling, and his eyes were wet. He clutched his old straw hat with both hands at his waist, and he was so ashamed that he just looked at the ground. I'd never seen a poorer, dirtier, or more broken man.

I looked at my mother. She, too, had wet eyes. I glanced at my father. I'd never seen him cry, and he wasn't about to at that moment, but he was clearly touched by Mr. Latcher's suffering. My hard heart melted in a flash.

'Let's get a move on,' Gran said with authority. 'We'll get the barn ready.'

We sprang into action, the men loading into the truck, the women heading for the barn. Just as she was walking away, Gran pulled Pappy by the elbow and whispered, 'You bring Libby and that baby first.' It was a direct order, and Pappy nodded.

I hopped into the back of the truck with Mr. Latcher, who squatted on his skinny legs and said nothing to me. We stopped at the bridge, where my father got out and began walking along the edge of the river. His job was to find Mr. Jeter's boat at the Cockleburr Slough, then float it downstream to where we'd be waiting at the bridge. We crossed over, turned onto the Latchers' road, and went less than a hundred feet before we came to a quagmire. Ahead of us was nothing but water.

'I'll tell 'em you're comin',' Mr. Latcher said, and with that he was off through the mud, then the water. Before long it was up to his knees. 'Watch out for snakes!' he yelled over his shoulder. 'They're everywhere.' He was trudging through a lake of water, with flooded fields on both sides.

We watched him until he disappeared, then we returned to the river and waited for my father.

We sat on a log near the bridge, the rushing water below us. Since we had nothing to say, I decided it was time to tell Pappy a story. First, I swore him to secrecy.

I began where it started, with voices in our front yard late at night. The Spruills were arguing, Hank was leaving. I followed in the shadows, and before I knew what was happening, I was trailing not only Hank but Cowboy as well. 'They fought right up there,' I said, pointing to the center of the bridge.

Pappy's mind was no longer on floods or farming or even rescuing the Latchers. He glared at me, believing every word but quite astonished. I recounted the fight in vivid detail, then pointed again. 'Hank landed over there, right in the middle of the river. Never came up.'

Pappy grunted but did not speak. I was on my feet in front of him, nervous and talking rapidly.

When I described my encounter with Cowboy minutes later on the road near our house, Pappy cursed under his breath. 'You should've told me then,' he said.

'I just couldn't. I was too scared.'

He got to his feet and walked around the log a few times. 'He murdered their son and stole their daughter,' he said to himself. 'My oh my.'

'What're we gonna do, Pappy?'

'Let me think about it.'

'Do you think Hank'll float to the top somewhere?'

'Nope. That Mexican gutted him. His body sank straight to the bottom, probably got eaten by those channel cats down there. There's nothin' left to find.'

As sickening as this was, I was somewhat relieved to hear it. I never wanted to see Hank again. I'd thought about him every time I crossed the bridge. I'd dreamed of his bloated corpse popping up from the depths of the river and scaring the daylights out of me.

'Did I do anything wrong?' I asked.

'No.'

'Are you gonna tell anybody?'

'Nope, I don't think so. Let's keep it quiet. We'll talk about it later.'

We took our positions on the log and studied the water. Pappy was deep in thought. I tried to convince myself that I should feel better now that I'd finally told one of the adults about Hank's death.

After a spell Pappy said, 'Hank got what was comin' to him. We ain't tellin' nobody. You're the

436

only witness, and there's no sense in you worryin' about it. It'll be our secret, one we'll take to our graves.'

'What about Mr and Mrs. Spruill?'

'What they don't know won't hurt 'em.'

'You gonna tell Gran?'

'Nope. Nobody. Just me and you.'

It was a partnership I could trust. I did indeed feel better. I'd shared my secret with a friend who could certainly carry his portion of it. And we had decided that Hank and Cowboy would be put behind us forever.

My father finally arrived in Mr. Jeter's flat-bottomed johnboat. The outboard was missing, but navigation was easy because of the strong current. He used a paddle as a rudder and came ashore under the bridge, right below us. He and Pappy then lifted the boat from the river and manhandled it up the bank to the truck. Then we drove back to the Latchers' road, where we unloaded the boat and shoved it to the edge of the floodwaters. All three of us hopped in, our feet covered with mud. The adults paddled as we moved along the narrow road, two feet above the ground, rows of ruined cotton passing by.

The farther we went, the deeper the water became. The wind picked up and blew us into the cotton. Both Pappy and my father looked at the sky and shook their heads.

Every Latcher was on the front porch, waiting in fear, watching every move we made as the boat cut through the lake that surrounded their house. The front steps were submerged. At least a foot of water covered the porch. We maneuvered the boat up to the front of the house, where Mr. Latcher took it and pulled it in. He was chest-deep in the water.

I looked at all of the frightened and sad faces on the porch. Their clothes were even more ragged than the last time I'd been there. They were skinny and gaunt, probably starving. I saw a couple of smiles from the younger ones, and I suddenly felt very important. From out of the crowd stepped Libby Latcher, holding the baby, who was wrapped in an old blanket. I'd never actually seen Libby before, and I couldn't believe how pretty she was. Her light brown hair was long and pulled tightly behind in a ponytail. Her eyes were pale blue and had a glow to them. She was tall and as skinny as the rest. When she stepped into the boat, both Pappy and my father steadied her. She sat beside me with her baby, and suddenly I was face-to-face with my newest cousin.

'I'm Luke,' I said, though it was an odd time to make introductions.

'I'm Libby,' she said, with a smile that made my heart race. Her baby was asleep. He had not grown much since I'd seen him in the window the night he was born. He was tiny and wrinkled and likely hungry, but Gran was waiting for him.

Rayford Latcher came aboard and sat as far away from me as possible. He was one of the three who'd beaten me the last time I was on their property. Percy, the oldest boy and the ringleader of that assault, was hiding on the porch. Two more children were put into the boat, then Mr. Latcher jumped in. 'We'll be back in a few minutes,' he said to Mrs. Latcher and the others still on the porch. They looked as if they were being left to die.

The rain hit fast, and the winds shifted. Pappy and my father paddled as hard as they could, but the boat barely moved. Mr. Latcher jumped into the water, and for a second he completely vanished. Then he found his footing and stood up, covered from the chest down in water. He grabbed a rope attached to the bow and began pulling us down the road.

The wind kept blowing us into the cotton, so my father crawled out of the boat and began pushing from the rear. 'Watch for snakes,' Mr. Latcher warned again. Both men were soaking wet.

'Percy almost got bit by one,' Libby said to me. 'It floated up on the porch.' She was leaning over the baby, trying to keep him dry.

'What's his name?' I asked.

'Don't have one yet.'

I'd never heard of such nonsense. A baby without a name. Most of the ones born into the Baptist Church had two or three names before they ever got into the world.

'When's Ricky coming home?' she whispered.

'I don't know.'

'Is he okay?'

'Yes.'

She seemed anxious for any news about him, and this made me uncomfortable. However, it was not unpleasant sitting next to such a pretty girl who wanted to whisper to me. Her younger siblings were wild-eyed with the adventure.

As we neared the road, the water became shallow and the boat finally hit mud. We all scrambled out, and the Latchers were loaded into our truck. Pappy got behind the wheel.

'Luke, you stay with me,' my father said. As the truck backed away, Mr. Latcher and my father turned the boat around and began pushing and pulling it back to the house. The wind was so strong they had to lean into it. I rode alone, with my head bowed, trying to stay dry. The rain came down in cold pellets that grew harder by the minute.

The lake around the house was churning as we drew close. Mr. Latcher pulled the boat in again and began yelling instructions to his wife. A small Latcher was handed down from the porch and almost dropped when a gust of wind hit the boat and knocked it away. Percy thrust forward a broom handle, which I grabbed to help pull the boat back to the porch. My father was yelling this and that, and Mr. Latcher was doing the same. There were four remaining children, and all of them wanted to board at once. I helped them in, one at a time. 'Steady, Luke!' my father said a dozen times.

When the children were in the boat, Mrs. Latcher flung over a burlap sack stuffed with what appeared to be clothing. I figured it was a collection of their only possessions. It landed at my feet, and I clutched it as if it had a lot of value. Next to me was a shoeless little Latcher girl – not a one of them had shoes – with no sleeves on her shirt to cover her arms. She was freezing, and she clung to my leg as if she might be taken away by the wind. She had tears in her eyes, but when I looked at her she said, 'Thank you.' Mrs. Latcher climbed in, stepping among her children, yelling at her husband because he was yelling at her. With the boat fully loaded and all the Latchers accounted for, we turned around and headed back toward the road. Those of us on board cowered low to shield our faces from the rain.

My father and Mr. Latcher labored furiously to push the boat against the wind. In places they were only knee-deep in water, but within a few steps it would be up to their chests, making it hard for them to get any leverage. They fought to keep us in the center of the road and out of the cotton. The return leg of our little voyage was much slower.

Pappy wasn't waiting. He had not had enough time to drop off the first load and come back for the second. When we got to the mud, my father tied Mr. Jeter's johnboat to a fence post, then said, 'No sense waitin' here.' We trudged through more mud and fought the wind and rain until we came to the river. The Latcher children were terrified of the bridge, and I'd never heard such bawling as we crossed over. They clung to their parents. Mr. Latcher was now carrying the burlap sack. Halfway over the St. Francis, I looked down at the planks in front of me and noticed that, like her children, Mrs. Latcher had no shoes.

When we were safe on our side of the river, we saw Pappy coming to get us.

Gran and my mother were waiting on the back porch, where they had set up a makeshift assembly line of sorts. They welcomed the second wave of Latchers and directed them to the far end of the porch, where there was a pile of clothes. The

Latchers stripped down, some concerned about privacy, others not, and got dressed in Chandler hand-me-downs that had been in the family for decades. Once outfitted in dry, warm clothing, they were ushered into the kitchen, where there was enough food for several meals. Gran had sausage and country ham. She'd made two pans of homemade biscuits. The table was covered with large bowls filled with every vegetable my mother had grown in the last six months.

The Latchers packed around the table, all ten of them – the baby was asleep somewhere. For the most part they were silent, and I couldn't tell if it was because they were ashamed or relieved or just downright hungry. They passed around the bowls and occasionally said thanks to one another. My mother and Gran poured tea and made a fuss over them. I observed them from a doorway. Pappy and my father were on the front porch, sipping coffee and watching the rain dwindle down.

When the meal was well under way, we drifted to the living room, where Gran had built a fire in the fireplace. The five of us sat close to it, and for a long time we listened to the Latchers in the kitchen. Their voices were muted, but their knives and forks rattled away. They were warm and safe and no longer hungry. How could people be so poor?

I found it impossible to dislike the Latchers anymore. They were folks just like us who'd had the misfortune of being born sharecroppers. It was wrong of me to be scornful. Besides, I was quite taken with Libby.

I was already hoping that perhaps she liked me.

As we were basking in the satisfaction of our goodness, the baby erupted from somewhere in the house. Gran jumped to her feet and was gone in a flash. 'I'll see about him,' I heard her say in the kitchen. 'You finish lunch.'

I didn't hear a single Latcher move from the table. That baby had been crying since the night he was born, and they were used to it.

We Chandlers, however, were not. It cried all the way through what was left of lunch. Gran walked the floor with it for an hour as my parents and Pappy moved the Latchers into their new accommodations in the loft. Libby returned with them to check on the baby, who was still bawling. The rain had stopped, so my mother took it for a walk around the house, but the outdoors did nothing to satisfy it. I had never heard anything cry so violently without end.

By mid-afternoon we were rattled. Gran had tried several of her home remedies, mild little concoctions that only made matters worse. Libby rocked the baby in the swing, with no success. Gran sang to it as she waltzed around the house; more bawling, even louder, I thought. My mother walked the floor with it. Pappy and my father were long gone. I wanted to run and hide in the silo.

'Worst case of colic I've ever seen,' I heard Gran say.

Later, while Libby was again rocking the baby on the front porch, I heard another conversation. Seems that when I was a baby I'd had a rough bout with colic. My mother's mother, my grandmother, who was now dead and who'd lived in town in a painted house, had given me a few bites of vanilla ice cream. I had immediately stopped crying, and within a few days the colic was gone.

At some point later in my babyhood I'd had another bout. Gran did not normally keep store-bought ice cream in her freezer. My parents had loaded me up in the truck and headed for town. Along the way I'd stopped crying and fallen asleep. They figured the motion of the moving vehicle had done the trick.

My mother sent me to find my father. She took the baby from Libby, who was quite anxious to get rid of it, and before long we were heading for the truck.

'Are we goin' to town?' I asked.

'Yes,' my mother said.

'What about him?' my father asked, pointing to the baby. 'He's supposed to be a secret.'

My mother had forgotten about that. If we were spotted in town with a mysterious baby, the gossip would be so thick it would stop traffic.

'We'll worry about that when we get there,' she said, then slammed the door. 'Let's go.'

My father cranked the engine and shifted into reverse. I was in the middle, the baby just inches from my shoulder. After a brief pause, the baby erupted again. By the time we got to the river I was ready to pitch the damned thing out the window.

Once over the bridge, though, a curious thing happened. The baby slowly grew quiet and still. It closed its mouth and eyes and fell sound asleep. My mother smiled at my father as if to say, 'See, I told you so.'

As we made our way to town, my parents whispered back and forth. They decided that my mother would get out of the truck down by our church, then hurry to Pop and Pearl's to buy the ice cream. They worried that Pearl would be suspicious as to why she was buying ice cream, and only ice cream, since we didn't need anything else at the moment, and why exactly my mother was in town on a Wednesday afternoon. They agreed that Pearl's curiosity could not be satisfied under any circumstances and that it would be somewhat amusing to let her suffer from her own nosiness. As clever as she was, Pearl would never guess that the ice cream was for an illegitimate baby we were hiding in our truck.

We stopped at our church. No one was watching so my mother handed the baby to me with strict instructions on how to properly cradle such a creature. By the time she closed the door, its mouth was wide open, its eyes glowing, its lungs filled with anger. It wailed twice and nearly scared me to death before my father popped the clutch and we were off again, loose on the streets of Black Oak. The baby looked at me and stopped crying.

'Just don't stop,' I said to my father.

We drove by the gin, a depressing sight with its lack of activity. We circled behind the Methodist church and the school, then turned south onto Main Street. My mother came out of Pop and Pearl's with a small paper bag, and, not surprisingly, Pearl was right behind her, talking away. They were chatting as we drove past. My father waved as if nothing were out of the ordinary.

I just knew we were about to get caught with the Latcher baby. One loud shriek from its mouth and the whole town would learn our secret.

We looped around the gin again, and when we headed toward the church we saw my mother waiting for us. As we rolled to a stop to get her, the baby's eyes came open. His lower lip trembled. He was ready to scream when I thrust him at her and said, 'Here, take him.'

I scrambled out of the truck before she could get in. My quickness surprised them. 'Where you goin', Luke?' my father demanded.

'Y'all ride around for a minute. I need to buy some paint.'

'Get in the truck!' he said.

The baby cried out, and my mother quickly jumped in. I ducked behind the truck and ran as fast as I could toward the street.

Behind me I heard another cry, one not nearly as loud, then the truck started moving.

I ran to the hardware store, back to the paint counter, where I asked the clerk for three gallons of white Pittsburgh Paint.

'Only got two,' he said.

I was too surprised to say anything. How could a hardware store run out of paint? 'I should have some in by next Monday,' he said.

'Gimme two,' I said.

I was sure two gallons wouldn't finish the front of the house, but I gave him six one-dollar bills, and he handed me the change. 'Let me get these for you,' he said.

'No, I can do it,' I said, reaching for the two buckets. I strained to lift them, then waddled down the aisle, almost tipping over. I lugged them out of the store and to the sidewalk. I looked both ways for traffic, and I listened for the wail of a sick baby. Thankfully the town was quiet.

Pearl reappeared on the sidewalk in front of her store, eyes darting in all directions. I hid behind a parked car. Then I saw our truck coming south, barely moving, looking very suspicious. My father saw me and rolled to a stop in the middle of the street. I yanked the two buckets up with all the might I could muster and ran to the truck. He jumped out to help me. I leapt into the back of the truck, and he handed me the paint. I preferred to ride back there, away from the littlest Latcher. Just when my father got behind the wheel again, the baby let out a yelp.

The truck lurched forward, and the baby was quiet. I yelled, 'Howdy, Pearl!' as we sped past.

Libby was sitting on the front steps with Gran, waiting for us. When the truck stopped, the baby began bawling. The women rushed it to the kitchen, where they began stuffing it with ice cream.

'Ain't enough gasoline in Craighead County to keep that thing quiet,' my father said.

Fortunately, the ice cream soothed it. Little Latcher fell asleep in his mother's arms.

Because vanilla ice cream had worked when I'd had colic, this cure was taken as further evidence that the baby was part Chandler. I was not exactly comforted by this.

Chapter 35

Having a barn full of Latchers was an event that we certainly had not planned on. And while we were at first comforted by our own Christian charity and neighborliness, we were soon interested in how long they might be with us. I broached the subject first over supper when, after a long discussion about the day's events, I said, 'Reckon how long they'll stay?'

Pappy had the opinion that they would be gone as soon as the flood-waters receded. Living in another farmer's barn was tolerable under the most urgent of circumstances, but no one with an ounce of self-respect would stay a day longer than necessary.

'What are they gonna eat when they go back?' Gran asked. 'There's not a crumb of food left in that house.' She went on to predict that they'd be with us until springtime.

My father speculated that their dilapidated house couldn't withstand the flood, and that there'd be no place for them to return to. Plus, they had no truck, no means of transportation. They'd been starving on their land for the last ten

448

years. Where else would they go? Pappy seemed a little depressed by this view.

My mother mainly listened, but at one point she did say that the Latchers were not the type of people who'd be embarrassed by living in someone else's barn. And she worried about the children, not only the obvious problems of health and nutrition, but also their education and spiritual growth.

Pappy's prediction of a swift departure was batted around the table and eventually voted down. Three against one. Four, if you counted my vote.

'We'll survive,' Gran said. 'We have enough food to feed us and them all winter. They're here, they have no place else to go, and we'll take care of them.' No one was about to argue with her.

'God gave us a bountiful garden for a reason,' she added, nodding at my mother. 'In Luke, Jesus said, "Invite the poor, the crippled, the lame, the blind, and you will be blessed."'

'We'll kill two hogs instead of one,' Pappy said. 'We'll have plenty of meat for the winter.'

The hog-killing would come in early December, when the air was cold and the bacteria dead. Every year a hog was shot in the head, dipped in boiling water, and hung from a tree next to the toolshed, then gutted and butchered into a thousand pieces. From it we got bacon, ham, loin, sausage, and ribs. Everything was used – tongue, brains, feet. 'Everything but the squeal' was a line I'd heard all my life. Mr. Jeter from across the road was a fair butcher. He would supervise the gutting, then

449

perform the delicate removals. For his time he took a fourth of the best cuts.

My first memory of a hog-killing was that I ran behind the house and puked. With time, though, I'd come to look forward to it. If you wanted ham and bacon, you had to kill a hog. But it would take more than two hogs to feed the Latchers until spring. There were eleven of them, including the baby, who at the moment was living off vanilla ice cream.

As we talked about them, I began to dream of heading North.

The trip now seemed more appealing. I had sympathy for the Latchers, and I was proud that we'd rescued them. I knew that as Christians we were expected to help the poor. I understood all that, but I could not imagine living through the winter with all those little kids running around our farm. I'd start back to school very soon. Would the Latchers go with me? Since they would be new students, would I be expected to show them around? What would my friends think? I saw nothing but humiliation.

And now that they lived with us, it was just a matter of time before the big secret got out. Ricky would be fingered as the father. Pearl would figure out where all the vanilla ice cream was going. Something would leak somehow, and we'd be ruined.

'Luke, are you finished?' my father asked, jolting me from my thoughts.

My plate was clean. Everyone looked at it. They had adult matters to discuss. It was my cue to go find something to do.

'Supper was good. May I be excused?' I said, reciting my standard lines.

Gran nodded and I went to the back porch and pushed the screen door so that it would slam. Then I slid back into the darkness to a bench by the kitchen door. From there I could hear everything. They were worried about money. The crop loan would be 'rolled over' until next spring, and they would deal with it then. The other farming bills could be delayed, too, though Pappy hated the thought of riding his creditors.

Surviving the winter was much more urgent. Food was not a concern. We had to have money for such necessities as electricity, gas and oil for the truck, and staples like coffee, flour, and sugar. What if someone got sick and needed a doctor or medicine? What if the truck broke down and needed parts?

'We haven't given anything to the church this year,' Gran said.

Pappy estimated that as much as thirty percent of the crop was still out there, standing in water. If the weather broke and things got dry, we might be able to salvage a small portion of it. That would provide some income, but the gin would keep most of it. Neither he nor my father was optimistic about picking any more cotton in 1952.

The problem was cash. They were almost out of it, and there was no hope of any coming in. They barely had enough to pay for electricity and gasoline until Christmas.

'Jimmy Dale's holdin' a job for me at the Buick plant,' my father said. 'But he can't wait long. The jobs are tight right now. We need to get on up there.'

According to Jimmy Dale, the current wage was three dollars an hour, for forty hours a week, but overtime was available, too. 'He says I can earn close to two hundred dollars a week,' my father said.

'We'll send home as much as we can,' my mother added.

Pappy and Gran went through the motions of protesting, but everyone knew the decision had been made. I heard a noise in the distance, a vaguely familiar sound. As it drew closer, I cringed and wished I'd hidden on the front porch.

The baby was back, upset again and no doubt craving vanilla ice cream. I sneaked off the porch and walked a few steps toward the barn. In the shadows I saw Libby and Mrs. Latcher approaching the house. I ducked beside the chicken coop and listened as they went by. The constant wailing echoed around our farm.

Gran and my mother met them at the back porch. A light was switched on, and I watched as they huddled around the little monster then carried him inside. Through the window I could see my father and Pappy scramble for the front porch.

With four women working on him, it took only a few minutes to stop the crying. Once things were quiet Libby left the kitchen and went outside. She sat on the edge of the porch in the same place Cowboy had occupied the day he had shown me his switchblade. I walked to the house and said, 'Hi, Libby,' when I was a few feet away.

452

She jumped, then caught herself. Poor girl's nerves were rattled by her baby's colic. 'Luke,' she said. 'What're you doin'?'

'Nothin'.'

'Come sit here,' she said, patting the spot next to her. I did as I was told.

'Does that baby cry all the time?' I asked.

'Seems like it. I don't mind, though.'

'You don't?'

'No. He reminds me of Ricky.'

'He does?'

'Yes, he does. When's he comin' home? Do you know, Luke?'

'No. His last letter said he might be home by Christmas.'

'That's two months away.'

'Yeah, but I ain't so sure about it. Gran says every soldier says he's comin' home by Christmas.'

'I just can't wait,' she said, visibly excited by the prospect.

'What's gonna happen when he gets home?' I asked, not sure if I wanted to hear her answer.

'We're gonna get married,' she said with a big, pretty smile. Her eyes were filled with wonder and anticipation.

'You are?'

'Yes, he promised.'

I certainly didn't want Ricky to get married. He belonged to me. We would fish and play baseball, and he'd tell war stories. He'd be my big brother, not somebody's husband.

'He's the sweetest thang,' she said, gazing up at the sky.

Ricky was a lot of things, but I'd never call him

sweet. Then again, there was no telling what he'd done to impress her.

'You can't tell anybody, Luke,' she said, suddenly serious. 'It's our secret.'

That's my specialty, I felt like saying. 'Don't worry,' I said, 'I can keep one.'

'Can you read and write, Luke?'

'Sure can. Can you?'

'Pretty good.'

'But you don't go to school.'

'I went through the fourth grade, then my mother kept havin' all them babies, so I had to quit. I've written Ricky a letter, tellin' him all about the baby. Do you have his address?'

I wasn't sure Ricky wanted to receive her letter, and for a second I thought about playing dumb. But I couldn't help but like Libby. She was so crazy about Ricky that it seemed wrong not to give her the address.

'Yeah, I got it.'

'Do you have an envelope?'

'Sure.'

'Could you mail my letter for me? Please, Luke. I don't think Ricky knows about our baby.'

Something told me to butt out. This was between them. 'I guess I can mail it,' I said.

'Oh, thank you, Luke,' she said, almost squealing. She hugged my neck hard. 'I'll give you the letter tomorrow,' she said. 'And you promise you'll mail it for me?'

'I promise.' I thought about Mr. Thornton at the post office and how curious he'd be if he saw a letter from Libby Latcher to Ricky in Korea. I'd figure it out somehow. Perhaps I should ask my mother about it.

The women brought baby Latcher to the back porch, where Gran rocked it while it slept. My mother and Mrs. Latcher talked about how tired the little fellow was – all that nonstop crying had worn it out – so that when it did fall off, it slept hard. I was soon bored with all the talk about the baby.

My mother woke me just after sunrise, and instead of scolding me out of bed to face another day on the farm, she sat next to my pillow and talked. 'We're leavin' tomorrow mornin', Luke. I'm going to pack today. Your father will help you paint the front of the house, so you'd better get started.'

'Is it rainin'?' I asked, sitting up.

'No. It's cloudy, but you can paint.'

'Why are we leavin' tomorrow?'

'It's time to go.'

'When're we comin' back?'

'I don't know. Go eat your breakfast. We have a busy day.'

I started painting before seven, with the sun barely above the tree line in the east. The grass was wet and so was the house, but I had no choice. Before long, though, the boards dried, and my work went smoothly. My father joined me, and together we moved the scaffold so he could reach the high places. Then Mr. Latcher found us, and after watching the painting for a few minutes he said, 'I'd like to help.'

'You don't have to,' my father said from eight feet up.

'I'd like to earn my keep,' he said. He had nothing else to do.

'All right. Luke, go fetch that other brush.'

I ran to the toolshed, delighted that I'd once again attracted some free labor. Mr. Latcher began painting with a fury, as if to prove his worth.

A crowd gathered to watch. I counted seven Latchers on the ground behind us, all of the kids except Libby and the baby, just sitting there studying us with blank looks on their faces.

I figured they were waiting for breakfast. I ignored them and went about my work.

Work, however, would prove difficult. Pappy came for me first. He said he wanted to ride down to the creek to inspect the flood. I said I really needed to paint. My father said, 'Go ahead, Luke,' and that settled my protest.

We rode the tractor away from the house, through the flooded fields until the water was almost over the front wheels. When we could go no farther, Pappy turned off the engine. We sat for a long time on the tractor, surrounded by the wet cotton we'd worked so hard to grow.

'You'll be leavin' tomorrow,' he finally said.

'Yes sir.'

'But you'll be comin' back soon.'

'Yes sir.' My mother, not Pappy, would determine when we came back. And if Pappy thought we'd one day return to our little places on the family farm and start another crop, he was mistaken. I felt sorry for him, and I missed him already.

'Been thinkin' more 'bout Hank and Cowboy,' he said, his eyes never moving from the water in front of the tractor. 'Let's leave it be, like we agreed. Can't nothin' good come from tellin' anybody. It's a secret we'll take to our graves.' He offered his right hand for me to shake. 'Deal?' he said.

'Deal,' I repeated, squeezing his thick, callused hand.

'Don't forget about your pappy up there, you hear?'

'I won't.'

He started the tractor, shifted into reverse, and backed through the floodwaters.

When I returned to the front of the house, Percy Latcher had taken control of my brush and was hard at work. Without a word, he handed it to me and went to sit under a tree. I painted for maybe ten minutes, then Gran walked onto the porch and said, 'Luke, come here. I need to show you somethin'.'

She led me around back, in the direction of the silo. Mud puddles were everywhere, and the flood had crept to within thirty feet of the barn. She wanted to take a stroll and have a chat, but there was mud and water in every direction. We sat on the edge of the flatbed trailer.

'What're you gonna show me?' I said after a long silence.

'Oh, nothin'. I just wanted to spend a few minutes alone. You're leavin' tomorrow. I was tryin' to remember if you'd ever spent a night away from here.'

'I can't remember one,' I said. I knew that I'd been born in the bedroom where my parents now slept. I knew Gran's hands had touched me first, she'd birthed me and taken care of my mother. No, I had never left our house, not even for one night.

'You'll do just fine up North,' she said, but with little conviction. 'Lots of folks from here go up there to find work. They always do just fine, and they always come home. You'll be home before you know it.'

I loved my gran as fiercely as any kid could love his grandmother, yet somehow I knew I'd never again live in her house and work in her fields.

We talked about Ricky for a while, then about the Latchers. She put her arm around my shoulders and held me close, and she made me promise more than once that I'd write letters to her. I also had to promise to study hard, obey my parents, go to church and learn my Scriptures, and to be diligent in my speech so I wouldn't sound like a Yankee.

When she was finished extracting all the promises, I was exhausted. We walked back to the house, dodging puddles.

The morning dragged on. The Latcher horde dispersed after breakfast, but they were back in time for lunch. They watched as my father and their father tried to outpaint each other across the front of our house.

We fed them on the back porch. After they ate, Libby pulled me aside and handed over her letter to Ricky. I had managed to sneak a plain white envelope from the supply we kept at the end of the kitchen table. I'd addressed it to Ricky, via the army mail route in San Diego, and I'd put a stamp on it. She was quite impressed. She carefully placed her letter inside, then licked the envelope twice.

'Thank you, Luke,' she said and kissed me on the forehead.

I put the envelope under my shirt so no one could see it. I had decided to mention it to my mother but hadn't found the opportunity.

Events were moving quickly. My mother and Gran spent the afternoon washing and pressing the clothes we would take with us. My father and Mr. Latcher painted until the buckets were empty. I wanted time to slow down, but for some reason the day became hurried.

We endured another quiet supper, each of us worried about the trip North, but for different reasons. I was sad enough to have no appetite.

'This'll be your last supper here for a spell, Luke,' Pappy said. I don't know why he said that, because it sure didn't help matters.

'They say the food up North is pretty bad,' Gran said, trying to lighten things up. That, too, fell flat.

It was too chilly to sit on the porch. We gathered in the living room and tried to chat as if things were the same. But no topic seemed appropriate. Church matters were dull. Baseball was over. No one wanted to mention Ricky. Not even the weather could hold our attention.

We finally gave up and went to bed. My mother tucked me in and kissed me good night. Then Gran did the same. Pappy stopped for a few words, something he'd never done before.

When I was finally alone, I said my prayers. Then I stared at the dark ceiling and tried to believe that this was my last night on the farm.

459

Chapter 36

My father had been wounded in Italy in 1944. He was treated there, then on a hospital boat, then shipped to Boston, where he spent time in physical rehabilitation. When he arrived at the bus station in Memphis, he had two US Army duffel bags stuffed with clothes and a few souvenirs. Two months later he married my mother. Ten months after that, I arrived on the scene.

I'd never seen the duffel bags. To my knowledge they hadn't been used since the war. When I walked into the living room early the next morning, they were both half-filled with clothing, and my mother was busy arranging the other necessities to be packed. The sofa was covered with her dresses, quilts, and some shirts she'd pressed the day before. I asked her about the duffel bags, and she told me that they'd spent the last eight years in a storage attic above the toolshed.

'Now hurry and eat breakfast,' she said, folding a towel.

Gran was holding nothing back for our final meal. Eggs, sausage, ham, grits, fried potatoes, baked tomatoes, and biscuits. 'It's a long bus ride,' she said.

'How long?' I asked. I was sitting at the table, waiting for my first cup of coffee. The men were out of the house somewhere.

'Your father said eighteen hours. Heaven knows when you'll get a good meal again.' She delicately placed the coffee in front of me, then kissed me on the head. For Gran, the only good meal was one cooked in her kitchen with ingredients that came straight off the farm.

The men had already eaten. Gran sat next to me with her coffee and watched as I plowed into the feast she'd laid on the table. We went through the promises again – to write letters, to obey my parents, to read the Bible, to say my prayers, to be diligent so as not to become a Yankee. It was a virtual roll call of commandments. I chewed my food and nodded at the appropriate moments.

She explained that my mother would need help when the new baby arrived. There would be other Arkansas people up there in Flint, good Baptist souls who could be depended on, but I had to help with chores around the house.

'What kind of chores?' I asked with a mouthful of food. I'd thought the notion of chores was confined to the farm. I'd thought I was leaving them behind.

'Just house stuff,' she said, suddenly vague. Gran had never spent a night in a city. She had no idea where we would be living, nor did we. 'You just be helpful when the baby gets here,' she said.

'What if it cries like that Latcher baby?' I asked.

'It won't. No baby has ever cried like that.'

461

My mother passed through with a load of clothes. Her steps were quick. She'd been dreaming of this day for years. Pappy and Gran and perhaps even my father thought that our leaving was just a temporary departure. To my mother it was a milestone. The day was a turning point not only in her life but especially in mine. She had convinced me at an early age that I would not be a farmer, and in leaving we were cutting ties.

Pappy wandered into the kitchen and poured himself a cup of coffee. He sat in his chair at the end of the table, next to Gran, and watched me eat. He was not good at greetings, and he certainly couldn't handle farewells. The less said the better in his book.

When I had stuffed myself to the point of being uncomfortable, Pappy and I walked to the front porch. My father was hauling the duffel bags to the truck. He was dressed in starched khaki work pants, a starched white shirt, no overalls. My mother was wearing a pretty Sunday dress. We didn't want to look like refugees from the cotton fields of Arkansas.

Pappy led me into the front yard, down to a point where second base used to be, and from there we turned and looked at the house. It glowed in the clear morning sun. 'Good job, Luke,' he said. 'You done a good job.'

'Just wish we'd finished,' I said. To the far right, at the corner where Trot had begun, there was an unpainted section. We'd stretched the last four gallons as far as possible and had come up a little short.

'I figure another half gallon,' Pappy said.

'Yes sir. That's about right.'

'I'll get it done this winter,' he said.

'Thanks, Pappy.'

'When y'all come home, it'll be finished.'

'I'd like that.'

We all converged at the truck, and everyone hugged Gran for the last time. For a second I thought she was going to run through the list of promises again, but she was too choked up. We got ourselves loaded – Pappy behind the wheel, me in the middle, my mother by the window, my father in the back with the duffel bags – and we backed onto the road.

When we pulled away, Gran was sitting on the front steps, wiping her face. My father had told me not to cry, but I couldn't help it. I clutched my mother's arm and hid my face.

We stopped in Black Oak. My father had a small matter at the Co-op. I wanted to say good-bye to Pearl. My mother had Libby's letter to Ricky, which she took to the post office and sent on its way. She and I had discussed it at length, and she, too, felt that it was none of our business. If Libby wanted to write a letter to Ricky and break the news about their baby, we shouldn't stop her.

Pearl, of course, knew we were leaving. She hugged my neck until I thought it was going to break, then she produced a small paper sack filled with candy. 'You'll need this for the trip,' she said. I gawked at the endless supply of chocolate and mints and jawbreakers in the bag. The trip was already a success. Pop appeared, shook my hand as if I were an adult, and wished me luck.

I hurried back to the truck with my candy and

showed it to Pappy, who was still behind the wheel. My parents came back quickly, too. We were not in the mood for a grand send-off. Our leaving was due to frustration and crop failure. We weren't exactly anxious for the town to know we were fleeing North. It was mid-morning, though, and the town was still quiet.

I watched the fields along the highway to Jonesboro. They were as wet as ours. The road ditches were overflowing with brown water. The creeks and streams were over their banks.

We passed the gravel road where Pappy and I had waited to find hill people. There we had met the Spruills, and I had seen Hank and Tally and Trot for the first time. If another farmer had been there earlier, or if we'd arrived later, then the Spruills would now be back in Eureka Springs with their family intact.

With Cowboy driving, Tally had made this same trip in this same truck in the middle of a storm at night. Running away to a better life up North, just like us. It was still hard to believe she had fled like that.

I didn't see a single person picking cotton until we reached Nettleton, a small town close to Jonesboro. There the ditches were not as full; the ground wasn't as wet. Some Mexicans were hard at work.

Traffic slowed us at the edge of the city. I sat up high to take in the sights: the stores and nice homes and clean cars and people walking about. I could not remember my last visit to Jonesboro. When a farm kid made it to the city, he talked about it for a week. If he made it to Memphis, then he might go on for a month.

Pappy became visibly nervous in traffic. He gripped the wheel, hit the brakes, mumbled just under his breath. We turned onto a street, and there was the Greyhound station, a busy place with three shiny buses parked in a row to the left. We stopped at the curb near a DEPARTURES sign and quickly unloaded. Pappy wasn't much for hugs, so it didn't take long to say good-bye. But when he pinched my cheek, I saw moisture in his eyes. For that reason he hustled back to the truck and made a hasty getaway. We waved until he was out of sight. My heart ached as I watched his old truck turn the corner and disappear. It was headed back to the farm, back to the floods, back to the Latchers, back to a long winter. But at the same time, I was relieved not to be going back.

We turned and walked into the station. Our adventure was now beginning. My father placed the duffel bags near some seats, then he and I went to the ticket counter.

'I need three tickets to St. Louis,' he said.

My mouth fell open, and I looked at him in complete amazement. 'St. Louis?' I said.

He grinned but said nothing.

'Bus leaves at noon,' the clerk said.

My father paid for the tickets, and we took our seats next to my mother. 'Mom, we're goin' to St. Louis!' I said.

'It's just a stop, Luke,' my father said. 'From there we catch a bus to Chicago, then to Flint.'

'You think we'll see Stan Musial?'

'I doubt it.'

'Can we see Sportsman's Park?'

'Not this trip. Maybe the next one.'

After a few minutes I was released to roam around the station and inspect things. There was a small café where two army boys were drinking coffee. I thought of Ricky and realized I would not be there when he came home. I saw a family of Negroes, a rare sight in our part of Arkansas. They were clutching their bags and looked as lost as we did. I saw two more farm families, more refugees from the flood.

When I rejoined my parents they were holding hands and were deep in conversation. We waited forever, it seemed, then finally they called for us to board. The duffel bags were packed in the cargo section under the bus, and we, too, climbed on.

My mother and I sat together, with my father right behind us. I got the window seat, and I stared through it, missing nothing as we maneuvered through Jonesboro and then got on the highway, speeding along, going North, still surrounded by nothing but wet cotton fields.

When I could pull my eyes away from the window, I looked at my mother. Her head was resting on the back of her seat. Her eyes were closed, and a grin was slowly forming at the corners of her mouth.